I0644782

Goethe

Conversations of German Refugees
Wilhelm Meister's Journeyman Years

GOETHE

Selected Poems
Faust I & II
Essays on Art and Literature
From My Life: Poetry and Truth (Parts One to Three)
From My Life: Poetry and Truth (Part Four) • Campaign in France 1792 • Siege of Mainz
Italian Journey
Early Verse Drama and Prose Plays
Verse Plays and Epic
Wilhelm Meister's Apprenticeship
Conversations of German Refugees & Wilhelm Meister's Journeyman Years or The Renunciants
The Sorrows of Young Werther • Elective Affinities • Novella
Scientific Studies

Collected Works in 12 Volumes

Goethe's Collected Works, Volume 10

Johann Wolfgang von

GOETHE

Conversations of German Refugees

Translated by Jan van Heurck
in cooperation with Jane K. Brown

Wilhelm Meister's Journeyman Years, or The Renunciants

Translated by Krishna Winston

Edited by Jane K. Brown

Princeton University Press
Princeton and Oxford

The English edition was first published by Suhrkamp Publishers New York, Inc.

Published by Princeton University Press
41 William Street, Princeton, New Jersey 08540
99 Banbury Road, Oxford OX2 6JX

press.princeton.edu

GPSR Authorized Representative: Easy Access System Europe - Mustamäe tee 50, 10621 Tallinn, Estonia, gpsr.requests@easproject.com

First published 1989
First Princeton paperback printing, 1995
New paperback and e-book editions, 2026

Paperback ISBN 978-0-691-29237-3
ISBN (epub) 978-0-691-29690-6
ISBN (PDF) 978-0-691-29236-6

This is volume ten in the Collected Works of Johann Wolfgang von Goethe

Cover images: Courtesy of INTERFOTO / Alamy and Rawpixel

The Library of Congress has cataloged a previous edition of this book as follows:

Goethe, Johann Wolfgang von, 1749–1832
[Unterhaltungen deutscher Ausgewanderten. English]
Conversations of German refugees ; Wilhelm Meister's journeyman years, or, The renunciants / Johann Wolfgang von Goethe ; edited by Jane K. Brown.
p. cm.—(Princeton paperbacks)
Originally published: New York : Suhrkamp, 1989. (Goethe's collected works ; v. 10)
"Conversations of German refugees" translated by Jan van Heurck in cooperation with Jane K. Brown; "Wilhelm Meister's ourneyman years" translated by Krishna Winston.
ISBN 0-691-04345-0 (alk. paper)
1. Brown, Jane K., 1943– . II. Heurck, Jan van. III. Winston, Krishna.
IV. Goethe, Johann Wolfgang von, 1749–1832. Wilhelms Meisters Lehrjahre. English
V. Title. VI. Title: Wilhelm Meister's journeyman years. VII. Series: Goethe, Johann Wolfgang von, 1749–1832. Works. English. 1994 ; v. 10.
PT2026.A1C94 1994 Vol. 10
[PT2027.U6]
831′.6—dc20 95–34663
[833′.6]

Contents

Prefatory Note

The Princeton *Goethe's Collected Works* series generally follows the texts in the edition Goethe's Werke, ed. Erich Trunz (Hamburg: Christian Wegner, 1948–), the so-called *Hamburger Ausgabe.* This volume is no exception. However, it should be noted that for the edition of Goethe's collected works which the poet himself prepared before his death, the *Ausgabe letzter Hand,* he added the poems "Vermächtnis" after "Reflections in the Spirit of the Wanderers" and "Im ernsten Beinhaus" at the end of "From Makarie's Archives." They are not included in the *Hamburger Ausgabe* and are therefore missing from this edition as well, but can be found in volume 1 of this series (see pp. 266 ff. and 256 ff., respectively).

I would like to thank the College of Arts and Sciences at the University of Washington and the Center for the Applied Humanities at the University of Colorado for support of my work on this edition. I would especially like to thank my colleagues at Colorado, Paul Levitt and Elissa Guralnick, for their careful reading of the *Conversations of German Refugees,* Imke Meyer for her excellent proofreading, and my husband for his assistance with the entire project. In rendering the poems in *Wilhelm Meister's Journeyman Years* into verse, I have here and there drawn gratefully on the formulations of E.A. Bowring and Thomas Carlyle.

J.K.B.

Goethe
Conversations of German Refugees
Wilhelm Meister's Journeyman Years

Introduction

Goethe was the great master of the unexpected. We know from his autobiography what pleasure he took in practical jokes and disguises, the more elaborate the better. We also know from references in letters that getting the better of his readers was a crucial part of his enterprise: he once wrote that he would discontinue work on *Wilhelm Meister* immediately if he thought any of his readers could guess what would come on the following page. It is small wonder, then, that he was one of the most consistent and energetic innovators in European literature. The two works in this volume, *Conversations of German Refugees* and *Wilhelm Meister's Journeyman Years*, are outstanding examples of Goethe's drive to innovate and to mystify his readers.

So far were these two works ahead of their time that they have occupied a marginal place in the canon of Goethe's major work. The *Conversations* has always been overshadowed by Goethe's other works of the same decade, *Wilhelm Meister's Apprenticeship, Hermann and Dorothea*, and *Faust, Part I*—his acknowledged masterpieces. The *Journeyman Years* was considered, except by occasional admirers like Hermann Broch, a hasty redaction of Goethe's left-overs, for which he had to find a place in print before his death, and as clear evidence for the poet's supposedly failing powers in the last decade of his life, the decade of *Faust, Part II* and of some of his greatest lyric poems. Only since World War II has the *Journeyman Years* been widely recognized as a major work and a novel equal in artistry, thematic significance and importance to Goethe's three earlier novels. So long as romanticism was understood to be a movement interested in naive simplicity and fairy tales, neither of these works was likely to be popular as a whole, although the "Fairy Tale" at the end of the *Conversations* spawned a whole tradition of "aesthetic fairy tales." But as we have come to realize that romantic simplicity reconciles complex political, social, ethical and epistemological concerns, we have learned to read these works on their own terms, and to see the *Journeyman Years*, at least, as paradigmatic for the period.

Although *Wilhelm Meister's Journeyman Years* is the sequel to *Wilhelm Meister's Apprenticeship* (vol. 9 in this edition), there are good reasons to read it together with the *Conversations of German Refugees*, to which it also forms the sequel. Both works are cycles of novellas connected by a frame narrative with its own plot; indeed the plot of the *Conversations* is rather more clearly structured than that of the *Journeyman Years*, which is explicitly subtitled "novel." Both works address similar themes and social issues, and do so by experimenting with fragmented narrations and narrative perspectives. Taken together, then, they illuminate the range of Goethe's thinking and development in the area of prose narrative over the length of his mature career; they also delineate the range of possibilities open to romantic narrative in the first thirty years of the nineteenth century.

Each of these works was produced during a high point of Goethe's career, the first in the decade following the French Revolution, the second in the last decade of his life. Upon his return from Italy in the late spring of 1789, Goethe gave up many of his public and private relationships, which he had largely outgrown during his eighteen-month absence, for the life of the spirit, and devoted the next five years to studying optics, Kant, Plato, Homer, art theory and history. Even as he accompanied the Duke of Weimar on the allied campaigns against the French in the summers of 1792 and 1793 Goethe claims to have directed most of his energy to science and art. With the exception of the *Roman Elegies* (see vol. 1 of this edition) no significant new poetic projects were initiated, though the revisions of *Wilhelm Meister's Apprenticeship* were begun. Toward the middle of the decade Goethe's situation changed dramatically, as Weimar became for a time the intellectual center of the German nation. During the latter half of the decade Fichte, Schelling, Hegel, the Humboldts, the Schlegels, Tieck, Novalis, Brentano, Hölderlin, Kleist—essentially all the important German intellectuals of the romantic generation—either lived in or visited the tiny Duchy of Weimar, often as a result of Goethe's own efforts. Most important of all was Goethe's friendship with Friedrich Schiller, which began in 1794: for the first time since the early 1770s the poet had a close friend of equal intellectual stature and commitment with whom he could share ideas and aspirations. With Schiller Goethe discussed his final revisions of *Wilhelm Meister* and his plans for his other masterpieces of the decade, *Hermann and Dorothea* (see vol. 8 of this edition) and *Faust* (vol. 2). *Conversations of German Refugees* was the first product of this friendship, for it was Goethe's first contribution to Schiller's journal, *Die Horen*, where it appeared serially in 1794 and 1795. With this journal Schiller aspired, and Goethe increasingly along with him, to establish a literature that was classical in the sense that Greek literature of the fifth century was classical. In the Germany of the 1790s, such a literature had not only to speak both for and to its nation, but had indeed to found and constitute that nation from amidst the turmoil precipitated by the revolution in France. Such is the context of the *Conversations.*

The *Journeyman Years* resulted from a much longer development, but it was completed under not entirely different circumstances. No sooner had Goethe completed the *Conversations* than he began planning a sequel to it, another cycle of novellas. At the same time he planned a sequel to *Wilhelm Meister's Apprenticeship* as well. Some of the novellas for the continuation of the *Conversations* were executed in the first decade of the nineteenth century; one so intrigued its author that it developed into a full-blown novel, *Elective Affinities* (see vol. 11 in this edition). At some point the two plans coalesced, for in 1821 Goethe published, without much fanfare, the first version of *Wilhelm Meister's Journeyman Years,* which was, however, a cycle of novellas, and contained texts conceived for the sequel to the *Conversations.* 1821 falls in the middle of a period of withdrawal in Goethe's life rather like that of the early 1790s. Goethe's wife, Christiane, had died in 1816; in 1817 he gave up his last official function in the Duchy of Weimar, the directorship of the court theater. Most of his energy was going into working on his autobiography, ordering his papers, supervising the final edition of his compete works—that is, into putting the final touches on his image for posterity. But then around 1825 came a final creative period, which resulted in great poems, the "Novella" (see vol. 11 of this edition), most of the second part of *Faust,* and the final, much expanded, version of *Wilhelm Meister's Journeyman Years.* This time there was no Schiller to catalyze the process, nor any cataclysm comparable to the French Revolution. Nevertheless it is clear that Goethe had no illusions as to the value or stability of the society that had succeeded the suppression of the revolution, and the *Journeyman Years* offers us his final views on that continuing crisis.

In both works the novellas appear to treat a variety of topics, but all of them are subsumed under the theme of individuals in their relationship to the social order. To be sure there are few plots that cannot be understood at least to some extent in the context of such a broad theme, but this aspect of the novellas is certainly the one emphasized by the frame in both works. Nature, for example, the other great theme of the romantics, never appears in its wild state to be admired or communed with, but only as a locus for social activities, as an object of scientific study, as the object of human exploitation or cultivation, or as the threat of chaos. And in this respect these cycles are in a tradition that extends back to Boccaccio's *Decameron* and beyond to *The Golden Ass* of Lucius Apuleius. Storytelling in Boccaccio takes place in an enclosed garden, a *hortus conclusus,* to which the storytellers have withdrawn to escape the plague (uncontrollable nature) raging in Florence. The problem they confront is the disintegration of their society; they deal with it by reconstituting a microcosm of that society within the protection of their enclosed garden. Having made and kept their new laws for a brief period, they return to Florence, not because the plague has ended, but because they are fortified by their renewed commitment to social order. Boccaccio's novellas, to be sure, at least the most memorable ones, seem to work against such order, but such tension between stories and the "reality" of the frame is the lifeblood of the cycle as a form. Goethe was to exploit the tension between different levels of fiction with increasing sophistication in his own two cycles.

The "natural event" that sparks the flight of the refugees in the *Conversations* is the French Revolution. Goethe's refugees are German aristocrats fleeing their estates on the west bank of the Rhine. When they arrive at another property they own across the river, they are in a sorry social state, teasing, aggravating, and, finally, mortally offending one another. Within their ranks they represent the range of possible political positions open to the German upper classes at the time, and also a range of moral stances, from the good manners of the baroness and the patience of the Abbé to the immaturity of Carl and Louisa. Thus they constitute a microcosm of society, and at this level the revolution is represented by the bad manners and lack of sociability within the group. They shut out this social threat not only with the walls of their estate, but also with the baroness's stricture against political discussion when all are present and with the Abbé's decision to tell them stories. The effectiveness of these "walls" is periodically tested by small catastrophes analogous to the large one raging across the river—the sound of a shot from within the house (a desk cracking, as it turns out), the fire on their aunt's estate nearby, Carl's insistence on the anarchic autonomy of the imagination. Although the cycle is open-ended and does not return its figures to their original society, the increasing civility of their discussions, the increasing sophistication of the stories told them by the Abbé and of their responses to them, and especially the improved responses of Louisa, offer some measure of their spiritual fortification.

There are two mechanisms at work to effect this social improvement, one associated with each of the dominant members of the group. The one associated with the baroness is renunciation, a central theme of the *Journeyman Years*, which carries the subtitle "The Renunciants." In the *Conversations* what must be renounced is, in effect, excessive preoccupation with oneself and one's own concerns—Louisa must stop talking about her absent fiancé; Carl's understanding of liberty as the right to say and do whatever one pleases is the antithesis of this concept. Renunciation is the basis of the good manners that restore order to the baroness's circle. The Abbé's mechanism is telling stories. Except for the first evening, the only storyteller in the cycle is the Abbé, and while the stories of the others lack focus and deal with situations where renunciation might be called for but is not achieved, the Abbé's stories are highly focused presentations of successful renunciation. Like his more famous counterpart in *Wilhelm Meister's Apprenticeship* the Abbé is an educator of his society. In this respect he plays the role to which Goethe and Schiller aspired in the ambitious program of *Die Horen*—as poets they were to lead the nation to new levels of civilization and culture, literature and art were to be the guarantors and generators of society.

The "Fairy Tale" at the end of the *Conversations* is the high point of the Abbé's educational and artistic efforts. The work has always been a great riddle in that it has not been possible to unlock its symbols, that is, to assign a particular significance to a particular figure that holds consistently throughout the tale. Nevertheless it is not hard to see in it an allegory of the restoration of society by the same mechanisms that work in the frame of the *Conversations*. The disorder of the society at the beginning is symbolized by the rushing river that separates the two halves of its world, by its buried kings, and by the enchantment which causes the princess to kill everything she touches. At the end the river is spanned by a magnificent bridge alive with travelers, the temple with its buried kings has risen to the light of day and the princess is united with her prince. All of this has resulted from the irrepressible sociability of some visiting will-o'-the-wisps and the green snake's decision at the crucial moment to sacrifice her identity as snake to become the reconciling bridge; here are the good manners and renunciation demanded by the baroness. The process is orchestrated by the old man with the lamp (a sly self-portrait of the Abbé and his transforming stories), who knows precisely what must be done but depends on all the others to cooperate. The tale summarizes the concerns of the cycle and simultaneously raises them to a higher, almost religious level.

"The Fairy Tale" is an allegory, in the most basic sense of that word; it describes a process which consistently represents another process distinct from itself. It is, as I said, an allegory of the process depicted in the frame of the cycle itself. But it is also important to recognize that the frame of the *Conversations* is an allegory in exactly the same sense. It depicts a response to the French Revolution in a microcosmic version of the German society being impacted by that revolution. In this respect miniature might be a better term than allegory, and this term may also help us to understand the discomfort readers have sometimes felt with the cycle. Surely there is something inadequate about "cultivate good manners" as a response to the terrors of the revolution. It is, indeed, a miniature, a trivial response. Curiously enough, "The Fairy Tale" seems a less trivial response—obvious allegory distances the reader more effectively than does the miniaturization of this cycle: the frame is too realistic to be read in the allegorical mode that was probably intended. Goethe ran the same risk of trivializing miniaturization in *Hermann and Dorothea,* where again he presented a microcosmic version of the revolution with his band of refugees passing a small German town. But in *Hermann and Dorothea* the ironic use of Homeric language and forms achieves the narrative distance necessary to make us read the miniaturization properly as signifying something larger than itself.

With regard to the novellas themselves, this miniaturization was much more successful, for the *Conversations* established the novella as a genre in German literature. German narrative in the eighteenth century, such as it was, tended to be rambling. Before the *Conversations* the only tight, closed, small-scale narrative in the German tradition was Goethe's own relatively short novel *The Sorrows of Young Werther* (see vol. 11 of this edition), but in the nineteenth century the novella was to be the preeminent genre. The parallel between the formal order and closure of the novella and the pervading concern for social order in the *Conversations* must not be overlooked. If the success of the miniaturization as a vehicle for meaning remains questionable in the frame, there can be no question as to the triumph of the formal miniaturization Goethe achieved in establishing the novella as a significant genre in Germany. In this context the *Conversations* can thus be seen as an experiment that was misunderstood by all those who seized exclusively on the "Fairy Tale," a masterpiece, to be sure, but the cycle's most conservative element.

There is nothing miniature about *Wilhelm Meister's Journeyman Years,* despite the presence of both novellas and aphorisms in its fabric. And yet it would be hard to find another of Goethe's works that continues the thematic and formal concerns of the *Conversations* as cogently as this last great novel. Despite the superficial difference in social conditions at the time of writing—Europe was politically at peace in the 1820s—Goethe was a sufficiently profound observer to realize that the full sequence of events set in motion by the revolution had not yet worked itself out. Indeed, the *Journeyman Years* sees the disorder caused by the Revolution as a much broader and profounder phenomenon than that envisioned in any of the works of the 1790s. The situation is no longer understood as a single cataclysm that can be represented in the image of a thunderstorm or a fire; it is a change in the pace of time itself, as the aphorisms insist. So fundamental a change necessitates, as Goethe correctly perceives, a thorough rethinking of all social institutions. The model for this in the novel is the rearrangement of all the social structures that had been carefully constructed in

Wilhelm Meister's Apprenticeship. At the end of that novel Wilhelm was betrothed to the ideal woman, Natalie, and had been initiated into the Society of the Tower, whose members were to disperse to different countries in order to minimize the impact of any future revolutions on the Society as a whole. At the beginning of the *Jouneyman Years* Wilhelm's marriage to Natalie has been postponed into an indefinite future; Wilhelm has been required to part from her, and at the same time prevented from forming any new ties by an oath to the Society not to spend more than three days in any one place. The Society, in the meanwhile, is planning a new settlement in the American wilderness, a great utopian venture to cultivate and exploit the wealth of this hitherto untamed nature. No longer, as in the *Apprenticeship*, are its members to function autonomously, each as fully developed individuals, but each must develop a single skill to contribute to the unity of the whole. The new colony is a world of technocrats, where, we are told, administration is more important than justice, where there will be no libraries, and where the attitude of the authorities toward books remains problematic. This is hardly the sociable, cultivated world envisioned by the *Conversations*, where poets are to be legislators, nor is it the world of the *Apprenticeship*, where each individual is to cultivate himself to the fullest.

In such a world renunciation is as much a part of the problem as it is a solution. Far more must be renounced here than one's own bad habits or asocial tendencies. Wilhelm must renounce Natalie, the ideal that guided him, however inchoately, through his apprenticeship; he must renounce not only his theatrical aspirations, but now any value he attributed to his theatrical experience. He must renounce his aspirations to educate his countrymen and settle instead for the trade (not even profession) of surgeon, binding wounds and letting blood. At the end of the *Apprenticeship* he has solemnly undertaken the responsibility of educating his son Felix, and is still attempting to do so at the beginning of the *Journeyman Years*; but by the middle of the novel he deposits Felix in a boarding school, and the last contact shown with him is when Wilhelm lets his blood to save him from the consequences of a fall into the river: even family ties are reduced in this world to matters of professional activity. Renunciation dramatically chosen to achieve what the eighteenth century would have called virtuous ends can have bizarre consequences in the world of this novel, as novellas like "The Foolish Pilgrim," "Who Is the Traitor?" or "The Man of Fifty Years" readily show.

And yet, renunciation is not all bad. The first episode in the novel deals with the seemingly miraculous reappearance of the Holy Family in the world through which Wilhelm travels. The novel teems with images of rebirth and renewal, ending with Felix's recovery after almost drowning; in the final tableau he and Wilhelm embrace. Renunciation and rebirth are inseparable in the *Journeyman Years*. The world of the novel is full of rigid structures that seem most inhospitable compared to those of Goethe's earlier work—not just the American utopia, but also the Pedagogic Province, where Felix is educated, and the realm of the saintly Makarie—but these are mostly presented as agents for good and for order. So positively are they presented, indeed, that it is easy to overlook the elements of irony and common sense that undermine the superlatively enthusiastic presentations. And then there are, finally, certain elements that resist the totalitarian structures of the novel. Felix and Hersilie refuse to renounce their incomprehensible passion that is mysteriously tied to the casket whose contents are never revealed. Their triangular relationship with Wilhelm remains unresolved, but maintains a profound dignity to the end of the novel, whereas the various love relationships mediated by Makarie degenerate into banality. Similarly the line between fiction and reality in the novel remains unresolvable. Some of the novellas are presented as discreet units, others are presented in pieces—often at a remove from one another—others run into the frame narrative or touch it in unexpected ways. By demonstrating the limits to our understanding and to our control of our passions and imagination, the novel preserves a realm beyond the reach of its oppressive social structures: this is the most important and positive aspect of renunciation.

Renunciation determines the unusual and difficult structure of the novel. *Conversations of German Refugees* had placed certain limits on interpretation of the "Fairy Tale" and had by its nature required its readers to draw comparisons among novellas and between novellas and frame. The *Journeyman Years*, however, makes much more complex demands on its readers, and at the same time elevates this demand into a central theme. As society is fragmented in this novel into many one-sided individuals, so too the world we confront is fragmented into many different versions of reality. The novellas present many different versions of renunciation; but the reasons for their presentation and their relation to the frame are often left unarticulated. The novel also includes two collections of aphorisms, which some scholars believe should no longer be printed with the novel at all. But it is precisely the aphorisms that offer a clue to this apparent confusion. Early in the novel Wilhelm visits a house where aphorisms are lettered in gold above all the doorways. There we learn that the value of aphorisms is that they can be understood in different ways, that unraveling their possible meanings provides food for thought. Understanding is to be found not in what an aphorism says, but in the act of interpretation. Knowledge can always be supplemented by reflection, whether metaphoric, as in the above example, or concrete, as when Lucidor in "Who

Is the Traitor?" comprehends the full extent of his happiness only when he sees the reflection of himself embracing his beloved in the mirror. This, too, is the sense of Wilhelm's confusion in the opening chapters between the Joseph and Marie he meets and the sequence of paintings of the life of St. Joseph that the live Joseph proudly shows him. It is also the sense both of the multiple perspectives we are offered on particular stories as their characters move back and forth from novella to frame, and further of the pervasive narrative irony, which leaves us to understand such elements as the Pedagogic Province or Makarie both seriously and critically at the same time. Ultimately the validity of a particular perspective is not the issue: truth, or knowledge, such as it is, is ineffable, and our access to it is only through however many perspectives on it we can achieve.

In this context renunciation extends far beyond the social concerns of the *Conversations* to epistemology. Truth can only be known, indeed only *exists*, in its multiple manifestations and reflections. As a result art—the domain of the poet—takes on a more profound epistemological role as well. As we have seen, the society of the *Journeyman Years* leaves no room for the poet as legislator and civilizer. Instead, art has become a crucial provider of perspectives. From the paintings of the Holy Family in the first chapter to the anonymous authors of the various novellas to the budding artists in the Pedagogic Province, where religion is taught through pictures, to the sculptor-anatomist from whom Wilhelm learns his trade, this novel about the harsh practicalities of life in the ninteenth century cannot do without art, for its capacity to generate alternate perspectives, to be and to generate reflection, is the basis of all knowledge.

And if the artist is the generator of perspectives, so too is the reader. The model of reading offered in the novel is the discussion about aphorisms alluded to above. One cannot expect the plot of the novel to organize and relate the materials of the novel, for that would be to reduce the material of the novel to one perspective. The novellas have tight, organized plots, but they are set off within the novel as explicit fictions; where they issue into the novel, the plot is unresolved or treated with extreme irony. Wilhelm does little more in the novel than read and listen to stories; late in the novel he finally tells a story himself, one that is analogous to the others but does not embrace them. In this respect he embodies the true plot of the novel, which is the action of the reader as perceiving and reflecting consciousness. The formal complexity of the novel, then, and its apparent incoherence, understood as multiplicity of perspective, constitute its essential coherence. *Wilhelm Meister's Journeyman Years* is an experiment in narrative form whose success could only be recognized in the wake of novels like *Ulysses* or *The Waves.*

One final point about the complexity of perspectives in the *Journeyman Years* involves the use of parody in the novel. Goethe always places himself in a tradition by alluding to, exploiting, rewriting, not uncommonly even burlesquing other texts. I use *parody* here to refer to all of these options. His normal practice was to use major authors from the tradition—Homer, Aeschylus, Euripides, Dante, Shakespeare, Calderon are typical examples—and to use one per work. *Faust* and the *Journeyman Years* are special among Goethe's works in the enormous number of other writers and texts parodied. The novel connects itself not only to *Conversations of German Refugees* and *Wilhelm Meister's Apprenticeship*, but to many others in addition. "The Deranged Pilgrim" is a translation of an anonymous French novella; "Who Is the Traitor?" and "The Perilous Wager" parody works by August von Kotzebue, Goethe's popular contemporary. "The Nut-brown Maid" is based on a ballad from Bishop Percy's *Reliques of Ancient English Poetry* and Matthew Prior's poem "Henry and Emma." The figure of the silent barber in Book Three and much of the material in "The New Melusine" comes from a fairy tale by J.K.A. Musäus, a popular mid-century writer in Germany. The Pedagogic Province parodies the famous German educators Basedow and Campe in terms of their relation to Rousseau. The story of the drowned boy in Book Two evokes Goldsmith's *The Vicar of Wakefield*, and, finally, the aphorisms and much of the organization of the same story invoke Laurence Sterne. Goethe's attitude toward his various ancestors is largely sympathetic, even where there is substantial correction or travesty involved, as in the case of the Pedagogic Province. Toward Goldsmith and Sterne he is positively reverent, for he numbered these two among the handful of writers whom he considered to have influenced him most throughout his long career.

This is a diverse group of works in terms of quality, genre, and audience appealed to; what does connect them is their great popularity in the later eighteenth century, especially in the Germany of Goethe's early maturity. These works constitute, or perhaps represent, the milieu that produced *Wilhelm Meister's Apprenticeship* and the *Conversations of German Refugees* with their ideal of a human society grounded on the cooperation and goodwill of broadly educated individuals civilized by the efforts of the philosopher-poet. Like the occasional stubborn refusals to renounce, the goodwill with which these exponents of an earlier, more humane age are evoked contradicts the prevailing drive of the novel toward the practicality of the dawning industrial age. Above all these parodies bring into the novel a strong sense of nostalgia for the age whose sensibility and excessive focus on individual subjectivity Goethe himself had criticized so cogently in *The Sorrows of Young Werther*. If subjectivity was a problem for the young Goethe, now at the end of his life he sets a memorial to it, as an expression of regret, but also as a celebration of the age that discovered it as the irreducible core of human existence.

J.K.B.

Conversations of German Refugees

Translated by Jan van Heurck
in Cooperation with Jane K. Brown

Conversations of German Refugees

In those unhappy days that brought such misfortune to Germany, to Europe, indeed to the whole world, when the Frankish army burst into our land through a breach in our defenses, a noble family abandoned their property in the region and fled across the Rhine in order to escape the afflictions threatening everyone of any distinction. Their only crime was that they remembered their ancestors with pleasure and respect, and that they enjoyed advantages which any well-meaning father would be happy to provide for his children and descendants.

The Baroness of C - - - , a middle-aged widow, comforted her children, relatives and friends as resolutely and energetically during their flight as she had at home. Raised in a cosmopolitan atmosphere and educated by a variety of experiences, she was known as a model of domesticity, and her intelligence welcomed challenges of every kind. She wanted to help others: a wide circle of acquaintances enabled her to do so. Now, she was suddenly called upon to lead a little cavalcade, and she was able to guide them, look after them, and maintain good humor in their circle even amidst fear and distress. And indeed our refugees were often cheerful enough, for surprises and unfamiliar circumstances provided their overwrought spirits with ample material for joking and laughter.

The hasty flight had revealed the character of each refugee. One might be carried away by false fears, by unreasonable terror; another would succumb to unnecessary anxiety. One might go too far where another did not go far enough; one would be too compliant, another too hasty—and each time there was such teasing and poking fun at one another, that their unhappy journey was more enjoyable than any excursion they had ever made before.

Sometimes we can watch a comedy for a stretch without laughing at the comic antics, but in a tragedy we immediately laugh uproariously at something inappropriate; it is the same in the real world, where some ludicrous aspect of a terrible misfortune may make us burst out laughing—often instantly, certainly in retrospect.

Louisa, the Baroness's eldest daughter, was made to suffer most, because she was supposed to have completely lost her head at the first alarm. She was a vivacious, impetuous and, in better days, domineering young woman, but in her confusion, indeed in a kind of trance, she had in all seriousness gathered the most useless things to be packed and had even mistaken an old family servant for her fiancé. She was miserable enough to know that as a soldier in the allied army he was in constant danger and that the general disruption would delay, perhaps even entirely prevent, their marriage.

Her elder brother Frederick, a resolute young man, faithfully carried out everything his mother decided: he accompanied the procession on horseback, and served as courier, caravan leader, and guide all in one. The younger son, a promising lad, had a cultivated tutor who kept the Baroness company in the carriage. In another carriage Cousin Carl followed with an elderly Abbé, who had long since become the family's indispensable companion. They were accompanied by two female relatives, one elderly and one quite young. Chambermaids and valets followed in smaller conveyances. Several heavily loaded wagons, which fell behind at various stops along the way, concluded the cavalcade.

It is easy to imagine that they had all been unhappy to abandon their homes, but Cousin Carl found it especially painful to leave the far bank of the Rhine. This was not because he had perhaps left a mistress behind, as his youth, good looks, and passionate nature might have led one to believe. Instead, he had been seduced by that dazzling beauty who under the name of Liberty had won so many devoted admirers, first in secret and then for all the world to see. And no matter how badly she treated some of these admirers, she was ardently courted by all the rest.

Lovers are usually blinded by their passion, and Cousin Carl was no exception. They are bent on possessing one supreme happiness and imagine that they can do without everything else. Rank, wealth, social connections seem to vanish to nothing while the one desire reigns supreme. Parents, relatives, and friends become strangers, while what we have acquired absorbs the whole being to the exclusion of everything else.

Cousin Carl abandoned himself to his passion and made no attempt to conceal it from others. He considered himself all the more entitled to surrender to such sentiments, since he was an aristocrat and, though a younger son, stood to come into a sizeable fortune. This very property which he was one day to inherit now lay in the hands of the enemy, who were not taking the best care of it. Nevertheless Carl could not hate a nation that promised the world so many advantages—and whose convictions he judged by the public speeches and statements of a mere handful of its citizens. He often disturbed the peace of the group—to the extent that they still had any—by praising to the skies every act, whether good or evil, of the New Franks, and noisily rejoicing in their victories. This irritated the others all the more: they could not help but suffer more keenly when their troubles were doubled by the malicious joy of their friend and relation.

Frederick had several times fallen out with Carl and finally stopped speaking to him altogether. The Baroness skillfully managed to restrain him at least for short periods. Louisa gave him the hardest time by casting aspersions on his character and judgment—often quite unfairly. The tutor silently agreed with him; the Abbé silently disagreed. The chambermaids, attracted by his good looks and impressed with his liberality, loved to hear him talk. They felt that his convictions entitled them to look openly at him with those tender eyes that in the past they had modestly lowered.

Their daily needs, the obstacles of the journey, and the uncomfortable quarters usually kept their minds on the concerns of the moment. Everywhere they met crowds of French and German refugees who varied greatly in their behavior and their past experiences. This often made them reflect on the importance in these times of practicing all possible virtues, especially impartiality and forbearance.

One day the Baroness remarked that times of general confusion and distress showed more clearly than any other how badly brought-up most people were. "Our whole social system," she said, "is like a ship that can transport a good many people, old and young, healthy and sick, across dangerous waters even during a storm. Only at the moment when the ship founders do you find out who can swim, and under such conditions even good swimmers may drown.

"For the most part refugees carry their faults and absurd habits with them, and that amazes us. But just as the Englishman is never without his tea kettle when he travels in any of the four corners of the globe, so the rest of humanity trails along its presumption, vanity, intemperance, impatience, obstinacy, wrong-headedness, and joy in taking advantage. The thoughtless enjoy their flight as if they were on an excursion; the demanding insist, even though they are now beggars, that everything be at their beck and call. How rare are people of simple integrity, who are able to live and sacrifice themselves for others."

While they made numerous acquaintances who prompted reflections of this kind, the winter passed. Fortune once again favored German arms. The French had been pushed back across the Rhine, Frankfurt liberated, and Mainz surrounded.

Hoping for the continued progress of the victorious forces and eager to reclaim part of their property, the family hastened to an estate they owned, beautifully situated on the right bank of the Rhine. It refreshed them to see the lovely river once again flowing beneath their windows; joyfully they once again took possession of every part of their house. They greeted the family furniture, the old pictures, and all their household effects with affection; how precious seemed even the most trifling object long given up for lost. And how their hopes rose that even on the other side of the Rhine they might, in days to come, find everything just as they had left it.

No sooner had word of the Baroness's arrival spread through the neighborhood than all her former friends, acquaintances, and servants hastened to talk with her, recount the events of the past few months, and in many instances ask her advice and help.

In the midst of these visits, she was most pleasantly surprised when Privy Councillor von S--- arrived with his family. From earliest youth work had been a necessity to him; he deserved and possessed the confidence of his sovereign. He was a man of strict principles and independent judgment. He was precise in speech and in conduct, and demanded that others be the same. Consistent behavior seemed to him the highest virtue.

His prince, his country, he himself had suffered much from the French invasion. He had experienced the arbitrariness of a nation that constantly talked about law, and the tyranny of those who never stopped talking about freedom. He had observed that the mob remained true to its nature and, in this case as in so many others, with great fervor took words for deeds and appearance for actuality. His acuteness readily discovered the results of an unfortunate campaign as well as the effects of the sentiments and opinions now so widespread. Nevertheless it could not be denied that his view was often jaundiced and his judgments colored by emotion.

After so many hardships, his wife, a childhood companion of the Baroness, was blissful in the arms of her friend. They had been raised and educated together and had no secrets from one another. They had always confided everything either in person or by letter—their first loves, the more important concerns of marriage, the joys, cares and sorrows of motherhood—and had never lost touch. Only the recent political troubles had interrupted their mutual exchange. Their conversations, therefore, were all the livelier now, and they had more to say to each other than ever before. In the meantime the Privy Councillor's daughters exchanged confidences with Louisa.

Unfortunately their joy in the enchanting countryside was often disrupted by the cannon's roar, which the shifting wind carried more or less distinctly to their ears. With the rumors that continually streamed in, it was equally impossible to avoid political discussion. Both factions expressed their views very heatedly and often disrupted the momentary tranquillity. Intemperate people do not abstain from wine and rich foods even though they know from experience that it will make them ill; so most of the group could not now restrain themselves and gave in to the irresistible urge to hurt one another and thereby to make life unpleasant for themselves.

It is easy to imagine that the Privy Councillor led the faction that supported the old regime, while Carl championed the opposite side, which hoped that the changes at hand would heal and revitalize the old, ailing society.

At first the discussions were reasonably calm, due largely to the tactful remarks with which the Baroness managed to maintain a balance between the two factions. But as the blockade of Mainz became a siege, and as their concern grew for the lovely city and its remaining inhabitants, both sides expressed their views with unrestrained vehemence.

The chief topic of conversation was the Jacobin sympathizers who had remained there; everyone expected them either to be punished or released, depending on whether he condemned or approved their actions.

Among the first group was the Privy Councillor, whose arguments irritated Carl most when he attacked the judgment of these people and accused them of complete ignorance of the world and of themselves.

"How blind they must be," he exclaimed one afternoon when the discussion was getting especially heated, "to expect any sympathy from a vast, confused, war-torn nation that even in peaceful moments respects nothing but itself! They will be seen as tools, used for a while, and finally be thrown away, or at least totally neglected. They are mistaken indeed, if they think they will ever be accepted in the ranks of the French nation!

"Nothing is more ridiculous to the great and powerful than someone small and weak who, in the darkness of delusion, in ignorance of himself, his abilities and his situation, considers himself their equal. And do you really think that after the good luck it has enjoyed up until now the 'great nation' will be any less proud and overbearing than any other royal conqueror?

"How many of them who are now trotting about decked in official robes will curse the whole masquerade when, after helping to impose a detestable new regime on their countrymen, they find themselves mistreated by those whom they had entirely trusted? Indeed, I think it very probable that at the surrender of the town, which must soon take place, all these people will be abandoned or turned over to our forces. Then let them receive their just reward, then let them receive the punishment they deserve—and I am judging them as impartially as I can."

"Impartially!" exclaimed Carl. "If only I never had to hear that word again! How can we condemn these people out of hand? True, they have not spent their lives working in the time-honored way for the advantage of themselves and other members of the privileged classes. True, they have not taken over the few habitable rooms in the old structure, and made themselves at home. Instead they have suffered the discomforts of the neglected wings of your palace of state—all the more because they have been forced to spend their days there in misery and oppression. Their workaday routine has not seduced them into accepting things merely because they were used to them. No, they have had no choice but to look on in silence at the prejudice, disorder, negligence, and clumsiness with which your statesmen still pretend to earn respect; no, they could only secretly hope that effort and enjoyment might be more evenly apportioned! Who can deny that there are some well-intentioned and capable men among them who, though they may not be able to create universal happiness at this very moment, have at least succeeded in their efforts to alleviate evil and to prepare for a better future? And, since there are such people, who would not pity them, now the moment is fast approaching that will rob them, perhaps forever, of all their hopes!"

The Privy Councillor replied with a bitter joke about the tendency of young people to idealize everything; Carl, in turn, did not spare those who can think only in obsolete terms and automatically reject whatever does not fit into them.

The dispute grew ever more violent as accusations were hurled back and forth, and the two opposing parties aired every issue that had divided so many well-meaning circles in recent years. In vain the Baroness tried to negotiate a truce, if not actual peace, between the combatants. Even the Privy Councillor's wife, whose charm had won her some power over Carl, was unable to influence him, particularly as her husband continued to fling well-aimed shafts at youth and inexperience, and to ridicule the penchant of children to play with fire, which they could not control.

Carl, beside himself with rage, now declared openly that he wished the French army all the luck in the world; and that he called on every German to bring an end to traditional servitude; that he was convinced that the French nation would know how to value those noble Germans who had taken her part and, far from sacrificing or abandoning them, would regard them as her own and heap honors, goods, and confidence upon them.

The Privy Councillor asserted in response that it was absurd to think that in the event of a surrender or whatever, the French would give these people even a moment's thought; instead these people would surely fall into the hands of the Allies, and he hoped to see them all hanged.

Carl could not bear this threat and shouted that he hoped the guillotine would reap a rich harvest in Germany, too, and would not miss a single guilty head. He added a number of strong personal remarks, directed at the Privy Councillor, which were thoroughly offensive.

"Well then," said the Privy Councillor, "I must take leave of people who no longer honor anything normally considered worthy of respect. I regret that I should be exiled for the second time, and now by a fellow countryman. But I see that we can expect less mercy from him than from the New Franks, and I find the old proverb confirmed that it is better to fall into the hands of the Turks than of renegades."

With these words he rose and left the room. His wife followed him, and the company fell silent. The Baroness expressed her displeasure in brief but forceful terms; Carl paced back and forth. The Privy Councillor's wife returned in tears and reported that her husband was having their things packed up and had already ordered horses. The Baroness went to try to change his mind; meanwhile the young ladies cried and kissed each other, and were distraught at this hasty and unexpected parting. The Baroness returned; she had achieved nothing. They began to collect everything that belonged to the visitors and suffered bitterly the sorrows of separation and departure. All hope vanished with the last of the boxes and cases. The horses arrived and there were more tears.

The carriage drove off and the Baroness followed it with tears in her eyes. She left the window and sat down at her embroidery frame. Everyone was silent, indeed ill at ease, especially Carl, who sat in a corner leafing through the pages of a book and often glanced at his aunt. Finally he rose and picked up his hat, as if he intended to leave; but at the door he turned, approached the embroidery frame, and said with quiet dignity: "I have offended you, my dear Aunt, I have upset you. Please forgive my thoughtlessness, I acknowledge my fault and regret it deeply."

"I will forgive you," answered the Baroness, "and not hold it against you, for you are a good and noble man. But you cannot repair the damage you have done. Because of you I have lost the companionship of a friend whom misfortune itself had just restored to me after a long separation and with whom I could for hours forget our misery and what is still before us. For so long she had been driven about in fear and been hounded from place to place. Scarcely had she begun to relax with old and well-loved friends, in a comfortable home in pleasant surroundings, than she is again forced to take flight. And we lose the company of her husband who, eccentric as he may be in many ways, is nevertheless a fine and honorable man with an inexhaustible knowledge of people and the world, of events and circumstances, which he is always ready to share with ease and charm. Your vehemence has deprived us of all this happiness. How can you make up to us what we have lost?"

CARL. "Spare me, my dear Aunt. I am ashamed enough. Don't let me see the consequences quite so clearly!"

THE BARONESS. "On the contrary, you should see them as clearly as possible! This is not the time to spare you. The only question is whether you can change. It isn't the first time you have been guilty of this fault, and it will not be the last. Ah, you strange people! Can't the suffering that has driven you together under one roof, crowded you into a single tight place, make you tolerant of each other? Aren't the disasters that are continually crashing down on you and the people you care for enough to convince you? Can't you control yourselves and behave sensibly and moderately towards people who are not trying to take anything away from you or rob you? Must your tempers work so blindly and relentlessly, like political upheavals, like a thunderstorm or some other natural phenomenon?"

Carl did not answer. The tutor left the window where he had been standing, went over to the Baroness and said, "He will improve. This will serve as a warning to him, as to us all. Every day we shall review our behavior, and call to mind the pain you have suffered; we will show that we can practice self-control."

BARONESS. "How easily men can deceive themselves, especially where self-control is concerned! Control is such an attractive word, and it sounds so noble to want to control ourselves. Men are excessively fond of talking about it, and would like us to believe that they are prepared to practice it seriously; and I have never in my life met one single man who was capable of controlling himself in even the smallest detail! They make a great show of renouncing things they don't care about a bit; but if there is something they really want, they convince themselves and other people that it's marvellous, necessary, unavoidable, and indispensable. I don't think I know even one man who is capable of giving up anything at all."

TUTOR. "You are seldom unjust, and I have never seen you so overcome by irritation and anger as at this moment."

BARONESS. "At least I have no cause to be ashamed of my anger. When I think of my friend in her carriage, uncomfortable, in tears and remembering how we mistreated our guests, I am very angry with you all."

TUTOR. "Even in the greatest misfortune I have not seen you so troubled and exasperated."

BARONESS. "A small misfortune that follows a greater one can be the last straw. And it is not a small misfortune to lose a friend!"

TUTOR. "Calm yourself, and trust us all to improve and to do all we can to please you."

BARONESS. "No! None of you shall lure me into trusting you. In future I shall command and be mistress in my own home."

"Do command, and give us orders," said Carl. "You will have no cause to complain of disobedience."

"Now, now, I shan't be as strict as all that," the Baroness answered with a smile, pulling herself together. "I don't like to give orders, especially to such liberal-minded people. But I will give you some advice, and add a request."

TUTOR. "Both shall be inviolable laws."

BARONESS. "It would be foolish to try to divert into other channels the interest that all of us must feel in politics, whose victims we have, to our regret, now become. I cannot change the attitudes that develop, take root, become confirmed, and operate in each of us; and it would be both foolish and harsh to expect you not to communicate them. But I can ask of the company in which I live, that like-minded people come together quietly to talk in a civilized manner about matters they know they agree on. In your own room, on walks, or if you meet someone who shares your feelings, by all means reveal your thoughts, support this opinion or that, indeed revel in the joy of passionate conviction. But my dear friends, in the company of others let us not forget how much of our personal ways we had to give up in order to be sociable, even before all these issues came up; and let us remember that as long as the world lasts, everyone, at least on the surface, must practice self-control in order to be sociable. It is not in the name of virtue, but in the name of common courtesy, that I ask you to give to me and to other people the same consideration in these times that you have shown all your life to anyone you happened to meet on the street.

"In any case," the Baroness went on, "I don't know what has got into us, how all civilized behavior can so suddenly disappear. Everyone used to be so careful in public not to touch on a subject that might distress others. In the company of a Catholic no Protestant would ridicule a religious ceremony; the most zealous Catholic would never let the Protestant suspect that the old religion was a more certain path to eternal bliss. In the presence of a mother who had lost her son one did not show too much pleasure in one's own children; and if something tactless was said, everyone was embarrassed and tried to make amends. But don't we nowadays do just the opposite? We seem to seek every opportunity to bring up things that will irritate and shock the others. In future, my dear children and friends, let us return to the old ways! We have known so much sadness and soon perhaps smoke by day and fire by night will announce the destruction of the homes and belongings we have left behind. Let us not discuss even these tidings in anger, let us not harp continually on what has already caused us all such pain.

"When your father died, did you seize every occasion to remind me of this irreparable loss? Didn't you try to avoid everything that could recall his memory at an inopportune moment and to lighten our loss, to heal the wound by your quiet efforts and your kindness? Don't we now have an even greater need to practice that humane forbearance which often achieves more than well-meaning, but clumsy, help? Now, it is not an isolated misfortune here or there that wounds this man or that among a happy multitude, so that one sorrow is soon absorbed in the general well-being; but at the present time among a huge mass of unfortunates hardly anyone, whether through temperament or education, by accident or by effort of will, enjoys peace of mind."

CARL. "You have humbled us enough now, my dear Aunt. Won't you extend your hand to us again?"

BARONESS. "Here it is, but on condition that you accept its guidance. Let us declare an amnesty! The sooner the better."

The young ladies, who had been crying heartily ever since the departure, now came into the room, but could not bring themselves to give Cousin Carl a friendly look.

"Come here, children!" cried the Baroness. "We have had a serious discussion, which I hope will restore peace and harmony among us and bring back the manners that we have lacked for some time. It has perhaps never been more important for us to turn to one another and to distract ourselves a little, even if only for a few hours each day. Let us make a pact to ban all mention of current events when we are together. How long has it been since we had any interesting and cheering conversation! How long has it been, dear Carl, since you've told us about distant lands and people of whose ways and customs you know so much. How long has it been since you," she said to the tutor, "talked about earlier and recent history, and compared the different centuries and the people who lived in them. And what has become of the pretty poems that the girls so often brought for our enjoyment? Where have our free-wheeling philosophical speculations disappeared to? Have you lost all joy in taking walks and returning with some curious rock, some plant unfamiliar to us, or some strange insect—all these led at least to pleasant reflections on the grand unity of all creatures. At one time we did all this spontaneously; now let us agree to restore these conversations by intention, by a self-imposed rule! Try as hard as you can to be interesting, useful, and, especially, sociable! We must all abide by this rule even if everything in the world goes to rack and ruin; indeed then we shall need it even more than now. Children, promise!"

They promised eagerly.

"And now, go on out. It's a beautiful evening. Each of you enjoy it in your own way, and then, at supper, for the first time in weeks, let us enjoy the pleasure of friendly conversation!"

They all went their separate ways, leaving only Louisa sitting beside her mother. She could not readily forget the annoyance of losing her companion, and snappishly refused Carl's invitation to go for a walk with him. Mother and daughter had been sitting quietly side by side for some time when the Abbé returned from a long walk, ignorant of what had occurred in his absence. He put aside his hat and cane, sat down, and was about to tell them something, but Louisa, pretending that she had been engaged in conversation with her mother, cut him off by saying:

"Many people will find the law we have just made rather uncomfortable. Even when we lived in the country before, we often lacked topics of conversation; in the country you don't have the daily opportunity that you have in town to slander some poor girl or run down a young man's character. But at least we were still free to describe the silly antics of great nations, to say that the Germans were just as ridiculous as the French, and to accuse someone or other of being a Jacobin. If these topics are now to be banned, many of us will end up not saying a word."

"Is this attack aimed perhaps at me, young lady?" the old gentleman began with a smile. "Well, you know, I am happy occasionally to sacrifice myself for the rest. True, you are always a credit to the excellent woman who raised you, and everyone finds you pleasant, attractive, and charming. Nevertheless there seems to be a malicious little imp inside you who gets out of control and takes out his ill-will on me, to get even for the way you are always penning him up. Tell me, my lady," he went on, turning to the Baroness, "what happened during my absence, and what topics have been banned?"

The Baroness told him everything. He listened attentively and then answered: "This arrangement should not prevent us from amusing one another, and may even give some of us a bit of an edge."

"I'd like to see that," said Louisa.

"There's nothing onerous about this rule," he went on, "for people who look for entertainment to their own resources. In fact it will be a pleasure, for they can speak openly of interests they used to pursue surreptitiously. Please don't be offended if I say this, young lady, but isn't it society that breeds the tale-bearers, the busybodies, and slanderers? I have seldom seen people at a serious reading or a presentation intended to stimulate heart and mind look as attentive and thoughtful as when they listened to the latest gossip, especially if it was derogatory. Ask yourself and ask anyone: What makes news attractive? Not its importance, not its consequences, but its novelty. For the most part only what is new seems important, because without a clear context it arouses amazement, momentarily stirs our imagination, just grazes our emotions, and requires no mental effort whatever. Everyone can take a lively interest in such new things without the least trouble to himself. Indeed, since a series of news items continually pulls us from one subject to the next, most people find nothing more pleasant than this stimulus to ceaseless diversion, this convenient and never-ending opportunity to vent their malice and spleen."

"Well," exclaimed Louisa, "you seem to know what you're doing. You used to run down individuals; now you're taking on the whole human race."

"I don't ask that you ever be fair to me," he replied. "But this much I must say to you: those of us who are dependent on society must follow its dictates. Indeed, it is more acceptable to do something offensive than to impose, and nothing in the world is a greater imposition than to expect people to reflect and observe. We must avoid anything that tends in this direction, and in any case pursue in private what is unacceptable at public gatherings."

"In private you may well have downed a few bottles of wine and snoozed away many an hour of broad daylight," Louisa interrupted.

"I have never attached much importance to what I do," the old gentleman continued, "for I know that compared to other people I am very lazy. Nevertheless I have put together a collection that might afford many pleasant hours' entertainment to a company in our frame of mind."

"What kind of collection is it?" asked the Baroness.

"No doubt just a scandalous chronicle," Louisa chimed in.

"You are mistaken," said the old man.

"We'll see," replied Louisa.

"Let him have his say," said the Baroness. "And in any case don't get into the habit of speaking to people in a harsh and unfriendly way, not even if they pass it off as a joke. We have no reason to cultivate bad habits, even in fun. Tell me, my friend, what do you have in your collection? Will it provide suitable entertainment for us? Have you been collecting for long? Why haven't we heard about it before?"

"I will tell you about it," the old gentleman answered. "I have been in this world a long time and have always taken an interest in what happens to different people. I have neither the strength nor the courage to review the history of the world at large, and isolated historical episodes confuse me. But of the many personal histories, true and false, that circulate in public or are whispered about in private, some have a greater, more genuine charm than mere novelty; some amuse us by an ingenious twist; some reveal for a moment the innermost secrets of human nature; and others delight us by their bizarre absurdities. Countless stories attract our attention and our malice in ordinary life, and are as ordinary as the people who tell or live them. Of these I have collected the ones that I felt had some special quality that touched and intrigued my judgment, or my heart, and whose recollection gave me a moment of sincere, calm pleasure."

"I am very curious," said the Baroness, "to hear what kind of stories they are and what they are really about."

"As you can imagine," the old man replied, "they rarely deal with lawsuits or family problems. These subjects are usually of interest only to the people suffering from them."

LOUISA. "What are they about then?"

OLD MAN. "I will not deny that as a rule they treat of the feelings by which men and women are brought together or divided, made happy or unhappy, and more often confused than enlightened."

LOUISA. "Really? So you are trying to pass off a collection of lewd jokes as a refined entertainment? Forgive me, Mama, but it seems such an obvious conclusion, and after all, one ought to be allowed to speak the truth."

OLD MAN. "I hope that you will find in my whole collection nothing that I would term lewd."

LOUISA. "And what exactly do you term lewd?"

OLD MAN. "I cannot bear lewd talk or lewd stories, for they describe something that is vulgar, something not worth noticing or mentioning, as if it were remarkable and exciting, and they arouse spurious desires instead of occupying the mind with something pleasant. They conceal what we should either look at without veils or turn our eyes away from altogether."

LOUISA. "I don't understand you. Surely you intend to tell your stories with at least some elegance? You cannot plan to offend our ears with crude anecdotes? Is this to be a school for young ladies, and you think we should thank you in addition?"

OLD MAN. "Neither the one nor the other. In the first place, you will be learning nothing you did not know before, especially since for some time now I have observed that you never fail to read a certain kind of review in the journals."

LOUISA. "That was offensive."

OLD MAN. "You are to be married, and so I forgive you gladly. I simply wanted to show you that I, too, have arrows that I can use against you."

BARONESS. "I see what you're driving at, but make sure that she understands, too."

OLD MAN. "I need only repeat what I said at the beginning of our conversation. It appears that she hasn't the good will to listen."

LOUISA. "What does good will or all this chitchat have to do with it? However you look at it, they'll turn out to be scandalous stories, scandalous in one way or another, and nothing more."

OLD MAN. "Should I repeat, young lady, that a sensible person sees scandal only where he perceives malice or arrogance, the desire to do harm or unwillingness to help; and that he turns his eyes from sights like these? But he will be amused by minor faults and foibles, where a good person comes into mild conflict with himself, with his desires or intentions; where silly and conceited fools are shamed, reproved, or deceived; where presumption is punished in a natural, even casual way; where plans, desires, and hopes are first spoiled, blocked, and thwarted, and then quite unexpectedly furthered, fulfilled, and confirmed. But best of all he likes quietly to contemplate events in which chance plays with human weakness and inadequacy; and none of the heroes of those tales he preserves need fear his censure or expect his praise."

BARONESS. "Your introduction makes me eager to hear a sample. I was not aware—and we have generally moved in the same circles—that much had happened that would qualify for such a collection."

OLD MAN. "Of course, much depends on the observer and how he looks at it. But there again I won't deny that I have also taken many things from old books and traditions. Now and then you may enjoy meeting old friends in a new guise. But precisely this gives me an advantage, which I insist upon retaining: no one may interpret my stories!"

LOUISA. "But surely you won't forbid us to recognize our friends and neighbors and, if we like, decipher the riddle?"

OLD MAN. "By no means. But in such a case you must allow me in turn to pull out an ancient volume to prove that this story happened, or was made up, hundreds of years ago. In the same way you must allow me a secret smile if you take for an old fairy tale something that happened right before our eyes, but that you do not recognize in this form."

LOUISA. "You always have an answer. The best course is to make peace for this evening, and you can give us a quick little sample."

OLD MAN. "Please allow me in this case to be disobedient. I am saving this entertainment for the full assembled company. We must not deprive them of it, and I warn you ahead of time that nothing I will say has any intrinsic value. But if, after some serious conversation, people would like to relax a little while; if, after eating their fill of good things, they would fancy a light dessert, then I will be ready, and hope that the dish I serve will prove tasty."

BARONESS. "Then we will simply have to wait until tomorrow."

LOUISA. "I am extremely curious to find out what he will offer us!"

OLD MAN. "You ought not to be, Miss. High expectations are seldom gratified."

That evening after supper, while the Baroness retired early, the others remained together, talking about the latest news and rumors that were spreading. As is usual at such times they were uncertain what to believe and what to reject.

The old family companion said: "I think the most comfortable solution is to believe what pleases us and reject out of hand what does not, and to accept whatever else seems possible."

Someone remarked that this was how people normally behaved, and a few turns of the conversation brought them to the decided propensity of human nature to believe in the marvelous. They talked about the gothic and about the supernatural, and when the old man promised sometime to tell them good stories of this kind, Louisa replied: "It would be very nice of you, and we would appreciate it very much, if you would tell us one right now, since we are all together in the right mood. We would listen carefully and be very grateful."

Without needing to be asked twice, the Abbé began as follows:

"When I was living in Naples, an incident occurred that attracted a lot of attention, and about which peoples' verdicts were very different. Some claimed the story was a total fabrication, others that it was true but involved a fraud. The latter faction, in turn, was divided: they disagreed about who could have been the deceiver. Still others claimed that spiritual natures might well be able to influence physical bodies, and that miraculous occurrences need not invariably be regarded as either lies or frauds. Now for the story itself!

"A singer named Antonelli was in my time the darling of the Neapolitan public. In the flower of her youth, beauty, and talents, she lacked none of those qualities with which a woman charms and attracts the crowd, and delights a few chosen friends. She was not indifferent to fame and love, but being by nature moderate and sensible, she knew how to enjoy the pleasures of both without losing that self-control so essential to a woman in her position. All the young, wealthy, distinguished men flocked after her, but she accepted only a few. And although, in choosing her lovers, she generally followed her eyes and her heart, throughout her little adventures she displayed a firmness and strength of character that won respect from everyone who observed her closely. I had the opportunity to observe her for a time, while I was close to one of her favorites.

"Several years had passed and she had known plenty of men, and among them many fools, weak and unreliable. She had come to believe that a lover who in one certain respect fulfills a woman's every need, generally fails her precisely where she most needs his support: namely in personal crises, household affairs, or when quick decisions are needed. Indeed, she believed, he might actually harm her by thinking only of himself, and be driven in his selfishness to give her the worst possible advice and to lure her to the most dangerous steps.

"Her past relationships had generally failed to engage her intellect, and that too now required nourishment. She wanted finally to have a friend, and no sooner had she felt this need than there appeared among her suitors a young man in whom she immediately placed all her confidence, and who appeared in every way worthy of it.

"He was a Genoese who because of important business affairs was at the time living in Naples. The most careful education had enhanced his considerable natural talent. His knowledge was extensive, his mind and body fully developed, and his conduct was exemplary in that he never forgot himself, yet seemed always to forget himself in his interest for others. He had been blessed with the business acumen of his native city, and regarded all tasks from the long-term perspective. Yet his situation was far from ideal. His firm had embarked on some very risky speculations and was involved in dangerous lawsuits. As time went on, affairs grew even more complicated, and his concern about them lent him a melancholy air that was very becoming and gave our young woman the more courage to seek his friendship, because she felt that he too needed a friend.

"He had seen her so far only on public occasions. But at his first request, she allowed him to come to her home, indeed pressed him to visit her; and he did not fail to come.

"She wasted no time in revealing her confidence and her wish. He was amazed and pleased at her proposal. She earnestly begged him to remain her friend and to make none of the claims of a lover. She told him about a difficulty in which she was currently involved, and with his varied experience he was able to advise her most effectively and to act promptly to her advantage. He in turn confided his situation to her; and since she encouraged and comforted him, since ideas emerged in her presence that might otherwise not have occurred to him so quickly, she appeared to act as his adviser also. Thus a mutual friendship, based on the deepest respect and the noblest desires, had soon been established between them.

"But unfortunately when people accept conditions, they do not always consider whether they are possible. He had pledged to be only a friend and to make no claims to become her lover. Yet he could not deny that her accepted lovers were constantly in his way, and that he resented, indeed, utterly detested them. He found it especially painful when she capriciously entertained him with the good and bad points of one of them, all of whose faults she seemed to know clearly; and yet perhaps that very evening, as if to mock her esteemed friend, she might be resting in the arms of an unworthy man.

"Soon—whether fortunately or unfortunately—her heart again became free. Her friend observed this with pleasure and tried to show her that he most deserved the vacant place. She complied with his wishes, but not without resistance and reluctance. 'I fear,' she said, 'that by this concession I will lose the most valuable thing in the world, a friend.' She had predicted correctly. For scarcely had he functioned for a time in his dual capacity, than his demands became rather annoying. As a friend he required absolute respect; as a lover absolute affection; and as an intelligent and amiable man, constant entertainment. But this was by no means what the high-spirited girl had in mind. She had no vocation for self-sacrifice and no desire to concede exclusive rights to anyone. Therefore she tactfully arranged gradually to shorten his visits, to see him less often, and let him see that she would not give up her freedom for any price.

"As soon as he noticed, he was miserable, and unfortunately this blow did not fall alone, for his financial situation was deteriorating very badly. And he had only himself to blame, since from his youth he had treated his fortune as inexhaustible, and had neglected his business interests in order to travel and cut a more glamorous figure in society than his birth or income allowed. The lawsuits on which he set his hopes were costly and slow-moving. Because of them he went several times to Palermo, and during his last journey the shrewd girl made various changes in her living arrangements in order to detach him from her gradually. He came back to find her living at a different address, some distance from his own, and saw the Marquis of S - - -, who at that time exercised great influence in the theatrical world, coming and going freely from her home. This overwhelmed him, and he fell gravely ill. As soon as the news reached his mistress, she hastened to his bedside, looked after him, and arranged for his care. Learning that he was short of money, she left him a considerable sum, enough to reassure him for some time.

"By his presumptuous attempt to curb her freedom, her lover had already lost his attractiveness for her. As her affection for him decreased she observed him more closely; finally, the discovery that he had so grossly mismanaged his own affairs lowered her opinion of his good sense and character. In the meantime he did not notice the great change in her. Instead, her concern for his recovery, the constancy with which she spent half a day at a time at his bedside, seemed a sign of her friendship and love, rather than of her pity, and he hoped to be restored after his recovery to all his rights.

"How mistaken he was! In proportion as his health returned and his strength was renewed, her affection and confidence evaporated; indeed, he now seemed to her as tiresome as he had formerly been attractive. His temper, moreover, had, without his realizing it in the course of events, become extremely bitter and irritable; he cast all guilt for his troubles on others and insisted he had made no errors. He considered himself an aggrieved and troubled victim and expected compensation for all his wrongs and sufferings from the complete devotion of his mistress.

"He approached her with these claims as soon as he was able to go out and visit her. He demanded nothing less than that she devote herself exclusively to him, send away her other friends and acquaintances, give up the theater, and live with and for him alone. She showed him the impossibility of his demands, first playfully and then gravely, and in the end was unfortunately forced to tell him the sad truth that their relationship was completely at an end. He left and did not see her again.

"He lived a few years longer, seeing almost no one, indeed only a pious elderly lady who shared a house with him and lived on a small pension. During this time he won first one and, soon after, the other of his lawsuits; but his health had been undermined and his life's happiness lost. From some minor cause he again fell gravely ill; the doctor told him he would die. He heard the verdict without reluctance, but desired to see his beautiful mistress once more. He sent to her a servant who in happier times had brought him many favorable replies. He made his request; she refused. He sent a second time, imploring her to come; she persisted in her answer. Finally, it was already late at night, he sent a third time; she was upset and confided her difficulty to me, since I was just then having supper with the Marquis and several other friends at her home. I advised her and begged her to do her friend this final act of kindness; she seemed uncertain but after some reflection pulled herself together. She sent the servant away with her refusal, and he did not return.

"We sat talking freely after dinner and were all cheerful and in good spirits. It was around midnight when there suddenly sounded a plaintive, piercing, alarming, echoing cry. We started, looked at each other, and peered about to see what would happen next. The voice had emerged from the center of the room and seemed to die away along the walls. The Marquis stood up and sprang to the window, and the rest of us attended to the lady, who lay in a faint. Only slowly did she regain consciousness. No sooner had the jealous and impetuous Italian seen her eyes open than he bitterly reproached her. 'When you agree on signals with your friends,' he said, 'let them be less obvious and violent.' She replied with her usual presence of mind that as she had the right to see anyone in her home at any time, she would hardly choose to preface hours of pleasure with such melancholy and terrible sounds.

"And certainly the sound was incredibly frightening. Its long resounding vibrations had lingered in everyone's ears, indeed in our very limbs. She was pale, upset, and constantly on the verge of fainting; we had to stay with her half the night. Nothing further was heard. The next night the same company, not as cheerful as the day before, but calm enough; and—at the same hour the same violent, fearful sound.

"Meanwhile we had made countless conjectures about the nature and source of the cry and exhausted our ideas. Why should I go into detail? Whenever she dined at home, the cry was heard at the same time; sometimes it seemed louder and sometimes fainter. All Naples was talking about it. All the servants, all her friends and acquaintances were concerned, and the police were even called in. Spies and watchmen were posted. From the street the sound seemed to originate in the open air; inside the room, it was also heard right at hand. When she dined out nothing was heard; whenever she was at home the sound came.

"But even away from home she was not completely safe from this malicious companion. Her charm had gained her entry to the most distinguished houses. She was welcome everywhere as good company, and to elude her malevolent guest she had grown accustomed to spending her evenings out.

"A man respected for his age and position was driving her home one evening in his carriage. As she is parting from him outside her door the sound starts between the two of them, and the man, who knew the story as well as a thousand others, is lifted into his carriage more dead than alive.

"Another time a young tenor of whom she was fond is driving through the city with her in the evening to visit a friend. He had heard people talk about this strange phenomenon and, being a light-hearted sort, was skeptical about such a miracle. They talked about the situation. 'I'd like to hear the voice of your invisible companion, too,' he said. 'Call him up! After all there are two of us and we won't be afraid!' Recklessness or fearlessness—I don't know what impelled her—but she calls the spirit, and at that moment the deafening sound comes right from the middle of the carriage. It sounds quickly three times in a row, very loud, and disappears, with a whimpering echo. They were both found unconscious in the carriage outside her friend's house; it took some effort to revive them and find out what had happened.

"It was some time before she recovered. The constant fright undermined her health and the sonorous ghost seemed to grant her a reprieve; indeed, she even hoped, because it was silent for so long, that she was completely free of it at last. But this hope was premature.

"At the end of Carnival she took a trip with another woman and a chambermaid. She wanted to make a visit in the country; night fell before they could reach their destination, and when, in addition, something went wrong with the carriage, they had to spend the night in an uncomfortable inn and manage as best they could.

"Her friend was already in bed and, having lit a night light, the maid was just about to get into the other bed with her mistress when the latter said to her jokingly: 'Here we are at the end of the earth and the weather is dreadful; do you think he could find us here?' At once he was heard, louder and more terrible than ever. Her friend literally thought that the devil was in the room, jumped out of bed, ran down the stairs just as she was, and roused the whole house. No one closed an eye that night. Yet this was also the last time the cry was heard. Unfortunately, however, the uninvited guest soon found another, even more annoying way to make his presence known.

"He had kept quiet for some time when suddenly one evening at the usual hour, as she was dining with her guests, a shot, as if from a shotgun or heavily loaded pistol, came through the window. Everyone heard the report, everyone saw the flash, but careful inspection of the glass revealed no damage at all. Nevertheless they took the incident very seriously, and everyone believed that her life was in danger. They hurried to the police; the neighboring houses were investigated and when nothing suspicious was found, sentries were posted next day from cellar to attic. Her house was carefully searched, lookouts were assigned to the street.

"All these precautions were in vain. For three months in succession, the shot came at the same moment through the same windowpane without damaging the glass and—remarkably—always exactly one hour before midnight, despite the fact that Naples is on Italian time and no real account is taken of the midnight hour.

"People finally grew accustomed to this manifestation as they had to the other and paid little attention to the ghost's harmless mischief. Often the shot failed to frighten the company or to interrupt their conversation.

"One evening after a very hot day, without thinking about the time, she opened the window in question and stepped out onto the balcony with the Marquis. They had been standing outside for only a few minutes when the shot rang out between them and they were flung backwards into the room, where they reeled to the floor in a faint. When they had recovered he felt on his left cheek, and she on her right, the pain of a hard slap, and since they had suffered no further injury, the incident inspired a variety of witty exchanges.

"After that the shot was not heard again and she thought that she was at last truly free of her invisible persecutor; but one evening when she was out with a friend, an unexpected adventure once again completely terrified her. Their way led through the Chiaia, where her Genoese beloved had formerly lived. There was bright moonlight. The lady sitting beside her asked: 'Isn't that the house where Mr. ---- died?' 'As far as I know it's one of those two,' said the beauty, and at that moment the shot rang out from one of the two houses, and went right through the carriage. The coachman thought they had been attacked and drove off as fast as he could. At their destination the two women were lifted from the carriage, to all appearances dead.

"But this scare was also the last. The invisible companion changed his methods, and a few evenings later loud applause sounded outside her windows. As a popular singer and actress she was more accustomed to this sound. There was nothing inherently frightening about it, and it could more readily be attributed to one of her admirers. She took little notice of it; her friends were more concerned and posted sentries as before. They heard the sound but saw no one before or after, and most of them hoped that these phenomena would soon end completely.

"After a time this sound dissipated also, and changed to more pleasant tones. They were, to be sure, not actually melodious, but they were unbelievably pleasant and delightful. To the most careful observers they seemed to come from a nearby street corner, to float through the air up to the window, and then softly die away. It was as if a heavenly spirit wanted to draw attention by a beautiful prelude to a melody he was just about to perform. Even this tone finally disappeared and was not heard again after the whole strange affair had gone on for about a year and a half."

As the narrator paused for a moment, the others began to express their thoughts and doubts whether the story was true, whether it even could be true.

The old gentleman said that it must be true for anyone to find it interesting, since it had little enough merit as fiction. Then someone remarked that it seemed strange that no inquiries had been made about the deceased friend and the circumstances of his death, since this might perhaps have thrown some light on the affair.

"That did happen," the old man replied. "I myself was curious enough, right after the first incident, to go to his house and find a pretext to visit the lady who at the end had cared for him like a mother. She told me that her friend had had an unbelievable passion for the young woman, that at the end of his life he had spoken almost exclusively of her, and had talked about her sometimes as an angel, sometimes as a devil.

"As his illness overpowered him, she said, he had wished for nothing but to see her once again before he died, probably only in the hope of wresting from her some expression of tenderness, remorse, or some other token of love and friendship. Thus her persistent refusal had been dreadful for him indeed, and her last, decisive refusal had visibly hastened his end. In despair he had cried out: ‘No, nothing shall help her! She avoids me; but even after my death she shall have no peace from me!’ With these angry words he died, and we learned but too well that promises can be kept beyond the grave.”

Once again the company began to offer opinions and judgments about the story. At last brother Fritz said: “I have a suspicion, which, however, I don’t want to tell, until I have reviewed all the circumstances again and tested my conclusions.”

When they pressed him harder he tried to avoid a reply by offering to tell a story himself, one which was, he said, of course less interesting than the previous tale, but also of the sort that could never be explained with complete certainty.

“In the home of an upright nobleman, a friend of mine, who lived in an old castle with his large family, there was an orphan girl being raised. By the time she was fourteen she mostly attended the lady of the house and acted as her personal servant. They were perfectly satisfied with her, and she seemed to wish for nothing more than to show gratitude to her benefactors by her attentiveness and loyalty. She was attractive and there were suitors who approached her. The family did not think a match with any of them was likely to make her happy, nor did she manifest even the slightest desire to change her state.

“All of a sudden, whenever the girl went about the house doing her work, knocking was heard here and there under her feet. At first it seemed a coincidence, but since the knocking did not stop and accompanied virtually her every step, she grew nervous and hardly dared to leave her mistress’s room, the only place where she was left in peace.

“This knocking was heard by everyone who walked with her or stood nearby. At first it seemed funny, but finally it became unpleasant. The master of the house, a quick-witted man, now investigated the circumstances himself. The knocking was not heard until the girl walked, and moreover not when she put her foot down but only when she raised it to take the next step. But often the blows came irregularly, and they were especially loud whenever she walked diagonally across a great hall.

“The head of the family had some workmen there one day, and when the knocking was at its loudest, he had them tear up some floorboards right behind her. Nothing was found except that a few large rats were exposed, which were hunted with great commotion.

“Irritated by this event and by the confusion, the master seized on a harsh expedient; he took his largest hunting whip down from the wall, and swore to beat the life out of the girl, if the knocking were ever heard again. From that time on she went all over the house without a tap, and no further knocking was heard.”

"Which clearly shows," Louisa interrupted, "that the pretty child was her own ghost and for some reason had been playing this prank and pulling her master's leg."

"By no means," replied Fritz. "The people who attributed the effect to a ghost believed that a protective spirit wanted the girl out of the house, but did not wish her any harm. Others were more skeptical and thought that one of her lovers had been smart enough or clever enough to make the sounds, in order to drive the girl out of the house and into his arms. In any case the dear child almost wasted away over the incident and looked like a sad ghost, although once she had been brisk and cheerful, the happiest person in the house. But there is more than one way to explain a physical decline like that."

"It's a shame," Carl replied, "that cases like this are not investigated thoroughly, and that to judge events that interest us so much we must always waver among different probabilities, because not all the circumstances under which such wonders occur have been recorded."

"If only it were not so very difficult to investigate," said the old man, "and to keep all the points and issues that are truly important in mind, at the moment when something like this occurs, so that nothing escapes where deception and error could hide. Is it, after all, so easy to detect a conjuror's tricks, even though we know he's deluding us?"

Scarcely had he finished speaking when a very loud crack was suddenly heard in the corner of the room. Everyone jumped, and Carl joked, "Surely we are not hearing from a dying lover?"

He wished he could have taken back his words, for Louisa turned pale and confessed that she feared for her fiancé's life.

To distract her Fritz picked up the light and went over to the desk standing in the corner. Its curved top was cracked all the way across. They had found the source of the sound; nevertheless it seemed remarkable that this desk, which was an example of Röntgen's best workmanship and which had been standing for several years on the same spot, should have happened to split at just this moment. It had often been praised and exhibited as a model of outstanding and durable carpentry, and now it seemed odd that it should suddenly split without the slightest detectable change in the weather.

"Hurry," said Carl, "let's check this aspect first and look at the barometer!"

The mercury stood exactly where it had for the last few days; and the thermometer had dropped no more than was natural between day and night.

"What a shame we have no hygrometer," he exclaimed. "That's just the instrument we need!"

"It seems," remarked the old man, "that we are always missing the most necessary instruments, when we want to experiment on spirits."

Their reflections were interrupted by a servant who entered in haste and reported that a great fire could be seen in the sky but that no one knew whether it was in the town or their vicinity.

Since the preceding events had made them more susceptible to fright, they were all the more upset by the news than they might have been otherwise. Fritz hurried to the belvedere, where a detailed map of the country was drawn on a large horizontal disk; by this means the locations of various places could be determined fairly exactly even at night. The others waited together, not without anxiety and agitation.

Fritz came back and said: "I have bad news. In all probability the fire is not in town, but on our aunt's estate. I know the area very well and fear I am not mistaken." They lamented the beautiful buildings and calculated the loss. "All the same," said Fritz, "a peculiar notion has come to me that can at least reassure us about the strange portent of the desk. First of all we need to figure out the exact minute at which we heard the sound." They calculated back, and decided it might have been about eleven-thirty.

"Now, you can laugh if you like," Fritz continued, "but I am going to tell you what I suspect. You know that several years ago our mother gave a similar, indeed, one might say, identical, desk to our aunt. Both were made with extreme care at the same time, from the same piece of wood, by the same craftsman. Both of them have lasted splendidly until now, and I would wager that at this moment the other desk is burning up with our aunt's summerhouse and that its twin here is suffering with it. Tomorrow I shall go myself and attempt to verify this strange fact as well as I can."

Whether Frederick really believed what he said or was just trying to calm his sister's fears is unclear; nevertheless, they seized this opportunity to talk about many undeniable sympathies, and in the end decided that a sympathy between pieces of wood grown from one trunk, between works fashioned by one artist, was quite probable. Indeed, they agreed that phenomena of this sort were just as natural as others that occur repeatedly, that we can hold in our own hands and that even then we cannot explain.

"In any case," said Carl, "it seems to me that every phenomenon, like every fact, is interesting in and of itself. Anyone who explains it or relates it to other events really only does it for the fun of it and is teasing us, like a scientist, for example, or a historian. But in fact, a single action or event is interesting not because it is explicable or probable, but because it is true. If the flames destroyed our aunt's desk around midnight, then the strange crack in ours at the same time is a true event for us, regardless of whether it is explicable and what it may relate to."

Late as it was, no one felt any inclination to go to bed, and Carl offered to tell a story too, which, he said, was no less interesting than the previous ones, though it might perhaps be more readily explained and understood.

"Marshal de Bassompierre," he said, "tells it in his memoirs. Allow me to speak in his name:

"For five or six months I had noticed, whenever I crossed the little bridge (for at that time the Pont Neuf had not yet been built) and passed the Sign of the Two Angels, that a beautiful shopkeeper curtsied to me deeply and repeatedly and watched me as far as she could. Struck by her behavior, I returned her gaze and thanked her politely. Once I was riding from Fontainebleau to Paris, and as I once more crossed the little bridge, she stepped to the door of her shop and said to me as I rode by: 'Your servant, sir!' I returned her greeting, and as I looked back from time to time, I saw that she had leaned further out to watch me as long as possible.

"A servant was with me, as well as a postilion whom I intended to send back to Fontainebleau that very evening with letters to several ladies. At my order the servant dismounted and went to tell the young woman in my name that I had noticed how she watched and greeted me, and that if she wished to become better acquainted, I would visit her wherever she desired.

"She responded to the servant that he could not have brought better news, and that she would come to whatever place I appointed, with the sole condition that she be permitted to spend a night in the same bed with me.

"I accepted the offer, and asked the servant if he knew of some place where we could meet. He answered that he would take her to a certain procuress; but because there had been outbreaks of plague, he advised me to bring mattresses, blankets and sheets from my own home. I accepted his offer and he promised to prepare me a comfortable bed.

"That evening I went and found a very beautiful woman about twenty years old, in a dainty night-cap, a very fine nightgown, a short green woolen petticoat. She had slippers on her feet and a kind of loose robe thrown over her. I was enchanted, and when I tried to fondle her she politely declined my caresses and asked to lie with me between two sheets. I did as she wished and can say that I have never known a finer woman nor have ever had more pleasure from any. Next morning I asked if I couldn't see her again, since I wasn't leaving until Sunday and we had spent Thursday night together.

"She replied that she certainly wanted to even more than I did, but unless I stayed in town all day Sunday it was impossible, because she could not see me again until Sunday night. When I raised some objections she said: 'You are probably tired of me right now and would like to leave on Sunday; but soon you will remember me and will surely be willing to give up one day in order to spend a night with me.'

"I was easy to persuade and promised to stay Sunday and to come to the same place that evening. Then she answered: 'I know very well, sir, that I have come to a house of ill repute for your sake; but I did it by choice, and my desire for you was so overpowering that I would have agreed to anything. Passion brought me to this dreadful place, but I would consider myself an ordinary prostitute, if I came a second time. Let me die a miserable death if I have ever been available to any man besides my husband and you, and if I ever desire any other! But what would I not do for someone I love, and for a Bassompierre? For his sake I have come to this house, for a man who has made this place respectable by his presence. If you want to see me again, I will meet you at my aunt's house.'

"She described the house to me in great detail and continued: 'I shall expect you between ten and midnight; indeed the door shall be open even later. First you will find a small hallway; don't linger there, for my aunt's door opens on it. Right after comes a staircase, which will take you to the second floor, where I will welcome you with open arms.'

"I made my arrangements, sent on my servants and belongings, and waited impatiently for Sunday night, when I would see the beautiful creature again. By ten o'clock I was already at the appointed place. I found the door she had indicated at once, but it was locked tight, and in the whole house there was light, which seemed to flare up from time to time like a fire. Impatiently I began to knock to announce my arrival, but I heard a man's voice ask who was there.

"I went away and walked around in the streets. Finally desire drew me back to the door. I found it open and rushed through the corridor, up the stairs. But to my amazement I saw two people in the room burning bedstraw and, in the firelight which lit up the whole room, two naked bodies stretched out on the table. I hastily withdrew and on the way out bumped into a pair of gravediggers who asked me what I wanted. I drew my sword to keep them off and went home, not unshaken by this strange sight. Immediately I drank three or four glasses of wine, a remedy against plague that people swear by in Germany, and, after I had rested, began my journey to Lorraine the following day.

"Every effort that I made after my return to learn something about the woman was in vain. I even went to the shop of the Two Angels, but the tenants did not know who had been there before them.

"This encounter involved a person of the lower classes, but I do assure you that except for the disagreeable outcome it would have been one of the most charming I can recall. I have never been able to remember that beautiful little woman without regret."

"This riddle is not so easy either," replied Fritz. "It's never clear whether the nice little woman also died of plague in the house, or whether she only stayed away to avoid it."

"If she'd still been alive," replied Carl, "surely she would have waited for her lover on the street, and no danger would have kept her from seeking him again. I'm afraid she was lying with the others on the table."

"Hush!" said Louisa. "The story is too dreadful. What kind of night will we have if we go to bed with such ideas!"

"I just thought of another story," said Carl, "which is pleasanter and which Bassompierre tells about one of his ancestors:

"A beautiful woman who greatly loved this ancestor met him every Monday in his summerhouse, where he spent the night with her, letting his wife believe meanwhile that he spent this time hunting.

"For two years they had been meeting this way without interruption, when the wife became suspicious, stole to the summerhouse one morning, and found her husband sound asleep with his mistress. She had neither the nerve nor the will to awaken them; instead she took the veil from her head and spread it over the feet of the sleepers.

"When the woman awoke and noticed the veil she cried out, mourned aloud, and lamented that she would not be allowed to see her lover again nor indeed even to come within a hundred miles of him. She left him after she had presented him three gifts—a small fruit measure, a ring and a goblet—for the three daughters of his marriage and enjoined him to take the greatest care of these talismans. They were carefully preserved, and the descendants of the three daughters believed that their possession was the cause of many a stroke of good luck."

"This looks more like the story of beautiful Melusina and other fairy tales like that," said Louisa.

"But the same kind of tradition and a similar talisman has been preserved in our family," replied Frederick.

"What do you mean?" asked Carl.

"It's a secret," he answered. "Only the eldest son may learn it from his father and possess the precious object after his death."

"So you have it in safekeeping?" asked Louisa.

"I think I've already said too much," replied Frederick, lighting the candle and preparing to depart.

The family had breakfasted together as usual and the Baroness was again seated at her embroidery frame. After a few minutes of general silence their friend the Abbé began with a smile: "It is rare for singers, poets, and storytellers who promise to entertain a company to do so at the right time. Instead they usually have to be urged when they ought to be willing, and insist when people would rather decline their performance. So I hope I will be an exception when I ask if it would appeal to you to hear a story now."

"Yes indeed," replied the Baroness, "and I believe the others will all agree. But if you want to give us a sample story, I must tell you what kind I don't like. I do not enjoy stories in which, as in the Thousand and One Nights, one action is embedded within another and one interest is crowded out by the next, where the storyteller feels he must stimulate the curiosity he has thoughtlessly aroused by interruption, and, rather than reward attention with a rational sequence of events, use bizarre, cheap tricks to keep it at high pitch. I think it is wrong to try to transform stories that ought to approach the unity of a poem into mystical riddles, and so to corrupt taste more and more. The subject matter I leave entirely to you, but let us at least see by the form that we are in good society. Give us to begin with a story with few characters and events, imaginative and well-constructed, true-to-life, natural and not commonplace; with as much action as essential and as much sentiment as necessary. It should not be static nor move too slowly, but it should not move too fast either. The characters should be the kind of people we like, not perfect but good, not extraordinary but interesting and likable. Let your story entertain us in the telling, satisfy us when it is over, and leave behind some urge to reflect further upon it."

"If I didn't know you better, my lady," replied the Abbé, "I would believe it was your intention with these exalted and strict requirements to discredit my wares before I've even had a chance to display them. It must be rare indeed for anyone to meet your standards! Even now," he continued, when he had reflected a little, "I'll have to defer the story I had in mind, and I really don't know whether in my haste I may not be choosing badly, if right now on the spur of the moment I begin with an old story that I have always been rather fond of:

"In an Italian seaport there once lived a merchant who had been known from his youth for industry and shrewdness. He was also a good sailor and had amassed great wealth by sailing to Alexandria in order to buy or trade for costly merchandise, which he then sold again at home or shipped to the northern parts of Europe. His fortune grew from year to year, the more so because his business was his greatest pleasure and left him no time for expensive diversions.

"Into his fiftieth year he had been entirely absorbed in this manner and had learned little of the social amusements with which ordinary citizens season their lives. Nor, despite all the charms of his countrywomen, had the fair sex ever attracted his notice, except that he knew their love for jewelry and precious objects and could on occasion exploit it.

"He was scarcely prepared, therefore, for his change of heart when his ship entered his native port one day with a rich cargo, just at the time of an annual festival celebrated especially for children. After church, boys and girls gaily made their way through the city in all sorts of costumes, sometimes in processions, sometimes in crowds, and then, in a large open field, they played all kinds of games, performed tricks and feats of skill, and competed for small prizes.

"At first our sailor enjoyed this celebration. But as he watched the excitement of the children and the pleasure of the parents, and as he saw so many people enjoying both present happiness and the pleasantest of prospects, he was greatly struck, when he returned home, by his own solitary state. For the first time his empty house made him uneasy, and his thoughts were filled with self-reproach.

" 'What a miserable fool I am! Why have my eyes been opened so late? Why is it only in old age that I come to see what really makes a man happy? All that effort, all those dangers! And for what? My vaults are full of goods, my chests full of precious metals, and my cabinets full of jewelry and gems; yet none of these makes me happy or satisfied. The more of them I pile up, the more companions they demand: one gem calls for another, one gold coin demands the next. They don't recognize me as master; they call out imperiously: "Go hurry, fetch still more of us! Gold loves only gold, jewels only jewels." They have commanded me this way my whole life long, and only too late do I realize that this brings me no enjoyment. Only now, alas, as the years advance, do I begin to reflect and say to myself: You don't enjoy these treasures and no one will enjoy them after you! Have you ever adorned a beloved wife with them? Have you given them to a daughter as a dowry? Have you given a son the opportunity to win and hold the affection of a fine girl? Never! Of all your possessions neither you nor anyone who belongs to you has ever possessed a single one; and everything you have amassed with such effort will be squandered thoughtlessly by some stranger after your death.

" 'Oh, how different it is for those happy parents who will gather their children around the table tonight, praise their skill, and encourage them to do well. How their eyes were shining this afternoon; what hope the present moment seemed to give them! But should you really have no hope at all? Are you already a greybeard then? Isn't it good that I understand the omission, now, when there is still time? No, at your age it's still not foolish to think of marriage. With your wealth you will win a good wife and make her happy, and if you do have children in your home, these later fruits will bring you great happiness, unlike those that come from Heaven too soon, and become a burden and source of perplexity.'

"Having strengthened his resolve with this monologue, he sent for two members of his crew and told them his thoughts. Always ready and willing, they did not fail him now, and hurried into the city to discover the youngest and most beautiful girls; they were determined that their master, once he desired this new ware, should have the very best.

"He himself was no more idle than his deputies. He went out, asked questions, looked and listened, and soon found what he sought in a young woman who currently deserved to be called the most beautiful in the whole city. She was about sixteen, handsome and well brought up; her figure and manner seemed most attractive and promising.

"After a brief negotiation, which secured her a most advantageous position during the lifetime and after the death of her husband, the wedding was celebrated with great pomp and gaiety, and from this day on our merchant felt himself in true possession and enjoyment of his wealth for the first time. Now he joyfully used his finest and richest fabrics to clothe the beautiful body; the jewels shone far more brightly on the breast and in the hair of his beloved than in the jewel case, and his rings gained inestimable value from the hand that wore them.

"So he felt not merely as rich as before, but even richer, for his goods seemed to increase with sharing and use. In this way the couple lived for almost a year in the greatest contentment, and he seemed to have entirely exchanged his love of activity and wandering for the enjoyment of domestic bliss. But it is not easy to give up an old habit, and although we can be temporarily diverted from a course we embarked on when young, we can never leave it altogether.

"So our merchant often felt the stirrings of his old passion when he saw others boarding ship or returning happily to port. Even at home with his wife he frequently felt restless and dissatisfied. This desire increased with time and finally grew into such yearning that he became extremely unhappy and at last really ill.

" 'What will become of you now?' he said to himself. 'Now you've discovered how foolish it is to exchange late in life an old way for a new one. How can we drive what we've always done and struggled for out of our thoughts, out of our very bones? And look what's happening to me, who always loved water like a fish and the open air like a bird, now that I've shut myself up with all my treasures and with the flower of all riches, a beautiful young woman? I'd hoped to find contentment and enjoy my possessions; instead I seem to be losing everything by not adding any more. It's wrong to call people fools who work with restless activity to heap goods upon goods, for activity is happiness, and to those who can experience the joys of unremitting effort, the wealth they earn has no significance. I'm growing wretched from lack of activity, sick from lack of exercise, and if I don't decide on something, I'll soon be almost dead.

" 'Of course it is a risky undertaking to part from a young, charming wife. Is it fair to court an attractive and susceptible girl, and then leave her to herself, to boredom, to her sensations and her longings? Aren't there sleek young men already strolling up and down before my windows? Aren't they already trying, in church and in the parks, to catch my wife's attention? And when I am gone? Shall I believe that my wife might be saved by a miracle? No, at her age, with her constitution, it would be silly to hope that she could refrain from the joys of love. If you go away, on your return you will have lost your wife's love and her fidelity, along with the honor of your house.'

"Such considerations and doubts, with which he tortured himself for a while, made his condition much worse. His wife, his relatives, and his friends worried about him but could not discover the cause of his illness. Finally he again took counsel with himself and after some thought exclaimed: 'You fool! You're driving yourself mad trying to keep a wife whom, if your problem persists, you'll have left behind you for some other man anyway. Doesn't it at least make more sense to try to stay alive, even at the risk of losing that in her which is considered woman's most valuable possession? How many men can't prevent the loss of this treasure even by their presence, and patiently do without what they cannot preserve! Why shouldn't you have the courage to renounce such a thing, since your life depends on this decision?'

"With these words he took heart and summoned his crew. He ordered them to load up a vessel as usual and to have everything ready, so that they could be off at the first favorable wind. Then he explained to his wife as follows:

" 'Do not be concerned if you see a bustle from which you might conclude that I am planning to leave. Do not be distressed if I confess that I am planning to undertake another sea voyage. My love for you is still the same and will certainly remain so throughout my life. I know the value of the happiness I have till now enjoyed at your side, and I would enjoy it still more if I did not often have to reproach myself in secret for laziness and inactivity. My old habits are reviving, and my old life lures me once more. Let me see the market of Alexandria again; I will visit it now even more eagerly because I plan to get the most precious fabrics and the finest treasures there for you. I will leave you in possession of all my goods and my entire fortune; use it and enjoy yourself with your parents and family! The time of separation will also pass, and we shall meet again with joy.'

"Not without tears did the dear woman make him the tenderest reproaches, assuring him that she would not pass one happy hour without him; and, since she neither could nor would restrain him, she begged only that he remember her always, even in his absence.

"After he had discussed various matters and domestic affairs with her, he said, after a brief pause: 'There is one more thing which you must allow me to talk about freely; only I beg you please not to misinterpret what I say, but even in this concern to recognize my love for you.'

" 'I can already guess,' replied the lady. 'You are worried about me, because like all men you think our sex is unalterably weak. You have known me only to be young and gay, so now you think that in your absence I will be careless and led astray. I don't reproach you for this attitude; it's normal for you men. But as I know my own heart, I can assure you that nothing shall make an impression on me so easily, and that no impression can possibly be so deep as to tempt me from the path of love and duty that I have walked thus far. Have no fear; you will find your wife as tender and faithful at your return as you used to find her of an evening when you returned to my arms after a brief absence.'

" 'I believe that you mean this,' her husband answered, 'and hope you will persist. But let us consider the extreme case; why shouldn't we be prepared for that as well? You know how much your beauty and figure attract the gaze of our young fellow-townsmen. In my absence they will be after you even more than before; they will try everything to approach and to please you. The image of your husband will not always chase them from your door and from your heart, as his presence does now. You are a good and noble child, but the demands of nature are just and powerful; they are in constant conflict with reason, and usually carry off the victory. Don't interrupt me! You will certainly, in my absence, dutifully though you remember me, feel the desire whereby woman attracts man and is attracted by him. I will remain for a time the object of your desires; but who knows what circumstances, what opportunities may arise—and another man will reap in reality what imagination had intended for me. Don't be impatient; I beg you, hear me out!

" 'Should it come to pass—that which you think impossible and which I certainly do not wish to encourage—that you can no longer do without a man's company nor forego the joys of love, then promise me only not to choose in my place one of those thoughtless boys who, handsome though they may be, are more dangerous to a woman's honor, even, than to her virtue. Ruled more by vanity than by desire, they chase after any woman, and think nothing more natural than to sacrifice one for the next. If you feel like looking for a lover, look for one who deserves the name, one who can modestly and discreetly enhance the joys of love by the virtue of secrecy.'

"At this the beautiful woman hid her sorrow no longer, and her tears, which she had held back until now, flowed freely from her eyes. 'Whatever you may think of me,' she cried after a passionate embrace, 'nothing could be further from my thoughts than this crime that you apparently consider inevitable. If I ever so much as dream of such a thing, may the earth open and swallow me up, and may all hope of that bliss be snatched from me, which promises us such a joyous continuation of our existence. Lay aside your mistrust and leave me my pure virtuous hope that I will soon see you in my arms again!'

"After he had tried to calm his wife in every possible way, he set sail the next morning. His journey prospered and he soon reached Alexandria.

"Meanwhile his wife lived in tranquil possession of a large fortune with every pleasure and comfort, but in seclusion, seeing no one but her parents and relations; and while her husband's business was carried on by faithful servants, she lived in a great mansion in whose splendid rooms she daily renewed with pleasure the memory of her spouse.

"But however quiet and secluded the life she led, the young men of the city had not remained idle. They did not fail to pass frequently before her window and tried in the evening to attract her attention with music and song. At first the lonely beauty found these attentions disagreeable and annoying, but she soon grew used to them, and in the long evenings allowed herself to enjoy the serenades as a pleasant entertainment without worrying about where they came from. At the same time she could not help sighing for her absent loved one.

"Instead of gradually growing weary, as she had hoped, her unknown admirers seemed to increase their efforts and make them permanent. She could already distinguish the recurring instruments and voices, the repeated melodies, and soon could no longer resist the curiosity to know who the unknown men might be, and especially who were the most persistent. She could surely—as a pastime—allow herself such interest.

"So she began, from time to time, to look through her curtains and shutters out onto the street to see who was passing, and especially to note the men who gazed at her windows the longest. They were mostly handsome and well-dressed young people, who revealed in their gestures, however, as in their whole outward appearance, as much frivolity as vanity. In their attentions to her house they seemed more concerned to draw notice to themselves than to show devotion to her.

" 'Truly,' the lady sometimes said to herself jokingly, 'my husband knew what he was doing! With the condition under which he permits me a lover, he excludes everyone who is after me and who might appeal to me. He knows well that prudence, modesty, and discretion are qualities of maturity, qualities that our reason may value, but that have no capacity to stir our imagination or excite our affection. From these men who besiege my house with compliments I am safe, because they can awaken no trust; and those to whom I could give my trust, I find not the least bit appealing.'

"In the security of these thoughts she allowed herself more and more to enjoy the music and the appearance of the young men passing by, and without her noticing it there gradually grew a restless longing in her breast that she did not think to resist until it was too late. Loneliness and idleness, comfortable, easy, and rich living were a breeding-ground in which wayward desire could develop faster than the good child realized.

"Now she began, though with secret sighs, to admire, among her husband's other merits, his knowledge of the world and of human nature, and especially his knowledge of a woman's heart. 'So, it was possible after all, what I so vehemently denied,' she said to herself, 'and it really was necessary for me to be warned to be cautious and prudent in such a case! But what use are caution and prudence, when pitiless chance seems only to toy with a vague desire! How am I to choose a man I do not know? And once we are better acquainted, is there any choice left?'

"With such thoughts and a hundred others the lovely woman aggravated the malady, which had already spread far enough. In vain she tried to distract herself; every pleasant object excited her emotions, and even in the deepest solitude her emotions evoked pleasurable images in her imagination.

"Such was her state when her relatives told her, along with other gossip of the city, that a young lawyer who had been studying in Bologna had just returned to his native city. They could not say enough in his praise. With all his extraordinary knowledge he displayed a prudence and skill uncommon in young men, and with a very attractive appearance showed the greatest modesty. As an attorney he had soon won the confidence of the townspeople and the respect of the judges. Every day he appeared at the courthouse in order to see to his affairs and to further them.

"The fair one heard the description of such a perfect man not without desiring to meet him, and not without secretly wishing to find in him the man to whom she could give her heart according to her husband's own precept. How attentive she was, therefore, when she heard that he passed by her house daily; and how carefully she noted the hour when lawyers customarily assembled at the courthouse! Not without emotion did she finally see him pass, and although his handsome looks and his youth of necessity charmed her, it was his modesty, on the other hand, that caused her anxiety.

"For several days she had secretly observed him and could now no longer resist the desire to attract his attention. She dressed with care, stepped onto the balcony, and her heart pounded when she saw him come along the street. But how distressed, indeed ashamed, she was, when he passed as usual with measured pace, sunk in reflection and with downcast eyes, and continued on his way with the utmost propriety, without even noticing her.

"Vainly she tried several days in a row to gain his attention in the same way. Always he proceeded at his usual pace, without raising his eyes or looking to either side. The more she observed him, however, the more he seemed to her the very man she so needed. Her liking became more intense with each day, and was finally, as she did not resist it, utterly overwhelming. 'What!' she said to herself, 'after your noble, sensible husband foresaw your state in his absence, and now that his prediction has come true that you can't live without a friend and favorite, must you languish and pine away when fortune has shown you a young man—just to your taste, just to the taste of your husband—with whom you could savor the joys of love in impenetrable secrecy? It is foolish to let opportunity slip, foolish to resist overpowering love!' With these and many other thoughts she tried to stiffen her resolve, and only briefly did she toss about in uncertainty. Then finally, as often happens, a passion we have long resisted carries us suddenly away, and so enflames us that we scornfully dismiss as trifling all concern and fear, reserve and shame, circumstances and obligations. So all of a sudden she rashly resolved to send her young serving maid to the beloved man and, regardless of the cost, to have him.

"The girl hurried off, found him sitting at dinner with several friends, and punctually delivered the message as her mistress had instructed her. The young lawyer was not surprised at this message. He had known the merchant in his youth; he knew him to be away at present; and although he had heard only vaguely about his marriage, he surmised that in her husband's absence the wife probably required legal assistance in some important business matter. Thus he answered the girl most courteously, and promised that as soon as the meal was over he would wait upon her mistress without delay. With inexpressible joy the lady heard that she was soon to see and speak to her beloved. She hastened to dress in her best clothes and had her house and apartments quickly arranged as neatly as possible. Orange leaves and flowers were strewn, the sofa covered with the most exquisite tapestries. So the brief period of waiting passed busily, which would otherwise have dragged unbearably.

"With what emotion did she advance to meet him when at last he arrived, in what confusion, as she sank down upon the couch, did she bid him sit upon an ottoman right beside it! She was struck dumb in the presence of what she had so desired; she had not considered what she would say to him. He too was silent and sat modestly before her. Finally she took courage and said, not without anxiety and constraint:

" 'Sir, you've returned to your native city only recently, and already you are known everywhere as a talented and reliable man. I, too, am placing my trust in you, in an important and peculiar situation which, as I think about it, is perhaps more appropriate to a confessor than a legal adviser. For a year I have been married to an honorable and wealthy man, who, as long as we lived together, treated me with the greatest consideration; and I would have no complaints about him, if a restless desire to travel and trade had not some time ago torn him from my arms.

" 'Being a sensible and fair man, he realized the injustice he did me by going away. He understood that a young woman could not be stored like jewels and pearls; he knew rather that she resembled a garden full of beautiful fruit, which would be lost for everyone as well as for the master, if he stubbornly chose to lock its gates for several years. Before his departure, therefore, he spoke to me very seriously. He assured me that I would not be able to live without a lover; he not only gave me permission, but he urged me, and made me promise to follow the inclination that would develop in my heart freely and without reservation.'

"She paused for a moment, but soon an expressive look from the young man gave her courage enough to continue her confession:

" 'My husband placed only one restriction on his otherwise so generous permission. He recommended extreme caution, and explicitly required that I choose a sober, reliable, prudent, and discreet friend. Spare me from saying the rest, sir; spare me the embarrassment of confessing how much I am taken with you, and divine from this confidence my hopes and my desires.'

"After a short pause the amiable young man replied thoughtfully: 'I am indeed indebted to you for the trust with which you grant me such great honor and happiness! I long only to convince you that I am not unworthy of it. Let me answer you first as a jurist: as such, I confess that I admire your husband, who so clearly felt and understood his injustice, for it is certain, that any man who leaves a young wife to visit faraway lands must be regarded as one who completely abandons any other possession; by his actions he clearly renounces all claim to it. Just as the first comer may lawfully claim any such abandoned article, so I must regard it as even more natural and just for a young woman, under the same circumstances, to bestow her affection anew and to entrust herself without hesitation to a lover who seems pleasant and reliable.

" 'And if you have a case like this, where the husband himself, conscious of his injustice, explicitly permits to his abandoned wife what he cannot refuse her, then no doubt remains whatever, since no one suffers an injustice, if he has declared himself willing to bear it.

" 'If you now,' the young man continued with completely different looks and in the most passionate tone, as he took his lovely mistress by the hand, 'if you choose me as your servant, you acquaint me with a blessedness I never before dreamed of. Rest assured,' he exclaimed, kissing her hand, 'that you could not have found a more devoted, tender, faithful, and discreet servant!'

"How reassured she felt after this declaration. She did not hesitate to show him the most ardent evidence of her tenderness: she pressed his hands, nestled close to him, and laid her head upon his shoulder. They had not been very long in this position when he gently tried to withdraw from her and, not without distress, began: 'Could anyone be in a more peculiar situation? I am forced to withdraw from you and to exercise the greatest self-control, just when I should abandon myself to feelings of rapture. I may not at the moment take possession of the happiness that awaits me in your arms. Ah, if only the delay does not cheat me of my fondest hopes!'

"The beauty asked anxiously after the cause of this strange utterance.

" 'Just as I was completing my studies in Bologna,' he replied, 'and was driving myself hardest to prepare for my future calling, I fell into a grave illness, which threatened to destroy if not my life, at least my physical and mental powers. In the extreme of distress and pain I swore an oath to the Mother of God, that if she would let me recover, I would spend a year in strict fasting and abstain from all enjoyment of whatever kind. For ten months now I have kept my oath to the letter, and considering the great benefit I received, the time did not drag, since it was not hard for me to go without many habitual and familiar pleasures. But what an eternity have the two remaining months suddenly become to me, since a happiness that exceeds all conception can be mine only when they are past! Do not lose patience, and do not take back the favor you have so generously intended!'

"The lady, not especially pleased with this explanation, took heart once again when her friend, after some reflection, continued: 'I would hardly dare suggest to you the means by which I can be released earlier from my oath. If I were to find someone who would undertake to keep my vow as strictly and dependably as I do, and who would share half the remaining time with me, I would be free that much faster, and then nothing would interfere with our wishes. Would you not, my sweet friend, in order to hasten our happiness, be willing to remove part of the obstacle that stands in our way? I can transfer my vow only to someone completely reliable. It's strict, for I may eat daily only two meals of bread and water, and at night I may spend only a few hours on a hard bed, and despite my many duties I must say a great number of prayers. If, as happened today, I cannot avoid attending a banquet, I may not ignore my obligation on that account; instead I must try to resist all the enticing delicacies passed before me. If you can also resolve to observe all these rules for one month, then you will take greater pleasure in the possession of a lover, since you will have earned it yourself, so to speak, by such a praiseworthy undertaking.'

"The beautiful lady was not happy to hear of the obstacles opposing her passion; but her love for the young man had been so increased by his presence, that no trial seemed too hard to her, if only her possession of so precious a treasure could be thus assured. She said to him, therefore, in her sweetest tones: 'My darling friend! The miracle by which you recovered your health is so precious and venerable, that I make it my duty and my joy to take part in the vow that you are obliged to fulfill in return. I am glad to give you such a clear proof of my affection; I shall follow your instructions to the letter, and until you release me nothing shall deflect me from the course you set.'

"After the young man had settled in detail with her the conditions under which she could spare him half his vow, he departed, promising that soon he would visit her again and see if she was successfully persisting in her resolve. And so she had to let him go without a handclasp, without a kiss, and with scarcely a significant glance as he departed. The activity to which her odd resolution had committed her made her happy; and she had much to do to change her whole way of life. First all the beautiful leaves and flowers that she had strewn to welcome him were swept out; then, in place of the well-upholstered couch came a hard bed, where she lay down in the evening, for the first time in her life barely satisfied by a meal of only water and bread. The next day she was busy cutting out and sewing shirts, of which she had promised to make a certain number for a hospital and poorhouse. During this new and disagreeable task she occupied her imagination with visions of her attractive lover and with the hope of future rapture, and with these thoughts her meagre fare seemed to grant her heart-strengthening nourishment.

"So a week passed and by its end the roses in her cheeks were already beginning to fade somewhat. Gowns that once had fitted her well were too loose, and her once brisk and nimble limbs had grown languid and weak, by the time that her friend appeared again and infused her with new strength and vitality. He exhorted her to persist in her resolve, encouraged her by his example and hinted at uninterrupted enjoyment to come. He stayed only briefly and promised to return soon.

"The charitable work resumed with renewed vigor and the strict diet was in no way relaxed. But, unfortunately, she could not have been more depleted by a major illness. Her friend, who visited her again at the end of the week, looked at her with the greatest compassion and strengthened her with the thought that the trial was already half over.

"Now, the unaccustomed fasting, prayer, and work became more burdensome to her every day, and the excessive abstinence seemed to undermine completely the health of a body accustomed to rest and generous nourishment. She was finally no longer able to stand up, and was driven, despite the warmth of the season, to wrap herself in two and three layers of clothing in order to retain at least the last residue of body heat. Indeed, she was no longer able to sit upright, and finally was forced to stay in bed.

"To what reflections was she reduced by her state! How often did this peculiar situation pass before her soul and how it pained her when ten days passed without an appearance by the lover who cost her such extreme sacrifices! And yet these dark hours prepared for her full recovery, indeed brought it about. For when, soon after, her lover appeared and sat down by her bed on the very same ottoman where he had listened to her first declaration, and warmly, even rather tenderly, urged her to endure staunchly the brief time that remained, she interrupted him with a smile and said: 'No further persuasion is needed, my worthy friend, and I will keep my vow patiently for the few remaining days, in the conviction that you imposed it for my own good. I am now too weak to express to you the gratitude I feel. You have saved me for myself; you have restored me to myself, and I realize that from now on I owe my whole existence to you.

" 'In truth my husband was clever and prudent and knew a woman's heart; he was fair enough not to scold for an inclination that might arise in her bosom through his fault; indeed, he was generous enough to place his rights second to the demands of nature. But you, sir, *you* are rational and good; you have made me feel that besides inclination there is something else in us that can hold it in balance, that we are capable of renouncing every habitual pleasure and even of rejecting our most ardent desires. You have taught me this lesson by error and hope; but both cease to be necessary, once we have become acquainted with the good and mighty self, which dwells so still and quiet within us and which, until it gains mastery in the house, at least makes its presence known by constant gentle reminders. Farewell! Henceforth your friend will watch you with pleasure. Influence your fellows as you have done me; do not just unravel the perplexities that only too easily arise over property, but show them, too, by your gentle guidance and example, that in every breast the power of virtue sprouts secretly. The respect of all will be your reward, and you, more than the most distinguished statesman and the greatest hero, will deserve the title father of his country.' "

"I have to praise your 'Lawyer,' " said the Baroness. "He is neat, rational, entertaining, and instructive; so should all men be who want to hold us back, or help us recover, from some mistake. Really this tale deserves, before many others, that title of honor, moral tale. Give us more of this kind, and we shall certainly appreciate it."

OLD MAN. "If this story meets your approval, then I am indeed delighted, but I am sorry if you want still more moral tales; for this one is the first and the last."

LOUISA. "It does you little credit that in your collection you have only one story of precisely the best kind."

OLD MAN. "You misunderstand me. This is not the only moral tale I can tell; but they all resemble one another so closely that one always seems to be telling the same one."

LOUISA. "You really ought to give up these paradoxes once and for all; they only confuse the conversation. Explain yourself more clearly!"

OLD MAN. "Gladly! Only that story deserves to be called moral which shows us that man has in himself the power to act against his inclination from the conviction of what is right. This is what this story teaches us, and no moral tale can teach anything else."

LOUISA. "And so, in order to act morally, I must act against my inclination?"

OLD MAN. "Yes."

LOUISA. "Even if it is good?"

OLD MAN. "No inclination is good in itself, but only insofar as it results in something good."

LOUISA. "Suppose someone had an inclination to charity?"

OLD MAN. "Then he should forbid himself to be charitable, as soon as he sees that he is ruining his own household by it."

LOUISA. "And if someone had an irresistible drive to gratitude?"

OLD MAN. "Provision has already been made in the case of man that gratitude can never become a drive. But supposing it could, the man to value would be the one who preferred to show ingratitude rather than undertake something wicked out of love for his benefactor."

LOUISA. "So then there could actually be innumerable moral tales?"

OLD MAN. "In that sense, yes, but none of them would say anything beyond what my lawyer said, and therefore you can call it unique in terms of spirit, since you're right that the subject matter can vary greatly."

Louisa. "If you had expressed yourself more clearly we wouldn't have quarreled."

Old Man. "Nor spoken either. Mistakes and misunderstandings are the wellsprings of active life, and of conversation."

Louisa. "I still cannot agree with you completely. When a brave man rescues others at the risk of his own life, is that not a moral action?"

Old Man. "In my way of speaking, no. But if a timid person overcomes his fear and does the same, then it is a moral action."

Baroness. "I would prefer, my dear friend, that you gave us a few more examples, and came to terms with Louisa about the theory another time. It is true, a heart that tends to the good is, when we become aware of it, bound to delight us; but there is nothing in the world more beautiful than inclination guided by reason and conscience. If you have another story like this, we would like to hear it. I especially love parallel stories. One illuminates the other and explains its meaning better than many dry words."

Old Man. "I can probably tell a few more that belong here; I have always been particularly interested in these qualities of the human spirit."

Louisa. "There is only one thing I would like to request. I can't deny that I don't like stories that always drag our imaginations to foreign lands. Must everything take place in Italy and Sicily, or in the Orient? Are Naples, Palermo, and Smyrna the only places where anything interesting can happen? Fairy tales must be set in Ormus and Samarkand just to confuse our imaginations. But if you want to cultivate our minds, our hearts, give us local settings, give us family portraits; then we will recognize ourselves all the more readily and, when they seem accurate, beat our breasts with that much more emotion."

Old Man. "In this too you shall be obliged. But family portraits are peculiar things. They all look so alike, and we have already seen virtually every aspect of them well presented on the stage. All the same, I will take a chance and tell a story that is similar to something you already know about, and that might prove novel and interesting only in its precise depiction of emotional developments.

"In families it is often possible to observe that with regard to both mind and body children inherit sometimes from their father, sometimes from their mother; and so it often happens that a child combines the natures of both parents in a special and remarkable way.

"Of this a young man whom I shall call Ferdinand was striking proof. His physical appearance resembled that of both parents, and their temperaments could be precisely distinguished in his own. He had the gay and carefree disposition of his father, as also his tendency to live for the moment, and a certain impetuous way, on many occasions, of considering only himself. But from his mother, it seemed, came calm deliberation, a sense of justice and fairness, and a nascent capacity to sacrifice himself for others. It is easy to see why those who dealt with him, in order to explain his actions, often had to resort to the hypothesis that the young man must have two souls.

"I will skip over many scenes from his childhood and relate only one occurrence that illuminates his whole character and that marked a distinct epoch in his life.

"From childhood on he had enjoyed every comfort, for his parents were well-off, and lived and raised their children as people of their station ought to; and if his father spent more than was proper on parties, gambling, and fancy clothes, nevertheless his mother, as a thrifty housewife, knew how to limit their ordinary expenses, so that overall a balance was maintained and no shortage could ever develop. Moreover, the father prospered in business; a number of his riskier speculations succeeded, and because he liked being with people, he also had the benefit of many contacts and considerable assistance.

"Children, as developing personalities, usually take as a model whoever in the family seems to enjoy life most. In a father who knows how to have a good time they see the decisive rule for their own behavior, and, because they reach this conclusion so young, their appetites and desires usually develop out of all proportion to the resources of their families. They are constantly frustrated, the more so because each new generation makes new demands, and makes them at an ever younger age, whereas the parents normally would like to allow their children only what they themselves enjoyed at an earlier period, when everyone was content to live more modestly and simply.

"Ferdinand grew up with the unpleasant feeling that he often lacked what his playmates had. In clothing, and in a certain liberality of life and manner, he wished to stand second to none. He wanted to be like his father, whose example he saw daily before him and who appeared a model twice over: once because he was a father, whom a son is usually predisposed to favor; and then again, because the boy saw that the man lived a pleasant and enjoyable life, and at the same time was esteemed and loved by everyone. On this account Ferdinand had, as one might imagine, many quarrels with his mother, since he didn't want to wear his father's cast-off coats, but always wanted to be in fashion himself. So he grew, and his demands always grew a little ahead of him, with the result that at last, by the time he was eighteen, he had indeed completely lost touch with his circumstances.

"So far he had made no debts, because his mother had instilled in him an intense horror of them, had tried to preserve his confidence, and several times had gone to extreme lengths to grant his wishes or to rescue him from small embarrassments. Unfortunately, at the very time when, as a young man, he was more concerned with externals, when, because he was attracted to a very pretty girl, he became more involved in society and wished not merely to equal others, but to excel and to please—just at this moment she had to be tighter in her management than ever. Instead of satisfying his demands as before, she began to appeal to his reason, to his good heart, to his love for her; and because she convinced him without changing him, she truly reduced him to despair.

"He could not, without giving up what was as dear to him as his own life, change the circumstances in which he found himself. From earliest childhood on he had been growing toward this situation, becoming entwined with everything that surrounded him; he could not cut a single fiber of his relationships, parties, rambles, and excursions without also offending an old school friend, a playmate, a new, distinguished acquaintance and, what was worst, his love.

"How highly he valued his love is easy to understand when one learns that it flattered simultaneously his senses, his mind, his vanity, and his warmest hopes. One of the most beautiful, attractive, and wealthy girls in the city preferred him, at least for the moment, to his many fellow suitors. She allowed him to flaunt, so to speak, the service he devoted to her, and they seemed mutually proud of the chains with which they had bound one another. Now it was his duty to dance attendance upon her, to spend time and money in her service, and to show in every way how much he valued her love, how he had to possess her.

"Such companionship and such an endeavor cost Ferdinand more than would have been natural in other circumstances. She had actually been entrusted by her absent parents to the care of a rather eccentric aunt, and it took all kinds of stratagems and unusual arrangements to bring Ottilie, this ornament of society, into society. Ferdinand exhausted himself inventing ways to provide her the pleasure that she so much enjoyed and that she knew how to enhance for everyone around her.

"And at just this moment to be summoned by a loved and venerated mother to completely different obligations, to expect no help from her, to have such horror of debts, which would not have maintained his situation long in any case, to be regarded by everyone as well-off and generous and yet to experience daily urgent need of money, was surely one of the most painful situations in which a young temperament stirred by passion can be.

"Certain ideas, which had otherwise only flitted by, now held his attention; certain thoughts, which had troubled him only in passing, now lingered in his mind; and certain resentful feelings became more persistent and more bitter. If once he had taken his father as his model, now he envied him as his rival. Everything that the son desired, the father possessed; everything that caused the son anxiety, the father acquired with ease. Moreover, it was not as if it was a matter of necessities, but rather, of what both might well have given up. Thus the son felt that his father should sometimes go without, so that *he* might enjoy. But the father had entirely different views; he was the kind of man who is liberal with himself and who, as a result, deprives his dependents. He had set his son a fixed allowance and demanded from him an exact accounting, indeed a regular tabulation.

"Nothing sharpens people's eyes more than restrictions. This is why women are so much cleverer than men, and why subordinates so carefully watch superiors who do not practice what they preach. So the son carefully watched all his father's actions, especially those that involved spending money. He listened more carefully when he heard that his father had lost or won at gambling; he judged him more severely when the latter arbitrarily allowed himself something expensive.

" 'Isn't it strange,' he said to himself, 'that while parents stuff themselves with pleasure of every sort, spending at whim a fortune given them by chance, they exclude their children from every reasonable pleasure just at the age when we are most responsive to it! And what right have they to do it? And how did they get this right? Should it depend on chance alone, and can there be a right, where chance is at work? If my grandfather were still alive, who treated his grandchildren like his children, I would be much better off. He would not let me want for necessities: because isn't something a necessity, if we need it in the circumstances to which we were born and bred? Grandfather wouldn't let me live in want any more than he would tolerate my father's extravagance. If he had lived longer, if he had understood that his grandson also deserves some pleasure, then he would perhaps in his will have provided sooner for my happiness. I've even heard that my grandfather died unexpectedly, just as he was about to make his will, and so perhaps only chance has deprived me of my earlier share in a fortune that, if my father goes on spending like this, I may well lose forever.'

"These and other sophistries about ownership and justice—whether one had to obey a law or arrangement to which one had not consented, and to what extent a person might privately violate the laws of society—these occupied him often in those lonely, morose hours when, for lack of ready money, he had to decline an excursion or some other pleasant event. For he had already sold off the small things of value that he owned, and his usual allowance was certainly not sufficient.

"He withdrew, and one can say that at such moments he had no respect for his mother, who could not help him, and hated his father, who, in his opinion, constantly obstructed him.

"Just at that period he made a discovery that irritated him even more. He perceived that his father was not only a poor manager, but also a careless one. For he often took money from his desk in haste, without recording it, and later would sometimes recount and calculate, and seem annoyed that the sums did not tally with the cash box. The son noticed this several times, and was even more sensitive about it if, at the moment when his father was dipping into the till, he himself was distinctly short of cash.

"While he was in this mood there occurred a strange accident, which gave him an attractive opportunity to act on what had been only an obscure and indeterminate urge.

"His father gave him the task of looking through a crate of old letters and sorting them. One Sunday, when he was alone, he was carrying the box through the room that housed the desk where his father kept his money. The crate was heavy; he had not grasped it properly and wanted to put it down for a moment or, actually, to rest it on something. Unable to hold it, he banged into the corner of the desk, and its top flew open. He saw now lying before him all the rolls of money at which he had often cast a furtive glance, set down his box, and took, without thinking and without reflecting, a roll from the side where his father generally seemed to take the money for impulse purchases. He closed the desk again and tried hitting it: the top flew open every time, and it was as good as having the key to the desk.

"Impetuously he sought again every pleasure that until now he had had to give up. He played the swain with more energy; in all his undertakings he was more passionate; his vivacity and grace had turned into an almost wild impetuosity which, to be sure, did not suit him badly, but brought no one any good.

"What a spark is to a loaded gun, opportunity is to impulse, and every impulse that we satisfy against our conscience forces us to expend an excess of physical energy; we behave again as savages, and it is difficult to hide the outward effects of this exertion.

"The more his inner sensibility opposed him, the more specious arguments Ferdinand accumulated; and he seemed to act that much more boldly and freely, the more constrained he felt within.

"At this same time all sorts of trinkets of no real worth had come into fashion. Ottilie loved to wear jewelry; he looked for a way to supply it so that Ottilie herself would not actually know where the presents came from. Her suspicions fell upon an old uncle, and Ferdinand was doubly delighted when she expressed her pleasure at the gifts and her suspicions of the uncle at the same time.

"But to give himself and her this pleasure, he had to open his father's desk several more times, and he did so with rather less concern, because his father had on various occasions inserted or withdrawn money without recording it.

"Shortly afterwards Ottilie was to visit her parents for several months. The young people were very distressed at the prospect of parting, and one circumstance made their separation even more significant. Ottilie learned by accident that the gifts were from Ferdinand; she confronted him, and when he confessed, seemed very annoyed. She insisted that he take them back; and this demand pained him bitterly. He declared that he was neither able nor willing to live without her; he begged her to preserve her love for him, and implored her not to refuse him her hand as soon as he should be provided for and have a proper home. She loved him, she was touched, she consented to his wishes, and, in this happy moment, they sealed their promise with ardent embraces and a thousand heartfelt kisses.

"After her departure, Ferdinand felt very lonely. The company in which he had been accustomed to see her held no charm for him, now that she was absent. He continued only from force of habit to visit either friends or entertainments, and dipped only reluctantly a few more times into his father's till to defray expenses to which no passion compelled him. He was often alone, and his good soul seemed to gain the upper hand. He was amazed at himself, upon quiet reflection, that he could ever have devised those cold and distorted sophistries about justice and ownership, about claims on the property of others, and all the rest, in order to extenuate unacceptable conduct. It gradually became clear to him that only fidelity and faith make men worthy of esteem, and that the good man must actually live so as to put all laws to shame, even though another might either evade them or exploit them to his own disadvantage.

"In the meantime, before these true and good principles became completely clear to him and led to firm resolutions, he yielded yet a few more times to the temptation, in pressing cases, to tap the forbidden source. But he never did so without repugnance, and only as if an evil spirit were dragging him by the hair.

"Finally he took heart and resolved, before all else, to make the deed impossible and inform his father about the condition of the lock. He did this with cunning: he carried the box of now-sorted letters through the room in his father's presence, deliberately banged into the desk, and his father was indeed amazed when he saw the lid fly up! They both examined the lock and found that the catches were worn with age and the hinges loose. At once everything was repaired, and Ferdinand had not had for a long time so pleasant a moment as when he saw the money in such safe custody.

"But this was not sufficient. He immediately decided to collect together the sum that he had purloined from his father and that he still knew down to the penny, and, in one way or another, to return it. He began to live most frugally and to save as much of his allowance as was possible. To be sure, what he could recover this way was only a little, compared to what he had squandered before; nevertheless, the sum seemed great because it was the beginning of restitution for his wrong. And indeed, there is a vast difference between the last dollar one borrows and the first that one pays back.

"He had not pursued this virtuous course for long, when his father decided to send him on business affairs. He was to familiarize himself with a distant manufacturing arrangement. The plan was to establish an office of their own in an area where materials and labor were very cheap, settle a partner there, themselves earn the profits now lost to others, and with capital and credit, expand the business. Ferdinand was to investigate the situation on site and make a detailed report. His father allowed him money for travelling expenses and directed him to manage with it; the sum was generous and he had no cause to complain.

"Even on his journey Ferdinand lived frugally, calculated over and over, and found that if he continued to economize in every way, he could save one third of his travelling money. Moreover, he now hoped for an opportunity to attain the rest; and he found it. For opportunity is an indifferent goddess: she favors good as well as evil.

"In the district that he was to visit he found everything far more advantageous than anticipated. Everyone was proceeding mechanically in the same old rut. Either nothing was known of modern improvements, or none had been introduced. People invested only modest amounts, and were content with only modest profits; and he soon saw that with a certain amount of capital, with loans, with the wholesale purchase of raw materials, with the introduction of machinery under competent supervisors, they could establish a substantial and solid enterprise.

"He was elated at the thought of perhaps doing this himself. The magnificent countryside, where every moment the image of his beloved Ottilie hovered before him, made him wish that his father would assign him to this spot, entrust him with the new establishment, and thus make generous and unexpected provision for him.

"He observed everything more attentively because he already saw it as his own. For the first time he had an opportunity to use his knowledge, his intelligence, his judgment. Both the countryside and his affairs absorbed his interest. They were balm and healing for his wounded heart; for it pained him to recall his father's house where, as if in a kind of madness, he had been able to commit an act that now seemed to him the rankest crime.

"A family friend, a fine man but in poor health, who himself had first suggested the idea of such an enterprise in his letters, was his constant companion, showed him everything, told him his ideas, and was delighted when the young man responded to and even anticipated him. This man led a very simple life, partly by inclination, partly because his health required it. He had no children, but was cared for by a niece, to whom he intended to leave his fortune, and for whom he desired a worthy, enterprising husband. With the support of additional capital and fresh energy he hoped to see executed the idea he had conceived, but which his physical and economic circumstances prevented him from achieving himself.

"Scarcely had he set eyes on Ferdinand than the latter seemed to him just the man, and his hopes grew as he saw the young man's devotion to business and to the region. He let his niece see his thoughts, and she did not seem averse. She was a young, attractive, healthy girl, good-natured in every way. Caring for her uncle's household kept her active and busy, concern for his health always tender and obliging. No one could have desired a more suitable person for a wife.

"Ferdinand, who could think only of the charm and the love of Ottilie, overlooked the fine country girl, except perhaps to wish that if Ottilie one day lived here as his wife, he might find such a housekeeper and manager to assist her. He responded to the girl's friendliness and kindness without reserve, learned to know her better and to value her; soon he treated her with more respect, and both she and her uncle interpreted his behavior according to their wishes.

"By now Ferdinand had taken a careful look and acquainted himself with all the details. With the help of the uncle he had drawn up a plan and, careless as always, did not conceal his intention to execute it himself. At the same time he had paid the niece many compliments and said how lucky was the household that could be entrusted to so careful a mistress. Hence she and her uncle believed that he had serious intentions, and treated him more cordially than ever.

"Not without satisfaction had Ferdinand learned in his investigations that he had in the future much to expect from this place, that he could also make a profitable deal right now, and that he could, as well, restore the purloined sum to his father and so at once free himself from this crushing burden. He revealed the intended speculation to his friend, who was extraordinarily pleased and gave him all possible assistance; in fact, he even wanted to supply his young friend everything on credit, which however the latter did not accept. Instead, he paid part immediately with the excess from his travel allowance, and promised to pay the rest in a reasonable time.

"The joy with which he had his merchandise packed and loaded was inexpressible; the satisfaction with which he set out for home can be imagined. The most sublime feeling a person can have is when he overcomes and frees himself from a major fault, indeed from a crime, by his own effort. The good man who goes through life without noticeably departing from the proper path is like a peaceful, commendable citizen, but a man of the former type, on the other hand, deserves admiration and glory as a hero and conqueror. And this would seem to be the sense of the paradox that the Godhead itself rejoices more over one repentant sinner than over ninety-nine just men.

"But unfortunately Ferdinand could not, by his good resolutions, by his amendment and restitution, erase the sad results of his deed that now awaited him and that were about to wound anew his recently comforted spirit. During his absence a storm had gathered that was to break immediately upon his arrival in his father's house.

"Ferdinand's father was, as we know, not especially orderly about his personal finances; his business affairs, however, were conducted with the greatest correctness by a skilled and punctilious associate. The old man had not actually noticed the money his son had pilfered, but unfortunately it had included a packet of coins, uncommon in the neighborhood, that he had won gambling with a foreigner. These he did miss, and the circumstance troubled him. But what upset him in the extreme was that there were missing several rolls of a hundred ducats each, which he had lent out some time ago but was certain had been repaid. He knew that until recently the desk had opened at a blow, concluded that he had been robbed, and completely lost his head. His suspicion fell on all and sundry. With the most fearful threats and imprecations he told his wife; he wanted to search every inch of the house, question all the servants, maids, and children; no one was proof against his suspicion. The good woman did her best to calm her husband. She pointed out the embarrassment and discredit this affair would bring upon him and his household if it became public: no one would care about their misfortune except to humiliate them with their sympathy; in such a case neither he nor she would be spared; people would be able to make even more farfetched remarks if nothing came out of it all; in any case they might be able to discover the thief and, without ruining him for the rest of his life, recover the money. With these and similar arguments she finally persuaded him to be calm and to pursue a quiet investigation.

"And unfortunately the discovery came soon enough. Ottilie's aunt was informed of the young people's promises to each other. She knew about the gifts that her niece had accepted. The entire situation displeased her, and she had kept silent only because her niece was away. A secure match with Ferdinand seemed advantageous to her, but an uncertain adventure was intolerable. So, since she heard that the young man would shortly return, and since she also expected her niece again any day, she hastened to report what had happened to his parents and to hear their opinion about it, to ask whether to expect that Ferdinand would soon be provided for and whether they would consent to a marriage with her niece.

"The mother was not a little astonished, when she heard about these ties. She was horrified, when she learned what presents Ferdinand had given Ottilie. She concealed her amazement, requested the aunt to allow her a little time to discuss the matter at leisure with her husband, assured her that she considered Ottilie an advantageous match and that it was not impossible to make suitable provision for their son in the near future.

"When the aunt had departed, the mother did not think it advisable to confide this discovery to her husband. Her only concern was to clear up the unhappy mystery of whether Ferdinand had, as she feared, bought the gifts with the stolen money. She hastened to the dealer who specialized in jewelry of this sort, bargained for similar items, and finally told him he must not overcharge her, since he had let her son, for a similar order, have them for less. The tradesman insisted no, showed her the exact terms of sale, and added that it was also necessary to take account of the exchange on the currency in which Ferdinand had paid a part. He named, to her great distress, the currency; it was the one that the father was missing.

"After she had him write down, for the sake of appearances, his lowest prices, she left with heavy heart. Ferdinand's fault was too apparent, the sum that was missing was large, and she imagined, with her anxious disposition, the worst crime and the direst consequences. She had the good sense to conceal the discovery from her husband; she awaited her son's return, torn between fear and longing. She wished to know the truth, and feared to learn the worst.

"Finally he returned in high spirits. He could expect praise for his work, and at the same time secretly carried in his merchandise the ransom with which he planned to free himself from his secret crime.

"His father received his report well but not with as much applause as expected, because the affair of the money left him distracted and out of sorts, particularly since he had several large amounts to pay just then. His father's mood greatly oppressed him, still more the presence of the walls, the furnishings, the desk, which had been witnesses of his crime. All his joy was gone, his hopes and expectations; he felt he was a base, indeed a bad man.

"He was about to seek a quiet way to sell his goods, which were shortly to arrive, and by his activity extricate himself from his misery, when his mother drew him aside and charged him with his fault in grave and loving terms and left him not the slightest loophole for denial. His tender heart was wrung; in tears he cast himself at her feet, confessed, begged forgiveness, swore that only his love for Ottilie could have led him astray and that no other vices had ever accompanied this one. Then he told the story of his repentance, that he had deliberately shown his father how the desk could be opened, and that from savings on his journey and from a successful speculation he was in a position to replace all the money.

"His mother, unable to yield so easily, insisted upon knowing what he had done with such large sums, for the presents involved only the tiniest fraction. She showed him, to his horror, an accounting of what his father was missing; he couldn't take responsibility even for all of the silver, and he solemnly swore he had not touched any of the gold. At this his mother was enraged. She rebuked him, saying that at the very moment when he should be demonstrating his reform and conversion with sincere repentance, he was still trying to deceive his loving mother with denials, lies, and fairy tales. She knew well, she said, that anyone capable of the one theft was capable of all the rest. Probably he had accomplices among his dissolute companions, probably the deal he had transacted had been made with the stolen money, and doubtless he would never have mentioned it, if the crime had not accidentally come to light. She threatened him with his father's anger, with legal penalties, with total banishment; but nothing hurt him more than when she hinted that there had just been discussion of a marriage to Ottilie. Deeply moved, she left him in a terrible state. He saw his fault revealed, saw himself suspected of a greater crime. How could he convince his parents that he had not touched the gold? Given his father's violent temper, he had reason to fear public exposure; he saw himself the opposite of everything he might have been. His prospects for a useful life, for marriage to Ottilie, disappeared. He saw himself banished, a fugitive, and exposed in foreign lands to every privation.

"But even all this, which bewildered his mind, injured his pride, and insulted his love, was not the most painful aspect. Most deeply he was wounded by the thought that his sincere intention, his manly resolution, the plan he had pursued to repair the deed, should be completely misunderstood, completely rejected, and indeed interpreted as the very opposite. If those earlier thoughts reduced him to dark despair, since he had to admit that he deserved his fate, these others made the deepest impression, since he learned the sad truth that a bad deed has the capacity to ruin even good efforts. This communion with himself, this reflection that his noblest striving was to be in vain, weakened him; he no longer wished to live.

"In these moments his soul thirsted for higher assistance. He sank down at his prayer stool, which he wet with his tears, and demanded aid from the Divine Being. His prayer was worthy to be heard: that the person who overcomes sin on his own should have a claim upon immediate help; that one who has left no powers unused should be able, when they are exhausted, when they are no longer sufficient, to call upon the aid of his Father in Heaven.

"In this conviction, in this urgent entreaty, he persisted for some time and scarcely noticed that his door opened and someone came in. It was his mother, who approached him with a cheerful face, saw his confusion, and addressed him with words of comfort. 'How happy I am,' she said, 'to find that at least you are no liar and that I can regard your repentance as genuine. The gold has turned up; your father, when he received it back from a friend, gave it to the cashier to keep for him and, distracted by the many activities of the day, forgot it. Your tally of the silver was reasonably close; now the missing sum is much less. I could not hide the joy in my heart, and promised your father to recover what is missing, if he would promise to compose himself and to ask no more questions.'

"Ferdinand became at once supremely happy. He hastened to complete his transaction, soon turned the money over to his mother, even replaced what he had not taken, since he knew that it was missing only due to his father's carelessness in spending. He was happy and calm, but this entire episode had made a very serious impression on him. He had convinced himself that man has the power to desire and achieve goodness; he now also believed that man could thereby win God's favor and count on His assistance, as he had just directly experienced. With great excitement he now told his father his plan to settle in the area he had visited. He laid out the arrangement in its full value and scope; his father was not opposed, and his mother privately revealed to her husband Ferdinand's relationship with Ottilie. He was pleased with such a fashionable daughter-in-law, and found the prospect of being able to provide for his son without cost quite agreeable."

"This story appeals to me," said Louisa, when the old man had concluded, "and even though it is taken from ordinary life, I do not find it commonplace. For if we examine ourselves and observe others, we find that we are rarely moved on our own to renounce some wish or other; mostly it is external circumstances that compel us."

"I wish," said Carl, "that we never had to deny ourselves anything, but instead that we didn't even know about what we were not to possess. Unfortunately, in our way of life everything crowds in on us, every inch is planted, all the trees are heavy with fruit, and we are just supposed to go past underneath, settle for the shadow, and renounce the best part."

"Now," said Louisa to the old man, "let us hear the rest of your story!"

OLD MAN. "It is really already over."

Louisa. "Of course, we've heard the development, but now we'd also like to hear the end."

Old Man. "You're right in your distinction, and since you take an interest in my friend's fate, I will tell you briefly what became of him.

"Freed from the oppressive burden of such an ugly crime, not without a certain self-satisfaction, he now thought about his future happiness and yearned for Ottilie's return, so that he could declare himself and redeem his promise to the full extent. She arrived in company with her parents; he hastened to her, he found her more beautiful and gay than ever. Impatiently he awaited the moment when he could speak to her alone and lay out his prospects before her. The hour came, and with all the joy and tenderness of love he told her of his hopes, the nearness of his happiness, and his wish to share it with her. But how amazed, indeed dismayed, he was when she listened to the whole affair with indifference, indeed, one might almost say, contempt. She joked less than politely about the hermitage he had picked out, and about the fine figure they both would cut as shepherd and shepherdess huddling under a straw roof, and other things of that sort.

"Shaken and embittered he withdrew; her behavior had upset him, and for a moment he turned cold. She had been unjust to him, and now he noticed faults in her that had otherwise remained hidden from him. Furthermore, it did not take a very sharp eye to see that a so-called cousin, who had arrived with her, had captured her attention and won much of her affection.

"Despite the anguish that Ferdinand suffered, he soon took heart; the conquest that he had already achieved once, seemed possible to him a second time. He saw Ottilie often and made himself observe her. He was cordial, even affectionate, to her and she was no less so; but her charms had lost their greatest power, and he realized soon that her conduct rarely came from the heart, that she could rather be tender and cold, charming and dismissive, pleasant and capricious, as she chose. His heart detached itself gradually from her, and he decided to break the last remaining ties.

"This operation was more painful than he had anticipated. He found her alone one day, and plucked up the courage to remind her of her promise, and to recall those moments when the two of them, stirred by the tenderest feeling, had made an agreement about their future life. She was friendly, one might almost say tender; he softened and wished at this moment that everything might be different than he had thought. However, he pulled himself together and calmly and lovingly narrated the story of the establishment that awaited him. She seemed pleased and, as it were, only to regret that for this reason their union would be further postponed. She made it clear that she hadn't the slightest desire to leave the city; she voiced her hope that by a few years' work in that region he might enable himself to cut a distinguished figure among his present fellow-townsmen. She let him see plainly that she expected him in future to surpass his father and to prove in every way even more distinguished and upstanding.

"Only too clearly did Ferdinand sense that he could expect no happiness from such a match, and yet it was difficult to renounce so many charms. Indeed, perhaps he would have parted from her still undecided, if her cousin had not arrived in his turn and shown in his behavior rather too much familiarity with Ottilie. Ferdinand then wrote her a letter in which he again assured her that she would make him happy if she would follow him to his new calling, but that he did not consider it advisable for either of them to cherish a faint hope of future times and bind themselves to an uncertain future with a promise.

"Even to this letter he wished for a favorable answer; it came, however, not as his heart, but rather as his reason, had to approve. Ottilie released him gracefully from his promise without quite releasing his heart, and the note communicated the same for her sentiments; according to the sense, they were still bound, and according to the words, free.

"Why should I elaborate any further? Ferdinand hastened back to that peaceful countryside; his arrangements were soon made. He was orderly and diligent and only became all the more so when the good, natural girl whom we have already met blessed him as his spouse, and her old uncle did everything possible to make his domestic life secure and comfortable.

"I met him in later years, surrounded by a large, handsome family. He told me his story himself, and, as is often the case with people to whom in their early years something significant has happened, that episode had made such an impression on him that it had a profound influence on his life. Even as a husband and father he made a habit of often denying himself something that would have given him pleasure, simply in order not to get out of practice of such an admirable virtue; and his sole principle of education was, so to speak, that his children must be able, even on the spur of the moment, to renounce something.

"In a way that I could not initially approve, he would, for example, at dinner forbid one of the boys to eat a favorite food. To my surprise the boy remained cheerful, and it was as if nothing special had happened.

"And so the eldest, on his own initiative, often used to allow a special piece of fruit or some other delicacy to pass; and yet he allowed them, I would say, virtually everything, and there was no lack of good and bad conduct in his house. He seemed indifferent to everything and allowed them almost unbridled freedom, except that once a week he would get the notion that everything had to happen on the dot. Then first thing in the morning the clocks were synchronized, everyone received his orders for the day, chores and amusements were piled up, and no one was allowed to miss a second. I could entertain you for hours with his discussion and comments on this remarkable mode of education. He used to joke with me about my vows as a Catholic priest and claimed that everyone, actually, should vow both temperance to himself and obedience to others, in order to practice it not constantly, but rather at the proper moment."

The Baroness made a few comments, and confessed that friend Ferdinand was on the whole, probably right, for in a kingdom, too, everything depended on the executive power; the legislative one could be as rational as it liked, it would avail the state nothing, if the executive were not powerful.

Louisa jumped to the window, for she heard Frederick riding into the courtyard. She went to meet him and led him into the room. He seemed cheerful, even though he had just come from scenes of misery and devastation, and instead of entering into a detailed story about the fire that had struck the house of their aunt, he assured them that her desk had most certainly burned up at the very same hour when their desk had so violently cracked.

"At the very moment," he said, "that the fire was already approaching the room, the steward managed to save a clock standing on this very desk. While he was carrying it out, something in the works must have been jostled, and it stopped at eleven-thirty. So we have, at least with respect to the time, complete agreement." The Baroness smiled; the tutor claimed that just because two events occurred simultaneously, you couldn't conclude that they were related. Louisa, however, chose to connect the two incidents, especially since she had received word that her fiancé was well, and once again they gave their imaginations completely free rein.

"Can't you," Carl said to the old gentleman, "tell us a fairy tale? Imagination is a wonderful faculty, but I don't like to see it applied to what has really happened. The ethereal forms it creates are welcome to us as a breed all their own; united to truth, it usually brings forth only monsters and then, it seems to me, generally stands in opposition to common sense and reason. It must, I think, attach itself to no object, it must force no object upon us; it should, in producing art, simply play upon us as music does, move us within ourselves, and indeed in such a way, that we forget there is anything outside us that generates this emotion."

"Do not continue," said the old man, "to elaborate your demands on works of the imagination in more detail. It is also appropriate to the enjoyment of such works that we enjoy them without demands;

for imagination itself cannot demand, it must await what is granted it. It makes no plans, chooses no path, but instead it is borne and led by its own wings; and as it swings back and forth it traces the strangest courses, which constantly shift and change direction. Allow me first, during my usual walk, to revive in my soul those strange images that often entertained me in years past. This evening I promise you a fairy tale that will remind you of nothing and of everything."

They were glad to let the old gentleman go, the more so because each of them hoped to gather from Frederick news and reports of what had happened in the meantime.

The Fairy Tale

By the great river, which was newly swollen with heavy rain and overflowing, the old ferryman, weary from the toil of the day, lay in his little hut and slept. In the middle of the night loud voices wakened him; it seemed that travelers wanted to be ferried across.

Stepping outside he saw hovering over his moored boat two large will-o'-the-wisps, who insisted they were in a great hurry and wished they were already across. The old man pushed off without delay and rowed across the river with his usual skill, while the strangers hissed at one another in an unfamiliar, very animated language, and occasionally burst into loud laughter as they capered now about the sides and benches, now upon the bottom of the boat.

"The boat is rocking!" cried the old man. "And if you are so wild it might capsize. Sit down, you wisps!"

They burst into laughter at the very idea, mocked the old man, and were wilder than ever. He bore their mischief with patience and soon reached the other side.

"This is for your trouble!" cried the travelers, and as they shook themselves, glittering gold pieces tumbled into the damp boat.

"For heaven's sake, what are you doing?" cried the old man. "You'll ruin me! If a single piece of gold had fallen into the water, the river, which cannot abide this metal, would have risen in terrible waves and swallowed my boat and me. And who knows how you yourselves would have fared? Take back your money!"

"We can take back nothing we have shaken off," they replied.

"So you are giving me the extra trouble," said the old man, as he stooped and gathered the gold coins in his cap, "of having to collect them, take them on shore, and bury them."

The will-o'-the-wisps had leaped from the boat, and the old man cried: "What about my fare?"

"Anyone who refuses gold can work for nothing!" cried the will-o'-the-wisps.

"You must know I can be paid only with fruits of the earth."

"With fruits of the earth? We despise them and have never touched them."

"Even so, I cannot let you go until you promise me three cabbages, three artichokes, and three large onions."

The will-o'-the-wisps wanted to slip away playfully, but they felt themselves inexplicably riveted to the ground; it was the most unpleasant sensation they had ever had. They promised to pay his claim right away; he released them and pushed off. He was already far away, when they called after him: "Old man! Listen, old man! We have forgotten the most important thing!" He was gone and did not hear them. He had drifted downstream on the same side of the river, where, in a mountainous place that the water could never reach, he planned to bury the dangerous gold. There among towering rocks he found an enormous cleft, tossed in the gold, and returned to his hut.

In this cleft lay the lovely green serpent, who was awakened from her sleep by the coins clinking down. She no sooner caught sight of the shining disks than she immediately devoured them with great relish and carefully sought out every one scattered in the brush and the chinks of the rock.

No sooner were they swallowed than she felt the gold melting in her entrails and spreading through her whole body with the most pleasant sensation; and to her great joy she discovered that she had become transparent and luminous. Long ago she had been assured that this phenomenon was possible; but since she doubted that the light could last long, curiosity and the desire to safeguard her future drove her out from the rocks to find out who could have strewn the beautiful gold about. She found no one. But it was that much pleasanter for her, as she crept along among the plants and bushes, to admire herself and the attractive light that she diffused through the fresh greenery. Every leaf seemed made of emerald, every flower gloriously transfigured. In vain did she roam through the lonely wilderness; but her hopes increased when she came out onto the plain and in the distance glimpsed a radiance that resembled her own. "I find my own kind at last!" she cried and hastened toward the place. She ignored the difficulties of creeping through swamp and reeds. For though she preferred to live in dry mountain meadows or in rocky clefts, though she liked to feed on aromatic herbs and to still her thirst with delicate dew or fresh spring water, yet for the sake of the beloved gold and in hope of finding the glorious light, she would willingly have undertaken anything that was imposed upon her.

Tired out, she came at last to a bog, where our two will-o'-the-wisps were frolicking about. She shot over to them, greeted them, and was delighted to find two such charming kinsmen. They went flitting past her, danced over her and laughed in their fashion. "Dear Cousin," they said, "even if you do belong to the horizontal line of our family, it doesn't matter a bit. Of course we're related only on the luminosity side, for look here"—and at this, by sacrificing their entire breadth, the two flames made themselves as long and tapering as possible—"see how the long slender look becomes us gentlemen of the vertical line. Don't take it amiss, my dear friend, but what family can boast of the like? For as long as there have been will-o'-the-wisps, not one has ever sat down or lain flat."

The serpent felt exceedingly uncomfortable in the presence of these relatives, for however high she might lift her head, she realized that she still must lower it to earth again in order to move. And although she had been extraordinarily pleased with herself before in the dark grove, in the presence of these cousins her radiance seemed to diminish from one moment to the next, indeed she feared that it would at last die out altogether.

In her embarrassment she hastily inquired whether the gentlemen could not tell her whence came the glittering gold that shortly before had fallen into the chasm; she suspected it to be a shower of gold that had drizzled straight from heaven. The will-o'-the-wisps laughed and shook themselves, and a swarm of gold coins came tumbling about them. Swiftly the serpent lunged to devour them. "Bon appetit, dear Cousin," said the obliging gentlemen. "We can offer you more." And they proceeded to shake themselves several times more with great agility, so that the serpent could not gulp down the precious food fast enough. Her glow began to increase visibly, and truly she shone most gloriously, while the will-o'-the-wisps had become rather thin and small, without, however, losing an ounce of their good humor.

"I am forever in your debt," said the serpent, once she had caught her breath after her meal. "Ask of me what you will! Anything in my power I will do for you."

"Splendid!" cried the will-o'-the-wisps. "Tell us, where does the fair Lily live? Lead us as fast as you can to her palace and garden. We are dying of impatience to cast ourselves at her feet."

"This service," replied the serpent with a deep sigh, "I cannot perform at once. Unfortunately, the fair Lily lives on the other side of the river."

"On the other side of the river? And we came across on a stormy night like this? How cruel is the river that now divides us! Wouldn't it be possible to summon the old ferryman again?"

"It would be useless," replied the serpent. "Even if you found him on this side, he would not take you; he is allowed to bring everyone over here, no one the other way."

"Now we're in a pretty pickle! Is there no other way to cross?"

"A few, but not at this moment. I can take the gentlemen myself, but not until noon."

"That is a time when we do not like to travel."

"Well, in the evening you can cross on the shadow of the giant."

"How is that possible?"—"The great giant who lives not far from here can do nothing with his body: his hands couldn't lift a wisp of straw, his shoulders couldn't carry a bundle of twigs. But his shadow can do a great deal, in fact everything. That is why he is most powerful at sunrise and sunset. And so in the evening one need only sit upon the neck of the shadow; the giant walks gently toward the bank, and his shadow carries the traveler across the river. But if you want to come at noon to that wooded corner, where the underbrush grows right down to the riverbank, I can take you across and present you to the fair Lily; if, however, you're afraid of the noonday heat, you have only to look for the giant at sunset in that rocky cove. No doubt he will be pleased to oblige you."

With a graceful bow the young gentlemen took their leave. The serpent was happy to be rid of them, partly to enjoy her own light, partly to satisfy a curiosity that for some time had been tormenting her.

In the rocky clefts, where she often crawled about, she had made a remarkable discovery. Although she had to creep through these chasms without any light, she could distinguish objects well enough by touch. She was accustomed to encounter nothing but the irregular products of nature; sometimes she would wind her way between the sharp points of giant crystals, sometimes she would feel the snags and strands of pure silver and carry some precious gem with her out into the light. But to her great amazement, inside a rock enclosure sealed off on all sides, she had felt objects that revealed the forming hand of man. Smooth walls that she could not scale, sharp symmetrical angles, well-shaped columns, and, what seemed to her strangest of all, human figures, about which she had twined herself many times, and which she concluded must be made of metal or highly polished marble. All these perceptions she now wished to bring together at last through her sense of sight, and to confirm what she only conjectured. She believed she could now illuminate this wondrous subterranean vault with her own light, and hoped all at once to become fully acquainted with these peculiar objects. She hurried off on the usual way and soon found the fissure through which she was accustomed to slip into the sanctuary.

Once inside she looked about with curiosity; although her glow could not illuminate all the objects in the rotunda, the nearest ones appeared distinct enough. In amazement and awe she looked up into a glittering niche, in which stood the image of a venerable king, in pure gold. The statue was larger than life, yet it seemed the likeness of a small rather than a large man. Its well-shaped body was draped with a simple cloak, and a wreath of oak held the hair.

Scarcely had the serpent looked at this venerable image than the king began to speak, asking "Whence comest thou?" "From the clefts where the gold dwells," replied the serpent.—"What is more glorious than gold?" asked the king. "Light," answered the serpent. "What is more refreshing than light?" he asked. "Discourse," she answered.

As they spoke she had glanced to the side and seen in the next niche another splendid image. There sat a king of silver, a tall and somewhat delicate figure; his body was covered with an embroidered robe; crown, girdle, and sceptre were adorned with jewels. In his countenance shone the serenity of pride, and he seemed about to speak, when suddenly a dark vein running through the marble wall grew bright and spread a pleasant light throughout the temple. By this light the serpent saw the third king, who sat, a mighty form of bronze, leaning on his club, adorned with a laurel wreath, and seeming more rock than human. She was about to go look at the fourth king, who stood farthest from her, but the wall opened as the glowing vein flashed and disappeared.

A man of ordinary height, who stepped out, drew the serpent's attention. He was dressed as a peasant and carried in his hand a small lamp, into whose quiet flame it was pleasant to gaze, and which miraculously, without casting a single shadow, lit up the whole vault.

"Why have you come, when we already have light?" asked the golden king.

"You know I may not enlighten what is dark."

"Shall my kingdom come to an end?" asked the silver king. "Late or never," replied the old man.

In a booming voice the bronze king began to ask: "When shall I arise?"—"Soon," replied the old man. "With whom should I join?" asked the king. "With your elder brothers," said the old man. "What shall become of the youngest?" asked the king. "He shall be seated," said the old man.

"I am not tired," cried the fourth king in a rasping, uneven voice.

During this exchange the serpent had crept softly about the temple, had inspected everything, and was now examining the fourth king close at hand. He stood leaning on a column, and his imposing figure was heavy rather than handsome. In what metal he was cast, however, was not easy to determine. Examined closely, it was a mixture of the three metals from which his brothers were formed. But during the casting these materials seemed not to have fused properly; gold and silver veins ran irregularly through a bronze mass and gave the figure an unpleasant look.

Meanwhile the golden king was saying to the man: "How many secrets dost thou know?"—"Three," answered the old man. "Which is the most important?" asked the silver king. "The revealed one," answered the old man. "Wilt thou reveal it also unto us?" asked the bronze king. "As soon as I know the fourth," said the old man. "What do I care!" murmured the composite king to himself.

"I know the fourth," said the serpent; she approached the old man and hissed something in his ear. "The time is at hand!" cried the old man in a mighty voice. The temple echoed, the metal statues rang, and at once the old man sank toward the west and the serpent toward the east, and both passed with great swiftness through the clefts in the rocks.

All the passages through which the old man traveled at once filled up with gold after him; for his lamp had the miraculous property of transforming all stones into gold, all wood into silver, dead creatures into jewels, and of annihilating all metals. But to manifest this effect, it had to shine all alone; whenever there was another light, it produced only a lovely, bright luster, and all living things were always refreshed by it.

The old man entered his hut, which was built against the mountain, and found his wife in terrible distress. She sat by the fire and wept and would not be consoled. "How unhappy I am!" she exclaimed. "I knew I shouldn't have let you leave today!"—"What's wrong, then?" asked the old man calmly.

"No sooner were you gone," she said sobbing, "than two boisterous travelers arrived at the door. Foolishly I let them in; they seemed to be pleasant, proper people. They were dressed in light flames, you could have taken them for will-o'-the-wisps. No sooner were they in the house, than they began to flatter me shamelessly; finally they were so impertinent that I'm ashamed even to think about it."

"Well," replied her husband smiling, "the gentlemen were probably joking; considering your age, they ought surely to have confined themselves to common politeness."

"Age! What age!" cried the wife. "Must I always hear about my age? How old am I then? Common politeness! I know what I know. And just take a look at those walls; just look at the old stones, which I haven't seen these hundred years. They've licked off all the gold, you wouldn't believe how quickly, and they kept telling me the whole time it tasted much better than ordinary gold. After they had scoured the walls bare, they seemed in a very good mood, and really, in that short time they had gotten much taller, broader and brighter. Then they started in again with their nonsense, stroked me again, called me their queen, shook themselves, and gold coins went flying all over; you can still see them shining there under the bench. But what a disaster! Our pug ate some of them, and look, there he is lying dead by the hearth. The poor creature! I will never get over it. I didn't notice until after they had gone, otherwise I wouldn't have promised to pay their debt to the ferryman."—

"What do they owe him?" asked the old man.

"Three cabbages," said his wife, "three artichokes, and three onions. I promised to carry them to the river in the morning."

"You can do them this favor," said the old man, "for they may well help us sometime in return."

"I don't know whether they will help us, but they certainly promised and swore that they would."

Meanwhile the fire had burned down on the hearth. The old man spread a thick layer of ashes over the coals and cleared away the glittering gold pieces; and now once again his little lamp shone all alone with the loveliest radiance; the walls coated themselves with gold, and the pug had become the most beautiful onyx imaginable. The alternation of brown and black in the precious stone made it an extraordinary masterpiece.

"Take your basket," said the old man, "and put the onyx in it. Then take the three cabbages, the three artichokes, and the three onions, lay them around it, and carry them to the river. At noon let the serpent take you across, and visit the fair Lily; take her the onyx. She will bring it to life with her touch, just as, by her touch, she kills everything that is alive. She'll find him a faithful companion. Tell her she shouldn't grieve, her deliverance is near; tell her she may regard the greatest misfortune as the greatest good fortune, for the time is at hand."

The old woman packed her basket and set out when it was light. The rising sun shone brightly over the river glittering in the distance. She proceeded at a slow pace, for the basket weighed upon her head, and yet it was not the onyx that was so heavy. She never felt the weight of anything dead she carried; rather the basket would immediately rise into the air and float over her head. But to carry a fresh vegetable or a small living creature was extremely tiring. She had been walking along for a while, rather cross, when suddenly she stopped in fright: she had almost stepped on the giant's shadow, which stretched across the plain right up to her. Only now did she see the immense giant, who had been bathing in the river, step out of the water, and she didn't know how to avoid him. As soon as he noticed her, he began to greet her jokingly, and the hands of his shadow reached at once into the basket. With ease and dexterity they removed a cabbage, an artichoke, and an onion and carried them to the mouth of the giant, who then continued upriver, and left her path free.

She thought about whether she shouldn't return home and replace the missing vegetables from her garden, and with these doubts kept walking on, so that she soon arrived at the edge of the river. She sat a long time waiting for the ferryman, whom she finally saw crossing with a remarkable traveler. A noble, handsome young man, from whom she could not tear her eyes, stepped out of the boat.

"What have you got?" called the old man. "The vegetables the will-o'-the-wisps owe you," replied the woman and showed her wares. When the old man found only two of each kind, he was annoyed, and declared that he could not accept them. The woman implored him, told him that she couldn't go home now, and that the weight would be a burden on the errand she had before her. He still refused, insisting that it was not even up to him. "Whatever I have earned I must leave standing for nine hours, and I may take nothing until I have given the river one third." After much haggling the old man finally responded: "There is still a way. If you will make a pledge to the river and acknowledge yourself its debtor, I will accept the six vegetables; but there is some risk involved."

"Surely if I keep my word, I run no risk?"

"Not the least. Put your hand into the river," the old man continued, "and promise that in twenty-four hours you will pay what you owe."

The old woman did so; but wasn't she frightened, when she drew her hand out of the water coal black! She scolded the old man vigorously, protesting that her hands had always been her most beautiful feature and that in spite of hard work she had managed to keep these noble limbs white and delicate. She inspected her hand indignantly, then cried in despair: "This is worse yet! I can see that it's actually shrunk, it's much smaller than the other."

"It only appears so now," said the old man. "But if you don't keep your word, it may come true. The hand will gradually shrink away and finally vanish altogether, without your losing the use of it. You will be able to do anything with it, only no one will see it."

"I would rather not be able to use it, and have no one able to tell," said the old woman. "In the meantime, it makes no difference; I'll keep my word in order to get rid of this black skin soon, and this worry." Hastily she took up the basket, which rose of its own accord above her head and floated freely in the air; then she hurried after the young man, who was quietly and pensively walking along the river bank. His splendid form and his remarkable clothing had made a deep impression on the old woman.

His chest was covered with glittering mail, through which every motion of his handsome body was revealed. A purple mantle hung about his shoulders, beautiful locks of brown hair cascaded about his bare head. His graceful face was exposed to the sun's rays, as were his beautifully shaped feet. Barefoot he walked calmly across the hot sand, and some profound sorrow seemed to dull all outer impressions.

The chatty old woman tried to draw him into conversation; but he responded only in monosyllables, so that, his beautiful eyes notwithstanding, she finally got tired of addressing him without success, and took leave of him, saying: "You walk too slowly for me, sir; I must not miss the time to cross the river on the green serpent and bring the fair Lily my husband's splendid gift." With these words she proceeded rapidly; and just as swiftly the handsome youth pulled himself together and hurried after her. "You're going to the fair Lily!" he cried. "Then we are going the same way. What sort of present are you taking?"

"Sir," replied the old woman, "it is not fair, after you have declined my questions so brusquely, to inquire so eagerly into my secrets. If, however, you will agree to an exchange, and tell me your story, then I will not conceal from you what the situation is with me and my present." They soon reached agreement; the woman confided her circumstances, the story of the dog, and let him see the marvelous gift.

He immediately lifted the natural artwork from the basket and took in his arms the pug, which seemed to be resting quietly. "Fortunate creature," he cried. "You will be touched by her hands, you will be revived by her, while living things must flee her to avoid an unhappy fate. But what do I mean, unhappy? Isn't it far more distressing and frightful to be paralyzed by her presence than it would be to die by her hand? Look at me!" he said to the old woman. "At my age, what a wretched state I must endure! This armor, which I wore with honor in battle, this purple mantle, which I tried to deserve by governing wisely; these Fate has left to me: the one as an unnecessary burden, the other as a meaningless adornment. Crown, scepter, and sword are gone. I am otherwise as naked and needy as any other mortal, for so unholy is the effect of her beautiful blue eyes, that they drain all living creatures of their strength, and those whom the touch of her hand does not kill outright are transformed into living, wandering shadows!"

He continued to lament in this fashion, and by no means satisfied the curiosity of the old woman, who did not want to hear about his internal as well as his external circumstances. She learned neither the name of his father, nor of his kingdom. He stroked the hard pug, whom the sun's rays and the warm breast of the youth had warmed, so that it seemed alive. He asked a great deal about the man with the lamp and the powers of the sacred light, and seemed to expect from it in future great benefit for his melancholy state.

As they talked they saw in the distance the majestic arch of the bridge, which stretched from one bank to the other, shimmering most marvelously in the bright sunlight. Both were amazed, for they had never yet seen this structure so glorious. "What!" cried the prince. "Wasn't it already beautiful enough, when it stood before our eyes as if built of jasper and chalcedony? Must we not fear to set foot on it, now that it appears to be composed of emerald, chrysoprase, and chrysolite in the most enchanting variety?" Neither knew of the change that had come over the serpent; for it was the serpent, who every noon arched herself across the river to form a daring bridge. The travelers stepped onto it with awe and crossed in silence.

They had scarcely reached the far side, when the bridge began to sway and move. Soon it touched the surface of the water and the green serpent, in her characteristic form, glided onto the land after the travelers. The two of them had scarcely thanked her for permitting them to cross the river on her back, when they noticed that, besides the three of them, there must be others present whom they could not actually see. They heard their hissing, to which the serpent gave an answering hiss. They listened attentively, and were finally able to discern the following: "First we will have a look incognito around the fair Lily's park," said a pair of alternating voices, "and we will request you to introduce us at nightfall, as soon as we are at all presentable, to this perfect beauty. You will find us by the edge of the large lake."—"Agreed," replied the serpent, and a hiss died away in the air.

Our three travelers consulted now on the order in which they would appear before the fair one, for however many people might be with her, they had to come and go one at a time, if they were not to suffer severe pain.

The woman, with the transformed dog in her basket, approached the garden first and looked for her benefactress, who was easy to find, because she was just then singing to the harp. The delightful tones appeared first as rings on the still surface of the lake, then like a gentle breeze they stirred the grass and shrubbery. In a secluded glade, in the shadow of a magnificent grouping of different trees she sat, and at her first appearance she enthralled anew the eyes, ears, and heart of the woman, who approached her in rapture and vowed to herself that during her absence the fair one had only grown fairer than ever. Still at some distance the good woman called greetings and praises to the enchanting girl. "What a pleasure to see you! What a heaven does your presence spread around you! How beautifully the harp rests in your lap, how gently your arms encircle it, how it seems to long for your breast, and how delicately it sounds at the touch of your slender fingers! Thrice happy the young man who could take its place!"

With these words she had come nearer. The fair Lily raised her eyes, let her hands fall, and replied: "Do not distress me with untimely praise! I suffer only that much more. Look, here at my feet the poor canary is dead who accompanied my songs so beautifully. He used to sit on my harp and was carefully trained not to touch me. Today, after a refreshing sleep, as I began a peaceful morning hymn and my little singer poured out his harmonies more gaily than ever, a hawk swoops down over my head. The poor little creature, terrified, flies to my breast, and in that instant I feel the last twitches of his parting life.

To be sure, struck by my gaze, the robber is creeping about over there by the water, powerless; but how can his punishment help me? My favorite is dead, and his grave will only increase the mournful shrubbery of my garden!"

"Take heart, dear Lily!" cried the woman, as she dried off a tear drawn from her eyes by the tale of the unhappy girl. "Be brave! My old man says to tell you to calm your grief, to look on the greatest misfortune as the forerunner of the greatest happiness, for the time is at hand. And truly," the old woman went on, "strange things are afoot. Just look at my hand, see how it has turned black! Truly, it's already much smaller, I must hurry, before it disappears altogether! Oh, why did I have to do the will-o'-the-wisps a favor, why did I have to meet the giant, and why dip my hand in the river? Couldn't you give me a cabbage, an artichoke and an onion? Then I can take them to the river and my hand will be as white as before, so that I could almost compare it with yours."

"Cabbages and onions you could probably still find, but artichokes you will seek in vain. No plant in my huge garden bears either blossoms or fruits, though every sprig I break off and plant on the grave of a loved one at once turns green and shoots up. Alas, I have seen all these clumps, shrubs, and groves grow. The umbrellas of these pines, the obelisks of these cypresses, the colossal oaks and beeches—they were all little twigs planted by my hand as a sad memorial in otherwise unfruitful soil."

The old woman had paid little attention to this speech and only watched her hand, which in the presence of the fair Lily seemed to grow blacker and blacker, and smaller by the minute. She was about to take her basket and hurry off, when she realized that she had forgotten the best part. She lifted the transformed dog out at once and placed it in the grass not far from the fair one. "My husband," she said, "sends you this keepsake. You know that you can bring this jewel to life with your touch. The sweet, faithful creature will surely make you very happy, and my grief at losing him can only be cheered by the thought that you possess him."

The fair Lily looked at the engaging creature with pleasure and, as it seemed, amazement. "Many signs come together," she said, "to bring me some hope. But alas, isn't it only a delusion of our nature to imagine, when several misfortunes coincide, that the best is near?

What help are all good omens that appear:
The bird's death, my friend's black hand I see,
The pug of precious stone, has he indeed a peer?
And has the lamp not sent him here to me?

Sweet human joys, far distant, are no more,

And misery alone is now my friend,
Alas, why stands no temple on the shore?
Alas, why does no bridge its arch extend?"

The good woman had listened impatiently to this song, which the fair Lily accompanied with the pleasant tones of her harp, and which would have enthralled anyone else. She was just about to take her leave, when she was once again prevented by the arrival of the green serpent. The latter had heard the last lines of the song and confidently encouraged the fair Lily at once.

"The prophecy of the bridge is fulfilled!" she cried. "Just ask this good woman how splendid the arch now looks. What was once opaque jasper, mere chalcedony, through which the light glimmered at best only at the edges, has now become transparent gemstone. No beryl is so clear and no emerald so beautiful a color."

"I congratulate you for it," said Lily, "but forgive me if I do not yet believe the prophecy fulfilled. Over the high arch of your bridge only foot passengers can pass, and we have been promised that horses and carriages and travelers of all kinds shall cross back and forth over the bridge at the same time. And hasn't it been prophesied that great pillars will arise of themselves out of the river?"

The old woman had kept her eyes fixed constantly on her hand, interrupted the conversation here, and said goodbye. "Stay just one moment more," said the beautiful Lily, "and take my poor canary bird with you! Ask the lamp to change him into a beautiful topaz. I will revive him with my touch, and he, along with your good pug, will be my favorite amusement. But hurry as fast as you can, for at sunset corruption will seize the poor creature and destroy for ever the beautiful unity of his form."

The old woman laid the little corpse between soft leaves in her basket and hurried off.

"Be that as it may," said the serpent, resuming their interrupted conversation, "the temple is built."

"But it does not yet stand on the river," replied the fair one.

"It still rests in the depths of the earth," said the serpent. "I have seen the kings and spoken with them."

"But when will they arise?" asked Lily.

The serpent replied: "I heard the great words resound in the temple: 'The time is at hand!' "

A cheerful brightness suffused the beautiful countenance. "That is the second time that I have heard those happy words today. When will the day come that I shall hear them three times?"

She stood up, and at once a lovely maiden stepped from the shrubbery and took her harp. She was followed by a second, who folded the carved ivory chair on which Lily had been sitting and took the silver cushion under her arm. Then a third, carrying a large parasol sewn with pearls, took her place, to see whether Lily might need her on a walk. These three maidens were beautiful and engaging beyond all expression, and yet they only enhanced Lily's beauty, for it was plain to all that they could not be compared with her.

Meanwhile, the fair Lily had been looking kindly at the marvelous pug. She bent down, touched him, and instantly he sprang to his feet. Gaily he looked around, ran back and forth, and finally dashed over to greet his benefactress warmly. She took him in her arms and hugged him. "Cold as you are," she exclaimed, "and even though you are only half alive, I am glad to have you. I will love you tenderly, play with you nicely, pet you affectionately, and hug you tightly." Then she let him go, chased him away, called him back, teased him so sweetly, and played with him in the grass so gaily and innocently, that one had to watch with delight and share her joy, just as a short time before her grief had moved every heart to compassion.

This happiness, these pleasant games were interrupted by the arrival of the sad youth. He entered as we have already seen him, except that the heat of the day seemed to have fatigued him still further, and in the presence of his beloved he grew paler with every moment. On his hand he carried the hawk, which sat quiet as a dove, and drooped its wings.

"It is not kind," Lily called to him, "to bring that hateful creature before me, that monster who killed my little singer today."

"Don't blame the poor bird!" replied the youth. "Accuse yourself instead, and fate, and allow me to keep my companion in misery."

Meanwhile the pug continued to tease the fair one, and she responded to her transparent pet most affectionately. She clapped her hands to shoo him away; then she ran to make him follow her. She tried to catch him when he fled, and chased him away whenever he tried to jump up on her. The youth watched in silence and with growing irritation. But finally, when she took the ugly creature, which he found utterly repulsive, in her arms, pressed him to her white bosom, and kissed his black muzzle with her heavenly lips, he lost all patience and exclaimed in despair: "Must I, who am fated to live with you, perhaps forever, in absent presence, I, who through you have lost everything, even myself—must I see with my own eyes how such an unnatural freak can make you happy, win your love, and enjoy your embrace? Am I to keep going to and fro, treading out the weary circle back and forth across the river? No, there still lingers a spark of the old heroic mettle in my breast; now let it burst into a final flame! If stones can rest at your breast, let me be turned to stone; if your touch kills, then I will die at your hands."

With these words he made a violent movement. The hawk flew from his hand, but he lurched forward towards the fair one. She stretched out her hands to hold him off, and touched him all the sooner. Consciousness left him, and with horror she felt the dear burden on her bosom. With a cry she stepped back, and the handsome youth sank lifeless from her arms to the ground.

The misfortune had occurred! Sweet Lily stood motionless, and stared at the lifeless body. Her heart seemed to falter in her bosom and her eyes were without tears. In vain the pug tried to provoke some friendly gesture; the whole world had died with her lover. Her mute despair sought no assistance, for it knew of none.

The serpent, by contrast, bestirred herself all the more. She seemed intent on rescue, and really her strange action did stave off at least the most immediate dreadful effects of the disaster for a time. With her supple body she made a wide circle around the corpse, seized the end of her tail in her teeth and lay still.

It was not long before one of Lily's beautiful handmaidens came forward, bringing the ivory stool, and with kindly gestures made her sit down. Soon after came the second, who brought a flame-colored veil and with it adorned, rather than covered, her mistress's head. The third handed her the harp, and scarcely had she taken the magnificent instrument to her and enticed a few notes from the strings, than the first returned with a bright round mirror, placed herself opposite the fair one, caught her glances in the mirror, and showed to her the loveliest image to be found in nature. Grief enhanced her beauty, the veil her charms, the harp her grace; and much as everyone hoped to see her sad state change, they wished equally to preserve forever the image of her as she was now.

Gazing quietly into the mirror she would draw melting notes from the strings, then her grief would seem to increase, and the strings throbbed answer to her affliction. At times she opened her mouth to sing, but her voice failed her. Soon her grief melted into tears, two maidens caught her by the arms, the harp dropped from her lap; the swift handmaiden just caught the instrument and put it aside.

"Who will get us the man with the lamp before the sun sets?" hissed the serpent softly but audibly; the maidens looked at one another and Lily's tears increased. Just then the woman came back with the basket, breathless. "I am lost and mutilated!" she cried. "Look how my hand has almost completely disappeared! Neither the ferryman nor the giant would take me across, because I am still in debt to the water. In vain have I offered a hundred cabbages and a hundred onions; only those three will do, and there is not a single artichoke to be found anywhere around here."

"Forget your trouble," said the serpent, "and try to help here; perhaps at the same time you can be helped as well. Hurry as fast as you can to find the will-o'-the-wisps; it is still too light to see them, but maybe you'll hear them laughing and capering. If they hurry, the giant will still take them across the river, and they can find the man with the lamp and send him."

The woman hurried as fast as she could, and the serpent seemed to await the return of both as impatiently as Lily. Unfortunately, the rays of the setting sun were already gilding the highest summits of the trees in the thicket, and long shadows were drawing over lake and meadow. The serpent stirred impatiently and Lily dissolved in tears.

In this extremity the serpent looked all about her, for she feared that at any moment the sun would set, decay penetrate the magic circle, and inexorably attack the handsome youth. Finally, high in the air she caught sight of the crimson feathers of the hawk, whose breast caught the last rays of the sun. She trembled with joy at the good omen, and she was not deceived; for soon after the man with the lamp could be seen gliding across the lake, just as if he were skating.

The serpent did not change her position, but Lily stood up and called to him: "What good spirit sends you at the moment when we want you so much and need you so much?"

"The spirit of my lamp impels me," replied the old man, "and the hawk has led me here. The lamp sputters when I am needed, and I just look about in the sky for a sign; a bird or a meteor shows me in what direction I should head. Be calm, loveliest maiden! Whether I can help or not, I do not know; no one can help by himself, but only when he unites with many others at the right time. Let's wait and hope. Keep your circle closed," he went on, as he turned to the serpent, sat down on a mound beside her, and illuminated the dead body. "Bring the little canary here too, and lay him in the circle!" The maidens took the tiny corpse out of the basket, which the old woman had left behind, and obeyed the man.

The sun had meanwhile set, and, as the darkness increased, not only did the serpent and the old man's lamp begin to shine, each in its own way, but Lily's veil also diffused a soft light that, like the delicate glow of dawn, tinged her pale cheeks and her white garment with infinite grace. They gazed at one another in silent contemplation; care and sorrow were eased by sure hope.

Thus there was nothing unwelcome in the appearance of the old woman, accompanied by the two merry wisps, who, to be sure, must have been very prodigal in the interim, for they had again grown extremely thin. But they only behaved all the more courteously to the princess and the other young women. With great assurance and style they said rather ordinary things; they were especially responsive to the allure that the gleaming veil shed over Lily and her companions. Modestly the young women lowered their eyes, and the praise of their beauty actually made them more beautiful. Everyone was content and calm except for the old woman. Despite her husband's assurance that her hand could shrink no further so long as the lamp shone upon it, she asserted more than once that if things went on like this, by midnight this noble member would vanish completely.

The old man with the lamp had been listening carefully to the conversation of the will-o'-the-wisps, and was glad that Lily had been distracted and cheered by this recreation. And indeed, midnight had come, no one knew how. The old man looked at the stars and then began to speak: "We are met at a fortunate hour. Everyone perform your office, everyone do your duty, and communal good fortune will assuage individual griefs just as communal misfortune devours individual joys."

After these words there arose a wondrous murmur, for everyone present spoke to himself and said aloud what he had to do. Only the three maidens were silent; one had fallen asleep beside the harp, the second beside the parasol, the third beside the chair, and no one could blame them, for it was late. The fiery youths had, after a few brief courtesies to the handmaidens, in the end attended exclusively to Lily as the most beautiful of all.

"Take the mirror," said the old man to the hawk, "and with the first rays of the sun illuminate the sleeping women and awaken them with light reflected from above!"

The serpent now began to move; she opened the circle and undulated slowly in great rings toward the river. Solemnly the two will-o'-the-wisps followed her, and they could have passed for the most serious of wisps. The old woman and her husband took hold of the basket, whose soft light had hardly been noticed up to now; they pulled from both sides and it grew steadily larger and brighter. Then they lifted the corpse of the youth into it and placed the canary on his breast. The basket rose into the air and floated above the old woman's head, and she followed at the heels of the will-o'-the-wisps. The fair Lily took the pug in her arms and followed the old woman; the man with the lamp concluded the procession, and the landscape was most oddly illuminated by these varied lights.

But with no little amazement the company saw, as they arrived at the river, a splendid arch spanning it; the benevolent serpent had prepared them a glittering path. If by day they had admired the transparent gems of which the bridge seemed composed, at night they were astounded by its shining glory. Above, the brilliant arc stood out sharply against the dark sky, but below, vivid rays flickered towards the center and revealed the airy strength of the structure. The procession crossed slowly, and the ferryman, looking out from his hut in the distance, regarded with amazement the shining circle and the strange lights passing over it.

Scarcely had they arrived on the far bank than the arch began to sway in its characteristic way and to undulate toward the water. Soon after the serpent reached the land, the basket settled to the ground, and the serpent again made her circle around it. The old man bowed down before her and spoke: "What have you decided?"

"To sacrifice myself before I am sacrificed," replied the serpent. "Promise me that you will not leave a single stone on land!"

The old man promised, and then said to the fair Lily: "Touch the serpent with your left hand and your beloved with your right!" Lily knelt down and touched the serpent and the corpse. Instantly the youth seemed to come to life; he stirred inside the basket, indeed rose up to sitting position. Lily was about to embrace him, but the old man restrained her; instead he helped the youth stand up and guided him as he stepped from the basket and the circle.

The youth stood upright, the canary fluttered on his shoulder; there was again life in them both, but the spirit had not yet returned. The handsome lover had his eyes open and did not see; at least he seemed to look at everything without interest. And scarcely had their astonishment at this circumstance subsided somewhat, than they noticed how strangely the serpent had been transformed. Her beautiful, slender body had separated into thousands and thousands of shining gems. In reaching for her basket, the old woman had carelessly bumped into her, and nothing more was to be seen of the serpent's shape: only a beautiful ring of glowing gems lay in the grass.

The old man immediately set about to gather the stones into the basket, at which task his wife had to assist him. Both of them then carried the basket to an elevated spot on the bank, and he poured the entire load, not without opposition from Lily and his wife, who would have liked to select a few for themselves, into the river. Like shining, twinkling stars the stones floated down with the waves, and it was impossible to tell whether they were lost in the distance or sank to the bottom.

"Gentlemen," the old man then said deferentially to the will-o'-the-wisps, "now I will show you the way and open the passage. But you will be doing us the greatest favor, if you will open the portal of the sanctuary, through which we must this time enter, and which none but yourselves can unlock."

The will-o'-the-wisps bowed decorously and remained behind. The old man with the lamp went ahead into the rock, which opened before him. The youth followed him as if mechanically; silent and uncertain Lily stayed some distance behind him; the old woman did not want to be left behind and stretched out her hand, so that the light from her husband's lamp would shine on it. The will-o'-the-wisps brought up the rear, bending the tips of their flames together and seeming to talk to one another.

They had not been walking long when the procession reached a great brazen portal whose leaves were bolted with a golden lock. The old man immediately summoned the will-o'-the-wisps, who needed little encouragement; with their sharpest flames they energetically consumed lock and bolt.

The bronze rang loudly as the portals suddenly sprang open, and in the sanctuary the stately images of the kings, illuminated by the entering lights, came into view. Everyone bowed before the venerable sovereigns, and especially the will-o'-the-wisps did not fail to make the most elaborate reverences.

After a pause the golden king asked: "Whence do ye come?"—"From the world," answered the old man. "Whither do ye go?" asked the silver king. "Into the world," said the old man. "What do ye want here with us?" asked the bronze king. "To accompany you," said the old man.

The composite king was just about to speak, when the golden king said to the will-o'-the-wisps, who had come too close: "Get you behind me; my gold is not for feeding you!" Next they turned to the silver king and nestled against him; his robe shone beautifully with their yellow reflection. "I welcome you," he said, "but I cannot nourish you. Eat your fill elsewhere and bring me your light!" They moved away and stole past the bronze king, who did not seem to notice them, to the composite one. "Who shall rule the world?" asked this king stuttering. "He who stands on his feet," the old man answered. "I am he!" said the composite king. "That shall soon be revealed," said the old man, "for the time is at hand."

The fair Lily threw her arms around the old man's neck and kissed him warmly. "Holy Father," she said, "I thank you a thousand times over, for I am now hearing those prophetic words for the third time." She had scarcely finished speaking, when she held on to the old man even tighter, for the ground was beginning to heave beneath their feet. The old woman and the youth also clung to one another; only the nimble will-o'-the-wisps noticed nothing.

They could distinctly feel the whole temple move, like a ship gently leaving harbor when the anchors are weighed. The depths of the earth seemed to open before it as it passed. It struck nothing, no rock stood in its path.

For a few moments a fine rain seemed to drizzle through the opening of the dome. The old man held the fair Lily more tightly and said to her, "We are under the river, and soon at our goal." Not long after, they thought they had stopped, but they were mistaken: the temple was rising.

Then there arose a strange clatter over their heads. A shapeless assemblage of boards and rafters came crashing in through the opening of the dome. Lily and the old woman jumped aside, the man with the lamp seized the youth and stood fast. The ferryman's little hut—for this was what the temple had dislodged and engulfed in its upward progress—gradually sank to the floor and covered the youth and the old man.

The women screamed and the temple shuddered, like a ship unexpectedly running aground. Anxiously the women wandered in the half-light around the hut; the door was locked and no one answered their knocking. They knocked harder and were not a little amazed, when at length the wood began to ring. By the power of the lamp sealed inside, the hut had turned to silver from within. Before long it even changed form; for the noble metal abandoned the chance configurations of planks, posts, and beams and extended itself to form a magnificent housing of chased silver. Now there stood a magnificent small temple in the middle of the large one, or, if you like, an altar worthy of the temple.

By a staircase leading upward from the inside, the noble youth now mounted aloft; the man with the lamp lighted his path, and he seemed to be supported by another man, who emerged in a short white garment and carried a silver oar in his hand. They recognized him immediately as the ferryman, the erstwhile occupant of the transformed hut.

The fair Lily climbed the outer stairs from the temple to the altar, but she still had to remain apart from her beloved. The old woman, whose hand had continued to grow smaller and smaller as long as the lamp was concealed, cried: "Shall I be lost after all? Among so many miracles, is there no miracle to save my hand?" Her husband pointed to the open door and said: "Look, day is breaking, hurry and bathe in the river!"—

"What advice!" she cried. "That would make me turn black all over and disappear completely; after all, I still haven't paid my debt!"—

"Go ahead," said the old man, "and do as I say. All debts have been paid."

The old woman hurried away, and at that moment the light of the rising sun appeared at the rim of the dome. The old man stepped between the youth and the maiden and cried in a loud voice: "Three things there be that rule on earth: wisdom, appearance, and power." At the first word the golden king stood up, at the second the silver one, and at the third the bronze king slowly arose, while the composite king abruptly and clumsily sat down.

Despite the solemnity of the moment, the onlookers could hardly refrain from laughing, for he did not sit, he did not lie, he did not lean: he had simply collapsed formlessly.

The will-o'-the-wisps, who until now had been busy with him, stepped aside. Although pale in the morning light, they seemed once again well nourished and in the best of flame. They had skillfully licked the golden veins out of the colossal figure with their pointed tongues, even the tiniest ones. The irregular hollow spaces thus produced stayed open for a while, and the figure retained its former shape. But when at last even the most delicate veins were consumed, the statue suddenly collapsed, unfortunately at just those places that hold their shape when one sits down; whereas the joints, which ought to have bent, remained stiff. There was no choice but to laugh or look away; this cross between form and lump was a hideous sight.

The man with the lamp now led the handsome, but still rigidly staring, youth down from the altar and straight to the bronze king. At the feet of the mighty sovereign lay a sword in a brazen sheath. The youth girded it on. "The sword at the left, the right hand free!" cried the powerful monarch. They went then to the silver king, who extended his scepter to the youth. The latter grasped it with his left hand, and the king said in a gracious voice: "Tend the sheep!" When they came to the golden king he pressed the oak wreath on the young man's head with a gesture of paternal blessing and said: "Know the highest!"

During this circuit the old man had carefully observed the youth. After he had girded on the sword, his chest swelled, his arms stirred, and he walked with a firmer step. When he took the scepter in his hand, his strength appeared to be tempered and to become, through some indescribable allure, even more powerful. But when the oak wreath adorned his locks, his face came alive, his eyes shone with ineffable spirit, and the first word of his mouth was "Lily."

"Dear Lily!" he cried, hastening up the silver stairs to meet her, for she had viewed his tour from the top of the altar. "Dear Lily! What more precious thing can a fully-endowed man wish for, than the innocence and the quiet love your heart offers me?—Oh my friend," he went on, turning to the old man and regarding the three holy statues, "glorious and secure is the kingdom of our fathers, but you have forgotten the fourth power, which has ruled the world longer, more universally, more securely: the power of love." With these words he threw his arms around the fair maiden. She had thrown off her veil, and her cheeks were suffused with the loveliest, most imperishable blush.

The old man responded, smiling, "Love does not rule; but it forms, and that is more."

Amid this solemnity, this happiness, this rapture they had not noticed that it was broad daylight, and now suddenly, through the open portal, the most unexpected objects met their eyes. A large space surrounded by columns formed the forecourt, at the end of which they saw a long and splendid bridge spanning the river with many arches. It was provided with splendid arcades on both sides for the comfort of foot travelers, of whom many thousands had already appeared and were passing busily to and fro. The great highway in the center was alive with herds and mules, riders and carriages that flowed freely back and forth like a river on both sides. They all seemed to admire the comfort and splendor, and the new king and his consort were as delighted by the movement and life of this great populace, as they were made happy by their mutual love.

"Remember the serpent and honor her!" said the man with the lamp. "You owe her your life, your people owe her the bridge, by which alone these neighboring shores have been brought to life as countries and united. Those floating and shining jewels, the remains of her sacrificed body, are the foundations of this magnificent bridge; upon them it has built itself and will maintain itself."

They were about to demand from him the explanation of this wonderful mystery, when four beautiful maidens entered the portal of the temple. By the harp, the parasol, and the folding chair they at once recognized Lily's attendants, but the fourth, fairer than the other three, was a stranger, who, joking in sisterly fashion, hurried with them through the temple and mounted the silver stairs.

"Will you believe me from now on, dear wife?" said the man with the lamp to the beautiful girl. "Happy are you and every creature that bathes in the river this morning!"

The rejuvenated and beautified old woman, of whose shape not a trace remained, embraced with eager, youthful arms the man with the lamp, who responded with affection to her caresses. "If I am too old for you," he said smiling, "you may choose another husband today. From today on no marriage is valid that is not joined anew."

"Don't you know," she replied, "that you also have grown younger?"

"I am glad, if to your young eyes I appear to be a sturdy youth. I'll marry you again and gladly live on with you into the next millennium."

The queen welcomed her new friend and descended into the altar with her and her other companions, while the king, between the two men, looked towards the bridge and attentively regarded the teeming multitude.

But his satisfaction did not last for long, for he saw an object that caused him some annoyance. The great giant, who seemed to have not yet fully awakened from his morning nap, came staggering across the bridge, causing great chaos. As usual he had risen still drowsy and intended to bathe in the familiar cove of the river. Instead of that he found dry land and groped along the broad pavement of the bridge.

Even though from the first he trod clumsily among the people and animals, his presence was to be sure astonishing to those about him, but as yet unfelt. When, however, the sun shone into his eyes and he raised his hands to rub them, the shadow of his monstrous fists behind him flew back and forth among the crowd so powerfully and clumsily, that people and animals collapsed together in great masses, were injured, and were in danger of being hurled into the river.

The king, when he saw this outrage, involuntarily reached toward his sword, but he reflected, and looked quietly first at his scepter, then at the lamp and the oar held by his companions. "I can guess your thoughts," said the man with the lamp, "but we and our forces are powerless against this powerless one. Be calm! He is doing harm for the last time, and fortunately his shadow is turned away from us."

Meanwhile the giant had come nearer and nearer; in amazement at what he saw with his own eyes, he let his hands drop, did no more harm, and entered the forecourt gaping.

He was heading straight for the door of the temple, when he was suddenly stuck fast to the ground in the middle of the courtyard. He stood there as a colossal, mighty statue of ruddy shining stone, and his shadow told the hours inlaid on a circle on the ground, not as numbers, but as noble and significant images.

The king was not a little pleased to see the monster's shadow turned to a useful purpose; the queen was not a little amazed when, ascending from the altar with her handmaidens, dressed with great magnificence, she glimpsed the strange image that almost completely obscured the view from temple to bridge.

Meanwhile, the people had come crowding after the giant, now that he stood still; they surrounded him and marveled at his transformation. From there the crowds turned toward the temple, which they seemed only now to perceive, and thronged to the door.

At that moment the hawk hovered with the mirror high above the dome, caught the light of the sun in it and shed it upon the group standing on the altar. The king, queen, and their companions appeared in the twilit vault of the temple illuminated by a heavenly radiance, and the people prostrated themselves. By the time they had recovered and risen to their feet, the king and his followers had descended into the altar to make their way by hidden passageways to his palace, and the people dispersed through the temple to satisfy their curiosity. They gazed at the three standing kings with amazement and reverence, but were even more curious to know what sort of lump might be hidden beneath the carpet in the fourth niche; for, whoever might have done it, well-meaning modesty had spread over the collapsed king a magnificent covering that no eye could penetrate and no hand dared remove.

The people would never have tired of looking and marveling, and the advancing crowds would have crushed one another to death inside the temple, had their attention not again been drawn back to the great court.

Unexpectedly gold coins were falling, as if from the air, ringing on the marble pavement; the closest travelers rushed to seize them. This miracle was repeated intermittently, now here, now there. It is easy to conceive that the departing will-o'-the-wisps were at it again and merrily squandering the gold from the limbs of the collapsed king. Greedily people continued to run about for a while, jostling and fretting even when the gold coins stopped falling. At last they gradually dispersed, set out on their journeys, and to this day the bridge teems with travelers, and the temple is the most frequented in the entire world.

Wilhelm Meister's Journeyman Years or The Renunciants

Translated by Krishna Winston

Translator's Note

I wish to acknowledge my gratitude to Jane Brown for translating the poems into rhymed verse and for translating several pages in the fifth chapter of Book Three that describe the technical aspects of spinning and weaving. For checking the accuracy of those passages I am very grateful to Laura Frenzel of Middletown, Connecticut.

I should like to dedicate this translation to the memory of my parents, Richard and Clara Winston, whose literary sensitivity and consummate skill at transferring the spirit of a text from one language and culture to another inspire me and set a standard against which I constantly measure my own work.

K.W.

Book One

Chapter One

The Flight into Egypt

Overshadowed by a mighty cliff, Wilhelm was sitting at a fearsome, significant spot, where the precipitous mountain path turned a corner and began a swift descent. The sun was still high in the sky, illuminating the tops of the spruces in the rocky ravines below. He was just making a notation in his writing tablet when Felix, who had been scrambling about, approached him with a rock in his hand. "What is this stone called, Father?" the boy asked.

"I do not know," Wilhelm replied.

"Could this be gold, the shiny part?" the boy wondered.

"No, it is not," the father responded, "and now I remember that people call it fool's gold."

"Fool's gold?" said the boy with a smile, "And why is that?"

"Probably because whoever takes it for gold is a fool."

"I will remember that," said the lad and stowed the rock away in his leather pouch. But he promptly produced another object and asked, "What is this?"

"A fruit of some sort," his father replied, "and to judge by its scales it must be related to the pine cone."

"But it does not look like a cone; it is round."

"Let us ask the huntsman; those fellows know everything about the forest and all the fruits. They know how to sow, to plant, and to wait; then they let the shoots grow and develop as they can."

"The huntsmen know everything; yesterday the guide showed me where a stag had crossed the path; he called me back and pointed out the spoor, as he called it. I had skipped right past it, but now I clearly saw the imprint of hooves—it must have been a large stag."

"I heard you interrogating the guide."

"He knew a lot, and he is not even a huntsman. But I wish I could be a huntsman. It is so wonderful to be in the forest all day long, to hear the birds, to know their names and where they nest, to know how to remove their eggs or their young, how to feed them or capture the parents: that is such a lark."

He had barely concluded when a curious sight appeared on the rugged path. Two boys, as lovely as a summer day, in bright little jackets that looked almost like open shirts, came gamboling downhill, one after the other.

Wilhelm had an opportunity to inspect them more closely when they stopped short at the sight of him and stood motionless for a moment. The older boy's head was wreathed in thick golden curls, the first feature that struck the observer; next one noticed the boy's clear blue eyes, and finally one became absorbed in his beauty. The second lad, in appearance more a friend than a brother, was graced with straight brown shoulder-length hair, whose color seemed mirrored in his eyes.

Wilhelm had no time to examine further these two remarkable beings, so unexpected in the wilderness, for he heard a man's voice calling in serious but friendly tones from around the corner, "Why have you stopped? Do not block the way!"

Wilhelm looked up the path, and surprised though he had been by the children, he was amazed at what now presented itself to him. A sturdy, capable young man, not overly tall, in shirtsleeves, with bronzed skin and black hair, came striding firmly yet cautiously down the mountain path, leading a donkey. At first only its well-nourished and well-groomed head could be seen, but then its lovely burden came into view, a gentle, appealing woman mounted on a large, ornamented saddle. Nestled in the blue cape that enveloped her was an infant, which she pressed to her bosom and gazed down at with ineffable sweetness. The leader responded as the children had: he paused in surprise when he spied Wilhelm. The animal slowed its steps, but the slope was too steep, the passers-by could not stop, and Wilhelm watched in astonishment as they vanished around the projecting cliff.

It was only natural that this rare apparition should distract him from his train of thought. Filled with curiosity, he stood up and looked down below to see whether they might not come into view again. And he was just about to descend and greet these strange wayfarers, when Felix came back up the path and said, "Father, may I go home with the children? They want to take me with them. And you are to come, too, the man told me. Come! They are waiting down there."

"I will speak with them," Wilhelm replied.

He found them at a spot where the path was not quite so steep, and devoured with his eyes the extraordinary figures that had so caught his attention. Only now could he make out particular details. The robust young man was in fact carrying an adz on his shoulder and a long, slender iron square. The children held large bundles of reeds, as if they were palm fronds, and if they resembled angels in this respect, they also carried little baskets of food, and thus resembled the guides who daily ply back and forth over the mountains. And the mother wore, as he saw when he regarded her more closely, a rosy, delicately tinted shift beneath her blue cloak, so that our friend to his amazement found the Flight into Egypt, which he had so often seen painted, here before his very eyes.

They exchanged greetings, and since Wilhelm was so astonished and fascinated that words failed him, the young man remarked, "Our children have already made friends in this short moment. Would you care to come along with us, to see whether good relations may not also spring up among the adults?"

Wilhelm reflected briefly and then replied, "The sight of your little family procession awakens trust and liking, and, let me at once admit, in equal measure both curiosity and a lively desire to be better acquainted with you. Indeed, one wonders at first whether you are real travelers or merely spirits that delight in enlivening these inhospitable mountains with pleasant apparitions."

"Then come along with us to our dwelling," the young man said. "Come along!" shouted the children, as they pulled Felix away with them. "Come along!" said the woman, turning her expression of sweet friendliness from the infant to Wilhelm.

Without hesitation Wilhelm replied, "I am sorry that I cannot follow you at once. This night at least I must still spend up above in the border lodge. My portmanteau, my papers—everything is still up there, unpacked and unguarded. But to demonstrate my wish and my willingness to accede to your kind invitation, I shall give you my Felix as security. Tomorrow I will join you. How far is it from here?"

"We will reach our home before sundown," the carpenter replied, "and from the border lodge you have only another hour and a half. Your boy shall join our household for tonight; tomorrow we will expect you."

The man and the beast started off. Wilhelm was pleased to see his Felix in such good company; he was now able to compare him with the dear little angels, from whom Felix stood out markedly. He was not large for his years, but sturdy, with broad chest and powerful shoulders; his nature was an odd combination of leader and follower: he had already snatched up a palm frond and a little basket, which seemed to express both qualities. The procession was on the point of vanishing again around an escarpment when Wilhelm pulled himself together and called out, "How shall I ask the way?"

"Just ask for Saint Joseph," rang out from below, and the entire apparition had vanished behind the blue walls of shadow. From the distance a devout song floated up, sung in several parts, and Wilhelm thought he could distinguish the voice of his Felix.

He ascended the path and in this manner delayed the sunset. The heavenly body, which he had lost more than once, shone upon him again as he mounted, and it was still day when he reached his lodging. Once more he gazed with pleasure on the magnificent mountainscape, and then withdrew to his chamber, where he promptly took up his pen and passed part of the night in writing.

Wilhelm to Natalie

Now at last the summit has been reached, the summit of the mountain range that will separate us more powerfully than all the regions traversed thus far. To my mind, we are still near our loved ones so long as the rivers still run from us to them. Today I can still imagine that the twig I toss into the forest brook might well float down to her, might in a few days' time wash ashore at the foot of her garden; and thus our soul sends its images, the heart its sentiments, more easily downwards. But on the other side, I fear, a dividing wall will obstruct my imagination and emotions. Yet perhaps my anxiety is too hasty: in all likelihood it will be no different on the other side. What could separate me from you! from you, to whom I belong forever, even if a singular fate parts me from you and unexpectedly bars the gates of the paradise to which I had come so near. I had time to compose myself, and yet no time would have sufficed, had I not received this composure from your mouth, from your lips, in that decisive moment. How could I have torn myself away, had not the enduring thread been spun that shall bind us for all time and all eternity? But I may not speak of this. I do not wish to violate your gentle commandments; on this summit let it be the last time I utter the word separation before you. My life is to become a journey. I must undertake the strange obligations of the journeyman and undergo trials meant for me alone. How I smile sometimes when I read over the conditions that the league, that I myself established! Some of them are observed, some violated, but even as I violate them, this document, this record of my last confession, my last absolution, serves in place of a stern conscience, and I return to my path. I watch my step, and my errors no longer tumble one over the other like the mountain waters.

Yet I will freely admit that I often admire those teachers and leaders of men who impose only external, mechanical tasks upon their disciples. They make it easy for themselves and for the world. For it is precisely this portion of the requirements, which at first seemed to me the most irksome, the most strange, that I now regard as the most comfortable and hold most dear.

I am not to remain more than three days under the same roof. I am not to leave my lodging without traveling at least one mile from the spot. These commandments are calculated to make my years true journeyman years and to forestall the least temptation to settle anywhere. Until now I have observed this rule strictly, indeed have not made use of the leeway accorded me. This is actually the first time I have lingered, the first time I shall sleep for a third night in the same bed. From here I dispatch to you assorted information, observations, impressions I have collected, and then tomorrow begin the descent to the other side, first to visit an extraordinary family, a holy family I might call it, about which you will find more in my journal. For now, farewell, and lay this letter aside with the sense that it has only *one* thing to say, wishes to repeat only *one* thing, over and over again, but will not say it, will not repeat it, until I have the good fortune to kneel once more at your feet and to pour out my heart to you for the great deprivation I have endured.

In the morning.

Everything is packed. The guide is strapping my portmanteau onto the pack frame. The sun has not yet risen, mists billow up from every ravine; but the heavens above are clear. We are about to descend into the dark depths, which will also soon clear up above our heads. Let me send my last sigh across to you! Let my last gaze in your direction be filled with involuntary tears! I am bound and determined: you shall hear no more laments from me; you shall hear only of the wanderer's encounters. And yet, even as I make ready to close this letter, a thousand thoughts, wishes, hopes, and intentions crowd upon me again. Fortunately I am being driven away. The guide is calling, and the innkeeper has already begun to tidy up, as if I were gone, just as unfeeling, thoughtless heirs take no pains to conceal from the departing that they are about to take possession.

Chapter Two

Saint Joseph the Second

Following close on the heels of the guide, the wanderer had already left steep cliffs behind and above him; already they were traversing gentler hills and hastening through many a fine stand of trees, over many a pleasant meadow, ever onwards, until they finally found themselves on a slope looking down into a carefully cultivated valley, ringed all around by hills. The eye was immediately drawn to a large monastery, part of which lay in ruins, the other part of which was well preserved. "This is Saint Joseph," said the guide; "a terrible shame about the beautiful church! See how well the columns and pillars are preserved, showing through brush and trees, even though the church has lain in ruins for hundreds of years."

As they spoke, they had passed through the open gate into the spacious courtyard which, surrounded by stately, well-maintained structures, revealed that order and calm reigned here. Wilhelm at once spied his Felix and the angels of the previous day busy around a pack basket which a sturdy woman had set down beside her; they were buying cherries, but Felix, who always carried some money with him, was doing the actual dickering. Now he, the guest, promptly played host, giving fruit generously to his playmates, and even his father was glad of this refreshment in the midst of these barren, mossy woodlands, where the colorful, gleaming fruit looked all the more luscious. She had to carry the cherries up from a large orchard far below, the woman said in defense of her price, which her buyers had thought rather high. Their father would be back soon, the children said; Wilhelm should go right into the hall and rest.

But how astonished Wilhelm was when the children led him into the room they called the hall. A wide door opened directly into it from the courtyard, and the wanderer found himself inside a very clean, well-preserved chapel, which, however, as he at once saw, was arranged for daily domestic use. On one side stood a table, an armchair, and several chairs and benches, on the other a handsomely carved hutch filled with gay crockery, pitchers, and glasses. There were also several chests and trunks, and tidy though everything was, the room still had the inviting air of a place that was lived in. Light entered through high windows in the side walls. But what most struck the wanderer were colorful pictures painted on the walls, extending like hangings over three sides of the room, reaching from just below the windows down to the wainscot that covered the rest of the wall to the floor. The paintings portrayed the story of St. Joseph. Here you saw him busy at his carpentry; here he encountered Mary, and a lily sprouted from the ground between them, while several angels hovered attentively around them. Here he is being married, then comes the Annunciation. Here he sits disgruntled, surrounded by unfinished work, his adz idle as he considers parting from his wife. But next the angel appears to him in a dream, and his circumstances change. He gazes with reverence upon the newborn child in the manger at Bethlehem and worships it. Soon afterward comes a strangely beautiful picture. It shows several pieces of worked wood about to be assembled; by chance, two of the pieces form a cross. The child has fallen asleep on the cross, while the mother sits beside him, gazing on him with deep devotion, and the foster father pauses in his work so as not to disturb the infant's slumber. The Flight into Egypt follows next. It evoked a smile from the contemplative wanderer as he saw the living tableau of the previous day repeated here on the wall.

He had little time to pursue his reflections, for soon his host entered; Wilhelm at once recognized him as the leader of the holy caravan. They greeted one another most warmly, and conversation on various topics ensued; but Wilhelm's attention remained fixed on the paintings. His host noticed his interest and began with a smile, "Surely you are wondering at the correspondence between this building and its occupants, whom you encountered yesterday. But it is perhaps even more curious than one might suspect: in actuality the building created its occupants. For if the inanimate is full of life, it can bring forth something alive."

"Oh, yes," Wilhelm replied, "it would surprise me to hear that the spirit that worked with such force in these desolate mountains hundreds of years ago and attracted to itself such a mighty body of buildings, estates, and privileges, from which the blessings of culture spread through the region—it would surprise me if it did not still exert a vital influence on living beings even from amidst these ruins. But let us not dwell too long on the general; acquaint me with your own story, that I may understand how, without frivolity or presumption, the past could come alive again in you and that which had passed on reappear."

Just as Wilhelm was expecting an explanation from the lips of his host, a friendly voice in the courtyard called out the name Joseph. The host listened and went to the door.

"So his name is Joseph, too," Wilhelm said to himself. "That is certainly odd enough, and yet not so odd as the fact that he portrays his saint in his own life." At this moment he looked toward the door and saw the man talking with the Mother of God from the previous day. At last they separated, and the woman started for the dwelling across the way. "Marie," he called after her, "just one more thing!"

"So she is even named Marie," Wilhelm thought; "I almost feel as though I had been transported back eighteen hundred years." He contemplated the solemn, secluded valley to which he had come, the ruins and the stillness, and an extraordinary sense of antiquity stole over him. It was just as well that his host and the children entered. The children invited Wilhelm for a walk, while the husbandman attended to a few matters. They strolled among the ruins of the church, with its many pillars; its towering gables and walls seemed to have been reinforced in wind and weather, for stout trees had long ago taken root atop the thick walls and, along with grasses, flowers, and moss, presented the appearance of exotic hanging gardens. Gentle meadow paths followed the course of a lively brook, and from a little higher the traveler could overlook the entire structure and its site, viewing it with the greater interest inasmuch as its occupants had become yet more remarkable to him, and their harmony with their surroundings had awakened his intense curiosity.

The little group returned and found a table laid in the consecrated hall. At its head stood an armchair in which the mistress of the house took her place. Next to her was a large basket in which lay the infant; then came the father to her left and Wilhelm to her right. The three children occupied the lower end of the table. An old serving woman brought in a carefully prepared repast. The dishes and goblets likewise evoked earlier times. The children provided occasion for conversation, while Wilhelm did not tire of contemplating the form and demeanor of his holy hostess.

After dinner the company broke up. The host led his guest to a shaded part of the ruins where, from an elevated spot, they had a pleasing view down the entire valley and saw the lower mountains beyond spreading into the distance with fertile slopes and wooded ridges. "It is only proper," began the host, "that I should satisfy your curiosity, the more so as I sense that you can take a serious view of things that appear odd, so long as they prove serious at bottom. This religious institution, whose remains you see, was consecrated to the Holy Family, and used to be a famous place of pilgrimage because of the many miracles that took place here. The church was dedicated to the Mother and the Son. It was destroyed several centuries ago. The chapel, dedicated to the Holy Foster Father, survived, as did the usable section of the monastery buildings. For many years now the revenues have gone to a secular prince, who maintains a steward here, and that is who I am, the son of the previous steward, who likewise followed his father in the position.

"Although all religious observances ceased here long ago, St. Joseph was always so generous to our family that it is not surprising we had a particular fondness for him; thus it was that I was christened Joseph and thereby more or less had my life's course set for me. As I grew up, I often joined my father when he went to collect the rents, but it gave me even greater pleasure to accompany my mother, who regularly dispensed charity, to the extent her means allowed, and was known and loved throughout the mountains for her kindness and her good deeds. She dispatched me hither and yon to make deliveries, give instructions, look after things, and I took readily to this pious calling.

"On the whole, there is something more humane about life in the mountains than in the flatlands. The inhabitants are closer to one another and, if you will, also farther apart; their needs are simpler but more pressing. Each person must rely more upon himself, must learn to depend on his own hands, his own feet. Workman, courier, porter—all are combined in one person; everyone is also closer to his neighbor, sees him more often, and is engaged with him in a common venture.

"While I was still young, and my shoulders could not bear heavy loads, I had the idea of equipping a little donkey with baskets and driving him up and down the steep footpaths. In the mountains the donkey is not the contemptible animal he is in the flatlands, where the farmhand who plows with a horse considers himself superior to one who draws his furrows with oxen. And I had even fewer compunctions about making my rounds with the donkey because I had already noticed in the chapel that this animal had had the honor of carrying Our Lord and His mother. But this chapel was not yet in the condition in which it is now. It was used as a shed, almost as a stable. Firewood, poles, implements, barrels and ladders, and what have you were crammed in any which way. It was sheer good fortune that the paintings are so high and that the wainscoting can take mistreatment. But even as a child I loved to climb around on the lumber and look at the pictures, which no one could really interpret for me. It was enough to know that the saint whose life they depicted was my patron saint, and I rejoiced in him as I would have in an uncle. I was growing up, and because it was stipulated that the person who aspired to the lucrative office of steward must have a trade, my parents, who hoped to pass on to me this excellent living, urged me to learn a trade, and one that would be useful in maintaining the household up here.

"My father was a cooper, and whenever work of this sort needed doing, he attended to it himself, a most advantageous arrangement for all concerned. Yet I could not decide to follow him in it. I was irresistibly drawn toward carpentry, the tools for which I had since my childhood seen so painstakingly and accurately depicted beside my saint. I declared my wish; no objections were raised, the more so because we often needed a carpenter for all sorts of construction, and a carpenter with a taste and a talent for fine work might easily find himself—especially in forest regions—doing cabinetry and even carving. What strengthened me in my aspiration was one painting, which by now is unfortunately almost wholly obliterated. Once you know its subject matter, however, you will be able to decipher it when I show it to you. St. Joseph received no less a commission than to make a throne for King Herod. The great seat is to be positioned between two existing columns. Joseph carefully measures the length and width and builds a magnificent royal throne. But how astonished he is, how chagrined, when he delivers the splendid seat: it is too high and too narrow. As we know, King Herod was not one to be trifled with; the devout master carpenter is sorely troubled. The Christ Child, who accompanies him everywhere, carrying his tools in humble child's play, sees his need and at once comes to his aid. The miraculous child directs his foster father to take hold of one side of the throne, while he himself grasps the carving on the other, and both begin to pull. Quickly and easily, as if made of leather, the throne extends in breadth, loses height proportionately, and now fits perfectly into place, to the immense relief of the master carpenter and the complete satisfaction of the king.

"In my youth that throne could still be made out clearly, and from what remains of one side you will be able to see that no pains were spared with the carving—which of course must have been easier for the painter than it would have been for a carpenter, if anyone had demanded it of him.

"But none of this gave me a moment's pause; indeed, I so greatly respected the trade to which I had dedicated myself that I could hardly wait to be placed as an apprentice. This proved easy, because a master carpenter lived nearby; he did work for the entire region and could employ several journeymen and apprentices. So I remained close to my parents and to an extent continued my previous life, devoting my free time and holidays to the charitable errands on which my mother continued to send me."

The Visitation

"Thus several years passed," the man continued his story. "I soon recognized the advantages of my trade, and my body, molded by work, could meet all the demands made in the course of it. In addition, I performed my previous service to my good mother, or rather, to the sick and needy. I traveled throughout the mountains with my donkey, distributed my cargo conscientiously, and brought back from shopkeepers and merchants what we lacked up here. My master was content with me, as were my parents. On my journeys I already had the satisfaction of passing a number of houses that I had helped to build, that I had decorated. For the final notching of the beams, carving simple designs, burning decorative figures into the wood, accenting grooves in red—all these humble arts which give a wooden chalet its cheery appearance—were assigned to me, because I was the most skillful at them, since I had ever before my mind's eye Herod's throne and its ornamentation.

"Among the needy persons for whom my mother had a particular concern, young women with child occupied a special position; I gradually came to realize this, although in such cases the actual missions were kept secret from me. I was never given a direct assignment; instead, everything was done through a good woman who lived a short distance down the valley and was called Dame Elisabeth. My mother, herself skilled in that art which has rescued for life so many children as they tottered on the threshold, maintained a cordial exchange with Dame Elisabeth, and I often heard from all sides that many a one of our sturdy mountain folk owed his existence to these two women. The secretiveness with which Dame Elisabeth always received me, the laconic answers to my puzzled questions, which I myself did not wholly comprehend, filled me with a curious awe of her, and her house, which was spotlessly clean, seemed to me a small sanctuary of sorts.

"In the meanwhile my competence and craftsmanship had gained me a certain influence in the family. As my father, in his capacity as cooper, had equipped the cellar, I now attended to the roof over our heads, and repaired many dilapidated sections of the old buildings. In particular I managed to restore a number of tumbledown barns and sheds for household use; and as soon as these were done, I began to clear out and clean my beloved chapel. In a few days it was in order, almost as you see it now; I took great pains to restore the missing or damaged sections of the wainscoting to match the rest. And you probably think that the double doors at the entrance are original, but in fact they are my work. I spent several years carving them in my leisure hours, having first carefully assembled them from stout oaken planks. Those sections of the paintings which had not faded or been damaged have been preserved, and I helped the master glazier with a new building, on the condition that he make stained-glass windows for me.

"If previously the pictures and thoughts about the life of the saint had occupied my imagination, they impressed themselves even more vividly upon me now that I could regard the space once more as a sanctuary and could linger there, especially in summertime, pondering what I saw or surmised. I felt an irresistible urge to follow in the footsteps of this saint, and since similar circumstances could not be conjured up at will, I wished at least to begin to resemble him in the fundamental details, as indeed I had long since begun to resemble him through my beast of burden. I was no longer content with the little creature I had used hitherto; I found myself a much finer pack animal, procured a handsomely made saddle equally suited to a rider or a load. I purchased a pair of new panniers; and a web of colorful cord, tufts, and tassles with little jingling metal disks adorned the neck of the long-eared beast, which now could hold its own with its model on the chapel wall. No one dreamt of mocking me as I journeyed through the mountains thus outfitted, for people readily concede charity's right to an eccentric guise.

"In the meantime, war, or rather its consequences, had drawn near our region. Several times dangerous bands of marauding deserters came together and committed here and there acts of violence or malice. Thanks to the local militia, to patrols and heightened vigilance, the evil was soon contained; but people too quickly let down their guard, and before we knew it, new mischief broke out again.

"It had been peaceful in our region for some time, and I was calmly plying the accustomed paths with my pack mule, when one day I crossed the freshly seeded clearing and came upon a female figure seated, or rather lying, on the edge of the surrounding ditch. She seemed to be asleep or in a swoon. I busied myself about her, and as she opened her lovely eyes and sat up, she exclaimed eagerly, 'Where is he? Have you seen him?' 'Whom?' I asked, and she replied, 'My husband.' Given her youthful appearance, the answer was unexpected, but I offered her my assistance all the more gladly, and assured her of my concern. I learned that because of the bad roads the two travelers had left their carriage and set out by a more direct footpath. Near this spot they had been attacked by armed men. Her husband had drawn his sword and attempted to drive the ruffians off. She had not been able to keep up with him, and had remained lying there, she knew not how long. She begged me to leave her and hasten after her husband. She rose to her feet, and the most beautiful, appealing figure stood before me; but I could easily see that she was in a condition that would soon require the ministrations of my mother and Dame Elisabeth. We disputed for a short while, for I insisted that I first bring her to safety, while she insisted that she first have news of her husband. She refused to leave his trail, and all my urgings would probably have come to naught if a squad of militia had not come riding toward us through the forest just then, they having heard that trouble was afoot. I told them what had occurred, made the necessary arrangements with them, agreed on a rendezvous, and thus settled the matter for the present. I quickly concealed my panniers in a nearby cave which I had often used for storage, converted my saddle to a comfortable seat, and, not without a peculiar sensation, lifted the lovely burden onto my willing animal, which could follow the familiar paths on its own, and thus gave me the opportunity to walk alongside.

"You can imagine, without lengthy descriptions, how strange I felt. I had actually found that which I had so long sought. It was as if I were dreaming, and then again as though I were awakening from a dream. This divine figure, which I seemed to see floating in the air and moving against a backdrop of green trees, was like something out of a dream generated in my soul by those paintings in the chapel. At moments these pictures seemed to have been merely dreams, which now gave way to an exquisite reality. I asked her a number of questions, and she answered gently and pleasantly, in a tone befitting one who is properly downcast. Several times when we reached a treeless elevation she asked me to stop, to look around, to listen. She asked with such grace, with such fervent pleading in her eyes, with their long, dark lashes, that I did everything possible; I even scaled a tall, branchless spruce that stood alone. Never had I been more grateful for this special skill of my trade; never had it given me greater satisfaction to retrieve a ribbon or silk scarf from a similar treetop at a fair or festival. But this time, alas, I came away without a prize; even from my high perch I saw and heard nothing. Finally she herself called me to come down, and even beckoned vigorously. Indeed, when I slid down, and let go at a fair height and leaped to the ground, she uttered a cry, and a look of sweet goodwill spread over her face when she saw me standing before her unharmed.

"Why should I tell you at length the hundreds of attentions I showered upon her, trying to win her favor and distract her. And indeed how could I! For it is the nature of true attentiveness that it transforms mere nothings into everything. To me the flowers I plucked for her, the distant parts I pointed out to her, the mountains, the forests I identified for her, were like so many precious treasures I wished to bestow on her, in order to forge a bond between us, as one tries to do with gifts.

"She had already won my heart forever when we reached the village and the door of that good woman, where I knew already that I faced a painful parting. Once more my eyes traveled over her entire form, and when they reached her feet, I bent over, as though to adjust the girth, and kissed the most charming little shoe I had ever seen, but without her noticing it. I helped her down, dashed up the steps, and called in through the front door, 'Dame Elisabeth, you are receiving a visitation!'

"The good woman came out, and I watched over her shoulders from the doorway as the lovely creature mounted the steps with a sweet air of sorrow and innate dignity, then embraced my excellent old woman, and allowed herself to be escorted to her best room. They closed the door behind them, and I stood there outside with my donkey like someone who has just unloaded precious wares, and finds himself as poor a drover as before."

The Lily Stalk

"I was still hesitating to depart, for I was undecided as to what I should do, when Dame Elisabeth came to the door and requested that I summon my mother to her, then go out and if possible bring back tidings of the husband. 'Marie beseeches you to do this,' she said. 'Can I not speak with her myself, just once more?' I responded. 'That may not be,' Dame Elisabeth said, and we parted.

"In a short while I reached our home; my mother was ready to go down that very evening and assist the young stranger. I hurried down to the valley, hoping I could obtain reliable information from the bailiff. But he himself was still in uncertainty, and because he knew me, he bade me pass the night with him. That night was interminably long, and through it all I saw before me that lovely form, swaying on the animal's back and looking down at me with such a sorrowful, friendly expression. Every moment I hoped for news. I did not begrudge the good husband his life, I wished it for him, and yet I did so like to think of her as a widow.

"The roving patrol gradually reassembled, and after various contradictory rumors, it finally became certain that the coach had been rescued, but that the unfortunate husband had died of his wounds in the neighboring village. I also learned that, as previously agreed, some of them had gone to bring this sad news to Dame Elisabeth. That meant that I had nothing more to do or to accomplish there, and yet boundless impatience, immeasurable longing, drove me through mountains and forests back to her door. It was night, the house shut tight. I saw light in the rooms, saw shadows moving across the curtains, and so I sat on a bench across the way, always on the verge of knocking and always restrained by various considerations.

"But why should I recount in such detail what is really of no interest. To be brief, on the following morning I was not allowed in either. The sad news was known, I was superfluous; I was to return to my father, to my work. My questions remained unanswered; my presence was not wanted.

"This treatment continued for a week, until finally Dame Elisabeth called me inside. 'Come on tiptoe, my friend,' she said, 'but do come in!' She led me to an immaculate room, where through half-drawn bedcurtains in the corner I could see my fair one, sitting upright. Dame Elisabeth went to her, as if to announce me, lifted something from the bed, and brought it toward me: swaddled in the whitest linen, the most beautiful little boy. Dame Elisabeth held him exactly halfway between me and the mother, and at once there occurred to me the lily stalk in the picture, rising from the earth between Mary and Joseph in testimony of their purity. From that moment all burdens were lifted from my heart; I felt certain of my cause, of my happiness. I could approach her freely, speak with her, bear her heavenly gaze, take the boy in my arms and press a heartfelt kiss on his brow.

" 'How I thank you for your affection for this orphaned child!' the mother said. Without a moment's reflection, I exclaimed, 'He is an orphan no longer, if you are but willing!'

"Dame Elisabeth, more prudent than I, took the child from me and sent me on my way.

"Memories of that time still serve as my happiest entertainment when I am obliged to travel through our mountains and valleys. I can still recall the smallest circumstance, though I shall spare you the details, as is proper. Weeks passed; Marie had recovered, and I was permitted to see her quite often. My intercourse with her was a succession of services and attentions. Her personal circumstances allowed her to live where she wished. First she remained with Dame Elisabeth; then she visited us, to thank my mother and me for so much and such friendly assistance. She enjoyed being with us, and I flattered myself that it was partly on my account. But that which I would so gladly have spoken and yet did not dare to speak found expression in a curious and charming fashion when I led her into the chapel, which I had already transformed into a livable space. I showed her the pictures and explained them one at a time, dwelling on the duties of a foster father in such a lively and heartfelt manner that tears came to her eyes and I could not finish my exposition. I was confident of her affection, although I was not so presumptuous as to expect to obliterate her memories of her husband so soon. The law imposes a year of mourning on widows, and such a period, which comprehends the cycle of earthly change, is certainly necessary for a feeling heart to overcome the painful impressions of a great loss. One sees the blossoms fade and the leaves fall, but one also sees fruit ripen and new buds swell. Life belongs to the living, and he who lives must be prepared for change.

"I now spoke with my mother about this matter, so close to my heart. She thereupon revealed to me how painfully Marie had been affected by her husband's death, and how only the thought that she must live for her child's sake had sustained her. My love had not remained hidden from the women, and Marie had already accustomed herself to the idea of living with us. She lingered in the neighborhood a short while longer; then she came up to us, and we continued for a while in the most devout and blissful betrothal.

"At last we were married. That first feeling that had brought us together did not wane. The duties and joys of a foster father and a father were joined; and though to be sure our little family surpassed its model in number as it grew, nevertheless the virtues of that ideal image of fidelity and purity were revered and practiced by us. And so we preserve as a pleasant custom the outward appearance, upon which we happened by chance, and which corresponds so well to our inner inclinations: for although we are all good walkers and sturdy bearers, the beast of burden remains ever with us, to carry some load or another, whenever a transaction or visit takes us through these mountains and valleys. As you found us yesterday, so we are known throughout the region, and we are proud that our way of life is such as to bring no shame upon those holy names and figures to whose imitation we dedicate ourselves."

Chapter Three

Wilhelm to Natalie

I have just completed a pleasant, almost miraculous tale, which I transcribed for you from the mouth of a most excellent man. If the words are not exactly his, if here and there I have expressed my own sentiments as his, that is only natural, given the affinity I feel for him. The reverence for his wife—does it not resemble that which I feel for you? and does not the very coming together of these two lovers bear a resemblance to ours? But he has the good fortune to walk beside the beast that bears the doubly beautiful burden; when evening comes, he can accompany his family procession through the old cloister gate; he is inseparable from his beloved, from his dear ones. For all that I may be permitted to envy him in secret. But I am not even permitted to bemoan my fate, since I promised you to keep silent and endure, as you also took upon yourself.

I must pass over many a lovely feature in the shared lives of these devout and serene people, for how could I write it all? A few days have passed pleasantly for me, but now the third admonishes me to be on my way.

Felix and I had a little tiff today, for he tried to induce me to violate one of the commitments I made to you. It is my failing, my misfortune, my fate that willy-nilly the company around me grows, that I often take on a new burden that I am thenceforth obligated to carry, or drag, along with me. Now, on this journey no third person is supposed to become our constant companion. We desire and ought to be but two, and should remain so, and just now a new and not altogether gratifying liaison seemed to be in the making.

The children of the house, with whom Felix has enjoyed playing these last few days, were joined by a lively little poor boy, who allowed himself to be used and misused as the game required, and who quickly won Felix's favor. And I could already guess from various remarks that Felix had chosen a playmate for the coming journey. The boy is well known about these parts, is tolerated everywhere because of his high spirits and receives occasional alms. But I did not like him, and

I asked the master of the house to send him on his way. That was then done, but Felix was cross about it, and there was a little scene.

On this occasion I made a pleasant discovery. In one corner of the chapel, or hall, stood a box of stones, which Felix, who has developed a passionate interest in rocks since our journey through the mountains, eagerly pulled out and inspected. There were some beautiful and striking pieces. Our host said the child might choose what he liked. The stones were left over from a large quantity which a stranger had recently shipped from here. He called him Montan, and you can imagine that I was delighted to hear this name, under which one of our best friends is traveling, a man to whom we owe much. I enquired as to the time and the circumstances, and can now hope to encounter him soon on my journey.

The news that Montan was in the vicinity had made Wilhelm reflective. He considered that it ought not be left to chance whether he should see such a valued friend again, and therefore he inquired of his host whether anyone knew which path the traveler had taken. No one had any precise information, and Wilhelm had already decided to continue according to his original plan, when Felix exclaimed, "If you were not so stubborn, Father, we could find Montan easily." "How so?" Wilhelm asked. Felix replied, "Little Fitz said yesterday that he could probably trace the gentleman who had the beautiful rocks with him and knew so much about them." After some discussion back and forth, Wilhelm finally decided to make the attempt, but to keep an even closer eye on the questionable boy. He was soon found, and when he learned what was intended, brought along a mallet and chisel, and a sturdy hammer, as well as a small sack, and darted merrily on ahead in his miner's garb.

Their way took them off to the side, again up the mountain. The children bounded from rock to rock, up hill and down dale, over brooks and springs, and without any path before him Fitz pressed quickly onward, glancing to right and left. Since Wilhelm and especially the guide with his heavy pack could not follow so quickly, the boys kept getting ahead and running back, singing and whistling. The form of some unfamiliar trees caught Felix's attention; he now made his first acquaintance with the larch and the arolla pine, and he was fascinated by the wonderful gentians. And so there was no lack of entertainment on the arduous journey.

Suddenly little Fitz stood still and listened. He beckoned the others to him: "Do you hear tapping?" he said. "It is the sound of a hammer striking the rock." "We hear it," answered the others. "That is Montan!" he said, "or someone who can give us word of him." As they followed the sound, which was repeated from time to time, they came to a clearing and saw a steep, high, bare cliff towering over everything, leaving even the tall trees far below. On the summit they spied a person. He was too far away to be recognized. The children promptly set out to climb the steep path. Wilhelm followed with some difficulty, even danger; the person who goes up a cliff first is always safer, because he can seek out the best way, while the one who follows behind sees only what spot the other has reached, but not how he got there. The boys soon reached the summit, and Wilhelm heard a loud cry of joy. "It is Jarno!" Felix called down to his father, and Jarno at once stepped out onto a jagged promontory, offered a hand to his friend, and pulled him up. They embraced and greeted each other with delight under the open heavens.

But they had barely released one another when vertigo overcame Wilhelm, not only for himself, but because he saw the children hanging over the vast abyss. Jarno noticed and bade them all sit down at once. "Nothing is more natural," he said, "than that we should experience vertigo before an unexpected grand view, for it confronts us simultaneously with our own smallness and our grandeur. Yet there cannot be any true pleasure, except where one is at first overcome."

"Are those the high mountains down there that we have already climbed?" Felix asked. "How small they look! And here," he continued, prying a piece of rock loose from the summit, "is that fool's gold again; I suppose it is everywhere?" "It occurs far and wide," Jarno replied, "and since you ask about such things, you should note that you are now sitting on the oldest mountain formation, the oldest rock in the world." "Wasn't the world made all at once?" Felix asked. "Hardly," Montan replied; "Rome was not built in a day." "And so down there is an entirely different kind of rock," Felix said, "and another kind over there, and another and another!" as he pointed from the nearest mountains to the more distant ones and on down into the plain.

It was a very beautiful day, and Jarno made them survey the glorious view in detail. Here and there rose several peaks, similar to the one on which they sat. A mountain formation of medium height seemed to strive upward, but never approached their own elevation. Farther away the land grew flatter, but there, too, curious formations suddenly jutted up. In the far distance lakes and rivers became visible, and a fruitful plain stretched toward the horizon like an ocean. As the eye drew back, it plunged into fearsome depths, where waterfalls roared in a labyrinth of gorges.

Felix did not tire of asking questions, and Jarno was gracious enough to answer every one of them. Yet Wilhelm thought he detected that the teacher was not being entirely truthful and straightforward. When, therefore, the restless boys began to scramble about again, Wilhelm said to his friend, "You did not speak with the child about these things the same way you speak with yourself about them." "That is asking a great deal," Jarno replied, "for after all, one does not always speak with oneself as one thinks, and it is one's duty to tell others only what they can comprehend. People understand only what suits them. The best one can do for children is to hold them to the present, to supply them with a label, a category. They will ask about causes soon enough in any case."

"You cannot blame them for that," replied Wilhelm. "The diversity among objects confuses everyone, and it is easier, instead of connecting them, to ask quickly, 'Where from?' 'Where to?' " "And yet," said Jarno, "since children see objects only superficially, you can also speak with them only superficially about development and purpose." "Most people," responded Wilhelm, "remain their whole life long in this condition and never reach that glorious stage in which what is easy to understand seems common and foolish." "You may well call it glorious," Jarno replied, "since it is a condition halfway between despair and deification." "Let us stay with the boy," Wilhelm answered, "who matters more to me now than anything else. He has become very interested in rocks since we have been traveling. Can you not communicate to me enough so that I can satisfy him, at least for a while?" "That is not possible," said Jarno. "In each new realm you must begin again as a child, attack the thing with passionate interest, enjoy the outer shell first, until you have the good fortune to reach the inner kernel."

"So tell me," replied Wilhelm, "how did you come by your knowledge and insight? It is not so long ago that we parted!" "My friend," Jarno replied, "we had to renounce, if not forever, at least for quite a while. The first thing that occurs to an able person under such circumstances is to begin a new life. New objects are not enough; they are good only for distraction. He requires a new whole, and promptly locates himself in the middle of it." "But why, then," Wilhelm interrupted, "this oddest, this most solitary of pursuits?" "For the very reason that it is reclusive," Jarno exclaimed. "I wanted to avoid people. There is nothing to be done for them, and they keep us from doing anything for ourselves. If they are happy, you are supposed to let them alone in their silliness; if they are unhappy, you are supposed to save them without interfering with that silliness; and no one ever asks whether *you* are happy or unhappy."

"It is not really all that bad," replied Wilhelm with a smile. "I do not wish to deny you your happiness," Jarno said. "Continue on your way, you second Diogenes. Do not let your lantern go out in broad daylight! Down there a new world lies before you; but I'll wager it is just like the old one behind us. If you cannot pander and pay your debts, you are of no use to them." "They still seem more entertaining to me," replied Wilhelm, "than your lifeless cliffs." "Not at all," replied Jarno, "for these at least are not to be comprehended." "You are looking for an excuse," replied Wilhelm; "it is not like you to occupy yourself with things no one can hope to comprehend. Be honest and tell me what you have found in this cold and lifeless pastime!" "That is difficult to say for any pastime, especially for this one." Then he thought for a moment and said, "The letters of the alphabet are fine things, but they are inadequate to express sounds; we cannot do without sounds, and yet they are by no means sufficient to express actual meaning; in the end, we cling to letters and sounds, and we are no better off than if we did without them altogether. Everything we communicate, everything that is transmitted to us, is always only the obvious, not worth the effort at all."

"You are evading the question," Wilhelm said, "for after all, what does this have to do with these cliffs and peaks?" "But suppose I treated these very fissures and crevasses as letters, attempted to decipher them, shaped them into words, and learned to read them, would you have any objection to that?" "No, but it seems to me a rather diffuse alphabet." "More coherent than you think; but you must learn it, like any other. Nature has only one script, and I do not need to load myself down with all sorts of scribblings. Here I have no fear, as can happen if I work long and lovingly on some parchment, that some clever critic will come along and assure me that I have merely read my own meaning into it." With a smile his friend replied, "And yet even here someone may question your reading." "For that very reason I discuss it with no one," he answered, "and precisely because I am fond of you, I prefer not to continue this empty and false exchange of words."

Chapter Four

The two friends had descended, not without care and effort, to rejoin the children, who were resting below in a shady spot. The rock samples they had collected were unpacked by Montan and Felix almost more eagerly than the provisions. The latter had many questions, the former many names to provide. Felix was delighted that Montan knew all the names, and he quickly committed them to memory. Finally he brought out one more and asked, "And what is this one called?" Montan looked at him in wonder and said, "Where did you get that?" Fitz replied quickly, "I found it, it comes from here." "It does not come from this region," answered Montan. Fitz was delighted to see this superior man in doubt. "You shall have a ducat," said Montan, "if you can take me to where it outcrops." "That will be easy to earn," Fitz replied, "but not right away." "Well, then, tell me the exact place, so that I can be sure of finding it. But that is impossible, because it is a cross-stone from Santiago de Compostela, which some foreigner lost, if indeed you did not filch it from him because it looks so remarkable." "Hand over your ducat to your traveling companion for safekeeping," said Fitz, "and I will confess truthfully where I got the rock. In the ruins of the church at St. Joseph is an altar, also in ruins. Beneath the stones on top, which have all split apart, I discovered a layer of this stone, which served as a base for the other, and I broke off as much as I could. If all the upper stones were moved out of the way, there would certainly be much more."

"Take your gold coin," Montan replied. "You deserve it for this discovery. It is certainly a nice one. We are pleased, and with reason, when inanimate Nature produces a likeness of that which we love and revere. She appears to us in the form of a sibyl, who testifies in advance to what has been determined in all eternity and will come to be only in the passing of time. On this rock, as on a miraculous, sacred base, the priests had founded their altar."

Wilhelm, who had listened for a while and had noticed that certain names, certain terms recurred, repeated his earlier wish that Montan might impart to him such knowledge as he would need for the initial instruction of the boy. "Give it up," Montan replied. "There is nothing worse than a teacher who knows no more than what his pupils should know. One who would instruct others may often withhold the best of his knowledge, but he must not have only partial knowledge." "But where are such perfect teachers to be found?" "You can find them easily," Montan replied. "But where?" asked Wilhelm with some disbelief. "Where the subject that you wish to study has its home," Montan replied. "You obtain your best instruction from complete immersion. Do you not learn foreign languages best in their own countries? where only the one language and no other reaches your ear?" "And so you arrived at your knowledge of the mountains here in the mountains?" Wilhelm enquired. "That is obvious." "Without dealing with human beings?" "At least only with such human beings," Montan replied, "as had absorbed the spirit of the mountains. Where pygmies, drawn by veins of metal, burrow through the rock, make the inside of the earth accessible and use all means to solve the most difficult tasks, that is where the thinking man, thirsty for knowledge, should take his place. He sees actions, deeds, does not interfere, and enjoys the successes and the failures. What is useful is only part of what is significant. To possess something wholly, to master it, you must study it for its own sake. But while I speak of lofty and ultimate questions, to which one ascends only late in life, after developing a rich variety of insights, I see the boys there before us; for them it is completely different. The child wants to try everything, because any thing done well looks easy. 'The first step is always the hardest!' That may be true in some sense, but in general one can say: the first step is always the easiest, and it is the last steps that are achieved least often and with the greatest difficulty."

Wilhelm, who had been thinking, asked Montan, "Can you really have embraced the conviction that all activities should be approached separately, both in practice and in instruction?" "That seems to me the best and only way," Montan responded. "Anything a person is to accomplish must emanate from him like a second self, and how would that be possible if his first self were not completely permeated by it?" "But a liberal education has generally been considered advantageous and necessary." "That it may certainly be, at the proper time," Montan replied. "Liberality merely establishes the context within which the specialist can work effectively, since only that gives him adequate space. Yes, the day for specialization is come; fortunate is he who comprehends this and labors in this spirit for himself and others. In certain areas it is completely and immediately apparent. Practice to become a good violinist, and you may be sure that the conductor will be delighted to assign you a place in his orchestra. Make a receptive organ of yourself, and wait to see what position humanity will benevolently grant you in the overall scheme of things. Let us end here! He who does not believe it may go his own way, and may even succeed occasionally. But I say: to start serving at the bottom is necessary everywhere. To restrict oneself to a craft is the best thing. For the lesser mind it will always be a craft, for the better one an art, and for the best, if he does *one* he does all, or, to be less paradoxical, in the one thing he does properly, he sees the likeness of all that is done properly."

This conversation, of which we have conveyed only the outlines, went on until sunset, which, glorious though it was, made the company give thought to where they might pass the night. "I would not know of any shelter," Fitz said, "but if you are willing to spend the night with a kindly old charcoal burner, sitting or lying in a warm place, you are welcome." And so they all followed him along strange pathways to the quiet spot where each was soon to feel at home.

In the middle of a modest clearing stood the neatly rounded charcoal kiln, smoking and exuding warmth, and to one side a hut of pine boughs, with a bright little fire before it. Our friends sat down and made themselves comfortable. The children at once gravitated to the charcoal burner's wife, who hospitably set about dipping slices of toasted bread in butter, letting the tasty fat soak into the bread, to make delectable snacks for the ravenous travelers.

After this the boys played hide-and-seek among the dimly lit trunks of the fir trees, howling like wolves, barking like dogs, so that even a stouthearted wanderer might well have been alarmed. Meanwhile the friends conferred quietly about their circumstances. Among the curious obligations of the renunciants was the following: that if they encountered one another they should speak neither of the past nor the future, but only of the present.

Jarno, whose mind was filled with mining projects and the requisite knowledge and skills, passionately delivered the most precise and complete account of what gains he expected in both worlds, the old and the new, from such insights and technical skills; his friend, however, who had always sought his true treasures in the human heart alone, could scarcely form an idea of all this; finally he responded with a smile, "But you are contradicting yourself by starting only now, in your later years, to do what one should be trained up to from one's youth." "By no means," Jarno responded, "for I was raised as a child by a loving uncle, a high mining official, and I grew up among the pit boys, sailing little bark ships with them on the drainage ditch; that is what has brought me back to this world, where I now feel comfortable and rejuvenated. This charcoal smoke can hardly appeal to you as it does to me, who have drunk it in eagerly like incense since childhood. I have tried many things in the world, and always reached the same conclusion: comfort depends solely on custom; even disagreeable things to which we have become accustomed are dear to us. Once I suffered for a long time with a wound that would not heal, and when I finally recovered, it seemed very disagreeable that the doctor did not come by to change the dressing and have breakfast with me."

"But I should like to provide my son a freer view of the world than a narrow craft can give," replied Wilhelm. "Confine a man as you wish; the time will still come when he will gaze about him in his epoch; and how can he comprehend it if he does not know at least something of what has gone before? And would he not enter every spice shop with astonishment if he had no concept of the countries from which these indispensable rarities have made their way to him?"

"Why all the fuss?" Jarno replied. "Let him read the newspapers like any philistine and drink coffee like any old woman. But if you cannot let it be, and have set your heart upon a comprehensive education, I cannot understand how you can be so blind, how you can keep searching, how you fail to see that you are very close to a most excellent educational institution." "Very close?" Wilhelm asked, and shook his head. "Certainly!" the other replied; "what do you see here?" "Where do you mean?" "Right here in front of your nose." Jabbing with his forefinger, Jarno pointed and exclaimed impatiently, "What is that then?" "Oh, that," Wilhelm answered, "a charcoal kiln; but what does that have to do with it?" "Good! Finally! A charcoal kiln! And how does one go about building one?" "One piles split logs against and on top of one another." "And when you have done that, what comes next?" "It seems to me," said Wilhelm, "that in Socratic fashion you wish to do me the honor of making me comprehend, of making me admit, that I am thoroughly absurd and thickheaded."

"By no means!" Jarno replied. "Continue, my friend, to reply to each point. All right: what happens when everything has been piled neatly, with the logs close together, yet with air spaces in between?" "Well, then you light it." "And when it has all caught fire, when flames are licking out of every crack, what do you do? Do you let it keep burning?" "No indeed! You quickly cover the licking flames with turf and earth, with coal dust and whatever you have at hand." "To put it out?" "No indeed! To damp it down." "And so you leave it as much air as it needs to heat evenly, so that everything is completely charred. Then you seal up every crack, prevent any outbreak, so that gradually everything will go out, char, cool, and finally be dismantled and delivered as a saleable ware to smiths and locksmiths, to bakers and cooks, and when it has served sufficiently for the benefit of our beloved Christendom, the ash is used up by washerwomen and soapmakers."

"Well," Wilhelm replied, laughing, "with reference to this parable, how do you see yourself?" "That is not hard to say," Jarno responded. "I consider myself an old coal basket full of stout beech charcoal, but I allow myself the singularity of burning only for myself, for which reason I strike others as very peculiar." "And how about me?" Wilhelm returned, "How will you deal with me?" "At the moment," Jarno said, "I see you as a wanderer's staff, which has the remarkable quality of sprouting leaves in whatever corner one sets it, but of nowhere striking roots. Now extend the parable for yourself, and you will understand why neither forester nor gardener, neither charcoal burner nor cabinetmaker, nor any craftsman, can do anything with you."

During this discussion, Wilhelm drew from his bosom, for what purpose I know not, something that looked half like a wallet, half like a set of instruments; Montan spoke of it as something familiar from long ago. Our friend did not deny that he carried it with him as a sort of fetish, in the superstition that his fate depended to some degree on its possession.

But what it was, we may not confide to the reader at this juncture. We must say only this: it gave rise to a discussion that finally concluded with Wilhelm's admitting that he had long been inclined to devote himself to a certain special occupation, a truly useful art, provided that Montan would intercede with the league to revoke that most burdensome of rules, the prohibition on spending more than three days in one place, and to permit him to remain, here or there, as he wished, so as to attain his goal. Montan promised to see this done, after Wilhelm had solemnly sworn to pursue unceasingly the purpose that he had confided to him and to adhere most faithfully to his resolution.

Discussing all this earnestly, and replying to one another without interruption, they had left their refuge of the night, where little by little a strange, sinister company had gathered, and at daybreak they emerged from the woods into a clearing, where they found a few deer, which particularly delighted the responsive Felix. They prepared to part, for here the paths pointed in different ways. They asked Fitz about the various directions, but he seemed distracted and gave uncharacteristically confused replies. "You are a little scoundrel," Jarno remarked. "You knew all of those men who came and sat down around us during the night. There were woodsmen and miners; that was all right, but I think the others were smugglers, poachers, and the tall one, the very last one, who kept scratching marks in the sand and whom the others treated with some respect, was certainly a treasure hunter with whom you are in league."

"They are all good folk," Fitz retorted, "their means are scant, and if they sometimes do things that others forbid, it is because they are poor devils who have to take liberties just to stay alive."

But in fact the little scamp was pensive, because he had noticed the friends' preparations for parting. He was silently deliberating, for he was in doubt as to which of the two parties he should follow. He calculated the advantages: the father and son were careless with silver, but Jarno with gold; he decided it was best not to let go of him. Therefore he promptly seized a proffered opportunity, and when in parting Jarno said to him, "Now, when I come to St. Joseph, I shall see whether you are honest; I will look for the cross-stone and the ruins of the altar." "You will find nothing," Fitz replied, "and I will still be honest; the stone comes from there, but I took all the pieces away and have hidden them up here. It is precious stone, and without it no one can raise any treasure; they pay me very well for a small piece. You were perfectly right; that is how I was acquainted with that lean man."

Now there were new negotiations. Fitz pledged to provide Jarno, in return for another ducat, with a hefty piece of this rare material, to be had at a moderate distance from there, while at the same time he advised against venturing to the Castle of the Giants. But because Felix nevertheless insisted, Fitz impressed upon the guide not to allow the travelers too far inside, for no one had ever found his way out of those caves and crevices again. They parted, and Fitz promised to arrive in good time in the halls of the Castle of the Giants.

The guide strode on ahead, the two others followed; but the man had gone only a short stretch up the mountain when Felix noticed that they were not taking the path that Fitz had indicated. The guide replied, however, "I should know what I am about! Just a few days ago a violent storm knocked down this next section of the forest; trees are lying every which way, blocking the path. Follow me: I will bring you there safely." Felix enlivened the arduous path for himself by gamboling along and leaping from boulder to boulder, taking pleasure in his newfound knowledge that he was jumping from granite to granite.

Up he went, until finally he paused, balancing on toppled black columns, and suddenly saw before him the Castle of the Giants. Walls and columns towered up on a solitary peak; continuous palisades formed portal after portal, corridor after corridor. The guide issued a stern warning not to wander too far inside, and, noticing ashes left by his predecessors on a sunny spot that commanded an extensive view, he soon had a crackling fire going. While he prepared a frugal meal, as he was accustomed to do in such locations, and while Wilhelm studied the magnificent view of the region through which he intended to journey, Felix vanished; he must have strayed into the cavern. He did not answer their whistles and shouts, and did not reappear.

Wilhelm, however, was prepared, as is fitting for a pilgrim, for many eventualities, and now took from his hunting pouch a ball of string, attached it firmly, and entrusted himself to the guiding sign by which he had intended to lead his son inside. He moved forward, blowing his whistle from time to time, but long in vain. Finally a piercing whistle sounded from the depths, and soon after that Felix's head popped up from a fissure in the black rock. "Are you alone?" the boy whispered suspiciously. "All alone!" the father replied. "Hand me some wood! Hand me heavy sticks!" the boy exclaimed, took them, and disappeared, after calling anxiously, "Let no one into the cave!" But after a while he popped up again, asking for longer and stronger sticks. The father waited eagerly for the answer to this riddle. Finally the bold child climbed nimbly out of the crevice, carrying a small casket, no larger than a small octavo volume, old and splendid in appearance. It seemed to be of gold ornamented with enamel. "Hide it, and do not let anyone see it!" Then he described hastily how, in response to a mysterious inner urging, he had crawled into that crevice and had found below a dimly illuminated room. In it stood, as he said, a large iron chest; it was not locked, to be sure, but the top was too heavy to lift, almost too heavy to open even a crack. To master it, he had asked for the sticks, using some as props under the lid, forcing some in as wedges; finally he had found, though the chest was empty, the splendid little book in a corner of it. They promised each other to keep this a deep secret.

Noon was past, they had eaten, but still Fitz had not come as he had promised. Felix, however, was especially restless, longing to leave this place where his treasure seemed exposed to terrestrial or subterrestrial demands that it be returned. The columns seemed to him darker, the caverns deeper. A secret weighed on him, a possession—rightful or wrongful? safe or unsafe? Impatience drove him from the spot; he thought he would be free of care if he changed location.

They took the way toward the large estates of that great landowner of whose wealth and eccentricities they had heard so much. Felix no longer bounded along as he had that morning, and all three proceeded in silence for hours. Several times he wanted to look at the casket, but his father, indicating the guide, bade him be still. At one moment he longed to see Fitz. Then he dreaded the rogue again. First he whistled to give him a sign, then he regretted having done it, and thus he continued to waver, until finally Fitz sounded his little whistle in the distance. He excused his absence from the Castle of the Giants; he had lost time with Jarno, he said, and the fallen trees had held him back. Then he inquired in detail how they had fared among the columns and caverns, how far inside they had penetrated. Felix told him one tale after the other, half cocky, half ill at ease. He smiled at his father, plucked at him furtively, and did everything possible to let on that he had a secret and was hiding something.

They had finally reached a wagon road which was to lead them easily to the estate, but Fitz claimed to know a shorter and better way; the guide refused to accompany them, and continued along the straight, broad road on which they had started. The two wanderers trusted the roguish lad, and believed they had done well, for the path led steeply down the mountain, through a forest of very tall, slender larches, which, thinning out, finally allowed them to see the most beautiful estate imaginable, in brilliant sunlight.

It was a great plantation, dedicated, it appeared, entirely to productive use. Despite the profusion of fruit trees, it lay spread out clearly before their eyes, for it was laid out in symmetrical segments over a generally sloping area, which, however, was varied with rises and depressions. There were several dwellings scattered in such a fashion that the place seemed to belong to several owners, although, as Fitz assured them, it was governed and used by a single lord. Beyond the plantation they could see an immense landscape, amply cultivated and planted. They could clearly distinguish lakes and rivers.

They had come ever nearer down the mountainside, and expected to enter the grounds any minute now, when Wilhelm stopped short and Fitz made no effort to hide his malicious glee: a sudden chasm at the foot of the mountain opened before them, revealing a hitherto invisible high wall on the other side. From the outside it looked forbidding enough, although on the inside the ground was level with its top. A deep moat thus separated them from the plantation, into which they could look directly. "We have to go a fairly long way around," Fitz said, "if we want to reach the road that leads in. But I know an entrance from this side which is a good bit closer. The tunnels through which the water pouring off the mountains during rain storms is diverted into the gardens start near here; they are high enough and wide enough that it is possible to get through them fairly comfortably." When Felix heard tunnels mentioned, he was burning to try this entrance. Wilhelm followed the children, and together they climbed down the thoroughly dry, steep steps of the aqueduct. They found themselves alternately in light or in darkness, depending on whether light streamed in through the openings or was blocked by columns or walls. At length they reached a somewhat level stretch, and were advancing slowly when suddenly a shot rang out quite near them, two concealed iron gratings closed simultaneously, and they were trapped from both sides. Not the entire party, to be sure: only Wilhelm and Felix were caught. For Fitz, as soon as the shot sounded, had jumped back, and the grating had caught only his wide sleeve as it clanged shut; but he, quickly slipping out of his jacket, had fled, without a moment's delay.

The two prisoners barely had time to recover from their astonishment when they heard human voices that seemed to be approaching slowly. Presently armed men bearing torches approached the gratings, looking curiously to see what sort of catch they had made. They at once asked whether the two were willing to surrender peaceably. "There can be no talk of surrender here," Wilhelm replied; "we are in your power. We should rather ask whether you are willing to spare us. I shall hand over to you the only weapon we have with us," and with these words he passed his flintlock through the bars. The grating opened promptly, and the new arrivals were led calmly onward, and when they had been conducted up a spiral staircase, they found themselves in a peculiar place; it was a clean, spacious room, lit by small windows just below the ceiling; despite the heavy iron bars, they admitted ample light. Chairs, bedsteads, and whatever else one might need in a modest lodging were provided, and anyone finding himself here would seem to lack for nothing but freedom.

Upon entering Wilhelm had at once sat down to consider the circumstances; Felix, however, once recovered from his initial astonishment, fell into a terrible rage. These steep walls, these high windows, these strong doors, this isolation, this confinement, were completely new to him. He looked around, he ran back and forth, stamped his feet, wept, rattled at the doors, beat upon them with his fists, and was even about to run at them with lowered head if Wilhelm had not seized him and held him fast.

"Just look at all this calmly, my son," the father began; "impatience and violence will not help us out of this situation. The mystery will be cleared up, but I am sorely mistaken if we have not fallen into good hands. Look at these inscriptions: 'For the Innocent, Freedom and Reparation; for the Misguided, Compassion; for the Guilty, Justice with Mercy.' All this shows that these arrangements are the work of necessity, not of cruelty. Man has all too much reason to protect himself against man. There are many of ill will, not few of ill deeds, and to live as one ought, it is not always enough to practice kindness."

Felix had pulled himself together, but at once threw himself down on one of the cots, without further utterance or response. His father did not desist, but continued, "Let this experience, which you have made while you are still young and innocent, stand as vivid testimony to you of the century into which you have been born, and of how perfect it is. What a road did not mankind have to travel before it reached the stage at which it could treat the guilty with gentleness, the criminal with tolerance, the inhumane with humanity! Surely they were men of divine nature who first preached such tolerance, who dedicated their lives to making its practice possible and to hastening its acceptance. Humans are seldom capable of the beautiful, more often of the good; and in what high respect must we not hold those who seek to further it at great sacrifice."

These comforting and instructive words, which precisely expressed the intended meaning of these surroundings, had gone unheard by Felix; for he lay in deepest slumber, more beautiful and fresher than ever, for a passion to which he was seldom prone had brought his innermost emotions to his smooth cheeks. His father stood gazing on him with pleasure, when a handsome young man entered. After regarding the new arrival amiably for a while, he began to question him about the circumstances that had led him on his unusual route and into this trap. Wilhelm recounted the incident simply, handed him a few papers that served to establish his identity, and cited as witness the guide, who would soon be arriving from another direction, by the proper route. When matters had been clarified to this extent, the official besought his guest to follow him. Since Felix could not be awakened, the attendants bore him on the sturdy mattress out into the fresh air, like the unconscious Ulysses in his time.

Wilhelm followed the official to a lovely garden pavilion, where refreshments were laid out for him to enjoy, while the official went to report to his superiors. When Felix awoke and noticed the table laid with fruit, wine, and pastry, and also the cheering sight of the open door, he was overcome with a curious sensation. He runs outside, he comes back, he thinks he must have been dreaming; and soon, with the excellent fare and the pleasant surroundings, he had forgotten his previous terror and distress, as one forgets a bad dream in the bright light of morning.

The guide had arrived; the official returned with him and another, elderly, even friendlier man, and the matter was explained as follows: the owner of this estate, a benefactor in the noble sense that he inspired all those around him to be active and creative, had for some years now given away saplings from his extensive nurseries, free to industrious growers, for a certain price to neglectful ones, and likewise to those who wished to market them, though at a modest price. But the two latter groups also demanded to receive gratis that which the worthy growers received gratis, and when their demand was not met, they tried to steal the saplings. By a number of means they had succeeded. This vexed the owner all the more because the nurseries were not only plundered but also ruined by their careless haste. There were indications that they had entered by way of the water conduit, and therefore the trap with the iron grating had been installed, with an automatic shot intended only as a signal. The little boy had appeared in the gardens several times under various pretexts, and nothing was more natural than that his audacity and roguery should have caused him to lead the strangers by a path that he had earlier scouted for another purpose. They had hoped to capture him; in the meantime, his little jacket was being saved along with other pieces of evidence.

Chapter Five

On the way to the manor house, our friend, to his amazement, found nothing resembling an older pleasure garden or a modern park; fruit trees planted in straight rows, fields of vegetables, large beds of medicinal herbs, and anything that might be useful in any way—all this he could observe with one glance over the gently sloping land. A courtyard shaded by tall lindens formed the dignified entry to the imposing structure, and a long avenue leading from it, with trees of similar size and dignity, provided at any hour of the day an opportunity to stroll and enjoy the open air. Entering the manor house he found the walls of the vestibule adorned in a singular manner: large geographical representations of the four corners of the earth caught his eye; the stately walls of the stairwell were likewise decorated with maps of individual kingdoms, and, once admitted to the great hall, he found himself surrounded by views of the most notable cities, framed above and below by depictions of the landscapes in which they are situated, all of this done with great artistry, such that details were clearly visible, and yet an unbroken continuity remained evident.

The master of the house, a small, vivacious man well along in years, welcomed the guest and asked without further ceremony, indicating the walls, whether perhaps one of these cities might be familiar to him, and whether he had ever passed time there. Our friend was able to render a satisfactory account of a number of matters and prove that he had not only seen many cities but had also carefully noted their circumstances and special characteristics.

The host rang and ordered that the two new arrivals be assigned a room and later shown down to supper; this was done. In a large hall on the ground floor two ladies greeted Wilhelm. One addressed him with great cheerfulness: "You will find little company here, but it will be good. I, the younger niece, am called Hersilie, and this, my older sister, is named Juliette. The two gentlemen are father and son, stewards, whom you have met, friends of the family who receive all confidence, as they deserve. Let us be seated!" The two ladies placed Wilhelm between them, the stewards sat at both ends, with Felix on the other side of the table, where he immediately moved to the seat opposite Hersilie and did not take his eyes off her.

After some preliminary pleasantries, Hersilie took occasion to say, "That the stranger may become acquainted with us more quickly and be initiated into our circle, I must confess that we read a good deal here, and that through chance, individual taste, and probably also a spirit of contradiction, each of us has chosen a different literature. Our uncle likes Italian, the lady here does not object to being taken for the perfect Englishwoman, I myself prefer the French, so long as they are lighthearted and graceful. And Papa steward here enjoys the older German literature, while his son, as is fitting, turns his attention to the newer, more recent writings. According to this arrangement you shall judge us, shall join in, agree, or take issue with us; in every sense you will be welcome." And in this spirit the conversation grew more lively.

Meanwhile the direction of the handsome Felix's fervent glances had by no means escaped Hersilie; she felt surprised and flattered, and sent him the tastiest morsels, which he received with joy and gratitude. But now, during the dessert, as he gazed at her across a bowl of apples, the luscious fruit seemed to her like so many rivals. No sooner thought than done: she seized an apple and passed it across the table to the budding adventurer. He, hastily seizing it, at once began to peel it; but, keeping his eyes fixed upon his charming neighbor, he cut deeply into his own thumb. Blood spurted out; Hersilie leapt up and attended to him. When she had stopped the bleeding, she bound the wound with sticking plaster from her kit. Meanwhile the boy had thrown his arms around her and would not let her go. The disturbance spread to the rest of the company; they all rose from the table and prepared to take leave of one another.

"You also read before you go to sleep, do you not?" Hersilie asked Wilhelm; "I shall send you a manuscript, a translation from the French that I did myself, and you must tell me if you have ever encountered anything more charming. A mad girl appears in it! That may not sound like a great recommendation, but if I should ever go mad, as I am sometimes tempted to do, it would be in this fashion."

The Deranged Pilgrim

Monsieur de Revanne, a wealthy gentleman of private means, owns the finest estates in his province. Together with his son and his sister, he occupies a chateau that would be worthy of a prince; and indeed, inasmuch as his park, his water, his tenantries, his manufactures, and his household nourish half the inhabitants for six miles around, by virtue of his good name and the benefits he confers, he is truly a prince.

Some years ago he was strolling on the highway along the wall surrounding his park, and he took a notion to rest in a pleasant grove where travelers like to stop. Tall trees tower above young, dense underbrush; one is protected from wind and sun; a neatly lined spring sends its water over roots, stones, and grass. As was his wont, the gentleman had a book and his flintlock with him. Now he tried to read, agreeably distracted, often by the singing of the birds, sometimes by other walkers' footsteps.

A lovely morning was passing thus when a woman, young and charming, approached him. She left the road, seeming to expect peace and refreshment from the cool spot where he sat. His book fell from his hands, so surprised was he. The pilgrim, with the loveliest eyes in the world and a face pleasantly flushed from the exercise, was so distinguished in figure, gait, and comportment that he involuntarily rose from his place and looked toward the road, expecting to see her entourage following. The figure further caught his attention by bowing to him with a noble air, and he greeted her respectfully in return. The lovely traveler seated herself by the rim of the spring, without saying a word, merely sighing deeply.

"The curious workings of sympathy!" exclaimed M. de Revanne as he recounted the incident to me. "In the silence, I echoed this sigh. I stood there, not knowing what to do or to say. My eyes were unable to take in all her perfections. Lying there, resting on one elbow, was the loveliest figure of a woman one could imagine! Her shoes gave me cause for reflection; covered with dust, they indicated a long journey on foot, and yet her silk stockings were as neat as if they had just come out from beneath the iron. Her gathered-up dress had no wrinkles, her hair seemed to have been freshly curled that very morning; fine linen, fine lace; she was dressed as if she were going to a ball. Nothing about her suggested the vagabond, and yet she was one; but one worthy of pity, one worthy of honor.

"At last I took advantage of a few glances she cast at me to inquire whether she were traveling alone. 'Yes, Sir,' she replied, 'I am alone in the world.' 'How is that, Madame? Can it be that you have no parents, no acquaintances?' 'No, that I did not wish to say, Sir. Parents I have, and acquaintances aplenty; but no friends.' 'For that,' I continued, 'you cannot possibly be to blame. You have a figure and surely a heart as well to which much may be forgiven.'

"She perceived the gentle reproach my compliment concealed, and I formed a favorable impression of her breeding. She looked at me with two heavenly eyes of the deepest, purest blue, transparent and shining; and she responded in a noble tone: that she could not take it amiss when a man of honor, such as I appeared to be, harbored certain suspicions toward a young woman he found traveling alone on the road. She had encountered similar suspicions several times before. But although she might be strange, although no one had a right to question her, she begged me to believe that the purpose of her journey was consistent with the most exacting virtue. Reasons for which she was obliged to account to no one compelled her to carry her sorrows about with her in the world. She had discovered that the perils generally feared for one of her sex were imaginary and that a woman's virtue was endangered, even among highwaymen, only when her heart and principles faltered.

"Besides, she ventured forth only at those times and on those roads which she thought safe; she did not speak with just anyone she chanced to meet, and at times she would stay at suitable places where she might earn her keep by performing services of the sort to which she had been bred. Here her voice sank, her eyelids drooped, and I saw a few tears run down her cheeks.

"I replied that I in no wise doubted the quality of her origins, any more than I doubted her virtue. I regretted only that some necessity compelled her to serve when she seemed so worthy of being served. I did not wish to press her further, I continued, despite my lively curiosity, but rather hoped to convince myself through nearer acquaintance with her that she was as concerned for her reputation as for her virtue. These words seemed to wound her again, for she replied that she concealed her name and native land precisely for the sake of her reputation, which, however, in the end usually involves less reality than speculation. When she offered her services, she showed references from the households where she had most recently made herself useful, and she did not disguise her wish not to be questioned about her native land and her family. People decided accordingly, trusting to Heaven or her own word for the blamelessness of her entire life and for her honesty."

Statements of this sort aroused no suspicion that the lovely adventurer might be suffering from mental confusion. M. de Revanne, who could not well comprehend such a decision to run off into the world, now surmised that she was perhaps to have been married against her will. It then occurred to him that it might even be unrequited love, and strangely enough, but as is often the case, from thinking she loved another, he fell in love himself and feared that she might continue her journey. He could not turn his eyes from the beauty of her face, which was enhanced by the greenish half-light of the grove. Never, if nymphs had ever existed, had a more beautiful one appeared stretched out upon the grass, and the rather romantic quality of this encounter exerted a charm that he was incapable of resisting.

Without more careful consideration of the matter, therefore, M. de Revanne persuaded the lovely stranger to let him lead her to his chateau. She raises no objection, she goes along and proves herself well acquainted with the genteel world. Refreshments are served, and she accepts them without false courtesy but with gracious expressions of gratitude. In the time before luncheon, she is shown around the house. She comments only upon things that deserve to be singled out, whether furniture, paintings, or the ingenious arrangement of the rooms. She comes upon a library, recognizes the good books, and speaks of them with taste and modesty. No idle chatter, no awkwardness. At table an equally noble and natural bearing and a most charming tone in conversation. Thus far everything she says is sensible, and her character appears to be as charming as her person.

After luncheon a little obstinate trait made her even lovelier; turning to Mlle de Revanne with a smile, she says: it is her custom to pay for her midday meal with some bit of work. Whenever she lacks for money, she asks the hostess for sewing needles. "Permit me," she added, "to leave a flower in one of your embroidery frames, so that at the sight of it you may remember this poor stranger."

Mlle de Revanne replied that she was most sorry to have no canvas prepared and would therefore have to forego the pleasure of observing her skill. At once the pilgrim turned her eyes toward the piano. "In that case," said she, "I shall pay my debt with wind coin, as was the custom among strolling minstrels." She tried out the instrument with two or three preludes that bespoke a practiced hand. They doubted no longer that she was a young woman of high station, endowed with all the most winning accomplishments. At first her playing was lively and brilliant. Then she moved to more serious tones, to tones of profound sorrow that could also be read in her eyes. They filled with tears, her face was transformed, her fingers ceased to move; but suddenly she surprised everyone with a mischievous song, which she performed in a merry and droll manner, with the loveliest voice imaginable. Since later events gave reason to believe that this burlesque romance had some closer connection with her own story, I may be forgiven for including it here:

Who comes in haste, his cloak awry,
When scarce the east is growing gray?
Perhaps our friend, 'neath windy sky
As pilgrim comes abroad today?
Who can have torn away his hood?
Does he by choice thus barefoot go?
How came he to this somber wood,
To barren heights adrift with snow?

Lost hopes of joy—a bitter joke—
Now driven from his cozy spot
And had he also lost his cloak,
What great disgrace would be his lot!
Thus did that naughty scamp betray
The lad, and took his clothes away.
Our friend set out upon his road
Like Father Adam all unclothed.

But why went he upon that road
To seek the apple full of woe,
Which in the miller's garden glowed,
As once in Paradise it shone!
He'll not repeat this venture soon.
He scampered quickly from the house,
And now beneath the waning moon
In bitterest lament breaks out:

"In her deep glances' burning light
No word of treachery could I read.
Our love seemed nothing but delight,
Yet she was plotting this cruel deed!
How could I, locked in her embrace,
Divine the treason in her breast?
She bade swift Cupid slow his pace;
He did his part to make us blest.

To take her pleasure in my ardor

All through that long and lovely night,
And not to call or rouse her mother
Before she saw the dawn's first light!
In swarmed all her kith and kin,
A veritable stream, a tide!
Brothers, cousins, aunts pressed in,
All clamoring that she be my bride.

What raging, what appalling clamor!
Each seemed a different beast to be,
Insisting I return the flower,
With horrid shouts assaulting me:
'But why attack with insane pleasure
Thus cruelly this guiltless youth!
To be the first to rob such treasure
I was not quick enough in truth.

Swift Cupid knows no other will
But his own joy at working woe:
He'd not let flowers at the mill
Full sixteen summers untouched grow.'
They snatched my clothing from my side,
And would have had the mantle too.
How could so small a house thus hide
So many men, so cursed a crew!

Then up I leapt, and raged and swore,
Intent my way past all to dare,
Gazed at the wicked girl once more,
And she, alas, was still so fair.
They all gave way before my anger,
Though many a shout still filled the air;
So raging with a voice of thunder
At last I fled the evil lair.

As ladies of the town we flee,
We'll shun you maidens of the village!
Leave it to ladies of quality,
Their humble servingmen to pillage!
But if you're one of those 'of skill,'
And tender duties you'd evade,
So change your lovers, if you will,
But never let them be betrayed."

Thus sings he in the winter night,
No blade of grass upon the mead,
I laugh to see his sorry plight,
For it was well-deserved indeed;
And may this be the fate of all
Who treat by day their true loves ill,
And with foolhardy boldness crawl
By night to Cupid's faithless mill.

It was undoubtedly worrisome that she could forget herself in such a fashion, and this episode might serve as an indication of a mind not always equally composed. "But," M. de Revanne told me, "we, too, forgot all the observations we might have made, I do not know exactly how. We must have been captivated by the inexpressible grace with which she performed these antics. She played in a teasing manner, yet with feeling. Her fingers obeyed her perfectly, and her voice was truly enchanting. When she had finished, she appeared as self-possessed as before, and we thought she had intended simply to enliven the time for digestion.

"Soon afterwards she requested permission to continue on her way, but at a sign from me, my sister said: if she were in no hurry and our hospitality were not displeasing to her, it would indeed be delightful for us to have her several days with us. I intended to offer her some occupation, since she agreed to stay. But on this first day and on those that followed we merely showed her around. She never once belied herself; she was the soul of reason, endowed with every grace. Her spirit was refined and acute, her memory well stocked, and her disposition so lovely that she often aroused our admiration and held our attention completely. At the same time she knew the rules of good conduct and practiced them toward every one of us, and no less toward several friends who came to call. So perfectly did she comport herself that we could not think how to reconcile those peculiarities with such flawless breeding.

"I really no longer dared to suggest service in my household. My sister, who liked her, likewise considered it her duty to spare the delicate feelings of the stranger. Together they attended to household matters, and here the good child quite often lowered herself to menial tasks and yet could equally well handle anything which demanded organization and calculation.

"In a short time she established a degree of order in the house that we had not even realized we lacked. She was a most capable housekeeper, and since she had begun by sitting down to table with us, she did not now withdraw out of false modesty, but continued to dine with us without scruple. But she would not touch a playing card, a musical instrument, until she had completed the tasks she had assumed.

"I must now confess that the fate of this girl had begun to touch me most deeply. I pitied the parents, who probably missed such a daughter a great deal; I sighed to think that such gentle virtues, so many qualities, should go to waste. She had already lived with us for several months, and I hoped that the trust we sought to inspire in her would at last bring her secret to her lips. If it was a misfortune, we could help. If it was a misstep, it was to be hoped that our mediation, our attestations, could procure forgiveness for a passing error on her part. But all our assurances of friendship, even our pleading, proved ineffective. Whenever she sensed our intention to obtain some clarification from her, she would take refuge behind general maxims in order to justify herself without revealing anything. For example, if we spoke of her misfortune, she remarked, 'Misfortune befalls both the good and the evil. It is a potent medicine, which attacks good fluids simultaneously with bad ones.'

"If we sought to discover the reason for her flight from her father's house, she would say with a smile, 'If the hind flees, that does not mean it is to blame.' If we inquired whether she had suffered persecution, 'It is the fate of many a girl of good birth to experience and endure persecution. She who weeps at an insult will encounter many such.' But how could she have decided to expose her life to the coarseness of the common throng, or at least to owe it sometimes to their mercy? At that she laughed again and responded, 'The poor man who greets the rich man at table does not lack for good sense.' Once, when the conversation became jocular, we spoke to her of lovers and asked her whether she were not acquainted with the frosty hero of her ballad. I still recall vividly how this question seemed to pierce her through and through. She looked at me wide-eyed, with a gaze so solemn and severe that my own eyes could not withstand it. And whenever love was mentioned thereafter, we could expect to see the grace of her being and the vivacity of her spirit dampened. She promptly fell into a reflectiveness that we took for brooding and was probably merely sorrow. Yet on the whole she remained cheerful, though without great vivacity, noble without pretension, upright without frankness, withdrawn without timidity, more long-suffering than meek, and more appreciative than warm in response to caresses and attentions. Certainly she was a lady bred to preside over a great household, and yet she seemed to be no older than twenty-one.

"Thus this young, inexplicable person, who had completely captivated me, continued to comport herself during the two years that it pleased her to tarry with us, until she concluded with a folly far stranger than her personal qualities were admirable and splendid. My son, younger than I, will be able to console himself. As for me, I am afraid I shall be so weak as to miss her always."

Now I must describe an intelligent woman's folly, so as to show that folly is often nothing but reason under another aspect. To be sure, a strange contradiction will be seen between the pilgrim's noble character and the odd ruse that she employed. But the reader is already familiar with two of her peculiarities: the pilgrimage itself and her ballad.

It must be obvious that M. de Revanne was in love with the stranger. Now, he did not place much trust in his fifty-year-old face, notwithstanding that he looked as fresh and vigorous as a man of thirty. But perhaps he hoped to please her with his pure, youthful good health, with the goodness, serenity, gentleness, generosity of his character; perhaps also with his fortune, although he was tactful enough to realize that one cannot purchase that which has no price.

But his son, on the other hand, charming, tender, passionate, threw himself head over heels into the adventure, with no more thought than his father. First he sought cautiously to win the stranger, whom he had come to esteem chiefly because of his father's and his aunt's praise and friendship. He strove in earnest for a charming woman, who to his passion appeared elevated far above her present condition. Her severity inflamed him more than her merits and her beauty. He dared to speak, to venture, to promise.

His father, without intending to do so, always lent his own wooing a somewhat fatherly aspect. He knew himself, and once he had recognized his rival, did not hope to triumph over him without resorting to means unworthy of a man of principle. Nonetheless he continued on his course, although he could not but know that kindness and even a fortune constitute attractions to which a woman may succumb with premeditation, but which remain powerless the moment love manifests itself paired with youth and its charms. M. de Revanne committed other errors as well, which he later regretted. Where a noble friendship already existed, he spoke of a permanent, secret, legal union. He may also have complained and uttered the word ingratitude. Certainly he revealed that he did not know the lady he loved when he told her one day that many a benefactor received ill in return for good. The stranger replied simply, "Many benefactors would like to buy all the rights of their protégés for a mess of pottage."

The lovely stranger, caught between two rival suitors, guided by unknown motives, seems to have intended nothing but to spare herself and others foolish nonsense when, under these trying circumstances, she resorted to a very peculiar solution. The son was pressing her with the boldness characteristic of his age, threatening, as youths will, to sacrifice his life if she would show him no mercy. The father, somewhat less unreasonable, was, however, equally insistent; both of them utterly serious. This charming creature could have secured for herself a situation she well deserved, for both of the de Revannes swear they intended to marry her.

But from the example of this girl let women learn that an upright soul, even if the mind has been confused by vanity or true madness, does not prolong the sufferings of those whom it does not wish to heal. The pilgrim felt herself in an extremity, in which it would not be easy to defend herself for long. She was in the power of two lovers who could excuse any impertinence on their own part by the purity of their intentions, since they had resolved to justify their temerity by a solemn union. Thus it was, and thus she perceived it.

She could barricade herself behind Mlle de Revanne, but she chose not to, doubtless out of delicacy, out of respect for her benefactress. She does not lose her composure, she conceives a plan to preserve everyone's virtue by letting her own appear questionable. She is mad out of faithfulness, which her lover certainly does not deserve if he fails to appreciate all her sacrifices, even if they should remain unknown to him.

One day, when M. de Revanne responded somewhat too vigorously to the friendship, the gratitude she evidenced toward him, she suddenly assumed a naive air that captured his attention. "Your kindness, Sir," she said, "alarms me, and let me reveal frankly to you why. I am fully sensible that I owe all my gratitude to you alone, and yet—" "Cruel maiden!" exclaimed M. de Revanne, "I understand you. My son has moved your heart." "Alas, dear Sir, that was not all! Only through my confusion can I express . . ." "What, Mademoiselle, could it be that you—" "I very much fear so," she said, with a deep curtsey, and shedding a tear. For women never lack a tear for their strategems, never an excuse for their missteps.

However much in love M. de Revanne might be, he had to be amazed at this new style of innocent honesty wearing a mother's mobcap, and he found her curtsey entirely fitting. "But Mademoiselle, I utterly fail to understand—" "I likewise," said she, and her tears flowed more copiously. They flowed so long that M. de Revanne, after some very morose reflection, with calm mien broke the silence and said, "This opens my eyes. I see now how absurd my demands were. I make you no reproach, and as the sole punishment for the pain you cause me, I promise you as much of his inheritance as is necessary to discover whether he loves you as much as I do." "Ah, dear Sir, take pity on my innocence and say nothing to him about it."

Demanding secrecy is not the way to secure it. After these steps the lovely stranger expected to see her lover before her indignant and enraged. Soon he appeared, with a look in his eye that presaged devastating words. Yet he stammered and could bring forth nothing but,

"What is this, Mademoiselle, is it possible?" "What do you mean, Sir?" she replied with a smile that in such a situation can drive a man to desperation. "What is this 'What do you mean?' Come along, Mademoiselle, you are a fine one! But at least one should not disinherit legitimate offspring. It is bad enough to accuse them. Yes, Mademoiselle, I see through your plot with my father. You both are giving me a son, and it is really my brother, of that I am certain!"

With the same calm, pleasant expression, the lovely but demented lady replied, "You are certain of nothing. It is neither your son nor your brother. Boys are naughty, I did not want one. It is a poor little girl whom I will take away, far, far away from people, evil, foolish, faithless people!"

And then with a deep sigh, "Farewell," she continued, "Farewell, dear Revanne! You have by nature an upright heart; hold fast to the principles of integrity. They are not dangerous when one has a well established fortune. Be kind to the poor. He who despises the plea of troubled innocence will one day plead himself and go unheard. He who has no compunction to despise the compunction of a defenseless maiden will fall prey to women without compunction. He who is not sensible of what an honorable maiden must feel when she is courted, does not deserve to receive her hand. He who defies all reason, all the intentions and plans of his family, to fashion projects to serve his passion deserves to be deprived of the fruits of his passion and to lose the respect of his family. I do believe you loved me honestly, but, my dear Revanne, the cat knows whose beard she licks. If ever you become the lover of a worthy woman, remember the mill of the faithless lover. Learn from my example to rely upon the loyalty and discretion of your beloved. You know whether I am unfaithful, and your father knows it, too. I thought to speed through the world and expose myself to all its perils. Certainly the greatest are those that threaten me in this house. But because you are young, I shall tell you alone, and in confidence: men and women are unfaithful only by choice. And that is what I wanted to prove to my friend from the mill, who will perhaps see me again when his heart is pure enough to understand what he has lost."

Young Revanne was still listening when she had finished speaking. He stood there as if struck by lightning. At length tears opened his eyes, and thus moved he ran to his aunt, his father, to tell them that Mademoiselle was leaving, Mademoiselle was an angel, or rather a demon, wandering about in the world to torture hearts. But the pilgrim had prepared everything so carefully that she was no longer to be found. And when father and son had revealed all to each other, there could no longer be any doubt as to her innocence, her talents, her madness. No matter what lengths M. de Revanne has gone to since that time, he has been unable to obtain the least intelligence of that lovely person who appeared as fleetingly as an angel, and quite as charmingly.

Chapter Six

After a long and thorough rest, of which the wanderers certainly had need, Felix sprang energetically out of bed and hurried to dress himself with more care than usual, the father thought. Nothing fit him snugly or neatly enough; he would also have liked to have everything newer and fresher. He bounded down to the garden, snatching on the way only a little of the light refreshment that the servant had brought for the guests because the ladies would not appear in the garden for another hour.

The servant was accustomed to entertaining strangers and to giving tours of the house. And so he conducted our friend to a gallery filled only with portraits, hanging or propped on easels, all of persons who had been active in the eighteenth century, a large and glorious company; paintings as well as busts, when possible by great masters. "You will find," the custodian explained, "no picture in the entire manor that refers even obliquely to religion, tradition, mythology, legend, or fable; our master wishes the imagination to be encouraged only in order that it may take cognizance of the true. 'We spin fables enough without having to intensify this dangerous propensity of our minds by external stimuli,' he is wont to say."

Wilhelm's question as to when he might present himself to him was answered with the following intelligence: the master had ridden off very early, as was his custom. He was wont to say, "Alertness is the soul of life!" "You will see this and other mottos that reflect his views inscribed above the doorways, as here, for example, we find 'From the Useful by Way of the True to the Beautiful.' "

The ladies had already arranged breakfast under the linden trees, and Felix was clowning about, trying to outdo himself in foolish tricks and daredevil behavior, so as to call attention to himself and catch a warning or a reprimand from Hersilie. Now the sisters attempted through candor and communicativeness to gain the confidence of their reticent guest, who appealed to them. They told of a beloved cousin, who, three years absent, was now expected back at any moment, of a worthy aunt, who lived not far off in her castle and might be regarded as the guardian spirit of the family. She was described as withered by illness in body, blooming with health in spirit, as if the voice of an ancient sibyl, now become invisible, spoke pure, divine words of the greatest simplicity about human affairs.

Now the new guest directed the conversation and questions to the present. He desired to know the noble uncle better in his decisive activity. He brought up the suggested progression from the Useful by way of the True to the Beautiful, and sought to interpret the words in his own way, in which he proved successful, thereby having the good fortune to earn Juliette's approbation.

Hersilie, who had until then listened in silence with a smile, now remarked, "We women find ourselves in a peculiar situation. We are forever hearing men's maxims repeated, indeed, we must see them inscribed above our heads in golden letters, and yet in secret we girls might very well say the opposite, and it would be valid too, as is here the case. The *Beauty* finds admirers, also suitors, and finally even a husband; then she attains to the *True,* which may not always be entirely pleasing, and if she is sensible, she dedicates herself to the *Useful*, tends her house and children, and contents herself with that. Or at least I have often found that to be so. We girls have time to observe, and we usually find that which we did not seek."

A messenger arrived with word from the uncle that the entire company was invited to dine at a nearby hunting lodge and might ride or drive there. Hersilie chose to ride. Felix pleaded to be given a horse as well. It was agreed that Juliette should drive with Wilhelm, and that Felix as a page might owe his first ride to the lady of his young heart.

Meanwhile Juliette drove with her new friend through a series of plantations, all suggesting usefulness and pleasure; indeed, the innumerable fruit trees made it seem doubtful whether all of the fruit could be consumed.

"You came into our company by way of such an odd antechamber and encountered things that are really unusual and curious, so I take it you wish to know how they are all connected. All of this is based on the spirit and intentions of my excellent uncle. The prime of this noble person coincided with the era of Beccaria and Filangieri; the maxims of a general humanitarianism were influential everywhere. This general notion, however, was developed by Uncle's ambitious spirit and firm character according to his own sentiments, which were oriented strictly toward the practical. He did not deny that he had altered the liberal motto, 'the best for the most' according to his own ideas to 'the desirable for the many.' The 'most' cannot be found or recognized, and what the 'best' is, can even less be determined. 'The many,' however, are always around us; what they desire, we can discover, what they ought to desire, we can consider, and thus something significant can always be done and accomplished. It is in this spirit," she continued, "that everything you see here has been planted, built, organized, and indeed all for an immediate, easily grasped purpose; all this was done to benefit the large mountainous region nearby. This excellent man, having both energy and fortune, said to himself, 'No child up there shall lack for a cherry, an apple, which children rightly crave; the housewife shall suffer no lack of cabbage or turnips, or any other vegetable for her pot, so that our wretched consumption of potatoes may at least be held in check.' In this spirit, in this manner he seeks to accomplish what his possessions make possible, and thus for many years now vendors of both sexes have prepared themselves to deliver fruit to the deepest ravines in the mountains."

"I myself enjoyed it as much as a child," Wilhelm replied; "there, where I would not have expected to encounter it, among pines and bluffs, I was less surprised to discover a true spirit of piety than refreshing, fresh fruit. The gifts of the spirit are everywhere at home; the gifts of Nature are sparingly distributed over the earth."

"Furthermore our worthy lord brought various necessities from afar to the mountains; in those buildings near their feet you will find stores of salt and spices. He lets others worry about tobacco and brandy; these are not necessities, he says, but addictions, and for them purveyors enough will turn up."

Once arrived at the appointed place, a spacious forester's lodge in the woods, the company gathered and found a small table already set. "Let us be seated," Hersilie said; "this is our uncle's chair, to be sure, but he will doubtless not come, as usual. In a sense I am glad that our new guest, as I hear, will not stay long with us; for it would surely be tiresome to make the acquaintance of our cast of characters. It is the one eternally repeated in novels and plays: an eccentric uncle, one gentle and one merry niece, a wise aunt, household companions of the usual stripe; and if the nephew were to return now, he would meet a whimsical traveler, who might perhaps bring an even stranger companion with him, and so the whole dreary play would be complete and translated into reality."

"We should respect our uncle's idiosyncrasies," Juliette remarked. "They burden no one, but rather contribute to everyone's well-being. A set hour for dining happens to be irksome to him; seldom does he observe it; indeed he asserts that one of the finest inventions of recent times is dining à la carte."

Among many other subjects, they came to speak of the worthy gentleman's proclivity for having inscriptions everywhere. "My sister," Hersilie said, "can interpret them all; she and the curator vie with one another in understanding them; but I find that you can reverse them and that they are then just as true, if not more so."

"I do not deny," replied Wilhelm, "that there are sayings among them that seem to cancel themselves out; I saw, for example, prominently inscribed: 'Possessions and Common Property'; do not those two concepts negate each other?"

Hersilie joined in: "Our uncle seems to have borrowed such inscriptions from the Orientals, who venerate the sayings from the Koran on all their walls more than they understand them." Juliette, without allowing herself to be distracted, responded to Wilhelm's question: "If you paraphrase those few words, their meaning will at once shine forth."

After several other comments, Juliette continued to explain what was meant: "Let each seek to value, to preserve, to increase the property allotted him by Nature, by Fate; let him reach as far about him with all his skill as he is able, but let him always consider how others may participate in it: for the wealthy are valued only insofar as others reap benefits through them."

When they then tried to think of examples, our friend found himself in his element; they vied with one another, outdid themselves in their eagerness to find those laconic words quite true. Why, it was asked, is a ruler revered, if not because he can put each subject to work, further him, favor him, and in a sense let him share in his absolute power? Why do all look to the wealthy man if not because he, the neediest, always seeks others to participate in his surplus? Why do all men envy the poet? Because his nature makes communication necessary, indeed is itself communication. The musician is more fortunate than the painter; he gives welcome gifts directly of himself, whereas the latter gives only when the gift has been separated from himself.

Now they proceeded to generalize: a man should cherish every sort of possession, should make himself the center from which all common property can issue forth; he must be an egoist, lest he become an egotist, must conserve, that he may contribute. What good is it to give goods and possessions to the poor? It is more laudable to act as an administrator for them. That is the meaning of the maxim "Possessions and Common Property": the capital should not be touched, for in the course of events the interest will in any case belong to everyone.

It was revealed in the discussion that some people had reproached the uncle because his estates did not bring in what they ought. He replied, however, "I regard the reduction in earnings as an expenditure that affords me pleasure, because I make life easier for others; I do not even have the bother of handling this contribution myself, and thus everything balances out."

In this manner the ladies conversed with their new friend on a multitude of subjects, and as mutual trust increased, they came to speak of the cousin who was expected soon.

"We think his curious behavior has been arranged with our uncle. For several years he has not been heard from; instead he sends charming gifts that hint at his whereabouts. Now he suddenly writes from very close by, but will not come until we have given him a report of our circumstances. This behavior is not natural; and we must discover what lies behind it before his return. This evening we shall give you a bundle of letters from which you can gather the rest." Hersilie added, "Yesterday I introduced you to a foolish vagabond, and today you shall hear about a demented traveler." "You must admit," added Juliette, "this communication is not without an ulterior motive."

Hersilie was just asking rather impatiently what had happened to the dessert, when a message came that the uncle was expecting the company to join him for dessert in the arbor. On the way they caught sight of a field kitchen, the cook busy packing up the spotlessly washed casseroles, bowls, and plates with considerable clatter. In a roomy arbor they found the old gentleman sitting at a large, round, freshly laid table, where the most beautiful fruit, tempting pastries, and the finest sweetmeats were being served in profusion as the company took their seats. At the uncle's inquiry as to what had been happening and how they had amused themselves, Hersilie broke in impetuously, "Our dear guest might have been confused by your laconic inscriptions, had Juliette not come to his aid with a running commentary."

"You are forever teasing Juliette," the uncle replied, "but she is a good girl, who still wants to learn and understand more."

"I should like to forget much of what I know, and what I have understood is not worth much," Hersilie replied merrily.

At this Wilhelm spoke up, remarking thoughtfully, "I have great respect for pithily formulated sayings, especially when they prompt me to ponder the opposite position and to bring the two into agreement."

"Quite right," the uncle responded, "indeed, reasonable men have no more fitting occupation for an entire lifetime."

In the meantime the table was gradually filling up, so that latecomers could hardly find a place. The two stewards had come, huntsmen, horse trainers, gardeners, foresters, and others whose calling was not immediately evident. Each had something to tell and communicate about his most recent experiences; the old gentleman enjoyed these narratives, and even elicited them by asking sympathetic questions. But at length he rose, and taking leave of the company, which was not to stir, departed with the two administrators. All had partaken of the fruit, and the young people, though somewhat wild in appearance, had enjoyed the sweets. One after another stood up, saluted those who remained, and went on his way.

The ladies, who perceived that the guest was observing the goings-on with some wonderment, explained as follows: "Here you again see the effect of our worthy uncle's idiosyncrasies; he asserts that no invention of the present century deserves more admiration than that at inns one can now eat à la carte at separate tables; as soon as he became aware of this he sought to introduce it in his family for himself and others. When he is in especially good humor, he likes to give a lively description of the horrors of a family dinner, where everyone comes to the table engrossed in his own thoughts, unwilling to listen, speaking distractedly, or sitting in glum silence, and should ill luck have it that small children are present, creating most unnecessary tension with improvised pedagogical measures. 'There are so many evils we have to put up with,' he says, 'but from this one I have managed to liberate myself.' He appears seldom at our table and then occupies his place but briefly. He takes his field kitchen with him, usually dines alone, letting others fend for themselves. But when he does offer breakfast, dessert, or other refreshments, then all the scattered members of the household gather and enjoy what is placed before them, as you have witnessed. That gives him pleasure; but no one may come who does not bring a good appetite, and each must rise when he has had his fill; in this way our uncle is assured of always being surrounded by people who are enjoying themselves. 'If one wishes to give pleasure,' I have heard him say, 'one must strive to bestow upon people that which they can seldom or never obtain for themselves.' "

On the way home an unexpected mishap threw the company into some agitation. Hersilie said to Felix, who was riding beside her, "Look over there—what kind of flowers are those? They have covered the entire southern slope of the hill; I have never seen them before." Felix at once spurred his horse, galloped off, and was returning with a great bunch of blooming crowns, which he waved from afar, when he and the horse suddenly vanished. He had fallen into a ditch. Two riders promptly broke away from the company and raced toward the spot.

Wilhelm wanted to alight from the carriage, but Juliette forbade it: "Help has reached him already, and our rule in such cases is that only he may go who brings help; the surgeon is already there." Hersilie reined in her horse. "Yes," she said, "for a general physician there is seldom need, but there is for a surgeon at every moment." Already Felix came galloping up with his head bandaged, holding his blooming booty and waving it high in the air. Well pleased with himself, he handed the bouquet to his lady, and in return Hersilie gave him a bright-colored light kerchief. "That white bandage does not suit you," she said; "this will be gayer." And so they reached home, reassured, but in a more thoughtful mood.

It was now late, and they parted, cordially looking forward to seeing each other on the morrow; the following exchange of letters, however, kept our friend awake and preoccupied for several hours more.

Lenardo to the Aunt

After three years, here at last is the first letter from me, dear Aunt, true to our agreement, which was certainly peculiar enough. I wanted to see the world and surrender myself to it, and for this period I wanted to forget my homeland, from which I came and to which I hoped to return. I wanted to retain a complete impression, and details were not to confuse me in foreign parts. Meanwhile the necessary signs of life passed back and forth from time to time. I received money, and little gifts for my near and dear were delivered to you for distribution. From the goods I sent, you could tell where I was and how I was faring. From the wines Uncle could certainly taste out my whereabouts; and the laces, the knick-knacks, the steel implements marked my path through Brabant to Paris to London for the ladies. And so I shall find on your writing, sewing, and tea tables, on your negligées and ball gowns, many a reminder to which I can attach my account of my travels. You accompanied me without hearing from me, and perhaps you are not even eager to hear more. For me, on the other hand, it is extremely urgent to be apprised through your good offices of how things stand in the circle I am about to rejoin. I should like to arrive from foreign parts like a real foreigner, who, in order to be pleasant, first informs himself about the wishes and likings of the members of the household, and is not so vain as to think that he will be well received simply for his beautiful eyes or hair. Please write to me, then, about my good uncle, about the dear nieces, about yourself, about our relations, both near and distant, and also about the old and new servants. Enough, let your practiced quill, which you have not dipped on your nephew's behalf in so long a time, for once hold sway over the paper for his benefit. Your informative missive will also serve as the letter of introduction with which I shall announce myself as soon as I have received it. Seeing me in your arms thus depends on you. One changes much less than one thinks, and circumstances usually remain fairly constant as well. Not what has changed but what has remained, what has gradually waxed or waned is what I want to recognize again at a glance, and I want to discover myself once again in a familiar looking glass. Please give my warm greetings to all our dear ones, and do believe that the odd manner of my absence and return implies an affection sometimes lacking where constant involvement and lively communication are maintained. A thousand greetings to each and all!

Postscript

Please do not fail, dear Aunt, to send me word also of our men of affairs, and how things stand with our magistrates and tenants. What has become of Valerine, the daughter of the tenant whom our uncle dismissed shortly before my departure, with justification, to be sure, but still, it seems to me, rather harshly? You see, I still recall many details; probably I remember everything. You shall examine me on the past, once you have informed me about the present.

The Aunt to Juliette

Finally, dear Children, a letter after three years of silence. How very odd these odd people are! He believes his wares and tokens are as good as a single good word that a friend may write or speak to a friend. He actually imagines we are in his debt, and now wants us to do what he himself in so harsh and unfriendly a manner refused to do. How should we proceed? For my part, I would promptly accommodate his wishes with a long letter, if my headache had not set in, which scarcely allows me to finish this note. We all long to see him. Do take over this task, my Dear Ones. If I have recovered before you have finished, I shall do my share. Select the persons and circumstances you prefer to describe. Divide the task between you. You will do everything better than I would myself. The courier will bring word from you, I trust?

Juliette to her Aunt

We read your letter at once, considered it, and are giving our opinion by way of the courier, each of us separately, having first assured you together that we are not so kindly disposed as our dear Aunt toward that spoiled nephew. While he kept his cards hidden from us for three years, and still keeps them hidden, we are supposed to show ours and play an open game against his secret one. That is by no means fair, and yet it may pass; for the cleverest person often cheats himself by trying to protect too much. It is only about the ways and means that we are in disagreement, about what we should send to him, and how. To write what one thinks of one's own relatives strikes us, at least, as a peculiar task. Normally one thinks about them only in specific cases, when they give reason for particular pleasure or particular annoyance. Otherwise everyone leaves everyone else to his own devices. You alone could do it, dear Aunt, for you possess both the insight and the fair-mindedness. Hersilie, who, as you know, is easily inflamed, gave me on the spur of the moment a humorous review of the entire family; I wish I had it down on paper to coax a smile from you despite your pain, but not to send to him. My suggestion, however, is to share with him our correspondence of the last three years. He can read his way through it, if he has the courage, or he can come and see for himself what he does not want to read. Your letters to me, dear Aunt, are in perfect order and are at your disposal. Hersilie does not concur; her excuse is the disorder in her papers, etc., as she herself will tell you.

Hersilie to her Aunt

I will and must be very brief, dear Aunt, for the courier is making a rather rude show of haste. I consider it excessive good nature and altogether improper to share our letters with Lenardo. Why should he know the nice things we said about him, why should he know the bad things we said about him, to learn from the last even more than from the first that we are fond of him! Keep him on a short rein, I beg of you! There is something so calculating and arrogant in this demand, in this conduct, such as men usually display when they arrive from foreign parts. They never take those who have stayed at home quite seriously. Use your migraine as an excuse. He will come anyway; and if he did not come, we should simply wait a while longer. Perhaps then he will think of a way to introduce himself into our midst in an unusual, mysterious manner, to make our acquaintance without being recognized, and who knows what else might be part of a clever man's plan. Wouldn't that be charming and delightful! It would bring all sorts of relationships to light that he could never expect to discover with the highly diplomatic entry into the family that he now intends.

The courier! The courier! Govern your old servants better, or send young ones! This one can be distracted neither with flattery nor with wine. A thousand good wishes!

Postscript upon Postscript

Tell me: what does our cousin want with Valerine in his postscript? That question caught my attention on two accounts. She is the only person he mentions by name. The rest of us are merely nieces, aunts, agents, not people but categories. Valerine, the daughter of our magistrate! To be sure, a beautiful blond girl who may have caught the eye of our fine cousin before his departure. She is married, well and happily; that I need not tell you. But he knows that no more than he knows anything else about us. Do not forget to inform him, likewise in a postscript, that Valerine grew more beautiful by the day and therefore also made an excellent match. She is the wife of a wealthy landowner. The beautiful blond is married. Make that perfectly clear to him. But now, dear Aunt, that is not all. How he could remember the blond beauty so accurately and at the same time confuse her with the daughter of that miserable tenant, a hoyden of a brunette called Nachodine, of whose whereabouts I know nothing—that is completely incomprehensible to me and especially intrigues me. For it does seem certain that our dear cousin, while boasting of his good memory, mixes up names and persons in a curious fashion. Perhaps he senses his weakness and wants to refresh his faded impressions by means of your account. Keep him on a short rein, I beg of you; but try to discover what is afoot with Valerine and Nachodine, and whatever other -ines, -trines, may still occupy his fancy, while the -ettes and -ilies have all vanished. The courier! The accursed courier!

The Aunt to the Nieces (dictated)

Why dissemble toward those with whom one must pass one's life! Lenardo, for all his peculiarities, deserves our trust. I am sending him your two letters; from them he will become acquainted with you, and I hope the rest of us will unconsciously take an opportunity also to present ourselves to him soon! Farewell! I am in great pain.

Hersilie to the Aunt

Why dissemble toward those with whom one passes one's life! Lenardo is a spoiled nephew. It is revolting that you are sending him our letters. He will not come to know us through them, and all I hope for is an opportunity to present myself soon in another light. You make others suffer by suffering yourself and loving blindly. A rapid recovery from your pain! Your love cannot be helped.

The Aunt to Hersilie

I would have put your last note into the packet for Lenardo, had I held to the intention prompted by my incorrigible fondness, my pain, and my desire for convenience. Your letters have not gone off.

Wilhelm to Natalie

Man is a sociable, talkative being; he derives great pleasure from exercising the abilities that have been given to him, even if nothing more should come of it. How often people complain in society that one person does not let another get a word in edgewise, and likewise one could say that one person does not let another get a letter in edgewise, if writing were not usually an enterprise that one must undertake by oneself and alone.

We have absolutely no idea how much people write. I shall not even mention what gets printed, although that is already enough. But how much circulates in the form of letters and messages and stories, anecdotes, descriptions in letters and essays of current circumstances of individuals, that can be imagined only if one passes some time with cultivated families, as I am now doing. In the sphere in which I presently find myself, they spend almost as much time communicating to their friends and relatives what they are doing as they spend actually doing it. This observation, which has thrust itself upon me in the last few days, is one I am the more glad to make in that my new friends' passion for writing allows me to become acquainted with their circumstances rapidly and from all sides. They trust me, they hand me a packet of letters, a few notebooks of travel journals, the confessions of a soul not yet at peace with itself, and so I am at home in no time. I know those with whom they regularly associate and those whom I shall soon meet, and I know almost more about them than they do themselves, for they are caught up in their circumstances, while I hover above them, always guided by your hand, discussing everything with you. And it is my first stipulation, before I accept any confidences, that I be allowed to communicate everything to you. So here are a few letters, which will introduce you to the circle in which I am currently revolving, without breaking my vow or circumventing it.

Chapter Seven

Very early in the morning our friend made his way alone to the gallery and took pleasure in the many familiar faces; a catalogue conveniently at hand identified those whom he did not recognize. Portraits, like biographies, have an interest all their own; a significant person, who cannot be conceived without a context, steps forward separately and places himself before us as before a mirror. We are asked to give him our undivided attention, to occupy ourselves exclusively with him, as he is contentedly occupied with himself before the glass. It may be a general, who now represents the entire army, while behind him the very kings and emperors for whom he fights recede into the gloom. The adept courtier stands before us, as if he were paying court to us, and we do not think of the great world for which he actually cultivated such grace. Our visitor was surprised by the similarity of many figures long dead to living persons whom he knew and had seen in the flesh, indeed, their similarity to himself! And why indeed should identical twins be born to only one mother? Why should not the great mother of the gods and men be able to bring forth the same image from her fruitful womb simultaneously or at intervals?

And finally the sensitive observer could not deny that many attractive but also many repelling images passed before his eyes.

In such reflections the master of the house came upon him, and Wilhelm discussed these matters with him freely, seeming thereby to gain his favor more and more. For he was kindly escorted to the inner chambers, where he saw precious paintings of prominent men from the sixteenth century, fully present, just as they had lived and breathed, without regarding themselves in a glass or in the viewer, self-reliant and self-sufficient, impressive for their sheer presence, not for any will or intention.

The master of the house, pleased that the guest could fully appreciate such a richly evoked past, showed him autographs by several of the people about whom they had spoken earlier in the gallery. Finally he even showed him relics which the original owners were known to have used, to have touched.

"This is my sort of poetry," the master of the house said with a smile. "My imagination needs something to cleave to; I can scarcely believe that a thing has existed if it is no longer present. For such relics of the past I try to get the most reliable evidence, otherwise they would not be included in the collection. Written documents receive the most stringent examination, for I may well believe that a monk wrote a certain chronicle, but that to which he attests I seldom believe." Finally he placed before Wilhelm a blank sheet of paper, requesting him to write a few lines, but without a signature. Thereupon the guest was shown out into the hall through a tapestry-covered door, and found himself at the side of the curator.

"I am pleased," said the curator, "that our master values you. The fact that you have come out through this door proves it. But do you know what he takes you for? He thinks you are a practical pedagogue, and the boy he takes for a young man from a noble family who has been entrusted to your guidance, that he may be initiated directly into the world and its multiplicity of circumstances, according to sound principles, at an early age."

"He does me too much honor," our friend replied, "but I shall not have heard your words in vain."

At breakfast, where he found his Felix already busying himself about the ladies, they revealed to him their wish that, since he could not be detained, he should make his way to their noble aunt Makarie, and perhaps from there to their cousin, to clear up his mysterious hesitation. He would thereby at once become a member of the family, do a decided favor to all of them, and without much preparation enter into an intimate relationship with Lenardo.

Wilhelm, however, replied, "Wherever you send me, I will gladly go; I set out to see and to think; in your home I have experienced and learned more than I could have hoped, and, on the path being charted for me, I am convinced that I shall discover and learn more than I can expect."

"And you, you little n'er-do-well, what will you learn?" Hersilie asked, to which the boy replied boldly, "I will learn to write, so that I can send you a letter, and to ride like no one else, so that I can always come right back to you." To this Hersilie replied thoughtfully, "Things have never worked out well with admirers of my own age; it seems as though the next generation will soon make amends for that."

But now we feel with our friend how painfully the hour of leave-taking approaches, and we should like to convey a clear idea of the idiosyncrasies of his excellent host, of the peculiarities of this extraordinary man. But lest we judge him falsely, we must direct our attention to his origins and to the formation of this worthy person, already advanced in years. What we were able to discover is the following:

His grandfather lived in England as an active member of an embassy, just in the last years of the sublime William Penn. The lofty benevolence, the pure intentions, the unflagging efforts of such an excellent man, the conflict in which he therefore found himself with the world, the perils and pressures to which the noble man seemed to succumb, aroused in the receptive mind of the young man a decided interest. He made common cause with the undertaking and finally moved to America himself. The father of our gentleman was born in Philadelphia, and both of them took pride in having contributed to the increased general freedom of religious practice in the Colonies.

Here the maxim developed that a self-contained nation, which had traditionally been in agreement about religion and morals, should guard itself against foreign influences and against all innovation. But in new territory, where it is desirable that people come together from many quarters, the most unconstrained economic activity possible and the greatest freedom in matters of morality and religion should be permitted.

The lively urge to get to America was widespread at the beginning of the eighteenth century, since everyone who felt at all uncomfortable over here hoped to make himself free over there. This urge was nourished by the desirable lands one could acquire, before the population had spread farther west. Entire so-called counties were still for sale along the boundaries of the inhabited territory, and the father of our gentleman had also established himself there with significant holdings.

But as there often develops in sons opposition to their fathers' ideas and arrangements, so it was here, too. Our host, arriving in Europe as a youth, felt like a different person; this priceless culture, born thousands of years ago, which had grown, expanded, been diminished, oppressed but never entirely suppressed, which had drawn new breath, revived, and continued to generate boundless activity, gave him an entirely new concept of what mankind can hope to accomplish. He preferred to accept his share of these great, incalculable advantages and to submerge himself in the orderly, active mass, rather than to remain across the sea, playing the role of Orpheus and Lycurgus centuries too late. He said, "A man needs patience everywhere, he must have consideration for others everywhere, and I would rather come to terms with my king, that he may allow me this or that prerogative, would rather compromise with my neighbors, that they may release me from certain restrictions if I yield to them on some other matter, than thrash around with the Iroquois in order to drive them away, or defraud them with contracts in order to expel them from their swamps, where one is tortured to death by mosquitoes."

He took over the family estates, administering them liberally, organizing them productively, shrewdly annexing large, seemingly useless, adjoining lands, and so, within the cultivated world, which in a certain sense can also often be called a wilderness, he amassed considerable holdings and shaped them, which, for those confined conditions, is still utopian enough.

Freedom of religion is therefore natural in this district, the public ritual being viewed as a voluntary profession of faith that people belong together in life and death; but accordingly, great care is taken to see that no one stays aloof from the others.

In each settlement one sees a moderately large building; this is the space that the landowner owes the community. Here the elders come together to take counsel, here the members gather to receive instruction and pious encouragement. But the building is also intended for merrymaking; here wedding dances are held and holidays are concluded with music.

Nature herself can show us the way to such practices. In good weather we will usually see gathered under the same linden tree the elders in council, the community for edification, and the youth dancing. Against life's somber background, merriment stands out so beautifully; solemnity and holiness moderate pleasure, and only through moderation do we sustain ourselves.

Should the community have other wishes and money sufficient to realize them, it is free to dedicate separate structures to the separate activities.

But if all this serves the interests of public life and common morality, true religion remains something inward, indeed individual, for it has to do with the conscience alone, which is to be aroused or placated. Aroused when it broods along dully, inactively, ineffectively; placated when it threatens to embitter life with remorseful restiveness. For the conscience is closely related to care, which threatens to turn to anguish when we are to blame for having brought some evil upon ourselves or others.

But since we are not always disposed toward reflections such as are required here, nor do we always wish to be prodded into them, Sunday is set aside as a day on which anything weighing on a person in a religious, moral, social, or economic sense must be discussed.

"If you were to stay with us for a time," remarked Juliette, "our Sunday here would certainly not displease you. The day after tomorrow you would notice a great stillness in the morning; everyone stays alone and applies himself to a prescribed subject of reflection. Man is a limited creature; and Sunday is devoted to considering our limitations. If they be physical ills which we perhaps scarcely noticed in the whirl of the week's affairs, then we must seek out the physician at the beginning of the new week. If our limitations are financial and in the larger sense social, then our officials are required to hold meetings. If what oppresses us is spiritual, moral, we are to turn to a friend, to someone well disposed toward us, to request his advice, his intervention. In short, it is the rule that no one may carry over into the new week any matter that disturbs or torments him. From burdensome duties only the most conscientious execution can free us, and what cannot be solved at all we leave finally to God, as the Being who establishes and looses all constraints. Our uncle himself does not fail to conduct such an examination, and there have even been times when he discussed with us in confidence a matter which he could not master at the moment. But for the most part he consults with our noble aunt, whom he visits from time to time for such assistance. He also regularly asks on Sunday evenings whether everything has been confessed and disposed of. From this you can see that we exercise great care not to be taken into your order, the community of the renunciants!"

"A fine life!" Hersilie exclaimed. "If I resign myself for one day a week, I have the benefit of it for all three hundred sixty-five!"

But before his departure our friend received from the younger steward a package with a missive enclosed, from which we excerpt the following passage:

"It seems to me that every nation has its own prevailing inclination, whose satisfaction is necessary for its happiness, and indeed one can observe this in different people as well. When a person loves to listen to full, gracefully arranged notes, seeking mental and spiritual pleasure from them, will he thank me if I present him with the most splendid painting? And a devotee of painting wants to see and will reject attempts to stir his phantasy with a poem or a novel. Who is so talented that he can enjoy in a variety of ways?

"But you, transient friend, struck me as such a person, and if you could appreciate the charm of a refined French aberration, you will not, I hope, disdain the simple, faithful honesty of German circumstances and will forgive me if, true to my nature and way of thought, to my upbringing and position, I can find no more pleasing image than that presented by the German middle class in its simple domesticity.

"May you enjoy this tale and think of me."

Chapter Eight

Who Is the Traitor?

"No! No!" he exclaimed, as he strode hastily and angrily into his assigned chamber and put down the lamp. "No! It is not possible! But where should I turn? For the first time I am of another mind, have different feelings, other wishes than his.—Oh, Father! if you could be here invisible and could look straight through me, you would convince yourself that I am still the same, still your loyal, obedient, loving son.—To say no! To oppose my father's fondest, long cherished wish! How do I break the news? How do I express it? No, I cannot marry Julie.—I shudder even to speak the thought aloud. And how can I go to him and reveal this to him, my dear, good father? He will stare at me in amazement and shake his head without a word; that perceptive, intelligent, learned man will be speechless. Oh, woe is me!—I know very well to whom I would confide this pain, this embarrassment, whom I would choose to speak for me! Of all those I know, you, Lucinde, are the one! And first I should like to tell you how much I love you, how I surrender myself to you, and beseech you: 'Speak for me, and if you can love me, if you will be mine, then speak for us both!' "

Short though this heartfelt and passionate soliloquy was, it will take many words to explain it.

Professor N. of N. had one little boy of remarkable beauty, whom he left in the care of his wife, a most worthy woman, until the lad was eight years old; she it was who directed the child's hours and days toward living, learning, and good conduct at all times. She died, and in that moment the father felt personally incapable of devoting the same care to the child's upbringing. Until then everything had been agreed upon by the parents; they both worked toward the same end, decided jointly what should be done in the immediate future, and the mother was adept at carrying it out. The widower's sorrow was now double and triple, for he knew well, and daily saw proof of it, that for the son of a professor to acquire a good education at the academy required a veritable miracle.

In this distress he turned to his friend, the chief bailiff in R., with whom he had earlier discussed plans for closer ties between their families. This friend had good advice for him and was able to arrange for the boy to be admitted to one of the fine schools flourishing in Germany where attention is given to the whole person, to body, soul, and mind.

Now the boy was safely established, but the father found himself terribly lonely: deprived of his wife, deprived of the pleasant company of his boy, whom he had seen being educated as he wished, with no effort of his own. Here, too, the friendship of the chief bailiff stood him in good stead; the distance between their dwellings vanished in the face of his pleasure and delight in movement and distraction. And here the orphaned scholar found in a likewise motherless family two beautiful daughters growing up, each appealing in her own way; and both fathers became more and more attached to the thought, the prospect, of eventually seeing their families united in the most gratifying fashion. They lived in a fortunate principality; the able bailiff was secure in his position for life and would probably be able to choose his successor. Now, in accord with a sensible family and ministerial plan, Lucidor was to prepare himself for the important position occupied by his future father-in-law. And in fact he progressed from stage to stage. No pains were spared to impart to him all the knowledge, to develop in him all the skills of which the state always has need: attention to those laws strictly enforced by the courts and also to those laxer ones for whose administration intelligence and resourcefulness are important; accounting for daily use, not excluding more complicated auditing procedures, but all of it directly connected with life, as would certainly and inevitably be needed.

In this spirit Lucidor had completed his schooling, and now his father and his benefactor prepared him for the academy. He displayed the finest talent for everything, and Nature had also endowed him with the rare good fortune of being motivated by love for his father and respect for his friend to develop his abilities in precisely those directions they indicated, first out of obedience, later out of conviction. He was sent to an academy abroad, and both his own letters and the reports of his teachers and tutors testified that he was following the course that would lead to the desired goal. The only criticism was that in some cases he had shown himself too impatiently upright. At this his father shook his head, and the chief bailiff nodded. Who would not have wished to have such a son!

In the meanwhile the two daughters, Julie and Lucinde, were growing up. Julie, the younger one, playful, charming, unsettled, most entertaining; the older one difficult to categorize, for she embodied precisely those qualities of honesty and purity which we find desirable for all women. The two families visited each other in turn, and in the house of the professor Julie found inexhaustible sources of entertainment.

Geography, which he enlivened with topography, was part of his specialty, and no sooner had Julie discovered one of the Homann volumes, of which the professor owned a whole series, than she set about studying all the cities, evaluating them, preferring some and rejecting others. All ports enjoyed her special favor; if other cities wished to secure even partial approval, they had to display a profusion of towers, domes, and minarets.

Her father left her for weeks at a time with his trusted friend; she genuinely gained in knowledge and insight, and became conversant with the principal features, particulars, and places of the inhabited world. She also paid close attention to the native dress of foreign nations, and when her foster father sometimes asked her jokingly whether any of the many handsome young people passing by outside the window might not appeal to her, she would say, "Oh yes, if he looks very exotic!" And since students at our academies are not known for the conventionality of their appearance, she often had occasion to take interest in one or the other; she was reminded at the sight of him of some foreign national costume, but in the end she always insisted that anyone to whom she should give her special attention would have to be at the very least a Greek, in full national regalia, for which reason she longed to visit the Leipzig Fair, where such sights could be seen in the streets.

After his dry and sometimes irritating work, nothing provided our teacher such happy moments as when he jestingly instructed the girl and secretly triumphed that he was training such a charming daughter-in-law, ever entertained and entertaining. The two fathers had agreed, by the bye, that the girls were to have no inkling of their intentions, and Lucidor, too, was kept in the dark.

Thus years passed, as they so easily do; Lucidor presented himself, accomplished, successful on all the examinations, even to the satisfaction of his higher superiors, who wished no more than to fulfill with good conscience the hopes of worthy old servants who enjoyed and deserved favor.

And so the matter had proceeded in orderly fashion to the point where Lucidor, having conducted himself admirably in lower-ranking positions, was about to enter a most advantageous situation, suited to his achievements and his desires, and located exactly halfway between the academy and the home of the chief bailiff.

Until this time the father had but hinted to his son about Julie, but he now spoke of her as his fiancée and spouse, without further doubts or reservations, emphasizing the young man's good fortune at having acquired such a living gem. In his mind's eye he pictured his daughter-in-law visiting again from time to time, busy with maps, plans, and engravings of cities; his son, for his part, recalled the lovable, merry creature who in his childhood had always delighted him with her teasing and her friendly ways. And now Lucidor was to ride over to the chief bailiff's to have a closer look at the fully grown beauty and spend several weeks reestablishing his familiarity and acquaintance with the entire household. If, as was hoped, the young people should speedily reach an accord, Lucidor's father was to be notified, whereupon he would appear at once, so that a solemn betrothal might seal the hoped-for bliss.

Lucidor arrives; he enjoys the friendliest possible reception. He is assigned a room, unpacks, and comes down. There he finds assembled, in addition to the members of the family with whom we are already acquainted, a half-grown son, quite spoiled but clever and good-natured, so that, if one wished to consider him the jester, he was not ill-suited to the rest of the company. To the household belonged also an elderly but sound and cheerful man, quiet, refined, and intelligent, devoting his remaining years to helping others here and there. Shortly after Lucidor, another stranger arrived, a man no longer young, of distinguished appearance, dignified, polished, and most entertaining because of his knowledge of distant parts of the world. They called him Antoni.

Julie received her prospective bridegroom decorously but obligingly, while Lucinde did the honors for the household, as her sister did for herself. And so the day passed most agreeably for all, with the exception of Lucidor; he, who was in any case shy, felt compelled to ask questions from time to time, so as not to fall into complete silence; and no one appears to his advantage in such a situation.

He was thoroughly distracted, for from the first moment he had felt neither dislike nor aversion for Julie, but estrangement; Lucinde, on the other hand, attracted him so much that he trembled when she turned her large, clear, calm eyes upon him.

In this distress he reached his chamber the first evening and poured out his heart in that monologue with which we began. But to explain it, as well as how such a passionate flood of speech fits with what we already know of him, a brief communication is in order.

Lucidor was a young man of deep feeling, and was usually preoccupied with something other than what the immediate present required, for which reason he was never very adept at pleasantries or conversation. He was aware of this and became reticent, except on certain subjects which he had studied thoroughly and for which he commanded the necessary facts. Furthermore, both in school and later at the university he had been mistaken in his friends and had bared his soul in the wrong place; he was reluctant, therefore, to communicate anything; and reluctance renders any true communication impossible.

Toward his father he was wont to express only assent; accordingly, he poured out his heart in monologues as soon as he was alone.

The following morning he had pulled himself together, and yet he was almost jolted out of his composure when Julie's manner toward him became still friendlier, gayer, and freer. She besieged him with questions about his journeys on land and water, how as a student he had hiked through Switzerland with his bundle on his shoulder, and even crossed the Alps. Then she wished to hear all about the lovely island in the large southern lake; then, working backwards, the Rhine had to be traced from its point of origin, first through very inhospitable regions, then downstream through richly varied landscapes, until finally, between Mainz and Koblenz, the moment comes to release the great river with honor from its last constraints and let it flow out into the wide world, toward the sea.

Lucidor felt much relieved at this, and he told his story so willingly and so well that Julie exclaimed, quite enchanted, that these sights should be enjoyed in the company of another. At which Lucidor again took fright, for he thought he detected an allusion to their common journey through life.

But he was soon rescued from his duties as narrator, for the stranger they called Antoni rapidly eclipsed all the mountain springs, cliffs at water's edge, constrained or liberated rivers: he made straight for Genoa; Livorno lay not far off, the most interesting features of the countryside were, so to speak, snatched in passing; one had to have seen Naples before one died, but then there was still Constantinople, which should likewise not be missed. Antoni's description of the wide world captured the imagination of all his listeners, although he could summon less passion for his narrative. But Julie, quite beside herself, was still by no means satisfied—she still longed to hear about Alexandria, Cairo, but especially the Pyramids, of which she had acquired considerable knowledge from her presumed father-in-law's instruction.

That evening Lucidor (he had hardly closed his door, not yet set down his candle) exclaimed, "Think what you are doing! This is serious. You have studied serious matters and thought them through; but what good is training in justice if you do not act justly? Look upon yourself as a legal representative, forget yourself and do what you would be obligated to do for another person. Everything is tangled in the worst way! The stranger is apparently here for Lucinde's sake, and she shows him the finest, noblest social and domestic attentions; the little madcap would like to go dashing through the world with almost anyone, at the drop of a hat. Besides that she is a rogue; her interest in cities and countries is a farce to reduce us to silence. But why do I find this business so confused and complicated? Is not the chief bailiff a most understanding, perceptive, loving intermediary? Tell him how you feel and think, and he will be able to follow your thoughts, if not your feelings. He can persuade Father of anything. And are not both his daughters? And what does that Anton Rover want with Lucinde, who is born for domesticity, to be happy and to bring happiness there to others? Why not attach that bouncing quicksilver to the wandering Jew—that would make a charming pair!"

In the morning Lucidor went downstairs, fully resolved to speak with the father and therefore to approach him directly during his usual hour of leisure. How great was his sorrow, his perplexity, when he learned that the chief bailiff had departed on business, and was not expected back until the day after next. Julie seemed to have chosen this as her day for travel; she stuck close by the world traveler, and with some joking references to domesticity, left Lucidor to Lucinde. If previously our friend had observed the noble maiden from a certain distance, forming a general impression, and had already taken her into his heart, he now had an opportunity in close proximity to discover two and three times over that which had first attracted him in general.

The good old friend of the family now stepped to the fore, in place of the absent father. He, too, had lived and loved, and now, after many a bruising in the arena of life, lived restored and cherished with the friend of his youth. He enlivened the conversation, and dwelt especially on errors in the choice of a spouse, recounting remarkable examples of prompt and belated declarations of love. Lucinde shone in her full glory. She confessed that in life chance occurrences of every sort could produce the best of results, in marriages as well; and yet it was finer and more edifying when a person could say he owed his happiness to himself, to the calm, quiet conviction of his heart, to noble intentions and prompt decisions. Tears came to Lucidor's eyes as he applauded these sentiments, after which the ladies soon withdrew. The elderly gentleman was disposed to exchange stories, and so the conversation broadened to comic anecdotes, which, however, touched our hero so personally that only a youth as well bred as he could control himself sufficiently not to burst out; but that occurred as soon as he was alone.

"I restrained myself!" he exclaimed. "I will not worry my good father with such confusion; I kept myself in check, for I regard this worthy friend of the family as the deputy of both fathers. I shall speak to him, reveal everything, he will surely mediate; indeed, he has already almost voiced my own wishes. Will he reprove in the individual case what he approves in general? Tomorrow first thing I shall seek him out; I must find relief from this distress."

At breakfast the old gentleman did not appear; he had, it was said, talked too much the previous evening, had sat up too long and drunk a few more drops of wine than was his custom. Much was recounted in his praise, and indeed just such speeches and actions as made Lucidor despair at not having turned to him at once. His discomfiture was only intensified when he learned that after such attacks the good old man sometimes remained out of sight for a full week.

A country setting has considerable advantages for sociability, particularly when the hosts are thoughtful, sensitive individuals, who have been impelled over the years to come to the aid of the natural potential of their surroundings. Such had successfully been done here. First alone, then in a long, happy marriage, with his own means, in a lucrative post, following his own vision and insight, the inclinations of his wife, even, finally, the wishes and whims of his children, the chief bailiff had first laid out and cultivated larger and smaller separate areas, and these, by degrees tastefully linked with plantings and paths, presented to anyone who strolled among them a charming, varied, and characteristic progression of scenes. The younger members of our family had their guest begin just such a pilgrimage, as indeed we all enjoy showing our grounds to a stranger, that we may view with fresh eyes that which has become ordinary to us and retain a favorable impression of it forever.

The immediate and also the more distant surroundings were very well suited to modest plantings and even to rustic details. Fertile hills alternated with well-watered meadows, so that from time to time the entire landscape was visible, without its being flat; and if the land seemed principally devoted to useful purposes, attractiveness and charm had not been forgotten.

Adjacent to the residence and the utility buildings lay pleasure gardens, orchards, and mowings; thence one wandered unexpectedly into a wood, through which a lane broad enough for driving wound back and forth. At its center, at the highest elevation, had been constructed a hall with adjoining chambers. Entering by the main door, one saw in a great mirror the finest view the entire region had to offer, then quickly turned around to recover with the help of reality from the unexpected tableau. For the approach was artfully designed and everything ingeniously hidden to achieve this surprise effect. No one entered without turning with pleasure back and forth from the mirror to Nature and from Nature to the mirror.

Once underway on this most beautiful, sunny, and lengthy day, they made a reflective tour around and through all the grounds. Here their good mother had sat of an evening, where a glorious beech had maintained a clear space all around itself. Soon afterwards Julie half-teasingly indicated the site of Lucinde's morning devotions, by a little brook among poplars and alders, with meadows sloping down on one side, cultivated fields mounting on the other. It was indescribably beautiful! One felt that one had seen this everywhere before, but nowhere with such meaningful and welcome simplicity. On the other hand, the squire pointed out, half against Julie's will, the diminutive bowers and childish flower beds, which, next to a cozy mill, were scarcely noticeable any more. They harked back to a time when Julie, about ten years of age, had taken it into her head to become a miller and, after the death of the two old folks, to take over the mill herself and find an honest millhand to wed.

"That was at a time," Julie exclaimed, "when I knew nothing of cities built on rivers or better yet on the ocean, like Genoa etc. Your kind father, Lucidor, converted me; since then I have scarcely come here." She sat down coquettishly on a little bench, which barely held her, beneath an elder bush that had bent over too far. "Fie on crouching like this!" she exclaimed, leaped up, and darted ahead with her merry brother.

The other couple lagged behind, conversing sensibly, and in such cases good sense tends imperceptibly toward emotion. Walking past varied simple natural objects and reflecting calmly upon them, they could discuss in detail how a thoughtful, intelligent person can produce something from them, how insight into what is available, along with a sense of needs, can work wonders in making the world habitable, then populating it, and finally overpopulating it. Lucinde accounted for everything, and despite her modesty could not conceal that the convenient and pleasing links between separate parts of the grounds were her achievement, under the guidance, direction, or encouragement of her revered mother.

But since even the longest day eventually gives way to evening, they had to think about their return, and as they were planning an agreeable roundabout way, the merry brother demanded that they take the shorter path, even though it was less pleasant and indeed more fatiguing. "For," he exclaimed, "you have been showing off your plantings and landscaping, and how you have beautified and improved the landscape for artistic eyes and tender hearts; but now let me have some credit as well."

Now they had to make their way across plowed fields and along bumpy paths, even across swampy spots on stones scattered at random; some distance off they spied all sorts of machinery piled high in confusion. Examined more closely, this proved to be a large pleasure ground, arranged with a certain sense for popular taste. And so there stood at proper intervals the great wheel, where the ascending and descending seats remained calmly horizontal; other swings of various kinds; swinging ropes, see-saws, bowling and ninepin alleys, and everything imaginable in a large pasture to occupy and entertain crowds of people in a variety of equally interesting ways. "This," he exclaimed, "is my own invention and design. And although my father contributed the funds and a clever fellow provided his brains, without me, whom you often call foolish, mind and means would never have come together."

Thus in a cheerful frame of mind all four returned home at sundown. Antoni made an appearance, but the young lady, who had still not had enough from such an eventful day, ordered the horses and rode off through the countryside to visit a friend, desperate at not having seen her for two days. The four who remained behind unexpectedly felt ill at ease, and it was even said that the father's absence disquieted the household. The conversation was beginning to flag when suddenly the merry squire sprang up and, quickly returning with a book, offered to read aloud. Lucinde did not refrain from asking how he came by such an idea, which he had not had for years; he replied cheerfully, "Everything occurs to me at the right moment, which is more than you can say for yourself." He read a series of authentic fairy tales, the sort which lure a person out of himself, gratify his wishes, and make him forget all the restrictions that hem us in, even at our happiest moments.

"What do I do now?" Lucidor exclaimed, when he was finally alone; "time is short; I have no confidence in Antoni, he is so remote; I do not know who he is or how he got into this house, or what he is seeking. He seems attentive toward Lucinde, so what could I hope from him? I have no choice but to approach Lucinde herself; she must know my feelings, she first of all. And that was my first instinct; why do we let ourselves be led astray down the paths of cleverness! The first shall now be the last, and I hope to reach my goal!"

On Saturday morning Lucidor was dressed early, pacing back and forth in his room, considering what he should say to Lucinde, when he overheard a sort of playful quarrel outside his door, which promptly flew open. The merry squire shoved in a boy with coffee and pastry for the guest, while he himself brought cold meats and wine. "You should go ahead of me," cried the squire, "the guest must be served first, and I am used to serving myself. My friend! Today I come rather early and noisily; let us enjoy our breakfast in peace, and then see what to do, for we cannot expect much from the rest of the company. The little one has not yet returned from visiting her friend; those two must pour out their hearts to each other at least once in a fortnight to keep them from bursting. On Saturdays Lucinde is of no use, she always prepares her household accounts punctually for our father. I was supposed to be involved in that, too, but heaven forbid! If I know what something costs, I cannot enjoy a single bite. Guests are expected for tomorrow, the old man has not yet recovered his equilibrium, Antoni has gone off hunting, so let us do likewise!"

Muskets, pouches, and hounds were ready for them when they came into the courtyard, and soon they were off to the fields, where a young hare and a poor, insignificant bird were all they shot. In the meantime, they chatted about their domestic and social circumstances. Antoni was mentioned, and Lucidor did not fail to inquire further about him. The merry squire assured him, with a certain complacency, that he had already seen straight through that strange man, despite his mystifications. "He is," he continued, "surely the son of a rich mercantile family that went bankrupt just when he, in the fullness of youth, thought to turn his strength and enthusiasm to large business dealings, and also to partake of the many pleasures the world had to offer. Dashed from the height of his hopes, he pulled himself together and achieved for others what he could no longer do for himself and his family. Thus he traveled all over the world, becoming thoroughly acquainted with its ways and mutual exchange, and did not overlook his own interests in the process. Tireless activity and proven integrity won him the full and unswerving confidence of many. Thus he made acquaintances and friends everywhere, and indeed it is clear that his fortune is distributed around the world, wherever he has friends, for which reason his presence in all four corners of the world is required from time to time."

The merry young squire had recounted all this more naively and circumstantially, adding many humorous asides, as though he wished to spin out his tale as long as possible.

"How far his association with my father goes back! They think I do not notice anything because I do not bother with anything. But I see it all the more clearly precisely because it is none of my business. He has deposited a good deal of money with my father, who has invested it soundly and profitably. Just yesterday Antoni slipped the old man a jewel case; I have never seen anything simpler, more beautiful, or more precious, even though I had only a glimpse of it, because it is being kept hidden. Probably it is intended to be bestowed on his bride for her pleasure, joy, and future security. Antoni has placed his trust in Lucinde. But when I see the two of them together, I cannot think them a well-matched pair. The harum-scarum one would be better for him, and I think she would rather have him, too, than the older girl would; really, sometimes she looks at the old curmudgeon so gaily and with such interest, as if she would love to jump into a coach with him and fly away." Lucidor contained himself. He did not know what to reply. Everything he heard was greatly to his liking. The squire continued: "In general, the girl has a perverse fondness for older people; I think she would as gladly have married your father as the son."

Lucidor followed his companion wherever he led, up hill and down dale. They both forgot about hunting, which held little promise in any case. They turned in at a farmhouse, where, warmly received, one of our friends refreshed himself with food, drink, and gossip, while the other lost himself in thoughts and deliberations as to how he might turn the discovery he had made to his best advantage.

After all these stories and revelations, Lucidor had gained enough confidence in Antoni that he asked after him at once as he entered the courtyard, and he hurried into the gardens, where Antoni was supposed to be. He hastened along every path in the park in the serene evening sunlight—but in vain. Not a soul was to be seen. Finally he stepped through the door of the great hall, and strangely enough, the setting sun, reflected in the mirror, blinded him in such fashion that he did not recognize the two persons on the sofa, but could at least distinguish a woman receiving a passionate kiss on her hand from the man seated beside her. How great was his horror when his eyes recovered and he saw Lucinde and Antoni before him. He would have liked to sink into the ground, but stood rooted to the spot while Lucinde welcomed him in the friendliest, most unconstrained fashion, moved over, and asked him to sit at her right. In a daze he sat down and as she spoke to him, asking him about his day, excusing her absence on the ground of household obligations, he could hardly bear her voice. Antoni rose and took his leave of Lucinde, whereupon she, also rising, invited the other to join her for a walk. Walking beside her, he was silent and embarrassed. She, too, seemed uneasy; and had he been only slightly in possession of his senses, her deep breathing would have betrayed that she was at pains to conceal heartfelt sighs. Finally, as they approached the house, she took her leave, but he continued walking, first slowly, then impetuously, out toward the open country. The park hemmed him in; he hurried through the fields, aware only of the voice of his heart, without feeling for the beauties of this glorious evening. As soon as he was alone and his feelings could be vented in a soothing gush of tears, he cried out: "Several times in my life, but never so cruelly, have I suffered the pain which now makes me utterly wretched: when the most longed-for happiness finally takes us by the hand, opens its arms and simultaneously announces eternal parting. I sat with her, walked by her side; her dress brushed against me, and I had already lost her! Do not remind yourself, do not twist the knife in the wound; be silent and be firm."

He had forbidden himself further words. In silence he pushed on, deep in thought, through fields, meadows, and undergrowth, not always on the easiest paths. But when he finally returned late at night to his room, he contained himself no longer and exclaimed, "I shall be off tomorrow morning early. I will not go through another day like this!"

And so he threw himself, fully clothed, onto his bed. Ah, fortunate, healthy youth! He fell asleep instantly; the exhausting exercise of the day had earned him a sweet night's rest. The first rays of the sun, however, woke him from comforting morning dreams. It happened to be the longest day of the year, which threatened to be all too long for him. As he had not been susceptible to the grace of the calming evening star, so, too, he felt the bracing beauty of the morning only to despair. To him, the world seemed as glorious as ever, for so it still was in his eyes. His inner being, however, denied it; all this no longer belonged to him, for he had lost Lucinde.

Chapter Nine

His portmanteau was soon packed; that he wanted to leave behind. He wrote no note. His absence from the dinner table, perhaps from supper as well, was to be explained in a few words by the groom, whom he had to wake in any case. But he found the groom already down by the stables, pacing up and down. "You do not wish to ride, I hope," exclaimed the usually good-natured fellow, with some irritation. "You won't mind my saying this, but the young master becomes more intolerable every day. Yesterday he was gadding about, so that one would think he might thank God for a rest on Sunday morning. But didn't he turn up this morning before daybreak, make a racket in the stables, and when I jumped out of bed, there he is, saddling and bridling your horse, and nothing I said could stop him. He swings himself up and calls out, 'Just think what a good deed I am doing. This creature does nothing but amble at a judicious trot. I'll spur him to a gallop with some life in it.' That was more or less what he said, among other extraordinary things."

Lucidor was doubly and triply upset; he loved the horse for the way it suited his own character, his own style of living. It annoyed him to think of the good, intelligent creature in reckless hands. His plan was ruined, his intention to flee in this crisis to an old university comrade, with whom he had enjoyed a happy, cordial friendship. His old sense of trust had reawakened, he did not count the miles that separated them, and he felt as though he were already receiving advice and comfort from this kindly and sagacious friend. This prospect was now cut off; yet not if he dared to reach his goal with his own two feet, which were still at his disposal.

He tried above all now to get out of the park into the open fields and to the road that would lead him to his friend. He was hesitating as to his direction, when he noticed to his left, rising above the shrubbery, the exotic structure of the hermitage, whose whereabouts had previously been kept secret from him. He also saw, to his great surprise, on the balcony under the pagoda roof, the good old man, who for several days had supposedly been ill, looking about him alertly. To his friendly greeting and pressing invitation to come up, Lucidor responded with excuses and hurried gestures. Only sympathy for the good old man, who, hastening down the steep steps with unsteady tread, threatened to fall, could induce him to approach and then let himself be drawn into the house. With amazement he entered the charming little room; it had only three windows, with a lovely view over the countryside; the other walls were adorned, or rather covered, with hundreds of portraits, some of them engravings, some drawings, mounted on the wall in a particular order, and separated from each other by colorful borders and spaces.

"This is a favor, my friend, that I would not do for everyone; this is the sanctuary in which I cozily spend my declining days. Here I recuperate from all the errors into which society lures me. Here I bring my dietary indiscretions back into balance."

Lucidor examined the entire room, and, well versed in history himself, soon perceived that a historical inclination underlay the arrangement.

"Up here, in the frieze," the old man remarked, "you will find the names of outstanding men of ancient times, and then from more recent times, likewise only the names of famous people, for their actual appearance would be difficult to ascertain. Here, in the main section, however, my own lifetime begins; here are the men whom I heard mentioned while I was still a boy. For the names of outstanding men survive some fifty years in the memory of the people—after that the names vanish or become legendary.—Although my parents were German, I was born in Holland, and for me, William of Orange, as regent and king of England, remains the model of all extraordinary men and heroes.

"But here you see Louis XIV right beside him, who"—how gladly would Lucidor have interrupted the good old man, had it been proper for him to do, as it is for us telling the tale, for he was threatened by recent and most recent history, as could be deduced from the pictures of Frederick the Great and his generals, at which he glanced furtively. Even though the good youth respected the old man for his lively interest in his own times and those immediately preceding them, and even though certain individual traits and views could not but strike him as worthwhile, he himself had attended lectures on recent and most recent history at the academies, and what one has heard once, one thinks one knows forever. His mind was elsewhere; he heard nothing; he barely saw, and was about to slip through the door in most uncouth fashion and clatter down the long, perilous stairway, when a loud clapping was heard from below.

While Lucidor hesitated, the old man's head poked out the window, and a familiar voice sounded from below: "Come down, Sir, for heaven's sake, from your historical picture gallery! Put an end to your fasting and help me placate our young friend—when he learns what has happened. I have been a bit rough with Lucidor's horse; it has lost a shoe, and I had to leave it behind. What will he say? It's just too absurd when a person is absurd."

"Come up!" the old man said, and turned to Lucidor: "Well, what do you say?" Lucidor remained silent, and the wild squire entered. The back and forth resulted in a long scene; suffice it to say, they decided to send the groom out at once to see to the horse.

Leaving the old man behind, the two young people hastened to the house, to which Lucidor was not entirely reluctant to be drawn. Let happen what might, at least his heart's sole desire was enclosed within these walls. In such desperate straits, our free will in any case fails us, and we feel a momentary relief when some external force or necessity takes over. Nevertheless, he had a very odd sensation when he once more stepped into his room, as when someone is unwillingly constrained to return to a chamber at an inn he has already left, because he has broken an axle.

The merry squire busied himself with the portmanteau, very neatly unpacking it, taking care to lay out whatever articles of clothing he found which, although suitable for traveling, were more formal. He made Lucidor put on shoes and stockings, arranged his curly brown locks, and dressed him up smartly. Then, stepping back and surveying our friend and the result of his meddling from head to foot, he commented, "Now, my young friend, you look like someone who might lay claim to pretty girls, and serious enough at that to look around for a bride. Just one moment, and you shall see that I can make a good showing when the hour strikes. I picked that up from the officers, at whom the girls always cast sidelong glances, and have myself joined the ranks of a certain soldiery, and now they look at me, too, and then look again, because no one knows what to make of me. That kind of looking back and forth, amazement and attention, can often lead to something quite nice, which, even if it is not lasting, still merits a moment's attention.

"But come along now, my friend, and do me a similar service. When you see me slip into my costume, piece by piece, you will not deny this flighty lad cleverness and ingenuity."

He took his friend in tow through the long, rambling corridors of the old manor. "I have bedded down way in the rear," he explained. "Without wanting to hide, I prefer to be alone; for you can never do things to others' liking."

They passed the chancellery, just as a servant was coming out, carrying an old-fashioned writing set, black, large, and fully equipped; paper, too, was included.

"I know what they are going to be scribbling," the squire remarked. "Go along and leave me the key. Have a look inside, Lucidor. It will keep you amused till I get dressed. To a friend of the law a place like that is not so detestable as to a horseman!" and with these words he pushed Lucidor into the courtroom.

The youth immediately felt himself in a familiar, congenial element, surrounded by memories of the days when he, keen on his profession, had sat at just such a table, and practiced listening and writing. It was also not lost upon him that this was a handsome old private chapel, converted, with the change in religious practices, to the service of the goddess Themis. On the shelves he found headings and documents that were already familiar; he had himself worked on these cases back in the capital. Opening a file, he found a document which he himself had copied, another which he himself had authored. The writing and the paper, the official seal and the presiding judge's signature, all recalled that period of honest striving and youthful hopes. And when he looked around and saw the bailiff's seat, which had been reserved and promised to him, such a fine position, such a worthy sphere of endeavor, which he was in danger of scorning and renouncing, the entire situation distressed him doubly and triply, while at the same time the figure of Lucinde seemed to recede from him.

He wanted to go outside, but found himself imprisoned. His peculiar friend had, out of either carelessness or mischief, locked the door after himself. Our friend did not long remain in this painful oppression, however, for the other returned, apologized and put him into genuine good humor through his odd appearance. A certain audacity in the colors and cut of his clothing was moderated by his natural taste; similarly we cannot withhold a certain admiration even from tattooed Indians. "Today," he exclaimed, "will compensate us for the tedium of the past few days. Good friends, merry friends, have arrived, pretty girls, roguish, amorous creatures, and then my father, and, wonder of wonders, your father as well! What a party it will be! Everyone is already gathered in the hall for breakfast."

Lucidor suddenly felt as though he were peering into a dense fog; all the familiar and unfamiliar new arrivals appeared to him as so many ghosts. But his character, in conjunction with his pure heart, sustained him, and in a few seconds he was ready for anything. He followed his hastening friend with firm tread, resolved to be patient, whatever might happen, and to declare himself, whatever might result.

Nevertheless he was taken aback as he crossed the threshold. In the large semicircle around the windows he at once spied his father, next to the bailiff, both splendidly dressed. The sisters, Antoni, and various other figures, known and unknown to him, he took in with a single glance, which threatened to become clouded. Faltering, he approached his father, who greeted him in the friendliest fashion, although with a certain formality, which was hardly conducive to intimate confessions. Standing there before so many people, he looked about for a suitable place; he could have stood next to Lucinde, but Julie, disliking stiff propriety, turned toward him, so that he was obliged to go to her; Antoni remained next to Lucinde.

At this critical moment Lucidor once more felt as if charged with a commission and, falling back on his entire legal training, called upon that fine maxim for his own benefit: "We should conduct the affairs entrusted to us by strangers as though they were our own; why not, then, conduct our own affairs in the same spirit?"—Practiced as he was in public speaking, he quickly ran through what he had to say. In the meanwhile the company, arranging itself in a formal semicircle, seemed to be outflanking him. He knew indeed the content of his speech, but could not think how to begin. Then he noticed, set out on a table in the corner, the great inkwell, with some notaries by it. The bailiff made a movement indicating that he was about to speak. Lucidor wanted to forestall him, and at that very moment Julie squeezed his hand. This completely destroyed his composure; he concluded that everything had been decided and that he was utterly lost.

Now it was no longer a matter of respecting existing circumstances, family ties, social custom, or etiquette. He stared straight ahead, pulled his hand from Julie's, and was out of the door so quickly that he was gone without anyone's realizing quite how, and once outside, he himself hardly knew where he was.

Shy of the sunlight, which blazed down upon him with full force, avoiding the gaze of those he encountered, fearful of those who might come looking for him, he walked on and reached the pavilion. There his knees threatened to give way. He stumbled inside and threw himself down disconsolately on the sofa beneath the mirror. To be overcome in the midst of a proper, well-bred company by such confusion, which still beat back and forth inside him like a wave! His past existence warred with the present. It was a dreadful moment.

And thus he lay for a time, his face buried in the cushion on which yesterday Lucinde had rested her arm. Still absorbed in his pain, he suddenly sprang up, feeling someone's touch, yet not having sensed the approach of any other person: there he saw Lucinde, who stood close by him.

Assuming she had been sent to bring him back, that she had been commissioned to lead him back with tactful, sisterly words to the company, to face his horrid fate, he exclaimed, "They should not have sent you, Lucinde, for you are the one who drove me away from there; I will not return! If you are capable of any pity, provide me with the opportunity and the means to flee. And, that you may testify why it was impossible to bring me back, accept this key to my conduct, which must strike you and everyone else as mad. Hear the pledge I made to myself and which I now repeat aloud irrevocably: with you alone do I wish to live, to use and enjoy the years of my youth and likewise a loyal, upright old age. Let this be as firm and sure as anything ever spoken at the altar, what I now swear as I leave you, I, the person most to be pitied on this earth."

He made a movement as if to slip by her, who stood so close in front of him, but she caught him gently in her arms. "What are you doing?" he cried. "Lucidor!" she exclaimed, "You are not to be pitied, as you imagine. You are mine, I am yours; I hold you in my arms; do not hesitate to put yours around me. Your father has agreed. Antoni is to marry my sister." He drew back from her in astonishment. "Could that be true?" Lucinde smiled and nodded, and he freed himself from her embrace. "Let me see at a distance once more what will be so near to me, what will belong to me most nearly." He took her hands, their eyes met. "Lucinde, are you mine?" She replied, "Yes, I am," with the sweetest tears in the truest of eyes. He embraced her and pressed his head to her shoulder, clinging like a shipwrecked man to a cliff; the ground was still heaving beneath him. But his entranced eyes, opening again, now fell upon the mirror. There he saw her in his arms, himself entwined by hers; he gazed again and again. Such feelings remain with a person for his entire life. At the same time, the mirror showed him the landscape, which yesterday had looked so dreary and ominous to him, now more brilliant and wonderful than ever, and himself in such a state, with such a background! Sufficient recompense for all his suffering.

"We are not alone," Lucinde remarked, and hardly had he recovered from his ecstasy than girls in finery, wearing wreaths, and boys carrying garlands appeared, blocking the doorway to the garden house. "It was all supposed to work out differently," Lucinde exclaimed. "We had everything so delightfully planned, and now everything is in chaos!"

A lively march sounded in the distance, and the company could be seen approaching the pavilion in gay and festive procession by way of the main avenue. He hesitated to go out to meet them, and seemed sure of his steps only when she held his arm. She stayed by his side, awaiting from moment to moment the solemn scene of reunion and of thanks for the forgiveness that had already been granted.

But it had been otherwise disposed by the willful gods: the cheerful blare of a postilion's horn, from the opposite direction, seemed to throw the whole arrangement into confusion. "Who could be coming?" Lucinde cried. Lucidor shuddered at the thought of a stranger's presence, and indeed the carriage seemed completely unfamiliar. It was a new two-seater in the very latest style! It drove right up to the pavilion.

A fine, well-mannered boy sprang down from the back and opened the door, but no one stepped out; the carriage was empty. The boy climbed in and with practiced hand threw back the hood. In a twinkling the most charming conveyance for gay pleasure trips stood ready, before the eyes of all those who had in the meantime reached the pavilion. Antoni, hurrying on ahead of the others, led Julie to the carriage. "Try it," he said, "and see whether this conveyance pleases you for traveling with me through the wide world on the best of its roads; I shall take you on no others. And should it be necessary, we will know how to improvise. Packhorses will carry us over the mountains, and the carriage as well."

"You are a dear," Julie exclaimed. The boy came forward and with a conjurer's dexterity demonstrated all the comforts, little luxuries, and conveniences of the light vehicle.

"There is no way on earth to thank you," Julie cried. "Only in this small mobile heaven, from this cloud into which you raise me, will I give you my hearty thanks." She had already leaped into the carriage, casting him a friendly kiss and glance. "For the moment you may not yet join me here, but there is someone else whom I intend to take along on this trial drive; he still has another trial to undergo." She summoned Lucidor, who, engaged in a conversation with his father and his father-in-law in which he had no voice, was glad to be forced into the carriage, since he felt an inescapable need to distract himself in some way, if only for just a moment. He sat down beside her, she told the postilion which way to go. Swiftly they rode off, enveloped in dust, out of sight of the astonished spectators.

Julie settled herself firmly and comfortably in one corner. "You take the other, dear brother-in-law, so that we can comfortably look into each other's eyes."

LUCIDOR. You sense my confusion, my embarrassment. I am still as in a dream. Help me out of it.

JULIE. Look at the fine peasants, how warmly they greet us. But during your visit you have not been in the upper village. All prosperous folk, who are all well disposed toward me. Not one is so rich that one cannot, now and then, do him a significant favor. This road, on which we are traveling so comfortably, was laid out by my father, as were these other excellent arrangements.

LUCIDOR. I can well believe that, and admit as much. But what have these extraneous matters to do with my inner confusion?

JULIE. Be patient, and I will show you the kingdoms of the world and the glory of them. Now we are on top. How clearly the level land is set off against the mountains! All of these villages have much to thank my father for, and probably my mother and us daughters as well. The commons of that little town, way over there, mark the boundaries of our holdings.

LUCIDOR. I find you in a very strange mood. You do not seem to be saying exactly what you would wish to say.

JULIE. Now look down here to your left; what a lovely composition that makes! The church with its tall linden trees, the bailiff's house with its poplars behind the village hill. We can also see the gardens from here, and the park.

The postilion was driving faster now.

JULIE. You recognize that pavilion; it looks as splendid from here as the surrounding countryside does from there. We shall stop here by the tree. From here we are reflected above in the great mirror, so that they can see us perfectly well from there, but we cannot see ourselves.—Drive on!—Not long ago a couple saw itself reflected in that mirror, and, if I am not greatly mistaken, with great mutual satisfaction.

Lucidor, irritated, made no reply; they drove on awhile in silence, the carriage whipping along. "Here," said Julie, "is where the bad road begins. There is a future good deed for you. Before we start down, look over there again, where the glorious crown of my mother's beech towers over everything. You will drive back by the bad road," she continued to the coachman; "we will take the footpath through the valley, and will be there before you." As she got out she said, "You must admit that the wandering Jew, that Anton Rover, knows how to make his pilgrimages comfortable enough, for himself and his companions; it is a very beautiful, comfortable carriage."

She was already down the hill; Lucidor followed, lost in thought, and found her seated on a well-placed bench; it was Lucinde's favorite spot. She summoned him to her side.

JULIE. Now we sit here, and are nothing to one another, since that was how it was to be. Little Quicksilver was not to your liking. You could not love such a creature; she was hateful to you.

Lucidor's astonishment increased.

JULIE. Ah, but Lucinde! She is the essence of all perfection, and the pretty little sister was once and for all out of the question. I see the question trembling on your lips: who informed us so accurately?

LUCIDOR. There is some treason here!

JULIE. Oh yes, there is a traitor involved.

LUCIDOR. Name him!

JULIE. He is quickly unmasked. You yourself!—You have the commendable or uncommendable habit of talking to yourself, and I will confess to you, in the name of all of us, that we took turns eavesdropping.

Lucidor (jumping up). A fine sort of hospitality, to lay traps for strangers this way!

Julie. By no means. We never thought of eavesdropping on you, any more than on anyone else. You know, your bed stands in an alcove in the wall; on the other side is another ordinarily used for storage. A few days before, we had made our elderly friend sleep there, because we were worried about him in his isolated hermitage. Then your very first evening you launched into such a passionate soliloquy, whose contents he revealed to us most urgently the following morning.

Lucidor had no desire to interrupt her. He moved away.

Julie (standing up and following him). How useful this disclosure was! I will readily admit that though you were not exactly repugnant to me, the situation that awaited me was by no means desirable. To be Madame Bailiff, what a dreadful fate! To have a capable, good husband, who is to administer justice to people and is so preoccupied with justice that he cannot manage to be just! Who cannot do justice either to those above or to those below and, what is worst, cannot do justice to himself! I know what my mother suffered from the incorruptible, unbending nature of my father. Finally, alas after her death, a certain mildness developed in him; he seemed to feel more at one with the world, to adapt somewhat to its ways, which in the past he had always opposed in vain.

Lucidor (highly dissatisfied with the situation, provoked by the frivolous treatment, stood still). For an evening's jest it might have been all right, but to perpetrate such a humiliating mystification on an unsuspecting guest for days on end is not pardonable.

Julie. We all shared the blame; we all eavesdropped on you. Yet I alone am atoning for the guilt of listening.

Lucidor. All of you! All the more unpardonable! And how could you look at me by day without shame, when you had ignominiously and illicitly duped me by night? But now it is absolutely clear to me that your arrangements by day were intended only to make a fool of me. A fine family! And what happened to your father's love of justice?—And Lucinde!—

Julie. And Lucinde!—What sort of tone is this? You mean to say, do you not, how painful it is to think evil of Lucinde, to have to put Lucinde in the same class as the rest of us?

Lucidor. I do not comprehend Lucinde.

Julie. You mean to say: that this pure and noble soul, this calm, tranquil nature, goodness and kindness itself, this woman just as she ought to be, should join forces with a thoughtless company, with a madcap sister, a spoiled brother, and certain other mysterious persons: that surpasses understanding.

Lucidor. Yes, that surpasses understanding.

JULIE. Well, try to understand it! Like all of us, Lucinde had her hands tied. Had you been able to see her embarrassment, how she barely kept herself from revealing all to you, you would love her doubly and triply, if every true love were not already ten- and hundredfold. Let me also assure you: toward the end, the game became too long for us all.

LUCIDOR. Then why did not you put an end to it?

JULIE. That, too, can now be explained. After our father had heard about your first monologue and saw that all his children had no objection to such a switch, he decided to go to your father right away. The importance of the matter weighed on him. Only a father can truly feel what respect is owed to a father. "He must be informed first," my father said, "so that he shall not be compelled afterwards, when the rest of us are all agreed, to give an annoyed consent. I know him perfectly; I know how he clings to an idea, a preference, a project, and that worries me. He has thought so long about Julie in connection with his maps and drawings that he has already resolved to transfer everything here, when the day should come for the young pair to settle here and be unlikely to move. He wanted to devote all his vacations to us, as well as whatever other kindness and goodness he had in mind. He must learn what kind of joke Nature has played on us, before anything is actually declared or decided." He then made us all promise with a solemn handshake to watch you and prevent you from doing anything, no matter what. How his return was delayed, how much art, effort, and tenacity it took to win your father's consent, that you may hear from him. Enough, the matter is settled; Lucinde is yours.

And thus the two of them, moving briskly from where they had first been seated, talking as they went, pausing along the way, still talking, then strolling on, passed through the meadows and came to the hillock, where they reached another well laid roadway. The carriage came swiftly toward them. At this point Julie called her neighbor's attention to a strange spectacle. All the machinery of which her brother had been so proud was occupied and in motion; the wheels were transporting a crowd of people up and down; the swings were flying to and fro, and people were climbing the poles. What bold swings and leaps one saw above the heads of an enormous throng! The squire had set it all in motion so that the guests might be entertained after dinner. "Drive on through the lower village," Julie called. "The people wish me well and they must see how well it goes with me!"

The village was deserted, for the young people had already hurried to the amusement area. Old men and women appeared at doors and windows, roused by the posthorn. They all waved, blessed her, and cried, "Look at the handsome couple!"

JULIE. Well, there you have it! We would have been well suited after all; you may yet be sorry.

LUCIDOR. But as it is, dear sister-in-law!

JULIE. "Dear" now, when you are free of me, isn't that so?

LUCIDOR. Just one word! A heavy responsibility rests on you; why did you squeeze my hand, when you knew and felt my terrifying plight? Nothing in my life has ever seemed so thoroughly malicious.

JULIE. Thank the Lord, now everything is atoned for, everything is forgiven. I did not want you, that is true, but that you did not want me in the slightest, that is something no girl forgives, and that squeeze—mark this well—was for calling me a rogue. I admit it was more roguish than was proper, and I can forgive myself only by forgiving you, and so let everything be forgiven and forgotten! Here is my hand on it.

He clasped it, and said, "So here we are again! Once more in our park, and you will soon set off, around the wide world, and doubtless back again. We shall meet again."

They had reached the garden pavilion; it seemed empty; the company, discomfited by the long delay of dinner, had gone for a walk. But Antoni and Lucinde emerged. Julie sprang out of the carriage toward her betrothed, thanking him with a warm embrace, and wept for joy. A flush appeared on the cheeks of the worthy man, his features relaxed, his eye grew moist, and a handsome, distinguished youth emerged from his husk.

And so the two couples joined the party, with emotions beyond the loveliest dream.

Chapter Ten

Father and son, accompanied by a groom, had passed through a stretch of pleasant country, when the groom halted in view of a high wall that seemed to enclose a large area. He signified that they should now approach the great gate on foot, because no horse was allowed within these precincts. They pulled at the bell, the gate swung open without any human form becoming visible, and they set out toward an old building that gleamed from among ancient trunks of beeches and oaks. It was a remarkable sight, for although it seemed old from the style, it looked as if the masons and stonecutters had only just left the site, so fresh, complete, and crisp did the joints appear, as well as all the worked stone ornament.

The heavy metal ring on the handsomely carved front door invited them to knock, which Felix mischievously accomplished rather ungently. This door, too, sprang open and they discovered in the hall a woman in her middle years, occupied at her embroidery frame with a handsome piece of work. She greeted the newcomers at once as though they had been expected and began to sing a cheerful song, at which another woman emerged from a door nearby. What dangled from her belt identified her at once as the busy housekeeper and chatelaine. She too greeted the strangers in a friendly manner, led them up a staircase and showed them into a solemn hall; it was broad and lofty, with wainscoting all around, surmounted by a series of historical scenes. Two persons came toward them, a younger woman and an older man.

The woman at once welcomed the guest frankly. "You have been announced as one of us. But how shall I introduce this gentleman here in few words? He is the friend of the family in the finest and broadest sense, by day instructive company, by night astronomer, and at all times physician."

"And I," the man replied cordially, "commend this lady to you as tirelessly industrious by day, immediately at hand when needed by night, always the most cheerful companion."

Angela, for that was the name of this woman so beautiful in both body and spirit, now announced the arrival of Makarie. A green curtain rose, and an elderly, hallowed figure in an armchair was pushed in by two pretty young girls, while two others wheeled in a round table set with a welcome breakfast. Cushions were laid in a corner on the massive oak benches that ran all around the room, and the other three seated themselves here, with Makarie in her chair across from them. Felix consumed his breakfast standing, roaming around the room and studying with curiosity the knightly scenes above the wainscoting.

Makarie spoke to Wilhelm as to an intimate. She seemed to enjoy giving telling descriptions of her relations. It was as though she penetrated the inner nature of each through the individual mask covering him. Those with whom Wilhelm was acquainted stood before him as if transfigured: the benevolent insight of this inestimable woman had detached the outer husk and ennobled and revived the healthy kernel.

After these pleasant topics had been exhausted in the friendliest fashion, she said to the worthy companion, "You shall not make the presence of this new friend another pretext for deferring our promised discussion; he seems of the sort who might well participate in it."

But he replied, "You know how difficult it is to explain oneself in these matters, for the subject is nothing less than the misuse of excellent and widely applicable means."

"I agree," Makarie answered, "because you face a dilemma. If you talk about misuse, then you seem to impugn the dignity of the means themselves, since the means are always still implicit in their misuse; if you talk about means, then you can scarcely concede the possibility that their thoroughness and dignity might allow any misuse. However, since we are among ourselves and are not attempting to establish anything definitive or affect the outside world, but only to clarify things for ourselves, the discussion can still proceed."

"Yet we ought first to ask," replied the cautious old man, "whether our new friend even wishes to delve into a fairly abstruse matter, or whether he would not prefer to retire to his room for some needed rest. Could he enter with any enthusiasm into this topic of ours without any context or knowledge of how we came to it?"

"If I may explain to myself what you said through an analogy, then it seems rather like the case in which one attacks hypocrisy and can be accused of attacking religion itself."

"We may let the analogy stand," he replied, "for we are dealing with a combination of several important persons, a lofty science, significant art, and, to be brief, mathematics itself."

"I have always," Wilhelm answered, "even when listening to discussions of very unfamiliar subjects, been able to come away with something. After all, everything that interests one person will evoke some response in another."

"Assuming," the other replied, "that he has acquired a certain liberality of mind; and since we credit you with that, I for my part shall make no objection to your remaining."

"But what shall we do about Felix?" asked Makarie, "who, as I see, has already finished looking at the pictures and shows some signs of impatience."

"Allow me to say something privately to this lady," replied Felix, and whispered something to Angela, who then departed with him, but soon returned smiling, while the friend of the household began to speak as follows:

"When it comes to expressing criticism, finding fault, or even airing doubt, I do not willingly take the initiative; I look for some authority and take comfort in the knowledge that someone stands beside me. I praise without scruple, for why should I keep quiet when something appeals to me? Even if it reveals my limitations, I have nothing to be ashamed of. But if I criticize, it may happen that I reject something excellent and thus invite the disapproval of others who understand it better. Then I have to retract, once I have been enlightened. For this reason I have brought with me several texts, even translations, for in such questions I trust my nation as little as I do myself. Concurrence from afar and abroad gives me greater certainty." After receiving permission, he began to read as follows:

If, however, we find ourselves disinclined to let the worthy man read, our patrons will most likely be pleased, since what was said earlier against Wilhelm's presence at the conversation applies even more to the situation in which we find ourselves. Our friends have taken a novel into their hands, and if it has already been more didactic here and there than it should be, we find it advisable not to put the patience of our well-wishers further to the test. We intend to have the papers at our disposal printed elsewhere, and shall proceed with our history without further ado, since we ourselves are impatient to see the riddle before us finally explained.

Nevertheless we cannot forbear to mention a few more things that were said before this noble gathering dispersed for the evening. Wilhelm, who had listened attentively to the reading, spoke up very directly: "I have been hearing tell of great natural talents, abilities, and skills, and yet also of reservations about their application. If I were to sum up about it, I would exclaim: great ideas and a pure heart—that is what we should pray for from God!"

Applauding these sensible words, the gathering dispersed; the astronomer, however, promised to let Wilhelm enjoy fully the wonders of the starry heavens on this splendid clear night.

A few hours later the astronomer had his guest wind his way up the staircase to the observatory. He emerged alone on the bare platform at the top of a high round tower. A most serene night, with all the stars shining and twinkling, surrounded the observer, who thought he beheld the great dome of the heavens for the first time in all its glory. In ordinary life, quite apart from the unfavorable weather, which so often conceals from us the brilliant realm of the ether, our view of the sky is blocked at home by roofs and gables, on the road by forests and cliffs, but most of all, wherever we are, by the inner disturbances of the spirit which, obscuring our surroundings more than fog and bad weather, pull us hither and yon.

Overwhelmed and amazed, he covered both eyes. The colossal ceases to be sublime; it exceeds our power to understand, it threatens to annihilate us. "What am I in the face of the universe?" he asked his spirit. "How can I stand before it, stand in its very midst?" Upon brief reflection, however, he continued, "The result of our evening's discussion also solves the riddle of the present moment. How can man confront the infinite except by gathering all his spiritual forces, which are drawn in all directions, into the innermost, deepest part of his being, by asking himself: 'Have you the right even to imagine yourself in the midst of this eternally living order if there does not immediately manifest itself inside you something in continuous motion, revolving around a pure center? And even if it would be difficult for you to find this center in your own breast, you would recognize it because a benevolent, beneficent effect emanates from it and testifies to its existence.'

"But who should, who can, regard his past life without becoming somewhat confused, for he will usually discover that his intentions were good, his actions wrong, his demands blameworthy, and his achievement nevertheless desirable.

"How often have you not seen these stars shine, and have they not each time found you a different man? But they are always the same and say always the same thing: 'We mark,' they repeat, 'by our orderly progression the day and the hour.' And this time I can reply: 'In the present circumstances I have no cause for shame. My purpose is to bring all the members of a noble family properly together again. My way is marked out. I am to investigate what keeps noble souls apart, and remove barriers, of whatever sort they may be.' This is what you may safely declare to these heavenly hosts; if they noticed you, they would doubtless smile at your limitations, but they would surely respect your intention and favor its fulfillment."

With these words or thoughts he turned to look about him, and caught sight of Jupiter, the planet of good fortune, shining as magnificently as ever. He took this as a favorable omen and continued to gaze joyfully for some time.

Immediately afterwards the astronomer summoned him to come down and let him look at this very planet through a telescope, significantly enlarged and accompanied by its moons, as a wonder of the heavens.

After our friend had remained absorbed for a long time, he turned to the stargazer and spoke: "I do not know whether I should thank you for bringing this star so very much nearer to me. When I saw it before, it stood in its proper relationship to all the other countless bodies of the heavens and to myself. But now it stands out disproportionately in my imagination, and I do not know whether I should want to bring the remaining hosts closer in the same fashion. They would crowd me, make me anxious."

Our friend continued in this vein, as was his custom, and in this context many unexpected things were discussed. Upon some response from the expert, Wilhelm replied, "I understand very well that for you stargazers it must be the greatest joy gradually to draw the immense universe as close as I have just seen and still see this planet. But allow me to say: I have discovered in life, altogether and on average, that these aids with which we enhance our senses have no favorable moral effect. Someone who sees through spectacles considers himself cleverer than he is, because his external senses have been thrown out of balance with his inner judgment; it requires a higher degree of cultivation, of which only superior people are capable, to balance to some degree their inner sense, the truth, with this false image drawn closer from outside. Whenever I look through spectacles, I am another person and do not like myself; I see more than I ought to see, and the sharper images of the world do not harmonize with my internal ones. I quickly put aside the glasses as soon as I have satisfied my curiosity about how this or that distant object is constituted."

In response to several joking comments of the astronomer's, Wilhelm continued, "We can as little ban these glasses from the world as we can machinery. But to the observer of morals, it is important to find out and to know how various things we deplore in humanity have crept in. Thus, for example, I am convinced that the custom of wearing spectacles is largely responsible for the arrogance of our young people."

During these conversations the night had far advanced, and the older man, himself accustomed to such vigils, suggested to his young friend that he lie down on the cot and sleep for a while, so that he might observe and greet Venus with fresher eye just before sunrise, for she was to display her full brilliance on this particular morning.

At this suggestion of the kindly, considerate man, Wilhelm, who to this moment had remained fully alert and awake, realized that he was truly exhausted. He lay down and in a moment had sunk into the deepest slumber. Awakened by the stargazer, Wilhelm jumped up and hurried to the window; there he stared in amazement for a moment, then exclaimed in rapture, "What magnificence! What a miracle!" Other words of delight followed, but the sight remained for him still a miracle, a great miracle.

"I could have predicted that this lovely star, which appears today in singular fullness and splendor, would come as a surprise to you, but I may well say, without being accused of coldness, that I see no miracle, no miracle at all."

"And how could you?" replied Wilhelm, "since I bring it along, since I carry it within me, since I do not know what is happening to me. Let me keep looking, dumbstruck and amazed, then you shall hear." After a pause he went on, "I was lying in a gentle but deep sleep, and found myself in yesterday's hall, but alone. The green curtain rose, Makarie's chair moved forward by itself, as if it were an animate being. It shone like gold, her clothing seemed priestly, a soft light radiated from her. I was about to prostrate myself. Then clouds billowed out around her feet, and rising, bore the sacred figure upward, as if they were wings. Finally I saw amidst the parting clouds, in place of her glorious countenance, a star twinkling, which was steadily carried aloft, and through the opened vault of the ceiling joined the entire starry sky, which seemed to keep spreading and encompassing everything. At that moment you wake me; drunk with sleep, I stagger to the window, the star still vividly in my eyes, and as I look out—there is the morning star, of equal beauty though perhaps not of equal shining splendor, truly before me! This real star, floating up there, takes the place of the dreamed one; it consumes the glory of the vision, yet still I gaze on and on, and you gaze with me, at what should actually have vanished from before my eyes together with the mist of sleep."

"A miracle, yes, a miracle!" the astronomer cried. "You do not know yourself what wondrous things you have spoken. But may this not foretell the departure of that glorious woman, to whom sooner or later such an apotheosis is destined."

The next morning Wilhelm hastened to find his Felix, who had slipped away early while all was still. Wilhelm came to the garden, which, to his astonishment, was being tended by a number of girls. All, if not pretty, were at least not homely, and not one seemed to have reached the age of twenty. They wore the costumes of their different villages, and they kept busy, greeting him cheerfully and continuing with their tasks.

He there encountered Angela, who was going about assigning the work and supervising. The guest expressed his astonishment at so pretty and bustling a colony. "This," she replied, "does not die out; it changes, but remains always the same. For in their twentieth year these girls, like all the girls in our establishment, leave us to enter active life, mostly to be married. All the young men in the neighborhood who want a stout helpmate pay attention to what is going on here. Moreover, we do not keep our pupils locked up; they have already looked about at various county fairs and have been seen, chosen, and betrothed. And so there are several families waiting to see when we have room, in order to place their daughters here." After this matter had been discussed, the guest could not conceal from his new friend his wish to look through again what had been read aloud the previous evening. "I grasped the main points of the discussion," he said, "but now I should like to become better acquainted with the specifics of the matter."

"Fortunately," she replied, "I am in a position to satisfy this desire at once. The intimacy with our innermost concerns that you were so quickly vouchsafed justifies me in telling you that those papers are already in my hands and are carefully preserved with other papers. My mistress," she continued, "is thoroughly convinced of the importance of spontaneous discussion. There passes before us, she says, what can be found in no book, and then again the best that books have ever contained. Therefore she has made it my duty to record individual good ideas that spring from an intelligent conversation, like seeds from a plant with many branches. 'Only if we can faithfully capture the present,' she says, 'can we truly appreciate what has come down to us, since we find there the finest thought already articulated, the most beautiful feeling already expressed. We come thus to contemplate the universal harmony to which man is summoned, to which he must often accede against his own will, since he is only too prone to imagine that the world began anew with himself.' "

Angela went on to confide to her guest that a significant archive had been assembled in this way, and that she sometimes read from it to Makarie on sleepless nights. On such occasions, remarkably enough, thousands of particular insights would spring forth, as when a glob of quicksilver falls and splits in all directions into the most various and innumerable droplets.

To his question about the extent to which this archive was kept secret, she revealed that, to be sure, only their closest circle knew of it, but that she would take the responsibility and, since he displayed interest, show him at once some of the notebooks.

During this conversation in the gardens they had reached the castle, and, entering the rooms in one of the wings, she said with a smile, "Since we are here, I have another secret to confide to you, for which you are not in the slightest prepared." She let him look through a curtain into an alcove, where he saw, with great astonishment, to be sure, his Felix sitting at a table and writing. At first he was unable to make sense of this unexpected industry, but he soon understood, when Angela revealed that Felix had disappeared the previous day for this purpose, declaring that writing and riding were his sole desire.

Our friend was then shown into a room, where he could see many well-ordered papers in the cabinets lining the walls. Labels of various sorts indicated the most diverse contents; everything radiated discernment and order. When Wilhelm praised these qualities, Angela attributed the entire merit to the friend of the household; he supervised with remarkable keenness not only the general scheme but in difficult cases the particular classification as well. Then she located the manuscripts of the previous evening and permitted our avid friend to make use of them, as well as of everything else, and not only to read the material but to copy it as well.

In this respect our friend had to hold back, for there was only too much he thought intriguing and worth having. He found the notebooks with brief, almost unconnected sentences particularly valuable. These were conclusions which, if we did not know what occasioned them, would seem paradoxical, but which make us go backwards, by a process of reversed intuition or invention, to reconstruct as best we can the filiation of such ideas from the bottom up.

Once again, we cannot allot space here for such matters, for the reasons alluded to above. Nevertheless we will not fail to take the first opportunity to present a selection from these acquired insights in a suitable place.

On the morning of the third day, our friend betook himself to Angela and stood before her, not without some embarrassment. "Today I am to leave," he said, "and should receive my final instructions from that admirable woman whom, unfortunately, I was not permitted to see all day yesterday. But there is something weighing on my heart, on my entire inner being, which I should like to have clarified. If it is possible, do me this kindness."

"I believe I understand you," Angela replied agreeably, "but go on."

"A wondrous dream," he continued, "some solemn words of the stargazer's, a separate, locked drawer in the cabinets, labeled 'Makarie's Particularities'—these suggestive elements join with an inner voice that tells me the study of those heavenly lights is not merely a scientific pastime, a striving to know the universe; rather one may suspect there lies hidden here a very special relationship between Makarie and the stars, one it would be most important for me to comprehend. I am neither curious nor prying, but this is such a significant case for the inquirer into things of the mind and spirit that I cannot forbear to ask whether, in addition to all that has been entrusted to me, this extra measure may not be vouchsafed as well."

"I am authorized to grant you this," the agreeable Angela replied. "To be sure, your remarkable dream has remained secret from Makarie, but the astronomer and I have contemplated and considered your strange spiritual intervention, your unexpected comprehension of our deepest mysteries, and we feel confident that we should lead you further. But let me speak first in similitudes. Where things are difficult to comprehend, one does well to help oneself this way.

"It is said of the poet that the elements of the visible world are buried in the depths of his nature, and have only to unfold gradually from within. Hence nothing in the world may come before his eyes that he has not already experienced intuitively. In the same way, it would seem, the conditions in our solar system existed within Makarie, completely innate from the beginning, at first dormant, then gradually developing, becoming increasingly clear. At first she suffered from these visions, but then she took pleasure in them, and with the years, her delight grew. However, she did not come to terms with them and achieve serenity until she had found support, the friend with whose merits you have already become well acquainted.

"As a mathematician and philosopher he was skeptical by nature, so for a long time he doubted whether her knowledge might not have been acquired. For Makarie had to admit that she had had the benefit of instruction in astronomy at an early age and had pursued it passionately. But she also reported to him that for many years she had compared these inner visions with her external observations, but could never bring them into agreement.

"The scientist then had her describe minutely what she saw, which was only occasionally very clear. He made calculations and concluded from them that she not only carried the entire solar system within her, but also that she moved within it spiritually as an integral part. He proceeded according to this hypothesis, and his calculations were confirmed in an incredible manner by her statements.

"For the moment, this is all I may confide to you, and I do so with the urgent plea that you not say a word of it to anyone. For would not every person of sense and reason, however well intentioned, take such statements to be phantasies, imperfectly understood recollections of previously acquired knowledge? Even the family knows none of these details; indeed these private sightings, these entrancing visions, are what passes with her relatives for an illness that temporarily prevents her from taking part in the world and its interests. Preserve all of this in silence, my friend, and let even Lenardo notice nothing."

Toward evening our traveler was again presented to Makarie. Much that was edifying was broached in a pleasant fashion, from which we select the following:

"By nature we possess no faults that could not become virtues, no virtues that might not become faults. The latter are the most disturbing. I am led to this consideration by my remarkable nephew, that young man of whom you have heard such strange tales in the family, and whom I, as my family asserts, treat more tolerantly and lovingly than is proper.

"From his youth he manifested a certain lively technical ability, to which he devoted himself entirely and which he successfully developed into considerable knowledge and mastery. Later on, everything that he sent back from his travels was always the most intricate, the cleverest, the finest, the most delicate of workmanship, indicative of the country where he happened to be and whose identity we were supposed to guess. From this one might surmise that he is and will remain a dry, detached person, preoccupied with externalities. In conversation, too, he was not given to joining in general moral observations. Yet he secretly and quietly possessed such a remarkably fine, pragmatic sense of good and evil, of what is praiseworthy and what is not, that I never saw him err toward either old or young, high or low. But this inborn conscientiousness, unregulated as it was, developed in certain cases into a capricious weakness; he was driven to discover obligations for himself where none existed, and would sometimes needlessly take blame upon himself.

"From the style of his travels, but especially from the preparations for his return, I believe that he thinks he once injured some woman in our circle, that her fate now worries him, and that he will feel free and absolved only when he learns that all is well with her. Angela will discuss the rest with you. Take this letter and prepare a happy reunion for our family. To speak frankly, I wish to see him once more upon this earth, and give him my heartfelt blessing as I depart."

Chapter Eleven

The Nut-brown Maid

After Wilhelm had transmitted his message accurately and in detail, Lenardo replied with a smile, "I am greatly indebted to you for what you have told me, yet I must still ask another question. Did not my aunt, at the end, ask you to report an apparently insignificant matter to me?" The other reflected for a moment. "Yes," he answered, "Now I recall. She made mention of a young woman whom she called Valerine. I was supposed to tell you that she is happily married and finds herself in enviable circumstances."

"You lift a stone from my heart," answered Lenardo. "Now I am glad to go home, because I need not fear that the memory of this girl will be a reproach to me once there."

"It would not be proper for me to ask what kind of relationship you had with her," said Wilhelm. "Enough, you may be at peace, if you are concerned at all in her fate."

"It is the strangest relationship in the world," Lenardo said, "in no way a love relationship, as one might think. I may trust you and tell you what is actually no story at all. But what must you think, when I tell you that my hesitant return, that my fear of coming home, that these peculiar arrangements and questions as to how things stood in our family, actually had this single purpose: to learn indirectly how things stood with this girl.

"For believe me," he continued, "I am well aware that you can leave people you know for a considerable time without finding them changed, and so I expect I shall soon feel quite at home among my family. My worry was for this single person, whose condition had to change, and has, thank heaven, changed for the better."

"You make me curious," said Wilhelm. "You lead me to expect something most unusual."

"I, at any rate, consider it so," replied Lenardo, and began his tale as follows:

"I had had the firm intention, cherished from boyhood, of making the traditional tour through civilized Europe while still a youth, but, as often happens, the execution of this plan was delayed time and time again. My immediate surroundings beguiled me, held me fast, and distant things lost more and more of their attraction, the more I read or heard about them. But finally, spurred by my uncle, enticed by friends, who had gone out into the world before me, the decision was taken, and indeed faster than we were all prepared for.

"My uncle, who had the most to do to make the journey possible, at once fixed his eye on this alone. You know him and his way of always aiming at one thing only and completing it, while everything else must stand aside for the time being and be silent; by which means he has, to be sure, accomplished a great deal that would seem beyond the power of a private individual. This journey came as something of a surprise to him, yet he was able to adjust his plans at once. Building projects he had undertaken, and even started on, were suspended, and since, as an intelligent manager of his finances, he never wants to touch his savings, he looked about for other resources. The obvious step was to call in outstanding debts, especially tenants' rents. For this too was a part of his character, that he was accommodating to debtors, so long as he himself did not reach the point of need. His steward received the list; the necessary steps were left to him. We learned nothing about the details. I only happened to hear in passing that the tenant of one of our farms, with whom my uncle had long had patience, was finally to be evicted, his deposit retained as a poor substitute for the loss, and the farm let to someone else. This man belonged to the sect called the 'The Silent Ones,' but was not, like his fellows, particularly prudent and hardworking. Though he was loved for his piety and kindness, yet he was faulted for his weaknesses as husbandman. After his wife died, his one daughter, who was known only as the nut-brown maid, was, although she already gave promise of becoming energetic and resolute, still much too young to take things in hand. In short, the man was on the downward path, and my uncle's clemency could not have altered his fate.

"My journey was uppermost in my mind and I had to approve whatever measures made it possible. Everything was ready, the packing and the leave-taking began, every moment counted. One evening I was wandering through the grounds for the last time, to say farewell to the familiar trees and bushes, when suddenly Valerine stepped into my path; for that was the girl's name, the other was only a nickname, because of her brown complexion. She stepped into my path."

Lenardo paused for a moment and reflected. "What is wrong with me? Was her name really Valerine? Oh, yes," he continued, "but her nickname was more common. Be that as it may, the brown skinned maid stepped into my path and begged me urgently to put in a good word for her father, for herself, with my uncle. Since I knew what the situation was and could see that it would be difficult, indeed impossible, to do anything for her at this juncture, I told her so honestly and represented her father's responsibility for his own misfortunes in an unfavorable light.

"She replied with so much clarity, and at the same time with so much filial forbearance and love, that she completely won me over, and if it had been my own money, I would promptly have made her happy by granting her request. But the rents belonged to my uncle, these were his arrangements, his orders; given his way of thinking, and what had already passed, there was nothing to hope for. I had always considered promises sacred. When someone asked me a favor, I was thrown into confusion. I had become so accustomed to refusing that I never even made promises that I intended to keep. This habit once more served me well. Her reasons were based on exceptional circumstances and affection; mine were based on duty and reason, and I cannot deny that in the end they seemed too rigid even to me. We had already repeated ourselves several times without convincing each other, when necessity made her more eloquent, and the inescapable ruin which she saw before her brought tears to her eyes. Her composure did not entirely desert her, but she spoke animatedly, with emotion, and while I continued to feign coldness and detachment, she gave vent to all her feelings. I wanted to put an end to the scene, but suddenly she was at my feet, had taken my hand, kissed it, and looked up at me so sweetly and imploringly that for the moment I did not know myself. Quickly I said, as I raised her up, 'I will do whatever is possible; calm yourself, my dear!' and with that I turned onto a side path. 'Do the impossible!' she called after me. I no longer know what I meant to say, but I replied, 'I shall . . . ,' and hesitated. 'Do!' she exclaimed, with an expression of heavenly hope. I said good-bye and hurried off.

"I did not want to approach my uncle first, for I knew only too well not to remind him of details when he had his mind fixed on the whole. I looked for the steward; he was off somewhere on his horse. Guests came for the evening, friends who wished to bid me farewell. We played games, we feasted until far into the night. They stayed the following day, and the distraction erased the image of the suppliant. The steward returned; he was busier and more harrassed than ever. Everybody wanted to see him. He had no time to hear me, but still I tried to detain him. Yet I had barely mentioned the pious tenant when he energetically stopped me. 'In God's name, say nothing of this to your uncle, if you do not want any unpleasantness.' The day of my departure was set. I had letters to write, company to receive, calls to make in the neighborhood. My attendants had served me adequately until now, but were by no means skilled at preparing for a long journey. Everything fell on me; and yet, when the steward gave me an hour late one evening to arrange money matters, I ventured once again to plead for Valerine's father.

" 'My dear baron,' said the energetic man, 'how can you think of such a thing? Even without this I had a difficult time with your uncle today. What you need in order to set out is far more than we had thought. To be sure, this is quite natural, but still troublesome. The old gentleman is particularly displeased when something seems settled and then new details crop up. But that is how it often is, and we others have to bear the brunt. Concerning the severity with which the outstanding debts are to be collected, he has imposed a binding principle on himself; he is in accord with himself about it, and it would be difficult to persuade him to be lenient. Do not try, I beg of you! It would be utterly in vain.'

"I allowed myself to be deterred from my petition, but not entirely. I urged him, since the execution, after all, rested with him, to be gentle and fair. He promised everything, as such people will in order to be left alone for the moment. He was rid of me; the haste, the distractions increased. I sat in the coach and turned my back on every involvement I might have had at home.

"A powerful impression is like any other wound; one does not feel it when one first receives it. Only later does it begin to hurt and fester. Thus it was with that encounter in the garden. Whenever I was lonely, whenever I was unoccupied, there rose before me the image of the imploring maiden, together with the entire setting, with every tree and shrub, the spot where she knelt, the path I took to escape from her, all merged in a single image, fresh before my mind. It was an inextinguishable impression, overshadowed, to be sure, by other images and sympathies, obscured, but never blotted out. With new vividness it returned in every quiet hour, and the more time passed, the more painfully I felt the guilt I had incurred, contrary to my principles, contrary to my habit, although not explicitly, and only in a stammered utterance, for the first time at a loss in such a situation.

"I did not fail, in my first letters to our steward, to ask what had happened. He put me off with his answers. Finally he proceeded to reply to my question. But his words were ambiguous, and in the end he fell silent on the matter. Distances grew; more things came between me and my home; many observations, many involvements claimed my attention. The image disappeared; of the girl hardly anything was left, save for her name. The memory of her came to the fore more rarely, and my whim of communicating with my family not through letters but only through tokens contributed to making my previous existence, with all its circumstances, fade almost entirely. Only now, as I draw nearer to home, and mean to repay my family with interest for what they have been deprived of, this strange remorse—I myself must call it strange—attacks me again with full force. The figure of the girl appears fresh before me, along with the figures of all my family, and I fear nothing more than to learn that she was undone by the misfortune into which I thrust her. For my negligence now seems to have been an act leading to her destruction, a compounding of her sad fate. I have already told myself a thousand times that this feeling is at bottom only a weakness, that I had been driven only by fear of remorse to that early principle of never promising anything, not by any nobler sentiment. And now this very remorse, from which I had fled, seems to be taking revenge upon me by seizing on this particular case, instead of a thousand others, to torment me. Yet at the same time, the image, the vision which tortures me, is so pleasant, so lovely, that I linger gladly over it. And when I think of it, the kiss she pressed on my hand still seems to burn there."

Lenardo fell silent, and Wilhelm replied quickly and cheerfully, "Then I could have done you no greater service than through the appendix to my report, just as the most interesting part of a letter is often contained in the postscript. To be sure, I know only a little about Valerine, for I learned about her only in passing. But there is no doubt she is the wife of a prosperous landowner and lives content, as your aunt assured me when I was leaving."

"Good," Lenardo said. "Now nothing holds me back. You have absolved me, and we must set out at once for my family, who have already been waiting longer than is proper." Wilhelm replied, "Unfortunately I cannot accompany you. For I am under a peculiar obligation not to stay anywhere longer than three days, and once I have left a place not to return to it for a year. Forgive me if I may not explain the basis for this peculiarity."

"I am sorry," Lenardo said, "that we must lose you so soon, and that I cannot help you with something in return. But since you are doing me favors, you would make me very happy if you would call on Valerine, inform yourself accurately of her situation, and then impart to me by letter or orally—for a third meeting place can surely be found—all you have discovered, to set my heart at rest."

This proposal was discussed further; Wilhelm had been told where Valerine lived. He undertook to visit her; a third location was fixed, to which the baron was to come and also bring Felix, who had remained in the meantime with the ladies.

Lenardo and Wilhelm had continued on their way, riding side by side through pleasant meadows, discussing all manner of things, when they approached the main road and caught up with the baron's coach, which, accompanied by its master, was to return home. Here the friends were to separate, and Wilhelm took leave with a few friendly words and once more promised the baron early news of Valerine.

"When I consider," replied Lenardo, "that it would be only a short detour if I went with you, why should I not seek out Valerine myself?

Why not convince myself of her happy circumstances in person? You were so good as to offer your services as a messenger; why not be my companion? For I must have a companion, a moral counsel, as one takes legal counsel when one does not feel adequate to handle a lawsuit."

Wilhelm's objections that he had been awaited at home for so long, that it would make a strange impression for the coach to return without him, and other arguments of this sort, had no effect on Lenardo, and in the end Wilhelm had to agree to act as companion, although, fearing the probable consequences, he was not at ease.

The servants were instructed as to what to say when they arrived, and the friends now took the road which led to Valerine's residence. The region seemed rich and fertile, an ideal setting for agriculture. And so too in the area that belonged to Valerine's husband the soil was excellent and cultivated with care. Wilhelm had time to observe the landscape well, since Lenardo rode beside him in silence. Finally Lenardo began, "Another man in my position would perhaps try to approach Valerine without being recognized; for it is always embarrassing to come face to face with someone you have injured. But I would rather do that and endure the reproach I fear from her first glances than protect myself by disguise and subterfuge. Subterfuge can lead to as much embarrassment as truth, and if we compare how often one or the other helps us, it would always seem worth the effort to choose the truth once and for all. So let us go forward confidently; I will give my name and introduce you as my friend and companion."

They had now reached the courtyard of the estate and dismounted in its precincts. A handsome man in simple dress, who could have been taken for a tenant farmer, came toward them and identified himself as the master of the house. Lenardo gave his name, and the owner seemed very pleased to see him and make his acquaintance. "What will my wife say," he exclaimed, "when she sees the nephew of our benefactor here? She never tires of recounting what she and her father owe to your uncle."

What strange thoughts swirled in Lenardo's mind! "Is this man, who looks so upright, hiding his bitterness behind a friendly manner and smooth words? Is he capable of giving his reproaches such an agreeable appearance? Did my uncle not make this family wretched? can this have remained unknown to him? Or else—" he thought with a rush of hope, "did it not turn out as badly as you think? After all, you never did receive definite information." Such suppositions darted back and forth, while the master of the house had a horse harnessed to fetch his wife, who was paying a call in the neighborhood.

"If I may entertain you in the meantime, until my wife comes, in my own fashion and at the same time attend to my affairs, take a few steps with me into the fields and see how I manage my farm. Surely for you, as a large landowner, nothing is of more consequence than the noble science, the noble art of agriculture." Lenardo did not disagree; Wilhelm was always glad to learn something new; and the farmer knew every detail of his land, of which he was full owner and manager. Whatever he undertook was in accord with his purposes; whatever he sowed and planted was in just the right place. He could give such clear explanations of the procedures and the reasons for them that anyone could understand and might think it possible to undertake the same thing and succeed, an illusion to which one easily succumbs when watching a master who is adept at everything.

The visitors expressed their delight and could bestow only praise and approval. He accepted this gratefully and cordially, but added, "Now I must show you my weak side, which to be sure is common to everyone who devotes himself completely to one object." He led them to his farmyard and showed them his tools—his array of them along with his collection of every conceivable implement and attachment. "I have often been criticized," he commented, "for going too far in this matter. However, I cannot find it reprehensible. Happy the man whose vocation also becomes his favorite pastime, so that he ends up playing at it and takes pleasure in that which his station also makes a duty."

The two friends were not remiss in asking questions and seeking information. Wilhelm particularly enjoyed the general observations to which this man seemed given, and was ready with his own rejoinders, while Lenardo, more withdrawn, was silently rejoicing in Valerine's happiness, which in this situation seemed certain. Yet he was aware of a slight uneasiness, for which he could not account.

They had already returned to the house when the cart returned with the mistress. They hurried out to meet her; but how astounded, how startled Lenardo was when he saw her dismount. She was not, it was not, the nut-brown maid, rather quite the opposite; she was, to be sure, a pretty, slender figure, but blond, with all the advantages natural to blondes.

Her beauty, her grace, startled Lenardo. His eyes had expected the brown girl; now quite another glowed before him. These features he recalled also; the way she addressed him, her bearing soon removed any doubt: she was the daughter of the magistrate, whom his uncle held in high regard, and so his uncle had contributed a good deal toward the dowry of the daughter and had been helpful to the newlyweds. The young woman joyfully referred to all of this and more in the course of her greeting, with unfeigned pleasure at the surprise of seeing Lenardo again. She asked whether he would have recognized her, and there was some discussion of the changes in appearance which are noticeable enough in persons of this age. Valerine was always pleasant, but she became positively charming when happiness plucked her out of her customary placidity. The company waxed talkative, and the conversation so lively that Lenardo could master himself and conceal his dismay. Wilhelm, whose friend had given him a hasty hint of the strange situation, did his best to assist Lenardo. And Valerine's touch of vanity at the baron's remembering her and visiting her even before returning to his own family, prevented the least suspicion that a different intention or a misconception was at work.

They remained together until late in the night, although the two friends longed to speak privately, which, then, they at once began to do when they were alone in the guest chamber.

"It would seem," said Lenardo, "that I am not to be rid of my agony. An unfortunate mix-up of names, I see, compounds it. I often saw this blond beauty playing with the dark girl, whom no one would have called pretty; in fact I, though so much older, used to roam about with them in the fields and gardens. Neither of them made the slightest impression on me; I have retained only the name of the one and attached it to the other. Now I find the one who means nothing to me, tremendously fortunate in her way, while the other is cast adrift in the world, who knows where."

The next morning the two friends were up almost earlier than the industrious country folk. The happy prospect of seeing her guests had also wakened Valerine betimes. She could not guess with what thoughts they came to breakfast. Wilhelm, who perceived that without some news of the nut-brown maid Lenardo would be in a most painful plight, brought the conversation around to earlier times, to playmates, to the locality with which he himself had become acquainted, to other recollections of that sort, so that by and by Valerine was naturally prompted to mention the nut-brown maid and to speak her name.

No sooner had Lenardo heard the name Nachodine than he recalled it perfectly; but with the name, the image of the suppliant returned as well, with such force that he found it quite intolerable when Valerine described with warm sympathy the eviction of the pious tenant, his resignation and his departure, and how he leaned upon his daughter, who carried a small bundle. Lenardo felt he must sink through the floor. Unfortunately, or fortunately, Valerine went into a certain amount of detail, which, though tearing at Lenardo's heart, nevertheless enabled him, with his companion's assistance, to muster a certain composure.

They departed amidst fulsome, sincere entreaties by the couple that they return soon, and half-hearted, disingenuous expressions of willingness by the guests. And as everything adds to the happiness of those who feel entitled to it, Valerine finally interpreted Lenardo's silence, his obvious distraction as he took leave, and his hasty departure, to her own advantage, and, faithful and loving wife of a manly farmer though she was, could still not but discover a certain pleasure in what she perceived as the freshly awakened or reborn affection of her former lord.

After this curious incident, Lenardo said, "Now that we, despite such bright hopes, have foundered so close to the harbor, I can console myself somewhat, calm myself for the moment and proceed to my family, only when I consider that Providence has brought you to me, you, whose unusual mission makes you indifferent to the road and purpose you follow. Take it upon yourself to find Nachodine and give me tidings of her. If she is happy, then I am satisfied; if she is unhappy, help her at my expense. Act without reservations; save, spare nothing."

"But to what quarter of the globe," asked Wilhelm with a smile, "should I bend my steps? If you have no idea, how am I to guess?"

"Listen," Lenardo replied, "last night, when you saw me in despair, restlessly pacing, as everything tumbled wildly through my heart and mind, an old friend came into my thoughts, a worthy man, who, though not exactly my tutor, nevertheless had a great influence upon my youth. I would have happily requested that he be my traveling companion, at least for part of the way, were he not strangely bound to his home by a collection of the most beautiful works of art and antiquities, which he leaves only for brief moments. This man, I know, enjoys an extensive acquaintance with everything in this world which is held together by noble ties. Hasten to him, tell him what I have told you, and it is to be hoped that his subtle intuition will suggest to him some place, some region, where she might be found. In my distress it occurred to me that the girl's father belonged to the Pietists, and at that moment I became pious enough to turn to the moral world order and beg it to show itself miraculously merciful to me this once."

"One further difficulty, however, remains to be solved," replied Wilhelm. "What shall I do with my Felix? I would not want to take him on such very uncertain pathways, and yet I would not willingly leave him, either. For I believe that a son develops nowhere better than in the presence of his father."

"Not at all!" Lenardo responded. "That is a touching fatherly error. A father always retains a certain despotic relationship to his son, whose virtues he does not recognize and in whose faults he takes pleasure. For which reason even the ancients used to say, 'The sons of heroes become good-for-nothings,' and I have seen enough of the world to be clear on this score. Fortunately our old friend, to whom I shall write a quick note, will also have excellent advice on this topic. When I last saw him a few years ago, he told me a great deal about a pedagogic association, which I could imagine only as a kind of utopia. It seemed to me that under the guise of reality he was presenting a series of ideas, thoughts, proposals, and intentions that were consistent, to be sure, but in the usual course of things could hardly occur together. But because I know him, because he likes to evoke the possible and the impossible through images, I listened seriously. And now that stands us in good stead; he can surely tell you the location and circumstances in which you can confidently leave your boy and hope for the best results from wise guidance."

Riding along and talking thus, the two saw before them a noble country residence, the buildings in sober yet friendly taste, with an open space in front of it and in the spacious, dignified surroundings stately trees. But all doors and sashes were locked, everything deserted, though apparently well tended. From an elderly man, who seemed to be busy at the entrance, they learned that this was the inheritance of a young man to whom it had just been left by his father, who had died only recently at an advanced age.

Upon further inquiry, they were informed that everything here was unfortunately too complete for the heir; he had nothing more to do here, and enjoying what was already there was not his nature; therefore he had sought out a place nearer the mountains, where he was building sod huts for himself and his companions, and wanted to establish a sort of hermitage for hunters. As for their informant himself, they learned that he was the castellan who had been inherited with the property, that he took utmost care to preserve and maintain it so that some future grandchild, sharing his grandfather's inclinations and property, would find everything as the latter had left it.

After they had proceeded on their way for a while in silence, Lenardo began with the observation that it was a peculiarity of people to want always to start afresh. His friend replied that this was easy to explain and forgive, because, strictly speaking, everyone actually does start from the beginning. "For no one," he exclaimed, "is ever exempt from the pains which his forefathers suffered. Can you blame him for not wanting to miss any of their pleasures?"

To this Lenardo replied, "You give me courage to confess that I would actually not want to devote my energy to anything but what I have created myself. I have never cared for a servant I did not raise from a boy, nor a horse I did not break myself. I must also tell you that as a result of this attitude, I am irresistibly drawn toward primitive conditions, that my travels among all the civilized countries and peoples could not dull these feelings, that my imagination seeks its pleasure across the seas, and that neglected family property in those fresh territories makes me hope that I may one day execute, in accordance with my wishes, a plan which I conceived in secret and which has gradually matured."

"I should have no objection to that," Wilhelm said. "Such a notion, directed toward the new and undefined, has something original and grand about it. I would merely ask you to consider that such a venture can succeed only if undertaken by a group. You will go over and find holdings already in the family, as I know. My associates have similar plans and have already settled there. Join these cautious, intelligent, and energetic people, and the enterprise will be simplified and enlarged for both of you."

Conversing thus, our friends had reached the place where they were again to part. Both of them sat down to write, Lenardo commending his friend to the above-mentioned remarkable man, while Wilhelm reported to the league the situation of his new companion, which report became, as was only natural, a letter of introduction. Toward the end he pressed his own case, as he had discussed it with Jarno, and once more explained why he wished to be released, as soon as possible, from the condition that stamped him as a Wandering Jew.

As they exchanged these letters, Wilhelm could not resist raising once more certain reservations with his friend.

"In my position," he said, "I consider it the most desirable of assignments to free you, my noble friend, from distress of mind and at the same time to rescue a human creature from misery, should that be her condition. One may view such a goal as a star, by which one navigates even without knowing what one may encounter, what one may meet along the way. Yet I cannot overlook the danger which still hangs over you. Were you not a man who always refuses to give his word, I would demand your promise never to see again this young woman who has cost you so much, but to be satisfied if I report that she is faring well, regardless of whether I really found her in a happy state or were able to further her happiness. Since, however, I neither can nor wish to extract promises from you, I implore you, by all that is precious and holy to you, for the sake of you and yours, and of me, your newly won friend, not to allow yourself to approach the lost one, under any pretext whatsoever. You must not ask me to describe or to specify where I have found her, or in what region I have left her: you must take my word that she is well; you must be absolved and set at rest."

Lenardo replied with a smile, "Do me this service, and I shall be grateful. What you desire to or can do shall be left up to you, and you must leave me to the influence of time, understanding, and, if possible, reason." "Forgive me," Wilhelm answered, "but knowing in what strange forms love can steal in on us, a person may well be anxious when he foresees that a friend might desire something that would necessarily bring unhappiness and confusion upon him, given his circumstances and relationships."

"I hope," said Lenardo, "that when I know the girl is happy, I shall be free of her."

The friends parted, each going his own way.

Chapter Twelve

After a short and pleasant ride Wilhelm had reached the town to which his letter was addressed. He found it cheerful and well built; only its new appearance showed all too clearly that it must recently have suffered from fire. The address on his letter led him to the small quarter which alone had been spared, to a house in an older, sober style but well maintained and of tidy appearance. The dark window glass, leaded with great artistry, promised wonderful color effects inside. And indeed the interior truly corresponded to the outside. Everywhere in immaculate rooms stood utensils that must already have served several generations, intermingled with a few new ones. The master of the house welcomed Wilhelm kindly in a room furnished in this fashion. These clocks had already struck the hour for many a birth and death, and the other pieces testified that the past could well pass on into the present.

The new arrival delivered his letter, but the recipient laid it aside without opening it and tried to make his guest's acquaintance directly, through pleasant conversation. They were soon at ease with one another, and as Wilhelm, contrary to his usual custom, let his eyes wander inquisitively about the room, the old man remarked, "My surroundings arouse your interest. Here you see how long something can last, and indeed one must see such things, as a counterbalance to all that is replaced and changes so rapidly in the world. This teakettle served my parents, and was a witness to our evening family gatherings; this copper fire screen still protects me from the fire which these massive old tongs stir up, and thus it is with everything. I have been able to turn my attention and efforts to many other things, since I did not bother with replacing these outward necessities, which consume the time and energy of so many people. Loving attention to one's possessions makes a man rich, in that he builds up a treasury of memories out of neutral things. I once knew a young man who, upon parting from the girl he loved, stole a pin of hers, fastened his neckcloth with it every day, and brought this cherished and protected treasure back from a long journey of many years' duration. This might well be considered a virtue for us ordinary folk."

"From such a long journey," Wilhelm replied, "many a man might also bring back a thorn in his heart, which he would perhaps prefer to be rid of." The old man seemed to know nothing of Lenardo's plight, although he had in the meantime opened and read the letter, for he returned to his former observations. "Our attachment to our possessions," he continued, "in many cases proves our greatest source of energy. I owe the preservation of my house to this persistence. When the town was on fire, they wanted to rescue what they could from my house and then flee. I forbade it, ordered the windows and doors to be shut, and with several neighbors turned against the flames. Our efforts succeeded in saving this tip of the town. The next morning everything still stood here as you see it now, and as it has stood for almost a century." "Despite all this," Wilhelm said, "you will grant that there is no resisting the changes time brings about." "To be sure," the old man said, "but he who holds out the longest has also achieved something.

"Indeed we are capable of preserving and securing things even beyond our own existence; we pass along knowledge, we bequeath ways of thinking as well as property, and now that my chief interest is for the latter, I have for some considerable time used extraordinary foresight, have thought out most unusual provisions. But only recently have I succeeded in fulfilling my wish.

"Usually the son scatters what the father has collected, and collects something else, or in a different manner. Yet if one can wait for the grandson, for the new generation, the same preferences, the same views will again come to the fore. And so, through the careful efforts of our pedagogic friends, I have acquired a capable young man who values even more than myself, if possible, possessions inherited from earlier times and has a passionate interest in strange objects. He won my confidence decisively by his tremendous exertions in keeping the fire away from our house. He has earned two and three times over the treasure I mean to leave to him; in fact, I have already handed it over to him, and since then our stores have increased in a remarkable fashion.

"But not everything you see here belongs to us. Rather, as you usually see many another person's jewel at the pawnbroker's, I can also show you valuables here which people have deposited with us, under a great variety of circumstances, for safekeeping." Wilhelm thought of the magnificent casket, which in any case he did not want to carry about with him on his journey, and did not refrain from showing it to his friend. The old man looked at it attentively, gave the probable date of its making, and brought out a similar one. Wilhelm raised the question of whether it should be opened. The old man did not think so. "To be sure, I suppose it could be done without undue harm. However, since you came by it through such a curious chance, you ought to try your luck on it. If you were born fortunate, and if this casket has any significance, then the key to it must turn up sometime, and precisely where you least expect it." "There probably are such cases," Wilhelm replied. "I have experienced several myself," answered the old man, "and here you see the most remarkable example before you: this ivory crucifix. For thirty years I owned the body with head and feet all in one piece, and because of its wonderful artistry kept the object in a most precious little box. About ten years ago I obtained the cross which belonged to it, along with the inscription, and I let myself be seduced into having arms attached by the most skillful carver of our times. But this good man lagged so far behind his predecessor! Still, I left it as it was, more for the sake of edifying reflections than out of admiration for the craftsmanship.

"But now imagine my delight! Not long ago I obtained the original arms, as you see them here refitted in the most exquisite union. Delighted by such a fortunate set of coincidences, I cannot but see in this the fate of the Christian religion, which, often enough dismembered and dispersed, must in the end always come together again around the Cross."

Wilhelm admired the image and its strange fate. "I shall follow your advice," he added. "Let the casket remain locked until the key turns up, even if it should stay that way to the end of my life." "Those who live long," said the old man, "see many things collected and many others dispersed."

The young joint owner appeared, and Wilhelm declared his intention of delivering the casket to their care. A huge book was fetched, and the entrusted article was entered. With many formalities and stipulations a receipt was issued, which would be valid regardless of who should present it, but would be honored only when the bearer gave an agreed-upon sign.

When all this had been completed, they reflected on the contents of the letter, conferring first on what accommodation should be made for the good Felix. In this connection, the old man without more ado delivered himself of certain maxims concerning the basis of all education.

"All living, all activity, all art must be preceded by technical skill, which can be acquired only through limitation. To know one thing properly and be adept at it results in higher cultivation than half-competence in a hundred different fields. Where I am sending you, all the fields of endeavor have been divided up. The pupil is tested at each step; thus the true bent of his nature can be ascertained, even though he may be turned from his path by competing desires. Wise men subtly help the boy find what suits him best. They shorten the detours by which we all too gladly tend to stray from our true calling.

"Afterwards," he continued, "I have reason to hope that from that splendidly established center someone will direct you to where you can find that good girl, who has made such a singular impression on your friend. His moral sense and concern have set so high a value upon an innocent and unfortunate creature that he was obliged to make her existence the aim and purpose of his life. I hope you will be able to reassure him, for Providence has a thousand ways to raise up the fallen and lift up the bowed. Often our fate resembles a fruit tree in winter. Who, seeing its dismal appearance, would ever think that these stiff branches, these jagged twigs could turn green again in the coming spring, blossom, and then bear fruit; yet this we hope, this we know."

Book Two

Chapter One

The pilgrims had followed instructions and found their way successfully to the border of the province in which many a marvel awaited them. As they rode into it, they at once saw before them a most fertile region, whose rolling hills favored field crops, its mountainous parts sheep raising, and the broad, level valleys cattle raising. It was shortly before harvest time, and everything at its most bountiful. Yet what instantly aroused their wonder was that neither women nor men were to be seen, but only boys and youths at work, preparing for a successful harvest, indeed making arrangements already for a joyous harvest feast. They greeted one and another of the boys and asked for the Superior, of whose whereabouts, however, no one could give any account. The address on their letter read: "To the Superior, or the Three." Here, too, the boys could not comply. They referred the travelers, however, to a supervisor who was just preparing to mount his horse. They explained their purpose; Felix's ingenuous manner seemed to please the man, and so they rode off down the road together.

Wilhelm had already noticed in the young people's clothing a diversity in cut and color that gave a singular aspect to the little community. He was just about to ask his guide about this, when an even more curious observation impressed itself upon him: all the children, no matter what they were engaged in, dropped their work and turned, with distinct but varied gestures, toward the party as it rode by, and it could easily be deduced that this was intended for the supervisor. The youngest ones crossed their arms over their chests and looked cheerfully heavenward, the middle ones put their hands behind their backs and looked smilingly down at the earth, the third group stood stiffly and bravely: with their arms at their sides they turned their faces to the right and formed themselves into a row, instead of each standing alone where he had been.

When the riders later stopped and dismounted, at a spot where several children were lining up in various postures and being reviewed by the supervisor, Wilhelm inquired after the meaning of the gestures. Felix interrupted to ask cheerfully, "What position should I be taking?" "In any case," the supervisor replied, "first your arms across your chest and gravely but joyfully looking upwards, without shifting your gaze." Felix obeyed, but soon exclaimed, "I do not like this much. I do not see anything up there. Must I do this long? But oh!" he exclaimed happily, "a pair of hawks is flying from west to east; that is surely a good omen?"

"However you take it, behave accordingly," the supervisor replied. "Now mingle with them, as they mingle among themselves." He gave a signal, and the children abandoned their positions, resuming their work or returning to their play.

"May you and can you explain the meaning," Wilhelm said, "of all this, which causes me such amazement? It seems clear to me that these gestures, these positions, are salutations, by which you are received." "Quite right," the other man replied, "salutations which at once indicate to me at which stage of his education each of these boys stands."

"Are you permitted to explain," Wilhelm continued, "the significance of this progression of stages? For it is quite evident that it is one." "That would be for persons higher than myself," the supervisor answered, "but of this much I may assure you: these are not empty posturings; rather the children have had imparted to them, not the ultimate significance, but at least a guiding meaning that is within their grasp. Yet each is told to keep to himself and to cherish whatever insight it has been judged good to convey to him. They must not chatter about it either with strangers or among themselves, and so our teachings can be adjusted to each individual. Furthermore, secrecy has great benefits. For if a person is always told at once what everything means, he will think there is nothing behind it. Certain mysteries, even if they could be explained, must be shown respect through veiling and silence, for this promotes modesty and good morals."

"I understand you," replied Wilhelm. "Why should we not practice what is so essential in regard to physical matters also in regard to the spiritual? But perhaps you can satisfy my curiosity in another connection. I have been struck by the great diversity in the cut and color of the clothing, and yet I do not see all colors, but only certain ones, in all their gradations, from the lightest to the darkest. Yet I observe that no indication of levels of age or merit can be intended, since the smallest and the largest boys seem intermingled as regards the color and cut of their dress, while those with the same gestures do not match each other in their clothing."

"Again I must refrain from saying what lies behind all this," the guide replied. "But I should be very much mistaken if you were not given as full an explanation as you wish before you take leave of us."

They now set out on the track of the Superior, whom they thought to have located. But the newcomer could not but be struck by a melodious singing that was heard ever more clearly the deeper they advanced into the country. Whatever the boys were engaged in, at whatever work one found them, they were always singing, and indeed the songs seemed particularly suited to each task, and the same song recurred wherever the same kind of work was underway. Where a number of children gathered, they accompanied one another in turn; toward evening the newcomers also saw dancers, whose steps were enlivened and regulated by children singing in chorus. Felix joined in from his saddle, and not at all badly, while Wilhelm was much diverted by this form of recreation, which enlivened the region.

"Apparently," he remarked to his companion, "much care is devoted to instruction in this activity, for otherwise the skill would not be so widespread and so highly developed." "Yes, indeed," was the reply. "We make singing the first stage of education. Everything else follows from it and is conveyed through it. The simplest pleasure as well as the simplest lesson is enlivened here through song and imprinted on the memory. Even our religious and moral teachings are communicated by way of song. Entirely different purposes derive immediate benefits from it as well, for when we train the children to write the notes they produce in symbols on their slates and on the basis of the symbols to find these notes again in their throats, and then to put the text to them, they are training hands, ears, and eyes simultaneously, and learn spelling and penmanship more quickly than one might think. And since all this must eventually be executed and imitated according to accurate measures and precise numbers, they grasp the high value of the arts of measurement and arithmetic far more quickly than in any other way. This is why we have chosen music, from among all the conceivable subjects, as the key element of our education, since smooth paths lead from it in all directions."

Wilhelm tried to learn more, and did not conceal his amazement that he heard no instrumental music. "We do not neglect this," his guide responded, "but it is practiced in a special district, isolated in the pleasantest of mountain valleys, and there, too, we see to it that each instrument is taught in a separate village. The wrong notes of beginners especially are confined to certain solitary spots, where they will not drive anyone to distraction. For you yourself will admit that to the well-regulated middle-class household there is hardly a more miserable torture to be suffered than that imposed by a beginning flutist or violinist in the vicinity.

"Our beginners betake themselves of their own accord into the desert, in the praiseworthy desire not to be burdensome to anyone. They stay away for a longer or shorter period, and in their isolation apply themselves zealously to their instruments, so as to be worthy of returning to the populated world. From time to time they are allowed to make a trial appearance, and it seldom goes awry, since we know how to foster shame and pride by this arrangement, as by all our others. That your son possesses a good voice pleases me greatly, for the rest will take care of itself that much more easily."

By now they had reached the place where Felix was to stay and prove himself in his surroundings, until it might be time to admit him formally. From some distance they heard a joyful song; it was a game with which the boys were amusing themselves, now that the workday was ended. A general chorus resounded, in which, at the nod of the conductor, each member of a large circle joined with his own part, joyfully, clearly, and vigorously. The conductor, however, often took the singers by surprise, suspending the chorale with a sign and calling upon some individual participant, whom he touched with his baton, to sing a suitable solo which took up where the other voices died away and carried on in the same spirit. The majority displayed considerable skill; some, who could not manage it, willingly surrendered their pledges without precisely being laughed at. Felix was child enough to plunge into their midst and acquit himself tolerably. Afterward he was directed to use that first salutation: he promptly crossed his hands on his chest and gazed upward, and yet with so waggish an expression that it was plain he was not yet aware of any secret meaning to the gesture.

The agreeable spot, the warm welcome, and the jolly playmates all pleased the boy so much that he was not greatly upset at seeing his father ride away. Watching his horse be led off was almost more painful to him. But he accepted it when he learned that he could not keep the horse in this district. He was promised in return that another, if not the same one, spirited and well trained, would later come his way when he least expected it.

Since the Superior was inaccessible, the supervisor said, "I must leave you now and attend to my duties. But I will take you to the Three, who preside over our sanctuaries. Your letter is directed to them as well, and together they represent the Superior."

Wilhelm would have liked to hear something about the sanctuaries in advance, but the other replied, "In return for the trust you have shown in leaving your son under our care, the Three will surely reveal to you the most important matters, as far as wisdom and discretion dictate. The visible objects of veneration, which I called our sanctuaries, are isolated in a special district, so that nothing may mix with them, nothing disturb them. Only at certain times of the year are the pupils allowed to enter there, depending on their level of development, in order to be instructed historically and visually, so that they may carry away a strong enough impression to live on for a while as they perform their tasks."

Wilhelm now stood at a gate in a high wall which surrounded a wooded valley. At a certain sign a little door opened, and a grave, imposing man received our friend. He found himself in a large, magnificently planted space, shaded by trees and shrubs of many varieties; he was scarcely able to glimpse the stately walls and handsome buildings through this luxuriant and tall greenery. A friendly reception by the Three, who made their appearance one by one, led to a conversation to which each contributed his thoughts, but whose content we shall summarize briefly.

"Since you are entrusting your son to us," they said, "we owe it to you to let you look deeper into our method. You have seen many external signs which do not immediately lend themselves to understanding. Which of these would you particularly want to have explained?"

"I have seen gestures and salutations which, while seemly enough, are nevertheless strange, and whose meaning I should like to learn. Among you, the outward surely refers to the inward, and vice versa; let me learn of this connection."

"Well-born, healthy children," they replied, "bring a great deal with them. Nature has endowed each of them with whatever he would need for time and duration. Our duty is to develop these things, though often they develop better on their own. But there is one thing that no one brings with him into the world, and yet it is this on which everything depends and by which man becomes human in the full sense. If you can identify it yourself, then speak its name." Wilhelm reflected for a short while, then shook his head.

The others, after a decent interval, exclaimed, "Reverence!" Wilhelm was startled. "Reverence!" they repeated. "Everyone lacks it, perhaps even you yourself.

"You have seen three sets of gestures, and we teach a threefold reverence, which reaches its greatest strength and effectiveness only when it flows as one and forms a whole. The first is reverence for that which is above us. That gesture, the arms crossed over the chest and a joyful gaze toward the sky, is what we require of young children, thereby demanding they testify that there is a God above who is reflected and manifested in their parents, teachers, and superiors. The second: reverence for that which is beneath us. The hands held behind the back, bound, as it were, and the lowered smiling glance say that one must regard the earth carefully and serenely; it affords nourishment, it furnishes unutterable delights, but it also produces disproportionate suffering. If someone suffers bodily injury, by his own doing or innocently, if others deliberately or inadvertently injure him, if the indifference of the earth inflicts some suffering upon him, let him consider it well, for this sort of peril remains with him his whole life long. But we liberate our pupil from this position as quickly as possible, as soon as we are certain that the lesson of this stage has had sufficient effect. Then we call upon him to take courage, to turn to his comrades and be guided by them. Now he stands up straight and bold, but not in selfish isolation; only in alliance with others like him does he form a front against the world. Beyond that, we would not know what to add."

"This makes sense to me," Wilhelm replied. "This is why the majority of people are in such bad straits, because they wallow in ill will and ill speaking. Whoever succumbs to this habit soon grows indifferent toward God, contemptuous toward the world, and spiteful toward his fellow men; his true, authentic, indispensable sense of himself is consumed by presumption and arrogance. Will you allow me, nevertheless," Wilhelm continued, "to raise one objection? Was not the fear which primitive people felt in the face of the powerful phenomena of Nature and other inexplicable, ominous experiences considered the germ from which a higher feeling, a purer way of thinking would gradually develop?"

To this the others replied, "As a response to nature, fear is appropriate, but reverence is not. One fears a known or unknown mighty being. The strong try to resist it, the weak to avoid it. Both wish to be free of it, and consider themselves fortunate when they have eliminated it for a short while, during which their own nature can to some degree reassert its freedom and independence. Natural man repeats this operation a million times over in his life; enmeshed in fear, he strives for freedom, and is driven from freedom back into fear again, and cannot break this cycle. To be fearful is easy, but painful; to cultivate reverence is difficult, but comfortable. Only with reluctance does a person commit himself to reverence, or rather, he does not commit himself to it. It is a higher sense that must be given to him, and that develops by itself only in certain specially favored natures, who from time immemorial have been called saints or gods on this account. Herein lies the majesty and the chief concern of all true religions, of which there are only three, to judge by the objects of their devotion."

The men paused, and Wilhelm, too, reflected in silence for a while. Since he could not presume to interpret their strange words, he asked the sages to continue their discourse, a wish to which they immediately acceded. "Among us," they said, "no religion based on fear is respected. When a person lets himself be governed by reverence, he preserves his honor in paying honor; he is not at odds with himself, as in the other case. The religion founded on reverence for that which is above us we call the ethnic religion; this is the religion of the multitude of peoples, and the first successful liberation from servile fear. All the so-called pagan religions are of this sort, whatever names they go by. The second religion, based on reverence for that which is equal to us, we call the philosophic religion, since the philosopher, who locates himself in the middle, must draw all the higher elements down to him, while elevating lower elements to his own level, and only in this middle position does he merit the name of sage. Since he can survey his relationship to his kind, and thus to all mankind, and his relationship to all other earthly contexts, essential and fortuitous, he alone lives the truth, in the cosmic sense. But now we must speak of the third religion, which is based on reverence for that which is below us. We call this the Christian religion, because in it that kind of attitude is most strongly manifested. It is an ultimate to which humanity could and had to attain. But what must it have required, not only to leave the earth behind and to claim a higher birthplace, but also to acknowledge lowliness and poverty, scorn and contempt, humiliation and misery, suffering and death, as divine, yes, to regard even sin and crime not as barriers but as furtherances to saintliness, to venerate them and cherish them! To be sure, there are traces of such a view throughout the ages, but a trace is not a destination, and this once reached, mankind can no longer go backward, and, one may say, the Christian religion, having once made its appearance, can never vanish again. Having once embodied itself in divine form, it may never again be dissolved."

"Which of these religions do you especially profess?" Wilhelm inquired. "All three of them," they replied, "for the three taken together actually produce the true religion. From the three reverences springs the highest reverence, reverence for oneself, and the others are born once again from this latter, so that the individual can arrive at the highest attainment of which he is capable, so that he may view himself as the finest thing that God and Nature have produced, yes, so that he can remain at this height without being dragged back again to a common level by presumptuousness and self-centeredness."

"Such a profession of faith, presented in such a way, does not appear strange to me," Wilhelm responded. "It agrees with everything one hears here and there in life, except that you are united by what drives others apart." To this the others countered, "This profession of faith is already articulated by a great portion of the world, albeit unknowingly."

"How so, and where?" Wilhelm asked. "In the Creed," the others exclaimed. "For its first article is ethnic and belongs to all peoples; the second is Christian, for those contending with suffering and glorified by suffering; the third, finally, teaches an inspired communion of saints, which is to say, persons of the highest wisdom and goodness.

Should not then the three divine figures, in whose image and name such convictions and such promises are expressed, by rights stand for the highest Unity?"

"I thank you," Wilhelm said, "for being willing to present all this so clearly and coherently to me, who, after all, am an adult and not unacquainted with the three attitudes. And when I consider that you convey this high doctrine to the children, first as physical gesture, then with certain symbolic echoes, and finally in its highest significance, I must give your undertaking the highest praise."

"Quite right," the sages replied. "But now you must learn more, so that you can convince yourself that your son is in the best of hands. But let this be saved for the morning hours. Rest and refresh yourself so that, early in the morning, restored and in full possession of your human faculties, you may follow us into the inner sanctum."

Chapter Two

Led by the eldest, our hero now entered through a handsome portal into a round, or rather octagonal, hall so richly adorned with paintings as to fill the newcomer with astonishment. He readily grasped that everything he saw must have a special meaning, even though he could not decipher it so quickly. He was on the point of questioning his guide about it when the latter invited him to step into a side gallery, which, open on one side, enclosed a spacious garden, with a profusion of flowers. Yet his eyes were more drawn to the wall than to this brilliant natural decoration, for it was completely covered with frescoes, and the newcomer could not walk far along it without realizing that the sacred books of the Hebrews had provided the subjects of these paintings.

"This is where we pass on that religion," said the eldest, "which I described for the sake of brevity as the ethnic one. Its import can be found in world history, as its husk can be found in individual events. From the repetition of the destinies of entire peoples, one can come to understand it."

"As I see," said Wilhelm, "you have honored the people of Israel by making its history the basis for this representation, or rather, you have made that history its chief subject matter."

"You see rightly," the old man replied, "for as you will notice, on the base of the wall and the friezes are painted motifs and events that are not only synchronous but also symphronic, since accounts with similar meaning and signification occur among all peoples. Thus when Abraham is visited by his gods in the shape of comely youths, in the main panel, in the frieze above you will see the scene of Apollo among Admetus' shepherds. Whence we may learn that when the gods appear among men, they usually walk unrecognized among them."

They continued on, contemplating the images. Wilhelm found mainly familiar objects, depicted, however, in a livelier, more significant way than he was accustomed to seeing. For a few details he requested some explanation. In this connection he could not forbear to ask once again why the history of the Israelites had been chosen over all others. To this the old man replied, "Among all the pagan religions—for such is also that of the Israelites—it has great advantages, of which I shall mention only a few. Before the ethnic judgment seat, before the judgment seat of the God of peoples, the question is not whether a nation was the best, the most admirable, but only whether it endured, whether it maintained its identity. The people of Israel was never worth much, as it was a thousand times admonished by its leaders, judges, chiefs, and prophets. It possesses few virtues and most of the faults of other peoples. But in self-reliance, constancy, bravery, and, should all these after all not matter, in tenacity, it has no equal. It is the most persistent people on earth; it is, it was, and it shall be, that it may glorify the name of Jehovah through the ages. That is why we have presented it here as a model, as the central subject, which the others only serve to frame."

"It does not behoove me to dispute with you," Wilhelm replied, "since you are in a position to instruct me. Explain to me therefore the other strengths of this people, or rather, of its history, its religion?"

"A principal strength," the sage replied, "is the splendid collection of its sacred books. They fit together so well that out of the most disparate elements a plausible whole can be constructed. They are sufficiently complete to be satisfying, sufficiently fragmentary to be intriguing, sufficiently barbaric to be challenging, sufficiently subtle to be soothing; and how many other paradoxical qualities can be celebrated in these books, in this book!"

The suite of pictures, as well as the connections to the smaller paintings that accompanied them above and below, gave the guest so much to think about that he scarcely listened to the profound observations by which his companion seemed more to distract his attention than to fix it on the objects. The latter, meanwhile, found occasion to remark, "Yet another strength of the Israelite religion I should mention here is that it does not represent its God in any corporeal form, and thereby leaves us free to give Him an exalted human form, and also, in contrast, to depict wicked idolatry in the form of animals and monsters."

Our friend had refreshed his memory of human history by a short stroll through these halls. He also perceived some new purpose to events. Through the arrangement of the pictures, and through the reflections of his companion, new insights had come to him, and he was pleased that Felix should be introduced to these great, momentous, and exemplary occurrences through such fine and vivid depiction, so that for his entire life they would seem real, and as though they had taken place close by him. In the end, he looked at the pictures entirely with the eyes of his child, and in this spirit was completely satisfied with them. And thus on their walk they had reached the grievous, troubled times and finally the fall of the city and the Temple, the massacre, exile, and enslavement of whole masses of this persistent nation. Their subsequent fate had been wisely represented in allegorical form, since a historical, realistic illustration lay outside the scope of true art.

At this point, the gallery through which they had been strolling was suddenly closed off, and Wilhelm was astonished to see himself already at its end. "I find," he remarked to his guide, "a gap in this historical panorama. You have had the Temple in Jerusalem destroyed and the people dispersed, without introducing that godly man who not long before had preached there, and to whom they had not long before refused to listen."

"To do this as you demand would have been an error. The life of the godly man whom you mention has no connection with the history of his time. It was a private life, his teaching a teaching for individuals. What publicly befalls entire peoples and their members belongs to world history, and to that world religion which we consider the first. What privately befalls the individual belongs to the second religion, to the religion of the sages; it was such a religion that Christ preached and practiced, for the time he was on earth. That is why the outward religion comes to an end here, and I shall now reveal the inward one to you."

A door opened, and they entered a similar gallery, where Wilhelm immediately recognized the images of the second Holy Scripture. They seemed to be the work of a different artist: everything was gentler—figures, movements, surroundings, light, and coloration.

"You see here," said the guide after they had passed some of the pictures, "neither deeds nor events, but miracles and parables. This is a new world, a new outward reality, different from the preceding one, and an inner reality that was entirely lacking there. Through miracles and parables a new world is revealed. The former render the ordinary extraordinary, while the latter render the extraordinary ordinary."

"Would you have the kindness," Wilhelm said, "to explain these few words at greater length, for I do not feel able to do so by myself."

"They have a straightforward meaning," the old man replied, "albeit a deep one. Examples will clarify it soonest. Nothing is more common or more familiar than eating and drinking. It is extraordinary, however, to so ennoble a drink or so multiply a meal that it could feed multitudes. There is nothing more common than sickness and bodily infirmity; but to cure them or ease them by spiritual means or those akin to the spiritual is extraordinary, and precisely herein lies the miraculousness of miracles, that the ordinary and the extraordinary, the possible and the impossible, become one. With similitudes and parables it is the reverse; here the meaning, the insight, the concept is the sublime, the extraordinary, the inaccessible. When this meaning becomes embodied in a common, familiar, apprehensible image, so that it confronts us in living, present, actual form, so that we can take possession of it, grasp it, hold it fast, so that we can treat it as our own kind, that is a second sort of miracle, properly ranked with the first, perhaps even preferred to it. Here the living doctrine is enunciated, the doctrine that elicits no contradiction. It is not an opinion on right and wrong; it is incontestably right or wrong itself."

This section of the gallery was shorter, or rather, it comprised only one quarter of the way around the inner court. However, though one merely walked past the frescoes in the first part, here one was inclined to linger; here one took pleasure in going back and forth. The subjects were not so striking nor so diverse, but for that very reason encouraged one to explore their deep and quiet meaning. Also, the two strollers turned around at the end of the corridor, while Wilhelm expressed his concern that the pictures went only as far as the Last Supper and the Master's farewell from his disciples. He inquired after the remaining portion of the story.

"We are happy to extract from every lesson, from every tradition, what can properly be extracted," the eldest answered. "For only in that way can the concept of what is significant develop in young people. Life mixes and mingles everything together without regard; so here, too, we have completely separated the life of this remarkable man from its end. In his life he appears a true philosopher—do not be shocked by this term—as a sage in the highest sense. He holds steadfastly to his principles; he travels his road undismayed, and when he raises up the lowly and allows the ignorant, the poor, the sick, to share in his wisdom, his wealth, and his strength, and seems thereby to place himself on their level, he does not deny on the other hand his divine origin; he dares to claim equality to God, yes, even to proclaim himself God. In this manner he astounds those around him from his youth, wins a certain number of them over to his side, arouses the others against him, and shows all who aspire to a certain sublimity in life and principles what they may expect from the world. And so his progress through the world is more instructive and fruitful for the noble part of mankind than his death; for everyone is called to the former tests, few to the latter. And in order that we may review everything that follows from this observation, consider the moving scene of the Last Supper. Here the sage, as always, is leaving his followers, utterly orphaned, behind, and while he cares for the good ones, he is at the same time feeding a traitor, who will destroy him and the better ones."

With these words the eldest opened a door, and Wilhelm was startled to find himself back in the first hall, by the entrance. They had, he now realized, made the entire circuit of the court. "I had hoped," said Wilhelm, "you would lead me to the end, and now you bring me back to the beginning." "For this time I can show you no more," said the eldest. "We do not let our pupils see any more, nor do we explain more than what you have just surveyed. Each can be instructed in the outward, commonly accessible aspect from childhood on, but the inward, spiritual and emotional aspect is conveyed only to those who have developed a certain reflectiveness. The rest, which is revealed but once a year, can be communicated only to those whom we release. As for that ultimate religion which springs from reverence for that which is beneath us, that worship of the repulsive, the hated, the shunned, we pass it along to each one merely as preparation for the world, that he may know where to find such a thing, should the need for it ever develop. I invite you to return after a year, to attend our school celebration and see how far your son has progressed. Then you, too, shall be initiated into the Sanctuary of Pain."

"Allow me one question," Wilhelm replied. "Have you, then, in addition to representing the life of this divine man as a lesson and example, also painted his suffering, his death, as a model of noble endurance?"

"By all means," said the eldest. "We make no mystery of this. But we draw a veil over his sufferings, precisely because we hold them in such respect. We consider it damnable impertinence to expose that martyr's scaffolding and the holy one suffering upon it to the gaze of the sun, which hid its face when a wicked world forced this spectacle upon it; it is a piece of insolence to play with, to trifle with, to make a show of these deep mysteries, in which the divine depths of suffering lie hidden, and to keep on until the most sacred matters appear commonplace and tasteless. For the time being, let this suffice to ease your mind about your son and to convince you that you will find him educated in some fashion, more or less, but certainly in a desirable way, and in any case not confused, vacillating, or unsteady."

Wilhelm hesitated, for he was gazing at the pictures in the entry hall and wished to have their meaning explicated. "This, too," said the eldest, "must be reserved for next year. We allow no outsiders to be present at the instruction we give the children in the meantime. But come then and hear what our best lecturers judge useful to be spoken publicly about these subjects."

Shortly after this exchange they heard knocking at the little gate. The supervisor of the previous day announced his presence; he had brought Wilhelm's horse around, and so our friend took his leave of the Three, who in parting commended him to the supervisor as follows: "This man now numbers among the trusted, and you are aware what you are to reply to his questions. For surely he will wish to be instructed about much that he has seen and heard here. Measure and purpose are not hidden from you."

Wilhelm did indeed have other questions on his mind, which he now promptly posed. As they rode through the grounds, the children comported themselves as they had the previous day, but today he noticed, although infrequently, that one or another of the boys did not greet the supervisor as he rode by, did not look up from his work, and let him pass unnoticed. Wilhelm inquired about the reason for this, and what this exception might signify. The other responded, "It is in fact highly significant, for this is the most severe punishment we impose on the pupils: they are declared unworthy of manifesting reverence, and required to show themselves rude and uncultivated. But they do their best to escape from this situation and throw themselves at once into every task. Should, however, a child obstinately make no effort to redeem himself, he is sent back to his parents, with a brief but telling report. Anyone who does not learn how to obey the laws must leave the territory where they hold sway."

Today as yesterday, another sight aroused the wanderer's curiosity. It was the variety of color and cut in the pupils' clothing. It seemed not to be a question of rank, since boys who saluted differently were dressed alike, while those giving the same salutation were clothed differently. Wilhelm inquired as to the reason for this apparent contradiction. "The answer is," the supervisor replied, "that it is a means to discover the individual temperaments of the boys. Despite the general strictness and order that otherwise prevail, in this matter we allow a degree of personal choice. Within the limits of our supplies of fabric and trimmings, the pupils may take their favorite colors, and, again within reasonable constraints, choose the cut and form of their clothing. We observe their choices carefully, for the color reveals the way of thinking, while the cut reveals the way of living. Yet there is a peculiarity of human nature which makes it somewhat difficult to judge these things more accurately. It is the spirit of imitation, the tendency to affiliate oneself with others. It is very rare for a pupil to arrive at something that has not yet been tried; for the most part they choose something familiar, which they see before them. Yet even this observation is not without utility, for through such outward manifestations they ally themselves with this or that party, they join this or that group, and so general attitudes become visible; we discover each child's inclination and the example to which he cleaves.

"There have been instances where the dispositions tended toward the general, where one style spread to all and every distinction was in danger of disappearing. We try by gentle means to check any such development; we let the supplies run out: this or that fabric, one or another trimming, is no more to be had. We substitute something new, something attractive, in its place. With bright colors and a short, snug cut we lure the bolder spirits, while with sober tones and comfortable, loose garments we appeal to the more circumspect, and thus gradually restore a balance.

"For we are completely opposed to uniforms. They conceal character and hide the children's unique qualities from the view of their instructors more than any other dissimulation."

Conversing on this and other topics, Wilhelm reached the border of the province, and in fact at the very spot where the wanderer was to leave it, according to his old friend's indications, to pursue his actual goal.

In saying farewell, the supervisor remarked that Wilhelm must now wait until the great festival was announced to all concerned, by a variety of means. All the parents were invited, and the proficient pupils were released into the freedom and contingencies of life. Then he would be able to tour the remaining sections of the province as he pleased, where, in suitable settings, the separate forms of instruction were imparted and practiced, each according to its own principles.

Chapter Three

To gratify the expectations of the worthy public, which for some time now has enjoyed taking its entertainment in small doses, we at first thought to offer the following tale in a number of installments. Its inner continuity, however, considered as to attitudes, emotions, and events, occasioned an uninterrupted presentation. May this latter fulfill its purpose and may it at the same time become evident, when the story is told, how the characters in this seemingly unconnected episode are intimately entwined with those others whom we already know and love.

The Man of Fifty Years

The major had ridden into the courtyard, and Hilarie, his niece, was already standing outside on the steps leading up to the manor house, waiting to receive him. He scarcely recognized her, for she had again grown taller and more beautiful. She flew to him, he pressed her to his breast with the feelings of a father, and they hurried in to her mother.

He was equally welcome to the baroness, his sister, and when Hilarie hurried off to attend to breakfast, the major said happily, "This time I may be brief, and report that our business is concluded. Our brother, the marshal, now recognizes that he can handle neither his tenants nor his stewards. He will convey his property in his own lifetime to us and our children; to be sure, the annual allowance that he stipulates for himself is large; but it is within our means. We are still gaining a good deal for the present and everything for the future. The new arrangement is to be settled soon. Since I expect my discharge at any moment, I shall take an active role again, which can bring decided advantages to us and our children. We look calmly on while they grow up, and it is up to us, and to them, to hasten their union."

"That would be all very well," the baroness replied, "if I did not have a secret to reveal to you, of which I myself have only just become aware. Hilarie's heart is no longer free; in that regard your son has little or nothing to hope for."

"What are you saying?" the major exclaimed. "Is it possible? When we are taking such pains to make financial provision for them, would inclination play us such a trick? Tell me, my dear, tell me quickly: who can have captured Hilarie's heart? Or is it really that serious? Might it not be a fleeting impression, which one may hope to extinguish again?"

"You must first think a bit and guess," answered the baroness, thereby increasing his impatience. This had reached its height when the entrance of Hilarie with the servants bringing breakfast made a quick solution of the riddle impossible.

The major himself felt that he was seeing the lovely girl with other eyes than shortly before. It was almost as if he were jealous of the lucky man whose image could have impressed itself upon so lovely a soul. Breakfast did not taste good to him, and he failed to notice that everything was prepared exactly as he liked it and normally requested.

With the major so taciturn and constrained, Hilarie herself almost lost her merry air. The baroness felt discomfited, and drew her daughter to the piano, but her spirited and expressive playing elicited scarcely any applause from the major. He wished both the lovely girl and the breakfast gone, the sooner the better, and the baroness was obliged to rise from the table and suggest to her brother a stroll in the garden.

No sooner were they alone than the major urgently repeated his earlier question, to which his sister after a pause replied with a smile,

"If you wish to find the lucky man whom she loves, you need not go far. He is very close by. It is you she loves."

The major was taken aback, then exclaimed, "It would be a very untimely joke if you wished to persuade me of something which, if true, would make me both embarrassed and unhappy. For although I need time to recover from my amazement, I can see at a glance how greatly our situation would be upset by such an unexpected occurrence. The only thing that consoles me is the belief that inclinations of this kind are illusory, that they are based upon self-deception, and that a sound and good soul will soon recover from such a mistake, either on its own, or with the assistance of sensible friends."

"I am not of your opinion," said the baroness, "because to judge by all the symptoms, it is a very serious feeling with which Hilarie is filled."

"I would never have imagined such a natural disposition capable of something so unnatural," the major remarked.

"It is not all that unnatural," his sister replied. "From my own girlhood I can recall a passion for a man older than you. You are fifty; that is no great age for a German, if perhaps other, livelier nations age more quickly."

"But how do you justify your suspicion?" the major asked.

"It is not a suspicion, it is a certainty. You shall learn the particulars by and by."

Hilarie joined them, and the major found his feelings, against his will, altered once again. Her presence seemed dearer and more precious to him than before; her manner appeared more loving, and he was already beginning to lend credence to his sister's words. The sensation was very pleasant, although he was inclined neither to admit it nor indulge it. To be sure, Hilarie was most charming, as her manner toward him combined the delicate shyness due a lover with the easy familiarity due an uncle. For she truly loved him, with her entire being. The garden was in its full spring glory, and the major, seeing so many old trees leafing out anew, could believe in a similar return of his own springtime. And who would not have been seduced into such thoughts in the presence of such a charming girl!

Thus they passed the day together; the various domestic rituals were carried out with greatest good cheer. In the evening, after dinner, Hilarie again sat down at the piano. The major listened with different ears than in the morning. One melody intertwined with another, one song flowed into the next, and even the arrival of midnight could hardly induce the little company to disband.

When the major reached his chamber, he found everything arranged for his comfort in the old, familiar manner; some engravings, before which he liked to linger, had even been moved here from other rooms.

With his awareness sharpened, he saw how he was being cared for and coddled, down to the smallest detail.

That night he needed but a few hours' sleep; his vital energies were roused early. But he now perceived all of a sudden that a new order of things brings many inconveniences in its train. His old orderly, who acted both as manservant and valet, had heard not a sharp word for several years, since everything was done in its accustomed way according to a rigid order. Horses were looked after and articles of clothing cleaned at the proper times. But today the master had awakened earlier, and nothing seemed to suit him.

Added to this was another circumstance, which increased the major's impatience and even ill humor. In the past, he had found no fault with himself or his servant. Now, however, stepping before the mirror, he did not find himself as he would have liked. He could not deny that there were gray hairs, and a few wrinkles had turned up as well. He scrubbed and powdered more than usual, but in the end he had to let it be. Nor was he satisfied with his clothing or its cleanliness. He claimed to find lint on his jacket and dust on his boots. The old servant did not know what to say, and was astonished to see his master so changed.

Despite all these hindrances, the major was out in the garden early enough. He had hoped to find Hilarie there, and so indeed he did. She came toward him with a nosegay, and he dared not kiss her as usual and press her to his heart. He found himself in the most delightful discomposure, and yielded to his feelings without thinking where they might lead.

The baroness also put in an early appearance and, showing her brother a note just brought by messenger, exclaimed, "You will never guess whose visit this note announces!" "Well, do not keep me in suspense," the major replied, and he learned that an old actor friend was passing not far from the estate and proposed to stop in briefly.

"I am curious to see him again," the major said. "He is no longer young, yet I hear that he still plays the youthful parts."

"He must be ten years older than you," the baroness replied.

"Certainly," the major answered, "from all I remember."

It was not long before a vigorous, trim, attractive man approached. There was a moment of hesitation at first. But very soon the friends recognized one another, and reminiscences of every sort enlivened the conversation. These gave way to stories, to questions, and accounts of the intervening years. They made one another acquainted with their present circumstances, and soon felt as though they had never been apart.

A secret source tells us that in earlier years this man, then a very handsome and attractive youth, had had the fortune or the misfortune to please a distinguished lady. As a result he found himself in great embarrassment and danger, from which the major happily rescued him at the very moment when he was threatened with a most sorry fate. He had always remained grateful to the brother and to the sister as well, for it was she who, by warning him in time, had put him on guard.

For a while before luncheon the men were left alone together. Not without admiration, indeed almost with astonishment, the major had inspected the outward appearance of his old friend, in general and in detail. He seemed not to have changed at all, and it was no wonder that he could still appear on the stage as a young lover.

"You are inspecting me more intently than is proper," he finally said to the major. "I greatly fear that you find me all too different from the old days."

"By no means," replied the major, "rather I am astonished to find your appearance fresher and younger than mine. For I know that you were a grown man when I, with the boldness of a foolhardy stripling, came to your aid in a certain extremity."

"It is your own fault," the other replied. "It is the fault of all your kind, and although you ought not to be scolded for it, you are nonetheless to be blamed. You think only of what is essential; you want to be, not to seem. That is perfectly fine, so long as you are something. But when finally the essence begins to depart along with the appearance, and appearance proves even more evanescent than essence, then one notices that it would have done no harm not to neglect the outward aspect of life entirely in favor of the inward."

"You are right," the major said, and could hardly suppress a sigh.

"Perhaps not entirely right," the aged youth countered. "In my profession, to be sure, it would be quite unforgivable not to keep up one's appearance as long as possible. But you others have reason to concentrate on other things that are more significant and more lasting."

"Still, there are occasions," the major said, "when one feels inwardly fresh and would very much like to freshen oneself up outwardly as well."

Since the visitor could not guess the major's true frame of mind, he took these words in the military sense and launched into a lengthy disquisition on the importance of outward appearances in the military, commenting how the officer who had to devote so much care to his clothing might also devote some attention to his skin and hair.

"For example, it is inexcusable," he went on, "that your temples are already gray, that wrinkles are forming here and there, and that your hair is growing thin. Look at me, old fellow that I am! See how well-preserved I am, and this without any witch's arts, and with far less care and effort than people expend daily to harm themselves or at least to bore themselves."

The major found this chance conversation too much to his advantage to break it off quickly, yet he went at the question delicately and with caution, even though he was dealing with an old acquaintance. "Unfortunately I have missed my chance," he exclaimed, "and the damage cannot be repaired. I must simply resign myself on this score, and you must not think any the worse of me for that."

"No chance has been missed," rejoined the other. "If only you serious-minded men were not so rigid and stiff, so quick to label as vain anyone who thinks about his appearance, and in the process ruin your own pleasure at being in attractive company and yourself being attractive."

"Even if there is no magic," the major said with a smile, "in the way you others keep yourselves young, still it involves some mystery, or at any rate secrets of the kind often touted in the newspapers, the best of which, however, you know how to ferret out."

"Whether you are joking or speaking in earnest," his friend replied, "you have hit the mark. Among the many things that have been tried through the ages to sustain our appearance, which often falters much sooner than our mind, there are some truly priceless substances, some simple, others complex mixtures. I obtained them from fellow actors, for money or by chance, and I have tested them on myself. I use them faithfully and shall continue to, without, however, abandoning my researches. This much I can tell you, and I am not exaggerating: I carry with me a dressing case beyond price, a casket whose effects I would gladly try on you, if we could but spend a fortnight together."

The thought that something of this sort was possible and that this possibility had chanced to come his way at just the right moment so lifted the major's spirits that he already looked fresher and more energetic. Cheered by the hope that he could bring his head and face into harmony with his heart, and animated by impatience to learn what must be done, he seemed quite another man at dinner. He received Hilarie's gracious attentions calmly, and looked at her with a degree of confidence that had still been altogether foreign to him that morning.

Since his actor friend was skilled at maintaining, stimulating, and heightening the good humor of the company with his reminiscences, anecdotes, and witty sallies, the major was greatly disconcerted when he threatened to leave and be on his way right after dinner. The major tried every means to prolong his stay, at least overnight, urgently promising fresh horses and the relay for the morning. In short, the restorative dressing case was not to leave the house until more had been learned of its contents and their application.

The major was well aware that there was no time to be lost and thus sought to speak privately with his old protégé right after dinner. Since he lacked the courage to go straight to the point, he approached it obliquely by returning to their previous conversation; for his part, he declared, he would gladly pay more attention to his outward appearance, were it not that others promptly concluded that anyone seen making such efforts was vain, and respected his moral being the less, the more they felt compelled to admire his physical being.

"Do not vex me with such talk," replied his friend. "These are phrases society has adopted without reflection, or, if one takes a harsher view, by which it expresses its hostile and malicious nature. If you examine it closely: what is this, after all, that is often decried as vanity? Everyone ought to delight in himself, and fortunate is he who does so. But if he does, how can he keep from showing this pleasant feeling? Why should he, in the midst of life, conceal that he delights in being alive? If polite society—for that alone is at issue here—frowned upon such manifestations only when they became too pronounced, when one man's delight in himself and his being interfered with the delight others might take and want to display, there could be no objection, and no doubt the blame originally arose from such excess. But what is the point of strange, severe strictures against the inevitable? Why not permit and tolerate conduct that one more or less allows oneself from time to time? In fact, polite society could not even exist without it, for the pleasure one takes in oneself and the desire to share this self-esteem with others makes one pleasing, the sense of one's own charm makes one charming. Would to heaven that all people were vain, but consciously so, in moderation and in the proper spirit. Then we in the cultivated world would be the happiest of people. Women, it is said, are vain from birth; but it becomes them, and they please us all the better for it. How can a young man shape himself if he is not vain? An empty, hollow character will at least know how to give himself some outward polish, while the man of parts will soon form himself from the outside inward. As for myself, I have reason to think myself the most fortunate of men, because my profession entitles me to be vain, and because the more I am so, the more I add to others' enjoyment. I am praised where others are blamed, and on this very score have the right and the good fortune to delight and enchant the public at an age at which others are compelled to leave the stage, or else stay on, but ignominiously."

The major heard these remarks out with scant pleasure. The little word "vanity," when he introduced it, was meant only to serve as a bridge to lead his friend smoothly to his own request. Now he was afraid that further discussion would displace the goal even more, and so he pressed directly to the issue. "As for me," he said, "I would be not at all disinclined to enlist under your banner, since you think that it is not too late, and that I can to some extent compensate for my past negligence. Share some of your tinctures, pomades, and salves with me, and I will make the attempt."

"Sharing these things," the other man replied, "is more difficult than you think. For example, it is not just a matter of pouring a certain amount from my vials and leaving you half of the best ingredients in my dressing case. The application is the chief difficulty. One cannot simply make these inherited substances one's own. How this one or that one fits, under what conditions, in what order they are to be used: all that requires practice and thought. In fact, even these may do no good, if one does not have an inborn talent for this particular undertaking."

"You would like, it appears," the major replied, "to retreat now. You are raising difficulties in order to rescue your rather fanciful assertions. You do not wish to give me a pretext, an opportunity, to put your words to the test."

"Your raillery, my friend," replied the other, "would not induce me to gratify your wish, had I not such good intentions toward you; I, indeed, made the offer first. Consider, my friend, that a person takes special pleasure in winning converts, in bringing to light in others, outside of himself, that which he values in himself, in having them enjoy what he enjoys, in finding himself and mirroring himself in them. In truth, even if this is egotism, it is the most lovable and laudable sort, the kind that has made us human and keeps us human. This, apart from the friendship I bear you, is the impulse behind my desire to make you a disciple in the art of rejuvenation. But because no master would want to train bunglers, I am at a loss as to how to begin. As I said before, neither the ointments nor any instructions are sufficient; the application cannot be taught in general terms. For your sake and for the joy of propagating my teachings, I am prepared for any sacrifice. I shall offer you at once the greatest I can for the moment: I will leave my servant with you. He is a sort of valet and a jack-of-all-trades, who, though he does not know how to concoct everything, is not initiated into every secret, still understands the entire treatment quite well and for the beginning will be of great use to you, until you have worked your way far enough in that I may reveal to you the higher secrets."

"What!" cried the major, "You have steps and grades in your art of rejuvenation? You have secrets even for the initiates?"

"Most certainly," the other replied. "It would be a sorry art that could be grasped all at once, and whose farthest reaches could be seen at once by one who first crossed its threshold."

Without more delay the servant was assigned to the major, who promised to treat him well. The baroness had to provide little boxes, canisters, and jars, for what purpose she knew not. Portions were doled out, and the men stayed together into the night, amid cheerful and spirited conversations. With the later rising of the moon, the guest drove off, promising to return after some interval.

The major was rather tired when he reached his chamber. He had risen early, had not spared himself during the day, and was eager to get to bed. He found not one servant waiting for him, however, but two. His old orderly speedily undressed him in the usual way. But now the new man came forward and gave him to understand that the proper time for applying rejuvenation and beauty preparations was the night, for their efficacy was greatest during peaceful sleep. Consequently the major had to submit to having his head salved, his face smeared, his eyebrows oiled, and his lips dabbed. Furthermore, various rituals were also required. He could not even put on his nightcap directly; instead, he had to have a net first, if not a soft leather cap!

The major lay down in bed with an unpleasant sensation, which, however, he had no time to define for himself, for he soon fell asleep. But if we may speak for his inner self, he felt rather like a mummy, a cross between a patient and an embalmed corpse. Yet the sweet image of Hilarie, surrounded by the brightest hopes, drew him quickly into refreshing slumber.

In the morning his orderly was on hand at the proper hour. Everything pertaining to the master's dress lay in the accustomed order on the chairs, and the major was just about to get out of bed when the new valet entered and protested vigorously against such haste. One must linger in bed, one must take one's time, if the undertaking was to succeed, if one was to reap the benefits of so much care and trouble. The master was then informed that he was to get up somewhat later, partake of a small breakfast, and then step into a bath that was already waiting. The directives could not be avoided; they had to be obeyed, and several hours were consumed by these activities.

The major shortened the rest period after the bath, and thought he would quickly throw on his clothes, for he was expeditious by nature, and moreover was eager to see Hilarie. But once again the new servant intervened, and made it clear to him that he must unlearn his habit of efficiency. Whatever one did must be carried out at a slow, comfortable pace, but especially the time for dressing should be regarded as a pleasant hour of communing with oneself.

The servant's ministrations corresponded exactly to his words. As a result, the major had the impression he really was better dressed than ever before when he stepped before the mirror and saw himself so smartly turned out. Without asking, the valet had even altered the major's uniform to bring it more up to date; he had spent the night on this transformation. Such an immediately visible rejuvenation put the major in a very cheerful state of mind; he felt refreshed both inwardly and outwardly, and with impatient longing hurried down to join his family.

He found his sister standing before the family tree, which she had had hung up, prompted by conversation the previous evening about various collateral relations, who, because they were unmarried, or had gone to live in distant lands, or had even totally disappeared, raised in greater or lesser degree the hope of large legacies either for brother and sister or for their children. They discussed the question for some time, without mentioning the fact that previously all family worries and endeavors had focused solely on their children. Hilarie's inclination had changed the entire picture, and yet at this moment neither the major nor his sister wished to consider the matter further.

The baroness withdrew, and the major remained alone before this laconic family portrait. Hilarie approached him, and leaning against him in childlike fashion, gazed at the chart and asked him whom of all these people he had known and who might be alive and still left.

The major began his account with the oldest ones, whom he remembered but dimly from his childhood. Then he went on, sketched the character of various fathers, the ways in which their children resembled or differed from them, observed that a grandfather often reemerged in a grandson, spoke as the occasion warranted of the influence of the women, who, marrying in from other families, often altered the character of entire lines. He praised the deeds of many a forefather and more distant relative, without concealing their faults. He passed over in silence those of whom there was cause to be ashamed. Finally he reached the bottommost rows. There were his brother the marshal, himself and his sister, and beneath them his son, with Hilarie next to him.

"These two certainly look each other directly in the face," said the major, and did not add what he had in mind. After a pause, Hilarie replied timidly, in a low voice and almost with a sigh, "And yet one will never reproach a person who gazes upward!" At the same time, she looked up at him with eyes in which her entire affection was expressed.

"Do I understand you rightly?" the major said, as he turned toward her.

"I can say nothing," Hilarie answered with a smile, "that you do not already know."

"You make me the happiest man under the sun!" the major exclaimed, and fell at her feet. "Will you be mine?"

"In God's name, stand up! I am yours forever."

The baroness entered. Without being surprised, she nevertheless started. "If this should turn out badly," the major said, "the fault is yours. If well, we shall be forever grateful to you."

The baroness had loved her brother since childhood so much that she had thought him superior to all other men, and perhaps even Hilarie's inclination had, if not sprung directly from this preference of her mother's, surely been fostered by it. All three were now joined in one love, one delight, and blissful hours sped by for them. But finally they became aware once more of the world around them, a world seldom in harmony with such sentiments.

Now they remembered the major's son. Hilarie had been destined for him, as he well knew. Upon concluding the agreement with the marshal, the major was supposed to visit his son in his garrison, to discuss everything and bring these matters to a happy conclusion. But now an unexpected occurrence had disrupted the entire situation; circumstances which in the past had fit together in such friendly fashion now seemed hostile, and it was difficult to predict what turn the affair would take, or what sort of mood might seize their spirits.

Meanwhile the major had to bestir himself to go see his son, to whom he had already announced his coming. Not without reluctance, not without foreboding, not without pain at leaving Hilarie, even for a short time, he set off, after considerable delay, leaving his orderly and his horses behind and accompanied only by his rejuvenation attendant, whom he could no longer do without. He made for the town where his son was stationed.

After so long a separation, father and son greeted each other and embraced most warmly. They had a great deal to say to each other, yet did not at once speak of what lay closest to their hearts. The son dwelt upon his hopes for a speedy promotion. The father in turn gave him a detailed report on what the elder members of the family had negotiated and settled with respect to the family fortune, the various estates, and the rest.

The conversation had begun to falter to some degree when the son plucked up his courage and said to his father with a smile, "You are treating me very gently, dear Father, and I thank you for it. You speak of holdings and fortunes and do not mention the condition under which these shall become mine, at least in part. You hold back Hilarie's name, waiting for me to utter it myself and express my desire to be united soon with the lovable child."

At these words of his son the major was in great confusion. But since he was disposed, partly by nature, partly by old habit, to feel out the disposition of the person with whom he was dealing, he said nothing and looked at his son with an ambiguous smile.

"You cannot guess, Father, what I have to tell you," the lieutenant continued, "and I shall speak my piece quickly once and for all. I can depend on your kindness, for I am sure that, having taken so many pains on my account, you have surely had my true happiness in mind. But it must be said, and so let it be said now: Hilarie cannot make me happy! I think of Hilarie as a charming relative, whom I should like to have as a dear friend all my life. But another woman has aroused my passion, has captured my heart. This inclination is irresistible; you will not condemn me to unhappiness, I know."

Only with difficulty did the major conceal the joy that wanted to light up his face. He asked his son with gentle earnestness who this person might be who could so utterly enslave him?

"You must see this creature for yourself, Father, for she is as indescribable as she is incomprehensible. I fear only that you yourself will be enraptured by her, as is everyone who comes near her. By God, I may yet see you as the rival of your son."

"Who is she, then?" the major asked. "If you are not able to convey her personality, then at least tell me something of her outward circumstances, for these are surely easier to state."

"Gladly, Father," the son replied, "though even these outward circumstances would be different if it were anyone else, and would have a different effect on another. She is a young widow, heiress to a rich old husband who died recently—she is independent and well fitted to be so, is surrounded by many, is loved by equally many, and courted by equally many, and yet, if I do not much deceive myself, has given her heart to me."

Confidently, since his father said nothing and gave no sign of disapproval, the son continued, recounting the fair widow's conduct toward him, extolling her irresistible charms, her delicate signs of favor toward him, one by one, in all of which his father of course recognized the easy complaisance of a universally sought-after woman, who always chooses some favorite among her many suitors without wholly committing herself to him. Under any other circumstances the major would surely have tried to point out to a son, even to a friend, that most likely self-deception was involved here. But in this case so much was at stake for him personally, if his son were not deceived and the widow were really to love him and decide as soon as possible in his favor, that he either felt no concern or thrust any such doubt from him, or perhaps merely kept it to himself.

"You are placing me in great embarrassment," began the father after a pause. "The entire agreement among the surviving members of our family rests on the assumption that you will be united with Hilarie. If she marries a stranger, then the whole fine and clever consolidation of a respectable fortune is shattered, and you especially will not be well provided for. To be sure, there might still be a way out, but one that sounds rather strange, and one by which you still would not gain much: old as I am, I would have to marry Hilarie, which could scarcely make you very happy."

"It would make me happier than anything else in the world!" exclaimed the lieutenant. "For who can feel a genuine passion, who can enjoy or hope for the happiness of love without wishing the same supreme happiness to every friend, to everyone dear to him! You are not old, Father; and how charming Hilarie is! and the very notion of offering her your hand testifies that your heart is still youthful, your courage still intact. Let us think through and work out this inspiration, this spontaneous suggestion of yours. For I could be truly happy only if I knew you were happy; then I could truly rejoice that you were so well and richly rewarded for the concern you have shown for my future. Only then could I take you to see my fair lady bravely, confidently, and with a truly open heart. You will approve of my feelings, because you feel similarly; you will place nothing in the way of a son's happiness because you go to meet your own happiness."

With these and other insistent words the son left the father no opportunity for the reservations he would have liked to interject, but hurried him off to the fair widow, whom they found in a large, well appointed house, engaged in conversation with a company not numerous but select. She was one of those feminine beings no man can resist. With incredible skill she made the major the hero of the evening. The rest of the company seemed to be her family, the major alone the guest. She knew his circumstances well, and yet could ask about them as though only he could give a proper account of them. Similarly, each of the guests had to show some sort of interest in the new arrival. One of the gentlemen had to have known his brother, another his estates, and the third something else again, so that the major always felt himself the center of the lively conversation. Also, he was seated next to the lovely lady; her eyes were upon him, her smile directed toward him. In short, he found himself so much at ease that he almost forgot the reason for his coming. Moreover, she barely mentioned his son at all, though the young man took a lively part in the conversation. As far as she was concerned, today he seemed to be there, like all the others, only for the sake of his father.

A woman's needlework, begun in public, and continued with seeming unconcern, can, through cleverness and grace, acquire considerable significance. Pursued unself-consciously and diligently, such efforts make a beautiful woman seem oblivious to those around her, and thus arouse in them a secret uneasiness. But then, as if she were just waking up, a word or a glance brings her back into the circle, and she seems newly welcomed. But if she lays her work down in her lap, and attends to a story someone is telling, or to an instructive discourse, of the sort men are so prone to give, it is highly flattering to the person she thus favors.

Our fair widow was working in such fashion on a splendid yet tasteful portfolio, which was, moreover, remarkable for its generous dimensions. This object was now discussed by the whole company, picked up by her nearest neighbor and passed around amidst effusive praise, while the artist herself talked of serious subjects with the major. An old habitué of the house went into raptures over the almost finished object. But when it was finally passed to the major, the lady seemed to want to keep it from him, as though it were not worthy of his attention, whereupon he found courteous words for the quality of the workmanship, while the other man claimed to see in it a never completed Penelopean project.

The guests strolled about the rooms and chatted in random groupings. The lieutenant approached the lady and asked her, "What do you say to my father?"

Smiling, she replied, "I think you might well take him for a model. Just see how well-dressed he is! And does he not carry himself and take care of himself better than his dear son!" She continued thus, praising the father to the detriment of his son, and evoking very mixed feelings of satisfaction and jealousy in the young man's heart.

Shortly afterward the son joined his father and told him what the widow had said, down to the smallest particular. The major's behavior toward the widow became even more cordial, and she assumed an even more lively and confidential tone toward him. In short, it may be said that when the time for departure came, the major already belonged to her and her circle just as much as all the others.

A heavy downpour prevented the guests from returning home as they had come. Some carriages drove up, into which those who had arrived on foot were distributed. The lieutenant, however, on the pretext that it was already too crowded, let his father be driven off, while he remained behind.

Back in his chamber, the major felt a kind of giddiness and inner uncertainty, such as overtakes someone precipitated from one situation into its opposite. The ground seems to move beneath the feet of one who disembarks from a ship, and light dances before the eyes of one who suddenly steps into darkness. In this wise, the major still felt himself surrounded by the presence of the lovely creature. He longed to see her still, to hear her, to see her again, to hear her again, and after some reflection he forgave his son and even considered him fortunate in being able to claim to possess a woman of such remarkable qualities.

He was jolted out of these feelings by his son, who burst rapturously in at the door, embraced his father, and exulted, "I am the happiest man on earth!" After these and similar exclamations, matters were finally clarified between the two. The father remarked that the lovely woman had not so much as mentioned the son in her conversation with him.

"That is simply her delicate, silent, half silent, half allusive manner, which makes you certain your wishes have been fulfilled, yet leaves you still in doubt. That is how she has been toward me up to now, but your presence, Father, has wrought a miracle. I gladly confess that I stayed behind solely to see her for another moment. I found her walking up and down through her brightly lit rooms. For I know it is her custom that when the guests depart no lights may be extinguished. She walks up and down alone in her enchanted salons when the spirits she summoned there are dismissed. She accepted the pretext under which I had returned. She spoke graciously, though of insignificant things. We walked up and down through open doors the whole length of the suite. Several times we had reached the last room of all, the little cabinet lit only by a dim lamp. If she was beautiful as she moved beneath the chandeliers, she was infinitely more so illuminated by the gentle light of the lamp. We had come there again, and before turning around stood still for a moment. I do not know how I found the audacity, I do not know how I could have dared in the midst of the most insignificant conversation suddenly to seize her hand, to kiss that delicate hand, to press it to my heart. It was not drawn away. 'Heavenly creature,' I cried, 'conceal yourself from me no longer! If your lovely heart has any inclination for the happy man who stands here before you, veil it no longer, reveal it, admit it. This is the best, the ideal time to do so! Banish me, or take me into your arms!'

"I do not know what all I said, I know not what I did. She did not withdraw, she did not resist, she did not reply. I dared to take her in my arms and ask whether she would be mine. I kissed her wildly; she pushed me away. 'Yes, yes,' she murmured, or something of the sort, as if bewildered. I started off, and called, 'I shall send my father; he will speak on my behalf.'—'Not a word to him about this,' she replied, following me a few more steps. 'Go away, forget what has just taken place.' "

What the major thought, we do not wish to enlarge upon. But to his son he said, "What do you think should be done now? As I see it, the issue has been adequately introduced, on the spur of the moment, so that we can go to work on a more formal basis. It is perhaps very appropriate for me to call tomorrow and ask for her hand for you."

"In God's name, Father," he exclaimed, "that would ruin the whole thing! That demeanor, that tone must not be disrupted, thrown out of tune, by any formality. It is enough, Father, that your presence has hastened this union, without your having to say a word. Yes, it is you to whom I owe my happiness! The respect my beloved feels for you has overcome her every doubt, and the son would never have found such a happy moment, had his father not prepared the ground."

This and similar communications occupied them far into the night. They agreed upon their plans: the major would make a parting call on the widow, purely for form's sake, and then go back to arrange his union with Hilarie. The son would further and hasten his own to whatever extent possible.

Chapter Four

Our major paid a morning call on the fair widow, in order to take his leave from her and, if it were possible, discreetly further his son's cause. He found her in elegant morning attire, and in the company of an older woman, who immediately won him by her highly proper and amiable manner. The charm of the younger woman was admirably balanced by the propriety of the elder, and their conduct toward one another certainly seemed to suggest that they were related.

The younger woman seemed to have just completed the portfolio familiar to us from yesterday. For after the customary greetings and courteous words of welcome, she turned to her companion and handed her the intricate work, as if reverting to an interrupted conversation: "So you see, I have finished it after all, although it did not look like it, with all these hesitations and delays."

"You have come at just the right moment, Major," the older lady said, "to settle our quarrel, or at least to declare yourself for one party or the other. I maintain that no one begins such an elaborate piece of work without having someone in mind for whom it is intended, and that no one finishes it without some such intent. Examine for yourself this work of art, for I may justly call it that, and say whether something of this sort can be undertaken without any purpose at all."

Naturally our major had to commend the work most warmly. Partly plaited, partly embroidered, it excited, along with admiration, desire to know how it was made. Colored silks predominated, but gold had also not been spared. In brief, one hardly knew what to admire more, its splendor or its good taste.

"There is still a bit left to do," remarked the fair widow, as she untied the ribbons that held it together and busied herself with the interior. "I do not want to quarrel," she continued, "but I should like to tell you how I feel during such work. As young girls we become accustomed to being precise with our fingers and to letting our thoughts wander. Both habits remain with us, as we gradually learn to complete the most intricate and delicate work, and I will not deny that I have always attached to each work of this sort thoughts of people, of situations, of joy and sorrow. And so a project once begun became dear to me, and the finished article, I may well say, precious. As such the humblest piece had some significance, the simplest of projects assumed worth, and the most challenging had more only because the memories bound up with it were richer and more complete. Thus I always felt I could offer such items to friends and loved ones, or to respected and eminent people. They recognized this, too, and knew that I was presenting them with some part of my self, which, though multifaceted and ineffable, was, when embodied in a pleasing gift, gladly received as a friendly greeting."

Such a charming confession, to be sure, hardly left room for an answer. Still, the companion was able to reply with some well-turned words. The major, however, who had long treasured the graceful wisdom of Roman writers and poets and had committed their luminous formulations to memory, recalled several lines that would have been fitting here, but took care not to recite them or even mention them, lest he seem a pedant. Not to appear tongue-tied and lacking in wit, however, he attempted on the spur of the moment a paraphrase in prose, which, however, was not very successful, with the result that the conversation almost came to a halt.

The older lady therefore reached for a book she had put down at the arrival of the caller. It was a collection of poems with which the two friends had just been occupied. This provided an opportunity to speak of the art of poetry, but the discussion did not long remain general, for the ladies soon admitted confidingly that they were informed of the major's poetic talents. His son, who did not conceal his own aspirations to the honorable title of poet, had spoken to them of his father's poems and even recited a few, his underlying purpose being to adorn himself with a poetic legacy and, as is youth's wont, discreetly portray himself as advancing and surpassing the abilities of his father. But the major, who sought to retreat, since he wished to be known simply as a man of letters and a dilettante, sought, since no escape was left to him, at least to dodge the attack by characterizing the type of poetry at which he had tried his hand as second-rate and almost spurious. He could not deny that he had made some attempts at what has been called descriptive and, in a certain sense, didactic verse.

The ladies, especially the younger one, championed this type of poetry, saying, "If we want to live reasonably and calmly, which is, ultimately, everyone's wish and intention, what use have we for hustle and bustle which arbitrarily stirs us up without giving us anything, which makes us restless, only to abandon us to ourselves after all. Since I, for my part, would not willingly dispense with poetry, I find immeasurably more pleasant poems that transport me into serene regions, where I seem to rediscover myself, and make me feel the deep value of the simple pastoral life; they lead me through bushy groves to the forest, and imperceptibly to a height overlooking a lake, where, on the other side, first cultivated hills, then more distant tree-covered slopes, and finally blue mountains would form a satisfying picture. When all of this is offered to me in clear rhythm and rhyme, I on my sofa am grateful that the poet has evoked a picture in my imagination that I can enjoy with more tranquility than if I had actually set eyes on it after a fatiguing hike, and possibly under other adverse circumstances."

The major, who saw the present conversation merely as a means to further his ends, tried to turn again to lyric poetry, in which his son's achievements were truly commendable. The ladies did not precisely contradict him, but sought to divert him jokingly from the path on which he had embarked, especially since he seemed to be alluding to passionate poems with which his son had attempted to express, not without force and skill, his steadfast devotion to the incomparable lady. "I do not care for poems by lovers," said the fair one, "whether read aloud or sung. Happy lovers arouse our envy before we know it, and the unhappy ones are always tedious."

At this, the older woman took up the conversation. Turning to her lovely friend, she remarked, "Why do we digress so much, and waste time on formalities toward a person we honor and love? Should we not confide to him that we have already had the pleasure of becoming partly acquainted with that delightful poem of his which presents the gallant passion for the hunt in all its particulars, and ask him not to withhold the rest of it from us? Your son," she continued, "has recited various sections from memory with enthusiasm, and made us curious to see how it fits together."

When the father wished to return once again to his son's talents and underscore them, the ladies made this impossible by interpreting it as an obvious stratagem for indirectly refusing to fulfill their request. Nor did he escape until he had promised unconditionally to send them the poem. After this, the conversation took a turn that hindered him from saying any more on his son's behalf, especially since the latter had advised against any importunities.

Since it seemed time for him to take his leave, and our friend made gestures in that direction, the pretty widow said with a sort of embarrassment, which only increased her loveliness, as she carefully straightened the freshly tied bow of the portfolio, "Poets and lovers have long had the reputation, alas, that their promises and assurances are not very trustworthy; forgive me, therefore, if I dare to cast doubt on the word of a man of honor and, instead of requiring a pledge or earnest money from you, rather give you one of my own. Take this portfolio; it has some resemblance to your hunting poem: many memories are attached to it, and much time went into its making, and now it is finally completed. Use it as a courier to deliver your delightful work to us."

The major was deeply touched by this unexpected offering. The delicate splendor of the gift had so little relation to what usually surrounded him, to the other things he used, that even when it was proffered, he could hardly take possession of it. However, he collected himself, and since his memory never lacked for some traditional gem, a classical passage sprang instantly to mind. To quote it would have been pedantic, but he was inspired to improvise a clever paraphrase, combining cordial thanks with a delicate compliment. And so the scene ended in a manner gratifying to all the participants.

He thus saw himself, not without embarrassment, involved in a pleasant relationship. He had agreed, had promised to send the poem, to write. If the circumstances seemed to some degree displeasing, he nevertheless had to consider it fortunate that he should maintain pleasant relations with a lady who, with all her remarkable qualities, was to be so closely tied to him. He took his leave, therefore, not without some inner satisfaction, for how should a poet not feel encouraged when the fruit of his assiduous labor, which has lain for so long unnoticed, receives quite unexpectedly kindly attention.

Upon his return to his quarters, the major sat down to write to his good sister and inform her of everything. As was only natural, his description bore traces of a certain exaltation that he himself was experiencing, heightened moreover by the periodic interruptions of his son.

The letter made a very mixed impression on the baroness. Even though the situation, which seemed to promote and hasten the union of her brother with Hilarie, ought to have satisfied her completely, she did not care for the fair widow, although she would not have bothered to analyze the reasons. On this occasion we make the following observation:

A man should never confide his enthusiasm for any woman to another one. They know each other too well to feel themselves worthy of such exclusive adoration. In their view, men are like customers in a shop, where the shopkeeper has the advantage of knowing his wares, and can take the opportunity to present them in the best light. The customer, by contrast, always enters the shop with a kind of innocence. He needs the wares, wants them, and thinks them desirable, but seldom knows how to examine them with expert eyes. The former knows full well what he is offering, but the latter not always what he is receiving. But this is one of those elements in human life and society that cannot be changed; indeed, it is as praiseworthy as it is necessary, since all our wishing and wooing, all our buying and trading, depends upon it.

Guided by instinct more than reflection, the baroness could feel entirely satisfied neither with the passion of the son nor with the favorable account of the father. The happy turn of events took her by surprise, but a premonition based on the double disparity in ages could not be dismissed. Hilarie is too young for her brother, the widow not young enough for the major's son. Nevertheless, the affair has begun its course, and cannot be halted. A devout wish that all might go well vented itself in a gentle sigh. To ease her heart, she took up her pen and wrote to a friend already known to us, wise in human affairs. Having filled in the history, she wrote as follows:

"This sort of young, seductive widow is not unfamiliar to me. She seems to shun female company and tolerates about her only a woman who can do her no damage, who flatters her and, should her unspoken qualities fail to shine forth clearly enough, knows how to call attention to them with words and skillful management. The audience and the participants for such a performance must be men; thence arises the necessity of attracting men and holding them fast. I think no ill of the pretty woman; she seems respectable and prudent enough. But such an avid vanity may well make concessions to circumstances, and the worst aspect of it, in my opinion, is that not everything is considered and deliberate; a certain happy instinct guides her and protects her. In such a born coquette nothing is more dangerous than audacity spawned by innocence."

The major, having returned to the family estates, devoted his waking hours to inspections and investigations. He now had occasion to observe that any grand concept, however correct and carefully formulated, is subject in its realization to so many obstacles and so much unpredictable interference that the original idea almost disappears and at times seems to have perished utterly, until in the midst of all the confusion, the possibility of success once more appears, when we see time, as the best ally of unbending persistence, extend a helping hand.

And so here, too, the sorry sight of handsome, extensive, neglected, abused estates might have seemed a hopeless situation, had not the sensible observations of perceptive agronomists made it possible to predict that a few years' intelligent and honest management would suffice to restore life to that which had withered and motion to that which was stagnating, so that at last, through order and industry, one might reach one's goal.

The ease-loving marshal had arrived, accompanied by a solemn solicitor, who, however, gave the major fewer worries than his client. For the latter belonged to that species of men who have no goals, or, if they see any goal before them, reject the proper measures to achieve it. Daily and hourly comfort was an absolute necessity of his life. After long hesitation, he was finally ready to rid himself of his creditors, to shake off the burden of his estates, to set his disorderly household to rights, and to enjoy a respectable and secure income in peace, but not to relinquish the least of his previous usages.

In general, he acceded to everything that would place the brother and sister in unambiguous possession of the estates, particularly of the principal estate. But he would not completely relinquish his claim to a certain pavilion on the grounds, where every year on his birthday he gathered his oldest friends and newest acquaintances, or, furthermore, to the ornamental garden that linked the pavilion with the main building. All the furniture was to remain in this pleasure house. The engravings on the walls, as well as the fruit from the espaliers, were to be reserved for him alone. Peaches and strawberries of the choicest varieties, large and tasty pears and apples, but especially one sort of small, drab apple, which he had been wont for many years to present to the widowed princess, were to be faithfully delivered to him. Other stipulations followed, of little significance, but uncommonly troublesome to the master, tenants, stewards, and gardeners.

The marshal was, by the bye, in the best of humors, since he persisted in thinking that at last everything would work itself out according to his wishes, as his frivolous nature had envisioned. So he ordered excellent meals, spent several hours a day in unstrenuous hunting for the sake of exercise, told story after story, and showed a cheery face throughout. He took his leave in the same genial manner, thanked the major heartily for his brotherly conduct, asked for another small sum of money, and had the little drab golden apples, which had been especially good this year, carefully packed, and, with this treasure, which he intended as a welcome gift for the princess, he set off for the widow's residence, where he indeed found a gracious and friendly reception.

The major, for his part, was left with the very opposite feelings, and would have despaired at the constraints imposed upon him, had he not been aided by that feeling which buoys up a man of action when he is called to resolve a tangled situation and may hope to see it disentangled.

Fortunately the solicitor was an upright man, who, since he had so much other business to attend to, brought this matter quickly to a close. Fortunately, too, a servant of the marshal's came forward, who, for modest recompense, promised to help in the operations, which boded well for their successful outcome. But gratifying though all this was, as a man of integrity the major felt that in working his way through this affair he had to dirty his hands considerably in order to clean it up.

When a break in the work left him some leisure, he hurried to his estate, where, mindful of the promise that he had made to the fair widow and that he had not forgotten, he took out his poems, which were put away in good order; at the same time he came upon many albums and commonplace books containing excerpts from his reading of both ancient and modern authors. Given his fondness for Horace and the Roman poets, the majority of the quotations were from these, and it struck him that the quotations referred mostly to regret for time past, for situations and feelings now flown, never to return. The following quotation may stand for many others:

Heu!
Quae mens est hodie, cur eadem non puero fuit?
Vel cur his animis incolumes non redeunt genae!

How comes it that today my mood
Is cheerful, and so clear my mind!
When, with the fresher blood of youth,
I felt so wild, in gloom confined?
But when old age its victim tweaks
However calm I may remain,
I think back on those rosy cheeks,
And wish that they were mine again.

Having quickly found his hunting poem among his well-ordered papers, our friend looked with pleasure at the carefully lettered fair copy he had painstakingly penned years before, in Latin script and octavo format. The generous proportions of the precious portfolio easily accommodated it, and an author could hardly have found his work more splendidly bound. It was essential to enclose a few lines, but prose would scarcely do. The Ovid passage came once more to mind, and he now thought that a verse paraphrase, as previously one in prose, would best serve his turn. The passage went:

Nec factas solum vestes spectare juvabat,
Tum quoque dum fierent; tantus decor adfuit arti.

Translated:

I saw it once in expert fingers
—That moment gladly I recall—
It first unfolds, then finished lingers

In glory which surpasses all.
Now it belongs to me, 'tis true,
And still I inwardly confess:
I wish there yet were more to do,
To me the making was the best.

But our friend was only momentarily satisfied with this translation. He chided himself for having substituted a dreary abstract noun for the elegant inflected verb *dum fierent*, and was vexed that no matter how he pondered he could not improve those lines. His preference for the ancient languages suddenly reawakened, and the luster of the German Parnassus, to which he had in fact secretly aspired, seemed to grow dim.

At last, however, when he had decided that this pretty compliment was after all well-turned, as long as it was not compared to the original, and that a lady would doubtless take it kindly, another scruple occurred to him: that one could not be gallant in verse without seeming to be in love, so that, as a prospective father-in-law, he would be playing an odd role. The worst, however, was still to come: Ovid's lines are spoken by Arachne, a weaver as skilled as she is lovely and delicate. Since however, Arachne had been transformed into a spider by jealous Minerva, there was the danger that a pretty woman compared to a spider, even indirectly, might be seen as hovering in the middle of her web. He could imagine that among the cultivated company that surrounded the lady a learned man might be found who would ferret out the reference. How our friend extricated himself from his perplexity we do not ourselves know, and we must consider this one of those cases over which even the Muses permit themselves the roguery to draw a veil. Suffice it to say that the hunting poem was dispatched, but of the poem itself we have a few more words to add.

The reader of it is entertained by the unabashed love of the hunt and whatever may further it. Pleasure is taken in the change of the seasons, which arouses and stirs the hunter's enthusiasm. The peculiarities of all the creatures that are stalked and hunted, the various types of men who surrender to the pleasures and the hardships of the chase, the chance circumstances that help or hinder—all of this, especially in regard to fowl, was set forth in most spirited fashion, and with great originality.

Nothing was omitted, from the way the wood grouse spreads its tail, to the second migration of the snipe, to the construction of a blind—all was accurately seen, clearly recorded, ardently traced, and presented in a light, witty, often ironic tone.

Nevertheless, an elegiac theme pervaded the entire poem. It had been composed more as a farewell to these particular joys of life, a stance which, to be sure, lent the poem an aura of pleasurable experience and had a most salutary effect, but ultimately, like the Latin maxims, left a feeling of emptiness after the enjoyment. Whether from looking through these papers, or from a momentary indisposition, the major did not feel happy. At the parting of the ways where he now stood, he suddenly became acutely aware that the passing years take away one by one the fine gifts they once brought. Missing his visit to the baths, having the summer slip by without any enjoyment, lacking his customary regular exercise—all this brought on physical discomforts that he took for real infirmities and regarded perhaps more impatiently than was proper.

Even as women find extremely painful the moment when their previously undisputed beauty first comes into question, so men of a certain age, although still in their full vigor, experience the slightest sense of waning powers as extremely disagreeable, indeed, alarming.

Another occurrence, however, which should have proved disquieting, helped him recover his good mood. His cosmetic valet, who had not left his side even on this country visit, seemed for some time to be taking a different tack, required by the major's early rising, his daily rides and rounds, and the presence of many busy people, and, when the marshal was there, of many who were not busy. For some time now he had spared the major all the petty measures that only an actor might justifiably bother with. But he insisted all the more sternly on a few crucial points that had previously been obscured by trivial hocus-pocus. Everything that did not merely further the appearance of health but truly preserved health was stressed, especially moderation in all things and relaxation after eventful times, as well as the care of the skin and hair, of eyebrows and teeth, of hands and nails, to whose elegant shaping and appropriate length the expert had been attending for some time. In the process moderation was forcefully urged again and again in anything that might upset his equilibrium. Hereupon this mentor in the preservation of beauty asked to be dismissed, since he was no longer of any use to the gentleman. It might be deduced that the man was eager to rejoin his previous patron, so that he might continue to share in the varied and numerous pleasures of the theatrical life.

In truth it did the major much good to be his own master again. An intelligent man needs only to observe moderation, and he will be happy. He could once more freely indulge in his customary exercise of riding, hunting, and all that went with it, and in such moments of solitude, the image of Hilarie would once more appear joyfully before him, and he slipped into the role of a bridegroom, perhaps the pleasantest one permitted us within the bounds of polite society.

For several months now the members of the family had remained without particular news of one another. The major was busy in the capital with the final negotiations for permits and certifications related to the disposition of the estate. The baroness and Hilarie were devoting their energies to preparing the finest, most ample trousseau. The major's son, passionately serving his lovely lady, seemed forgetful of all else. Winter had arrived, and surrounded all the country houses with dismal rainstorms and early darkness.

Had someone lost his way in the vicinity of the manor on a dreary November night and by the faint light of a clouded moon beheld fields, meadows, groves, hills, and bushes spread out dimly before him, but suddenly turning a corner had caught sight of an entire row of lighted windows in a long building, he would surely have expected to meet a festively attired company within. But how astonished he would have been when, conducted up the lighted staircase by a few servants, he had seen only three ladies—the baroness, Hilarie, and a chambermaid—sitting surrounded by cheerful furnishings in the well-lit chambers with bright walls, warm and cozy.

Since we may imagine that we have surprised the baroness in a festive moment, it must be observed that this brilliant illumination is not to be considered unusual here, but is one of the customs the lady had retained from her earlier life. As the daughter of a chief lady-in-waiting, brought up at court, she was accustomed to prefer winter to all other seasons, and to make the luxury of generous lighting an essential element of all her pleasures. Wax candles were never in short supply, but in addition, one of her oldest servants was so fond of technical advances that no sooner was a new type of lamp invented than he tried to introduce it somewhere or other in the manor. Thus it was that in some areas the lighting had gained considerably, but in others partial darkness prevailed.

The baroness had given up the condition of a lady at court to marry, for love, and in full realization of the consequences, a large landowner and serious farmer. Her perceptive husband, seeing that rural life at first did not appeal to her, had, with the agreement of his neighbors and even the sanction of the government, had the roads for several miles around so much improved that there were no better connections with neighboring estates anywhere. Yet the chief aim of this laudable enterprise was to enable the lady to travel about wherever she liked, especially in good weather. Winters, on the other hand, she would spend happily at home with him, since he contrived lighting to make the nights as bright as day. After the death of her husband, the baroness found sufficient employment in devoted care of her daughter, while the frequent visits of her brother supplied affectionate conversation, and the accustomed brightness of the surroundings comfort that might be taken for true contentment.

But on this particular day the lighting was truly fitting. For in one of the rooms we see what seem to be Christmas gifts, striking to the eye and splendid. The clever chambermaid had persuaded the servant to increase the lighting, and had collected and spread out everything that had been prepared thus far for Hilarie's trousseau, actually with the sly intention of calling attention to what was still lacking, rather than to display what had already been accomplished. All the necessities were there, in the best materials and the finest workmanship. There was also no lack of whimsical luxuries, despite which Ananette contrived to point out one gap after another, where one might just as well have seen perfect completeness. Though the eye was dazzled by all the household linens, imposingly laid out, though the cambrics, muslins, and all the many delicate stuffs of that sort, whatever they may be called, threw off an abundance of light, there were no colored silks, the purchase of which had been wisely postponed, since fashions in these fabrics were always changing, and the ladies wanted the newest thing to crown and complete the collection.

After this pleasant viewing, they returned to their customary, though varied, evening amusements. The baroness, who knew well what lends a young lady, wherever fate may lead her, not only a beautiful exterior but also inward grace, and knew what makes her presence sought after, had managed in these rural circumstances to introduce such diverse and educational occupations that Hilarie, despite her youth, seemed at home with everything, found no discussion beyond her, yet still behaved fully in accordance with her years. To explain how this was achieved would take us too far afield; suffice it to say that this evening fulfilled the pattern of their previous life. Interesting reading, charming piano-playing, lovely singing whiled away the hours, as always in pleasing and orderly manner, but now with special significance. A third person was in their thoughts, a beloved and respected man, for whose sake these and many other things were practiced, to give him a most loving reception. It was a bridal feeling, which inspired not only Hilarie with the sweetest sensations; her mother, with her delicate sensibility, innocently shared in it, and even Ananette, usually merely clever and energetic, succumbed to certain distant hopes that made her imagine her absent sweetheart as returning, as present. In this manner the sentiments of all three women, each lovable in her way, had come into accord with the surrounding brightness, the soothing warmth, and the pervading sense of well-being.

Chapter Five

Loud pounding and shouts at the outermost gate, demanding and threatening voices, arguing, the glare of lights and torches in the courtyard, interrupted the gentle singing. The commotion died down before its cause could be known, yet all was not quiet; on the stairway there was noise and the agitated voices of men coming nearer. The door sprang open without any warning; the women were horrified. Flavio plunged into the room. His aspect was terrifying, his hair in disorder, some of it bristling, some hanging limp in rain-soaked strands. His clothes were in tatters, as though he had been storming through thorns and thickets, and horribly dirty, as though he had waded through mud and marsh.

"My father!" he cried, "Where is my father?" The women stood there, transfixed. The grizzled huntsman, his oldest and most devoted attendant, entering close behind him, exclaimed to him, "Your father is not here, calm yourself! Here is your aunt, here is your cousin! Look!"

"Not here! Then let me go, so I can look for him. He alone must hear it, then I die. Away with these lights, this daylight—it blinds me, it destroys me."

The household doctor appeared, took the young man's hand, carefully feeling his pulse; several servants stood about anxiously. "What am I doing on these carpets? I am spoiling them, destroying them. My misery drips down on them, my vile fate sullies them." He pushed his way toward the door, and they used this attempt to lead him away and bring him to the distant guest room, which his father usually occupied. Mother and daughter stood paralyzed. They had seen Orestes pursued by the Furies, not idealized by art, but in dreadful, revolting reality, which, in contrast to the comfortable rooms gleaming with candlelight, was all the more terrible. Paralyzed, the women looked at one another, and each thought she saw in the eyes of the other the terrifying image that had printed itself so deeply on her own.

Half recovered, the baroness dispatched servant after servant to bring back word. They were somewhat reassured to hear that Flavio had been undressed and dried, and was being tended to. Half aware, half unconscious, he did not resist. In reply to their repeated inquiries, patience was urged.

Finally the anxious women learned that he had been bled and pacified by every means possible. He was quiet now; it was hoped he would sleep.

Midnight approached, and the baroness wanted to see him if he was asleep. The doctor opposed it, the doctor gave way. Hilarie pressed in with her mother. The room was dark; only one candle glimmered behind its green shade. Little could be seen, nothing heard. The baroness approached the bed; Hilarie, full of longing, seized the light and illuminated the slumbering figure. He lay with his face turned away, but one delicate ear, a rounded cheek, now rather pale, peeped charmingly from amidst the once more curling locks; the still hand, with its long, strong, yet sensitive fingers drew her unsteady glance. Hilarie, herself breathing softly, thought she could hear soft breaths. She brought the candle nearer, like Psyche in danger of disturbing the healing sleep. The doctor took the candle from her and lighted the ladies to their rooms.

How these good people, worthy of all sympathy, passed the hours of the night, remains a secret from us. The next morning, however, from early on, both seemed very impatient. Their questions were endless, their wish to see the sufferer restrained but urgent. Only toward noon did the doctor allow them a short visit.

The baroness approached, and Flavio extended his hand: "Forgive me, dearest Aunt, have patience, perhaps not for long." Hilarie stepped forward, and to her, too, he offered his right hand: "Greetings, dear Sister." The words pierced her to the heart, and he did not release her hand; they gazed at one another, the loveliest of pairs, a contrast in the best sense. The young man's glittering black eyes harmonized with his dusky, tousled hair. She, on the other hand, seemed to stand there in heavenly peace, though in fact the shattering experience was now compounded by the portentous present. The title "Sister"—her deepest feelings were in turmoil.

The baroness spoke: "How are you feeling, dear Nephew?"

"Not too badly, but I have been ill-treated."

"In what way?"

"They bled me; that was cruel. They got rid of it; that was shameless. It does not belong to me; it belongs to her, all of it." With these words his entire being seemed transformed, but with burning tears he buried his face in the pillow.

On Hilarie's face her mother saw an expression of horror. It was as though the dear child were seeing the gates of Hell open before her and for the first time and forever beheld something monstrous. In passionate haste she ran the length of the great hall and threw herself on the sofa in the alcove at the farthest end. Her mother followed her and asked the question whose answer she unfortunately already knew. Looking about her strangely, Hilarie cried, "The blood, the blood—it belongs to her, all to her, and she is not worthy of it. The poor, unhappy boy!" With these words her heart found release in a flood of bitter tears.

Who would be so bold as to reveal the circumstances that developed out of what had gone before, to bring to light the inner calamity that grew out of this first encounter? It had been highly damaging to the patient as well, or so at least the doctor asserted, who came often enough to report and give comfort, but felt obliged to prohibit any further contact. This order was willingly obeyed, for the daughter did not dare wish what her mother would not have allowed, and so the command of the sagacious man prevailed. However, he brought the reassuring news that Flavio had asked for writing materials, and had written something down, but quickly hidden it under the bedclothes. Now curiosity was added to the prevailing restlessness and impatience; those were trying hours. After some time, however, he brought them a page written in a fine, flowing hand, though in haste. The lines ran as follows:

The birth of wretched man is fraught with wonder,
In wondering erring man goes far astray.
And toward what dark, mysterious, hidden threshold
Feel out uncertain steps the unmarked way?
Then, in the midst of heaven's light and glory
I see, I feel dark night, and death, hell's fury.

Here the noble art of poetry could once more demonstrate its curative powers. Inwardly fused with music, it heals the heart's sorrows from the very core by intensifying them, evoking them, and dispelling them in cathartic pain. The doctor was certain that the young man would soon be cured; physically sound, he would soon recover his spirits if the passion weighing on his mind could be removed or alleviated. Hilarie meditated on a response; she sat at the piano and tried to set the sufferer's lines to music. She did not succeed; nothing in her own soul echoed to such deep sorrow. Yet in this attempt rhythm and rhyme gradually adapted themselves to her own disposition, so that she could respond to the poem with soothing serenity, taking time to compose and polish the following stanza:

Although in pain and torment yet you wander,
Youth's happiness still lies along your way.
With bold and manly footsteps cross that threshold,
Approach the realm where friendship's light holds sway.
There, in the midst of those who love you dearly,
Let waters from life's fountain now flow clearly.

The family doctor delivered the message. It succeeded; the youth responded more calmly. Hilarie continued gently, and little by little a brighter view and clearer ground seemed to be gained. Perhaps it will be granted to us one day to communicate the entire course of this delightful cure. Suffice it to say that some time passed very agreeably in such pursuits, and the way was prepared for a calm reunion, which the doctor did not intend to postpone any longer than necessary.

In the meantime, the baroness had engaged herself with ordering and arranging old papers, and this occupation, so suitable for present conditions, had a remarkable effect on her agitated mind. She looked back over many years of her life, in which threatening misfortunes had not come to pass; to contemplate them strengthened her courage for the moment. She was especially moved by the memory of a lovely friendship with Makarie at a time when circumstances were trying. The splendor of that unique woman once more came to mind, and she promptly decided to turn to her now as well, for to whom else could she confide her feelings, to whom reveal her hopes and fears?

While tidying up, she also came upon, among other things, a miniature of her brother, and sighed with a smile at the resemblance to his son. Hilarie surprised her at this moment, took possession of the portrait, and she, too, was strangely moved by the resemblance.

Thus some time passed; finally, with the doctor's approval and in his company, Flavio came, announced, to breakfast. The ladies had been apprehensive of this first appearance. But often in significant, even terrible moments, something cheerful, even comic will occur, and this happened now. The son came entirely in his father's clothing. Since his own clothes were unusable, he had drawn on the major's outdoor and indoor wardrobes that were kept at his sister's for his convenience in hunting and family activities. The baroness smiled and maintained her composure. Hilarie was overcome in a way she did not understand. She turned her face away, and in this moment the young man could not utter either a friendly word or a polite phrase. To help the gathering out of its embarrassment, the doctor began a comparison of the two figures. The father was somewhat taller, he remarked, hence the coat was rather too long; the son, however, was broader in the shoulders, for which reason the coat was too tight. Both discrepancies gave the masquerade a comical cast.

By dwelling on these details, they got past the danger of the moment. Yet for Hilarie, the resemblance between the youthful image of the father and the vivid living presence of the son remained uncanny, even oppressive.

But now we would dearly wish to have the next period described in all particulars by some delicate feminine hand, since we ourselves are restricted by our own manner and style to the most general aspects. For at this point the influence of poetry must once again be spoken of.

It could not be denied that our Flavio had a certain talent, but he required passionate, tangible emotion in order to produce something truly excellent. For that reason, then, almost all the poems dedicated to that irresistible woman appeared powerful and praiseworthy, and now, read aloud expressively in the presence of a lovely and charming girl, were bound to achieve no little effect.

A woman who sees another woman loved passionately falls easily into the role of confidante. She harbors a secret, scarcely conscious feeling that it would not be displeasing to be gently elevated to the place of the adored one. Their conversation, indeed, became more and more significant. It touched upon dialogue poems, of the sort a lover likes to write, since he can have his beloved reply more or less what he would wish her to say, albeit in modest form, and what he could hardly expect to hear from her own lovely mouth. Such poems also were read aloud with Hilarie, and since they read from only one manuscript, at which they both had to look in order to come in on cue, and therefore both had to hold the booklet, it happened that, as they were sitting side by side, their bodies and their hands gradually moved ever nearer, until finally their wrists touched, quite naturally, under cover of the papers.

But in this agreeable state of affairs, with all the charming pleasure that flowed from it, Flavio was tormented by a painful worry, which he concealed but poorly. Continually longing for his father to arrive, he let it be seen that he had something of the greatest importance to confide to him; with a little thought this secret would not have been difficult to divine. In a moment of high emotion the importunate youth must have pushed matters to extremes, and the charming lady must have decisively rejected him and abolished and destroyed the hopes to which he had clung so obstinately. We would not presume to describe the scene that must have taken place, for fear we might lack the requisite youthful ardor. Suffice it to say that he was so beside himself that he impetuously fled his garrison without leave and, in order to find his father, desperately struck out through night, storm, and rain toward the estate of his aunt, arriving as we recently saw him. With the restoration of sober thoughts, he now saw vividly the consequences of such a step, and, in the continued absence of his father, his only possible hope of intercession, he had no notion how to compose himself or rescue himself.

How astonished and overcome he was, therefore, when a letter from his colonel was handed to him. He broke the familiar seal with fear and trembling, only to find himself addressed in the most friendly manner, and to learn that his leave was being extended for an additional month.

However inexplicable this kindness seemed, he was nevertheless freed of a burden which had begun to weigh on his mind even more alarmingly than his rejection in love. He could now fully appreciate the happiness of being so well cared for by his kindly relatives; he could enjoy the presence of Hilarie, and after a short time was once again possessed of all those pleasant and sociable qualities that for a time had made him indispensable to the fair widow and her circle, and which had been obscured only by his peremptory demand for her hand.

In such a mood it was far easier to await the arrival of his father, and in any case intervening natural events stirred them to greater activity. Incessant rain, which until now had confined them to the manor, was falling everywhere in great quantity and had flooded river after river. Dams had burst, and the area below the manor lay like a smooth lake, from which villages, farms, larger and smaller estates, set as they were on high ground, stuck out like islands.

They were prepared for such rare, though foreseeable, situations. The mistress gave orders, and the servants carried them out. After the first, general, rescue measures, bread was baked, cattle were slaughtered, and fishing boats plied back and forth, bringing aid and provisions to the far corners of the land. All went well; the kindly offerings were received gladly and gratefully, and in only one place were the local selectmen distrusted in their distribution. Flavio took over the project, and steered his fully laden boat quickly and successfully to its destination. The simple task, handled simply, was accomplished splendidly. Our young man also performed an errand which Hilarie had entrusted to him as he set out. At the very time of these misfortunes, a woman in whom Hilarie had taken particular interest was due to deliver a baby. Flavio found the new mother, and brought home both general gratitude and her particular thanks. Expeditions of this sort were bound to produce many stories. Although no deaths had occurred, there was much to tell of miraculous escapes, of strange, amusing, even comical events: interesting descriptions were given of many perilous situations. Suffice it to say that Hilarie suddenly felt an irresistible desire to undertake such an expedition too, to visit the new mother, bring gifts and spend a few pleasant hours with her.

After some resistance on the part of her good mother, Hilarie's eagerness for the adventure prevailed. We freely admit that when we first learned of this incident we were rather worried that some danger might be lurking—the boat running aground, capsizing, mortal danger to the fair one, a dramatic rescue by the brave youth, so that the loose bond between them might be tightened. But there was no question of any of this; the excursion went smoothly; the new mother was visited and received her gifts, and the presence of the doctor was not without good effect. If now and then a slight obstacle arose, if an apparently dangerous moment seemed to unnerve the rowers, it ended in jest, with each accusing the other of an anxious expression, greater nervousness, or a frightened gesture. Meanwhile their mutual trust had increased considerably; the habit of seeing each other and being together under all circumstances had grown stronger, and the dangerous position, in which kinship and inclination seemed to justify drawing closer and holding fast to one another, grew ever more acute.

Yet they were to be lured pleasantly farther and farther along this path of love. The skies cleared, and intense cold, appropriate to the season, set in. The waters froze before they could recede. Suddenly the theater of the world changed before all eyes. What once the flood had separated was now connected by the frozen ground. Immediately there came to mind the wonderful art invented in northern climes to glorify the first, brief winter days and to bring new life to the frozen world. The storeroom was opened, and they all looked for their labeled skates, each eager, despite the risk, to be the first to step out on the clean, smooth ice. Among the residents of the manor were many in whom practice had developed great skill, for this sport could be enjoyed almost every year on nearby lakes and the network of canals, though this year offered a much expanded surface.

Now Flavio for the first time felt healthy through and through, and Hilarie, taught by her uncle from her earliest years, proved herself both graceful and strong on the newly created ground. Merrily and more merrily still they glided, now together, now alone, now separated, now united. Parting, normally such sorrow, was converted into an amusing little game, as they fled one another, only to come together again a moment later.

But in the midst of this pleasure and merriment, there was still a multitude of needs. Some places had still been but partially supplied: and now sleighs, drawn by sturdy horses, sped back and forth with the most essential goods; and, what was even more to the region's benefit, the many agricultural products from outlying farms too far from the main road could now be transported to the warehouses in the towns and villages, from which in turn all sorts of goods could be brought back. Thus a region stricken and in bitter need could now be liberated and supplied once more, joined together by a smooth surface open to the skilled and the bold.

The young pair, too, in the midst of their pleasures did not fail to be mindful of various obligations of charity. They visited the new mother, bringing her everything she needed. They visited others as well: old people, whose health had given cause for concern; pastors, with whom they were accustomed to hold edifying conversations, and whom they found even more admirable in this time of trial; small landowners, who in earlier times had rashly chosen to build on dangerously low spots, but this time, protected by well-constructed dikes, had remained unharmed, and after boundless anxiety were now doubly thankful to be alive. Every farm, every house, every family, every individual had a tale to tell; each had become an important person both to himself and to others, and thus each tended to break into the other's story. But talk and action, coming and going, were all conducted in haste, for there was always the danger that a sudden thaw might destroy the entire happy circle of welcome mutual aid, threatening hosts and cutting guests off from their homes.

If their days were spent in such lively and engaging activities, the evenings provided pleasant hours of quite another sort. For ice-skating has the advantage over all other physical exercise that it neither overheats nor tires its devotees. Our limbs seem to become more supple, and every expenditure of strength produces fresh strength, so that finally a blissfully active peace comes over us, and we are tempted to glide on forever.

On this particular day our young pair could not tear itself away from the smooth ice. Each dart toward the illuminated manor, where a large company had already gathered, was abruptly reversed in favor of a return into the distance. They did not want to separate, for fear of losing each other, and each took the other by the hand to be quite certain of the other's presence. But the sweetest variation of all was when their arms rested on one another's shoulders, and their fingertips secretly played with one another's curls.

The full moon rose in the glowing, starry sky, and crowned the magic of the surroundings. They could see one another distinctly again, and each sought in the eye of the other the usual response, but something seemed different. Out of their depths a light seemed to shine forth, hinting at what the mouth wisely left unspoken. Both had a sense of festive well-being.

All of the tall willows and alders along the ditches, all of the low-growing shrubs on hills and hilltops were clearly visible. The stars blazed, the cold had intensified. They felt none of it, and skated down the long glittering reflection of the moon, directly toward the silver planet itself. Then they looked up and saw in the glitter of the reflection the figure of a man floating back and forth. He seemed to be following his shadow; his dark form, surrounded by light, proceeded toward them. Instinctively they turned around, for meeting someone would have been disagreeable. They avoided the figure, which still forged ahead; the figure seemed not to have seen them, and was taking a direct route toward the manor. Then it abandoned this direction and circled several times around the couple, who were now almost frightened. With some cunning they tried to reach the shadows. In full moonlight the other sped toward them. He was very near them now. There was no mistaking Flavio's father.

Hilarie, braking herself in surprise, lost her balance and fell. Flavio was instantly down on one knee, cradling her head in his lap. She hid her face, not knowing what had come over her.

"I will go for a sled. One is just passing down there. I hope she is not hurt. I will meet you here, by these three alders." So spoke the father, and was off and away.

Hilarie pulled herself up, holding onto the youth. "Let us flee!" she cried, "I cannot bear it." She sped off toward the back of the manor house at such a pace that Flavio caught up with her only with difficulty, pleading with her in the most affectionate words.

There is no describing the inner state of the three, astray and adrift on the slippery surface in the moonlight. Suffice it to say, they reached the manor late, the young couple separately, not daring to touch one another, to come close to one another, the father with the empty sled, after he had solicitously hunted far and wide in vain. The music and dancing had already begun. Hilarie, under the pretext of painful injuries from a bad fall, hid herself in her room. Flavio willingly left the leadership of the festivities to some young friends who had already taken charge in his absence. The major did not put in an appearance. He found it peculiar, though not completely unexpected, that his room seemed occupied, with his clothes, linen, and personal effects lying about, but in less order than that to which he was accustomed. The mistress carried out her duties as hostess with exemplary self-control, and how glad she was when all the guests were properly accommodated and finally left her time to clarify things with her brother. That was soon done, but time was needed to recover from the surprise, to comprehend the unexpected turn of events, to dispel doubts, to assuage worries. It was still too early to think of loosing the knot or setting the mind at rest.

Our readers will surely understand that from this point on, in presenting our story, we can no longer offer scenes, but must narrate and reflect if we wish to penetrate the characters' states of mind, on which everything now depends, and portray these adequately.

Thus we shall first report that the major had, since we lost sight of him, been devoting all his time to that family affair, which, though it appeared to be running smoothly, still encountered many unanticipated little obstacles. And indeed, it is not so easy to untangle an old muddle and wind its many threads onto a single spool. Since he often had to be on the move, to attend to the affair in various places and with various people, his sister's letters had reached him but slowly, and not always in order. The news of his son's derangement and illness had been the first to arrive. He then heard something about a leave, which he did not understand. That Hilarie's affection was undergoing a change had been concealed from him, for how could his sister have apprised him of that!

At the tidings of the flood he had hastened his return, but had reached the ice fields only after the frost, whereupon he had equipped himself with skates, and sent his servants and horses toward the manor by a detour. Having proceeded at a smart pace, he was close enough to see the illuminated windows in the distance when he came upon that distressing sight in the brilliant moonlight and fell into the most dreadful confusion.

The transition from inner truth to outer reality is always painful because of the contrast, and should not loving and cleaving fast have the same rights as parting and renouncing? And certainly, when one is wrenched from the other there opens up in the soul a dreadful abyss, in which many a heart has been lost. For as long as love's illusion lasts, it is imbued with invincible truth, and only strong, manly spirits are ennobled and strengthened by the recognition of a mistake. Such a discovery lifts them out of themselves. They stand elevated above their former selves and, since the old road is closed to them, quickly search out a new one on which they may at once embark with renewed courage.

Countless are the perplexities a man finds himself confronting at such a moment. Countless are the means which a resourceful nature can find among its own capabilities, or, if these are not sufficient, which it can identify outside its own sphere.

Fortunately, however, the major had been prepared deep within for such an eventuality by a half-conscious knowledge which had come to him unbidden. Since dismissing the cosmetic valet, and lapsing back into his natural way of life, renouncing his pretensions to the appearance of youth, he had found his sensation of physical well-being somewhat diminished. He sensed how disagreeable it was to change from young lover to tender father; and yet more and more the latter role forced itself upon him. Concern for the future of Hilarie and his family always came first to his mind, while feelings of love, affection, longing to be with her, developed only later. And when he imagined Hilarie in his arms, what he cared about was the happiness he wished to provide her, rather than the bliss of possessing her. Indeed, if he wanted to think of her with unalloyed pleasure, he had first to remember her divine expression of affection and to summon up the moment when she had so unexpectedly pledged herself to him.

But now, when in clearest night he had seen a united young couple before him, had seen his beloved collapse, cradled in the youth's lap, had seen how both ignored his promised return with help, did not wait for him at the clearly designated place, vanished into the night, while he was left in the deepest melancholy—who in the major's place would not feel despair to the depths of his soul?

The family, habitually united and hoping for even closer union, kept apart in dismay; Hilarie stubbornly stayed in her room, while the major braced himself to hear from his son what had led up to this moment. The calamity had been occasioned by an act of feminine wantonness on the part of the fair widow. Lest she lose her hitherto passionate admirer Flavio to another beauty, who betrayed interest in him, she shows him more apparent favor than is proper. Excited and emboldened, he seeks to press his suit to improper lengths, causing first offence and quarrels, then a definitive break, bringing the entire relationship irreparably to an end.

When children commit mistakes that lead to sad consequences, paternal kindness has no choice but to sympathize and, where possible, set matters right, and, should these mistakes prove more trivial than had been feared, to forgive and forget. After brief consideration and discussion, Flavio went off to attend in his father's stead to various matters on the newly acquired estates, and was to stay there until the expiration of his leave, then rejoin his regiment, which had meanwhile been reassigned to another garrison.

For several days the major was occupied with opening the letters and packages which had arrived at his sister's during his prolonged absence. Among the rest he found a communication from his cosmetic friend, the well-preserved actor. He, having been informed by the dismissed servant of the major's condition and of his intention to marry, blithely outlined the reservations to be considered in such an undertaking. He treated the affair in his own terms and suggested that for a man of certain years the most dependable cosmetic method was to abstain from the fair sex and enjoy an honorable and comfortable freedom. With a smile the major handed the letter to his sister, with a playful remark, to be sure, but pointing out the importance of its message seriously enough. In the meanwhile he had also composed a poem, whose metrical rendering we cannot give at the moment, but whose content, conveyed through elegant similes and graceful phrasing, went as follows:

"The waning moon, which shines well enough at night, pales before the rising sun. The infatuation of old age disappears in the presence of passionate youth. The spruce, which appears fresh and strong all through the winter, in spring looks brown and discolored beside the newly greening birch."

We would not, however, credit either philosophy or poetry with being the critical help in bringing about a final resolution. For as a small event can have the weightiest consequences, it can often tip the balance, when minds are wavering and the decision can go either way. The major had recently lost one of his front teeth, and feared he might lose the other. An artificial replacement was unthinkable, given his convictions, and to court a young beloved with such a defect began to seem thoroughly humiliating, especially now, when he found himself under the same roof with her. Either earlier or later such an occurrence might perhaps have had little effect, but precisely at this moment such an event must be extremely distasteful to one accustomed to a sound body. It is as though the keystone of his physical being were gone, and the entire structure now threatened to collapse, piece by piece.

In any case, the major soon spoke understandingly and sensibly with his sister about the apparently so confused situation. They both had to admit that by this detour they had actually reached the goal, or were very close to it, from which, through a chance external factor, the mistake of an inexperienced child, they had thoughtlessly strayed. They found nothing more natural than to persist on this course, to arrange a union of the two children, and then to devote to them, loyally and unceasingly, all the parental solicitude for which they had been able to procure the means.

In full agreement with her brother, the baroness went to Hilarie in her room. She was sitting at the piano and singing to her own accompaniment. When her mother entered, she invited her with a bright look and a nod of her head to listen. The song was a pleasant, soothing one, expressing a mood that could not have been more to the mother's liking. When she had finished, Hilarie stood up, and before the judicious older woman could begin what she had to say, she began to speak. "Dearest Mother! It was good that we kept silent for so long on the most crucial matter. I am grateful that until now you have not touched this chord. But now it is high time that we declare ourselves, if that suits you. How do you see the situation?"

The baroness, well pleased to find her daughter's mood so tranquil and mild, at once began a circumspect review of the past, and of her brother's personality and merits. She conceded that the one superior man with whom she was closely acquainted was bound to make a strong impression on a young girl's unattached heart, and that the girl might come to feel not childlike respect and trust but inclination, love, and finally passion. Hilarie listened attentively and by affirmative expressions and gestures indicated her full agreement. Her mother went on to the son, and the other lowered her long eyelashes. Since the speaker could not find such flattering arguments for the son as for the father, she focused on their similarity and upon the advantages conferred on the son by youth, so that he, once chosen as a completely suitable life companion, promised in time to live up fully to his father's example. Here, too, Hilarie seemed in agreement, though a somewhat graver look and a cast-down eye betrayed an emotion entirely natural in this case. The lecture now proceeded to the external favorable circumstances, which seemed virtually decisive. The newly reached settlement, the fine income for the present, the prospects opening up in several directions—all these points were set forth fully in accordance with the truth, since, finally, there had been no lack of hints (as Hilarie herself must be able to recall) when she and her cousin had been growing up together, that they were betrothed, if only in play. From all that had been said, the mother drew the obvious conclusion that the union of the young people could now take place without delay, with the full approval of herself and Hilarie's uncle.

Hilarie, with serene gaze and voice, replied that she could not immediately accept this conclusion, and beautifully and sweetly took issue with it on grounds with which any sensitive person will sympathize, and which we shall not attempt to express in words.

Rational people, when they have thought out a sensible way to eliminate this or that problem and reach this or that goal, and have clarified and weighed all the conceivable arguments, find it most disagreeable when those who should be helping to further their own happiness turn out to be of quite another mind, and for reasons hidden deep in the heart oppose what is both commendable and necessary. They exchanged arguments without convincing one another. Reason could make no inroads on feeling, while feeling would not bow to the demands of utility and necessity. The discussion grew heated, and the sharpness of common sense pierced the already wounded heart, which no longer spoke moderately but passionately revealed its true condition, until the mother retreated, astounded at the nobility and dignity of the young girl, who energetically and truthfully articulated the unseemliness, nay, the infamy of such a union.

The reader may well imagine in what perplexity the baroness returned to her brother. Perhaps he may also infer, though not completely, how the major stood before his sister, inwardly flattered by this determined refusal, without hope and yet consoled, freed of any humiliation and feeling compensated by this event, in his innermost soul, for what had become a most delicate question of honor. For the moment he concealed his reaction from his sister and hid his painful satisfaction by saying what was perfectly natural in this situation: that they must not rush anything, but must allow the good child time to choose the newly opened path, which was now more or less obvious, of her own accord.

But we can hardly expect our readers to deduce from the intense inner states of our characters what would be their outward actions, upon which now so much depended. While the baroness left her daughter complete freedom to pass her days pleasantly with music and singing, with drawing and embroidery, and to entertain herself and her mother with reading and reading aloud, the major occupied himself, as spring was approaching, with putting the family affairs in order. His son, who now saw himself as a future landowner and, as he could hardly doubt, the happy spouse of Hilarie, began for the first time to feel a military urge for the glory and rank to be gained if the threatening war should break out. And so in this momentary lull it seemed likely that the predicament, which now appeared to hinge solely on a whim, would soon be resolved.

Unfortunately this apparent peace afforded no peace of mind. The baroness waited daily, but in vain, for a change of heart in her daughter, who, modestly and infrequently, but, when the occasion warranted, clearly, indicated that she held firm to her resolve, as only someone can who is possessed of an inner truth, whether it is in harmony with the surrounding world or not. The major was ambivalent; he would always feel hurt if Hilarie were really to decide in favor of his son, but were she to decide in his own favor, he was equally convinced that he must refuse her hand.

Pity this good man, with these cares, these torments hanging over him everlastingly, like a drifting mist, sometimes as background for the realities and the urgent tasks of the day, sometimes coming to the fore and obscuring all present concerns. There was a floating and wavering before the eyes of his soul; and if the demands of the day summoned him to swift and effective action, he would awake in the night and feel all sorts of distressing thoughts, constantly forming and re-forming, dancing within him in a horrible round. These ever recurring, inescapable visions reduced him to a state we might almost call despair, for activity and productivity, which normally would prove the best cures for such a condition, in this case hardly allayed his misery, let alone satisfied him.

In such plight our friend received a note in an unknown hand, inviting him to the inn in the nearby town, where a traveler in a hurry urgently wished to speak with him. The major, accustomed to such messages from his complex business affairs and social connections, was all the less inclined to delay because the hasty, free flowing script seemed somehow familiar. Calm and composed as usual, he betook himself to the assigned place, where, in the familiar, almost rustic parlor, he encountered the fair widow, prettier and more charming than he had left her. Whether because our imagination is not capable of retaining the exact particulars of the highest excellence, or because agitation had truly lent her greater beauty, in any case, a double measure of poise was necessary for the major to hide his astonishment and his confusion beneath the guise of ordinary courtesy; he greeted her politely with a coldness born of embarrassment.

"No, no, my dear friend!" she exclaimed, "Not for this have I summoned you to these whitewashed walls, to this highly inelegant setting. Such humble surroundings do not call for such courtly intercourse. I am here to free my heart from a heavy burden by saying, confessing, that I have created much havoc in your family."

The major drew back in amazement. "I know all," the widow continued. "There is no need for explanations. You and Hilarie, Hilarie and Flavio, your good sister—I am sorry for all of you." Words seemed to fail her; her magnificent eyelashes could not hold back the overflowing tears, her cheeks flushed, and she was more beautiful than ever. The noble man stood before her in extreme confusion, overwhelmed by an unfamiliar emotion. "Let us sit down," the lovely creature said, wiping her eyes. "Forgive me, have pity on me, you see how I am punished." She covered her eyes with her embroidered handkerchief to hide how bitterly she was weeping.

"Enlighten me, gracious lady," he hastened to say.

"Not gracious lady," she responded, with an angelic smile. "Call me your friend, for you have no truer one. And so, my friend, I know everything. I know all the circumstances of the entire family, am familiar with all your intentions and sufferings."

"How could you have learned so much?"

"From personal confessions. This hand will not be strange to you." She showed him several opened letters.

"My sister's hand! Letters, a sheaf of them, written, to judge by the careless script, to an intimate. Have you and she been acquainted, then?"

"Not directly, but indirectly for some time. See, here is the address: To ***."

"Another mystery! To Makarie, the most silent of all women."

"But for that reason also the confidante, the confessor to all troubled souls, to all who have lost themselves and wish to find themselves again but know not how."

"Thank God," he exclaimed, "that such mediation has been found. For me to supplicate her would not have been seemly. I bless my sister for doing so. For I, too, know of instances in which that admirable woman has held up a magic mirror of morality to some unhappy person and shown him the true, resplendent inner form behind his outwardly distorted one, and so suddenly put him at peace with himself and summoned him to a new life."

"This boon she conferred on me as well," replied the fair one, and in that moment our friend felt, if indistinctly yet with certainty, that from this remarkable person, previously self-absorbed, had emerged a being of moral beauty, sympathetic and generous. "I was not unhappy, merely restless," she continued. "I was no longer at one with myself, and that ultimately means not being happy. I was no longer pleased with myself; no matter how I fussed before the looking glass, I always seemed to be preparing myself for a masked ball. But ever since Makarie held up her mirror to me, since I became aware of how one can adorn oneself from within, I seem quite beautiful to myself again." She said all this half smiling, half in tears, and was, it must be admitted, more than charming. She seemed to merit esteem and to be worthy of a lifetime's true devotion.

"And now, my friend, let us be quick. Here are the letters. For you to read them and reread them, to reflect, to prepare yourself, should take you at least an hour—or more, if you wish. Then all of our circumstances can be decided with few words."

She left him and walked back and forth in the garden. He now unfolded the correspondence between the baroness and Makarie, whose content we shall summarize. The baroness complained about the fair widow. The letter shows how one woman looks at another and passes severe judgment on her. In fact, only outward appearances and utterances are discussed; no thought is given to inner feelings.

Then from Makarie's side, a milder judgment. Description of such a being from within. The outward manifestations appear as a series of accidents, hardly to be blamed, perhaps to be forgiven. Then the baroness reports her nephew's ravings and madness, the growing affection of the young pair, the arrival of the father, Hilarie's determined refusal. Everywhere there are replies from Makarie of impeccable fairness, arising from the strong conviction that all of this must result in moral improvement. Finally she sends the entire correspondence to the fair widow, whose angelically beautiful nature now emerges, and begins to glorify her outward being. It all concludes with her grateful reply to Makarie.

Chapter Six

Wilhelm to Lenardo

Finally, my dear friend, I can say that she is found, and, I may add, to ease your mind, in circumstances that leave nothing to be desired for the good soul. Let me speak in general terms; I am writing from the very spot, where I have before my eyes everything of which I am to give account.

Household based on piety, enlivened and sustained by industry and order, not too restricted, not too broad, the best possible match of duties to abilities and strengths. She is the center of a group of manual workers in the purest, most original sense; here dwell restraint and far-reaching effectiveness, caution and moderation, innocence and diligence. I have seldom experienced a more agreeable atmosphere, with such bright prospects for the immediate and more distant future. These considerations all together should be sufficient to reassure everyone concerned with her.

I may, therefore, in remembrance of all that we agreed upon, most earnestly beseech you to leave it at this general account, perhaps elaborating the picture in your thoughts, but to refrain from any further investigation, and dedicate your full energies to the great life task into which you have probably already been completely initiated.

Am sending one copy of this letter to Hersilie, and another to the Abbé, who, I would guess, knows best where to find you. Am writing a few lines to this tested friend, always as dependable in secret matters as in public; he will share them with you. Especially request that what concerns me be considered with sympathy, and my purpose furthered with devout and faithful wishes.

Wilhelm to the Abbé

If I am not wholly mistaken, Lenardo, highly deserving of our esteem, is at present in your midst; I am therefore sending a copy of a letter, so that it may be sure to reach him. May this excellent young man become involved in your circle in uninterrupted, significant work, since, as I hope, he has found inner peace.

As for myself, after extended alert self-scrutiny, I can only repeat all the more earnestly the petition presented long since by Montan. The desire to complete my journeyman years with more composure and stability is growing ever more urgent. In the expectation that my arguments will be accepted, I have completed my preparations and made my arrangements. Once I have taken care of my worthy friend's affair, I trust I shall be free to embark on my further course under the conditions already mentioned. As soon as I have made one last holy pilgrimage, I plan to arrive in ***. There I hope to find your letters waiting for me, and, in harmony with my inner urge, to begin afresh.

Chapter Seven

After our friend had dispatched the foregoing letters, he proceeded on, passing through several neighboring mountain ranges, ever farther, until the glorious valley opened before him where he meant to resolve so many things before commencing a new way of life. Here he unexpectedly met up with a young and lively traveling companion, through whose presence his endeavors and his pleasures were to flourish. He finds himself thrown in with a painter, like many such in the wide world and even more who frequent and haunt the pages of novels and plays, one who proved this time to be an excellent artist. They soon take to one another, and confide tastes, opinions, and plans to one another; then it develops that the admirable painter, who can decorate watercolor landscapes with clever figures, drawn and executed well, is infatuated with Mignon's fate, figure, and being. He had often imagined her, and had now set out on this journey to copy from Nature the surroundings in which she had lived, to portray the lovely child in all the surroundings and moments of her life, both happy and unhappy, and so to summon her image, which lives in all feeling hearts, before the eye.

The friends soon reach the great lake, and Wilhelm endeavors to find the indicated places one after another. Splendid country houses, rambling abbeys, ferry crossings and inlets, capes and landing places were sought out, nor did they overlook the dwellings of brave and good-natured fishermen, any more than the cheerful little towns along the lake shore or the small castles on the neighboring hills. All of these the painter successfully captures, matching lighting and color to the mood of the episode in question, so that Wilhelm passed the days in intense emotion.

In many of the pictures Mignon stood in the foreground, in perfect likeness, since Wilhelm could assist his friend's power of imagination with exact details, and embed his general conception of her in the specific features of her identity.

And so one saw the boyish girl portrayed in various settings and significations. Beneath the columned portal to the splendid country house she stood, gazing thoughtfully at the statues in the entry hall. In one sketch she was rocking and splashing in the moored skiff, in another climbing the mast like a bold sailor.

But one picture stood out amongst the rest, one the painter had done on his way, before he encountered Wilhelm; it plumbed Mignon's character. Amidst stark mountain scenery the graceful child, dressed as a boy, stands shining, surrounded by sheer cliffs, sprayed by waterfalls, in the midst of a band difficult to describe. A horrifying, steep, ancient chasm was perhaps never decorated by a more charming or significant crew. The colorful, gypsy-like company, at once crude and fantastical, exotic and ordinary, too casual to inspire fear, too outlandish to awaken trust. Sturdy packhorses plod along, now on corduroy roads, now on steps hewn out of the rock, loaded with a jumble of baggage. From it dangle all the musical instruments which are needed for a bewitching concert, and which now and then molest the ear with discordant tones. In the midst of all this the dear child, withdrawn into herself, without defiance, reluctant but unresisting, led but not dragged. Who could have failed to enjoy this remarkable, fully executed picture? The grim defile within the rocky mass was powerfully rendered, the series of black gorges cutting through everything, piled together, threatening to bar any exit, were it not that a boldly suspended bridge suggested the possibility of establishing contact with the outside world. With a clever knack for creating an aura of truth, the artist had also indicated the mouth of a cave, which one might imagine as the workshop where Nature produces giant crystals or the den of a brood of fabulous, frightful dragons.

Not without reverent awe did the friends visit the palace of the Marquis. The old man was not yet returned from his journey, but since the two knew how to conduct themselves toward authorities spiritual and secular, in these precincts, too, they were welcomed and treated kindly.

Wilhelm, indeed, was grateful that the master of the house was absent, for although he would have been glad to see the worthy man again and would have greeted him cordially, he shrank from the Marquis's grateful generosity and from being compelled to accept some reward for service he had rendered out of loyalty and affection and for which he had already received the sweetest remuneration.

And so the friends skimmed in a pretty bark from shore to shore, crossing the lake in every direction. In this finest of seasons they missed neither sunrise nor sunset, nor any of the thousand shadings the heavenly body lavishes on its firmament and thence over land and water, reaching its own full glory only in the reflection.

Luxuriant vegetation, sowed by Nature, tended and propagated by human art, surrounded them on all sides. The first chestnut groves had already bid them welcome, and now, reclining beneath the cypresses, they could not suppress a sorrowful smile as they saw laurel growing, pomegranates reddening, orange and lemon trees burgeoning with blossom even as fruits gleamed forth from the dark foliage.

But Wilhelm's spirited companion provided him with a new pleasure. Nature had not endowed our old friend with a painter's eye. Hitherto receptive to visual beauty only in human form, he now suddenly became aware that the world around him had been unlocked by this friend, who, though similar in outlook, had been trained to quite different tastes and talents.

From conversation about the ever changing glories of the region, but even more from concentrated imitation, Wilhelm's eyes were opened, and he was freed of his previous, stubbornly held doubts. He had always distrusted portrayals of Italian landscapes; the sky seemed to him too blue, the violet tones of the alluring distances were lovely, to be sure, but not real, and the various shades of green were simply too vivid. But now he merged his responses completely with his friend's, and, sensitive as he was, learned to see the world with the other's eyes. And when Nature disclosed the open secret of her beauty, it was impossible not to feel an unquenchable longing for art as the most worthy interpreter.

But quite unexpectedly his friend obliged him in another way. He had sometimes sung a cheerful song, and thereby movingly enlivened and accompanied quiet hours of traveling hither and yon through the waves. Now it happened, however, that the painter found an unusual instrument in one of the palaces, a small lute, powerful, resonant, convenient to play and carry around. He could soon tune the instrument and play it so well, to the great pleasure of those present, that, like a new Orpheus, he softened the heart of the castellan, otherwise a stern, dry man, and gently compelled him to lend the instrument to the singer for a while, with the proviso that he faithfully return it before departing and also in the meanwhile come on a Sunday or holiday and entertain the family.

From then on the water and the shore were enlivened in quite a different manner. Boats and skiffs vied for their company; even barges and ships bound for market lingered in their vicinity. Processions of people followed them along the shore, and whenever they landed, they were at once surrounded by a lighthearted crowd; when they departed, everyone called out blessings, contented yet full of yearning.

At length a third party, observing the friends, could have noticed that their missions were actually complete. All the places and locales associated with Mignon had been sketched, some done in light, shadow, and color, some faithfully completed in the heat of the day. To achieve this they had moved from place to place in a singular fashion, because Wilhelm's vow was often troublesome. They managed to evade it now and then, however, by the interpretation that it held only on land and did not apply on the water.

Wilhelm himself felt also that their actual purpose had been accomplished. But he could not deny that the desire to see Hilarie and the fair widow must still be satisfied if he was to leave the region with his mind at rest. His friend, to whom he confided the story, was no less curious, and was glad he had left a splendid empty space in one of the paintings that he now planned to adorn with the figures of such lovely persons.

They began to crisscross the lake, watching the points where newcomers were wont to enter this paradise. They had told their oarsmen that they hoped to meet friends here, and it was not long before they saw a handsome, luxurious vessel gliding along, to which they gave chase, and did not hesitate to grapple it eagerly. The ladies, somewhat alarmed, recovered their composure as soon as Wilhelm presented his note, and they both unhesitatingly recognized the arrow they themselves had drawn on it. The friends were trustingly invited to come aboard the ladies' ship, which they promptly did.

And now imagine the four of them, in the most charming space, seated face to face in this happiest of worlds, cooled by gentle breezes, rocked on sparkling waves. Imagine the two women, as we saw them described not long ago, and the two men with whom we have been sharing a journey for several weeks, and after some reflection we may see them all in the most pleasant, but also the most perilous, of situations.

For the three, who willingly or unwillingly are already numbered among the renunciants, the worst is not to be feared. The fourth, however, might find himself enrolled in that order only too soon.

After the lake had been crossed several times, and the places of greatest interest both along the shores and on the islands had been pointed out, the ladies were brought to the place where they were to pass the night, and where an experienced guide, engaged for the trip, had arranged for their every comfort. Here Wilhelm's vow was a proper but irksome master of ceremonies, for the friends had only recently spent three days at just this spot and had exhausted whatever was worth seeing in the vicinity. The artist, whom no vow constrained, asked leave to see the ladies safely to land, but since the ladies declined, they parted at some little distance from the harbor.

Hardly had the singer leaped into his boat, which hastily drew away from shore, when he reached for his lute and began to sound that wondrous, plaintive song which the Venetian boatmen send echoing from land to sea, from sea to land. He was well practiced at it, and this time it was specially tender and expressive. In proportion to their increasing distance he augmented the volume, so that the listener on shore seemed to hear the departing singer always at the same distance. At last he let the lute fall silent, trusting to his voice alone, and had the satisfaction of seeing that the ladies, instead of withdrawing indoors, chose to linger by the shore. So inspired was he that he could not cease, even when night and distance effaced the sight of all objects, until finally his calmer friend pointed out that even if the darkness enhanced the music, the boat had by now long since moved beyond that region where the singing might have any effect.

As agreed, the parties met again the following day out on the lake. Flying past, they became acquainted with the succession of beautiful views spread so remarkably before them, sometimes arranged in a row, sometimes displacing each other; doubled in the reflection in the lake, they afforded the most varied pleasure on such trips along the shores. And the artistic copies on paper made it possible to sense and guess at that which could not be viewed directly on the day's excursion. For all of this the quiet Hilarie seemed to possess a clear and open sensibility.

But toward noon something strange occurred again; the ladies disembarked alone, while the men cruised back and forth outside the harbor. Now the singer tried to adapt his performance to their proximity, hoping to achieve a happy effect not only with a prevailing tone of yearning, tender with a lively yodel, but also with cheerful, delicate insistence. Occasionally one or another of the songs, which we owe to beloved characters in the *Apprenticeship*, almost floated of their own accord from the strings and from his lips, but he restrained himself out of kindly consideration, of which he himself was in need. Instead, he ranged among unfamiliar images and emotions, to the benefit of his performance, which was rendered all the more appealing. Thus blockading the harbor, the two friends would have given no thought to food or drink, had the considerate ladies not sent over some delicacies, to which a drink of the choicest wine made the perfect accompaniment.

Every separation, every restriction which comes in the way of our budding passions quickens them rather than dulling them. This time, too, it may be presumed that the brief absence aroused equal longing on both sides. And indeed, before long the ladies could be seen setting out in their gleaming, gay gondola.

The word gondola must not, however, be understood in its melancholy Venetian sense. Here it refers to a cheerful, comfortable, and attractive boat which, had our little circle been twice as large, would still have been roomy enough.

Several days passed in this odd manner, between meeting and parting, between separating and coming together. Even as they enjoyed the most delightful companionship, loss and renunciation hovered always before their agitated spirits. In the presence of new friends, older friends came to mind; when they missed their new friends, they had to admit that these, too, had already established a strong claim upon remembrance. Only a composed and tested spirit like our fair widow could maintain her equilibrium in hours such as these.

Hilarie's heart had been too sorely wounded for her to be able to accept a new, clear impression. But when the beauty of a magnificent region soothingly surrounds us, when the kindness of sensitive friends begins to affect us, something peculiar comes over our minds and hearts, calling what is past, what is absent, back to us like a dream, while the present, wraithlike, recedes as though it were but an illusion. Thus rocked back and forth, attracted and repelled, approaching and retreating, they ebbed and flowed for several days.

Without judging the situation more closely, their guide, a skilled and experienced man, still thought he detected some alteration in the previously calm behavior of his heroines. When at last the reasons for the capriciousness of the situation became clear to him, he managed even here to bring about a most gratifying outcome. When the time arrived for the ladies to leave once more for the place where their meal awaited them, they were met by another decorated boat, which, pulling alongside theirs, displayed a well-laid table with all the essentials for a little feast. Thus they could expect to spend several more hours together, and only nightfall brought the customary parting.

Fortunately, the two men, on their previous excursions, had neglected to visit the most artfully decorated of the islands, out of a certain fetish for Nature. Even now they had not thought of showing their lady friends the island's contrivances, which were by no means well maintained, before the glorious natural scenes were completely exhausted. But suddenly something dawned on them! They took the guide into their confidence; he was at once able to expedite the excursion, and they thought it the most wonderful of all. Now, after so many interrupted pleasures, they could hope for and look forward to spending three entire heavenly days together, in a secluded place.

Here we must particularly praise the guide; he belonged to that energetic and skilled sort who, accompanying various parties, cover the same routes often. Well acquainted with the country's conveniences and inconveniences, they know what to avoid and what to seek out, and, without neglecting their own interest, are able to conduct their clients through the country more economically and more pleasurably than they would have managed on their own.

At the same time a lively maidservant of the ladies took an active part in the preparations for the first time, so that the fair widow could set the condition that the two gentlemen stay with her as guests, and accept her modest hospitality. Here, too, everything took the most favorable turn possible; for the clever guide had, on this occasion as on previous ones, made such wise use of the ladies' letters of introduction and credit that, in the absence of its owner, the castle and its grounds on the island were made available. Not only the kitchen was at their disposal; there was even some suggestion that the cellar might be open to them. So well did everything fall into place that from the very first moment they could not but feel at home, as though they were the born masters of this paradise.

The travelers' entire baggage was forthwith brought onto the island, which resulted in great comfort for the company. The greatest advantage achieved, however, was that all the portfolios of the excellent artist, in one place for the first time, gave him the opportunity to show the fair ones the route he had followed, in exact sequence. All were delighted with his work. Here was no need for the mutual canonization customary between artists and connoisseurs; here an excellent man received the most sincere and perceptive praise. But lest we be suspected of hoodwinking the credulous reader with generalities about something we cannot actually show him, we insert the judgment of an expert, who some years later lingered with admiration over the works in question, as well as similar and related ones:

"He succeeds in capturing the serenity of quiet views of the lake, where cozy, clustered houses reflected in the clear waters seem to be bathing; shores, rimmed with verdant hills, behind which rise wooded mountains and glacier-covered peaks. The coloration in such scenes is bright, and gaily fresh, with the distances as if suffused in softening mist that, grayer and denser, eddies forth from streams running through gorges and valleys, and marks their course. His ability is no less to be praised in the views from valleys closer to the high mountains, where densely forested slopes descend and clear streams rush by the foot of the cliffs.

"He has admirable skill at differentiating the various species of mighty shade trees in the foreground, both in the form of the whole and in the arrangement of the branches, and even in the individual groupings of the leaves. Nor is he less skilled in the many nuances of green in which the gentle breath of soft breezes seems to rustle and the light seems to dance.

"In the middle ground of his paintings the rich green tones gradually fade and, in the pale violet of the distant mountain peaks, unite with the blue of the sky. Yet our artist is most successful of all in his portrayal of high Alpine regions: their simple vastness and stillness, the extensive meadows on the slopes, clothed in the brightest green, where dark, isolated firs rear up from the sward and foaming brooks plunge from high rock walls. Whether he equips his meadows with grazing cattle or his narrow mountain path winding along cliffs with laden pack horses and mules, the animals are all drawn well and expressively. Always applied in suitable places and in not too great abundance, they adorn and enliven these pictures without disturbing, or even diminishing, their calm solitude. The bold hand of a master is evident in the execution, which is brief, accomplished with few, sure strokes, yet fully realized. Later on he used bright English permanent pigments on paper; therefore these paintings are of a remarkably florid coloration, bright yet strong and rich.

"His representations of deep chasms, where only barren rock projects, and the rushing stream thunders in the depths, spanned by a daring bridge, are to be sure, less attractive to the eye than the previous paintings, but their truthfulness stirs us. We admire the powerful effect of the whole, evoked sparingly with a few telling strokes and patches of color.

"He can portray with similar accuracy those heights where neither tree nor shrub can grow, but where, among jagged rocks and snowy summits, sunny spots are clothed in tender grass. Lovely and verdant and inviting though he makes such places appear, he wisely forbears to place grazing herds on them, for these are fields where only the chamois feed, and wild hayers go about their perilous business."

We are not departing from our aim of acquainting our readers as fully as we can with the character of such wild regions if we briefly explain the term wild hayers. It refers to the poorer inhabitants of the high mountains who undertake to cut hay from grassy spots which are utterly inaccessible to cattle. For this purpose they put climbing irons on their feet and scale the steepest, most dangerous cliffs, or, if necessary, let themselves down on ropes from rock walls onto the grass. After cutting the hay and letting it dry, they toss it from the heights down to the valley floor, where it is collected and sold to livestock owners, who bid for it gladly, knowing that this hay is of the choicest quality.

Hilarie especially looked with care at these pictures, which, to be sure, would have captivated anyone. Her remarks revealed that she herself was no stranger to the subject. This was certainly not lost on the painter, who valued the approbation of this most charming of persons above anyone else's. Accordingly, her older friend no longer remained silent, but reproached Hilarie for hesitating again, as always, to come forward with her own talent. Here it was not a question of praise or reproach but of learning. A finer opportunity might never present itself again.

Now that she was compelled to display them, her pictures revealed how much talent lay hidden in this quiet, delicate being. Her ability was innate, and had been diligently developed. She possessed a good eye and a neat hand, such as can transform women's toilette and attire into a higher art. There was, to be sure, some uncertainty in her strokes, and therefore a lack of distinctive character in her subjects, but the care with which they were executed was admirable. Yet the entire composition was not approached in the most advantageous fashion and lacked the final stamp of artistry. She fears, it seems, that she would profane the object if she did not remain wholly true to it, and therefore she is timid and gets lost in details.

But now the painter's great, free talent and bold hand stimulate, awaken the feeling and taste slumbering within her. It becomes clear to her that she need only take courage and follow seriously and punctiliously a few guiding principles which the painter repeatedly articulated in friendly but urgent tones. Her strokes take on decisiveness; she comes to dwell less on the parts than on the whole, and so a pleasing talent unexpectedly blossoms into accomplishment, like the rosebud that scarcely attracts our notice in the evening, but in the morning, with the rising sun, bursts open before our eyes, so that we imagine we can see with our own eyes the living quiver with which the splendid phenomenon reaches out toward the light.

This aesthetic education was not without moral consequences; for the recognition of heartfelt gratitude toward someone who has taught us a significant lesson makes a magical impression on the pure heart. This was the first joyous feeling to emerge in Hilarie's soul in some time. To see the glorious world spread out before her for days on end, and now suddenly to experience a fuller power to represent it! What bliss, to approach the inexpressible through lines and colors! She felt swept up by new youth, and could not but harbor a special fondness for the person to whom she owed this happiness.

So they sat side by side; it would not have been possible to say whether the one was more eager to transmit artistic techniques or the other to seize the suggestions and carry them out. They embarked on a happy rivalry, such as seldom arises between teacher and pupil. Sometimes the painter seemed to want to make some alteration on her drawing with a firm stroke, but she would gently refuse and hurry to do what was wanted, what was essential, always to his astonishment.

The last evening had now arrived, and a brilliant full moon shining forth made the transition from day to night imperceptible. The party had gathered on one of the highest terraces, so as to have a clear view of the lake, some of whose length stretched out beyond their sight, but whose entire breadth was visible, with reflected illumination from every side glittering on its calm surface.

No matter what people might discuss in such circumstances, they could not fail to dwell once more upon the delights of this sky, this water, this earth, under the influence of a more powerful sun, a milder moon—all discussed a hundred times before, now glorified in lyric effusions.

But what went unmentioned, what could scarcely be acknowledged, was the deep, painful feeling stirring in each heart, with greater or lesser intensity, but with equal truth and delicacy. The anticipation of parting hovered over everything. The gradual lapse into silence became almost painful.

Then the singer made bold to strike up his instrument, casting aside the discretion he had earlier observed. The image of Mignon rose before him with the first bars of the lovely child's delicate song. Forgetting all restraint, plucking the resonant strings with a force born of yearning, he began to sing:

Know you the land where lemon blossoms blow,
And through dark leaves— —

Hilarie rose in great agitation and hurried away, covering her brow. Our fair widow gestured with one hand in warning to the singer, while with the other she grasped Wilhelm's arm. The thoroughly bewildered youth set out after Hilarie, while the more self-possessed widow drew

Wilhelm after them. And when all four stood facing one another in the brilliant moonlight, the general emotion could no longer be concealed. The women threw themselves into each other's arms, the men embraced, and Luna stood witness to the noblest, chastest tears. Only slowly did some composure return, and they drew apart, in silence, moved by strange feelings and wishes, which, however, were already shorn of hope. Now our painter, who had been carried off by his friend, was initiated, beneath the majestic sky, in that solemn and lovely night hour, into all the pangs of the first order of the renunciants. His friends had already passed beyond this order, but now saw themselves in danger of being sorely tested once more.

The young men had gone to bed late; awakening betimes, they took heart and believed themselves strong enough to bid farewell to this paradise. They conceived various plans which would enable them to linger in the vicinity without injury to their obligations.

They intended to present these proposals, when they were surprised with the tidings that the ladies had departed at the break of day. A letter in the hand of our queen of hearts offered some insight. It would be difficult to say whether the note expressed more prudence or goodness, more love or friendship, more testimony to their merit or bashful partiality. Alas, it ended with the stern demand that they neither follow their friends nor seek them out, and even if by chance their paths were to cross, they were faithfully to avoid meeting.

Now the paradise was transformed as if by a stroke of magic into a desolate waste, and they themselves would certainly have smiled, had they realized at the moment how very unfair and ungrateful they were all of a sudden toward so beautiful and remarkable a place. No self-centered hypochondriac could have more cruelly and maliciously censured and criticized the dilapidated buildings, the neglected walls, the crumbling towers, the overgrown paths, the dying trees, the mossy mouldering of the grottos, and whatever else there was of that sort to notice. But then they took themselves in hand as well as they could; the artist carefully packed up his work, and both embarked together. Wilhelm accompanied him to the upper reaches of the lake, whence, as previously agreed, the artist was to find his way to Natalie, to carry her with his paintings to regions where she herself might not set foot for a long time to come. He was also authorized to confess to her the unexpected episode that had qualified him to be kindly accepted among the members of the order of renunciation, where through loving treatment he would be, if not healed, at least consoled.

Lenardo to Wilhelm

Your letter, dearest friend, found me in the midst of an activity which I might call confusion, were not its purpose so high, its success so certain. My connection with your people is more important than either party could have guessed. I must not even begin to write of that, for it immediately becomes obvious how incommensurable the whole thing is, and how ineffable the interconnection. For now our watchword must be: act and say nothing. A thousand thanks for the half veiled allusion to such a pleasing secret at a great distance; I do not begrudge the good creature so simple and happy a lot, while I myself am driven about in a whirl of complications, yet not without a guiding star. The Abbé has undertaken to report the rest to you; I must concentrate on what is essential; longing evaporates in deeds and accomplishments. You have done me—and now no more. Where there is enough to do, no room remains for reflection.

The Abbé to Wilhelm

Your well-meant letter, quite contrary to your intentions, came within a hair's breadth of doing us great harm. Your description of the long-lost young woman is so cheerful and appealing that our strange friend might have dropped everything to seek her out himself, were our now joint plans not so comprehensive and far-reaching. But he has now passed the test, and it is confirmed that he is fully imbued with the importance of our undertaking, and that it alone has the power to hold him.

In this new relationship, whose initiation we owe to you, there turned out to be, upon closer scrutiny, far greater advantages both for the others and for ourselves than had been expected.

For recently a canal has been proposed for a region poorly favored by Nature, where some of the lands turned over to him by his uncle are located. The canal will also pass through our holdings, with the result that their value, when we join forces, will be incalculably increased.

Here he can very easily pursue his overwhelming desire to make a completely fresh start. To either side of the new waterway uncultivated and uninhabited land can be found in plenty. Here spinners and weavers may settle; masons, carpenters, and blacksmiths may build them and themselves modest workshops. Everything may be destroyed by the first person to come along, while we others, however, are engaged in solving the more complicated issues and promoting a change in activity.

This, then, is our friend's next assignment. Complaint after complaint has been reaching us from the mountains that food shortages are getting out of hand; these areas are also said to be overpopulated. He will look around there, assess conditions and people, and select truly industrious ones, the ones who are useful to themselves and to others, for our colony. In addition, I can report of Lothario that he is preparing for the final step. He has set out on a journey to the Pedagogues, to ask them for able artists, only a very few. The arts are the salt of the earth; as salt is to food, so are the arts to technical science. We want from art only enough to insure that our handicrafts will remain in good taste.

All in all, a permanent link with that pedagogic institution will prove very useful and helpful to us. We must labor, and cannot be concerned with education. But to attract educated people to us must be our highest obligation.

A thousand and one reflections come to mind here. But allow me, as is our old custom, to offer just one more general thought, occasioned by a passage in your letter to Lenardo. Devotion to family is a principle from which we do not wish to withhold the praise it deserves. It forms the basis of the individual's security, upon which ultimately rest the stability and the dignity of the whole. But it is no longer sufficient. We must form the concept of devotion to the larger world, put our genuine humanitarian concerns into practice on a broad scale, and further the good not only of those close to us but of all mankind.

And now, finally, to come to your petition; I have this to say: Montan presented it to us promptly. Strange fellow that he is, he refused to explain just what you intended, but gave his word as a friend that it made sense and, if successful, would be most useful to society. And so you are forgiven for likewise treating it as a secret in your missive. In short, you are hereby released from all restrictions, as you should have been informed before this, had we known your whereabouts. I therefore repeat in the name of us all that on the basis of our confidence in Montan and yourself, we approve your goal, albeit undisclosed. Travel about, stop when you wish, move along again, abide! Whatever you achieve cannot fail to be good. May you form yourself into the most essential link in our chain!

In conclusion, I am sending along a little chart which should enable you to find the shifting center of our communications. In it you will see clearly laid out where your letters should be sent at each season of the year. They should preferably be conveyed by trustworthy couriers, of whom enough are designated in various places. Similarly you will find signs indicating where you are to seek out one or another of our company.

Interpolation

At this point we find ourselves in the position of announcing to the reader an intermission, and indeed one of several years, for which reason we should have liked to end the volume here, had that been compatible with the typographic conventions.

However, the space between two chapters will doubtless suffice to carry us over the appropriate span of time, since we are long accustomed to allowing that sort of thing to happen between the falling and the rising of the curtain in our presence.

In this second book we have seen our old friends' relationships significantly enhanced, and have also made new acquaintances. The prospects are such that it may be hoped that all will turn out as desired for each and every one, provided they find their way into life. We may therefore look forward to encountering them again one after the other, mingling and separating, on paths rough and smooth.

Chapter Eight

If we once more seek out our friend, who for some time has been left to himself, we find him entering the Pedagogic Province, which he has approached from the plains. He traverses pastures and meadows, circles the rim of many a small lake, sees slopes covered more with brush than with trees, and everywhere open vistas of largely undisturbed land. On such paths he was not long in doubt that he was in horse-raising country, and here and there he spied larger or smaller herds of these noble beasts of various breeds and ages. But suddenly the horizon is covered by a frightful cloud of dust which rapidly sweeps nearer and nearer, until it overspreads the entire area. But finally, swept off by a brisk wind from the side, the dust reveals the tumult at its heart.

A horde of the noble beasts is galloping toward him at top speed, driven and kept together by mounted herdsmen. The wild throng thunders past the wanderer, a handsome boy amongst the herdsmen looks at him with astonishment, reins in, jumps down, and embraces his father.

There is so much to ask, so much to tell; the son reports that he had a difficult time in the probationary period, missed his horse, and had to drag around on foot in field and meadow. Nor did he adapt well to the quiet, toilsome farming life, against which he had protested in advance. To be sure, he enjoyed the harvest festival quite well, but not the subsequent ploughing, harrowing, digging, and waiting. He occupied himself with the necessary and useful domestic animals, but always carelessly and grumpily, until he was finally promoted to the more lively stables. The business of caring for the mares and foals was sometimes tiresome enough, except that seeing a spirited little animal that in three or four years' time might gaily carry one off made it seem quite a different thing from fussing with calves and piglets, whose whole purpose in life was to be well fed and, once fattened, done away with.

The father could be well pleased with the way the boy had grown, lengthening out to a real youth, with his healthy bearing and with his frank and sprightly, not to say witty, conversation. Both hurried their horses on after the speeding herd, past isolated, extensive farmsteads, until they reached the town or village where the great market was held. There an unbelievable hurly-burly prevails, and it is impossible to say whether the merchandise or the sellers raise more dust. Eager buyers from all over assemble here to acquire creatures of noble pedigree and careful breeding. One thinks one can hear all the world's languages. Amidst the hubbub resounds the lively blare of wind instruments, and everything bespeaks animation, strength, and life.

Once again our wanderer encounters the supervisor he had met previously. He is in the company of other capable men who quietly and inconspicuously maintain propriety and order. Wilhelm, who takes all this for yet another example of exclusive activity and, despite its breadth, a restricted way of life, wishes to learn in what other areas the pupils are trained, lest, engaged in such wild and rather crude occupations as feeding and rearing animals, they should themselves become wild animals. And so he was very glad to hear that precisely this violent and apparently rough vocation was linked with that most refined of studies: the practice and cultivation of languages.

At that moment the father missed his son at his side, but glimpsed him through gaps in the crowd, engaged in lively bargaining with a pedlar boy over some trifles. A short time later, he had disappeared entirely. When the supervisor inquired why he seemed somewhat anxious and distracted, and learned that it was because of his son, the man reassured the father, "Let it go, he is not lost. But you shall see how we keep our charges together." At this he blew hard upon a little whistle hanging around his neck, and promptly dozens of answers sounded from every side. The man continued: "I shall leave it at that. It is only a signal that the supervisor is nearby and wants to know approximately how many can hear him. At the second signal they keep silent but make ready, at the third they answer and rush to me. These signals, by the bye, exist in all sorts of variations, and are particularly useful."

All at once some space had developed around them, and they could speak more freely as they strolled toward the nearby hills. "We had to introduce the study of languages," the supervisor continued, "because we draw boys from all quarters of the globe. In order to prevent what tends to happen abroad, namely that compatriots join together and form factions that isolate them from the other national groups, we try to unite them through facility with languages.

"But most important is general language study, for at this market every foreigner should be able to find ample enjoyment in his own tone and idiom, and also to conduct his bargaining and selling with the utmost ease. But to avert Babylonian confusion and ruination, each month one particular language is universally spoken, the principle being that one should concentrate entirely on whatever element one is to master.

"We view our students," the supervisor said, "all as swimmers who discover to their amazement that the element they expect to engulf them makes them lighter, buoys them up and carries them along, and so it is with every thing that man undertakes.

"Should one of our boys demonstrate a particular fondness for one language or other, in the many quiet, leisurely, solitary, and even tedious hours in what seems like a tumultuous life, careful and thorough instruction is provided. You would find it difficult to recognize our mounted grammarians, some of whom are even real pedants, among these bearded and beardless centaurs. Your Felix has settled upon Italian, and since, as you already know, melodic song pervades all we do, you would hear him sing many a song with delicacy and feeling, during the tedious stretches of his herdsman's life. Activity and industry are much more compatible with sustained study than is generally believed."

Since every region celebrates its own festival, the guest was escorted to the district for instrumental music. Bordering on the plain, it consisted of agreeable and pleasantly varied dales, clusters of slender young trees, and tranquil brooks flowing between occasional mossy rocks. Scattered houses nestled among shrubs were visible on the hillsides, while in gentle hollows the houses pressed closer together. Those pleasantly isolated cottages were far enough apart that neither chords or discord could travel from one to the other.

They approached a wide space, surrounded by buildings and shade trees, where people, crowded shoulder to shoulder, seemed to be waiting with great eagerness and anticipation. Just as the guest arrived, an orchestra of all the instruments was performing a mighty symphony, of astonishing power and delicacy. Opposite the broad platform on which the orchestra was seated was another, which drew special notice. Upon it were students, some older and some younger, all holding their instruments ready, but not playing; they were the ones who were not able or did not dare to join in with the rest. It was touching to see how they held themselves in readiness, and to hear the proud statement that a festival like this seldom ended without one or another's talent suddenly coming to the fore.

When voices were heard singing along with the instruments, there could be no doubt left that this was also favored. In response to his query as to what other branch of study had a special affinity with music, the wanderer learned that it was poetry, specifically lyric poetry. The chief consideration was that both arts be cultivated, each alone and for its own sake, but then also in conjunction and in contrast with each other. The pupils learn each of these arts within its own constraints; then they are taught how they mutually determine one another, and then again how each liberates the other.

The musician uses measures and rhythm to correspond to meter in poetry. But here music quickly proves its superiority to poetry, for if in poetry, as is right and necessary, quantity is kept as pure as possible, for the musician few syllables are unequivocally long or short. He destroys the most carefully wrought lines of the poet as he likes; he can even convert prose into song, which opens up the most remarkable possibilities. The poet would soon feel himself reduced to nought, did he not know how to inspire respect in the musician through the lyrical delicacy and boldness of his art, and how to evoke new emotions, now in the gentlest succession, now by the most abrupt of transitions.

The singers found here are mostly poets themselves. The elements of dance are also taught, so that all these accomplishments may be distributed evenly through every region.

When the guest was escorted across the next border, he suddenly saw a completely different manner of building. Here the houses were no longer scattered, no longer cottage-like; rather they were grouped together in a regular pattern, their exteriors splendid and handsome, their interiors spacious, comfortable, and elegant. One became aware of a generously laid out, solidly constructed town, befitting the natural setting. This was the home of the plastic arts and the related crafts, and a special calm reigned in these spaces.

The plastic artist regards all of man's deeds and thoughts as his province, yet his profession is solitary and, by the strangest of contradictions, demands lively surroundings perhaps more than any other. Here each shapes in silence what will soon occupy men's eyes forever. A Sabbath stillness prevails through the entire town, and did one not hear the stone mason's pick now and then or the measured hammer blows of the carpenters busily working to complete some magnificent building, not the slightest sound would have stirred the air.

Our wanderer was struck by the earnestness, the remarkable rigor with which both beginners and more advanced pupils were treated. It seemed as though no one accomplished anything by his own powers, but as if a mysterious spirit animated each and every one, and guided them toward a single lofty end. Nowhere did one see rough designs or sketches; every line was drawn with deliberation. When the wanderer asked his guide for an explanation of the entire procedure, he was told: the imagination in itself is a vague, unstable faculty, whereas the merit of the plastic artist is that he learns to make it precise, to hold it fast, and finally to imbue it with reality.

Mention was made of the necessity for firm principles in other arts. "Would the musician allow a student to pluck the strings wildly, or to invent intervals at his own whim and pleasure? What is striking here is that nothing is left to the free will of the learner. The element in which he is to function is already fixed, the tool he is to employ is handed to him, even the manner in which he is to use it—I mean the fingering—is prescribed, so that the fingers do not get in each other's way, but each prepares the way for the next. Only this regulated co-ordination, finally, makes the impossible possible.

"But the greatest justification for our strict demands and our insistence on definite rules is this: that it is precisely the genius, the person with inborn talent, who grasps them most promptly and obeys them most willingly. Only the mediocre talent wishes to enthrone his limited individuality in the place of the absolute and gloss over his bungling by pretending it represents ungovernable originality and independence. But we do not allow this sort of thing; we guard our students from all those missteps by which a good portion of life, and sometimes an entire life, can be thrown into confusion and fragmented.

"We like best dealing with the genius, for this sort is always blessed with the ability to recognize promptly what is good for him. He understands that art is called art precisely because it is not Nature. He is able to respect even what one might call conventional; for what does this mean other than that the most outstanding men have agreed to consider as best that which is essential, indispensable. And is this standard not always conducive to happiness?

"Here, as elsewhere in our realm, the task of the teacher is greatly aided by the three forms of reverence, and by their signs, which have been introduced and impressed on the pupils, with slight modifications according to the prevailing activity."

As our wanderer was shown around, he was astonished that the city seemed to stretch on and on, with one street leading to another, affording a great variety of vistas. The exteriors of the buildings expressed their purpose unambiguously; they were dignified and stately, beautiful without being ornate. The more noble and solemn ones at the center of the city gave way to buildings of a brighter character, until finally charming suburbs in a graceful style extended into the open fields, ending in a scattering of summerhouses.

The wanderer could not help remarking that the dwellings of the musicians in the previous region were in no way to be compared in beauty and size to these houses inhabited by painters, sculptors, and architects. He was told that this lay in the nature of the case. The musician had always to be turned in on himself, to cultivate his inner sensibility, in order to project it outward. "He does not have to please his sense of sight. For the eye tends to take precedence over the ear, and lures the spirit out of itself. The artist, by contrast, must live in the external world and express his inner spirit almost unconsciously, in and through visible forms. Plastic artists must live like kings and gods; how else could they build and decorate for kings and gods? They must ultimately raise themselves so far above anything common that the entire community feels itself ennobled in and through their work."

Our friend then sought the explanation of another paradox: why, when the other regions were celebrating these festival days in such stimulating, tumultuous fashion, did such silence reign and work not cease?

"A plastic artist," he was told, "needs no festival, for to him the entire year is a festival. If he has created something excellent, it stands there before his own eyes, before the eyes of the entire world. There is no need for repetition, for renewed exertion, for fresh realization, such as plagues the musician, who consequently must be allowed to have the most splendid of celebrations before the largest of audiences."

"Still," Wilhelm replied, "it would be desirable to have an exhibition during this period, where the progress of the best students over the past three years could be contemplated with pleasure and evaluated."

"In other places," the answer was, "an exhibition may be necessary, but not here. Our entire nature and existence is exhibition. You see here buildings of every sort, all of them the work of our students, constructed, to be sure, from plans discussed and reconsidered hundreds of times; for the builder must not be groping about and experimenting. Whatever is to remain standing must stand properly, and must at least suffice, if not for eternity, then for a long time. To err is human, but errors must not be built.

"Sculptors we treat more leniently and painters most leniently of all; they may try out one thing or another, each according to his genre. It is up to them to choose a space they wish to decorate, whether on the insides or outsides of the buildings, or in the public squares. They propose their ideas to us, and if they are reasonably acceptable, they are allowed to execute them, and in one of two possible ways: either with the dispensation that sooner or later the work may be removed if the artist himself is displeased with it, or with the condition that once installed it cannot be moved. Most of our students choose the first alternative, and take advantage of that permission, which is always the most advisable course. The second case occurs more rarely, and it is evident that the artists then feel less sure of themselves and hold long conferences with their fellows and with experts, and thereby manage to produce real works of lasting value."

After all this, Wilhelm did not fail to inquire what other subject might be paired here, and was told that it was poetry, specifically epic poetry.

But it did seem strange to our friend when he learned further that the pupils were not allowed to read or to recite the completed poems of ancient or more modern poets. They were given only laconic versions of a series of myths, traditions, and legends. In the artistic or poetic treatment of such material one can quickly recognize the unique generative qualities of a talent devoted to either of those arts. Poets and plastic artists both draw from the same source, and each tries to channel the stream toward his side, to direct it to his own advantage, to further his own ends; he succeeds far better this way than by reworking something that has already been worked.

Our traveler had the opportunity to see this in practice. A group of painters was at work in a room, while a sprightly young comrade narrated a very simple story in great detail, using almost as many words as the others did brush strokes, so as to round out his presentation as completely as possible.

Wilhelm was assured that while working together the students entertained each other delightfully, and thus often improvisers emerged who could stimulate great enthusiasm for this double approach.

Our friend now turned his inquiries back to the plastic arts. "Since you have no exhibitions," he asked, "have you also no competitions?" "In fact we do not," his informant replied, "but here nearby we can let you see what we consider more useful."

They entered a large hall, pleasingly illuminated from above. Here they saw first a large circle of busy artists, in the center of which rose a monumental group, admirably arranged. Powerful figures of men and women in drastic postures recalled that glorious battle between the youthful heroes and the Amazons, in which hatred and enmity were ultimately resolved in mutual trust and assistance. The intricately entwined figures of the group showed to equal advantage from every angle. Artists sat or stood all about around the monument, each at work in his own way, painting at the easel, sketching at the drawing board, modeling in the round or in bas relief. There were even architects designing the pedestal on which such a work of art would later be mounted. Each participant reproduced the subject in his own fashion. The painters and sketchers developed the group in one plane, but carefully, so as not to spoil it but to preserve as much as possible. The reliefs were handled in the same way. Only one artist had repeated the group on a smaller scale, and he seemed to have even surpassed the original sometimes in the shaping of the limbs and the rendering of certain movements.

It now emerged that this one was the master, who would eventually execute the piece in marble. Before doing so, he was submitting the model to a practical examination, carefully observing and incorporating, after full consideration, and to his own benefit, all that his fellow artists had perceived, preserved, or altered in it. Thus when the great work was finally completed in marble, even though it had been undertaken, designed, and executed by a single person, it would seem to belong to all of them.

The greatest silence reigned in the room, but the supervisor raised his voice and called, "Which of you here, in the presence of this static object, will rouse the imagination with well chosen words, so that everything we see fixed here may become fluid again, without losing its character, in order to prove to us that what the sculptor has captured is the most worthy image?"

Called upon by all, a handsome youth left his work, and stepping forward, commenced a quiet discourse, in which he seemed at first merely to describe the sculpture before them. It was not long, however, before he plunged into the actual realm of poetry, diving into the midst of the action and commanding this element admirably. Little by little his glorious declamation brought the performance to such a pitch that the rigid group seemed to revolve on its axis, and the figures seemed to double and triple in number. Wilhelm stood there entranced, and at length exclaimed, "Who can resist breaking into song and metrical verse!"

"I should object to that," the supervisor replied, "for if our excellent sculptor is honest, he will admit that he finds our poet hard to take, precisely because these two artists are the farthest apart. On the other hand, I would wager that one or another of the painters has appropriated certain lively touches from it.

"But I would like to let our friend hear a gentle, convivial song, one that you all sing so solemnly and sweetly. It ranges over all of art, and I myself am always edified when I hear it."

After a pause in which they waved to each other and conferred by gestures, there resounded from all sides the following noble song, uplifting to heart and mind:

To invent, to make decisions,
Artist, solitude is best;
To take pleasure in your mission,
Gather gaily with the rest!
Now, together, see and hear
What your own life's course has been,
And the deeds of year on year
In your fellow man be seen.

First the thought, and then the sketching,
Then the figures fitly massed,
One the other clearer etching,
And declare an end at last!
Well conceived with shrewd device,
Fairly shaped and smoothly done,
Artists in such artful wise
Ever have their power won.

Nature in her many guises
Shows a single God to man,
Through art's many enterprises
Weaves but one eternal strand.
This is nothing but the Truth;
Decked alone with Beauty bright,
She awaits eternal youth,
Clarity and highest light.

Orators' and poets' raptures
Issue forth in rhyme and prose,
So the painter's canvas captures
All life's beauty in the rose—
Sisters round about her gleaming,
Harvest fruit on either side,
Showing forth the secret meaning
Of the world where we abide.

Thousandfold in beauty bright
Form on form flows from your hand,
Joyous wonder's your delight:
God in human form's at hand.
And whatever tool you wield,
Stand together brothers all;
And as song our off'rings yield,
Rising from the altar tall.

Wilhelm was willing to grant all of this, although it seemed to him thoroughly paradoxical, indeed, had he not seen it with his own eyes, completely impossible. Since it was all presented to him frankly and freely, however, in clear order, there was scarcely need for questions in order to learn more. Nevertheless, in the end he did not refrain from addressing his guide as follows: "I see that wise provision has been made for everything that may seem desirable in life. But tell me: in which of your regions is a similar concern shown for dramatic poetry, and where might I learn more about that? I have looked around at all your buildings and find none that seemed intended for such a purpose."

"In response to this question, we cannot conceal that no such building exists in our entire province. For the drama assumes an idle crowd, perhaps even a mob, such as does not exist amongst us; riffraff of this sort, if it does not leave in disgust on its own, is transported over the border. You may be sure, however, that so important a point was carefully considered, since our institute aims at the general welfare. But no region seemed right; everywhere significant reservations appeared. Who among our pupils would lightly undertake to induce false and unsuitable emotions in his fellows with sham merriment or feigned grief, and all to produce varying, but always dubious pleasures. We found such impostures thoroughly dangerous, and could not reconcile them with our serious purpose."

"But it is said," Wilhelm replied, "that this all-embracing art furthers the others."

"By no means," was the response. "It makes use of all the others, but corrupts them. I do not blame the actor for taking up with the painter; but in such company the painter is lost.

"The actor will unscrupulously utilize for his ephemeral purposes whatever art and life offer him, and with no little profit. The painter, on the other hand, would also like to gain some advantage from the theater, but finds himself always at a disadvantage, and the same is true of the musician. The arts seem to me like siblings, most of whom incline toward good management, except for one frivolous one who wants to appropriate and consume the family's entire worldly goods. Such is the case with the theater. It has dubious origins, which it can never completely deny, whether as an art, as craft, or as pastime."

Wilhelm looked down with a deep sigh, for he was suddenly reminded of all the joys and sorrows he had experienced in and from the theater. He blessed the pious men who had been wise enough to spare their charges such pain, and out of conviction and principle had banished these dangers from their domain.

His companion, however, did not leave him much time for such reflections, but continued, "Since our highest and most sacred principle is not to misdirect any ability or talent, we cannot conceal from ourselves that among so great a number some will have a natural gift for mimicry. It manifests itself in an irrepressible joy in imitating the characters, figures, movement, and speech of others. We do not encourage this, to be sure, but we observe the pupil closely, and should he remain true to his nature, we have established connections with great theaters the world over and will forthwith send a boy of proven abilities there, so that, like a duck in water, he can be initiated on the boards without delay into his future of waddling and quacking."

Wilhelm listened to this patiently, but was only half convinced and perhaps somewhat annoyed. For man is so oddly constituted that he may indeed be convinced of the worthlessness of some beloved object, may turn from it and even execrate it, but nevertheless does not want to see it treated in similar manner by others. And perhaps the spirit of contradiction that dwells in all men never shows itself more vigorously and effectively than in such a case.

The editor of these pages might himself confess that he has allowed this odd passage to slip by with some reluctance. For has not he also in various senses expended more life and energy on the theater than is proper? And is he now to be persuaded that this was an unforgivable error, a fruitless effort?

But we have no time to dwell on such painful memories and afterthoughts, for our friend is agreeably surprised to see one of the Three, and in fact an especially engaging one of them, coming toward him. Sympathetic mildness, expressive of the purest peace of mind, emanated from him. Our wanderer could approach him with trust and feel his trust reciprocated.

Now Wilhelm learned that the Head was presently at the sanctuaries, and was there giving instruction, teaching and dispensing blessings. The Three had meanwhile dispersed to visit the various regions, and in each place, after consulting with the subordinate supervisors and acquainting themselves thoroughly with the facts, they furthered what had been initiated and put the directives into effect; they thereby faithfully carried out their high responsibility.

This same excellent person now gave him a more general overview of their internal situation and outside connections, as well as some knowledge of the interactions of the various regions. It also became clear how, after a longer or shorter period, a pupil might be transferred from one region to another. Suffice it to say that all this coincided perfectly with what Wilhelm had already heard. At the same time, the report on his son gave him great pleasure, and the plan for the latter's further education earned his complete approbation.

Chapter Nine

Wilhelm was now invited by the assistant and the supervisor to a miners' festival that was about to be celebrated. They ascended the mountain with some difficulty, and Wilhelm even thought he noticed that the guide moved more slowly as evening set in, as if not fearing the darkness would place an even greater impediment in their path. But when a deep night surrounded them, this mystery was solved: for he saw tiny flames flickering and bobbing out of clefts and valleys, extending into lines that swarmed over the mountaintops. Here was a phenomenon far friendlier than when a volcano erupts, spewing out a tumult that threatens whole regions with destruction, and yet the light gradually blazed brighter, spreading and intensifying, twinkling like a river of stars, mild and lovely, to be sure, but extending boldly over the entire region.

After his escort had enjoyed for a time the astonishment of his guest—for their faces and figures were illuminated by the distant light, as was their path—he began to speak: "You see before you, to be sure, an odd spectacle. These lights, which burn and work underground night and day all year long, assisting in the extraction of hidden, scarcely accessible treasures of the earth, now they are welling up and streaming forth from their recesses, and lighting up the apparent night. Few have ever witnessed so delightful a parade, in which this useful enterprise, dispersed underground far from all eyes, emerges in all its amplitude and reveals a large, secret association."

Amidst such talk and observations, they had reached the place where the rivulets of flame converged to form a lake of fire around a brightly lit island of space. The traveler stood now in the blinding circle, where thousands of dancing lights formed a portentous contrast to the black wall of bearers lined up in a row. At once the merriest music rang out to accompany hearty singing. Hollow masses of rock advanced mechanically, opening to disclose a glittering interior to the delighted eyes of the beholder. Pantomime and whatever else might amuse the multitude at such a moment combined to arouse and simultaneously satisfy the attention.

But what amazement filled our friend when he was introduced to the dignitaries and saw among them friend Jarno, in solemn imposing miner's garb. "Not for nothing," the other exclaimed, "have I traded my previous name for the more significant one of Montan. You find me here initiated into mountain and chasm, and happier in this limitation, beneath and above the earth, than anyone could imagine."

"Now that you are so expert," replied the wanderer, "you will be more generous with explanations and instruction than you were toward me back on those peaks and cliffs."

"By no means," answered Montan. "The mountains are silent masters, and they train silent pupils."

After the ceremony the crowd dined at many tables. All of the guests, whether invited or uninvited, were of the trade, so that at the table where Montan and his friend had seated themselves, a conversation proper to the place sprang up; there was extensive discussion of mountains, veins and deposits, of the types of veins and ores in the region. But the conversation soon became more general, and then the talk was of nothing less than the creation and origin of the earth. But here the conversation did not long remain peaceful, but rather developed at once into a lively dispute.

Several wanted to derive the present form of our earth from the gradual recession of the waters covering the world; in support they cited the remains of once living inhabitants of the oceans to be found in the highest mountains, as well as on plateaus. Others, of more violent disposition, began with heating and melting, even an all-pervading fire, which, when it had done its work on the surface, retreated into the depths, where it still manifested itself in volcanos raging on land and sea, and formed the highest mountains through successive eruptions and repeated discharges of lava. They urged those of the other camp to consider that there could be no heat without fire, and that an active fire always presupposed a source. However much this corresponded to experience, some were not satisfied with it. They maintained that mighty formations already completed in the bowels of the earth had been extruded through the earth's crust by irresistible elastic forces; and in the course of these convulsions various pieces of them had been shattered and strewn near and far. They adduced many phenomena that could not be explained without this assumption.

A fourth, if perhaps not numerous, party, scoffed at all these futile attempts and maintained that many features of the earth's surface could never be explained unless it was allowed that greater and lesser segments of mountain could have fallen from the sky and covered great broad stretches of the landscape. They adduced the larger and smaller masses of rock found strewn over many lands, which even in our own day were believed to have fallen from above.

Finally two or three quiet guests invoked a period of fierce cold, when glaciers descended from the highest mountain ranges far into the land, forming in effect slides for ponderous masses of primeval rock, which were propelled farther and farther over the glassy track. In the subsequent period of thaw, these rocks had sunk deep into the ground, to remain forever locked in alien territory. In addition, the transport of huge blocks of stone from the north might have been made possible by moving ice floes. However, the somewhat cool views of these good people did not make much headway. The general opinion was that it was far more natural to have the world be created with colossal crashes and upheavals, wild raging and fiery catapulting. And since the heat of the wine was now adding its strong effect, the glorious celebration might almost have ended in fatal clashes.

Our friend felt quite bewildered and dejected, for he had long secretly cherished the spirit moving over the waters and the great flood which had risen fifteen ells above the highest mountaintop. After this strange talk his well-ordered, fertile, and populated world seemed to collapse into chaos before his mind's eye.

The following morning he did not fail to question the serious Montan about it, exclaiming, "I could not understand you yesterday, for among all those strange things people were saying, I hoped to hear at last your opinion and your position. Instead you were now on one side, now on another, always attempting to bolster the arguments of whoever was talking at the moment. But now tell me seriously what you think and what you know about all this."

Hereupon Montan replied, "I know as much as they do, and prefer not to think about it at all."

"But," Wilhelm objected, "there are so many contradictory opinions, and we are always told that the truth lies in the middle."

"By no means," Montan answered. "The problem lies in the middle, unfathomable perhaps, perhaps also accessible, if you give it a try."

After they had discussed a little more back and forth in this fashion, Montan said confidingly, "You reproach me with supporting everyone in his opinion, as indeed there is always an additional argument to be found for everything. It is true, I added to the confusion, but in fact I cannot take the human race very seriously anymore. I am thoroughly convinced that everyone must cherish for himself, with utmost seriousness, that which he holds dearest, which is to say, his convictions. Each of us knows what he knows only for himself, and he must keep it secret. As soon as he articulates it, contradiction rears its head, and when he engages in conflict, he loses his inner equilibrium, and his best qualities are, if not extinguished, at least badly disturbed."

Challenged by Wilhelm's response, Montan explained further: "Once you know what truly matters, you cease to be loquacious." "But what does truly matter?" inquired Wilhelm impetuously. "That is easily said," the other replied. "Thought and action, action and thought, that is the sum of all wisdom, known from time immemorial, practiced from time immemorial, not realized by all. Both must always alternate in life, like breathing out and breathing in. Like question and answer, neither should occur without the other. Whoever takes as his law what the spirit of human reason whispers in the ear of every newborn babe, to test action by thought and thought by action, cannot go astray, or if he should, he will soon find his way back to the right path."

Montan now gave his friend a tour of the mining area, and they were greeted everywhere with a hearty "Good fortune to ye," which greeting was cheerily returned. "I should sometimes like," Montan remarked, "to answer them with 'Good sense to ye,' for sense is better than fortune. Yet the masses always have sense enough, if their superiors are blessed with it. Since I am here, if not to command, at least to advise, I have endeavored to learn the characteristics of this range. The metals it contains are passionately sought after. I have tried to explain their occurrence, and have succeeded. It is not good fortune alone, but sense, which summons good fortune to regulate it. How these mountains here came to be, I do not know, nor do I care to. But I seek continually to wrest from them the secret of their individuality. The search is on for the lead and silver hidden in their bosom. I know how to discover them. The how I keep to myself, and merely indicate where to find what is sought. At my word the attempt is made, it succeeds, and I am called lucky. What I understand, I understand for myself; where I succeed, the success accrues to others. And no one imagines that he could succeed in the same way. They suspect me of having a divining rod, but they do not notice that they contradict me when I make a sensible proposal—not realizing that they are closing off the road to the Tree of Knowledge, where these prophetic branches are to be cut."

Encouraged by these discussions and persuaded that, in his own previous thoughts and actions, he had successfully met the spirit of his friend's principles in a very different profession, Wilhelm now gave Montan an account of how he had employed his time since receiving the dispensation to arrange his assigned journey not by days and hours but in accordance with his true goal of obtaining thorough training.

As it fell out, there was no need of much talk, for a significant occurrence gave our friend an opportunity to apply his acquired talent cleverly and successfully, and to show himself truly useful to society.

But in what manner this was, we may not at the moment disclose, although the reader will soon be sufficiently informed, indeed before he puts down this volume.

Chapter Ten

Hersilie to Wilhelm

For many years I have been reproached by all and sundry that I am an odd, capricious girl. If I am, it is not my fault. People had to have patience with me, and now I must have patience with myself, with my imagination, which parades father and son, now together, now alternately, back and forth before my eyes. I see myself as an innocent Alcmene, continuously plagued by two beings who represent one another.

I have a great deal to tell you, yet it seems to me I write to you only when I have an adventure to recount; all the rest is, to be sure, adventurous enough, yet not an adventure. So now for today's:

I am sitting under the tall lindens, putting the finishing touches on a little portfolio, an exquisite one, without exactly knowing who should have it, the father or the son, but surely one or the other. Along comes a young pedlar with baskets and caskets. He modestly identifies himself with an official certificate permitting him to hawk his wares on estates. I look over his things, down to the endless trifles which no one needs and which everyone buys out of a childish urge to possess and to squander. The boy seems to be observing me attentively. Beautiful dark eyes, somewhat cunning, well-shaped eyebrows, rich curls, gleaming rows of teeth, in short, you understand, an oriental type.

He asks various questions concerning members of the family to whom he might possibly sell something. Through all sorts of maneuvers, he manages to make me say my name. "Hersilie," he says modestly, "will Hersilie forgive me if I deliver a message?" I look at him in wonder, and he brings out the tiniest of slates with a little white frame, such as children in the mountains use when first learning to write. I take it, see writing on it, and read the following inscription, neatly lettered with a sharp stylus:

"Felix
loves
Hersilie.
The equerry
will soon come."

I am taken aback, am greatly astonished at what I hold in my hand, see with my own eyes, but most of all at the fact that Fate seems about to prove itself even odder than I am myself. "What is this supposed to mean?" I ask myself, and the little rogue is more present to me than ever; indeed, it is as though his image were boring itself into my eyes.

Now it is my turn to ask questions, and I receive strange, unsatisfactory answers. I interrogate and learn nothing. I ponder and cannot make sense of my thoughts. At last I piece together from statements and contradictions this much, that the young pedlar had passed through the Pedagogic Province, that he had won the confidence of my young admirer, who had written the inscription on a slate he had purchased, and had promised him the finest gifts in return for a word of reply. He thereupon handed me a similar slate, of which he had several in his pack, as well as a stylus, and pressed and besought me so sweetly that I took them both, thought, thought again, could think of nothing, and wrote:

"Hersilie's

greeting
to Felix.
May the equerry
be well."

I looked at what I had written and was annoyed at its ineptness. Neither tenderness nor intelligence nor wit, merely embarrassment, and why? I was standing before a boy, writing to a boy—should that upset me? I do believe I sighed and was about to erase what I had written, but the boy took it so charmingly from my hand and asked me for some protective wrapping, and so it happened—I know not how it happened—that I put the slate into the portfolio, tied its ribbon, and handed it, thus enclosed, to the boy, who received it gracefully and, with a deep bow, hesitated a moment, so that I had just time to press my little purse into his hand, while reproaching myself that I was not giving him enough. He departed with all due speed, and when I looked after him, he had already vanished, I could not tell quite how.

Now it is over; I am already back on the usual dull ground of everyday existence again, and can hardly believe in the apparition. Yet do I not hold the slate in my hand? It is quite charming, the lettering beautifully and carefully done. I think I might have kissed it, did I not fear to obliterate the writing.

I have given myself some time, after writing the above; but no matter how I think about it, I remain at an impasse. Certainly there was something mysterious about the figure. There is hardly a novel these days without that sort of character; are we now to meet up with them in real life as well? Likeable, yet suspicious, strange, yet inspiring trust? Why did he leave before the confusion could be unraveled? Why did I not have sufficient presence of mind to detain him in some suitable way?

After an intermission I again take pen in hand to continue my confessions. This determined, persisting affection in a boy on his way to young manhood was flattering; but it occurred to me that it was not rare to be attracted at such an age to an older woman. Indeed, younger men are mysteriously drawn to older women. In other cases, when it did not involve me, I laughed at it and give it a spiteful construction: that it was a reminiscence of infantile or nursling tenderness, from which they had barely torn themselves away. Now it aggravates me to think about it in such terms; I reduce our good Felix to a child, and I, too, do not appear to myself in any too favorable light. Ah, what a difference it makes whether we are judging ourselves or others.

Chapter Eleven

Wilhelm to Natalie

For days now I have been going about, unable to resolve to take up my pen. There is much to say; in conversation one point would dovetail with the other, one subject would easily flow out of another. Since I am far away, let me begin with generalities; they will eventually lead me to the peculiar things I have to impart.

You have heard the story of the youth, who, strolling along the seashore, found an oarlock; the interest he took in it moved him to acquire an oar, as a necessary complement to it. But this, too, was of no use; he set his heart on a boat, and managed to get one. Yet boat, oar, and oarlock did not take him very far; he provided himself with masts and sails, and so little by little with everything requisite for speed and comfort in boating. Striving purposefully, he achieves greater knowledge and skill. Fortune smiles upon him, and he finally finds himself the master and owner of a larger vessel; his success multiplies, and he becomes prosperous, respected, and renowned among seamen.

Even as I give you occasion to reread this charming story, I must confess that it has bearing here only in the most remote sense; yet it smooths the way for what I have to say. Meanwhile I must proceed by way of matters even more distant.

The powers inherent in the human being may be divided into the general and the specific. The general are to be regarded as neutral, latent powers which in some circumstances come to life and are directed by chance toward one goal or another. The human gift of imitation is general—man wishes to emulate, to copy what he sees, even without the least internal or external means to the end in question. It is therefore natural to wish to accomplish what one sees others accomplish. But the most natural thing would be for the son to take up his father's occupation. Here everything comes together: powers whose specific character and original direction may perhaps be inborn, then consistent, step-by-step practice and a developed skill that would oblige us to continue on the chosen path, even though other urges might develop in us, and free choice might lead us to another calling, for which Nature has given us neither capacity nor persistence. Thus on average those people are the happiest who find the opportunity to cultivate hereditary family talent within a domestic circle. We know of such dynasties of painters; there were, to be sure, weak talents among them, but even these produced something that was useful and perhaps better than if they had chosen to work with their limited talents in some other field.

But since this, too, is not what I wished to say, I must try to approach my revelations from some other angle.

The sad thing about being far from friends is that we cannot instantaneously join and connect thoughts by means of those intermediary and auxiliary elements that develop on both sides and weave back and forth as quick as lightning when we are together. Here, then, to begin with, a story from my early youth.

We children, raised in an old, solemn town, had grasped the notions of streets and squares, of walls, and then also of ramparts, the glacis, and nearby walled gardens. But to take us, or even more themselves, out into Nature, our parents had long ago planned, but repeatedly postponed, an excursion to friends in the country. Finally at Whitsuntide came a more pressing invitation and suggestion, accepted only under the condition that everything be arranged so that we could return home by nightfall; for it seemed utterly impossible to sleep anywhere but in one's own accustomed bed. It was of course difficult thus to condense the pleasures of the day; two friends were to be visited and their claims for all too rare company satisfied. Nevertheless, it was hoped that with strict punctuality everything could be accomplished.

On the third day of Whitsun, then, everyone was up and ready at the crack of dawn; the carriage drew up at the appointed time, and we had soon left all the restriction of streets, gates, bridges, and moats behind us. A free, open world spread out before our unaccustomed eyes. The green of the grain fields and meadows, newly refreshed by the night's rain, the somewhat lighter green of the recently opened buds of bushes and trees, the blinding white of tree blossoms spreading in every direction—all of this gave us a foretaste of happy, blissful hours.

We arrived punctually at our first stop, the home of a worthy pastor. After the warmest of welcomes we soon realized that the benefits of the missed church celebration were not being denied to spirits in search of tranquility and freedom. With joyful interest I beheld a rural household for the first time. Plow and harrow, wagons and carts showed unmistakable signs of use, and even the disgusting looking manure seemed the most indispensable part of the entire operation—it had been collected carefully and stored almost daintily. But our eager attention to these new, yet comprehensible, sights was soon directed to more immediate pleasures: tasty cakes, fresh milk, and many other country delicacies drew our avid consideration. The children then left the little kitchen garden and the hospitable arbor and scampered off to the nearby copse, to carry out a task given them by a well-meaning old aunt. They were to gather as many cowslips as possible, and bring them faithfully back to town, where the resourceful matron was wont to prepare all kinds of wholesome beverages from them.

While we ran hither and thither over the meadows, banks, and hedgerows in this occupation, several village children joined us, and the lovely scent of the spring flowers we had gathered seemed to become ever more invigorating and fragrant.

By now we had picked such a mass of stalks and blossoms that we did not know what to do with them; we began plucking off the yellowish flower heads, for this was really the only part that mattered. Each tried to fill his hat or cap with as many as possible.

The older of the boys, however, only a little ahead of me in age, the son of the fisherman, did not seem to enjoy this fooling with the flowers. He was a boy to whom I had been especially drawn as soon as he had appeared, and he now invited me to go with him down to the river, which, already of considerable width, flowed not far off. We settled down with fishing rods in a shady spot where scores of little fish darted back and forth in the deep, still, clear water. He kindly showed me what to do, how to bait my line, and I succeeded a few times running in jerking the smallest of these delicate creatures against their will up into the air. As we sat there calmly, leaning against each other, he seemed to grow bored, and called my attention to a sandy spit that stretched out into the water on our side. It would make an excellent bathing place. He could not resist the temptation, he exclaimed, leaping to his feet, and before I knew it was down below, undressed, and in the water.

Since he was an excellent swimmer, he soon left the shallow spot, entrusted himself to the current, and came up toward me, in the deeper water. A very strange mood had come over me. Grasshoppers danced around me, ants scurried about, colorful beetles hung in the branches, and gold-glittering dragonflies, for so he had called them, hovered and fluttered, phantomlike, at my feet, just as the boy, pulling a large crab from a tangle of roots, held it up gaily for me to see, then skillfully concealed it again in its old place, ready for the catch. It was so hot and sultry all around that one longed to be out of the sun and in the shade, then out of the cool of the shade and down into the cooler water. So it was easy for him to lure me down. He did not have to repeat his invitation often, for I found it irresistible and felt, despite some fear of my parents, as well as wariness toward the unknown element, extraordinary excitement. But once I undressed on the sand, I cautiously ventured into the water, though no farther than the gently sloping bottom permitted. He let me linger there, moved away in the buoyant element, then swam back, and as he climbed out and stood up to dry off in the light of the sun, I thought my eyes were dazzled by a triple sun: so beautiful was the human form, of which I had never had any notion. He seemed to look at me with the same attention. Quickly dressed, we still faced each other without veils. Our hearts were drawn to one another, and with fiery kisses we swore eternal friendship.

Then running, running we reached the house, just in time, for the company was setting out on an hour and a half's walk along the pleasantest path imaginable through bushes and forest to the home of the magistrate. My friend accompanied me; we already seemed inseparable. But when at the halfway-point I asked permission to take him along to the magistrate's house, the pastor's wife refused, quietly remarking that it was not proper. Instead she commissioned him urgently to tell his father, when he returned, that she absolutely must have some fine crabs waiting when she returned, since she wished to give the guests this specialty to take back to town. The boy departed, but promised by word and gesture that he would await me late in the afternoon at this spot in the woods.

Then our party reached the magistrate's, where we encountered another country household, but of a higher order. The delay of the midday meal through the overzealousness of our hostess did not make me impatient, since the daughter of the house, somewhat younger than I, accompanied me to the well-tended flower garden for a walk that I found highly enjoyable. Spring flowers of all kinds stood in neatly laid-out beds, either filling them or decorating their borders. My companion was pretty, blond, and gentle; we were at ease with one another, soon took each other's hands and seemed to wish for nothing more. Thus we strolled past tulip beds, past rows of narcissus and jonquils; she showed me places where magnificent hyacinths had just finished blooming. But provision had also been made for the seasons to come: the foliage of the coming ranunculi and anemones was already growing green; the care lavished on the numerous staked carnations promised a rich flowering, while even earlier hope was budding in the many-flowered lily stalks judiciously interspersed among the roses. And so many arbors promised soon to offer glorious shade with honeysuckle, jasmine, grapes, and other vines!

When, after so many years, I consider my situation at that time, it seems truly enviable. At the very same moment I was seized by the premonition of friendship and love. For as I reluctantly took leave of the lovely girl, I was comforted by the thought that I could share these feelings with my young friend, confide in him and enjoy his sympathy simultaneously with these fresh, new emotions.

And if I may add another observation, I should confess that in the course of life that first blossoming of the external world struck me as a revelation of Nature herself, compared to which everything else that later touches our senses seems a mere copy, which, however closely it may approach it, still lacks that original spirit and meaning.

How we would despair, seeing the external world so cold, so lifeless, were it not that in our inner self something germinates that transfigures Nature in quite another way, by granting us the creative power to beautify ourselves in her.

It was already dusk when we once more reached the spot in the woods where my young friend had promised to await me. I strained my eyes to make out his presence; when I did not succeed, I impatiently dashed ahead of our slowly moving party, and ran back and forth in the bushes. I called out, I was worried; he was not to be seen and did not answer. For the first time in my life I experienced passionate pain, doubled and redoubled.

There had already sprung up in me an unreasonable need for confiding intimacy; I already had an irresistible longing to free my spirit of the image of that blond girl by talking about her, and to unburden my heart of the feelings she had awakened. My heart was full, my mouth was already murmuring, ready to overflow. Out loud I took that good lad to task for injuring our friendship, for neglecting a promise.

But heavier trials were in store for me. From the first houses of the village women rushed out wailing; howling children followed; no one would answer any questions. We saw a mournful procession round the corner; it moved slowly down the long street. It looked like a funeral procession, but a multiple one; there seemed to be no end of litters and stretchers. The wailing continued, swelled, the crowd grew. "They drowned, all of them drowned, every one. Him? Who? Which one?" The mothers who saw their children around them seemed relieved. But one grave man stepped forward and spoke to the pastor's wife. "Unfortunately I stayed away too long. Adolf drowned, all five of them. He wanted to keep his promise and mine." The man—it was the fisherman himself—passed on, following the procession; we stood shocked and paralyzed. Then a little boy came up, carrying a sack. "Here are the crabs, Mistress Pastor," he said, and held the sign high in the air. We shrank from it, as though from something unutterably destructive. There were questions, inquiries, and this much was learned: this last little fellow had stayed on the bank to gather the crabs thrown to him from below. Finally, but only after repeated questioning, it emerged that Adolf had gone down to and into the river with two sensible boys.

Two others, younger, had joined them unbidden, and were not to be restrained by any scolding or threats. The first group was almost past a stony, dangerous place; the others slipped, grabbed for the older ones, and each dragged down the one ahead of him. This finally happened to the first in line as well, and they all fell into the deep water. Adolf, who was a good swimmer, could have saved himself, but all the others clung to him in their fear, and he was pulled under. The little fellow had then run crying into the village, still clutching his sack of crabs. Along with others who were summoned, the fisherman, who by chance was returning late, rushed to the river. One after the other they were pulled out of the water, dead, and now they were being brought back.

The pastor and my father made their way somberly to the town hall. The full moon had risen and illuminated the paths of death. I followed, vehemently determined. I was not allowed in; I was in a dreadful state. I circled the building without pause. Finally I saw my chance and jumped in through an open window.

In the large hall, which is used for gatherings of every sort, the unfortunates lay stretched out on straw, naked, gleaming white bodies, brilliant even in the dim lamp light. I threw myself upon the largest, my friend. I would not be able to describe my state. I wept bitterly and flooded his broad chest with countless tears. I had heard something about rubbing being helpful in such a case, so I rubbed my tears in, and deceived myself with the warmth I generated. In my confusion I thought of blowing breath into him, but the rows of pearly teeth were firmly clamped shut, and the lips, on which our parting kiss still seemed to linger, refused the slightest sign of response. Despairing of any human help, I turned to prayer; I implored, I prayed; it seemed to me that at this moment I would have to perform a miracle, to call forth the soul still within him or to lure it back if it were still hovering nearby.

They tore me away. Weeping, sobbing, I sat in the carriage, and scarcely noticed what my parents were saying. Our mother, as I was to hear repeated so often afterwards, had accepted it as God's will. I, in the meantime, had fallen asleep and awoke late the next morning, dejected and in a puzzling, bewildered state.

But when I went down to breakfast, I found my mother, my aunt, and the cook, in grave consultation. The crabs were not to be boiled, not to be served; my father would not endure so direct a reminder of the recent misfortune. My aunt seemed most eager to get her hands on these unusual creatures, but still had time to scold me for forgetting to bring back the cowslips. But soon she seemed to calm down on this score, when the gruesome creatures, still alive and crawling all over each other, were placed at her disposal. She thereupon reached agreement with the cook on what to do with them.

But to illuminate the meaning of this scene, I must report some particulars about this woman's character and ways. From the moral point of view, her ruling qualities were in no way laudable; yet from the social and political point of view, they produced various good effects. She was genuinely parsimonious, for she begrudged every last penny that had to leave her hand, and was ever on the lookout for surrogates to supply her needs, either for nothing, by barter or by some other means. Thus the cowslips had been intended for a tea, which she thought healthier than any Chinese variety. God had bestowed on each land whatever it needed, be it for nourishment, seasoning, or medication; there was no need to turn to foreign lands for them. So she raised in her small garden everything which to her mind made food tasty and was wholesome for those who were ill; nor did she ever visit someone else's garden without bringing back something of this sort.

We gladly indulged her in this disposition and its consequent actions, because her diligently accumulated savings were eventually to benefit the rest of the family. Even my father and mother humored her and furthered her efforts in this regard.

But another passion of hers, an active one, which came ceaselessly and officiously to the fore, was the pride she took in being considered an important and influential personage. And she had indeed earned and achieved such fame, for she knew how to turn the otherwise idle, and often even harmful, gossip prevalent among women to her own advantage. She had detailed knowledge of everything that went on in town, and therefore also of the intimate affairs of families, and a dubious situation could hardly arise without her involving herself in it. This was all the easier for her because she aimed only to be of help, yet contrived to enhance her own fame and good name thereby. She had brought about many a marriage, with which at least one of the parties, perhaps, remained satisfied. But what occupied her most was furthering and promoting persons who were seeking some office or appointment. In this way she actually acquired a large number of clients, whose influence she was subsequently able to exploit.

As the widow of a not insignificant official, a strict and upright man, she had learned how trifles can win over those who cannot be swayed by significant offerings.

In order not to stray into further digressions, however, let me observe first that she had managed to obtain considerable influence with a man who occupied an important position. He was as stingy as she, and, unfortunately for him, also a gourmand with a sweet tooth. To bring him a delicious dish, under some pretext or other, was her chief concern. His conscience was not the most tender, but in dubious cases his courage and boldness had to be called on as well, if he was to overcome the resistance of his colleagues and to silence the voice of duty, which they invoked against him.

As it happened, my aunt was currently favoring an unworthy person. She had already done everything possible to insinuate him; the affair had taken a positive turn, and now the crabs, rarely seen here, came at just the right moment. They were to be fed carefully and brought, a few at a time, to the table of her highly placed patron, who customarily ate his sparse meals all alone.

It should be added that the unfortunate event gave occasion for much discussion and social stir. At that time my father was one of the first who was impelled by a general spirit of benevolence to extend his observations and concern beyond his family and city. He had worked with sensible doctors and police officials to eliminate the great obstacles that had originally stood in the way of vaccination against the smallpox. Better care in the hospitals, more humane treatment of prisoners, and whatever else might be included here constituted the preoccupation, if not of his life, at least of his reading and reflections. And indeed, he expressed his convictions everywhere and did much good thereby.

He viewed civil society, under whatever form of government, as a natural condition that had its good and bad aspects, its normal patterns of life, alternating fat years and lean, and its no less fortuitous and irregular hail storms, floods, and fires. The good was to be seized and put to use, the bad averted or endured. But nothing, he believed, was more desirable than to propagate general goodwill, independent of every other consideration.

As a result of such a disposition he was now impelled to bring forward again a beneficial measure he had previously promoted. This was the resuscitation of those given up for dead, no matter how they might have lost the external signs of life. Listening to these conversations, I learned that the opposite had been attempted and applied in the case of the drowned children, that indeed they had, as it were, been murdered; it was further believed that bleeding might have rescued all of them. In my youthful fervor I therefore vowed secretly to lose no opportunity to master everything that might be necessary in such situations, above all bleeding and other things of that sort.

But how soon ordinary life carried me off. The need for friendship and love had been aroused, and I was always looking for ways to satisfy it. Meanwhile my sensuality, imagination, and mind were excessively occupied with the theater; how far I was led and misled, I must not repeat.

But if after this involved story I have to confess that I still have not arrived at my intended goal and can hope to reach it only by a detour, what can I say! How shall I excuse myself? At all events, I could offer the following observation: if it is permissible for the humorist to throw together a hodge-podge of inconsequential details, if he brazenly leaves it to the reader to extract the half-meanings hidden in the confusion, should it not be incumbent upon the intelligent and reasonable person to strive in a seemingly curious fashion after many different points, until one can finally identify them, reflected and gathered into one focal point, and comprehend how the most diverse influences surrounding a person impel him to a decision which he could have made in no other way, neither out of inner impulse nor outward occasion?

Among the variety of things I still have left to say, I have a choice as to what I attempt first. But this does not matter, either; you will simply have to be patient, read, and read on, and in the end what would have struck you as most curious, had it been expressed in a word, will suddenly leap out at you and seem perfectly natural, so much so that afterward you will wonder why you had to give a moment's notice to these introductory remarks in the form of explanations.

But now to get somewhat back on course, I shall turn to that oarlock again, and recall a conversation that I by chance had with our true friend Jarno, whom I found in the mountains under the name of Montan, a conversation that had awakened especially strong feelings in me. The circumstances of our lives follow a mysterious course, which cannot be calculated. You surely remember the set of instruments your capable surgeon produced, when I lay wounded in the woods and you came to my aid? At the time, it glistened so before my eyes and made such a deep impression that I was utterly enchanted when, years later, I encountered it again in the hands of a younger man. The latter placed no particular value on it; all the instruments had been improved in recent times and made more functional. I acquired it all the more easily because that helped him to procure a new one. From then on, I carried it with me always, not for use, to be sure, but rather as a comforting memento: it was witness to the moment in which my happiness began, though I was to reach it only by a great detour.

By chance Jarno saw it the night we stayed at the charcoal burner's; he recognized it at once, and replied to my explanation, "I have nothing against setting up such a fetish, as a reminder of many an unexpected blessing, of the significant consequences of a random circumstance. It uplifts us, as something that points to the incommensurable, strengthens us in perplexity, and encourages our hopes. But it would be better if you had let yourself be prompted by these instruments to learn their use as well, and how to perform what they mutely demand of you."

"Let me admit," I replied, "that this has occurred to me hundreds of times. An inner voice spoke up inside me, allowing me to recognize in this my true vocation." I then told him the story of the drowned boys, and how I had heard at the time that they might have been saved, if they had been bled. I had resolved to learn how, but every hour effaced my resolution.

"Then take it up now," Montan said. "I have seen you occupied so long with matters that bear on and relate to the human mind, spirit, heart, and whatever else it is called. Yet what have you gained by it, for yourself and for others? The ills of the soul, into which we fall through bad luck or our own errors: common sense can do nothing to cure them, reason but little, time much, but decisive action most of all. Let everyone work with and on himself in this regard; that you have learned, both from your own experience and from that of others."

He attacked me with vehement and bitter words, as is his wont, and said many harsh things that I do not care to repeat. He concluded by saying that nothing was more worth learning or achieving than to help the healthy person when he was injured by some chance. With intelligent treatment, Nature would soon be restored. The sick should be left to physicians, but no one needed a surgeon so much as the healthy. In the tranquility of rural life, in the intimate circle of the family he was just as welcome as in the turmoil of battle and its aftermath; at the sweetest of life's moments as at its bitterest and most terrible. And meanwhile misfortune ruled everywhere, grimmer than death itself and just as relentless, indeed even more ruthless, spoiling life and its pleasures.

You know him and can imagine without much difficulty that he spared neither me nor the world. But he relied most on the argument that he brought to bear against me in the name of society as a whole. "It is all tomfoolery," he said, "your liberal education and all efforts in that direction. What counts is that a man understand one particular thing and do it supremely well, better than anyone else in the vicinity. That is self-evident, particularly in our league. You are just at an age when a person makes a thoughtful commitment, evaluates with insight what lies before him, approaches it from the proper angle, and directs his talents and skills to the proper goal."

Why should I continue to state the obvious? He made clear to me that I could receive a dispensation from the peculiar requirement of an unsettled life, though obtaining it would be difficult. "You are the kind of person," he said, "who takes easily to a place, but not easily to a vocation. An unsettled life is prescribed for everyone like that, in hopes that they find their way to a stable way of life. But if you will truly dedicate yourself to the most divine of professions, to heal without miracles and to perform miracles without words, then I will intercede for you." He said all this hastily, and added whatever else in the way of powerful arguments his eloquence could muster.

At this point I am inclined to end. But first you shall hear in detail how I have used the permission to stay longer in particular places, and how I have been able to enter into and train myself in the occupation to which I have always secretly been drawn. Enough! For the great project you are all undertaking, I will appear as a useful, a necessary member of the company, and will follow your paths with a measure of confidence, with a certain pride, for it is a praiseworthy pride to be worthy of you all.

Reflections in the Spirit of the Wanderers:
Art, Ethics, Nature

Everything clever has already been thought; one must merely try to think it again.

How can one come to know oneself? Through contemplation never, more likely through action. Try to do your duty, and you shall know at once what you are.

But what is your duty? What the day demands.

The rational world should be regarded as a great, immortal individual, who ineluctably brings about that which must be, and thereby gains mastery even over chance.

The longer I live, the more irked I am to see man, who actually occupies his high position in order to rule over Nature, in order to free himself and his loved ones from the harsh grip of necessity—when I see how, from some false preconception, he does the very opposite of what he wants, and then, because the undertaking as a whole is ruined, dabbles wretchedly in details.

Capable active man, earn and expect for yourself:
from the great—grace,
from the mighty—favor,
from the active and good—furtherance,
from the multitude—popularity,
from the individual—love.

Dilettantes, when they have done their best, are wont to excuse themselves by saying the work is not yet finished. Of course, it can never be finished, because it was never begun properly. The master presents his work as finished after only a few strokes; polished or not, it is nevertheless complete. The cleverest dilettante gropes in uncertainty, and as the work grows, the original insecurity becomes ever more perceptible. At the very end, the initial failure is revealed, when it cannot be corrected, and so of course the work cannot be finished.

For true art there can be no schooling, but certainly preparation. What is best, however, is for the humblest student to participate in the work of the master. Excellent painters have begun as a grinders of colors.

Another matter altogether is imitation, to which man's natural inclination toward activity can be drawn fortuitously by a significant artist, who executes difficult things with ease.

We are sufficiently convinced of the necessity of the plastic artist's doing studies from Nature and of their value in general; yet we cannot deny that we are often troubled when we become aware of the misuse of such a laudable endeavor.

To our mind, the young artist should embark on few, if any, studies from Nature without also thinking how he would develop each sketch into a whole, how he might transform this detail into a pleasing picture and enclose it in a frame, to present it to the art lover and connoisseur.

Many a beautiful thing stands isolated in the world, but it is for the mind to discover the connections and thereby create works of art.—The flower acquires its charm only from the insect that clings to it, from the dewdrop that moistens it, from the vase from which it draws its last nourishment. There is no bush, no tree, that cannot be given significance by the proximity of a rock or spring, or that would not gain greater appeal simply by being portrayed at a moderate remove. The same holds for human figures and animals of every sort.

The advantage the young artist derives from this is manifold. He learns to think, to join properly what belongs together, and if he composes cleverly in this fashion, he will not lack for what is called originality, the development of diversity out of a single element.

Should he meet the requirements of true art pedagogy itself in this respect, he has gained along the way the great additional benefit, which ought not to be sneered at, that he has learned to produce saleable drawings, graceful and pleasing to the collector.

Such a work need not be executed and polished to the highest degree. If it has been well observed, thought out, and completed, it may be more attractive to the collector than a more ambitious, elaborate work.

Let every young artist look through the studies in his sketch books and portfolio and consider how many of those drawings he might have made appealing and desirable in this manner.

This is not a question of aiming for the heights, though we might also speak of that; it is said only to warn against following a false path and to point to the higher way.

Let the artist try this out for only half a year and never reach for charcoal or brush without intending to make a completed picture of the natural object before him. If he has native talent, it will soon be revealed what purpose we had in mind with these suggestions.

Tell me with whom you associate, and I will tell you who you are. Once I know with what you occupy yourself, I know what you can become.

Every man must think in his own way, since he always finds on his path a truth, or a sort of truth, which helps him through life. Only he should not let himself go; he must keep watch over himself; naked instinct ill becomes a human being.

Unrestrained activity, of whatever kind, leads at last to bankruptcy.

In the works of man, as in those of Nature, we must attend first and foremost to intentions.

People go wrong, in regard to themselves and others, because they treat the means as an end, so that for sheer activity nothing happens, or perhaps something detestable.

What we think out, what we undertake, should be of such perfect beauty and purity that the world could only mar it. We would then have the advantage that we could adjust what has been disrupted and restore what has been destroyed.

With whole, half, and quarter mistakes it is exceedingly difficult and troublesome to put them right, to sift them, and to place their elements of truth in the proper context.

It is not always necessary for the truth to be tangible; it is enough if it hovers over us spiritually and produces harmony, if it wafts gravely and kindly through the air like the pealing of bells.

When I inquire of younger German painters, even those who have spent some time in Italy, why they assault our eyes with such ugly, glaring colors, especially in their landscapes, and seem to shun any harmony, they reply boldly and confidently: that is precisely how they see Nature.

Kant has made us aware that there is such as thing as a critique of reason, that this highest faculty possessed by man has cause to keep watch over itself. What great benefits this voice has brought us, I would hope everyone has observed in himself. In the same sense I should like to suggest that a critique of the senses is necessary if art, and especially German art, is ever to recover its vitality and move forward at a gratifying pace.

Though born a rational being, man needs much education, whether gradually imparted by the care of his parents and teachers, by gentle example, or revealed by stern experience. Likewise a *potential* artist is born, but not an *accomplished* one. He may look at the world with fresh eyes, he may have a good eye for form, proportion, movement; but for the higher aspects of composition, for placement, light, shadow, color, he may lack natural talent, without knowing it.

Unless he is inclined to learn from more highly trained artists of past and present days what he lacks in order to be a true artist, a false notion of preserving originality will lead him to look over his own shoulder. For not only what we are born with, but also whatever we can acquire belongs to us, and we are those things.

General notions and great arrogance are always poised to bring about dreadful misfortune.

"To play the flute, it is not enough to blow; you must also move your fingers."

Botanists have a category of plants they call *Incompletae.* One may also say that there are incomplete, unfinished human beings. They are those whose actions and achievements are not in proportion to their longing and striving.

The humblest person can be complete if he operates within the limits of his capacities and skills; but even great strengths are obscured, nullified, and destroyed if that indispensable moderation is lacking. We will see more of this evil in modern times, for who will be able to meet the challenges of this much more demanding age, and its rapid pace?

Only intelligent and active people, who know their own powers and utilize them with moderation and good sense, will go far in the world.

A great error: thinking oneself more than one is, and valuing oneself less than one is worth.

Now and then I encounter a youth who seems to need no alteration or improvement. But it alarms me when I see so many entirely ready to swim with the stream of the age, and this is the point I always wish to call to mind: that man is given the rudder of his fragile bark in order that he follow not the caprice of the waves but his own will, informed by insight.

But how is a young man to learn on his own to consider reprehensible and harmful things that everyone does, approves and encourages? Why should he not let himself and his instincts go along as well?

To my mind, the greatest evil of our time, which allows nothing to come to fruition, is that each moment consumes its predecessor, each day is squandered in the next, and so we live perpetually from hand to mouth, without ever producing anything. Do we not already have newspapers for each part of the day! Some clever soul could probably insert one or two more. The result is that everyone's deeds, actions, scribblings, indeed, all his intentions, are dragged before the public. No one is permitted to rejoice or sorrow except to entertain all the rest; and so everything leaps from house to house, from town to town, from empire to empire, and finally from continent to continent, always express.

As little as the steam engines can be throttled can anything similar be done in the moral realm. The liveliness of commerce, the continual rustle of paper money, the increase in debts to pay off other debts—all these are frightful elements that the young man of the present confronts. He is fortunate if he is endowed with a moderate, peaceable disposition that neither makes excessive demands on the world nor allows itself to be determined by it.

But the spirit of the day threatens him in every sphere, and nothing is more important than to make him aware early enough of the direction toward which his will must steer.

The significance of purity in word and deed grows with the years, and if I have someone around me for a longer period, I always try to alert him to the differences between straightforwardness, trust, and indiscretion, that in fact there are no distinct differences, but only subtle shadings, from the most innocent act to the most destructive, which must be observed, or rather, felt.

Here we must exercise our tact, or else we run the danger that we may unwittingly forfeit the good opinion of people just as we are trying to win it. One does come to learn this in the course of life, but only after paying a high tuition, which one can alas not spare one's descendants.

The relationship of the arts and sciences to life is very different, depending on the level at which they are situated, on the conditions of the time, and on thousands of other chance factors. For this reason no one can easily make sense of it as a whole.

Poetry has its greatest effect at the beginnings of situations, even if they are completely primitive, half cultivated; or at a turning point for a culture, as it becomes aware of a foreign culture, so that one might say in that case also that the effect of newness is making itself felt.

Music, in the best sense of the word, has less need of newness. In fact, the older it is, the more accustomed one is to it, the greater its effect.

The dignity of art appears perhaps most eminently in music, which has no content that must be discounted. It is entirely form and attitude and elevates and ennobles everything it expresses.

Music is either sacred or profane. The sacred is wholly suitable to its dignity, and here music exerts the greatest influence on life, an influence which remains constant through all periods and epochs. Profane music should certainly be cheerful.

Any music that mixes the sacred and the profane is godless, and halfhearted music which prefers to express weak, pitiful, wretched emotions is tasteless. For it is not serious enough to be sacred, and it lacks the chief characteristic of its opposite: cheerfulness.

The holiness of church music, the cheerfulness and playfulness of folk music are the two pivots about which true music revolves. At these two points it always displays an unfailing effect: devotion or dancing. Mixing causes confusion; the weakened form is flat, and if music turns to didactic or descriptive poetry and the like, it becomes cold.

Sculpture is effective only in its highest realization; anything mediocre can be impressive for more than one reason, but mediocre art works of this sort confuse more than they please. Sculpture must therefore seek some interesting content, and that it finds in the portrayal of important people. But here, too, it must attain a high degree of excellence if it is to be both true and dignified.

Painting is the most permissive and comfortable of all the arts. The most permissive because people give it a good deal of credit and take pleasure in it for the sake of its subject matter, even when it is only craftsmanship or scarcely art, partly because a soulless technical accomplishment arouses admiration in uneducated and educated viewers alike, so that it need merely approach true art in order to be warmly received. True colors, surfaces, relationships among the visible elements are pleasing in themselves, and since in any case the eye is accustomed to seeing everything, a misdrawn figure and thus a defective drawing are not so repugnant to it as a discord to the ear. One accepts the poorest copy, because one is accustomed to seeing even poorer objects. Consequently the painter need be only a middling artist to find a larger audience than a musician of the same stature. At any rate, the lesser artist can always function by himself, whereas the lesser musician must ally himself with others, to produce some effect through joint achievement.

To the question of whether in viewing artistic achievements one should or should not draw comparisons, we would reply as follows: the trained expert should draw comparisons, because he has the ideal hovering before him, has already grasped what can and cannot be achieved. The amateur, on the way toward acquiring such training, serves himself best when he draws no comparisons but considers each achievement separately; he thereby gradually develops his feeling and sense for general principles. The comparisons of novices are actually only a convenience to avoid making a judgment.

Love of truth manifests itself in this, that one can find and value the good everywhere.

A historical sense for mankind means one so well trained that when it evaluates contemporary accomplishments and merits, it also considers the past in its assessment.

The best thing we have from history is the enthusiasm it arouses.

Peculiarity elicits peculiarity.

One must take into account that there are a great many people who also want to say something important, but are not productive, and so the strangest things come out.

Profound and serious thinkers are not in good odor with the public.

If I am to listen to someone else's opinion, it must be expressed positively; I have enough problematic thoughts of my own.

Superstition is integral to man's being, and when we think we have banished it entirely, it takes refuge in the strangest nooks and crannies, from which, when it feels relatively safe, it suddenly emerges.

We would know a good many things better if we did not want to know them too precisely. After all, an object becomes comprehensible to us only at an angle of less than forty-five degrees.

Microscopes and telescopes actually confuse man's clear senses.

I keep still about many things, for I do not want to confuse people, and am quite content if they are happy when I am annoyed.

Everything that liberates the mind without giving us more self-mastery is harmful.

The *what* of a work of art interests people more than its *how*. They can grasp the former through details but cannot comprehend the latter as a whole. Hence the focus on specific passages, by which process, if one looks closely, the effect of the whole is still conveyed, but unbeknownst to all.

The question "where did the author get this?" likewise leads only to the *what*, while the *how* remains a mystery.

The imagination is regulated only by art, especially by poetry. There is nothing more frightful than imagination without taste.

Mannerism is idealism gone wrong, subjectivized idealism. Hence it seldom lacks cleverness.

The philologist must rely on the congruity of the written tradition. The basis of it is a manuscript, but a manuscript may contain actual gaps, copying errors which make for gaps in the sense, and whatever else may be a flaw in a manuscript. Now a second copy turns up, and a third. Comparison among these makes it possible to perceive more and more of what is sensible and rational in the transmitted texts. Indeed the philologist goes further and demands that his inner sense be increasingly able to grasp and portray the congruity of the material without external aids. Since a special tact, a special immersion in his long dead author are necessary for this, and a certain degree of ingenuity is required, we cannot blame the philologist if he takes it upon himself as well to make judgments of taste, in which, however, he does not always excel.

A poet must rely on representation. The latter is at its best when it vies with reality, i.e., when the descriptions are so lively in spirit that they seem actual to everyone. At its peak, poetry seems completely external; the more it withdraws into internal feelings, the more it is in danger of sinking.—Poetry that represents only internal feelings, without embodying them in external images, or that does not imbue these external images with internal feelings—both are the final stages from which poetry crosses into ordinary life.

Rhetoric relies upon all the advantages of poetry, all its privileges. It appropriates them and misuses them to obtain certain momentary outward advantages in civic life—whether moral or immoral.

Literature is the fragment of fragments; the least part of all that ever happened and was spoken was written down, and of what was written only the least part has survived.

Lord Byron is a talent fully developed in natural truth and grandeur, although wild and disturbing; and therefore there is hardly anyone comparable to him.

The special value of so-called folk songs is that their motifs are drawn directly from Nature. However, the educated poet could also avail himself of this advantage, if he knew how.

But here the former always have the advantage, in that natural people are better at laconic expression than the educated.

Shakespeare is dangerous reading for budding talents; he compels them to reproduce him, and they think they are producing themselves.

No one can pass judgment on history unless he has experienced history himself. This is true of entire nations. The Germans can pass judgment on literature only now that they have a literature themselves.

One is truly alive only when one enjoys the good will of others.

Piety is not an end but a means to rise to the highest level of culture through pure peace of mind.

That is why one can observe that those who set piety as their end and goal usually become hypocrites.

"When a man is old, he must do more than when he was young."

Duty fulfilled continues to feel like guilt because one has never done quite enough to satisfy oneself.

Only the unloving person perceives faults; therefore, in order to recognize them, one must become unloving, but no more than is necessary for this purpose.

The greatest happiness is the one that corrects our faults and makes good our errors.

If thou canst read, then thou shalt understand; if thou canst write, then thou must know something; if thou canst believe, then thou shalt comprehend; when thou desirest, thou wilt be obligated; when thou demandest, thou wilt not receive, and when thou art experienced, thou shalt be useful.

We acknowledge no one but he who is useful to us. We acknowledge our prince because we see our property secured beneath his aegis. We expect of him protection against disagreeable circumstances from without and within.

The brook is friends with the miller, to whom it is useful, and is glad to tumble over the mill wheels. What good is it to the brook to glide indifferently through the valley?

He who contents himself with pure experience and acts according to it has truth enough. The growing child is wise in this respect.

Theory in and for itself is of no use, except insofar as it makes us believe in the relatedness of phenomena.

All abstractions are brought closer to human understanding through application, and similarly, human understanding attains abstraction through action and observation.

He who demands too much or who rejoices in complexity is exposed to confusion.

There is nothing wrong with thinking by analogy; analogies have the virtue of not concluding and not aiming for ultimate answers. By contrast, induction is dangerous, since it begins with a foregone conclusion in view and in working toward it sweeps both falsehood and truth along in its path.

Ordinary perception, an accurate view of earthly things, is a legacy common to all ordinary human understanding.—*Pure* perception of outer and inner aspects is very rare.

The former manifests itself in practical good sense, in direct action; the latter symbolically, preeminently in mathematics, in numbers and formulas, in speech, primordially, in tropes, as the poetry of genius, as the proverbial expression of human understanding.

That which is absent affects us through tradition. Its usual form is what we call historical. A higher form, allied to the imagination, is mythical. Should one look beyond this one for yet a third form, some kind of meaning, it turns into mysticism. It is also apt to become sentimental, so that we appropriate only what we find agreeable.

The agencies to which we must attend if we wish truly to advance are those which:

prepare
accompany
contribute
aid
advance
strengthen
hinder
have lasting effects.

In thought as in action one must distinguish between what is accessible and what is inaccessible. Without this, little can be accomplished in life or in knowledge.

"Le sens commun est le Genie de l'humanité."

Common sense, which is supposed to be the guiding spirit of mankind, must be viewed first of all through its manifestations. If we examine what mankind uses it for, we discover the following:

Mankind is limited by its needs. If these go unmet, it becomes impatient; if they are met, mankind seems apathetic. The true human being therefore alternates between the two states, and he will use his understanding, his so-called common sense, to satisfy his needs. This done, he has the task of filling up the spaces left by apathy. If this remains confined to the nearest and most essential boundaries, he can succeed. But if his needs mount, if they overstep the limits of the ordinary, then common sense no longer suffices, is no longer a guiding spirit, and the realm of error stands open before mankind.

There is nothing so irrational that good sense or accident cannot set it straight, and nothing so rational that bad sense and accident cannot lead it astray.

Every great idea, as soon as it makes an appearance, exerts a tyrannical effect; hence the advantages it produces are transformed all too soon into disadvantages. Therefore one can defend and celebrate any institution when one recalls its beginnings and can show that everything that was true of it in the beginning still holds.

Lessing, who resented many kinds of constraints, has one of his characters say: No one must be compelled. A witty man, inclined to gaiety, said: To want is to be compelled. A third, to be sure an educated man, added: To the person of insight, wanting comes naturally. And so the whole circle of understanding, will, and obligation seemed to be taken care of. But on the whole, man's understanding, of whatever sort, determines his actions and omissions; for which reason nothing is more terrifying than watching ignorance in action.

These are two forces for peace: justice and propriety.

Justice emphasizes obligation, government authority seemliness. Justice deliberates and resolves, authority supervises and commands. Justice pertains to the individual, authority to the entirety.

The history of knowledge is a great fugue, in which the voices of the peoples come to the fore in turn.

In the natural sciences there are a number of problems which cannot be discussed properly without enlisting the aid of metaphysics—but not school wisdom and empty words; it is what was, is, and will be before, with, and after physics.

Authority, meaning that in the past something has happened, been said, or been decided, has great worth. But only the pedant would demand authority all the time.

Old foundations are to be honored, but we must not give up our right to lay new foundations again.

Stand fast where you are!—A maxim more necessary than ever, since on the one hand people are being swept into large parties; yet on the other hand each individual wants to make his mark according to his own insight and ability.

It is always better to say directly what one thinks without arguing too much, for all the arguments we present are merely variations on our opinions, and those who are opposed hear neither the one nor the other.

Since I am becoming increasingly acquainted with and immersed in natural science and following its day-to-day progress, many reflections have forced themselves upon me. In regard to the progress and regress that occur simultaneously, I shall make only one here:

that we *cannot eliminate even recognized errors from science.* The reason for this is an open secret.

I call it an error when some event is interpreted falsely, when it is related to something else falsely, when it is derived falsely. Now it can happen, however, in the course of experience and thought, that a phenomenon is seen in its logical relationship, and correctly derived. People are pleased, but ascribe no special importance to it, and calmly leave the error lying right next to it. I know of a whole little warehouse of errors that are being carefully stored.

Now since nothing really interests people except their own opinions, everyone with an opinion to express looks to the right and to the left for expedients to bolster himself and others. The truth is used as long as it serves the turn; but in the heat of rhetoric falsehoods are also seized upon wherever they can be used for the moment, to confuse the issue with half arguments, or to patch together fragments into an apparent whole. When I first discovered this, I was annoyed; then I was depressed, and now it gives me malicious pleasure. I have promised myself never again to unmask such a procedure.

Each thing that exists is an analogue for all that exists; thus being always seems to us separate and interconnected at the same time. If the analogy is pursued too far, everything becomes identical; if it is avoided, everything scatters into an infinitude of particulars. In both cases reflection stagnates, either overwhelmed by life or killed.

Reason is directed at that which is becoming, understanding at that which has become. The former does not ask "to what end?" nor the latter "whence?"—Reason delights in things unfolding; understanding would like to keep everything fixed, so as to make use of it.

It is an innate human peculiarity, and one intimately bound up with man's nature, that he finds what is most immediate insufficient for knowledge. Yet every phenomenon of which we become aware ourselves is what is most immediate at the moment, and we can demand an explanation of it, if we try hard to penetrate it.

But men will not learn this, since it goes counter to their nature. For this reason even educated people, when they have identified something true right on the spot, cannot refrain from connecting it not only with what is most immediate but also with the most distant and faraway things, so that error is piled on error. The immediate phenomenon is connected with the distant one only in the sense that everything is based upon a few great laws that manifest themselves everywhere.

What is the universal?
The individual case.
What is the particular?
Millions of cases.

There are two errors analogy must avoid: the first, lapsing into witticisms, where it evaporates into nothingness; the other, veiling itself in tropes and images, which, however, is less harmful.

Neither mythology nor legends are to be tolerated in science. Leave these to the poets, whose calling it is to employ them for the benefit and pleasure of the world. Let the man of science confine himself to the most immediate, clearest actuality. Should he, however, occasionally want to step forth as a rhetorician, let that not be forbidden to him.

To save myself, I regard all appearances as independent of one another and try to isolate them strictly. Then I regard them as correlates, and they join together and acquire a life of their own. I apply this primarily to Nature. But this form of observation is also fruitful with respect to the most recent violent developments in world history that encompass us.

Everything we call invention or discovery in the higher sense is the significant exercise or enactment of a basic feeling for truth, which, having long since developed unobtrusively within us, unexpectedly leads to a fruitful insight with lightning swiftness. It is a revelation from within in response to something from without that gives man a presentiment of his godlike nature. It is a synthesis of world and spirit, offering blissful assurance of the eternal harmony of existence.

Man must cling to the belief that the incomprehensible is comprehensible; otherwise he would not undertake research.

Every particular is comprehensible if it can be applied in some way. In this manner the incomprehensible can become useful.

There is a tender empirics that enters into so intimate an identification with its object that it actually becomes a theory. But this heightening of intellectual capacity is characteristic of a highly developed age.

The most obnoxious are the niggling observers and capricious theorists; their experiments are petty and complicated, their hypotheses abstruse and peculiar.

There are pedants who are also rogues, and these are the worst of all.

One need not travel around the world to know that the sky is blue everywhere.

The universal and the particular come together; the particular is the universal appearing under various conditions.

One need not have seen and experienced everything for oneself; but if you choose to trust someone else and his representations, bear in mind that now you are dealing with three elements: with the object and two subjectivities.

The fundamental property of the living entity: to divide, to unite, to dissolve in the universal, to persist in its particularity, to metamorphose, to assert its specificity, and, since anything alive can manifest itself under thousands of conditions, to emerge and disappear, to solidify and to melt, to freeze and to flow, to expand and contract. Since all these processes are taking place in the same moment, anything and everything can occur at the same time. Origination and extinction, creation and destruction, birth and death, joy and sorrow—everything interacts, in equal sense and equal measure, for which reason even the most particular event always appears as the image and likeness of the universal.

If all existence is an eternal parting and uniting, then it follows that human beings, in view of this overwhelming situation, will also be forever parting and coming together.

A clear distinction must be drawn between physics and mathematics. The former must exist in complete independence and endeavor to penetrate Nature and the sacred secret of life with all its loving, reverent, pious powers, quite untroubled by what mathematics achieves and does for its part. Conversely, mathematics must declare its independence of everything external to itself, must follow its own great intellectual course and develop itself more purely than is possible if, as formerly, it concerns itself with what is at hand and attempts either to gain from it or adapt to it.

Natural science requires a categorical imperative as much as moral science; however, one must remember that that is not the end but only the beginning.

The highest wisdom would be to comprehend that everything factual is already theory. The blue of the sky reveals to us the primary law of chromatics. Do not look for anything behind the phenomena; they themselves are the lesson.

In the sciences there are many certainties, as soon as one does not allow oneself to be led astray by the exceptions and learns to show proper respect for the problems.

When I finally come to rest at the primal phenomenon, that, too, is merely resignation. Still, there is a vast difference between resigning myself to the limits of human existence itself and accepting the hypothetical limitations of my narrow individuality.

When one examines the problems treated by Aristotle, one is astounded by his powers of observation and by all the Greeks had eyes for. But they commit the mistake of being overhasty, proceeding directly from the phenomenon to its explanation, as a result of which wholly inadequate theoretical assertions appear. This, however, is a universal mistake, still committed today.

Hypotheses are lullabies with which the teacher rocks his students to sleep. The thoughtful, faithful observer learns more and more to recognize his limitations. He sees that the farther knowledge extends, the more problems appear.

Our mistake consists in doubting certainties and wanting to pin down uncertainties. My maxim in scientific research is: to hold onto the certainties and to be alert to the uncertainties.

Venial hypotheses are the ones proposed almost as a joke to be disproved by sober Nature.

How could anyone hope to appear as a master in his field if he taught nothing useless?

The height of folly is that everyone thinks he must pass on what is believed to be known.

Because didactic presentations must offer certainty, since the student does not want to have anything uncertain passed on to him, the teacher must not leave any problem unsolved, or even skirt it at some distance. Things must be immediately pinned down ("bepaalt," as they say in Dutch), and so for a while one believes one possesses the unknown territory, until someone else pulls the stakes out again, and promptly stakes out another, larger or smaller, area.

Lively inquiry into the cause, mistaking cause for effect, and resting content with a false theory do great harm, not to be dwelt on here.

If many people did not feel obliged to repeat what is untrue simply because they had said it before, they would have developed into very different people.

The false has the advantage that people can always gabble about it; the truth must be put to use at once, or else it is not there.

Anyone who does not comprehend how truth simplifies practical life, may fuss and fret all he likes in order to gloss over his misguided, laborious blunderings a little.

The Germans, and not they alone, possess the talent of making the sciences inaccessible.

The Englishman is a master at putting a new discovery to immediate use, until it leads again to new discoveries and fresh applications. Is it any wonder that they are ahead of us in everything?

The thinking man has the strange characteristic that he likes to conjure up an imaginary picture on the spot where an unresolved problem lies, a picture that continues to haunt him even when the problem has been solved and the truth revealed.

A particular cast of mind is required to conceive of a formless reality in its unique nature and to distinguish it from chimeras, which have a way of obtruding themselves upon us with a certain vivid reality.

In observing Nature on both a large scale and a small, I have unceasingly posed the question: is it the object or is it you yourself finding expression here? And in this spirit I observe both my predecessors and my colleagues.

Every man sees the finished and regulated, formed, complete world only as an element from which he is trying to create a particular world suitable to him. Capable people set to without hesitation and try to manage as best they can. Others waver on the brink; some even doubt of its existence.

Anyone thoroughly imbued with this basic truth would quarrel with no one, but would simply regard the other's way of thinking, as well as his own, as a phenomenon. For we witness almost daily that one person can comfortably entertain thoughts that are impossible for someone else to think, and indeed not only in things that have any influence at all on our weal and woe, but in things that are of no consequence.

One actually knows what one knows only for oneself. If I speak with someone about what I believe I know, he at once believes that he knows better, and I must always withdraw into myself with my knowledge.

Truth is constructive. From error nothing comes; it only entangles us.

Man finds himself surrounded by effects and cannot but inquire into the causes. For the sake of convenience he seizes upon the nearest as the best, and contents himself with that. This is especially true of the common run of human understanding.

If anyone sees an evil, he immediately addresses it directly, i.e., he immediately tries to treat the symptoms.

Reason has mastery only over what is alive; the already existent world, with which geognosy deals, is dead. Hence there can be no geology, for reason has no role here.

When I find the fragments of a skeleton, I can gather them and put them together. For here eternal reason speaks to me through an analogue, even if the skeleton be a giant sloth.

What no longer comes into existence we cannot imagine as coming into existence; we do not comprehend that which has already come into existence.

The widespread new vulcanism is actually a bold attempt to link the incomprehensible world of the present to an unknown bygone world.

Identical, or at least similar, effects are produced in various ways by natural forces.

Nothing is more odious than the majority, for it consists of a few strong leaders, of scoundrels who accommodate themselves, of weaklings who assimilate, and of the masses, who trundle along behind without knowing in the least what they want.

Mathematics, like dialectics, is an instrument of the inner higher sense, while in practice it is an art like rhetoric. For both of these, nothing has value but form; content is immaterial. Whether mathematics is adding up pennies or guineas, whether rhetoric is defending truth or falsehood, makes no difference to either.

Here, however, it is a matter of the nature of the person who follows such a trade, practices such an art. An effective lawyer in a just cause, a brilliant mathematician before the starry firmament, both appear equally godlike.

What is exact in mathematics but exactitude? And this latter, is it not the result of an inner sense of truth?

Mathematics has no power to dispel prejudice; it cannot temper self-will, nor calm factional spirit. It can do nothing at all in the moral sphere.

The mathematician is complete only insofar as he is a complete human being, as he is sensible in himself of the beauty inherent in truth. Only then will his work be thorough, transparent, perceptive, pure, clear, graceful, even elegant. All that is needed if one would be like La Grange.

Aptness, effectiveness, and grace reside not in language itself but in the spirit embodied in it. Thus, it is not left to the individual to confer these desirable qualities on his calculations, speeches, or poems. It is a question of whether Nature has endowed him with the requisite spiritual and moral qualities. Spiritual: the gifts of sight and insight; moral: that he may fend off the evil demons that could prevent him from paying due honor to the truth.

The desire to explain the simple by the complex, the easy by the difficult, is a mischief that pervades the entire body of knowledge. It is probably acknowledged by those with insight, but not always admitted to.

Subject physics to thorough study, and it will be found that the phenomena and experiments on which it is based vary in value.

Everything depends on the primary, the original experiments, and the chapter built upon them stands firm and secure. But there are also secondary and tertiary ones, etc. If they are given the same credence, they only confuse what had been clarified by the first ones.

A great evil in science, indeed in all realms, is that people who possess no capacity for ideas venture into theory, because they do not comprehend that even a great deal of knowledge does not justify such a step. They set to work with a laudable degree of human understanding, but this latter has its limits and risks becoming absurd when they are exceeded. The allotted sphere and legacy of the human understanding is the realm of action and practical affairs. So long as it is active, it will seldom go wrong. The higher reaches of thought, however, drawing conclusions and forming judgments, are not its territory.

Experience is at first useful to science, then becomes harmful, because experience makes laws and exceptions visible. The average of the two by no means yields truth.

It is said that between two opposing opinions the truth lies in the middle. By no means! The problem lies between them, the unseeable, eternally active life, contemplated in tranquility.

Book Three

Chapter One

After all of this and what might ensue from it, Wilhelm's first concern was to seek renewed contact with the members of the league and to meet somewhere with some section of it. Accordingly he consulted his little chart and set out on the road that seemed most likely to bring him to his goal. But since he had to cut across country in order to reach the most favorable point, he found it necessary to make the journey on foot and to have his baggage carried along behind him. At every step, however, he was richly rewarded for his trouble, in that he unexpectedly encountered the loveliest regions, of the sort formed where foothills merge into the plain: shrub-covered hills, their gentler slopes thriftily cultivated, every surface green, nothing rugged, barren, and untilled to be seen anywhere. He now reached the principal valley, where all the tributaries flowed together. This too was carefully planted and formed a pleasant prospect. Slender trees marked the windings of the river and the brooks flowing into it, and when he took out the map which was his guide, he saw to his amazement that the plotted line cut right through this valley, and that he was therefore on the right road, at least for the moment.

An old, well maintained castle, renovated at different periods, appeared on a wooded hilltop. At its foot sprawled a cheerful hamlet, the inn conspicuously prominent. He made his way toward it, and was received cordially enough by the host, but with apologies that he could not be lodged there without the permission of a group who had reserved the entire inn for some time, for which reason he had to direct all other guests to the older hostel farther up the hill. After a brief conversation, the man seemed to reconsider and said, "At the moment no one is in, but it is Saturday, and it cannot be long before the prefect turns up to settle the weekly score and make arrangements for the coming week. Truly, an admirable order prevails among these men, and it is a pleasure to deal with them, even though they are particular;

if one makes no great profit from them, at least it is a sure one." With this he bade the new guest wait in the large antechamber upstairs and see what might happen next.

Upon entering, he found a spacious, clean room, completely bare but for benches and tables. He was the more astonished to see a large plaque fastened above one of the doors, on which could be read these words in golden letters: "Ubi homines sunt modi sunt," which we may explain in our own language as meaning that wherever men come together in society, the manner in which they may function and remain together at once develops. This saying started our traveler thinking. He took it as a good omen, since it confirmed what he himself had often found to be sensible and productive. It was not long before the prefect appeared, who, prepared by the innkeeper, after a brief conversation with no special interrogation, accepted him under the following conditions: that he stay three days, that he participate freely in all that went on, and, whatever might occur, not ask for the reason, nor on departing ask for the score. Our traveler had to agree to all of this, for the deputy could not yield on any of the points.

The prefect was just about to leave when the sound of singing floated up the staircase. Two handsome young men approached, singing, to whom the prefect intimated with a simple gesture that the guest had been accepted. Without interrupting their song, they greeted him cordially and continued their charming duet. It was easy to tell that they had practiced thoroughly and were masters of their art. As Wilhelm showed lively interest, they ended and asked whether he did not sometimes think of a song as he walked along and sing it to himself. "Nature has, to be sure, denied me a good voice," Wilhelm replied, "but often a secret spirit seems to whisper something rhythmical into my ear, so that I move in time as I stride along and imagine I hear soft sounds accompanying a song that comes to me in one way or other."

"If you can recall one of them, write it down for us," they said; "let us see whether we can accompany your singing spirit." At this he took a sheet of paper from his writing tablet and then handed them the following:

From the mountains to the hillsides,
Through the valley wide and long,
There's a sound as if of wingbeats,
There's a movement as of song;
On this urging from above
Follows pleasure, follows aid;
And thy striving be in love,
And of deeds thy life be made.

After brief consideration the two struck up a cheerful duet in hiking tempo, which swept the listener along with progressive repetition and interweaving. Wilhelm could not say whether this was his own melody, his own earlier theme, or whether the melody had only now been fitted to it so that no other rhythm was conceivable. The singers had continued contentedly in this way for some time when two sturdy young fellows arrived who, by all their attributes, were at once recognizable as masons, while the two who followed seemed to be carpenters. These four quietly set down their tools and listened to the song; soon they joined in, surely and resolutely, so that it seemed as if a whole band of hikers were tramping over hill and dale, and Wilhelm thought he had never heard anything so pleasant and so uplifting to the spirit. This pleasure, however, was to be increased and raised to its utmost when a gigantic figure came climbing up the stairs, trying in vain to moderate his strong, firm tread. He at once set his heavily laden packframe in a corner and himself upon a bench, which began to creak, at which the others laughed, without, however, missing a note. But Wilhelm was very surprised when this son of Enoch likewise joined the chorus in a thundering bass. The room shook, and it was significant that he immediately changed the refrain in his own way, singing

In thy life postpone no duty,
And thy life be deed on deed.

It also soon became evident that he was slowing down the tempo and obliging the others to follow him. When at last they had concluded and had enough of the song, they accused him of trying to throw them off. "Not at all!" he exclaimed, "it was you who wanted to throw me off; you wanted to make me change my pace, which must be measured and deliberate if I am to march with my burden up hill and down dale and still arrive at the appointed time to satisfy you all."

One by one they now reported to the prefect in another room, and Wilhelm could tell that they were settling accounts, about which he was not allowed to inquire. In the meantime a pair of lively, handsome boys came in and quickly laid the table, setting out moderate servings of food and wine. The prefect now came out and invited all of them to sit down with him. The boys waited on the others, but did not neglect themselves, taking their share standing up. Wilhelm recalled similar scenes from the days when he still lived among the actors, but the present company struck him as graver, their merriment not for show but directed toward significant purposes in life.

The conversation of the craftsmen with the prefect gave the guest clear insight into the situation. The four sturdy young men were employed in the neighborhood, where a lovely country town had been reduced to ashes in a terrible fire. He also gathered that the worthy prefect was busy obtaining lumber and other building materials, which puzzled the guest the more because all of the men proclaimed themselves in every other respect not as natives but as itinerants. At the end of the meal, St. Christopher, for so the others called the giant, fetched a glass of good wine that had been set aside as a sleeping draught, and a cheerful song kept the company together as far as Wilhelm's ear was concerned, when it had already dispersed before his eyes. Wilhelm was then shown to a most pleasantly situated room. The full moon was already up, illuminating a lush meadow, and awakened in our traveler's breast memories of similar moments. The spirits of all his dear friends passed before him, but Lenardo's image was so particularly vivid that he imagined he saw him right there in front of him. All this had soothingly prepared him for slumber when the strangest of sounds almost gave him a fright. It issued from the distance, and yet seemed to be within the house itself, for the house shook several times, and the beams reverberated when the sound reached its loudest. Wilhelm, who normally had a keen ear for distinguishing sounds, could not make out what this was. He compared it to the rumbling of a great organ pipe, which for sheer volume cannot produce a definite note. Whether this night terror abated toward morning, or whether Wilhelm gradually became accustomed to the sound and was no longer sensitive to it, is difficult to determine; in any case, he fell asleep and was pleasantly awakened by the rising sun.

Hardly had one of the serving boys brought him his breakfast when a figure entered whom Wilhelm had noticed at the supper table but had not been able to place clearly. Though well built and broad-shouldered, he moved nimbly, and by the implements he now set out revealed himself to be a barber, ready to render Wilhelm a most welcome service. Otherwise he said nothing, and the operation was carried out deftly without his making a sound. Hence Wilhelm began, and said, "You are a master of your trade; I do not know that I have ever felt a more gentle razor on my cheek. At the same time, you seem to adhere strictly to the laws of your society."

Smiling roguishly, his finger to his lips, the silent barber slipped out the door: "Truly," Wilhelm called after him, "You must be old Red Mantle, or if not he himself, at least a descendant. It is fortunate that you do not expect me to reciprocate, or you would have found yourself ill served."

Hardly had this singular man gone away when the prefect entered to deliver an invitation for that noon, which likewise sounded rather strange. The *bond*, so he said specifically, bade the stranger welcome, summoned him to the midday meal, and took pleasure in the expectation of closer acquaintance. Inquiry was also made as to the guest's well-being and whether he was satisfied with the accommodations. The latter had nothing but praise for all that he had encountered. To be sure, he would have liked to inquire of this man, as previously of the silent barber, about the dreadful noise in the night, which had, if not frightened him, certainly disturbed him. Recalling his pledge, however, he refrained from questions, in the hope that without pressing the issue he might learn what he wished to know through the good will of the company or by chance.

Not until our friend was alone did he wonder about the mysterious person from whom the invitation had come, and he could not tell what to make of it. To announce one superior or several by a neutral term seemed questionable indeed. Moreover, everything was so quiet round about that he thought he had never experienced a more quiet Sunday. He left the house, heard the pealing of bells, and went toward the village. Mass had just ended, and among the villagers and country folk thronging out of the church he spied three of yesterday's acquaintances: a journeyman carpenter, a mason, and one of the boys. Later he noticed the other three among the Protestant worshippers. How the rest attended to their devotions was not evident, but there seemed good reason for him to conclude that in this society a decided freedom of religion prevailed.

Toward noon the prefect met him at the castle gate. He led Wilhelm through a series of halls into a large antechamber, where he bade him sit down. Many people passed by and entered an adjacent hall. Among them were those he had already met; even St. Christopher strode past. They all saluted the prefect and the newcomer. What struck Wilhelm most was that he seemed to see only artisans, all dressed in the usual fashion, but their clothes were spotlessly clean; there were a few he might have taken to be connected with the chancellery.

When there were no more guests crowding in, the prefect led our friend through the stately doorway into a spacious hall. Here an immense table was set, and he was conducted past the lower end toward the head, where he saw three persons standing at the head. But he was seized with amazement as he came near and, almost before Wilhelm had recognized him, Lenardo threw his arms around his neck. He had scarcely recovered from this surprise when a second man ardently embraced him and turned out to be the eccentric Friedrich, Natalie's brother. The delight of the friends spread to all present; a cry of joy and blessing rose up from the entire table. But suddenly, when they were seated, all fell silent, and the banquet was served and partaken of with a certain solemnity.

Toward the close of the meal, at a sign from Lenardo, two singers rose, and Wilhelm was astonished to hear his song of the previous day repeated. Because of what is to follow, we find it necessary to insert it again here:

From the mountains to the hillsides,

Through the valley wide and long,
There's a sound as if of wingbeats,
There's a movement as of song;
On this urging from above
Follows pleasure, follows aid;
Let thy striving be in love,
And of deeds thy life be made.

Hardly had this duet, pleasantly accompanied by a small chorus, approached its end, when two singers on the other side of the table leaped to their feet and with earnest vehemence took up the song, giving it an entirely different turn. To Wilhelm's astonishment, they now sang:

For the bonds are ripped asunder,
Trust no longer carries weight.
Can I say, or even wonder,
Why, exposed to cruel fate,
I must part now, I must wander
Like the widow full of woe,
Not as once, but with another,
Now forever on must go.

The chorus, taking up this strophe, grew ever larger, ever more powerful, yet one could soon distinguish the voice of St. Christopher, who sat at the far end of the table. Toward the end the lament swelled almost unendurably; a defiant courage, combined with the singers' skill, evoked a fugue-like quality that seemed dreadful to our friend. All present seemed truly of one mind, and to be mourning their own fate on the eve of departure. The most remarkable recapitulations, the repeated revival of an almost exhausted song finally struck the bond itself as perilous. Lenardo stood up, and the others quickly took their seats, breaking off the hymn. Lenardo began with kindly words:

"I cannot reproach you for dwelling constantly on the fate that awaits us all, so that you may be prepared for it at any time. If old men, weary of life, remind their fellows, 'Give thought to your death,' we lusty younger folk may well encourage and exhort one another with the words, 'Give thought to your journey.' At the same time, we do well to speak with moderation and serenity of those things we either choose to do or feel we must do. You yourselves know best what is fixed among us and what remains flexible. Celebrate this, too, with cheering, heartening notes; to that I now drink with this farewell draught." He emptied his goblet and sat down. The four singers at once stood up and began, in a variation on the previous melody:

Cling not to your homeland's charms,

Take fresh courage, freely roam!
Strong and daring heads and arms
Everywhere can be at home.
Where we gladly greet the sun
Every care is gone at last;
Each a different course may run,
Therefore is the world so vast.

As the chorus was repeated, Lenardo rose, and all the rest followed; a gesture from him formed the entire company into a singing procession; those at the lower end marched from the hall in pairs, with St. Christopher in the lead. Their marching song became ever gayer and freer, but it sounded especially fine when the company, gathered on the terraced castle grounds, gazed out over the broad valley, in whose luxuriant beauty it would have been a pleasure to wander. As the crowd dispersed in various directions, each according to his wishes, Wilhelm was introduced to the third person who had presided. This was the steward, who had placed the count's castle, lying as it did among several other noble estates, at the disposal of this society for as long as it wished to tarry here, and had contrived to provide it with many advantages. Clever man that he was, he also knew how to make use of the presence of such unusual guests. For while he opened his orchards to them at low cost and supplied them with whatever else they required in the way of food and necessities, he took the opportunity to have long neglected roof shingles replaced, rafters repaired, walls given new footings, floorboards leveled, and other defects put to rights, so that this long neglected, dilapidated property of fading families displayed the happy appearance of active use and comfort, and testified that life begets life, and he who helps others thus constrains them to help him in return.

Chapter Two

Hersilie to Wilhelm

My situation reminds me of a tragedy by Alfieri: since confidantes are wholly lacking, everything must be dealt with in monologues. And indeed, a correspondence with you is exactly like a monologue. Your replies merely take up my syllables, like an echo, only to let them die away. Have you even once given a reply to which a reply could be given in turn? Your letters simply parry mine, keeping them at a distance. When I rise to come toward you, you point me back to my seat.

The above was written a few days ago; now a new urgency has arisen, and an opportunity to deliver this to Lenardo. This letter will find you there, or someone will know where to find you. But wherever it reaches you, I have this to say: if after reading this note, you do not immediately leap from your seat and, like a good traveler, promptly make your way to me, then I declare you the most masculine of men, that is to say, one totally devoid of the most charming of all qualities of our sex; by that I mean curiosity, which at the moment torments me sorely.

To be brief: the key to your splendid little casket has been found. No one must know this but you and I. Now you shall hear how it fell into my hands.

A few days ago our magistrate received an inquiry from a distant office, asking whether a boy had not been loitering around our neighborhood at such and such a time—playing all sorts of pranks, and finally, in the course of a foolhardy act, losing his jacket.

From the description of this rascal, there could be no doubt that it was Fitz, about whom Felix used to tell us so much, and whom he often wished to have back as a playmate.

The officials were now asking for the piece of clothing in question, if it were still available, because the boy, who had come under investigation, cited it as evidence. Our magistrate mentioned this suspected connection to us by chance, and showed us the jacket before he sent it off.

Some spirit good or evil induces me to reach into the breast pocket; a tiny, sharp object is in my grasp; I, usually so apprehensive, squeamish, and timid, clasp it; clasp it and say nothing, and the garment is dispatched. At once I am seized by the strangest of sensations. At the first, furtive glimpse I see, I guess, that it is the key to your casket. Then I was attacked by odd pricks of conscience, all sorts of moral scruples. To reveal what I had found, to surrender it, was impossible. Why should the courts have it when it could be so useful to my friend! Then rectitude and duty tried to raise their voices again, but they could not win me over.

So now you see to what a pass friendship has brought me; what a splendid new faculty is suddenly born in me, for your sake; what an odd thing to have happen! May it be no more than friendship that holds my conscience in check! I am strangely disquieted, between guilt and curiosity. I invent notions and phantasies by the hundreds of what might follow from it; justice and the courts are not to be trifled with. Hersilie, uninhibited, occasionally cheeky creature that she is, involved in a criminal case, for that is where it will end, and what can I do but think of the friend for whose sake I suffer all this! Even without this, I used to think of you, but with pauses; but now I think of you constantly. Now when my heart pounds and I think of the Seventh Commandment, I must turn to you as to the saint who gave rise to the crime and can probably also absolve me; nothing can calm me but opening the casket. My curiosity is now twice as powerful. Come as fast as you can, and bring the casket with you. Together let us decide before what judge the secret belongs. Until then, it remains between us; let no one know of it, whoever he may be.

But now, my friend, what do you say to this depiction of the riddle? Does it not remind you of a barbed arrow? Lord have mercy on us! But the casket must first stand unopened between you and me, and then, once opened, decree what should follow. I hope there will be nothing inside it, and what else I might hope and what else I could tell you—but let that be withheld, that you may set out all the more speedily.

And now, in girlish fashion, another postscript! What right have you and I to the casket? It belongs to Felix; he found it, he claimed it for his own. He is the one we must fetch; we should not open it without his presence.

And so here is a whole new set of problems; for two steps forward there are three steps back.

Why are you roaming about in the world? Come! Bring the dear boy with you, whom I, too, would like to see again.

And so we are back where we started, the father and the son! Do what you can, but come, both of you.

Chapter Three

This singular letter had been written long since and carried hither and yon before it could finally be delivered as addressed. Wilhelm resolved to answer it kindly but in the negative, by the first courier to be dispatched. Hersilie seemed not to take distance into account, and he was at the moment too engaged with serious matters to be tempted by the slightest curiosity as to what might be in the casket.

In addition, several accidents that befell the most impetuous members of the hardworking company gave him the opportunity to demonstrate his mastery in his chosen art. And as one word leads to another, so, even more happily, one action gives rise to another, and if, finally, all this leads back to words again, they are all the more fruitful and uplifting to the spirit. The conversations were as edifying as they were entertaining, for the friends reported to one another what they had hitherto been learning and doing, from which a degree of education had resulted that produced mutual astonishment, so much so that they had to come to know one another all over again.

So one evening Wilhelm began to tell his story. "In order to pursue my studies in surgery, I first sought out a large hospital in the largest city, for there alone is it possible, and I at once turned eagerly to anatomy as the basic field of study.

"In a curious way that no one would guess I was already far advanced in my knowledge of the human form because of my theatrical career; since, all things considered, physical man plays the main role in that world—a handsome man, a handsome woman! If the director is lucky enough to get them, his authors of comedies and tragedies have nothing to fear. The freer conditions under which such a company lives make its members more familiar with the true beauty of unveiled limbs than would any other environment. Various costumes even require that which is usually veiled to be exposed. I could say a great deal about this, as well as about physical defects which the intelligent actor must recognize in himself and others, in order at least to hide them, if not correct them. And so I was sufficiently prepared to pay steady attention to the anatomical lectures that taught the external features in detail; the inner features were likewise not unfamiliar to me, since I had always had a certain intuition about them. An annoying hindrance to these studies was the constant complaint at the lack of specimens, the shortage of cadavers to come under the scalpel for such high purposes. To provide as many as possible, though not enough, harsh laws had been enacted, so that not only criminals, who had forfeited their individuality in every sense, but also other poor wretches, victims of physical or mental ills, were claimed for this use.

"As the need grew, so did the stringency, and with it the opposition of the people, who, on moral and religious grounds, cannot surrender their own person and that of their loved ones.

"Nevertheless the evil continued to spread, becoming so distressing that people had to fear even for the peaceful graves of their dear departed. Not age, not dignity, neither high nor low was safe in its resting place. The mound adorned with flowers, the inscriptions intended to preserve memory were no protection against profitable robbery. The most sorrowful farewell seemed cruelly disrupted, and even as the mourner walked away from the grave, he had to dread the possibility that the body of the beloved person, adorned and laid to rest, might be dismembered, dragged off, and dishonored.

"All this was repeatedly discussed and threshed out, without anyone's suggesting a remedy or being able to think of one, and the complaints grew more and more widespread, as young men who had attentively followed the lectures felt the need to verify with hand and eye what had been previously seen and heard, and to imprint this essential knowledge more deeply and vividly upon their minds.

"In moments such as these there arises a sort of unnatural scientific hunger which demands to be satisfied by fair means or foul.

"For some time now, this obstacle and impediment had preoccupied and engaged those intent on scientific discovery and activity, when finally a certain case threw the city into such commotion that one morning the pro and contra were discussed with great intensity for several hours. A very beautiful girl, distraught from an unhappy love affair, had sought death in the river and found it. The department of anatomy took possession of her. In vain were all the efforts of her parents, relatives, and even her lover, whom false charges had caused to appear suspect. The higher authorities, who had just increased the severity of the law, could permit no exceptions. In any case there was great haste to use the booty as soon as possible and to distribute it for use."

Wilhelm, who was next in line, was likewise summoned, and found at his assigned place a dubious task, neatly covered on a clean tray. When he removed the cloth, there lay before his eyes the loveliest female arm that had ever been wound around the neck of a young man. He held his instrument case in his hand and dared not open it; he stood, and dared not sit down. His reluctance to mutilate this magnificent product of nature any further struggled with the demands which any man striving for knowledge must place on himself, and which everyone else in the room was busy satisfying.

At this moment there approached him an imposing man whom he had noticed as an infrequent but very attentive auditor and observer; indeed he had already made inquiries about him. No one, however, could give him precise information. It was generally agreed that he was a sculptor, but he was also held to be an alchemist, who lived in a large old house, where the first floor alone was accessible to visitors or those in his employ, while all the other rooms were locked. This man had occasionally approached Wilhelm, had left the class along with him, at the same time seeming to avoid any further connection or communication with him.

This time, however, he spoke with a certain frankness: "I see you hesitate; you marvel at the lovely form and cannot destroy it; forget the commands of your calling and follow me." With this he covered the arm again, made a sign to the attendant, and the two of them left the place. In silence they walked side by side until the semi-acquaintances stopped before a large portal, the small door in which he opened, urging our friend to enter. Wilhelm found himself in a courtyard, large and roomy, such as one sees in old mercantile establishments, where crates and bales are unloaded on arrival. Here stood plaster casts of statues and busts, as well as packing crates both full and empty. "All this looks rather commercial," the man said; "the possibility of shipping things by water from here is invaluable for me." All of this accorded well with the business of sculptor. Wilhelm found nothing to change this impression when his kindly host led him up a few steps into a spacious room adorned with high and low reliefs, with figures large and small, busts and even individual limbs of great beauty. Our friend surveyed all this with pleasure and listened gladly to the instructive words of his host, although he still could not fail to notice an enormous gulf between these aesthetic works and the scientific endeavors from which they derived. Finally the owner of the house said with some earnestness, "You will easily see why I brought you here. This door," he continued, as he turned to one side, "lies nearer to the entrance of the hall we just left than you might imagine." Wilhelm stepped inside and was indeed amazed when, instead of representations of living forms, as in the previous room, he found the walls covered with anatomical dissections. They must have been made of wax or some similar material, but in any case they had the fresh, colorful appearance of newly prepared specimens.

"Here, my friend," said the artist, "here you see an admirable alternative to those practices in which we engage—to the dismay of the public, at inappropriate times, often with feelings of disgust, and with great care—for destruction or for repulsive preservation. I have to pursue this activity in deepest secrecy, for you must often have heard men of the profession speak of it with contempt. I do not let that deter me, and am preparing something that is bound eventually to have a great effect. Surgeons, particularly when they achieve a plastic concept of form, will certainly be better able to assist eternally generative Nature in healing every injury; the physician himself would be improved in his practice by such a concept. But let us not waste words. You shall shortly discover that more can be learned by building up than by tearing down, more by joining than by separating, more by reviving the dead than by further killing what is already dead. In short, do you want to be my student?" And upon his assent, the expert set before his guest the skeleton of a woman's arm in the same position as the one they had recently seen before them. "I had occasion to notice," the master continued, "what attention you paid to the lectures on ligaments, and rightly so, since they are what first revive for us the clatter of old bones. Ezekiel must have seen his boneyard first reassemble and join in this fashion before the limbs could move, the arms feel, and the feet stand up again. Here you have material to model with, armatures, and whatever else might be necessary; now try your luck."

The new pupil collected his wits, and as he began to examine the segments of bone more closely, he saw that they were artfully carved out of wood. "I have a skillful man," the teacher explained, "whose art was going begging because the saints and martyrs that he was accustomed to carving were no longer in demand. So I set him to master the human skeleton and make faithful reproductions of it, large and small."

Our friend now did his best and earned the approval of his instructor. He enjoyed testing how strong or weak his memory was, and he discovered with pleasure that the task brought it all back to him. He conceived a passion for the work, and besought the master to take him into his house. Once there, he worked unceasingly; and the large and small bones of the arm were soon neatly assembled. But now the tendons and muscles were to be added, and it seemed a sheer impossibility to construct the entire body, in all its parts, accurately by this method. The master encouraged him, however, and showed him how to copy with casts, for in building up such pieces anew he was spurred to fresh efforts, fresh alertness.

Any task to which a man earnestly devotes himself becomes infinite; only through competitive activity can he help himself. Wilhelm, too, soon overcame the sense of inadequacy, which is always a form of despair, and found himself at ease with the work. "I am pleased," his master said, "that you are taking so well to this approach and proving how fruitful such a method can be, even if it is not acknowledged by the specialists in the field. To be sure, there must be schools, and they will be principally concerned with passing along tradition; whatever has been done before should continue to be done; that is good, and should and will be so. But where the schools fail should also be noted and recognized. We must take hold of the living organism, and practice upon it, but quietly, lest we be obstructed or obstruct others. You have felt vividly, and show through your work, that joining is better than separating, reproducing better than contemplating."

Wilhelm now learned that such models were already widely distributed, although without publicity. But to his greatest astonishment he learned that the current stock was to be packed up and shipped across the sea. This worthy artist had already established relations with Lothario and his friends. For such a school to be founded in the growing colony was considered especially fitting, indeed essential, especially among naturally moral, high-minded people, to whom actual dissection always has something cannibalistic about it.

"If you admit that most doctors and surgeons retain only a general impression of the dissected human body and believe that they can manage with that, then models like ours are certain to be sufficient to refresh their gradually fading mental images and keep alive what is essential for them. Yes, it requires but interest and inclination, and the most delicate results of the art of dissection can be reproduced. This can be achieved with nothing more than pen, brush, and stylus."

At this he opened a small cupboard and showed Wilhelm the nerves of the face, marvelously rendered. "This is the last work of a young assistant, who, alas, is no longer alive. I had great hopes that he would carry out my ideas and disseminate my wishes to the benefit of many."

There was much talk between the two of the various aspects of this approach, and its relationship to art also formed the subject of some remarkable conversations. In the course of such discussions there emerged a striking and beautiful example of how one should work forward and backward. The master had made a handsome cast in a plastic material of the classical torso of a youth, and was now judiciously attempting to strip the ideal form of its epidermis and transform the beautiful living figure into a demonstration model of muscle structure. "Here, too, means and end lie close together, and I freely admit that I have neglected the end in my concern with the means, though not entirely through my own fault. For only man without veils is truly man; the sculptor stands at the very side of the Elohim, when they fashioned that magnificent figure from formless, repulsive clay. He must harbor similarly god-like thoughts; to the pure all things are pure, so why not God's design in Nature? But we cannot ask that of our century, which cannot manage without fig leaves or animal skins, and even this is still much too little. I had scarcely learned anything when they demanded of me dignified men in dressing gowns with wide sleeves and countless folds. So I turned back, and since I was not allowed to employ what I knew to express beauty, I chose to be useful, and this, too, is of significance. Should my wish be fulfilled, should it be acknowledged as useful that, as in so many other things, copying and copies come to the aid of imagination and memory where the human spirit loses some of its freshness—then many a sculptor will doubtless, as I did, turn around and prefer to work along with you, rather than practice a hateful craft counter to conviction and feeling."

From this they went on to observe that it was good to see how art and technique always balance one another, and, closely related as they are, always incline toward each other, so that art cannot decline without turning into commendable handicraft, handicraft cannot rise without becoming artistic.

The two formed such a bond and grew so used to one another that they parted only with the greatest reluctance when it became necessary for each to embark on his own great purpose.

"Lest it be believed," the master said, "that we want to repudiate Nature and cut ourselves off from her, let us open up a fresh perspective. Across the sea where certain humane views are steadily gaining strength, the abolition of the death penalty has made it necessary to build extensive citadels, walled-in precincts, to protect peaceable citizens against crime, and prevent crime from reigning and raging with impunity. There, my friend, in those forlorn precincts, let us reserve a chapel for Aesculapius; there, as sequestered as the punishment itself, let our knowledge be continually refreshed from objects whose dismemberment will do no violence to our humane feelings, and whose sight will not, as happened to you with that lovely, innocent arm, make the knife falter in our hand and extinguish all desire for knowledge in the face of humane feeling."

"This," said Wilhelm, "was our last conversation. I saw the packed crates float downriver, and wished them a successful journey, and a happy time for us both at their unpacking."

Our friend concluded this account with as much spirit and enthusiasm as he had begun it, his language and voice, especially, livelier than had been usual with him in recent times. When he had come to the end of his story, however, he had the impression that Lenardo seemed distracted and absent-minded, and had not followed what he had said, while Friedrich had smiled and several times almost shaken his head. To our sensitive reader of faces, this lukewarm reception for what he considered extremely important was so noticeable that he could not refrain from taking his friends to task.

Friedrich was ready with a simple and frank explanation: he thought the undertaking laudable and good, to be sure, but not especially significant, and not in the least practicable. He tried to support this opinion with arguments of the sort that are more insulting than one might imagine to someone committed to a thing and intending to carry it out. Consequently, our sculptor-anatomist, after apparently listening patiently for a while, answered with vigor:

"You have excellent qualities, my good Friedrich, that no one could deny, least of all I, but here you speak in the ordinary way of ordinary people. In what is new they see only rarity, but to perceive the significant in something rare requires much more. For people like you everything must first be translated into deeds; it must take place, appear before your eyes as possible, as real—at which point you will accept it like anything else. Every argument you offer I have already heard repeated by experts and laymen, by the former on the basis of prejudice and convenience, by the latter out of indifference. A project like this one can perhaps be realized only in a new world, where men must take courage to devise new means to satisfy inescapable needs, because the conventional ones are entirely lacking. Then inventiveness awakens and is joined by boldness, and the perseverance of necessity.

"Every doctor, whether he works with medicines or with the scalpel, is nothing without accurate knowledge of the external and internal human organs, and it is by no means sufficient to have acquired in school a fleeting acquaintance with them, to have formed only a superficial conception of the shape, position, and relationships among the diverse parts of the inscrutable organism. Any serious doctor should make a daily practice of reviewing this knowledge and repeating these observations, should seek every opportunity to reestablish the coherence of this living miracle in his mind and eyes. If he knew what was best for him, since he would not have time for such exercises, he would hire an anatomist, who, under his guidance, would work for him in private, and who could be in touch, as it were, with all the complexities of life's involved processes and provide immediate answers to the most difficult questions.

"The more this is understood, the greater the vigor, energy, and passion with which studies in dissection will be pursued. But to that same degree the material for them will decrease; the objects, the cadavers, on which these studies are based, will not be available, will become rarer, more expensive, and a genuine conflict will arise between the living and the dead.

"In the old world everything moves at a sluggish pace, since people want to treat new developments in old ways, treat growing things by rigid rules. The conflict I foresee between the living and the dead will become a matter of life and death; people will be frightened, there will be investigations and laws passed, but in vain. Precautions and prohibitions are no help in such cases; one must start at the very beginning. And that is what my master and I hope to achieve in the new environment; in fact, it is nothing new, it is already there. But what is nowadays art must become handicraft, and what happens in individual cases must become universally possible, and nothing can spread abroad that is not first acknowledged. Our deeds and accomplishments must be acknowledged as the only solution to an obvious crisis that threatens large cities in particular. I will quote the words of my master, but listen well! One day he said to me in strictest confidence:

" 'The newspaper reader is intrigued and almost amused when he reads stories about resurrection men. At first they stole bodies in great secrecy. To prevent this, watchmen were posted. Now they come with armed bands and seize their booty by force. Nor dare I say out loud that matters will go from bad to worse, for I would be assumed to be if not an accessory, then at any rate privy to the crime by chance, and as such would be implicated in a very risky investigation, and would in any case have to be punished because I had not informed the authorities of the crime as soon as I learned of it. I will confess to you, my friend: murder has been committed in this city in order to supply the insistent anatomist who pays well for the object he needs. The lifeless body lay before us. I must not describe the scene. He discovered the outrage, and I did, as well; we looked at each other and said nothing; we looked away, said nothing, and went to work.—And it was this, my friend, that drove me to my wax and plaster. It is this that will surely keep you, too, faithful to the art that sooner or later will be appreciated by the world at large.' "

Friedrich jumped up, clapped his hands, and cheered so long that Wilhelm finally became angry in earnest. "Bravo!" exclaimed Friedrich, "now it is the old you again. The first time in ages that you have spoken like someone with something truly at heart. For the first time you have again been carried away by what you were saying, and shown yourself to be one who wants to do something and can speak with enthusiasm."

Lenardo now took the floor and clarified the previous small misunderstanding. "I may have seemed distracted," he said, "but only because I was especially attentive. In fact, I was recalling a large collection of this sort that I saw on my travels, and that interested me so much that the curator, who tried to get through quickly by reeling off his regular patter, soon dropped his role, and, since he was himself the artist, showed himself a knowledgeable demonstrator.

"It was remarkable to be in these cool rooms at the height of summer, with sweltering heat outside, seeing before me objects that one would hardly dare approach in the coldest of winters. Here everything conveniently served the search for knowledge. Calmly and in perfect order he showed me the wonders of the human frame and was pleased that he could convince me that such an arrangement was completely adequate for teaching the fundamentals and for refreshing the memory. Of course any student was free in the intermediate phase to turn to Nature and to take the opportunity to inform himself about some specific aspect or other. He asked me to recommend him. For only one large museum abroad had commissioned such a collection, while universities opposed the project altogether, because the masters in the field knew how to train prosectors, not prosculptors.

"Hence I thought this gifted man the only one in the world, and now we hear there is someone else pursuing the same course. Who knows where a third and fourth may turn up. For our part, we want to do what we can to promote this venture. The impulse must come from without, and in our new circumstances this useful enterprise will certainly prosper."

Chapter Four

Early the next morning Friedrich entered Wilhelm's room with a notebook in his hand, and offering it to him, said, "With all your virtuous doings, which you narrated in abundant detail, I had no room last night to speak of myself and my own accomplishments, on which I, too, may pride myself and which certify me as a worthy member of this great caravan. Have a look at this notebook and you will see a sample."

Wilhelm quickly skimmed the pages and saw, in easily readable though hastily written form, everything he had related the previous day about his anatomical studies, almost verbatim, at which he could not conceal his astonishment.

"You know," Friedrich explained, "the basic principles of our league; to claim membership you must be thoroughly grounded in some field. I was cudgeling my brains for what I might succeed at and could find nothing, though the answer was obvious—that no one could surpass me in memory, nor in rapid, ready, legible handwriting. You will recall these pleasant qualities from our theatrical days, when we wasted our powder on sparrows, so to speak, without considering that one shot, more sensibly aimed, would bring down a rabbit for the stew pot. How often have I not prompted without text, how often written out the parts from memory in a matter of hours. That was convenient for you and you took it for granted. I did, likewise, and it would not have occurred to me that it could serve me in such good stead. It was the Abbé who first made the discovery and saw that it was grist to his mill. He tried exercising me in it, and I enjoyed what came so easily and pleased a serious man. So now I am like a complete chancellery whenever it is called for, and furthermore we travel with a two-legged adding machine as well, and no prince with a whole corps of officials is better equipped than our leaders."

A cheerful conversation about such activities led their thoughts to other members of the society. "Would you ever think," said Friedrich, "that the most useless creature in the world, or so it seemed, my Philine, should become the most useful link in the great chain? Give her a length of cloth, place men, place women, before her, and without taking measurements she cuts everything out, and even uses all the snippets and scraps to the best advantage, all without a pattern. A gifted, penetrating eye tells her all this; she takes a good look at a person and cuts; he may then go wherever he likes; she keeps cutting and fashions him a coat that fits to a T. But this would not be possible had she not brought in a seamstress, Montan's Lydie, who has finally calmed down and remains calm, but who also sews more evenly than anyone else, stitch after stitch like pearls, like embroidery. That shows what can become of people. Usually we are weighed down by so much useless baggage, a ragged cloak patched together of habit, self-indulgence, distraction, and caprice. We can thus neither discover nor exercise the best of what Nature has implanted in us, nor even know what she wants of us."

General reflections on the benefits of this sociable connection that had so fortunately developed opened up the finest prospects.

When Lenardo now joined them, he was entreated by Wilhelm to speak of himself as well, to be so good as to give an account of the life he had been leading, and how he had furthered himself and others.

"You probably remember, my dear fellow," Lenardo replied, "in what a peculiar, overwrought condition you found me in the first moments of our acquaintance. I was absorbed, entangled, in the strangest yearning, in an irresistible desire; at the time it was a question only of the next few hours and of heavy suffering in store for me which I myself seemed intent on exacerbating. I could not acquaint you with my earlier youthful circumstances, as I now must do, to show you the road that has brought me here.

"Among the earliest of my abilities, which circumstances developed little by little, was especially a certain bent for the technical, which was daily nourished by the impatience people feel in the country during large building projects, and even more with small alterations, installations, whims, when they must do without one trade after another and would sooner push forward incompetently and sloppily on their own than slow down like a master. Fortunately there was a jack-of-all-trades who used to roam around our locality and, because he made out best with me, preferred helping me more than any of the neighbors. He set up a lathe for me, which he used on visits, more for his own purposes than for my instruction. I acquired carpenter's tools, and my taste for such work was intensified and quickened by the conviction widely expressed at that time that no one could venture into life unless he had some handicraft he might fall back on in an emergency. My enthusiasm received the approval of my tutors, since it accorded with their own principles; I can hardly remember playing, for all my free hours were devoted to building and making things. In truth, I may boast that even as a boy I spurred a smith, by my demands, to learn locksmithing, casting, and clockmaking.

"To achieve all this, it was of course necessary to create the tools, and we suffered not a little from the affliction of technicians who confuse means and end and would rather spend time on preparations and arrangements than on seriously applying themselves to execution. Where we could put our practical talents to work, however, was in designing the park, something no landowner could dispense with any longer. Many a hut covered with moss or bark, rustic bridges and benches testified to the energy with which we strove to represent primitive building forms in all their crudity in the midst of the civilized world.

"As I grew older, this bent led me to more serious interest in everything that is so useful to the world and indispensable to it in its present state, and lent my years of travel a particular focus.

"But since people tend to stay on the path that has brought them to where they are, I was less favorably disposed toward machinery than toward simple handwork, where strength and feeling operate in unison. Hence I was happiest to linger in isolated villages whose special conditions had made them the home of some special type of work. That sort of thing gives each community a special individuality, gives every family or group of families a distinctive character; people live with a clear sense of the living whole.

"I had also made it my habit to record everything, complete with drawings, and thus, not without a view to future use, pass my time pleasantly and commendably.

"I was best able to exploit this inclination, this developed gift, when the society gave me the important assignment of investigating the condition of the mountain dwellers and taking into our band the useful ones disposed to emigrate. Would you care to spend this lovely evening, when I have all sorts of pressing tasks, reading a section of my diary? I will not claim that it makes for especially pleasant reading; to me it always seemed interesting and somewhat instructive. After all, we always mirror ourselves in everything we produce."

Chapter Five

Lenardo's Diary

Monday the 15th

Late in the night, after a toilsome climb halfway up the mountain, I had reached a tolerably good inn, and before daybreak was awakened, to my great annoyance, from a refreshing sleep by a persistent tinkling and ringing of bells. A long line of packhorses passed by before I could manage to dress and hurry out ahead of them. Now I learned all too soon, as I set out, how unpleasant and irritating such company is. The monotonous ringing is deafening. The loads, which project far out on either side (they were carrying great sacks of cotton), tends to scrape against the cliffs, and when an animal, to avoid this, veers to the other side, his load teeters over the abyss, which causes the spectator fear and giddiness. But worst of all, in either case it is not possible to slip past them and gain the lead.

Finally I reached a ledge on one side, where St. Christopher, who was carrying my luggage on his powerful back, greeted a man who was standing there and apparently reviewing the procession. He was, in fact, its leader; not only did he own a considerable number of the pack animals, and had rented the others, along with their drivers, but a smaller portion of the wares also belonged to him. His chief business, however, consisted in attending to the safe transport of goods for bigger merchants. In conversation with him I learned that this was cotton which had come from Macedonia and Cyprus by way of Trieste. It was being brought by mule and packhorse from the base of the mountains to these altitudes and beyond to the far side of the mountains, where countless spinners and weavers scattered through the valleys and gorges prepared the material for a large trade in wares much sought after abroad. For convenience in loading, the bales weighed either one and a half or three hundredweight, the latter constituting the full load of a packhorse. The man extolled the quality of this kind of cotton, comparing it with that from the East and West Indies, especially from Cayenne, which was the best known. He seemed throughly knowledgeable in his field, and since I, too, was not altogether unfamiliar with it, we had a pleasant and profitable conversation. In the meantime the entire procession had passed us, and I looked with dismay at the rocky path winding its way up the mountain, at the endless line of laden creatures, behind which we would be creeping along, baking among the rocks as the sun rose higher. While I was grumbling to my guide about this, a squat, cheerful man approached, carrying a relatively light load on a fairly large packframe. Greetings were exchanged, and it was soon clear from their hearty handshakes that St. Christopher and the new arrival knew each other well. I at once learned the following about the man. For the more remote mountain regions, whose individual inhabitants find it too far to go to market, there is a sort of low-ranking dealer or collector called the Yarn Carrier. He makes his way through all the valleys and hamlets, visiting house after house, bringing the spinners small supplies of cotton, and either receives yarn in exchange or buys it, regardless of its quality; he then sells it at some profit to the manufacturers down below.

As the talk now turned again to the discomfort of dawdling along behind the mules, the man promptly invited me to descend with him into a side valley that branched off just there, forming a different watershed. The decision was soon made, and after we had climbed with some effort over a rather steep ridge, we saw the further slopes before us, at first quite forbidding, for the rock had changed and become slate-like. No vegetation enlivened the cliffs and rubble, and the descent threatened to be abrupt. Rivulets trickled together from several directions; we even passed a small lake surrounded by jagged cliffs. Finally single trees began to appear, and then clusters of pines, larches, and birches, then among them scattered rustic dwellings, to be sure of the most wretched sort, each hammered together by the inhabitants themselves out of interlocking logs, with the large, dark shingles on the roof weighted down with stones, so that the wind would not carry them off. Yet despite their forlorn exterior appearance, the confined interiors were not unpleasant; warm and dry, clean as well, they were in keeping with the happy look of the inhabitants, with whom one at once felt on a friendly rustic footing.

My guide seemed to be expected; people had even been watching for him through their little sliding windows, for he made it his custom to come on the same day of the week whenever possible. He bought the spun yarn, distributed new supplies of cotton; we then proceeded swiftly downhill to where several houses stand close together. As soon as they catch sight of us, the inhabitants come running to greet us; children join the throng and are delighted to receive a bun or a roll. There was joy everywhere, even more so when it turned out that St. Christopher, too, carried goodies in his load, and so likewise had the pleasure of garnering childish thanks. This was all the more pleasant for him because St. Christopher, like his companion, had a knack for getting on with little people.

The older folk, for their part, had all kinds of questions stored up; everyone wanted to hear about the war, which luckily was being waged far away, and even if nearer, would scarcely have threatened regions like these. They were glad, however, to be at peace, although another menace worried them. For it could not be denied that machine production was increasing throughout the land, and was gradually threatening to put their industrious hands out of work. But all kinds of reasons for hope and comfort could be adduced.

In the midst of this, our man was also asked for advice on various personal questions, and indeed had to serve not only as family counselor but also as doctor; he always carried a supply of miracle drops, salts, and balms.

As I entered the various houses I found an opportunity to pursue my old hobby and to learn about the technology of spinning. I noticed children carefully and diligently engaged in plucking the bolls of cotton apart and removing the seeds and fragments of the husk, along with other debris; they referred to this as "picking" the cotton. I asked whether this task was set aside for the children, but learned that during the winter evenings it was also undertaken by husbands and brothers.

The vigorous women who did the spinning next attracted my attention, as was proper. Their preparations are as follows: the "picked" or cleaned cotton is distributed evenly on the "cards," which in Germany are called "combs," and are then carded, during which the dust separates out and the fibers are all lined up in one direction. The cotton is then removed from the cards, twisted into hanks, and so made ready for the spinning wheel.

I was shown the difference between yarn twisted to the left or the right; the first is usually finer, and is produced by twisting the thread turned by the spindle around the whorl, as is clearly shown in the attached drawing (which like the rest, we unfortunately cannot include here).

The spinner sits before the wheel, not too high. Several of them held it steady between crossed feet, others only with their right foot, the left foot pulled back. She rotates the wheel with her right hand, stretching as high and far as she can, which produces beautiful movements and lets a slender figure, with body turning gracefully and nicely rounded arms, show to great advantage. The direction of the second method of spinning especially creates a picturesque contrast, so that our loveliest ladies would not have to fear any loss to their charm or grace, should they ever wish to take up the spinning wheel instead of the guitar.

In such surroundings, new, unaccustomed feelings pressed in upon me; the whirring wheels have a certain eloquence, the girls sing psalms and, though less often, other songs.

Siskins and goldfinches in hanging cages twitter along, and it would not be easy to find a picture of livelier activity than in a room where several spinners are at work.

Such wheel-spun yarn, however, is inferior to what is called "letter yarn." For this they use the best cotton, which has longer fibers than the other. Once it has been picked clean, instead of being carded it is placed on combs which consist of single rows of long steel teeth, and combed; then the longer and finer part is removed in bands with a blunt knife (the technical term is a "slice"). These are next wound up and placed in a paper envelope, and this is then fastened to the distaff. From such an envelope the cotton is now spun with a hand-held spindle, for which reason the process is called spinning from the letter, and the yarn is called letter yarn.

This work, which is done only by calm, careful individuals, gives the spinner a gentler appearance than does the use of the spinning wheel. If this last best becomes a woman of tall, slender figure, the hand-spinning is more flattering to a woman of delicate build and calm disposition. I saw these differing types in one room, engaged in different employment, and at length could not decide whether it was more to the work or to the workers that I should devote my attention.

But I cannot deny that the mountain women, stimulated by the rare presence of guests, were friendly and obliging. They were especially pleased that I asked such precise questions about everything they told me, noticed things, and sketched their implements and simple mechanical equipment. I even made quick, delicate drawings of their arms, hands, and pretty limbs, which you may see on the facing page. Then, as evening fell, the completed work was displayed, the full spindles laid aside in the cases intended for that purpose, and the entire day's work carefully put away. We were by now better acquainted, but the work continued; they now busied themselves with the yarn-winder, and were much freer than before in showing me first the equipment and then how to operate it, while I took careful notes.

The yarn-winder has a wheel and an indicator, so that with each rotation a spring is lifted that advances the indicator every time a hundred loops have been loaded onto the winder. A thousand loops are called a skein, and its weight is an index of the fineness of the yarn.

For right-spun yarn there are 25 to 30 to a pound, while for left-spun yarn 60 or 80, sometimes even 90. A loop on the winder will run about seven quarter ells or slightly more, and my slim, diligent spinner claimed that she spun 4 or even 5 skeins a day on her wheel, which would be 5000 loops, amounting to 8 to 9000 ells of yarn; she was willing to wager on it, if we would stay another day.

At this the shy, modest letter-spinner could not keep silent, and asserted that she could spin a pound of cotton into 120 skeins in a comparable time. (Letter-yarn spinning goes more slowly than spinning by wheel, but is better paid. With the wheel one perhaps spins about twice as much.) She had just filled her winder, and she showed me now how the end of the yarn was wound around a few times and knotted. She lifted off the skein, twisted it so that it looped around itself, drew the end through, and could display the completed work of a skillful spinner with innocent satisfaction.

Since there was nothing more to be observed here, the mother rose and said that since the young man was interested in seeing everything, she would show him dry weaving, too. Sitting down at the loom she explained just as good-naturedly that they did only this kind of weaving, because it was suited for nothing but coarse calico, where the weft is woven dry and not very tightly. She then showed me such dry-woven fabric; it is always simple, without stripes or checks or any other pattern, and only four to five and a half quarter ells wide.

The moon shone clear in the sky and the Yarn Carrier insisted that we continue our pilgrimage, since he had a schedule to maintain and had to arrive on time in every place. The footpaths were good and clear, he said, especially with such a torch as burned in the night sky. We for our part brightened the farewell with silk ribbons and kerchiefs, of which St. Christopher carried a sizeable packet. The gifts were given to the mother, to distribute among her family.

Tuesday the 16th, morning

The walk through the magnificent clear night was full of beauty and pleasure. We reached a somewhat larger cluster of cottages that might perhaps have been called a village; not far away a chapel stood on an open hill, and things began to look more inhabited and civilized. We passed enclosures which, to be sure, contained no gardens, but suggested sparse, carefully tended mowings.

We had reached a place where, along with spinning, weaving was more earnestly pursued.

Our journey of the day before, extended into the night, had consumed our sturdy and youthful energies. The Yarn Man climbed into the hay loft, and I was just about to follow him when St. Christopher handed me his packframe and went outside. I understood his kindly intention and let him have his way.

Yet first thing the following morning the entire family rushed together, and the children were strictly forbidden to step out the door, because a dreadful bear or some other monster must be lurking in the neighborhood. There had been such groaning and growling all through the night from the chapel that it was enough to make the very rocks and houses shake, and we were advised to be on our guard when we set forth today on our long foot journey. We tried our best to quiet these good people, but this appeared difficult in such lonely parts.

The Yarn Man now explained that he would finish his business as quickly as possible, then come and fetch us, since we had a long and arduous way ahead of us today; we would no longer be strolling along the valley but would have to clamber over a protruding mountain spur. I therefore decided to use the time as well as possible, and have my good hosts lead me into the antechamber of the art of weaving.

They were both elderly people, blessed late in life with two or three children; religious feelings and mystical ideas were evident in their surroundings, their activity, and manner of speech. I had arrived just at the beginning of a process that constitutes the transition from spinning to weaving, and since I found nothing else to distract me, I had them dictate the operation to me as it was in progress.

The first task, sizing the yarn, had been done the day before. The yarn is boiled in a dilute lime solution, consisting of starch and some carpenter's glue, which strengthens the threads. By morning the strands of yarn were already dry and preparations were made for spooling, that is for winding the yarn from the spool-winder onto spools. The old grandfather, sitting by the stove, performed this simple task; a grandson stood near him and seemed eager to handle the spool-winder himself. In the meantime the father, in preparation for warping, set the spools onto a rack divided by horizontal rods; they moved freely around strong perpendicular wires and allowed the thread to unwind. Spools with coarser or finer yarn are set up in the order demanded by the pattern, or rather the stripes, in the weaving. An instrument (the warping paddle), shaped rather like a sistrum, has holes on both sides through which the threads are drawn. This is held in the right hand of the warper; with his left he holds the threads together and places them, going back and forth, on the warping reel. Once down from the top and once up from the bottom is called a turn, and depending on the set and width of the weaving many turns are made. The length runs either 64 or else only 32 ells. At the beginning of each turn one or two threads are passed over the fingers of the left hand, raising them up, with the alternate threads allowed to drop, and these are called the cross; in this pattern the joined threads are placed on the two pegs at the top of the warping reel. This is done so that the weaver can keep the threads even and in correct order. When the warping is complete, all the crosses are secured and each turn separated so that nothing can get tangled; then marks are made on the last turn with dissolved verdigris so that the weaver can reproduce the right length; finally it is all taken down and all wound up in the form of a large skein called the warp.

Wednesday, the 17th

We had set out early, before daybreak, and enjoyed magnificent lingering moonlight. The brightness breaking forth with the rising sun made a more inhabited and better cultivated land visible before us. If up above we had encountered nothing but stepping stones or occasionally a narrow plank bridge with a railing on only one side for crossing streams, here the ever widening waters were spanned by stone bridges. Harmonious elements seemed gradually to couple with the wilder ones, and a pleasing impression was experienced by all the wanderers.

Over the other side of the mountain, from a different watershed, a slender man with black locks came striding and, having good eyes and a strong voice, called from afar, "Greetings, in God's name, brother Yarn Carrier!" The latter let him come nearer, then, he, too called with astonishment, "God's thanks to you, brother Harness-Fixer! From what parts do you come? what an unexpected meeting!" The other replied as he approached, "For two months now I have been tramping about the mountains to mend the harnesses for the good people and set up their looms so that they can work on for a while without interruption." At this the Yarn Man, turning to me, said, "Since you, young sir, show such love and devotion for this business and pay such careful attention to it, this man has come at just the right time. Indeed, I have been wishing him here the last few days; he would have explained everything to you better than the girls, for all their good will. He is a master of his trade and understands everything involved in spinning and the like—can describe, perform, maintain, and repair as necessary and to everyone's satisfaction."

I spoke with him, and as I reviewed some of what I had learned in the last few days and asked him to clear up some doubtful points, discovered a very intelligent man, even educated in a certain sense, entirely competent in his metier. I also told him about what I had seen yesterday of the first stages of weaving. He exclaimed happily, "It could not be better; I have come at just the right time to give such a worthy, dear gentleman necessary information about the oldest, most wonderful art, which first sets man apart from the beasts. We will come today to good, skilled folk, and I am no Harness-Fixer if you do not immediately comprehend the craft as well as I do myself."

He received heartfelt thanks, the conversation continued in various directions, and, after a rest and breakfast, we reached a somewhat helterskelter, though better built group of houses. He directed us to the best of these. As agreed, the Yarn Man went in first with me and St. Christopher; then, after the first greetings and a few pleasantries, the Harness-Fixer followed, and it was striking what joyful surprise his arrival produced in the family. Father, mother, daughters, and children gathered around him; the shuttle, about to fly through the warp, faltered in the hand of a handsome girl at the loom, and she also stopped working the treadles, stood up and at length came to offer her hand, slowly and shyly. Both the Yarn Man and the Harness-Fixer soon reestablished themselves with jests and anecdotes on the footing proper to friends of the family, and when all had enjoyed themselves a while, the good man turned to me and said, "We must not neglect you, my dear sir, in our joy at this reunion. We can chatter for days on end; you must be gone tomorrow. Let us introduce the gentleman to the mysteries of our art. He knows about sizing and warping; let us show him the rest; the maidens here will surely assist me. I see this loom is being dressed." It was the younger girl's loom around which they gathered. The older one sat down again at her loom and pursued her lively work with calm, affectionate mien.

I now observed the dressing closely. For this purpose the turns of the warp are run in order through a large comb exactly the width of the warp beam on which the dressing is to take place. This latter is provided with a slot fitted with a rod that runs through the end of the warp and is fastened in the slot. A small boy or girl sits under the loom and holds the warp tightly while the weaver vigorously turns the warp beam with a handle and simultaneously sees that everything ends up in order. When everything is wound on, one round and two flat sticks, lease sticks, are slipped through the cross so that it holds, and then the beaming begins.

About a quarter of an ell of the previous weaving is left on the second warp beam, and from this about three quarters of an ell of threads run through the reed in the beater and through the heddles. Onto these threads now the weaver carefully ties the threads of the new warp, one after the other, and when she is finished, everything tied on is drawn through at the same time so that the new threads reach to the cloth beam, which is still empty. The torn-off threads of the previous weaving are knotted, thread is wound onto small bobbins that will fit into the shuttle, and the final preparation for weaving is made, namely finish sizing.

For the whole length of the loom the warp is thoroughly moistened with a lime solution prepared from glove leather and brushed on; then the lease sticks mentioned above that hold the cross are pulled back, all the threads arranged in exact order, and everything fanned with a goose wing tied to a stick until it is dry. And now the weaving can be begun and continued until it is necessary to size it again.

Sizing and fanning are usually left to young people who are being trained for the weaver's trade, or in the leisure of a winter evening a brother or lover performs this service for the pretty weaver, or these last at least prepare the bobbins with the weft thread.

Fine muslins are woven wet, that is to say, the skein of the weft thread is dipped in lime, wound on the small bobbins while still wet and immediately woven, which allows the cloth to be woven more evenly and look smoother.

Thursday, September 18th

Altogether I discovered something busy, indescribably vital, domestic, peaceful in the atmosphere of such a weaving room; several looms were in motion, spinning wheels and spool-winders were turning, and by the stove the old folk sat and chatted with visiting neighbors or friends. Occasionally there was singing to be heard, usually Ambrosius Lobwasser's four-part psalms, less frequently secular songs; now and then gay, ringing laughter breaks out when cousin Jacob has made some clever remark.

An especially nimble and diligent weaver can, if she has help, produce a 32-ell piece of not particularly fine muslin in one week; that, however, is very rare, and if there are other household chores, it is usually two weeks' work.

The beauty of the cloth depends on the even operation of the treadles, on the even pressure of the beater, and also on whether the weft is laid in wet or dry. Completely even and strong tension also contributes, to which end the weaver of fine cotton cloth hangs a heavy stone from the nail of the cloth beam. If the cloth is pulled very tight during the weaving (the technical term is high tension), then it lengthens noticeably, by 3/4 of an ell per 32 ells, and about 1 1/2 ells per 64. This excess is the property of the weaver; she is paid extra for it or she saves it for kerchiefs, aprons, etc.

In the clearest, mildest moonlight, such as reigns only in the high mountains, the family and its guests sat out of doors in animated conversation. Lenardo was engrossed in thought. Even amidst the weaving and working and so many technical reflections and observations, the letter of reassurance from friend Wilhelm had again come to mind. The words he had so often read, the lines at which he had repeatedly gazed, reappeared before his inner eye. And as a favorite melody, before we realize it, all at once sounds softly in our innermost ear, so that gentle message was repeated in the calm soul, at one with itself.

"Household based on piety, enlivened and sustained by industry and order, not too restricted, not too broad, the best possible match of duties to abilities and strengths. She is the center of a group of manual workers in the purest, most original sense; here dwell restraint and far-reaching effectiveness, caution and moderation, innocence and diligence."

But this time the memory was more stimulating than soothing. "Does not this general and laconic description," he said to himself, "fit perfectly the circumstances that prevail here? Is there not here also peace, piety, ceaseless diligence? Only the far-reaching effectiveness does not strike me as entirely applicable. The good creature may well enliven a similar circle, but a wider, better one. She may feel as contented as these people here, perhaps even more contented, and look about her with more serenity and freedom."

But now, as the conversation of the others grew more animated, and his attention was drawn more closely to what they were discussing, an idea he had been harboring for some hours came to the fore. Would not this very man, with his masterful command of tools and apparatus, be the most useful member of our society? He considered this and all the excellent qualities of the man that had already impressed themselves upon him. He therefore guided the conversation in that direction, and, as if in jest, but all the more directly, put the proposition to him whether he would be willing to join an important society and try the experiment of emigrating across the sea.

The man excused himself, insisting cheerfully that he was doing well here, and he expected to do even better; he was a native of the region, was used to it, known far and wide and received everywhere with trust. In general there would be no inclination to emigrate found in these valleys; no want threatened the inhabitants, and the mountains held their people fast.

"That is why I am surprised," the Yarn Man remarked, "that it is rumored Dame Susanna is going to marry the foreman, sell her property, and cross the ocean with her good money." Upon inquiry our friend learned that this was a young widow in comfortable circumstances who carried on a thriving trade in the products of the region. The traveler would be able to confirm this for himself, since their route tomorrow would bring them in good time to her door. "I have already heard her mentioned a few times," Lenardo replied, "as active and charitable in the valley, and forgot to inquire about her."

"But now let us take our rest," said the Yarn Man, "so that we may be up early tomorrow, to use what promises to be a fine day."

Here the manuscript ended, and when Wilhelm asked for the continuation, he was informed that it was not currently in the possession of his friends. It had been, he was told, sent to Makarie, who was to straighten out certain complications mentioned in it by means of love and intelligence, and undo certain troublesome knots. Our friend had to resign himself to this interruption and prepare to find pleasure in a sociable evening, in cheerful conversation.

Chapter Six

As evening fell and the friends were sitting in an arbor overlooking the countryside, an imposing figure stepped over the threshold, whom our friend instantly recognized as the barber of the morning. To the man's profound, silent obeisance, Lenardo replied, "You come, as always, most opportunely, and will not fail to entertain us with your talent. I suppose I may tell you," he continued, turning to Wilhelm, "something of the society whose bond I am proud to be. No one enters our circle unless he can display certain talents that would be useful or pleasing to any society. This man is a rough and ready surgeon, who in difficult cases, where resolve and physical strength are demanded, can readily assist his master. To his skill as a barber you yourself can testify. In this capacity he is as necessary to us as he is welcome. But since this occupation usually carries with it a great and often annoying loquacity, in the interest of self-improvement he has accepted a condition, as everyone who wishes to live with us must restrict himself in one respect, that he may enjoy greater freedom in other respects. Thus he has renounced speech, insofar as it expresses ordinary or inconsequential things. But from this a talent in a different sort of speaking has developed, one that seems purposeful, clever, and pleasing, that is to say, the gift of storytelling.

"His life has been rich in remarkable experiences, which he used to fritter away in ill-timed chatter, but can now, under compulsion of silence, review in peace and put into order. Here the imagination comes into play and lends life and movement to events. With particular art and skill he recounts truthful fairy tales and fairy tale happenings. These often captivate us at a fitting time, when his tongue is released by me, as is now the case. I must also say in his praise that he has never repeated himself in the considerable while I have known him. And now I hope that this time, too, he will particularly excel, for the sake of our beloved and honored guest."

Red Mantle's face assumed a look of sprightly intelligence, and with no more ado he began to tell the following story.

The New Melusine

Honored gentlemen! Since I am aware that you do not particularly care for long speeches and introductions, I shall say no more than that I hope this time to perform exceptionally well. I have, to be sure, presented you with many a true story, to great and general satisfaction, but today, I may say, I have one to tell that far surpasses the others, and the memory of which, though it happened to me several years ago, still causes me some agitation when I remember it, and still gives hope of a final resolution. You could scarcely find its like.

I must first concede that I did not always conduct my life in such a way as to be entirely confident of the near future, or even of the next day. In my youth I was not a good manager, and often found myself in various difficulties. Once I set out upon a journey that was to bring me great profit, but I began a little too lavishly, and after starting in a first-class post chaise and then continuing for a while in the regular one, I at last found it necessary to face finishing it on foot.

As a lively fellow I had always been in the habit of looking around for the innkeeper's wife as soon as I arrived at an inn, or for the cook, and flattering her a little so that my score was usually reduced.

One evening, just as I was entering the posthouse of a small town, intending to proceed in my usual fashion, a fine two-seater drawn by four horses came clattering up to the door right behind me. I turned and saw a young woman alone, without maid, without manservant. I hastened to open the carriage door and ask how I might be of service. As she stepped out, I saw a beautiful figure, and her lovely face was, on close observation, enhanced by a slight touch of sadness. I asked her again whether I might be of service to her in any way. "Oh, yes," she replied, "if you would very carefully take out the casket sitting on the seat and carry it inside. But I must beg you to hold it perfectly level and not to move or shake it in the slightest." I lifted the casket with care, she closed the carriage door, and together we went up the steps. She told the servants that she would spend the night here.

Now we were alone in the room, and she bade me set the casket on the table near the wall; as I could tell from some of her gestures that she wished to be alone, I took my leave, pressing a respectful but ardent kiss on her hand.

"Order supper for both of us," she said, and you may imagine with what pleasure I carried out this assignment, in my high spirits scarcely casting a glance at the innkeeper, his wife, or the servants. Impatiently I awaited the moment that would finally bring me to her again. Supper was served, we sat down opposite each other, I regaled myself for the first time in a good while with a fine meal, as well as with so entrancing a sight. It seemed as though she were growing more beautiful with every minute.

Her conversation was pleasant, yet she sought to deflect anything relating to affection and love. The table was cleared; I lingered, and tried all sorts of tricks to break her reserve, but in vain. She held me back with a sort of dignity I could not withstand. Against my will, I had to part from her at an early hour.

After a mostly wakeful night and troubled dreams I was up early, and inquired whether she had ordered horses. I heard she had not, and went out into the garden. Seeing her standing dressed at the window, I hurried in to her. When she came toward me, so lovely and even lovelier than yesterday, I was seized with desire and reckless boldness; I rushed to her and caught her in my arms. "Angelic, irresistible being!" I exclaimed, "Forgive me, but I cannot help myself." With incredible agility she escaped from my embrace, and I was not even able to plant a kiss on her cheek. "Control such sudden bursts of passion," she said, "if you do not want to forfeit a happiness that lies within your reach, but can be possessed only after several trials."

"Demand what you will, angelic spirit," I cried, "but do not cast me into despair!" She replied, smiling, "If you would devote yourself to my service, hear the terms. I have come here to visit a friend, and plan to spend several days with her. In the meantime I would like my coach and this casket to proceed on ahead. Would you see to that? There is nothing for you to do but to lift the casket in and out of the coach with care, and when it is in the coach, sit beside it and watch over its safety. When you reach an inn, it is to be placed on a table, in a separate room, in which you may neither stay nor sleep. Each time you are to lock the room with this key, which locks and unlocks all doors and gives the lock the special property that it cannot be opened by anyone in the interval."

I looked at her, feeling most peculiar. I promised to do all this if I might hope to see her again soon, and if she would seal this hope with a kiss. She did so, and from that moment on, I was her slave. I should now order the horses, she said. We discussed the route I should take, and the places where I should stop and wait for her. Finally she pressed a purse of gold into my hand, and I pressed my lips onto her hands. She seemed moved at parting, and I no longer knew what I was doing, or should do.

When I returned from my errand, I found the door locked. I immediately tried the master key, and it passed the test perfectly. The door sprang open, and I found the room empty, with only the casket standing on the table where I had placed it.

The coach had rolled up; I carried the casket downstairs carefully, and placed it beside me. The innkeeper's wife asked, "But where is the lady?" A child answered, "She has gone into town." I said farewell to the people and drove away as if in triumph from the place where I had arrived the previous evening on foot, with dusty leggings. Now that I had leisure, you may well imagine that I considered this affair from every angle, counted the money, made various plans, and kept glancing occasionally at the casket. I proceeded straight ahead, did not stop at several stations, and made no pause until I had reached a stately town, to which she had directed me. Her instructions were carefully obeyed, the casket placed in a separate room and two wax tapers next to it, unlit, as she had ordered. I locked the room, settled myself in my own, and saw to my own comfort.

For a while I could occupy myself with memories of her, but very soon the time began to hang heavy. I was not accustomed to live without companionship, which I soon found to my taste at taverns and other public places. Under these circumstances my money began to melt away, and disappeared entirely from my purse one evening when I imprudently gave in to passionate gambling. When I returned to my room, I was beside myself. Stripped of money, but with the appearance of a rich man, I could expect a tidy bill, and, uncertain as to whether, or when, my fair lady would reappear, I was in the worst of straits. I longed for her with redoubled intensity and thought I could no longer live without her and her money.

After supper, which I scarcely enjoyed because I had to partake of it alone, I paced up and down the room, talked to myself, cursed myself, threw myself on the floor, tore my hair, and carried on wildly. Suddenly I hear a soft movement in the locked room next to mine, and shortly after a knock on the bolted door. I pull myself together, reach for the master key, but the double doors fly open of themselves, and in the gleam of those lighted tapers my fair one comes toward me. I cast myself at her feet, kiss her dress, her hands; she raises me up, and I dare not embrace her, scarcely dare to look into her eyes. Nevertheless I frankly and ruefully confess my error.

"That is forgivable," she said, "only you have postponed, alas, your happiness and mine. Now you must travel another stretch into the world before we see each other again. Here is more gold," she said, "which should last you, if you manage it at all sensibly. But if wine and gambling have brought you into difficulties this time, be careful now of wine and women, and let me hope that our next meeting will be more joyful."

She stepped back over the threshold, the doors flew shut. I knocked, I pleaded, but nothing more was to be heard. When I asked for my score the following morning, the waiter smiled and said, "Now we know why you lock your doors in so artful and mysterious a fashion that no master key can open them. We imagined you had all sorts of money and valuables in there; but now we have seen your treasure descending the stairs, and it seemed in every sense worthy of being well guarded."

I made no reply to this, paid my bill, and climbed into the coach with my casket. I journeyed forth into the world once more, with the firmest intention of abiding in future by the warning of my mysterious friend. Yet I had hardly arrived in a large city again when I made the acquaintance of attractive young ladies, and simply could not tear myself away from them. They seemed to place a high price on their favor, for even as they kept me always at a certain distance, they drew me into one expenditure after another, and since my sole aim was to assure their pleasure, I once more failed to think of my purse, but paid and treated constantly, as circumstances dictated. But how great was my amazement and delight when, after a few weeks, I noticed that the purse had not lost its fullness, but was as round and plump as ever. Wanting to make sure of this wonderful quality, I sat down and counted, and wrote down the exact sum. I now began to live as merrily as before with my companions. There was no lack of outings, on land and on water, of dance and song and other pleasures. But now it required no great powers of observation to become aware that the purse was truly dwindling, as if by my accursed counting I had robbed it of its virtue of being uncountable. In the meantime, once embarked upon the life of enjoyment, I could not turn back, yet I soon came to the end of my cash. I cursed my situation, inveighed against my lady, who had thus led me into temptation, was cross that she did not make another appearance, in my anger repudiated all my obligations toward her, and resolved to open the casket, to see whether it held anything that might be of help. Though it was not heavy enough to contain money, there might still be jewels inside, and these also would have been most welcome to me. I was about to carry out my purpose, but postponed it until night, in order to undertake the operation in peace and quiet, and hurried off to a banquet that had just been announced. Once again the merriment was in full swing, and we were powerfully stimulated by wine and the blare of trumpets when I had an unpleasant surprise. During the dessert an earlier admirer of my favorite beauty, returning from a journey, walked in unexpectedly, sat down by her side, and without much ceremony sought to assert his former rights. This soon led to anger, recriminations, and conflict; we both drew our swords, and I was carried home, sorely wounded and half dead.

The surgeon had bandaged me and departed; it was far into the night, and my attendant had fallen asleep. The door to the next room opened, my mysterious friend entered, and sat down at my bedside. She inquired how I was feeling; I did not reply, for I was weak and ill-humored. She continued speaking sympathetically, and rubbed my temples with a balm, so that I quickly felt much stronger, so strong that I could lose my temper and berate her. In a vehement tirade I cast all blame on her for my misfortunes, on the passion she had aroused in me, on her appearances, on her disappearances, on the boredom, and on the longing I was bound to feel. I became more and more vehement, as if overcome by fever, and at last swore that if she would not be mine, would not let me possess her and bind herself to me, I had no wish to go on living. I demanded a definite answer. As she hesitated to declare herself, I took leave of my senses completely and tore off the double and triple dressing on my wounds, determined to bleed to death. But how amazed I was to find my wounds all healed, my body spruce and gleaming, and my darling in my arms.

We were now the happiest pair on earth. We each begged the other's forgiveness, and hardly knew why. She promised to journey on with me, and soon we were seated together in the coach, with the casket across from us in place of the third person. I had never mentioned the casket to her. Even now it did not occur to me to speak of it, though it sat there in full sight, and by tacit agreement we both looked after it, as circumstances might require, though I alone lifted it in and out of the coach and took care of locking the doors, as before.

As long as there was still something in the purse, I had continued to pay; when my money ran out, I let her know. "That is easily helped," she said, and pointed to a pair of small pockets attached high up to the side of the coach, which I had noticed earlier but had never used.

She reached into one and drew out some gold pieces, likewise from the other some silver coins, and thus showed me the possibility of maintaining any degree of luxury we chose. So we journeyed on, from city to city, from country to country, and were happy together and with others, and I gave no thought to her ever leaving me again, the less so since for some time now she had been unmistakably with child, which only increased our happiness and our love. But alas, one morning I did not find her there, and because staying without her held no charms, I once more set out with the casket, tested the power of both the pockets, and found it undiminished.

All went well with my journey, and if previously I had not been inclined to reflect on my adventure, because I expected the strange state of affairs to take a perfectly natural turn, what now happened filled me with astonishment, anxiety, and even fear. Since I was accustomed to travel both day and night in order to keep moving, it often happened that I traveled in the dark, and when the lanterns chanced to go out, it would be completely black inside my coach. Once, in just such a dark night, I had fallen asleep, and when I awoke I saw light shining on the ceiling of the coach. I studied it and found that it issued from the casket, which seemed to have developed a crack as a result of the hot, dry weather that had come with summer. My thoughts of jewels revived, and I surmised there might be a carbuncle in the casket, and wanted certainty in the matter. I bent down as best I could to put my eye directly to the crack. But how great was my astonishment when I looked into a room, brightly lit by candles and furnished with excellent taste, indeed luxury, as if I were looking through an opening in a vault down into some royal apartment. To be sure, I could see only a part of the room, which let me guess at the rest. A fire seemed to be burning in the fireplace, by which stood an armchair. I held my breath and continued to observe. Presently from the other side of the room a woman appeared with a book in her hand, whom I at once recognized as my wife, although transformed into the tiniest of miniatures. The fair one sat down to read in the chair by the hearth, poked the fire with the sweetest little tongs, and as she moved, I could see that the darling little creature was likewise with child. But now I had to shift my uncomfortable position, and soon after, when I wanted to look in again and convince myself that it was no dream, the light had disappeared, and I looked into empty darkenss.

It may be imagined how amazed and even terrified I was. A thousand notions about this discovery went through my head, yet I could not make any sense of it. Thus preoccupied, I fell asleep, and when I awoke, believed I had dreamed it all. Yet I felt somewhat estranged from my beloved, and even as I handled the casket with still greater care, I did not know whether I should wish for her return in full human size, or dread it.

After some time my beautiful beloved did return one day toward evening, dressed in white. Since the room lay in shadow, she seemed taller than I expected, and I recalled that all those belonging to the race of the nixies or gnomes gain noticeably in height as night approaches. She flew into my arms as always, but I could not press her with unalloyed joy to my troubled breast.

"My dearest," she said, "I can feel in your welcome what I alas already know. You have seen me in the meantime; you are now aware of the condition in which I find myself at certain times. Your happiness and mine has suffered a blow, is even at the point of being completely destroyed. I must leave you, and do not know if I shall ever see you again." Her presence, the grace with which she spoke, drove away almost every memory of the sight which had already appeared to me as but a dream. I embraced her with energy, convinced her of my passion, assured her of my innocence, told her how the discovery had been sheer accident, and in short did so much that she seemed reassured and attempted to reassure me.

"Examine your heart," she said, "to see whether this discovery has not impaired your love, whether you can forget that I am with you in two different forms, whether the diminution of my being will not also reduce your affection."

I gazed at her; she was more beautiful than ever, and I thought to myself, "Is it such a misfortune to have a wife who from time to time becomes a dwarf, so that one can carry her about in a casket? Would it not be much worse if she became a giant and tucked her husband into the chest?" My good spirits had returned. I would not have given her up for anything in the world. "Dearest heart," I replied, "let us stay and be as we were. Could either of us be better off? Use your comfortable little arrangement, and I promise you that I will carry the casket all the more carefully. How could the sweetest thing I have ever seen in my life make a bad impression on me? How happy lovers would be, could they possess such miniature images! And in the end, it was merely such an image, a little sleight-of-hand. You are testing me and teasing me, but you shall see how steadfast I remain."

"The matter is more serious than you think," replied my fair one, "although I am quite pleased that you take it so lightly, since it can still have the happiest outcome for both of us. I will trust you and for my part do everything possible, only promise me never to make a reproach of this discovery. To this I add another urgent request: be more careful than ever about wine and wrath."

I promised what she requested, and would have promised more and more. But she herself turned the conversation to other things, and all went on as before. We had no reason to change our place of residence; the town was large, the company varied, and the season gave occasion for many country and garden festivities.

At all such events my wife was most welcome, indeed in demand with men and women alike. Polished, ingratiating conduct coupled with a certain nobility made her liked and respected by everyone. In addition, she played the lute magnificently and sang to her own accompaniment, and every sociable evening had to be crowned by her talents.

I must confess that I have never been able to make much of music, that, in fact, it has an unpleasant effect on me. My lady love, who had soon observed this, never tried to entertain me in this fashion when we were by ourselves, but she seemed to compensate herself in society, when she usually found a throng of admirers.

And now, why should I deny it, our last discussion, despite my best intentions, had not been sufficient to put the matter to rest for me; rather, it had worked very strangely on my feelings, without my being fully aware of it. One evening, in the midst of a large party, the suppressed rancor burst forth, resulting in the most serious loss for me.

Now that I think about it, I loved my beauty much less after that unfortunate discovery, and presently I grew jealous of her, which had never occurred to me earlier. One evening at dinner, where she and I sat diagonally across from each other at some distance, I was enjoying myself with both of my table partners, a pair of damsels whom I had found attractive for some time. Amidst joking and flirting, the wine flowed freely, while on the other side of the table a pair of music lovers had taken possession of my wife and were encouraging and leading the company in song, individually and in chorus. This put me in a bad humor. The two amateurs seemed too forward; the singing made me irritable, and when they demanded a solo verse from me as well, I became really incensed, emptied my glass, and brought it down hard on the table.

I was soon mollified, to be sure, by the charms of my neighbors, but it is a bad business with anger, once it has been aroused. It seethed away in secret, although everything should have disposed me to pleasure and compliance. On the contrary, I became more spiteful when a lute was produced and my beauty played and sang, to the admiration of all the rest. Unfortunately, general silence was called for. So I was not even allowed to chatter anymore, and the chords set my teeth on edge. Was it any wonder, then, that finally the smallest spark ignited the powderkeg?

The singer had just finished a song, to the greatest applause, when she looked in my direction, truly in the most loving manner. Unfortunately her gaze did not penetrate my anger. She saw me down a cup of wine and pour myself another. She shook her right forefinger at me, in tender warning. "Remember that it is wine," she said, no more loudly than was necessary for me to hear it. "Water is for nixies!" I exclaimed. "My good ladies," she said to my neighbors, "wreathe the cup with your graces, that it may not be emptied too often." "You are not going to let yourself be ordered around," hissed one of them in my ear. "What does the dwarf want?" I shouted, gesturing wildly so that I knocked over the cup. "How much has been spilt here!" cried the wondrous beauty, and she struck a chord on her lute, as though she wished to draw the attention of the company away from this disturbance and back toward herself. She succeeded, the more so when she stood up, as if to play more comfortably, and continued her prelude.

When I saw the red wine running over the tablecloth, I came back to my senses. I recognized the great mistake I had made, and was filled with remorse. For the first time the music spoke to me. The first strophe she sang was a friendly farewell to the company, which could still feel itself united in good fellowship. In the next strophe, it was as if the group were dissolving, each felt himself alone, isolated, no one seemed present any longer. But what shall I say of the last strophe? It was directed toward me alone, the voice of wronged love, which takes leave of sullenness and selfishness.

In silence I escorted her home, expecting the worst. But hardly had we reached our room when she showed herself most friendly and charming, even playful toward me, and made me the happiest of men.

The next morning I said to her, in all confidence and affection, "You have often sung at the request of company, as for example that touching song of farewell last night. Now sing for me for once, a pretty, cheerful greeting for this morning hour, so that we may feel as though we were first coming to know one another."

"That I cannot do, my friend," she replied gravely. "Yesterday's song referred to our parting, which must now take place at once. For I can tell you only that your insult contrary to promise and pledge has the worst consequences for us both. You have squandered a great happiness, and I, too, must renounce my dearest wishes."

As I now pressed her and begged her to explain herself better, she replied, "That I can now do, alas, for my time with you is at an end. Hear, therefore, what I should have preferred to conceal from you to the last. The form in which you saw me inside the casket is my true and natural form. For I belong to the line of King Eckwald, the powerful ruler of the dwarfs, of whom the true history has so much to report. Our people are industrious and busy today, as they were of old, and hence are easy to govern. But you must not imagine they are backward in their work. In the past they were most famous for making swords that followed the enemy when they were hurled at him, invisible chains that mysteriously bound up one's adversaries, impenetrable shields, and the like. Nowadays, however, they occupy themselves chiefly with objects of convenience and ornament, and surpass every other people on earth in this respect. You would be amazed if you were to go through our workshops and warehouses. All would be well, if it were not that the entire nation, but especially the royal family, is affected by a particular circumstance."

Since she paused for a moment, I besought her to reveal more about this curious secret, with which she obliged me straightaway.

"It is well known," she said, "that God, as soon as he had created the world, and the earth had dried out and the mountains stood there, mighty and magnificent—that God, I say, at once created the dwarfs, before all else, so that there might be intelligent beings who could marvel at and revere His wonders in tunnels and chasms deep inside the earth. It is further known that this little race later rose up and thought to assert mastery over the earth, for which reason God created dragons, to drive the dwarfs back into the mountains. But since the dragons settled into the large caverns and crevices themselves and lived there, and many belched fire and spread much other devastation, that caused the little dwarfs great distress and trouble, so much so that they did not know what to do, and turned in humble entreaty to the Lord, and beseeched Him in fervent prayers to exterminate this unclean race of dragons. Although in His wisdom He could not bring Himself to destroy His own creature, still the plight of the poor little dwarfs so touched His heart that He promptly created the giants, who would do battle with the dragons and, if not extirpate them, at least reduce their numbers.

"But when the giants had fairly well finished off the dragons, they, too, fell prey to pride and presumption, and began perpetrating many outrages, especially against the good little dwarfs, who then again turned to the Lord in their distress, who in His sovereign power then created the knights, who battle the giants and the dragons and live in perfect harmony with the dwarfs. With that, this phase of the Creation was concluded, and it is the case that since then giants and dragons, like knights and dwarfs, always stick together. From this you can see, my friend, that we belong to the oldest race on earth, which, to be sure, represents a great honor, but also carries great disadvantages.

"But since nothing on earth can exist forever, but everything which was once great must become small and dwindle, we, too, are in the situation that since the creation of the world we have been constantly dwindling and growing smaller, but most of all the royal family, which, because of its pure blood, is the first to undergo this fate. Therefore many years ago our wise men thought of a solution: that from time to time a princess of the royal house should be sent out into the world to wed an honorable knight, so that the race of dwarfs should be renewed and saved from utter ruin."

While my fair one spoke these words with utmost sincerity, I looked at her with distrust, for it seemed as if she wanted to pull my leg in some way. As to her tiny origins I had no doubt, but that she had chosen me instead of a knight aroused some mistrust, since I knew myself too well to believe that my ancestors had been directly created by God.

I concealed my astonishment and doubts and asked her kindly, "But tell me, my dear child, how do you come by this large and imposing form? For I know few women who could match you in magnificence of shape." "That you shall learn," replied my fair one. "Since time immemorial it has been customary in the council of the dwarf kings that every extraordinary step should be avoided as long as possible, which I also find right and proper. They would perhaps have delayed even further before sending a princess out into the world, had not my younger brother been born so tiny that the nurses lost him out of his swaddling clothes, and no one knows what has become of him. In this case, utterly unheard of in the annals of the dwarf kingdom, the wise men were gathered, and, to be brief, it was decided to send me out wooing."

"It was decided!" I exclaimed, "That is all well and good. People can decide, people can resolve, but to give a dwarflet such a divine form—how did your wise men manage that?"

"That, too," she said, "was anticipated by our ancestors. In our royal treasury lay an enormous gold ring. I am describing it as it seemed to me when it was shown to me in its place when I was still a child, for it is the very one I have here on my finger. The task was undertaken in the following fashion: I was instructed in everything that lay in store for me, and taught what to do and what to avoid.

"An exquisite palace, patterned after the favorite summer residence of my parents, was constructed: a main building, two wings, and whatever else one could wish for. It stood at the entrance of a great rocky cleft, and it adorned it beautifully. On the appointed day, the court assembled there, and my parents brought me. The army paraded, and twenty-four priests bore, not without difficulty, the miraculous ring on an elaborate litter. It was placed on the threshold of the building, just inside, where one would have to step over it. Various ceremonies were performed, and after heartfelt farewells I set to work. I stepped forward, placed my hand upon the ring, and at once began to grow perceptibly. In a few moments I had reached my present size, and promptly placed the ring on my finger. In the twinkling of an eye, windows, doors, and gates closed, the wings withdrew into the main building, and instead of the palace, a casket stood beside me, which I picked up forthwith and carried away with me, not without distinct pleasure in being so tall and strong, though still, to be sure, a dwarf compared to trees and mountains, rivers and landscapes, but nevertheless a giant compared to grass and plants, and especially to the ants, with whom we dwarfs do not always have the best relations, and by whom, therefore, we are often plagued terribly.

"How I fared on my pilgrimage before I met you would take long to tell. Suffice it to say, I tested many a man, but none but you seemed worthy to renew and immortalize the stock of the magnificent Eckwald."

As she told me all these tales, my head often wobbled of itself, without my actually having shaken it. I asked various questions, without receiving any proper answers to them, but rather learned, to my great sorrow, that after what had happened she absolutely had to return to her parents. To be sure, she hoped to come back to me, but for now she had to present herself at court without fail, else all would be lost for her, as well as for me. The purses would soon stop paying, with all kinds of other consequences.

When I heard that our money might run out, I did not ask what more might happen. I shrugged and fell silent, and she seemed to understand me.

We packed up and settled ourselves in the coach, the casket, in which I could not make out any features of a palace, across from us. Thus we proceeded for several way stations. Fares and tips were easily and generously paid from the pouches left and right, until finally we reached a mountainous region, and had barely got out when my fair one went on ahead and I followed with the casket at her command. She led me by fairly steep paths to a narrow meadow, through which the waters of a spring wound, now coursing swiftly, now flowing quietly. She pointed out a hummock, bade me set the casket down there, and said, "Farewell! You will easily find your way back; remember me; I hope to see you again."

At this moment I felt as though I could not part from her. This was one of the days—or one of the hours, if you will—when her beauty was at its height. To be alone with such an exquisite being, on the green turf, amidst grass and flowers, sheltered by cliffs, the water gurgling: what heart could have remained unfeeling? I wanted to take her by the hand, to embrace her, but she thrust me away and threatened me, though still lovingly enough, with great danger if I did not depart at once.

"Is there no possibility at all," I exclaimed, "for me to stay with you, for you to keep me with you?" I accompanied these words with such sorrowful gestures and tones that she seemed moved, and after some hesitation admitted that a continuation of our union was not entirely impossible. Who could have been happier than I! My insistence, which became ever more vehement, finally forced her to come out with what she had in mind, and to reveal to me that, if I were to decide to become as small with her as I had seen her, then I could stay with her even now, and enter her home, her kingdom, her family. This proposal was not altogether to my liking, but at this moment I simply could not tear myself away from her. Having been in any case accustomed to miraculous occurrences for some time now, and being of an impulsive nature, I agreed, and said she might do with me as she liked.

Without further ado I had to hold out the little finger of my right hand; she rested her own against it, and with her left hand gently drew the gold ring from her finger and let it slip over my own. No sooner had this happened than I felt a violent pain in my finger, as the ring contracted, pinching me horribly. I gave a great cry and involuntarily reached out for my fair one, but she had vanished. I can find no words to express my inner state at that moment; I have nothing else to say, except that I soon found myself a tiny little person in a forest of grass stalks beside my lady. Our joy at seeing each other after so short, yet so strange, a separation—or, if you prefer, at our reunion without separation—was boundless. I threw my arms around her, she returned my caresses, and the small pair felt as happy as the large one.

With some effort we now climbed up a hill, for the turf had become an almost impenetrable forest for us. But finally we reached a clearing, and how surprised I was to see there a massive, ordered shape, which I soon recognized as the casket, in the condition in which I had placed it there.

"Go up to it, my friend, and knock on it with the ring, and you shall see a real wonder," said my beloved. I stepped up to it, and hardly had I knocked when I truly experienced the greatest wonder. Two wings emerged, and at the same time various parts peeled off like chips and scales, revealing doors, windows, colonnades, and everything that a complete palace requires.

Anyone who has seen one of Röntgen's ingenious writing desks, where at a single touch many springs and hinges come into motion, so that the writing surface and implements, pigeonholes for letters and money appear simultaneously, or in quick succession—anyone who has seen one can imagine how that palace unfolded, into which my sweet companion now drew me. In the main hall I instantly recognized the fireplace that I had previously seen from above, and the armchair in which she had sat. And when I looked up, I really believed I could still detect the crack in the vault through which I had peeped in. I will spare you description of the rest; suffice it to say that all was spacious, luxurious, and tasteful. Hardly had I recovered from my amazement when I heard military music in the distance. My lovely partner jumped for joy and announced with delight the approach of her honored father. We stepped onto the threshold and beheld a brilliant procession emerging from a great fissure in the rock. Soldiers, attendants, house officials, and a brilliant court followed one another. Finally a golden throng appeared, and in it the king himself. When the entire procession was arrayed before the palace, the king and his retinue stepped forward. His loving daughter hastened toward him, pulling me along with her; we cast ourselves at his feet, he raised me up most graciously, and as I stood before him, I noticed for the first time that I naturally had the most imposing stature in this tiny world. We entered the palace together, where the king delivered a well-phrased speech in the presence of his entire court, in which he expressed his surprise at finding us here, bade us welcome, accepted me as his son-in-law, and set the next day for the wedding ceremony.

How dreadfully upset I was when I heard him speak of marriage: until now I had feared it almost more than music itself, which otherwise seemed to me the most hateful thing on earth. Those who make music, I used to say, at least imagine that they are at one with each other and working in harmony. When they have tuned long enough and abused our ears with all sorts of dissonances, they firmly believe that the situation is under control and each instrument is in tune with the next. Even the conductor shares this happy delusion, and so they go at it hammer and tongs, jarring on the ears of the rest of us. With marriage, on the other hand, not even this is the case; even though it is only a duet and one might think that two voices, or two instruments, could be harmonized to some extent, that happens but seldom. For if the husband sounds one note, then the wife immediately takes it higher, and the husband higher still, so that the whole thing passes from chamber music to full chorus and yet higher, until at last even the wind instruments cannot follow. And so, since harmonic music remains repugnant to me, no one can mind if I find the disharmonic variety intolerable.

Of all the festivities that filled the rest of the day, I am neither willing nor able to give an account, for I paid scant attention to them. Neither the rich food nor the fine wines tasted good to me at all. I brooded and pondered what I might do. But the possibilities were few. I decided simply to slip away at nightfall and hide myself somewhere. I succeeded in reaching a crack in the rocks into which I could squeeze and be fairly well hidden. My first concern after this was to get the wretched ring off my finger, but I could not manage it. Instead I felt it grow tighter and tighter as soon as I tried to pull it off, so that I suffered terrible pain, which, however, decreased as soon as I desisted from my intention.

I awoke early—for my small person had slept soundly—and wanted to look about me, when I felt something like rain starting. Great quantities of something like sand and grit seemed to be falling through grass, leaves, and flowers. But how horrified I was when everything around me came alive, and an innumerable host of ants came tumbling down upon me. No sooner had they noticed me than they attacked me from every side, and although I defended myself stoutly and bravely enough, they finally swarmed all over me, pinched and tormented me so much that was I was glad when I heard a call for me to surrender. I did indeed surrender, and instantly, upon which an ant of distinguished stature approached, and politely, even with respect, commended himself to me. I learned that the ants had become allies of my father-in-law, and that in the present case he had called them up and charged them to bring me back. So here I was, a little creature in the hands of still smaller creatures. I saw the marriage looming and had to thank God if my father-in-law was not angry with me or if my fair one was not vexed.

Let me pass over the ceremonies in silence; in short, we were married. However merrily and enjoyably things went with us, there nevertheless came those solitary hours in which one is lured into reflection, and something happened that had never happened to me before; what that was, and how it came about, you shall hear.

Everything about me was completely suited to my present shape and needs; the bottles and glasses were correctly scaled for a small drinker, indeed, if you will, somewhat better than among us. The delicate bites of food tasted wonderful to my small palate, a kiss from my wife's little mouth was absolutely delicious, and I would not deny that novelty made all these conditions highly agreeable. But for all this I had unfortunately not forgotten my previous state. I still retained some sense of my former size, which made me restless and unhappy. For the first time I comprehended what philosophers mean when they speak of those ideals which supposedly cause mankind such mental torment. I had an ideal of myself and sometimes appeared to myself in dreams as a giant. In short, a wife, the ring, my dwarfish stature, and so many other constraints made me thoroughly unhappy, so that I began to plan in earnest for my liberation.

Since I was convinced that the entire magic lay in the ring, I decided to file it off. To this end, I purloined some files from the court jeweler. Fortunately I was left-handed and all through my life had never done anything right. I kept at the task bravely. It was not easy, for the tiny gold band, though it looked slender enough, had grown thicker in proportion to its loss of diameter. I devoted all my free hours in secret to this job, and was clever enough to step outside when the metal was almost filed through. That proved wise, for all at once the gold band sprang violently from my finger, and my body shot up so vigorously that I truly thought I would bump into the sky and would in any case have burst the vault of our summer palace, would, in fact, have destroyed the entire building in my new clumsiness.

There I stood once more, to be sure much bigger than I had been, but also, so it seemed to me, much more stupid and clumsy. And when I had recovered from my confusion, I saw the coffer standing near me. I found it rather heavy when I lifted it and carried it down the path to the posthouse, where I immediately ordered horses and set off. Once in motion, I promptly tried the little pouches to either side. In place of the money, which seemed to have run out, I found a little key. It belonged to the coffer, in which I found a passable substitute. As long as that lasted, I used the coach; afterward the coach was sold to pay my way in the post chaise. The coffer was the last to be disposed of, for I kept hoping it would replenish itself, and so, ultimately, I came, though by something of a detour, to the good woman's hearth where you first made my acquaintance.

Chapter Seven

Hersilie to Wilhelm

Acquaintances, though they may seem of no particular significance when they begin, often have most important consequences, especially yours, which from the first moment was not insignificant. The peculiar key came into my hands as a strange pledge; now I possess the casket as well. Key and casket—what do you say to that? What can one say? Hear how it came about:

A refined young man calls on my uncle and tells him that the curious dealer in antiquities who was long in contact with you died recently, and left him all of his remarkable estate, but at the same time charged him to return without delay everything belonging to others that had merely been deposited with him. As the old man said, one's own property was no worry, since one bore the loss of them alone. But he permitted himself to keep other people's possessions only in special cases. He did not wish to burden the young man with this responsibility; indeed, he forbade him, with paternal love and authority, to assume it. And with this he brought out the casket, which, though I knew it already from description, still struck me as quite exceptional.

My uncle, after he had examined it from every side, gave it back, and said that he, too, had made it a principle to act in the same spirit and not to burden himself with any antique, however beautiful and wonderful, if he did not know to whom it had belonged previously and what historical curiosities were connected with it. Since this casket bore neither letters nor numerals, neither a date nor any other indication by which one might infer who had owned it or made it, it was utterly useless and without interest for him.

The young man stood there in great perplexity, and after some reflection asked whether he would allow him to leave it in the custody of the court. Uncle smiled, and turning to me, said, "This would be a nice business for you, Hersilie. You have all sorts of jewelry and precious little objects, too. Add this to the rest. For I would wager that our friend, toward whom you were not indifferent, will return one of these days and fetch it."

I must write all this, if I want to tell the truth, and I must also confess I looked at the casket with envious eyes, and a certain covetousness seized hold of me. It pained me to think of this magnificent little treasure chest, which Fate had destined for our dear Felix, sitting in the rusty old vault of the courthouse. Like a divining rod, my hand reached for it; what little good sense I have held my hand back. I already had the key, but this I could not reveal, and was I to torture myself by leaving the lock unopened, or else surrender to the forbidden audacity of opening it? At any rate, I do not know whether it was wish or premonition: I imagined you were coming, were coming soon, would already be here when I went back to my room. In short, I felt so strange, so odd, so flustered, as I always do when I am startled out of my calm good humor. I shall say no more, shall offer neither description nor apologies; let it suffice that the casket lies before me in my coffer, the key beside it, and if you have a spark of sensitivity or sympathy, you will imagine what I am feeling, how many passions are warring inside me, how I wish you here, and probably Felix as well, so that this may end, or that at least some interpretation be provided for all this mysterious finding, refinding, separation and reuniting; and even if I should not be rescued from all this confusion, I still wish fervently that all this may be clarified, be ended, even if, as I fear, something worse should befall me.

Chapter Eight

Among the papers before us for editing, we find this anecdote, which we may include here without further introduction, since our affairs are becoming ever more serious, and we are unlikely to have room further on for irregularities of this sort.

All in all, the reader may find some pleasure in this tale, as it was told by St. Christopher one pleasant evening to a circle of merry companions.

The Perilous Wager

It is well known that as soon as things are going well for people and are more or less to their liking, they do not know what to do with their high spirits. So it was that bands of mischievous students would spend their holidays traveling about the country and playing pranks of all sorts, which, of course, did not always have the best of consequences. They were of very different sorts, such as student life brings and joins together. Despite differences in birth and fortune, in intellect and education, they swarmed along in a common love of fun, full of merry doings. They often chose me as a companion; for if I could carry heavier loads than any of them, they also had to honor me with the title of a great prankster, and this chiefly because I carried out my capers more rarely, but all the more effectively, as the following will demonstrate.

In the course of our wanderings we had reached a pleasant mountain village, which, although out of the way, had the advantage of a post-house and, in great solitude, a pair of pretty girls as inhabitants. We wanted to rest, while away our time, flirt, live more cheaply for a while, and thus have more money to squander.

It was right after dinner, when some felt themselves in a heightened state, others in a depressed one. The latter went to bed and slept off their tipsiness, while the others would have liked to give it free rein in some mischief. We had a couple of large rooms in the wing, giving on the courtyard. A fine equipage with four horses clattered up, drawing us to the window. The lackeys leaped from the box and helped a gentleman of dignified and distinguished appearance to descend. Despite his years, he still moved vigorously enough. I was struck first by the newcomer's large, well-formed nose, and I cannot say what evil spirit possessed me that I instantly conceived the maddest sort of plan, and without further thought began to execute it at once.

"What do you think of this gentleman?" I asked the others. "He looks like someone who tolerates no nonsense," one of them replied. "Yes, yes," said another, "he has quite the look of a high and mighty Touch-me-not." "In spite of that," I countered boldly, "what will you wager that I will tweak his nose without any ill effects to me, that, in fact, I will earn his polite thank-you for it?"

"If you bring it off," said Rowdy, "everyone will give you a louis d'or."

"Collect the money for me," I exclaimed, "I am counting on you."

"I would rather pluck a hair from a lion's muzzle," remarked Tiny.

"I have no time to lose," I replied, and ran down the stairs.

At the first sight of the stranger I had noticed that he had a heavy growth of beard, and suspected that none of his attendants knew how to shave. I now encountered the waiter and asked him, "Hasn't the new arrival asked for a barber?" "So he has," the waiter answered, "and it is urgent. For the past two days the gentleman's valet has not been with him. The gentleman absolutely insists on being rid of his beard, and our only barber is off God knows where in the neighborhood."

"Then present me," I replied. "Introduce me as barber to the gentleman, and I will do you credit." I took the shaving kit they had in the inn and followed the waiter.

The old gentleman received me with gravity, looked me up and down, as if he could guess my skill from my physiognomy. "Do you know your trade?" he said to me.

"I do not like to boast," I replied, "but there are not many equal to me." Moreover I was on sure ground, for I had practiced the noble art from an early age, and was especially known for shaving with my left hand.

The room in which the gentleman was making his toilette gave on the courtyard, and was so situated that my friends could conveniently see in, especially if the windows were open. Nothing more was needed by way of preparations. My client had seated himself and covered himself with his towel. I stepped forward modestly and said, "Your Excellency, in the exercise of my art, I have noticed the oddity that I shave better and give more satisfaction with humble folk than with those of high station. I have thought a long time about this and have sought the reason now here, now there, but have finally determined that I do my job much better out in the open air than in closed rooms. If Your Excellency would therefore give me leave to open the window, you would soon enjoy the beneficial effect, to your own satisfaction."

He agreed, I opened the window, gave my friends a sign, and began to lather the strong beard with style. With equal adroitness and lightness I scraped the stubble from his skin, and when I came to the upper lip did not fail to take my patron by the nose and bend it conspicuously back and forth, placing myself so that my friends would have to see it, to their great delight, and acknowledge that their side had lost the wager.

With great dignity the old gentleman moved to the mirror; it was evident that he was looking at himself with no little pleasure, and truly, he was a very handsome man. Then he turned to me with an intense, dark, but friendly look and said, "You deserve, my friend, to be praised above many of your tribe, for I find in you fewer annoying habits than in others. You do not pass two or three times over the same place, but manage with a single stroke. Nor do you, as many do, wipe the razor on your palm and spread the dirt all over a person's nose. Your skill with your left hand is especially admirable. Here is something for your pains," he said, handing me a gulden. "There is only one thing you should learn: one does not take persons of rank by the nose. If in the future you eschew this peasant custom, you might well prosper in the world."

I bowed deeply, promised all sorts of things, besought him, if he should by any chance return, to honor me again, and hurried as fast as I could to our young friends, who had begun to cause me some anxiety. They had been making such a racket and laughing so loudly, had been cavorting about the room as though mad, clapping and calling, waking the sleepers and retelling the incident with ever renewed laughter and tumult, so that I myself, when I entered the room, closed the windows before all else and begged them in God's name to quiet down. But finally I had to laugh myself over the ridiculous performance that I had carried out with such solemnity.

When at last the tumultuous waves of laughter had somewhat subsided, I considered myself fortunate; I had the gold pieces in my pocket, along with my well-earned gulden, and thought myself well provided for, which was all the more welcome, since our party had decided to break up the following day. But we were not destined to leave in a decorous and orderly manner. The story was too delightful to keep to ourselves, however much I had entreated and beseeched the others to be still, at least until the old gentleman had departed. One of us, nicknamed Blabbermouth, had an affair going with the daughter of the house. They had a rendezvous, and God knows if he had no better way to entertain her, but in any case, he told her of the prank, and the two of them laughed themselves sick over it. Nor was that all; the girl spread the tale around, and it must finally have reached the ears of the old gentleman, just before he retired for the night.

We were sitting more quietly than usual, for we had been riotous enough all day long, when suddenly the little waiter, who was very devoted to us, dashed in, crying, "Run for it, they're coming to kill you!" We jumped up and wanted to hear more, but he was already out of the door. I ran to slide the bolt. But already we heard knocking and pounding; we even thought we heard it being splintered by an ax. Mechanically we withdrew into the second room. We had all fallen silent. "We are betrayed," I exclaimed. "The devil has us all by the nose."

Rowdy reached for his sword, while I once again demonstrated my enormous strength and all by myself pushed a heavy dresser in front of the door, which fortunately opened inward. But we could already hear the din in the adjacent room, and violent blows on our door.

Rowdy seemed determined to defend himself, but I repeatedly called to him and the others, "Save yourselves! You will get not only a good drubbing but also a tongue-lashing, which is worse for those of good birth." The girl rushed in, the same who had given us away, now desperate at the thought that her lover's life was in danger. "Away, away!" she cried. "I'll lead you through the attics, sheds, and passageways. Come, all of you, and the last one pull up the ladder."

Now they all crowded through the back door, while I stayed behind to lift a chest onto the dresser to hold back the already broken panels of the besieged door. But my steadfastness and fighting spirit would be my downfall.

When I ran after the others, I found the ladder had already been drawn up, and saw myself deprived of any hope of saving my skin. There I stand, the true culprit, with no prospect of escaping in one piece, with bones unbroken. And who knows—but leave me standing there thinking, since I am here to tell the tale. I will only add that this foolhardy prank brought terrible results.

The old gentleman, mortified at having endured ridicule without revenge, brooded over it, and it is claimed that this incident resulted in his death, if not directly, then at least in conjunction with other factors. His son, seeking to track down the perpetrators, unfortunately discovered that Rowdy had been involved, and, achieving certainty only years later, challenged him to a duel. The wound that handsome man received disfigured and afflicted him for the rest of his life. For his antagonist, too, this affair ruined several good years, because of chance events that issued from it.

Since every tale is actually meant to teach something, all of you will find the direction in which this one points abundantly clear.

Chapter Nine

The day of great moment had dawned; today the first steps were to be taken toward the general emigration; today would decide who would actually go out into the world and who would prefer to stay on the contiguous soil of the old world and seek his fortune.

A merry song rang through all the streets of the cheerful town. Groups formed; the individual members of each craft joined together and, all singing with one voice, proceeded into the hall, according to an order determined by lot.

The leaders, as we shall designate Lenardo, Friedrich, and the bailiff, were about to follow the others and take their rightful seats, when a personable man approached them and requested permission to join the assembly. It would have been impossible to refuse him anything, so well-bred, civil, and amiable was his manner, which made his imposing figure, suggestive of the army as well as of the court and society, appear most pleasing. He entered with the others, and they assigned him a place of honor. All had been seated; Lenardo remained standing and addressed them as follows:

"When we, my friends, look at the continent's most populous provinces and kingdoms, we find that whenever useful land appears, it has been cultivated, planted, ordered, beautified, and to the same degree desired, taken possession of, secured, and defended. This should convince us of the high value of land ownership and make us regard it as the first and best asset man can acquire. If, upon closer inspection, we now find that love for parents and for children, intimate ties to fellow inhabitants of countryside and town, as well as the general feeling of patriotism, are all founded directly on the soil, then that urge to grasp and lay claim to space, on large scale and small, appears as ever more significant and estimable. Yes, Nature has ordained it so! A man, born on the land, comes through habit to belong to it; the two grow together, forming the most beautiful ties. Who, then, would be so monstrous as to disturb this basis of all existence, or deny the worth and dignity of so unique and beautiful a gift of Providence?

"And yet one may say: even though a man's property is of great worth, even greater worth must be ascribed to his deeds and achievements. Hence, in the larger perspective, we may consider landholding as a smaller part of the blessings granted to us. Most of these, and the best of them, are actually to be sought in a life of movement and in that which is gained through such an active life.

"It is especially imperative for us younger people to look about us. For if we had the desire, inherited from our fathers, to remain and persist, we would still find ourselves challenged on all sides not to close our eyes to further aspects and prospects. So let us hasten to the edge of the sea and with one glance convince ourselves that immeasurable spaces lie open to action, and let us admit that we are stirred in unexpected fashion by the mere thought of them.

"Still, we do not want to lose ourselves in such boundless distances, but turn our attention to the contiguous broad expanses of so many lands and kingdoms. There we see great stretches of country roamed by nomads whose cities are movable, and whose living, nourishing property, their herds, can be led all about. We see them in the midst of the desert, at large, green oases, like ships at anchor in a safe harbor. Such movement, such wandering, has become a habit with them, a need; in the end they regard the earth's surface as though it were not dammed by mountains or cut through by rivers. Have we not seen the northeast moving toward the southwest, one people driving another before it, with patterns of authority and land ownership utterly transformed?

"In the course of history the same thing will happen again, starting in the overpopulated regions. What we can expect from strangers would be hard to say. But it is curious that we feel an inner pressure from our own overpopulation, and without waiting to be driven out, we drive ourselves out, and ourselves issue the sentence of banishment against one another.

"Now is the time and place to indulge a certain restlessness in our breasts without annoyance or discontent, and not to suppress the impatient desire that drives us to a change of scene. But let whatever we plan and intend spring not from passion, nor from any other compulsion, but from conviction based on the best reasons.

"It has been said and repeated: 'Where I am well off is my fatherland!' But this comforting saying would be even better formulated if it went, 'Where I am useful is my fatherland!' At home a person can be useless without its being noticed immediately; out in the world, the useless person is at once obvious. If I now say, 'Let each strive to be useful to himself and others in all ways,' it is neither a doctrine nor advice, but the maxim of life itself.

"Now let us survey this planet and leave the ocean aside for the moment, let us not be distracted by the swarms of ships, but fix our eyes on the dry land and wonder at how a teeming race of ants swarms across it. The Lord Himself sanctioned this, when, in disrupting work on the Tower of Babel, He scattered the race of man through all the world. Let us praise Him for this, for this blessing has passed to all mankind.

"Let us now observe with pleasure how natural movement is to youth. Since instruction is available neither at home nor nearby, young people rush off to countries and cities that lure them by their reputation for knowledge and wisdom. Having quickly assimilated some moderate degree of education, they feel impelled to look even farther afield in the wide world, to see whether here or there they may not discover and seize some useful experience that will further their purposes. May they try their luck! We, however, pay homage to those accomplished, excellent men, those noble scientists, who knowingly face all hardships and dangers to open the world to the world, and prepare a path and track through the uncharted wilderness.

"But see how along the smooth highways the dust is stirred up, rising in long clouds, marking the course of comfortable, heavily packed conveyances, in which the high-born, the wealthy, and so many others roll along, people whose different ways of thought and intentions Yorick has so charmingly analyzed for us.

"Let the sturdy artisan on foot look calmly after them, he on whom his fatherland has imposed the duty to acquire foreign skills and not to return to the family hearth until he has succeeded. More commonly, however, we meet upon our ways traders and dealers. Even a small retailer, from time to time, must not fail to leave his shop to visit fairs and markets, where he can rub shoulders with wholesalers and increase his modest profits by following their example, by taking part in the boundless realm. But the main and side roads are even more thronged with the horde of those riding alone on horseback who have designs on our purses, whether we wish to buy or not. They besiege us both in towns and country houses with samples of every sort and with price lists, and wherever we may try to flee, they busily seek us out, offering bargains which no one would think of looking for on his own. But what shall I say of the race which above all others has adopted the role of the eternal wanderer, and, through constant movement and activity, contrives to outsmart settled shopkeepers and outdo its fellow itinerants? We may speak neither good nor evil of it: not good, because the league is on its guard against them, not evil because the wanderer is obligated to treat everyone he meets in friendly fashion, and be mindful of mutual advantage.

"But above all we must think with sympathy of the artists, for they, too, are implicated in this worldwide movement. Does not the painter journey from portrait to portrait with his easel and palette? And are not his fellow artists also summoned hither and yon, since everywhere there is building and forming to be done? The musician strides along even more briskly, for he it is who serves up new surprises for new ears, fresh sensations for fresh minds. And then the actors, even if they spurn Thespis' cart, are still always on the move in smaller companies, and their portable world is thrown up quickly enough in every spot. Likewise individual actors like to change from place to place, even sacrificing serious and advantageous connections, the excuse and the impetus being heightened talent and the heightened demand. They usually prepare themselves for this by leaving no significant stage in the fatherland untrodden.

"Next we are admonished to consider the teaching profession: you will find it, too, constantly on the move, appearing on one podium after another to sow the seeds of rapid education profusely on all sides. Even more assiduous and farther reaching, however, are those pious souls who, to bring salvation to all peoples, disperse to every quarter of the globe. Others, on the contrary, make pilgrimages to obtain salvation for themselves; whole troops of them stream to sacred sites of miracles, where they seek and receive what was not vouchsafed their spirit at home.

"If none of these cause us amazement, since most of their doings would be unthinkable without wandering, we should assume that at least those who devote their effort to the land will be tied to it. Far from it! Cultivation is conceivable even without ownership, and we see a hardworking farmer leave a plot that has yielded him profit and pleasure for many a year while he leased it; avidly he searches for equal or greater advantages, whether far or near. Yes, even the proprietor abandons his newly cleared land as soon as he has made it inviting to a less able owner by his cultivation; he pushes on anew into the wilderness, once again makes a space for himself in the forests as reward for his first efforts, two or three times as large, where he likewise may not intend to remain.

"Let us leave him there, fighting it out with bears and other wild beasts, and return to the civilized world, where we find things no calmer. Consider any large, well-ordered kingdom, where the most competent man must conceive himself as the most flexible. At a nod from the prince, at a directive from the council, the useful person is transferred from one place to the other. To him also our motto applies: 'Make yourself useful everywhere, and you will be at home everywhere.' But when we see important statesmen leaving their high posts, albeit unwillingly, then we have reason to pity them, since they qualify neither as emigrants nor as wanderers. Not emigrants, because they are giving up a desirable situation without any prospect of finding better conditions. Nor are they wanderers, since it is seldom granted to them to be useful in some way in other places.

"The soldier is committed to a special life of wandering. Even in peace he is assigned first to one post, then another. He must always be ready to move near and far to fight for the fatherland, and not only for immediate safety, but also at the will of peoples and rulers he must turn his footsteps to every quarter of the globe, and only to few it is granted to settle anywhere. Since bravery is esteemed as the soldier's highest virtue, and is always linked with loyalty, we often see certain peoples renowned for their reliability summoned from their homeland to serve as bodyguards for secular and spiritual rulers.

"Yet another class, always on the move and indispensable to the state, can be seen in those men of business who, dispatched from court to court, swarm around princes and ministers and form a network of invisible threads over the entire populated world. Of them, too, not a single one is secure in one place for even a moment. In peacetime the most capable of them are sent from one part of the world to the other; in war, they follow the conquering armies, or pave the way for the retreating forces. In either case they are ever prepared to leave one place for another, for which reason they always carry with them a large supply of farewell cards.

"If up to now we have honored ourselves at every step by claiming the finest of the active people as our fellows and partners in fate, now, dear friends, in conclusion the greatest distinction still awaits you, that of finding yourselves in brotherhood with emperors, kings, and princes. Let us first summon up the blessed memory of that noble imperial wanderer, Hadrian, who on foot, at the head of his army, traversed the entire populated world, all subject to him, and thus first truly took possession of it. Let us recall with a shudder the conquering hordes, those armed wanderers, against whom no resistance availed, and walls and ramparts could not shield harmless peoples. Finally let us accompany with sincere sympathy those unfortunate exiled rulers, who, descending from the pinnacle of power, could never be admitted into even the modest guild of active wanderers.

"Now that we have surveyed all this and clarified it for one another, no small-minded melancholy, no impassioned gloom can hold sway over us. The time is past when people ran off into the world for adventure's sake. Through the efforts of scientific explorers, who have given us thoughtful descriptions and artistic representations, we are well enough informed that we have some idea of what to expect anywhere.

"Yet no individual can achieve complete clarity. Our society, however, is based upon the principle that each should be enlightened according to his capacities and purposes. Should anyone have a land in mind to which he feels drawn, we try to make clear to him in detail what had been but vaguely imagined. Giving one another an overview of the inhabited and habitable world is our pleasantest, most rewarding entertainment.

"In this sense we may view ourselves as involved in a world confederation. The concept is at once grand and simple; with intelligence and vigor it can easily be realized. Unity is all-powerful, therefore there is no dissension, no conflict among us. Insofar as we have principles, they are common to all of us. A man, we say, must learn to think of himself free from lasting external relations. He must seek consistency not in circumstances but within himself; there he will find it, protect it, and cherish it. He will educate and organize himself to be at home anywhere. He who dedicates himself to that which is most essential will achieve his goal with greatest certainty. Others, by contrast, who seek something higher and more refined, must be more cautious even in their choice of direction. But whatever a man may take up and pursue, he cannot manage as a lone individual; society remains a capable man's highest need. All useful men should stand in relation to one another, as the builder looks to the architect, and the latter to the mason and the carpenter.

"And so you all know how and in what fashion our league was formed and founded. We have no one among us who cannot usefully practice his occupation at any moment, who is not assured that wherever chance, inclination, or even passion might bring him, he will find himself well recommended, received, and encouraged, indeed rescued from misfortunes as far as that is possible.

"We have also taken upon us two strict duties: to honor every form of worship, since they are all more or less expressed in the Creed; in addition, to accept the validity of all forms of government, and, since all of them require and promote useful activity, to work within each according to its will and desire for however long it may be. Finally, we consider it our duty to practice and promote morality without pedantry or prudishness, as, indeed, reverence for ourselves demands, a reverence stemming from the three reverences to which all subscribe, and from the higher wisdom into which all of us have had the good fortune and happiness to be initiated, some of us since our youth. In this solemn hour of parting, let us once more consider all of this, explain it, hear it, and acknowledge it, then also seal it with an affectionate farewell.

Cling not to your homeland's charms,
Take fresh courage, freely roam!
Strong and daring heads and arms
Everywhere can be at home.
Where we gladly greet the sun
Every care is gone at last;
Each a different course may run,
Therefore is the world so vast."

Chapter Ten

During the final song many of those present rose quickly and filed out of the hall two by two, their voices ringing loudly. Taking a seat, Lenardo asked the guest whether he meant to present his request here in public, or whether he required a special session. The stranger stood up, greeted the company, and began the following recital:

"It is here, in just such a gathering, that I would like to declare myself without further ado. Those who have remained quietly behind, apparently stout men all, have clearly signified by staying that they wish and intend to continue allegiance to their native soil and country. I greet them all warmly, for I must explain that I am in a position to offer everyone who has so commited himself a good day's work for some years to come. I would like us to assemble again, but only after a short interval, since it is necessary first of all to reveal my undertaking in confidence to these worthy leaders, who have until now held these stout men together, and to convince them of the reliability of my mission. It will then be proper for me to speak individually with those who will remain, to learn with what contributions each would respond to my handsome offer."

At this Lenardo requested a recess, in order to attend to the most pressing business of the moment, and once this was approved, the throng of those remaining behind rose up with decorum and likewise left the hall in pairs, joining their voices in measured song.

Odoard then discovered his intentions and plans to the two leaders who had stayed, and showed them his authorization for the same. But he could not give further account of the matter in discussion with such superior men without considering the human basis on which the entire enterprise rested. As a result, the conversation proceeded to mutual explanations and confessions of profound matters of the heart. Until late in the night they remained together and became ever more entangled in the labyrinth of human dispositions and destinies. In the course of this Odoard was gradually moved to offer fragmentary accounts of the affairs of his heart and mind, for which reason only incomplete and unsatisfying reports of this conversation have been conveyed to us. Yet here again we are indebted to Friedrich's happy talent for seizing and retaining for this evocation of an interesting episode, as well as for some enlightenment on the career of an excellent man, who has begun to interest us, even though these are merely hints of what may later be reported, perhaps more thoroughly and in context.

Not Too Far

It had struck ten in the night, and everything was ready at the appointed hour: in the garlanded parlor a large table was prettily set for four, with elegant dessert and sweetmeats laid out between gleaming candles and flowers. How the children were looking forward to these refreshments, for they were to sit at the table with the adults; in the meantime, they crept about in costumes and masks, and since children cannot be disfigured, they seemed like the most adorable of twin fairies. Their father summoned them, and they recited the dialogue composed for their mother's birthday, with only a little prompting.

Time wore on, and from quarter hour to quarter hour the good old woman did not refrain from increasing our friend's impatience. Several of the lamps on the steps were about to go out, she said, and various dishes, choice favorites of the mistress, might, she feared, be overcooked. The children became first unruly out of boredom, and finally unbearable out of impatience. Their father pulled himself together, yet his usual composure failed him. He listened longingly for carriages; several rattled by without stopping. A certain annoyance began to stir in him. To pass the time, he made the children recite again; but they, inattentive from weariness, distracted and clumsy, muddled the words, made all the wrong gestures, and exaggerated, like actors who have no feeling. The good man's torment increased with every moment. It was already past ten-thirty. We shall leave it to him to describe what followed:

"The clock struck eleven; my impatience had intensified to despair. I no longer hoped, but feared. I was afraid that she would come in, hastily excuse herself with her usual easy charm, declare that she was very tired, and act as if to accuse me of curtailing her pleasures. Everything went around and around inside me, and many things I had borne in patience for years oppressed my spirit anew. I began to hate her, I could not think how to conduct myself in welcoming her. The dear children, dressed up like little angels, were sleeping peacefully on the sofa. The ground seemed to burn beneath my feet; I could not comprehend, could not understand myself, and had no choice but to flee, if only to survive the next few moments. I rushed, lightly and elegantly dressed as I was, to the door. I do not know what pretext I stammered out to the good old woman. She pressed a cloak upon me, and I found myself in the street, in a state which I had not known for years. Like a youth overcome with passion who has no idea where he is going, I ran up and down the streets. I would have made for the open fields, but a cold, damp wind blew strongly and unpleasantly enough to set limits to my anger."

We have, as this passage strikingly shows, usurped the rights of the epic poet, and plunged the willing reader all too swiftly into the midst of a passionate recital. We see an eminent man in domestic distress, without having learned anything more about him. In order to clarify the situation somewhat, let us join the old servant for a moment, listening in as she murmurs to herself in her trouble and confusion or exclaims out loud:

"I knew it long ago, I foretold it, I did not spare my lady, I warned her often, but it is stronger than she is. If the master wears himself out during the day in the chancellery, in town, or in the country, looking after business, in the evening he finds either an empty house, or company he does not care for. But she cannot stop. If she does not have people around her, men around her, if she does not drive hither and yon, dress and undress and change her clothes, it is as if she could not breathe. Today, on her birthday, she drives off early into the country. Good! We get everything prepared here in the meanwhile. She promises faithfully to be back home at nine o'clock; we are ready. The master listens to the children recite the nice poem they have memorized; they are all dressed up. Lamps and candles, fricassees and roasts—nothing is missing, but still she does not come. The master has great self-control; he hides his impatience, but it breaks forth. He leaves the house at so late an hour. Why is clear enough, but where to? I have often threatened her with rivals, openly and honestly. Till now I never noticed anything amiss with the master, though one beauty has been lying in wait for him a long time, lavishing attentions on him. Who knows how he has been struggling. Now it is breaking out; this time despair at seeing how his good intentions go unappreciated is driving him from the house in the middle of the night. Now I think that all is lost. I told her more than once that she should not push it too far."

Let us seek out her friend again and hear what he says himself:

"In the best inn I saw a light downstairs, knocked at the window and asked the waiter who looked out whether any strangers had arrived or were expected. Recognizing my voice, he opened the door promptly, but answered no to both my questions, even as he bade me come in. I found it suited my situation to continue with the charade, and requested a room, which he at once made ready on the third floor; the ones on the second, he indicated, would be reserved for the travelers I was expecting. He hurried off to arrange things; I let him go and promised to pay the bill. So far I had survived, but I relapsed into my agony; I recalled each and every detail, exaggerated, then moderated the situation, blamed myself, then tried to compose myself, to calm myself. After all, in the morning a new beginning could be made. I imagined myself going about the day in my accustomed way. But then my anger burst forth again violently; I would never have believed I could be so unhappy."

Our readers have doubtless become sufficiently concerned with this noble man, whom we have unexpectedly discovered so passionately agitated by an apparently trivial incident, that they wish to receive more detailed information about his circumstances. We shall make use of the intermission which now ensues in this night's adventure, while he continues to pace silently and fiercely up and down the room.

We learn that Odoard is a descendant of an old family, to whom the noblest merits were passed down through a succession of generations. Educated at a military academy, he acquired a polished manner which, combined with most admirable intellectual gifts, lent a particular grace to his conduct. A short period of service at court gave him insight into the way affairs are conducted in the highest circles, and when, as a result of quickly won favor, he was attached to an ambassadorial mission and had the opportunity to see the world and acquaint himself with foreign courts, the clarity of his understanding and his superior memory for events, down to the smallest details, but especially his earnestness in every sort of endeavor, came rapidly to the fore. His facility of expression in several languages, along with his open but not overbearing personality, led him from one rung to another. He achieved success on every diplomatic mission, because he won people's goodwill and thereby gained the advantage of being able to settle misunderstandings, and he was especially adept at satisfying the interests of both sides by fair consideration of all the pertinent arguments.

The prime minister was intent upon making so excellent a man his own; he married his daughter to him, a young lady of the most glowing beauty and skilled in all the higher social virtues. But as the course of all human happiness always encounters some dam that blocks its flow, such was the case here. Princess Sophronie was being raised as a ward of the princely court. She was the last sprig of her family tree, and her property and expectations, even though her lands and tenants were to revert to her uncle, were still considerable. For this reason, in order to avoid prolonged debate, it was deemed desirable to marry her to the crown prince, who, to be sure, was far younger than she.

Odoard was suspected of an inclination for her. It was thought that he had paid her, under the name Aurora, too passionate homage in a poem. This was compounded by a slip on her part, for she had, with her usual strength of character, replied boldly to certain teasing on the part of her companions, saying she would have to have no eyes at all to be blind to such merits.

The suspicion was, to be sure, dispelled by Odoard's marriage, but it was kept alive and occasionally stirred up again by secret enemies.

The question of the succession and the inheritance, although everyone tried to refer to it as little as possible, did sometimes come up. Both the prince and his prudent councillors thought it advisable to let the matter rest, while the secret partisans of the princess wanted it settled, so that the noble lady might enjoy a greater degree of freedom, especially since the elderly neighboring king, a relative of Sophronie's and well disposed toward her, was still alive and had at times shown himself ready to exert a paternal influence on her behalf.

Odoard came under suspicion of having tried, on a purely ceremonial mission to that court, to further the business that others were trying to retard. His adversaries made use of this incident, and his father-in-law, whom he had convinced of his innocence, had to exert all his influence to procure him a sort of governorship in a remote province. He was happy there; he could set all his talents to work; there were necessary, useful, good, fine, and great tasks to be done; he could achieve lasting effects without sacrificing himself, instead of destroying himself, as people sometimes do, by involvement, against his own principles, with affairs of no consequence.

His wife felt differently about it, for she felt truly alive only in wider circles, and followed him only after an interval, and under duress. He conducted himself toward her with the utmost consideration, and encouraged every surrogate for her erstwhile happiness: in the summer, outings in the surrounding countryside, in winter, amateur theatricals, balls, and whatever else she chose to initiate. He even tolerated a "friend of the family," a stranger who some time earlier had insinuated himself, although Odoard by no means liked the man, since with his keen eye for character he was convinced he perceived a certain falseness in him.

All that we have recounted may have passed through his mind in the present critical moment, some of it darkly and hazily, some of it clearly and distinctly. Suffice it to say that when we turn to him again, after these intimate revelations, whose substance was provided by Friedrich's excellent memory, we find him again pacing fiercely up and down the room, his gestures and exclamations expressing an inner struggle.

"With such thoughts I paced fiercely up and down the room. The waiter had brought me a cup of bouillon, which I badly needed, since in my careful preparations for the party I had not eaten, and a delicious supper waited untouched at home. At that moment I heard the pleasant sound of a post horn coming up the street. 'That one is from the mountains,' the waiter said. We ran to the window and saw by the light of two bright carriage lanterns an elegant, well-packed carriage drawn by four horses. The servants sprang down from the box. 'Here they are,' the waiter cried, and hurried to the door. I stopped him to impress upon him that he must not say I was there, must not reveal that orders had been given; he promised, and rushed off.

"In the meantime I had failed to see who had arrived, and a new impatience seized me: the waiter seemed to be taking much too long to bring me news. Finally I learned from him that the guests were ladies, an older woman of distinguished appearance, a younger one of incredible charm, and a chambermaid after everyone's heart. 'She started out,' the waiter told me, 'with orders, continued with flattery, and, when I flirted with her, assumed a merry, saucy manner, which in all probability was the most natural to her.' "

"I quickly noticed," he continues, "that they were astonished at finding me so alert and the house so ready to receive them, the rooms lit, the fires burning. They made themselves comfortable; a cold supper was waiting for them in the dining room; I offered bouillon, which seemed welcome."

Now the ladies were seated at table. The older one hardly ate, the beautiful, attractive one not at all. The chambermaid, whom they called Lucie, ate with gusto and praised the inn, admiring the bright candles, the fine table linen, the porcelain, and all the accoutrements. She had earlier warmed herself at the blazing fire, and now asked the waiter, when he returned, whether they were always so well prepared to serve guests who arrived unexpectedly at any hour of the day or night. The nimble young fellow reacted in this case as children do, who may well keep a secret but cannot conceal that some secret has been entrusted to them. At first he answered ambiguously, then came closer to the truth, and finally, driven into a corner by the chambermaid's spirit and repartee, confessed that a servant, a gentleman had come, had gone away, had returned, but finally he let slip that the gentleman was indeed upstairs, and was restlessly pacing back and forth. The young lady jumped up, and the others did the same. "It must be an elderly gentleman," they exclaimed. The waiter assured them that on the contrary, he was young. Now they doubted him again, but he swore to the truth of his assertion. Their confusion and uneasiness increased. "It must be my uncle," the beautiful woman maintained. "But this is not like him," the older woman countered. No one but he could have known that they would arrive here at this hour, the young woman insisted. The waiter, however, swore again and again that the person in question was a young man, handsome and vigorous. Lucie swore it must be the uncle; they should not believe the waiter; the rogue had already been contradicting himself for the past half hour.

After all this the waiter had to go up and urgently request the gentleman to come down quickly, under the threat of the ladies' coming to thank him themselves. "It's the very devil of a mess," the waiter continued. "I don't understand why you hesitate to let yourself be seen. They think you are an old uncle, whom they passionately long to embrace. I beg you, go down. Are these not the people you were expecting? Do not rashly shun such a delightful adventure; the young beauty is well worth seeing and hearing, they are thoroughly respectable people. Hurry downstairs, or they will march in on you in your chamber."

Passion begets passion. Agitated as he was, he longed for something different, unfamiliar. He descended, hoping that, in pleasant conversation with the newcomers, he might explain himself, clarify his own state of mind, learn of others' circumstances, distract himself; and yet he felt as if he were about to encounter a familiar, ominous situation. Now he stood before the door. The ladies, believing they heard the uncle's footsteps, ran to meet him. He entered the room. What an encounter! What a scene! The beautiful woman gave a cry and buried her face in the older woman's shoulder. Our friend recognized them both, started back, then was driven forward—he was at her feet, touching her hand, which he quickly let go again, with the most modest of kisses. The syllables "Au-ro-ra" died on his lips.

If we now turn our gaze to our friend's home, we shall find most unusual circumstances. The good old woman was at her wits' end. She kept the lamps burning in the vestibule and on the steps. She had removed the food from the fire, some of it hopelessly ruined. The chambermaid had remained with the sleeping children and watched over the many candles, her movements about the room as quiet and patient as the other's had been disgruntled.

Finally the carriage rolled up, the lady descended and heard that her husband had been called away a few hours earlier. As she mounted the stairs, she seemed to take no notice of the festive illumination. The old woman now learned from the manservant that an accident had occurred on the way: the carriage had fallen into a ditch, with all the attendant circumstances.

The lady came into the room. "What sort of masquerade is this?" she asked, pointing to the children. "You would have greatly enjoyed it," the maid replied, "had you returned a few hours earlier." The children, shaken out of their slumber, jumped up, and seeing their mother before them, began their memorized speech. It proceeded for a while, with embarrassment on both sides, but then, in the absence of encouragement or prompting, it faltered, then came to a complete halt, and the dear children were sent off to bed with a few caresses. The lady, now alone, threw herself down on the sofa and burst into bitter tears.

However, it now becomes necessary to offer more information about the lady herself and about the rural festivity which had apparently taken an unfortunate turn. Albertine was one of those women to whom one finds nothing to say in private, but who is well liked in larger gatherings. There they appear as true ornaments to society and enliven any dull moment. Their charm is of the sort that needs a certain space in which to manifest itself and operate comfortably; to achieve an effect they require a large audience. They must be surrounded by an element which buoys them up, which obliges them to be charming. They hardly know how to behave toward one person alone.

The friend of the family had won and retained her favor simply because he was skilled at introducing one activity after another, and could always keep in constant motion a circle, which if not large, was at least merry. When parts were being assigned, he always chose the role of tender father, and with his respectable and solemn bearing managed to outshine the younger first, second, and third admirers.

Florine, who owned a major estate in the neighborhood and wintered in town, was indebted to Odoard, because his economic planning had, fortuitously but fortunately, greatly benefited her lands, which promised to increase their yield considerably in the future. She spent summers on her estate, and made it the scene of all sorts of respectable amusements. Birthdays in particular were never overlooked, and parties of all sorts were held.

Florine was a lively, playful creature, seemingly fancy-free and neither welcoming nor desiring any special attachment. A passionate dancer, she valued men only to the extent that they could move in time to the music. Always a lively conversationalist, she could not abide anyone who stared into space for even a moment and seemed to reflect. She also played most charmingly the merry soubrette, needed for every play or opera, for which reason no rivalry arose between herself and Albertine, who always took the virtuous parts.

To assure that the impending birthday was celebrated in good company, the best people from the city and the countryside had been invited. The dancing commenced immediately after breakfast, continued after dinner; it went on too long, they set out late, and were overtaken by darkness before they realized it, on bad roads, doubly treacherous for being under repair; the coachman lost control, and the carriage fell into the ditch. Our beauty, along with Florine and the friend of the family, were all tangled up together. The friend extricated himself quickly; then, bending over the carriage, called, "Florine, where are you, my dear one?" Albertine thought she was dreaming. He reached inside and pulled out Florine, who was lying on top in a faint, tried to revive her, and finally bore her in his strong arms along the proper road. Albertine was still trapped in the carriage; the coachman and the servant helped her out, and supported by them, she tried to proceed. The going was rough, not meant for dancing slippers; although the lad helped her along, she stumbled repeatedly. But within her all seemed even wilder, even more desolate. She did not know, could not grasp what had happened to her.

But when she reached the inn, and saw Florine on the bed in the small room, the landlady and Lelio looking after her, she was certain of her misfortune. A secret relationship between her unfaithful companion and her treacherous friend was revealed in a flash when Florine, opening her eyes, threw her arms about Lelio, with the rapture of newly revived, tenderest possessiveness. She saw how her black eyes shone again, and a fresh bloom suddenly tinged her pale cheeks; she really appeared rejuvenated, charming, most lovely.

Albertine stood staring, alone, hardly noticed. The other two recovered, pulled themselves together, but the damage had already been done. And now they had to seat themselves once more in the carriage, and in Hell itself souls so hostile to one another could scarcely be more tightly packed in together, the betrayers with the betrayed.

Chapter Eleven

For some days both Lenardo and Odoard were extremely busy, the one providing the emigrants with all they needed, the other becoming acquainted with those staying behind, assessing their skills, and informing them adequately of his aims. In the meanwhile, there was time enough for Friedrich and our friend to talk in peace. Wilhelm had the general plan outlined for him, and once the landscape and region had become sufficiently familiar to him, and the hope had been discussed that a large number of inhabitants could be quickly settled in an extensive area, the talk finally turned, as was natural, to what actually binds men together: to religion and morality. On these matters merry Friedrich could give sufficient information, and we would doubtless earn thanks if we could communicate the discussion in its entirety, as it twisted its way in exemplary fashion by way of questions and answers, objections and corrections, often wavering this way and that, as it moved toward its actual goal. However, we may not take so much time, and will rather present the conclusions at once than commit ourselves to letting these principles gradually evolve in our readers' minds. The following represents the quintessence of what was discussed:

That man must accommodate himself to the inevitable, all religions insist on; each tries in its own way to come to terms with this task.

The Christian religion offers gentle assistance in the form of faith, hope, and charity. From these springs patience, a sweet feeling that existence remains a priceless gift, even when, instead of the desired enjoyment, it is burdened with the most hideous suffering. We adhere firmly to this religion, but in a peculiar way; we teach our children from youth on about the great benefits it has brought us; only much later, however, do we acquaint them with its origin and history. Only then do we come to love and value its founder, and any accounts that refer to Him become sacred. In this sense, which might perhaps be called pedantic, but whose consistency must be acknowledged, we tolerate no Jews among us. How can we grant them participation in the highest culture when they repudiate its origin and source?

Our moral teachings are entirely separate from all this; they are purely pragmatic and can be summed up in these few rules: moderation where there is choice, industry where there is necessity. Let everyone put these laconic words to use in his life in his own way, and he will have a rich text with limitless applications.

The greatest respect is instilled in everyone for time as the highest gift of God and Nature, and the most attentive companion of our existence. We have a multiplicity of clocks among us, which all mark the quarter hours with both hands and chimes. To multiply these signs as much as possible, the telegraphs set up in our country, when they are not being used otherwise, indicate the course of the hours both by day and by night, and do so by means of a very ingenious mechanism.

Our moral system, which is thus entirely practical, mainly enjoins circumspection, and this is greatly furthered by the organization of time, by attentiveness to every hour. Every moment must be well employed, and how could that happen if one did not attend to the task as well as to the hour?

In view of the fact that we are just beginning, we lay great stress on family circles. We plan to assign heavy obligations to fathers and mothers. The matter of rearing becomes easier the more each must be answerable for his or her own self, the farmhand and the maid, the male and female servants.

Certain things, to be sure, must be taught with a certain uniformity. The Abbé is taking over the task of teaching the multitude to read, to write, and to figure with ease. His method is reminiscent of alternating instruction, yet it is more ingenious. But actually everything depends on educating teacher and student at the same time.

But there is yet another form of mutual instruction I want to mention: practice in attacking and defending. Here Lothario is in his element; his maneuvers somewhat resemble those of our sharpshooters, but he cannot help being original.

In this connection I might remark that in our civilian life we have no bells, in our military no drums. There as here, the human voice, combined with wind instruments, is sufficient. All that has existed before and still does; the proper application of it, however, is entrusted to that mind which would probably have invented it in any case.

The greatest need of any state is courageous leadership, and ours shall not be deficient in this. We are all impatient to commence the enterprise, ready and convinced that one must simply begin. Therefore we concern ourselves not with justice but rather with police powers. The principle will be enunciated firmly: no one shall inconvenience the others. Anyone who proves a nuisance shall be removed until he understands how to behave so as to be tolerated. If there is anything counter to life or good sense involved, this, likewise, will be removed.

Every district has three police directors, who relieve each other in eight-hour shifts, as in mining operations, which likewise cannot stop; and one of our men must always be on hand, particularly during the night.

They are empowered to issue warnings, to censure, to reprimand, and to remove offenders. Should they find it necessary, they summon a larger or smaller number of jurymen. If the vote is tied, the decision is not left to the foreman, but lots are drawn, since we are persuaded that when opinions are equally divided, it does not matter which wins out.

As for majority rule, we have our own special views on that; we allow it to prevail, of course, in the necessary course of things, but in the higher sense we place little trust in it. On that question, however, I may not expatiate further.

If anyone inquires about the higher authority that directs everything, it is never to be found in one spot. It constantly moves about, in order to maintain uniformity in the most important matters, and to let everyone have his own will in less crucial ones. This practice has its precedent in history: German emperors traveled about, and this arrangement best accords with the spirit of free states. We are afraid of a capital city, even though we can already see the spot in our lands where the greatest number of people will congregate. But we keep this a secret, for it will develop gradually and soon enough in any case.

These are, in the most general terms, the points on which we are largely agreed, but whenever several, or even a few, of our members come together, these matters are always discussed anew. The chief thing, however, will be when we are actually there. The new conditions, which are meant to be lasting, will actually be determined by the law. Our penalties are mild: the right to issue warnings is open to every citizen of a certain age; only the acknowledged eldest may disapprove and reprimand; only a duly summoned jury may impose punishment.

It has been observed that severe laws very soon lose their force and gradually become more lenient, because Nature always asserts her rights. We have lenient laws, so that we can gradually become more severe. Our punishments consist initially in banishment from civil society—milder or more definitive, shorter or longer, according to the findings. Should the citizens' property gradually increase, then part of it will be pinched off, less or more, depending on how they deserve to suffer in this department.

All the members of the bond are instructed in these laws, and our examinations have shown that each person applies the main points to himself as is most suitable. The abiding principle is that we take the advantages of civilization with us, and leave its evils behind. Taverns and circulating libraries will not be tolerated among us; our attitude toward bottles and books I would rather not discuss; such things must be judged in practice.

In the same spirit the collector and arranger of these papers forbears to mention other dispositions which are still circulating as problems in the society, and which it will perhaps not be advisable to try out on the spot. The author might expect that much less applause, were he to dwell on them here.

Chapter Twelve

The time appointed for Odoardo to address the company had arrived, and when all had assembled and quieted down, he began to speak as follows: "The significant undertaking in which I have invited this throng of stalwart men to participate is not altogether unknown to you, for I have already discussed it with you in general terms. As my disclosures imply, there are in the old world, as in the new, areas which need better cultivation than they have previously received. Over there Nature has spread vast, wide spaces that lie untouched and wild, so that one hardly dares venture into them and engage them in battle. And yet it is easy for resolute men gradually to conquer this wilderness and assure themselves of partial possession. In the old world the opposite is true. Here every piece of land is already partially possessed, and the rights to it sanctified more or less from time immemorial. And if over there boundlessness seems an insuperable obstacle, here the many boundaries present obstacles even more difficult to overcome. Nature can be subdued through industry; men must be subdued through force or persuasion.

"If private property is held sacred by society as a whole, it is even more sacred to the owner of such property. Habit, youthful impressions, respect for one's forefathers, dislike of one's neighbor, and hundreds of other things are what make the landowners rigid and opposed to any alteration. The longer such conditions have prevailed, the more interlaced and fragmented the holdings, the harder it becomes to carry out any common venture, which, by taking something away from the individual, would bring to the whole and to each member unanticipated benefits through the effects of cooperation.

"For several years now I have governed a province in the name of my prince—a province which, separated from the rest of his lands, was for a long time not used as it might be. This very isolation or insularity, if you will, has prevented the development of any institution which might have allowed the inhabitants to disseminate what they can to the outside world and receive from the outside world what they need.

"I had unlimited authority to rule in this province. Much good could be done, but always within limits. Everywhere there were bars to improvement, and what was most desirable seemed to exist in an entirely different world.

"I had no other duty than to administer the province well. What could be easier! It is equally easy to eliminate abuses, to put human capabilities to work, to aid the ambitious. All this was readily accomplished with good sense and power; in a way it took care of itself. But what especially aroused my attention and my concern were the neighbors, who did not govern, or have their domains governed, in a similar spirit, let alone with similar convictions.

"I had almost resigned myself to the situation, making the best of it and relying on tradition to the extent possible, but I suddenly noticed that the spirit of the times was coming to my assistance. Younger administrators took office in the neighboring lands; they cherished similar ideas, though to be sure only in a general sense of benevolence, and gradually came to subscribe to my plans for cooperation on all sides, the more readily because it was my lot to concede the greater sacrifices without anyone's noticing that the greater benefit also accrued to my side.

"So now the three of us are authorized to rule over sizeable stretches of land, and our princes and ministers are persuaded that our suggestions are trustworthy and useful; for beyond a doubt it takes more to recognize one's advantage on a large scale than on a small one. Here necessity always shows us what we must do or not do, and this standard is sufficient if we apply it to present conditions. But there we are to create a future, and even if some keen intellect invented a plan for it, how can he hope that others will assent to it?

"As yet no individual could succeed at this. These times, which are liberating men's minds, are also opening their eyes to distant prospects, and in the larger perspective higher ideals are more easily recognized, and one of the worst obstacles to human action will be easier to eliminate. The problem lies in the fact that while people may often agree on goals, they agree much less on the means to attain them. For any truly great ideal raises us above ourselves and lights us on our way like a star. But when it comes to choosing the means, we are recalled to ourselves, and then the individual reverts to exactly what he was before, and feels just as isolated as if he had not previously joined in the whole.

"At this point we must reiterate: the times must come to our aid. The times must take the place of reason, and within our expanded hearts nobler motives must supplant baser ones.

"Let this suffice, and if for the moment it is too much, I shall remind every participant of it as we go on. Accurate surveys have been made, the roads charted, the points determined where inns are to be located, and eventually perhaps villages. There is an opportunity, indeed, a necessity, for every kind of building. Excellent architects and technicians are preparing everything. Plans and estimates are ready. The intention is to sign larger and smaller contracts, so that the available funds will be expended under close supervision, to the astonishment of the mother country. We live in the splendid hope of seeing unified activity develop in all directions from now on.

"However, what I must now call to the attention of all participants, since it might have some influence on their decision, is the arrangement, the form under which we mean to unite all our members and create for them a worthy position amongst themselves and toward the rest of the civilized world.

"As soon as we set foot in those designated lands, the crafts will immediately be declared arts, to be set apart and distinguished from the 'free' arts by the term 'rigorous.' For the moment we can consider only those occupations whose business is building; all of the men assembled here, young and old, belong to this group.

"Let us take these crafts in the order in which they erect a building and gradually prepare it for occupancy.

"First I name the stonecutters, who square off the foundation and cornerstones which, with the help of the mason, they will sink at the right spot, with perfect alignment. Next come the masons, who firmly attach the present and the future parts to this rigorously tested base. Sooner or later the carpenter comes by with the framing he has assembled, and thus the planned structure rises higher and higher. We hurriedly call in the roofer; on the inside we need joiners, glaziers, locksmiths, and if I name the painter last, that is because he can come in to do his work at all sorts of times, and in the end gives a pleasing finish to the entire structure, inside and out. I do not mention the various subsidiary crafts, but focus only on the principal ones.

"The stages of apprentice, journeyman, and master must be adhered to as strictly as possible; many gradations can be recognized within these, but the tests cannot be administered carefully enough. Anyone who enters knows that he is dedicating himself to a rigorous art, and must not expect lenient demands. A single link that breaks in a great chain destroys the whole thing. In great undertakings as in great dangers, frivolity must be banished.

"Precisely in this respect the rigorous arts must set an example for the free arts, and seek to put them to shame. If we examine the so-called free arts, which are to be understood and so named in a higher sense, it turns out to make no difference whether they are practiced well or badly. The worst statue stands on its feet with the best, a painted figure with misdrawn feet still strides forward briskly, while its misshapen arms reach out stoutly enough; figures may not be standing in correct perspective, yet the ground does not cave in on this account. With music it is even more striking; the screeching fiddle at the village tavern stirs stout limbs most powerfully, and we have seen believers edified by the most abominable church music. And if you wish to count poetry among the free arts, you will surely see that it, too, hardly knows its limits. And yet every art has its internal laws, though flouting them brings no harm to mankind; the rigorous arts, by contrast, can allow themselves no such liberties. The free artist may be praised, and one can derive pleasure from his merits, even if, upon closer scrutiny, his work does not pass muster.

"But if we consider both, the free as well as rigorous arts, at their best, the latter must be on their guard against pedantry and flatfootedness, the former against thoughtlessness and botched work. Those who guide them will point out these dangers, thus preventing abuses and carelessness.

"I shall not recapitulate, for our whole life will be a recapitulation of what I have already said. I note only the following: he who devotes himself to one of the rigorous arts must be faithful to it for life. Previously they were called handicrafts, quite suitably and correctly. Their practitioners are supposed to work with their hands, and the hand that performs such work must be animated by a life of its own, must be a being unto itself, with its own thoughts, its own will; and that cannot be spread over many skills."

After the speaker had concluded with a few more well-chosen words, all present rose, and instead of leaving, the crafts formed an orderly circle before the table of their acknowledged leaders. Odoard handed each of them a printed sheet, from which they sang, with measured cheerfulness, a trusting song set to a familiar melody:

Let staying, going, far or near,
Be one henceforth to him who strives.
And where a useful course we steer,
Then there's the place to build our lives.
To follow you is like child's play:
Obedience will show the way
To find a trusty fatherland.
All hail the leader! Hail the bond!

Our strength and burdens you distribute
And measure justly for each life;
You give the old ones peace and tribute
While youths are granted work and wife.
With mutual trust we live at one,
All building houses neat and snug,
Since each is closed by fence of wood,
No mistrust mars the neighborhood.

Along the smooth and well-paved ways
In taverns new the traveler rests,
The stranger there for all his days
Good land in ample portion gets.

There let us settle, join with others,
Let's hurry, hurry to our brothers,
To the trusty fatherland.
All hail the leader, hail the bond!

Chapter Thirteen

Perfect stillness followed the lively activity of the previous days. The three friends stayed on alone, and it was soon noticeable that two of them, Lenardo and Friedrich, were moved by an odd restlessness; they did not conceal their impatience at being prevented from taking part in the departure from this place. It seemed that they were waiting for some messenger, and in the interval nothing sensible, nothing decisive was said.

At last the messenger arrives, bringing an important packet, upon which Friedrich instantly throws himself, in order to open it. Lenardo stops him, saying, "Leave it be. Place it on the table before us. Let us look at it, think, and conjecture what it may contain. For our fate is closer to being decided, and if we are not ourselves masters of it, if it depends on the thinking or feelings of others, a yes or a no, a this way or that way is to be expected from outside, then it behooves us to be calm, to compose ourselves, to ask ourselves whether we would submit to it as if it were a so-called divine judgment imposed upon us to take our reason prisoner."

"You are not as calm as you wish to appear," Friedrich answered, "so stay alone with your secrets and deal with them as you please; in any case, they mean nothing to me. But let me in the meantime reveal the contents to this old and proven friend and present him with the dubious circumstances we have so long kept secret from him." With these words he whisked our friend off and was already on his way when he exclaimed, "She has been found, found long since! Now the only question is what is to become of her."

"I already knew that," Wilhelm replied, "for friends reveal most clearly the very things they do not say to one another. The last entry in the journal, where Lenardo deep in the mountains remembers my letter to him, called up before my mind's eye the entire spiritual and emotional sphere of that good creature. I could see him approach her the very next morning, recognize her, and whatever might follow from that. But I will say frankly that I was disquieted by your silence and reserve, not because I was curious, but because I had taken a genuine interest in her well-being."

"And in this respect," exclaimed Friedrich, "you are particularly affected by this packet that has arrived. The continuation of the journal was sent to Makarie, and we did not want to spoil the episode for you, in all its solemnity and charm, by telling it. But you shall have it right away. Lenardo has surely unpacked it by now and he does not need it himself."

With this Friedrich bounded off in his old way, bounded back, and brought the promised notebook. "But now I, too, must find out," he cried, "what will become of us." With that he was gone again, and Wilhelm read:

Lenardo's Diary (Continuation)

Friday the 19th

Since we could not delay if we wanted to reach Dame Susanna's in good time, we took a quick breakfast with the entire family, thanked them with discreet congratulations, and left behind with the Harness-Fixer, who was staying, the presents intended for the girls, somewhat richer and more bridal than those of the day before yesterday; we slipped them to him secretly, and the good man showed himself greatly pleased.

This time the road was put behind us early; after some hours we were looking down into a peaceful, not very wide, level valley, whose one rocky side was gently lapped and mirrored by the waters of a clear lake. There we saw solid, handsome houses, around which a more fertile soil, carefully tended, made some gardening possible in the sunny locations. Introduced to the main house by the Yarn Man and presented to Dame Susanna, I felt most strange when she addressed us kindly and assured us that she was very pleased that we had come on a Friday, the quietest day of the week; on Thursday evenings the finished goods were taken to the lake and from there to town. To the Yarn Man, who interjected, "I suppose Daniel always brings them down?" she replied, "Certainly; he manages the business as conscientiously and faithfully as if it were his own." "Indeed, there is not much difference," remarked the other. He received several commissions from the friendly hostess and hurried off to accomplish his business in the side valleys, promising to return in a few days and fetch me.

Meanwhile I was feeling most peculiar. Immediately upon entering, I had been overcome by a premonition that this was the long sought woman. When I looked at her closely, it was not she, and could not be, and yet when I looked away, or when she turned around, it was again, just as in a dream, memory and imagination vie with one another.

Several spinners who had fallen behind in their week's work brought it in; the mistress, with friendly admonitions to be industrious, bargained with them, but then, in order to converse with the guest, left the task to two girls, whom she called Gretchen and Lieschen. I observed them the more carefully as I wanted to see whether they corresponded to the description given by the Harness-Fixer. These two figures quite befuddled me and destroyed any resemblance between the woman I was seeking and the woman of the house.

But I observed the latter even more attentively, and she seemed to me the being most worthy and appealing of all I had beheld on my journey through the mountains. By now I knew enough about weaving to be able to speak knowledgeably with her about the business, which she understood well. My informed interest pleased her greatly, and when I asked where she procured her cotton—which I had seen being transported in bulk over the high mountains a few days earlier—she replied that this very shipment had brought her a substantial supply. The location of her village was very fortunate in this respect as well, for the highway leading down to the lake passed only fifteen minutes below her valley, so that she could receive either personally or through an agent the bales dispatched to her from Trieste, as had indeed occurred the day before yesterday.

She then led her new friend into a large, airy cellar, where her cotton supply was stored so that it should not dry out too much, and lose weight and pliability. I found assembled here all that I had already encountered separately; bit by bit she pointed out various things, and I took an intelligent interest in them. After a time she spoke less, and I could tell from her questions that she assumed I belonged to the trade. For she said that since the cotton had just arrived, she was expecting a clerk or a partner from the firm in Trieste, who, after discreetly looking over her situation, would collect the money due him; this lay ready for anyone who could show proper identification.

Somewhat embarrassed, I became evasive and watched her as she went through the room to give instructions; she seemed like Penelope among her handmaidens.

She returns, and I have the impression that she is troubled. "Then you are not a merchant?" she said. "I do not know why I should feel such trust, and why I venture to ask the same of you. I have no wish to compel you, but grant me to know what lies in your heart." With this, the face of a stranger with such familiar, penetrating eyes gazed at me, so that I felt myself pierced through, and could scarcely maintain my composure. My knees, my mind, were about to fail me when fortunately she was suddenly called away. I managed to recover, to strengthen my resolve of keeping my counsel as long as possible. For I had the feeling that another ill-fated relationship threatened me.

Gretchen, a calm, friendly girl, led me off to show me the elaborate forms of weaving. She did so with quiet intelligence, while I took notes to demonstrate my attentiveness; they are still in my notebook as testimony to a purely mechanical process, for I had something entirely different on my mind. They read as follows:

"The woof of treadled, as well as of hand-shuttled, woven fabric is composed, depending on what the pattern requires, of white, loosely twisted thread, the so-called fly yarn, occasionally also of yarns dyed Turkish red or blue, which are likewise used for stripes or flowers.

"When 'shearing' the fabric, they wind it on rollers that form a rectangular frame, around which several workers sit."

Lieschen, who was sitting among the shearers, stands up, joins us, and interrupts officiously, in such a way as to confuse the other girl with contradictions. And when, despite that, I paid closer attention to Gretchen, Lieschen began bustling about, fetching this and bringing that, and without being compelled to by the narrowness of the space, twice brushed me meaningfully with her soft elbow as she swept by, which did not especially please me.

The virtuous beauty (she deserves to be called this in any case, but particularly in comparison with the others) came to lead me into the garden, where we were to enjoy the evening sun before it hid behind the mountain peaks. A smile played about her lips, as it often will when a person is hesitating to say something agreeable. In me, too, this embarrassment produced an exquisite feeling. We walked side by side; I did not dare to take her hand, much as I would have liked to; both of us seemed fearful of words or signs by which the happy discovery might all too soon be revealed to be something vulgar. She pointed out some flower pots in which I recognized seedlings of cotton plants: "Thus do we tend and nourish the seeds, which are useless for our business, even bothersome, but have made such a long journey to us with the cotton. It is an act of gratitude, and there is a special satisfaction in seeing alive something whose dead remains quicken our existence. Here you see the beginning; you are already acquainted with the middle; and this evening, if fortune is kind, you shall see a happy conclusion.

"We manufacturers in person, or through an agent, bring the week's accumulation of goods to the market boat on Thursday evening, and, in the company of others on the same errand, reach town very early on Friday morning. Here each one takes his goods to the wholesale merchants and tries to dispose of them for the best possible price, occasionally even taking the necessary supply of raw cotton in place of payment.

"But our people do not bring only supplies of raw materials for production and cash earnings back from town; they also furnish themselves there with all sorts of other necessities or luxuries. When someone from the family has gone off to market in town, they leave behind them expectations, hopes, and wishes, and often even anxiety and fear. Storms and showers may arise, and people worry that the boat may come to grief. The avaricious wait around, eager to hear how the sale of wares came out, and calculate in advance the amount of pure profit. The inquisitive wait for the latest gossip from town, the lovers of finery for the clothing or fashionable fripperies that the traveler was commissioned to bring back, the lovers of food and especially the children for the comestibles, be they only white rolls.

"The departure from town is usually delayed almost until evening; then the lake gradually comes alive, and boats glide over its surface, sailing or propelled by the strength of oars; each strives to get ahead of the others, and those who succeed jokingly mock those condemned to lag behind.

"That trip on the lake is a delightful, beautiful spectacle, when the water mirrors the surrounding mountains, turns rosy with them in the sunset, then gradually settles deeper and deeper into shadow; the stars come out, the vesper bells sound, and lights appear in the villages by the shore, to be reflected in the water, and then the moon rises, and casts its shimmer over the barely rippled surface. The fertile terrain flies past; village after village, farmstead after farmstead is left behind, and when finally you near home, a horn is sounded, and at once you see lights twinkling here and there on the mountain, moving down toward the shore; every house that has a family member aboard sends someone to help with the bundles.

"We live farther up, but each of us has made this trip often enough, and we are all equally involved in anything connected with the business."

I had listened, amazed at the goodness and beauty with which she spoke, and could not withhold the frank observation: how could she have attained such cultivation in this rude part of the world, in such a mechanical trade? She replied, looking straight ahead with a charming, almost roguish smile, "I was born in a more beautiful, gentler land, governed and inhabited by superior people. Although as a child I showed myself headstrong and wild, still the influence of gifted landowners on their surroundings was unmistakable. The greatest influence on a young being, however, came from a religious upbringing which developed in me a certain sense of what was right and proper, of being nurtured by the omnipresence of divine love. We emigrated"—the delicate smile departed from her lips, she blinked back a tear—"and we wandered, far, far, from one land to another, following hints and recommendations from godly people. Finally we arrived here, in this hardworking place. The house in which you find me was the home of fellow believers; they kindly took us in; my father spoke the same language, was of the same mind, and before long we seemed part of the family.

"I joined industriously in all the housework and handiwork, and whatever you now see me presiding over I learned, practiced, and mastered step by step. The son of the family, a few years older than I, a well-built, handsome boy, came to love me and made me his confidante. By nature he was industrious, but also sensitive. The piety practiced in the house did not appeal to him, did not satisfy him; in secret he read books that he managed to obtain in town, the sort of books which guide the mind in a freer, more universal direction. Since he perceived a similar urge, a similar disposition in me, he endeavored to share with me little by little that which so absorbed him. Finally, since I entered into everything, he no longer hesitated to reveal his entire secret to me. We were truly a very odd pair, whose conversation on our solitary walks was only of the principles that make a person independent, and whose genuine affection seemed based only on mutually reinforcing ideas whose effect otherwise is to estrange people from one another completely."

Although I did not look at her directly, but only glanced up from time to time, as if by chance, I nevertheless observed with wonder and sympathy that her features faithfully expressed the meaning of her words. After a momentary silence her face brightened. "I must," she said, "answer your original question with a confession, that you may better understand my eloquence, which may sometimes seem not entirely natural.

"Unfortunately we both had to dissemble before the others, and although we were very careful not to lie and be false in the crude sense, yet in a subtler sense we were, in that we could never find excuses to absent ourselves from the well-attended meetings of the Brethren. Since we had to listen there to much that went against our convictions, he soon taught me to understand and perceive that not everything came straight from the heart, but that much of it was sheer verbiage: images, metaphors, conventional turns of phrase and oft-repeated lines, forever revolving around a single axis. I now paid closer attention and made the language so much my own that eventually I could have delivered a homily as well as any of the leaders. At first the good youth found this amusing, but finally too much of it made him impatient, so that, to pacify him, I took the opposite course, listened to him all the more carefully, and could repeat to him even a week later his own heartfelt, honest discourse, with at least comparable freedom and a not dissimilar spirit.

"And so our relationship grew into an intimate bond; a passion for something true and good, and a longing to put these ideals into practice were what actually united us.

"As I now consider what might have caused you to start me off on such a tale, it was my vivid description of a successfully concluded market day. Do not be surprised at that; it was precisely cheerful, heartwarming contemplation of beautiful and sublime scenes from Nature that occupied me and my betrothed most in quiet hours of leisure. Fine native poets had awakened and nurtured this feeling in us: Haller's 'Alps,' Gessner's 'Idylls,' Kleist's 'Springtime' were often recited, and we regarded the glorious world around us sometimes as picturesque, sometimes as sublime.

"I still recall with pleasure how we two, keen-eyed and farsighted, would vie with one another in trying to point out quickly the significant phenomena of the earth and the sky, seeking to outpace and surpass one another. This was the finest relaxation, not only from our daily work, but also from those serious discussions which often plunged us only too deeply into ourselves and threatened our peace of mind.

"At this time a traveler came among us, probably under an assumed name. We do not pry further, since he immediately wins our confidence by his ways, since he conducts himself with complete uprightness, and is also properly attentive in our assemblies. Guided by my friend through the mountains, he proves himself serious, intelligent, and knowledgeable. I, too, join in their discussions of moral questions, in which everything of import to the inner man is eventually addressed; here he quickly detects a certain vacillation in our attitudes toward divine questions. Religious expressions had become trivial to us; the kernel they were supposed to contain had been lost. He made us aware of our perilous state, of how serious it was to be estranged from the tradition to which so much had been connected from childhood on; it was particularly dangerous given the incompleteness of our own inner nature. To be sure, piety practiced daily and even hourly could ultimately become a mere pastime, and function as a sort of police over one's outward conduct without any longer affecting one's deeper being. The only countermeasure was to derive from one's own breast moral principles that were equally valid, effective, and soothing.

"Our parents had tacitly taken our union for granted, and, I do not quite know how it came about, the presence of our new friend hastened our betrothal. It seemed his wish to celebrate the confirmation of our happiness within our quiet circle, in the course of which he had to hear the leader take the occasion to remind us of the Bishop of Laodicea and of the great danger of lukewarm faith, which the community thought to have remarked in us. We discussed these problems once more, and our friend left us a page about them which I later often found cause to consult.

"Then he departed, and it was as though all good spirits had withdrawn with him. It is not a new observation that the appearance of a superior person in a circle has an epoch-making effect, and that his departure leaves a void, into which some chance misfortune often rushes. And now let me draw a veil over what followed. An accident abruptly destroyed the precious life of my betrothed and his magnificent form. He stalwartly used his last hours to be united to me, disconsolate as I was, and to secure for me the rights to his inheritance. But what made this occurrence even more painful to his parents was that they had lost a daughter shortly before, and now saw themselves orphaned in the full sense; their tender natures were so crushed that they did not long survive. They soon followed their loved ones, and yet another misfortune befell me when my own father suffered a stroke and, although he retained full perception of the world, lost all intellectual and physical capacity. And so, in my great need and solitude, I truly required all that self-sufficiency which I had earlier practiced in the expectation of a good marriage and happy life together, and in which I had recently been confirmed by the pure, lifegiving words of the mysterious traveler.

"Yet I must not be ungrateful, since in my plight I still have a capable assistant, who as my agent manages everything that is considered a man's task in our business. If he comes back from town tonight and you meet him, you will learn of my remarkable relationship to him."

I had responded from time to time and sought through my approval and sympathy to make her open her heart more and more and keep her story flowing. I did not avoid touching closely on what had not yet been fully expressed. She, too, was drawing ever closer, and we had reached a point where at the slightest pretext the open secret would have been put into words.

She stood up and said, "Let us go to Father." She hurried on ahead, and I followed her slowly; I was shaking my head at the peculiar position in which I found myself. She led me into a very clean back room, where the good old man sat motionless in a chair. He had scarcely changed. I approached him, and he looked at me, first blankly, then with more life in his eyes. His features brightened, he tried to move his lips, and as I reached out my hand to take his motionless one, he grasped mine of his own accord, pressed it, and rose from the chair, his arms outstretched toward me. "Oh God!" he cried, "Squire Lenardo! It is he, he himself!" I could not refrain from clasping him to my heart. He sank back into the chair, his daughter hurried over to assist him. She, too, cried, "It is he! You are Lenardo!"

The younger niece had come in; they led the father, who could suddenly walk again, to his room. Turning toward me, he spoke with perfect clarity, "How fortunate, how fortunate! We shall see each other again soon."

I stood there, looking at the floor and thinking; little Marie came back and handed me a paper which, she told me, was the one that had been mentioned. I recognized Wilhelm's hand at once, as earlier his figure had emerged from the description. Various strange faces swarmed about me, there was an odd commotion in the vestibule. And indeed, it is an unpleasant feeling to be led from the enthusiasm of a perfect reunion, the conviction of grateful remembrance, the acknowledgment of life's wondrous ways, and all the warmth and beauty that such an event may arouse in us, back to the harsh reality of mundane distractions.

This time Friday evening was not as cheerful and merry as usual; the agent had not returned from town on the market boat, but only reported in a letter that business would keep him there until tomorrow or the day after. He would return by some other means and bring everything that had been requested and promised. The neighbors, young and old, who had gathered to wait, as was their custom, made long faces, and especially Lieschen, who had set out to meet him, seemed to be in a very bad humor.

I had taken refuge in my room, still holding the paper, but without reading it, for I had been secretly vexed to learn from her account that Wilhelm had hastened the engagement. "All friends are like that, they are all diplomats; instead of honestly reciprocating our trust, they pursue their own views, go counter to our wishes, and lead our destiny astray." Thus I exclaimed, but soon abandoned my unjust reproach, admitted that my friend had been right, especially in light of the present situation, and no longer refrained from reading the following:

> "Every person, from the earliest moments of his life, finds, first unconsciously, then half consciously and finally wholly so, that he is continually limited, restricted in his position; but since no one knows the purpose and aim of his existence, but rather the hand of the Almighty conceals this mystery, he merely gropes about, snatches at what he can, lets go again, stands still, moves, hesitates, and rushes ahead; thus in a host of ways arise the errors that perplex us."
>
> "Even the most sensible soul is forced in his daily life to do what is prudent for the moment, and therefore generally does not achieve clarity. Seldom does he know with any certainty where he should turn next, and what he really should do or not do."
>
> "Fortunately all these questions and hundreds of other odd ones are answered by your unceasingly active way of life. Continue with direct attention to the task of the day, and always examine the purity of your heart and the firmness of your spirit. When you then catch

your breath in an hour of leisure and have room to contemplate higher matters, you will certainly achieve a proper attitude toward the Sublime, to which we must submit with veneration, regarding every occurrence with reverence, recognizing in it guidance from above."

Saturday the 20th

Engrossed in thoughts, through whose strange windings a sensitive soul will gladly and sympathetically accompany me, I was walking up and down along the lake at daybreak. The mistress—I was very pleased not to have to think of her as a widow—appeared, as I had hoped, first at the window, then at the door. She told me her father had slept well, awakened cheerfully, and announced in clear speech that he would like to stay in bed and see me not today, but tomorrow, after the worship service, by which time he would certainly feel stronger. She then told me that she would be leaving me alone for much of the day; it would be a very busy day for her. She came down and gave me an account of it.

I listened to her, simply to hear her, and concluded that she was completely absorbed by the business at hand, which appealed to her as a customary duty and as one in which she engaged by choice. She continued, "It is our established practice that the weaving should be finished by the end of the week and be brought on Saturday afternoon to the supervisor, who checks it over, measures it, and weighs it, and determines whether the work is correctly done and free of defects, and whether it conforms to standards in size and weight; if all is found to be right, he then pays the agreed upon weaver's fee. He for his part must now trim all dangling threads and knots from the cloth, lay it out nicely so that the best side with fewest defects lies uppermost, and thereby make the wares as attractive as possible."

In the meantime many weavers came down out of the mountains, bringing their wares into the house; among them I spied the one for whom our Harness-Fixer was working. She thanked me very sweetly for the gift I had left, and prettily recounted how the Harness-Fixer was at her house working on her empty loom while she was gone, and how he had assured her as she was leaving that Dame Susanna would at once see the difference in the weaving. She thereupon went into the house like the rest, and I could not forbear to ask my dear hostess, "For Heaven's sake, however did you come by that strange name?" "It is the third," she replied, "that has been imposed upon me. I allowed it gladly because my in-laws wished it; it was the name of their deceased daughter, whose place they allowed me to fill, and a name remains the finest, most living representative of a person." To this I replied, "You shall have yet a fourth, for were it up to me, I would call you Virtuous Beauty." She made a charming, modest curtsey, and was able to connect and enhance her delight at her father's recovery with her joy at seeing me again in such a way that I thought I had never heard or felt anything more flattering and more pleasing in my life.

The virtuous beauty, who had repeatedly been called back to the house, delivered me to an intelligent, well-informed man, who was to show me the sights of the mountains. The weather was splendid, and we traversed all sorts of terrain. But it may be imagined that neither cliffs nor forests nor waterfalls, much less mills or smithies, or even families of skilled wood-carvers could capture my attention. However, the expedition was planned to last the entire day. My guide carried a choice breakfast in his knapsack, and at midday we had a good meal at the company house of a mine, where no one could quite make me out, since to capable men nothing is more tiresome than an empty, hypocritical display of interest in their occupation.

But the guide understood me least of all, for the Yarn Carrier had commended me to him with great praise for my technical knowledge and my special interest in such matters. That good man had also talked about my constant writing and note-taking, for which the guide was fully prepared. My companion waited a long time for me to produce my notebook, and at last, with some impatience, inquired after it.

Sunday the 21st

It was almost noon before I was able to see my friend again. The worship service, at which she did not wish me to be present, had already been held; her father had attended, and, speaking the most edifying words clearly and intelligibly, had moved everyone present and herself to heartfelt tears. "They were," she said, "familiar sayings, verses, expressions, and phrases which I had heard hundreds of times, and had scorned as empty sounds. This time, however, they flowed forth so wonderfully melted together, gently glowing, free of dross, as when we see molten metal running from the crucible. I was in terror lest he consume himself in these outpourings, but he let himself be led back to bed quite cheerfully. He wanted, he said, to collect himself and would, as soon as he felt strong enough, have the guest summoned to him."

After dinner our conversation became livelier and more confiding, but for that very reason I could feel and see that she was holding something back, was struggling with disquieting thoughts, since she could not quite manage to present a bright face. After I had sought in various ways to make her speak out, I confessed honestly that I thought I detected a certain melancholy, an expression of worry, and if it was domestic or business cares, she should reveal them; I was wealthy enough to pay an old debt to her in any form.

Smiling, she denied that this was the case. "When you first arrived," she continued, "I took you for one of the gentlemen from Trieste who give me credit, and I was pleased with myself, since I knew my money was on hand, whether the whole sum was wanted or a part of it. But what weighs on my mind is a business matter, unfortunately not of concern for the moment; no, for the entire future. The increasing dominance of machine production torments and frightens me: it is rolling on like a storm, slowly, slowly; but it is headed this way, and it will arrive and strike. My husband was already full of this mournful feeling. People think about it, people talk about it, and neither thinking nor talking can help. And who likes to picture such calamities! But consider that there are many valleys winding through the mountains like the one through which you came down. The pretty, happy life you witnessed there must still be vividly before you, and the dressed-up crowd gathering from all sides yesterday was wonderful testimony. Think how all this will gradually collapse, wither, and the wilderness, enlivened and populated over centuries, will once more revert to its primeval solitude.

"Here are but two choices, one as sorry as the other: either to seize on the new development and thus hasten our ruin, or to set out, taking the best and worthiest people with us, and seek a kinder fate across the seas. Each has its own drawbacks, but who will help us weigh the principles that should prevail? I know perfectly well that people nearby are considering setting up machines and snatching the people's livelihood for themselves. I cannot blame anyone for thinking of himself first, but I would consider myself despicable if I were to plunder these good people and see them finally wander out into the world, poor and helpless. And wander they must, sooner or later. They sense this, they know this, they say this, and no one decides on any helpful steps. And yet, where should the decision come from? Is it not as difficult for everyone else as for me?

"My fiancé and I had decided to emigrate; he often discussed the ways and means of disengaging ourselves here. He kept an eye out for the better people whom we might gather around us, with whom we might make common cause, whom we could draw to us and draw away with us. We yearned, with perhaps all too youthful hope, for lands where that which would here be a crime would be regarded as rights and responsibilities. Now I am in the opposite situation: the honest assistant, who remained with me after my husband's death, admirable in all respects, devoted to me in tender friendship, is entirely of the opposite opinion.

"I must speak of him to you before you have had an opportunity to see him; I would rather have done so afterward, since personal presence solves many a riddle. Of about the same age as my husband, he formed a strong attachment, while still a poor little boy, to his well-to-do and well-meaning playmate and to the family, the house, and the trade. The two grew up together and stood by one another, and yet they were of two utterly different natures. One had a free and sharing spirit, while the other, crushed and constricted in earliest youth, clung to the slightest possession he could obtain, and though of pious disposition, thought more of himself than of others.

"I know that from the very first he had an eye on me, which he was entitled to do, for I was poorer than he; but he held back as soon as he noticed his friend's affection for me. Through unswerving industry, activity, and loyalty he soon became a partner in the business. My husband secretly intended to establish him here when we emigrated and entrust to him what we left behind. Soon after the death of that excellent man he drew closer to me, and some time ago did not conceal that he was asking me for my hand. But now the doubly peculiar circumstance crops up that he has always declared himself opposed to emigrating, and instead vigorously urges that we too install machinery. To be sure, his reasons are powerful, since there is a man living in our mountains who, if he should turn his back on our simpler tools and wish to build himself more complicated ones, could ruin us all. This man, who is highly skilled at his trade—we call him the Harness-Fixer—is devoted to a well-to-do family in the neighborhood, and one may well believe that he has it in mind to make good use of those progressive inventions for himself and those he favors. There can be no objection to the arguments of my assistant, for we have already in a sense lost too much time, and if the others should seize the advantage, we must do likewise, and now in an unfavorable position. It is this which worries and torments me, and that is why you, my dearest man, appear to me as a guardian angel."

I had little comfort to offer in reply; the case seemed so complicated that I asked for time to reflect. But she continued, "I have still more to tell you which will make my position appear even more peculiar to you. The young man, to whom I am not personally disinclined, but who can in no way replace my husband or win my real affection"—she sighed as she spoke—"has for some time been decidedly more insistent, and his speeches are as loving as they are sensible. The necessity of giving him my hand, the foolishness of considering emigration, and thereby losing the only true means of self-preservation, cannot be denied, and my resistance, my notion of emigrating, seems so little in accord with my usual prudence that in our last, somewhat heated, discussion, I could see his suspicion that my heart must be committed elsewhere." She brought forth the last words only with some hesitation, and cast down her eyes.

You can imagine what went through my soul at these words, and yet, upon reflection that followed like lightning, I realized that any word from me would merely compound the confusion. Yet at the same time I became fully conscious, as I stood before her, that she had become extremely dear to me, and that I would have to muster all the rational, reasonable strength of mind remaining to me in order not to offer her my hand at once. Let her leave everything behind, as long as she follows me! I thought. But the sorrows of previous years held me back. Should you nurture a new false hope, only to repent of it for the rest of your life?

We had both been silent for a while when Lieschen, whom I had not seen approaching, unexpectedly came up to us and requested permission to spend the evening at the neighboring hammer mill. It was granted without question. In the meanwhile I had pulled myself together, and now launched into a general account of my own: how on my travels I had seen all of this approaching long since; how with each day that passed the pressure and necessity for emigrating increased; yet such an adventure always remained the most risky imaginable. A hasty departure without adequate preparation would bring a sorry return. No other undertaking required so much caution and leadership. This consideration was not foreign to her; she had thought a good deal about all the circumstances, but at last she said, with a deep sigh, "During these days that you have been here, I have been hoping to gain comfort by confiding in you, but I feel worse off than before, and feel profoundly how unhappy I am." She looked up at me, but in order to hide the tears welling from her beautiful, kind eyes, she turned away and withdrew a few steps.

I do not wish to excuse myself, but the wish, if not to console, at least to distract this magnificent soul from her sorrows, gave me the idea of telling her about the strange union of wanderers and emigrants that I had joined some time earlier. Unwittingly, I had already let slip so much that I could hardly have held back when I realized how incautious my confidence might be. She calmed down, marveled, cheered up, revealed her whole being, and questioned me with such affection and good sense that I could no longer be evasive; I had to confess everything to her.

Gretchen came in and said we should come to Father. The girl seemed pensive and annoyed. As she was leaving, the virtuous beauty said, "I let Lieschen have the evening off. You take charge of things."

"You should not have let her go," replied Gretchen. "She is up to no good. You are too indulgent toward that scamp and trust her more than you should. I have just found out that she wrote him a letter yesterday. She eavesdropped on your conversation, and now she is going to meet him."

A child, who had been staying with the father in the interval, begged me to hurry; the good man was restive. We entered his room; he was sitting upright in bed, serene, even transfigured. "Children," he said, "I have spent these hours in continuous prayer. Not a single one of David's psalms of thanksgiving and praise have I left unrecited, and I add to them on my own with strengthened faith. Why does a man place his hopes only in the near future? There he should rather work and help himself, and place his hopes in the distant future, and trust in God."

He took Lenardo's hand and the hand of his daughter, and laying one on the other, said, "This shall be no earthly bond, but a heavenly one. Like brother and sister, love, trust, serve, and help one another, as unselfishly and purely as God may help you." When he had said this, he sank back with a blissful smile and was gone to his Maker. His daughter cast herself down by the bed, Lenardo beside her. Their cheeks touched, their tears united on the old man's hand.

At this moment the assistant rushes in, and is stunned by the scene. With a wild look, shaking his dark locks, the handsome youth exclaims, "He is dead! At the very moment when I desperately wanted to invoke his restored speech to decide my fate, the fate of his daughter, the being whom I love most, after God, for whom I would wish a sound heart, a heart that could feel the value of my affection. She is lost to me; she kneels beside another! Did he give you his blessing? Admit it!"

The splendid being had risen, Lenardo had stood up and recovered himself. She said, "I do not recognize you, the gentle, pious, now suddenly savage man. You know how I thank you, what I think of you!"

"Thanking and thinking are not the point," he replied calmly. "The issue is the happiness or unhappiness of my life. This stranger worries me. Looking at him, I do not trust myself to outweigh him. Overriding previous rights, loosing previous bonds is beyond my powers."

"As soon as you can be yourself again," said the virtuous woman, more beautiful than ever, "when we can talk as we always used to, then I will tell you, swear to you by the earthly remains of my transfigured father, that I have no understanding with this gentleman and friend beyond what you may know, approve, and share, and of which you must be glad."

Lenardo shuddered to the depths of his being; the three stood for a while, silent and reflective. The young man was the first to speak and said, "This moment is of too much significance not to be decisive. What I say is not spoken in haste; I have had time to think, so hear me out: the reason you refused me your hand was my refusal to follow you if you, through necessity or caprice, should emigrate. I hereby solemnly declare, before this legal witness, that I will place no obstacle in the way of your emigration, but will rather further it and follow you everywhere. In return for this declaration, which has not been wrung from me, but has only been accelerated by these very strange circumstances, I here and now demand your hand." He held out his own, standing firm and confident, while the other two, taken by surprise, involuntarily drew back.

"It is decided," said the young man, speaking quietly and with a certain pious dignity. "It was to be; it is for the best for all of us; God has willed it. But lest you think this was the result of haste or caprice, you should know that for love of you I had renounced mountains and cliffs and that just now in town I had set everything in motion so that I could live according to your wishes. But now I shall go alone, you will not deny me the means to do so, you will still have enough left to lose here, as you fear, and you are right to fear. For I have finally become convinced: the false, practical-minded rascal has moved into the upper valley, he is installing machines there, and you will see him taking all the livelihood for himself. Then perhaps, and all too soon, you will summon back a true friend, whom you are driving away."

Seldom have three people faced one another in greater embarrassment, all fearing to lose each other, and at the moment not knowing how they should hold onto one another.

With passionate resolve the young man rushed out the door. The virtuous beauty had laid her hand on her father's chilled breast: "We should not place our hopes in the near future," she exclaimed, "but in the distant future; that was his last blessing. Let us trust in God, in ourselves, and in each other; then everything will turn out for the best."

Chapter Fourteen

Our friend read the foregoing with great sympathy, but had to admit that by the end of the previous notebook he had sensed, even surmised, that the good soul had been found. The description of the rugged mountain region had first reminded him of those circumstances, but he was especially put on the trail by Lenardo's presentiment on that moonlit night, and then by the repetition of the passage from his own letter. Friedrich, to whom he explained all of this in detail, was pleased at the turn of events.

But here the task of communicating, portraying, amplifying, and pulling together becomes ever more difficult. Who does not feel that we are now nearing the end, where we are torn between the fear of losing ourselves in details and the wish not to leave anything unexplained. To be sure, we were informed of a number of things by the dispatch that just arrived, but the letters and their multiple enclosures contained various matters, not all of general interest. We are therefore inclined to summarize the things we knew or had learned of at that time, as well as that of which we were later informed, and in this spirit to bring the solemn business we have undertaken, of being a faithful chronicler, to a fitting conclusion.

Before all else, we must therefore report that Lothario, with Therese, his wife, and Natalie, who would not be parted from her brother, had really already gone to sea in the company of the Abbé. They set out with propitious omens, and it is to be hoped that a favorable wind will swell their sails. Only one unpleasant sentiment, a true moral grief, burdens them—that they were not able to pay a visit to Makarie first. The detour was too great, their undertaking too important. They were already reproaching themselves for delays, and had to sacrifice even a sacred duty to necessity.

We, however, from our narrating and portraying standpoint, should not allow these dear people, who earlier won so much of our affection, to disappear into so great a distance without our having conveyed a more precise account of their recent projects and actions, especially since we have had no detailed word of them for so long a time. Even so we shall omit this, because their activities up to now involved only preparations for the great enterprise on which we see them launched. We live, however, in the hope that we shall happily find them again in the midst of ordered activity that reveals the true worth of their various characters.

Juliette, the sensitive and virtuous one, whom we doubtless still remember well, had married, a man after her uncle's heart, who could work well with him and carry on after him in his spirit. Recently Juliette had spent a good deal of time with her aunt, where several of those on whom she had had a beneficent influence gathered, not only those who will remain devoted to the solid land, but also those who mean to cross the sea. Lenardo, however, had already said farewell, with Friedrich; their communication through messengers was all the livelier.

If the aforementioned noble persons were missing from the guest list, one could still find on it the names of many important ones who are well known to us. Hilarie came with her husband, now a captain and decidedly wealthy landowner. She, with her great charm and loveliness, was gladly forgiven here, as everywhere, for the excessive ease in moving from one interest to another of which we found her guilty in the course of our narrative. The men especially did not hold this greatly against her. A fault of that sort, if it be one, does not strike them as very objectionable, because each of them could wish and hope to have his turn.

Flavio, her husband, vigorous, cheerful, and charming enough, seemed to possess her love completely; she must have forgiven herself for the past; Makarie, too, found no reason to allude to it. Still an ardent poet, Flavio asked permission to read upon parting a poem he had composed in honor of Makarie and her circle during the few days of his sojourn. He was often seen pacing up and down outside, standing still a while, then with agitated gestures moving on again, writing in his tablet, deliberating, then writing once more. But he seemed to consider it finished when he conveyed his wish through Angela.

The good lady agreed, though unwillingly, and it was pleasant enough to listen to, although no one learned anything he did not already know, or felt anything he had not already felt. But the reading itself was light and pleasing, and here and there the phrasing and rhymes were original, even if one might have wished the whole thing somewhat shorter. Finally he presented it, very nicely lettered, with a pretty border, and everyone parted in mutual satisfaction.

This couple had just returned from a significant and well-employed journey to the south, in order to relieve their father, the major, at the house, since he, along with the irresistible lady, now become his wife, also wished to breathe some of that paradisal air for their own refreshment.

These two now came to take the other couple's place, and with Makarie, as everywhere, the remarkable woman enjoyed special favor, which particularly manifested itself in the lady's being received in the inner chambers and alone, a privilege the major was also to be granted afterward. This latter made an excellent impression as a cultivated officer, a good householder and landowner, a friend of literature, and even as a praiseworthy author of didactic verse, and was most welcome to the astronomer and the other members of the household.

He was also especially singled out by our old gentleman, the worthy uncle, who, residing at a moderate distance, came over more often than was his wont, although only for a few hours; he could not, in spite of the ample comforts offered him, be prevailed upon to stay the night.

His presence at brief gatherings of this sort, however, was very gratifying, because he then, as man of the world and of the court, assumed an obliging and mediating role, in which connection even a trace of aristocratic pedantry was not felt to be unwelcome. Besides, he was truly at ease this time; he was happy, as we all are when we have important matters to work out with intelligent and sensible people. The comprehensive project was now fully launched and was moving steadily along according to the arrangements agreed upon.

Of this only the chief points. He is, through his forebears, a large landowner over there across the sea. What precisely that signifies, anyone conversant with conditions over there may explain to his friends, since it would lead us too far afield here. These important estates had been leased out until now, and because of various difficulties brought in little. The society, with which we are sufficiently familiar, is now entitled to take possession there, in the midst of a perfect civil polity. From there, as an influential force in the state, it will be able to pursue its own advantage and expand far into the as yet undeveloped wilderness. This is where Friedrich, along with Lenardo, means to take an especially active part, in order to demonstrate how to start from the beginning and follow a path in conformity with Nature.

Hardly had the above-mentioned departed, fully satisfied, from Makarie's house, when guests were announced of quite another sort, though equally welcome. We might scarcely have expected to see Philine and Lydie in such a sacred spot, and yet they came. Montan, who for the time being lingered in the mountains, was to fetch them here and bring them to the sea by the most direct route. Both were very well received by the housekeepers, maids, and other women employed or living there. Philine brought with her a pair of darling children, and distinguished herself in her simple but most becoming clothing by a fairly large pair of English scissors that she wore hanging from a long silver chain attached to her flower-embroidered girdle; sometimes, as if to emphasize what she was saying, she would clip and snip at the air, to the amusement of all present. This soon led to the question whether, in a household of that size, there were not some dressmaking to be done. And it turned out that a pair of brides needed to be outfitted, a happy opportunity. Philine examines the local costume closely, has the girls stroll back and forth before her, and cuts away. Proceeding with cleverness and taste, she manages not to detract from the character of the local costume, yet contrives unobtrusively to blend its clumsy barbarity with such gracefulness that the girls looked better to themselves and to others and at the same time overcame their anxiety about diverging from tradition.

And now Lydie, who could sew with equal proficiency, precision, and speed, became the perfect assistant, and, with the other women helping, it could be hoped that the brides might be decked out more quickly than had been imagined. The girls could not absent themselves for very long, for Philine busied herself with them down to the smallest detail, treating them like dolls or like stage extras. The dozens of ribbons and other festive decorations customary in this region were smartly arranged, with the result that these strong bodies and pretty figures, usually covered up out of barbarian prudishness, now came into their own, and any remaining coarseness took on a special charm.

Yet those who are all too active become nuisances in a well-regulated setting. Philine with her voracious scissors had found her way into the rooms where cloth of all kinds was kept on hand to supply the wardrobe of the large household. The prospect of cutting up all that cloth filled her with rapture; she actually had to be led away and the doors locked, since she lacked any judgment or sense of proportion. For this reason Angela did not want to be announced as a bride, for she was afraid of such a cutter. Altogether, a good relationship between the two seemed impossible to achieve. But that issue can be taken up only at a later time.

Montan delayed his arrival, longer than anyone had expected, and Philine insisted that she be presented to Makarie. This was done, in the hope that they might then be rid of her sooner, and it was indeed singular to see the two sinners at the feet of the saint. They knelt on either side of her, Philine between her two children, whom she pushed down with lively grace. She spoke with her usual gaiety: "I love my husband, my children, and am happy to work for them, as well as for others; you will forgive the rest!" Makarie gave her blessing, and with a respectful curtsey Philine withdrew.

Lydie lay to the left of the saint with her face in her lap, wept bitterly, and could not utter a word. Makarie, understanding her tears, patted her soothingly on the shoulder, then kissed her head along the parting as it lay before her, fervently and repeatedly with pious intent.

Lydie raised herself up, first to her knees, then to her feet, and gazed at her benefactress with pure joy. "What has happened to me?" she cried. "What is this? The heavy, oppressive burden that robbed me of all thought, if not of all consciousness, has suddenly been lifted from my head. I can see freely into the higher regions, direct my thoughts to those heights, and," she added, after a deep breath, "I do believe that my heart wants to follow."

At that moment the door opened and Montan entered, as often a person who has been awaited all too long appears suddenly and unexpectedly. Lydie stepped up to him happily, embraced him with joy, and, as she led him to Makarie, exclaimed, "He must hear what debt he owes to this godly woman, and join me at her feet in gratitude."

Montan, moved, and, contrary to his wont, somewhat embarrassed, said, with a respectful bow toward the worthy lady, "It seems to be a great deal, for I owe you to her. This is the first time that you have come to me frankly and affectionately, the first time that you have pressed me to your heart, though I have long deserved it."

Here we must confide that Montan had been in love with Lydie from her youth, that the more engaging Lothario had carried her off, but that Montan had remained true to her and to his friend, and that he finally, perhaps to no little astonishment on the part of our earlier readers, made her his wedded wife.

These three, who perhaps might not feel altogether comfortable in European society, did not moderate their expressions of joy when the talk came around to the conditions expected in the New World. Philine's scissors were already quivering, for there was talk of retaining a monopoly on providing clothing to the new colonies. Philine gave a very pretty description of the great stores of cloth and linens, and snipped in the air, already seeing before her the harvest awaiting sickle and scythe, as she expressed it.

Lydie, on the other hand, only now reawakened by those felicitous blessings to shared love, envisioned her pupils increasing a hundredfold, and a whole race of housewives guided and inspired to precision and neatness. And serious-minded Montan has such a vision of the mountains there full of lead, copper, iron, and coal that he is sometimes tempted to declare all his knowledge and ability mere timid, groping attempts, with a rich and rewarding harvest to be had only over there, if he seize it boldly.

It was predictable that Montan would soon reach an understanding with the astronomer. The conversations they conducted in the presence of Makarie were most fascinating. We find, however, only little of them transcribed, since Angela had for some time now been less attentive in listening and more negligent in transcription. Furthermore, much of it may have been too general for her, and not readily grasped by a young woman. We therefore include in passing only a few of the observations made during those days, which did not even come down to us in her handwriting.

When we study the sciences, particularly those that deal with nature, it is as difficult as it is necessary to investigate whether that which has been passed down to us from earlier times and which our predecessors considered valid, is really well founded and dependable, to the extent that it can be further built upon, or whether a traditional article of faith has come to a standstill, and thus fosters stagnation rather than progress. One indication furthers this inquiry, namely if an assumption has retained its vitality and has influenced and furthered continuing endeavors.

It is just the opposite when new theories are being verified; there one must ask: is this assumption a real advance or merely obedience to fashion? For an opinion presented by energetic men spreads by contagion through the populace, and is then called unassailable—a claim that has no meaning to the true scientist. Church and state may possibly find cause for declaring themselves unassailable, for they have to deal with the recalcitrant masses, and so long as order is maintained, the means do not matter. But in the sciences the utmost freedom is required, for the scientist works not for today or tomorrow but for an inconceivable progression of ages.

But even if some falsehood does gain the upper hand in science, there will always be a minority for the truth, and if it shrank to a single soul, that would not matter. He will continue to work behind the scenes in silence, in obscurity, and a time will come when people will inquire after him and his convictions, or when the latter, as light becomes widespread and general, can venture forth once more.

What was less discussed in general terms, however, though it was incomprehensible and strange in the extreme, was Montan's revelation in passing that he was accompanied in his explorations of mountains and mining by someone who had quite remarkable faculties and a peculiar affinity for everything that might be called rock, mineral, indeed any kind of element. This companion could sense not only a certain emanation from underground streams, deposits, and veins of metal, as well as coal and whatever else might be massed together, but, what was more amazing still, would feel different with every change of place. The various types of mountains each had a special effect, which, ever since he had invented a peculiar but still adequate language, they had been able to communicate about and to verify in detail. His companion could pass any test quite remarkably, identify chemical as well as physical elements by intuition, and even tell the heavier elements from the lighter ones simply by looking. This person, whose gender he refused to reveal, had been sent ahead with our departing friends, and he had hopes of great discoveries to his advantage in the unexplored lands.

This confidence of Montan's made the astronomer open his own reserved heart, and with Makarie's approval, he revealed the latter's relationship to the cosmos. From subsequent reports by the astronomer, we are in a position to share, if not all one might like to know, at least the main points of their discussion on such important matters.

Here let us marvel at the similarity of these two cases, despite their great differences. One of our friends, lest he become a Timon of Athens, had buried himself in the deepest chasms of the earth, and there had come to realize that human nature contains something analogous to what is crudest and most rigid. The spirit of Makarie provided an opposing example to the astronomer; if in the former case staying in place, then here escape is the province of specially talented natures; we need not penetrate to the center of the earth nor escape beyond the boundaries of the solar system, for we are already sufficiently occupied and clearly directed toward activity, and charged to accomplish it. On and in the ground one finds material for the highest terrestrial necessities, a world of substances made available to man's highest ingenuity for fashioning. But along the other, spiritual path, sympathy, love, and disciplined, free effectiveness are always to be found. To move these two worlds toward one another, to manifest their reciprocal qualities in the transient phenomenon of life, that is the highest form toward which man must aspire.

At this point both friends made a compact and undertook not to conceal their experiences under any circumstances, because even someone who might smile at them as fairy tales, suitable perhaps for a novel, could still consider them a metaphor for the highest good.

The departure of Montan and his ladies followed soon after, and though the others would gladly have kept him and Lydie there longer, still the restless Philine had been bothersome to several of the other women, accustomed as they were to quiet and order, and especially to the noble Angela, in whose case special circumstances arose to exacerbate the discomfort.

We have already had cause to mention that Angela was no longer carrying out her duty of listening and recording, but seemed otherwise occupied. In order to explain this anomaly in an individual so devoted to order and accustomed to the most rarified circles, we must introduce yet another actor into this already populous drama.

Our old, tested business friend Werner, because his enterprises were growing, even expanding infinitely, as it were, was obliged to look about for new assistants, whom he did not take on without carefully testing them beforehand. He now sent such a one to Makarie, to negotiate for the payment of the considerable sums which that lady had designated and promised to contribute from her large fortune to the new undertaking, especially out of consideration for Lenardo, her favorite. The young man in question, now Werner's aide and journeyman, a vigorous and natural youth, who cut a remarkable figure, commends himself through one unique talent, an incredible aptitude for mental arithmetic, which is useful everywhere but especially among our entrepreneurs, engaged in their joint venture, since in the many aspects of the communal finances they must constantly deal with figures and reconcile them. Even in ordinary society, where discussions about worldly things often involve figures, sums, and balances, the presence of such a person must be equally welcome. Furthermore, he plays the piano most charmingly, his mathematical bent and his engaging naturalness combining and coming to his aid in the happiest manner. The notes flow lightly and harmoniously from his fingers, but at times he indicates that he could be at home in deeper regions; and so he is most attractive, even though he speaks but little and hardly any emotion shows in what he does say. In any case, he is younger than his years; one might almost find him childlike. Whatever his other qualities, he has won Angela's favor, and she his, to Makarie's great satisfaction, for she has long wished to see the noble young woman married.

Angela, however, always considering and feeling how difficult it would be to replace her, had surely already refused some loving offer, and perhaps even suppressed a secret inclination of her own. But since a successor was now conceivable, had even been all but appointed, she seems to have been overwhelmed by this attractive newcomer, and surrendered to him to the point of passion.

But we are now again in a position to reveal the most important development, inasmuch as all the matters we have long been discussing have gradually taken shape, dissolved, and assumed a new form.

It has now been decided that the virtuous beauty, otherwise known as the nut-brown maid, should come to Makarie's side. This plan, presented in general outlines and already approved by Lenardo, is very close to being realized. All participants agree; the virtuous beauty will transfer her entire property to her assistant. He will marry the second daughter of that hardworking family, and become the Harness-Fixer's brother-in-law. This makes possible the establishment of a new form of manufacture on a local and cooperative basis, and the inhabitants of that industrious valley will be employed in a different, more vital way.

The lovely woman is thereby freed; she will come to Makarie in place of Angela, who is already engaged to her young man. With this our report is finished for the present; what cannot be resolved will remain uncertain.

But now the virtuous beauty insists that Wilhelm come and fetch her. Certain circumstances must still be arranged, and she lays great value on Wilhelm's completing what he actually began. He first discovered her, and a strange fate put Lenardo on his trail; and now she wishes Wilhelm to ease her departure from there and thereby experience the joy and peace of mind that come from having picked up and joined some few of the intertwined threads of fate.

But in order to round off the spiritual and emotional elements of this tale, we must now reveal something even more secret, to wit: Lenardo had never spoken a word with the virtuous beauty concerning a closer tie. But in the course of the negotiations, with all the messages back and forth, delicate inquiries had been made as to how she regarded their relationship and what she might be disposed to do, should anything be said. From her response this much could be gathered: she did not feel worthy to return a love like that of her noble friend by giving her divided self. Affection of that sort deserved the entire soul, the complete powers, of a woman's being; but this she could not offer. The memory of her betrothed, her husband, and their mutual unity was still so vivid, still so absorbed her entire being, that no room could be found in her heart for love and passion; she could feel only the purest goodwill and in this case the greatest gratitude. It was left at this, and since Lenardo had not broached the matter, it was also not necessary to provide information or a reply.

A few general observations will, we hope, be in place here. The relationship to Makarie of all these persons passing through was marked by trust and respect; all felt the presence of a higher being, yet in her presence there remained to each the freedom to appear according to his own nature. Everyone shows himself as he is, more so than he ever did toward parents and friends, and with a certain confidence, for he was lured and encouraged to manifest only what was good, was best, in himself, for which reason well-nigh general satisfaction reigned.

However, we cannot conceal the fact that Makarie, during these somewhat distracting circumstances, remained preoccupied with Lenardo's situation. She spoke of it to those closest to her, to Angela and the astronomer. She believed she could see Lenardo's inner state clearly before her: for the moment he was at peace; the object of his worry is in perfect safety; Makarie had made provision for the future, come what might. Now he had to embark courageously upon the great undertaking and make a beginning, leaving the rest to the future and to fate. He would, presumably, be strengthened in his project chiefly by the thought that once he had secured a foothold, he would summon her to come over, if not fetch her himself.

In this connection people could not forego certain general observations. They gave close consideration to the rare phenomenon that manifested itself here: love arising from a troubled conscience. Other examples came to mind of impressions, once formed, undergoing strange transformations, of the mysterious development of inborn attraction and longing. They found it regrettable that in such cases there is little advice one can give; but it would be highly advisable to keep one's head as clear as possible and not yield unconditionally to one proclivity or another.

Having arrived at this point, we cannot resist the temptation to share a page from our archives concerning Makarie and the special quality with which her mind was endowed. Unfortunately, this essay was written from memory, long after its contents were communicated, and thus cannot be regarded as entirely authentic, as might be wished in so remarkable a case. Be that as it may, enough is presented here to provoke thought and make the reader consider whether anything similar or approaching this has ever been observed or recorded.

Chapter Fifteen

Makarie stands in a relationship to our solar system that one hardly dares to express. Not only does she harbor it, and see it in her mind, in her soul, in her imagination; she constitutes a part of it, as it were. She sees herself drawn along in those heavenly circles, but in her own particular way; since childhood she has moved around the sun, and, to be specific, as has now become clear, in a spiral course, moving ever farther from the center and circling toward the outer regions.

If one may assume that beings, insofar as they are corporeal, strive toward the center, while insofar as they are spiritual, they strive toward the periphery, then our friend belongs among the most spiritual. She seems born only to free herself from the terrestrial, in order to penetrate the nearest and farthest realms of existence. This trait, glorious though it is, has been a heavy burden, imposed since her earliest years. From the time she was little, she recalls her inner self as permeated by glowing being, illuminated by a light which even the brightest sunlight could not begin to equal. Often she saw two suns, an inner one, and one outside in the sky, two moons, of which the outer one remained the same size through all its phases, while the inner one grew smaller and smaller.

This gift drew her interest away from ordinary things, but her admirable parents made every effort for her education. All of her talents were awakened, all her activities were put to good effect, so that she satisfied every outward expectation, and while her heart and mind were wholly filled with superterrestrial visions, her actions and dealings always met the noblest moral standards. As she grew up, ever helpful, tireless in performing services large and small, she walked like an angel of God upon the earth, while her spiritual being moved around this world's sun, but in ever widening circles beyond this world.

The overwhelming richness of this state was somewhat mitigated by the fact that there seemed to be day and night inside her as well, so that, when her inner light was dimmed, she sought to fulfill her outward duties most conscientiously, and when her inner light blazed forth, she gave herself over to the most blessed rest. In fact, she claims to have observed a sort of cloud that enveloped her from time to time and temporarily obscured the sight of her heavenly companions, which interval she always managed to use for the well-being and happiness of those around her.

As long as she kept these visions secret, much was required to bear them; what she revealed of them was not acknowledged or was misinterpreted, so that in the course of her long life she passed them off as illness, and the family still speaks in those terms. Eventually, however, good fortune brought her the man whom you now see in our household, equally valuable as doctor, mathematician, and astronomer, in every respect a noble person who, however, first found his way to her out of curiosity. But as she gained confidence in him, and gradually described her states to him, linking the present to the past and establishing connections among the events, he was so taken with the phenomenon that he could no longer tear himself away, but daily strove to penetrate ever deeper into the mystery.

At first, as he gave her plainly to understand, he considered the entire thing a delusion. For she did not deny that from early youth she had diligently studied the stars and the heavens, that she had been well instructed and had missed no opportunity to clarify her image of the structure of the universe through the use of apparatus and books. Hence he would not be dissuaded that it was all the result of her learning. The workings of an imagination disciplined to a high degree, the influence of memory were to be suspected here, with the assistance of judgment, and above all a secret element of calculation.

He is a mathematician and therefore obstinate, an enlightened spirit, and therefore skeptical. He resisted for a long time, but noted exactly what she described, tried to get at the sequence of various years, and was especially astounded by her most recent declarations, which tallied exactly with the corresponding positions of the heavenly bodies, until finally he exclaimed, "Well, why should not God and Nature create and set up a living armillary sphere, a spiritual clockwork, that might be capable, as indeed clocks daily and hourly do for us, of following the movement of the stars in its own way?"

Here we dare go no further, for the unbelievable loses its value if one tries to examine it in greater detail. Yet this much we shall say—what served as the basis for the necessary computations was the following: to her, the seer, our sun appeared far smaller in visions than when she saw it by day; furthermore the unusual position this heavenly light occupied within the zodiac allowed certain inferences to be drawn.

On the other hand, doubts and errors arose because the visionary would indicate that some heavenly body or other appeared in the zodiac, when it could not be located in the sky. These were probably the minor planets, which had not yet been discovered at that time. For from other statements of hers it could be concluded that she had long since passed beyond the orbit of Mars and was nearing the orbit of Jupiter. Apparently she had been contemplating this planet for some time, from what distance it would be difficult to say, marveling at its extraordinary majesty and watching the play of its moons. But later she had seen it in the most amazing way as a waning moon, indeed, reversed, as the waxing moon appears to us. From this the conclusion was drawn that she was seeing it from the side, and was really about to cross its orbit and press on toward Saturn in infinite space. No one's imagination can follow her that far, but we hope that such an entelechy will not withdraw entirely from our solar system, but when she reaches its boundary will long again to return, in order to exercise her influence upon earthly life again, to the benefit of our descendants.

As we now conclude this ethereal fiction, hoping for indulgence, let us turn once more to that terrestrial fairy tale of which we earlier gave a passing hint.

Montan had declared, with the greatest appearance of honesty, that the extraordinary person who could identify differences among earthly substances so accurately by intuition was already far away with the first wanderers, a claim, however, which should have seemed improbable to anyone wise in the ways of men. For how could Montan and his sort allow such a convenient divining rod to stir from his side. And indeed, shortly after his departure, a suspicion gradually arose, fostered by talk back and forth and by strange tales told by the lower house servants. It seemed that Philine and Lydie had brought along a third woman, on the pretext that she was their servant, for which, however, she seemed utterly unsuited; and in fact she was never summoned when her mistresses were dressing or undressing. Her own simple garb clothed her sturdy and well-built figure very suitably, but suggested as did her entire person, a rustic quality. Her conduct, without being coarse, showed none of that social breeding of which ladies' maids usually present a caricature. She had also quickly found her place among the servants; she joined the gardeners and field hands, seized a spade, and worked for two or three. When she picked up a rake, it flew so skillfully over the ploughed soil that the widest expanse looked like a smooth planting bed. Otherwise she kept still and was soon held in general favor. People told one another how they had often seen her lay down her tool and go running clear across the field toward some hidden spring, where she quenched her thirst. She had repeated this practice daily, always finding a source of clean, running water when she needed to drink, wherever she might be.

So some evidence was left behind for Montan's assertions. He had probably decided to conceal the presence of so remarkable a person from his worthy hosts, who doubtless deserved to be taken into his confidence, in order to avoid troublesome experiments and inadequate tests. But we wanted to communicate what was known to us, incomplete as it is, so that we may kindly alert men of an inquiring mind to similar cases, which perhaps manifest themselves by some sign more often than one might think.

Chapter Sixteen

The steward of that castle which we recently saw enlivened by our wanderers, by nature an active and diligent man, always keeping in mind possible gain for his employers and himself, was sitting contentedly drawing up accounts and reports, taking pains to present and analyze, with some self-satisfaction, the great advantages that had accrued to his district during the presence of those guests. Yet, as he himself was convinced, this was the least of it; he had observed what beneficial effects could be had by active, skilled, free-spirited, and bold men. Some had departed to cross the seas, others to find a place for themselves on their continent; now he became aware of a third, secret, set of circumstances, which he promptly resolved to put to use.

As they were leaving it became apparent that, as might have been predicted and expected, quite a few of the vigorous young men had become more or less intimate with the pretty maidens of the village and the region. Only a few of them had enough courage, when Odoardo left with his followers, to declare that they had decided to stay. Of Lenardo's emigrants, not one had stayed behind, but several of them had averred that they would soon return and settle there, if they could be provided with a reasonably sufficient income and security for the future.

The steward, who was thoroughly acquainted with the character and the domestic circumstances of all who made up the little nation under his rule, gloated secretly like a true egotist over these events. Here were people going to such effort and expense to prove themselves free and active overseas or in the interior, and yet they were bringing him, sitting peacefully on his acres, extraordinary advantages for house and lands, giving him the opportunity to hold on to some of the best of them and gather them about him. His thinking, broadened by the present situation, found nothing more natural than that liberality well employed should have laudable, productive results. He at once resolves to undertake something similar in his own small domain. Fortunately, the prosperous inhabitants had been all but compelled to hand their daughters over legally to these premature bridegrooms. The steward persuaded them to view such a social mishap as good fortune, since in fact it was fortunate that precisely the most useful artisans had drawn this lot. So it was not difficult to make preparations for a furniture factory, which would require no great space or special conditions, but only skill and sufficient supplies of material. The steward promised this latter; the inhabitants contributed wives, space, and distribution, while the immigrants provided the skill.

All this the clever businessman had been quietly thinking through in the presence and commotion of the crowd, and could therefore set to work as soon as things had calmed down around him.

Calm, albeit a somewhat funereal calm, had settled over the streets of the village and the castle courtyard after this flood had receded, when a rider galloped up to the castle, summoning our businessman from his computations and calculations, and disturbing his peace. To be sure, the horse's hooves did not clatter—he was unshod—but the rider, who leaped down from the blanket—he rode without saddle or stirrups and controlled the horse only with a snaffle—shouted loudly and impatiently for the residents, for the guests, and was upset and astonished to find everything so still and dead.

The clerk did not know what to make of the new arrival; after some sharp words had been exchanged, the steward himself came out, and could also say no more than that everyone was gone. "Where to?" was the quick question of the spirited young stranger. Phlegmatically the steward specified the route taken by Lenardo and Odoard, as well as that of a third, ambiguous figure, whom they had sometimes called Wilhelm, sometimes Meister. This latter had embarked on the river a few miles away; he was going downstream, first to visit his son, and then to pursue some important business.

No sooner had the youth mounted his horse, and taken note of the quickest way to the river, than he was out the gate and speeding away so fast that the steward, who looked after him from an upper window, could hardly tell by a cloud of dust that the bewildered rider had taken the proper road.

The last of the dust had barely drifted off in the distance, and our steward was about to sit down again to his work, when a courier came dashing in by the castle's upper gate, and likewise asked after the group, to whom he had been hastily dispatched with one last thing to deliver. He had a fairly large package for them, but also a separate letter addressed to Wilhelm, known as Meister. A young woman had earnestly entrusted this letter to his special care and insisted he deliver it as soon as possible. Unfortunately, he, too, could receive no other reply than that the birds had flown, and that he had better proceed with utmost haste, so that he might hope either to catch up with all of them or to receive further directions.

We may not, however, withhold from our readers the letter itself, which turned up among the many papers confided to our care, and has great significance. It was from Hersilie, a young lady as remarkable as she is engaging; she has appeared but seldom in our communications, but has, at each appearance, surely proved irresistible to every reader of wit and sensibility. Her destiny is also probably one of the oddest that can befall a delicate soul.

Chapter Seventeen

Hersilie to Wilhelm

I sat in thought and could not tell you what I was thinking. But a pensive blankness sometimes comes over me, a sort of consciously felt indifference. A horse gallops into the courtyard and awakens me from my tranquility; the door flies open and in strides Felix, in youthful radiance like a young idol. He rushes up to me, wants to embrace me, I repulse him, he seems not to mind, keeps at a slight distance, and with unclouded cheerfulness praises the horse that brought him here, describes his studies and his pleasures, in detail and trustingly. Reminiscing about the past brings us to the splendid casket. He knows that I have it, and demands to see it; I give in, it was impossible to refuse. He looks at it, tells me in detail how he discovered it; I lose my head and betray that I am in possession of the key. Now his curiosity becomes extreme; that, too, he must see, if only from a distance. No one could have pleaded more earnestly and charmingly; he pleads as if he were praying, goes down on his knees, and implores with such fiery, beautiful eyes, with such sweet and flattering words, and so I was again seduced. I showed him the miraculous mystery from afar, but quickly he seized my hand and tore the key from it and jumped mischievously to one side, around a table.

"I have no benefit from the casket or the key," he exclaimed. "It is your heart I would wish to open, so that it should reveal itself to me, come to meet me, press me to itself, allow me to press it to my breast." He was infinitely handsome and lovable, and as I tried to approach him he kept pushing the casket before him along the table. Already the key was in; he threatened to turn it and really did turn it. The little key broke off, the outer half fell on the table.

I was more bewildered than one can be and should be. He takes advantage of my confusion, leaves the casket where it is, comes after me and takes me in his arms. I struggled in vain; his eyes drew closer to mine, and it is beautiful to see one's own image in the loving eyes of another. I saw this for the first time as he passionately pressed his mouth against mine. I must admit that I returned his kisses, for it is beautiful to make someone happy. I tore loose, the gulf between us seemed to me only too distinct. Instead of composing myself, I went too far; I pushed him away angrily. My confusion gave me courage and sense; I threatened, I scolded him, ordered him never again to appear before me; he took me at my word. "Good," he said, "I shall ride into the world until I perish." He threw himself onto his horse and galloped off. Still half dreaming, I go to put the casket away; the broken half of the key was lying there, and I found myself in double and triple perplexity.

O men, O humans, will you never cultivate reason? Was it not bad enough that the father should have sown so much mischief; did we also need the son to throw us into hopeless confusion?

I have kept these confessions here for a time, but now a curious circumstance has arisen, which I must report, and which clarifies and obscures the foregoing.

An elderly goldsmith and jewel merchant whom my uncle holds in great esteem arrives and shows us strange antique treasures. I am prompted to bring out the casket: he examines the broken key and points out what we had previously overlooked, that the break is not rough but smooth. On contact the two ends lock onto each other, and he draws the key out whole—they are magnetically joined and hold each other, but unlock only for the initiate. The man steps back some distance, the casket springs open, but he quickly snaps it shut again. Such secrets were better left untouched, he said.

You surely cannot imagine my incomprehensible state of mind, thank God, for how, if one is not oneself confused, can one recognize confusion. The significant casket stands before me, the key that does not unlock it is in my hand; I would gladly leave the casket unopened, could the key but unlock my immediate future.

It has been some time since you have worried about me, but I beg, implore, urgently recommend that you search for Felix. I have sent out in vain for any traces of him. I do not know whether I should bless or dread the day that will bring us together again.

At last, at last! The courier is insisting that he be dismissed. He has been kept here long enough; he is supposed to catch up with the emigrants with important dispatches. He will probably find you among this company, or be told where to look. In the interval I shall have no peace.

Chapter Eighteen

The boat was gliding down the river beneath the hot midday sun, while gentle breezes cooled the warm aether. Gentle banks to either side offered a simple but pleasant vista: wheat fields grew near the stream, and good soil came so close that swirling waters, throwing themselves up at spots, had mightily attacked the soft earth and swept it away, so that steep cliffs of considerable height had formed.

High above on the jagged edge of such an escarpment, where once the towpath must have run, our friend saw a young man, well-built and strong of frame, come trotting up. But before anyone could get a closer look at him, the grassy overhang broke loose, and the unfortunate rider, horse above, man beneath, hurtled abruptly into the water. There was no time to consider how or why; the boatmen rowed swift as an arrow toward the eddy, and in an instant had seized their beautiful booty. The noble youth lay as though lifeless in the boat, and after brief consideration the skilled men rowed to a sandbar that had formed in the middle of the river. Landing, carrying the body ashore, stripping and drying him was a matter of moments. Still not a sign of life to be seen; the lovely flower wilted in their arms.

Wilhelm immediately reached for his lancet to open a vein in his arm. A rich stream of blood sprang forth, and mingling with the winding, rippling waves, followed the course of the swirling stream. Life returned; the loving surgeon barely had time to fasten the bandage before the young man was already bravely getting to his feet, looking keenly at Wilhelm and crying, "If I am to live, let it be with you!" With these words he fell upon the neck of his rescuer, recognizing and recognized, and wept bitterly. Thus they stood in tight embrace, like Castor and Pollux, brothers who meet halfway along the road from Orcus to the realm of light.

They bade him calm himself. The stout men had already prepared a comfortable couch, half sunny, half shady, under light bushes and branches. Here he stretched out on his father's cloak, the fairest of youths. His brown hair, soon dry, once more crisped into curls; he smiled, reassured, and fell asleep. With pleasure our friend gazed down upon him, as he covered him. "You are always brought forth anew, glorious image of God!" he exclaimed, "and are always injured again straight away, wounded from within or without!" The cloak slipped over him, the milder rays of the sun gently warmed the young man's limbs through and through, his cheeks took on a healthy glow, and already he seemed fully restored.

The active men, rejoicing in anticipation of a happy outcome to a good action and the prospect of a generous reward, had already almost dried the youth's clothing on the hot sand so that when he awoke he could at once be restored to the condition most fitting for society.

From Makarie's Archives

The secrets of life's pathways cannot and may not be revealed; there will be stumbling blocks over which every wanderer must trip. The poet, however, points the places out.

It would not be worth the trouble of reaching the age of seventy if all the wisdom of the world were folly before God.

The truth is godlike; it does not appear directly but must be guessed from its manifestations.

The genuine student learns to derive the unknown from the known, and thus approaches mastery.

But people are not readily able to derive the unknown from the known, for they do not know that their intellect practices the same arts as Nature.

For the gods teach us to imitate their most special works; but we know only what we are doing, and do not recognize what we are imitating.

Everything is the same, everything is different, everything is beneficial and harmful, expressive and mute, reasonable and unreasonable. And what one claims to know of individual things is often contradictory.

For men have imposed laws on themselves without knowing what they were making laws about; but the order of Nature is given by the gods.

What men have ordained never fits, whether it be just or unjust. But what the gods ordain is always suitable, just or unjust.

But I want to show that the known arts of mankind are like natural occurrences, which take place openly or in secret.

The art of prophecy is of this kind: it perceives the hidden in the visible, the future in the present, life in death, and sense in nonsense.

Thus the initiate always has a firm grasp on human nature, while the uninitiated perceive it now one way, now another, and each emulates it in his own fashion.

When a man comes together with a woman, and a boy is begotten, something unknown has arisen from something known. On the other hand, when the dim mind of the boy absorbs things that are distinct, he becomes a man, and learns to know the future from the present.

The immortal is in no way comparable to the mortal, and yet even that which is merely alive has intelligence. Thus the stomach knows perfectly well when it is hungry and thirsty.

This is how the art of prophecy relates to human nature. And to the perceptive person, both are always right; to the limited person, however, they appear sometimes one way, sometimes another.

In the smithy iron is softened by fanning the fire and taking all the superfluous nourishment from the rod. Once cleansed, it is beaten and twisted and, with the nourishment of a different water, it again becomes strong. A person experiences the same thing with his teacher.

Since we are convinced that anyone who surveys the intellectual world and becomes aware of the beauty of true intellect can also observe its father, who is sublime above all thought, so we seek with all our might to understand and to express for ourselves—insofar as such things can be formulated—in what way we are capable of beholding the beauty of the mind and of the world.

Therefore imagine the following: two blocks of stone have been placed side by side, one crude and unworked, the other fashioned by art into a statue, whether of a god or a man. If a god, it might represent one of the Graces or the Muses. If human, it could not be any particular person, but rather someone whom art had distilled from all existing beauty.

Yet the stone which art has shaped into a beautiful figure will at once seem beautiful to you, not because it is a stone, for then the other block would also count as beautiful, but because it has a form imparted by art.

The material had no such form; but the form resided in the inventor before it reached the stone. It was in the artist not because he had eyes and hands, but because he was gifted with art.

It follows that much greater beauty was in art; for it is not the form inherent in art that gets into the stone; that form remains in art, and another, lesser version comes out, which is not there purely in itself, nor in accordance with the wishes of the artist either, but rather insofar as the material obeyed the commands of art.

If art produces the equivalent of what it is and possesses, and if it produces the beautiful according to the Idea which always guides it, then it is the one that possesses more, and more truly, a greater and more excellent beauty of art, more perfect than everything that appears in external things.

For insofar as form is diffused upon entering matter, it will be weaker than that which remains in unity. For anything that tolerates a dispersion of itself departs from its essence: strength from strength, warmth from warmth, power from power, and likewise beauty from beauty. Hence every cause must be more excellent than its effect. For it is not non-music that makes the musician, but music, and it is music beyond our senses that produces the music our ears can perceive.

If anyone should despise the arts because they imitate Nature, one can reply that natural things, too, imitate a number of other things, further, that the arts do not exactly imitate what can be seen with the eye, but reach back to those Ideas on which Nature is based, and according to which she functions.

Moreover, the arts generate many things out of themselves, and conversely add many elements that perfection lacks because they carry beauty in themselves. Thus Phidias could portray the god, even though he was not imitating anything visible, but rather had formed an image in his mind of how Zeus would look, were he to appear before our eyes.

One cannot blame the idealists of ancient and modern times for insisting so forcefully on consideration of the one question: whence everything springs and from what everything should be derived. For indeed the vital and ordering principle is so oppressed in the realm of appearances that it hardly knows what to do. Yet we restrict ourselves on the opposite side when we compress the formative principle and higher form itself into a unity that disappears before our inner and outer senses.

Expansion and movement are the conditions of our human existence; these two general forms are the ones in which all other forms, especially the sensory ones, manifest themselves. But a spiritual form is by no means diminished by emerging into appearance, provided that its emergence is a true procreation, true propagation. What is begotten is not inferior to the begetter, and indeed, the advantage of live begetting is that what is begotten can be superior to that which begets it.

It would be of great importance to expand on this further and make it completely clear, better still, in fact, to make it thoroughly useful. A detailed and logical exposition, however, might demand too much attention of one's audience.

You cannot get rid of what belongs to you, even if you throw it away.

The latest philosophy of our western neighbors gives testimony that a person, no matter how he tries, and likewise entire nations, will always revert to what is innate. And how could it be otherwise, when this is what determines his nature and way of life?

The French have renounced materialism and have ascribed somewhat more spirit and life to primal beginnings. They have freed themselves from sensualism and admitted that the deeper levels of human nature develop of their own accord; they grant a productive power to human nature and do not try to explain all art as the imitation of a perceived external reality. May they persist in such lines of thought.

Eclectic philosophy cannot exist, though, doubtless, eclectic philosophers can.

An eclectic is anyone who appropriates from the world around him and from the events around him whatever is compatible with his own nature; and in this sense everything known as culture and progress has validity, in either a theoretical or a practical sense.

Two eclectic philosophers could thus become the greatest of enemies, if, born with antagonistic temperaments, they extracted from all the traditional philosophies only that which was compatible with their particular natures. One has only to look around to see that everyone proceeds in this fashion and hence does not understand why he cannot convert others to his opinion.

Indeed it is rare that a person becomes a historic figure to himself in old age, and that his contemporaries also become historic to him, so that he no longer wishes to or can enter into controversy with anyone.

If you examine it more closely, it turns out that history does not readily become historic even to the historian: each historian always writes as though he himself had been there, not about what had gone before and what the moving forces were. Even the chronicler more or less hints at the limitations, at the peculiarities of his own city, of his monastery, as well as of his own epoch.

Various sayings of the ancients, which we are wont to repeat, had an entirely different meaning from what we have wanted to give them in later times.

The dictum that no one unacquainted with geometry, no stranger to geometry, should enter the school of the philosophers does not mean, for example, that one has to be a mathematician in order to attain worldly wisdom.

Geometry here means its first principles, as set forth in Euclid and as we require of every beginner. As such, it is the most perfect preparation, indeed introduction, to philosophy.

When the boy begins to comprehend that an invisible point must precede a visible point, or that the shortest distance between two points must be thought of as a straight line before it is drawn on paper with a pencil, he feels a certain pride and pleasure. And not without reason; for the source of all thought has opened to him, idea and realization—*potentia et actu*—have become clear to him. The philosopher will reveal nothing new to him, for the basis of all thought has already become clear to the geometrician.

If we now consider the weighty dictum "know thyself," we must not interpret it in the ascetic sense. It certainly does not refer to the heautognosis of our modern hypochondriacs, humorists, and heautontimorumens; it signifies quite simply: pay some heed to yourself, take notice of yourself, that you may become aware of how you stand with your fellows and with the world. For this no psychological agonizing is required. Every sensible person knows and learns what it means; it is good advice that brings everyone the greatest practical benefits.

One should see the greatness of the ancients, especially of the Socratic School, in their setting before our eyes the sources and guidelines for all living and doing, not as subjects of empty speculation but as a summons to life and action.

If our school curriculum always refers us to the ancients, and promotes the study of the Greek and Latin languages, we may congratulate ourselves that these studies, so important for a higher civilization, never decline.

When we confront antiquity and contemplate it with the serious intention of forming ourselves by means of it, we have the sensation that for the first time we are becoming truly human.

The schoolman, when he attempts to write and speak Latin, seems finer and more distinguished to himself than he can fancy in daily life.

A mind that is receptive to poetic and artistic creations feels itself transported by antiquity into a most graceful and ideal state of nature; and to this day the Homeric epics have the power to free us, at least for the moment, from the terrible burden inexorably imposed on us by a tradition of several thousand years.

As Socrates summoned ethical man to himself so that he might simply gain some insight into his own nature, so Plato and Aristotle approached Nature as authorized individuals, the former to assimilate himself to her with mind and soul, the latter to win her for himself with the researcher's eye and method. And so every step that brings us singly or collectively closer to these three is the happiest event we can experience and a powerful impetus to our education.

In order to rescue ourselves from the endless complexity, fragmentation, and intricacy of modern natural science and return to simplicity, we must always ask ourselves the question: how would Plato have conducted himself toward Nature as she now appears to us, in greater multiplicity despite her fundamental unity?

For we think we are certain that by following this same road we can arrive organically at the very last ramifications of knowledge, and from this base little by little build up and establish the pinnacles of every science. How the activity of our age furthers and hinders us is of course a question we must pose ourselves daily, if we are not to reject the useful and adopt the harmful.

The eighteenth century is celebrated for having devoted itself chiefly to analysis; for the nineteenth century there remains the task of uncovering the prevailing false syntheses and analyzing their content anew.

There are only two true religions, one of which acknowledges and worships the divinity that resides within us and around us, entirely without form, the other of which worships it in the most beautiful form. Everything in between is idolatry.

There is no denying that the human spirit attempted to liberate itself through the Reformation. Enlightenment about Greek and Roman antiquity awakened the wish, the yearning, for a freer, more decent, and more tasteful life. It was, however, furthered to no small degree by the fact that the heart sought to return to a certain simple state of nature, and that the imagination sought to become more focused.

All at once the saints were driven out of Heaven, and our senses, thoughts, and feelings were directed away from a divine mother with a tender child to the adult who performed good works and suffered undeservingly, was later transfigured as a demigod, acknowledged and worshiped as the true god.

He stood before a backdrop where the Creator had spread out the entire universe. A spiritual force emanated from him, took his sufferings as an example for themselves, and his transfiguration was the promise of eternal life.

Just as incense replenishes the life of an ember, so a prayer replenishes the hopes of the heart.

I am convinced that the Bible becomes ever more beautiful the better one understands it, that is to say, the more one realizes and sees that every word we take in a general sense and apply to ourselves specifically may have had, according to particular situations, according to circumstances of time and place, a unique, special, and directly individual reference.

Properly speaking, we should still be reforming ourselves daily, and protesting against others, even if not in the religious sense.

We have the inescapable, solemn goal that must daily be reaffirmed: to match what we have felt, observed, thought, experienced, imagined, and found reasonable to the word that most accurately captures it.

Let everyone examine himself and he will find that this is much more difficult than one would imagine; for unfortunately people normally use words as stopgaps; for the most part, a person thinks and knows things better than he expresses them.

But let us persist in the effort to purge ourselves, by exercising clarity and honesty, of everything false, improper, inadequate that may develop within or worm its way into us and others.

With the years our trials become more arduous.

When I must cease to be moral, my power is at an end.

Censorship and freedom of the press will always struggle with one another. The powerful demand and practice censorship; the weaker demand freedom of the press. The former do not wish to be hindered in their plans or in their activity by rude dissent, but to be obeyed; the latter would like to express their arguments, in order to legitimize disobedience. This will always be found to be true.

Yet it must also be said here that the weaker, suffering party likewise tries to suppress freedom of the press in its own fashion, specifically when it is engaged in conspiracy and does not wish to be betrayed.

One is never deceived, but rather deceives oneself.

Our language needs a word that would express the relationship of "peoplehood" to people as the word "childhood" relates to the word "child." The educator must hear the voice of childhood, not that of the child. The lawgiver and ruler must listen to the voice of peoplehood, not that of the people. The former always says the same thing, is rational, consistent, pure, and truthful. The latter is so full of demands that it never knows what it wants. And in this sense the law should and can be the generally articulated will of peoplehood, a will which the masses never articulate but which the intelligent ruler hears and the rational one knows how to satisfy and the good one gladly does satisfy.

We do not ask ourselves what right we have to govern—we govern. Whether the people has the right to depose us, that is something we do not worry about—we simply take care that it is not tempted to do so.

If death could be eliminated, we would have nothing against that; to do away with the death penalty would be a difficult task. If that happens, we will occasionally reinstate it.

If a society relinquishes the right to impose the death penalty, individuals immediately turn to self-help, and blood feuds are just around the corner.

All laws are made by old people and by men. Young people and women want exceptions, old people want rules.

It is not the intelligent man who governs, but intelligence; not the rational man, but reason.

When one praises a person, one places oneself on his level.

It is not enough to know, one must also apply one's knowledge; it is not enough to will, one must also act.

There is no patriotic art and no patriotic science. Both of these belong, like everything noble and good, to the entire world and can be advanced only through unfettered exchange among all those living in a given time, with constant reference to what remains and is known to us from the past.

The sciences on the whole are always moving away from life and return to it only by a detour.

For they are actually compendia of life; they bring outer and inner experiences together into a general picture.

Interest in them is aroused basically only in a special world, the scientific world; calling upon the rest of the world and informing it about the sciences, as is done in modern times, is an abuse and does more harm than good.

The sciences ought to affect the outer world only through their higher application: in fact all of them are esoteric and become exoteric only by improving some course of action. All other forms of participation lead nowhere.

Even within their inner circles the sciences attract instantaneous interest when a new discovery is made. A striking advance, especially something new and unheard-of, or at least extremely suggestive, excites general interest that can persist for years, and has proved most fruitful, particularly in recent times.

A significant fact, an inspired aperçu, spurs a large number of people, first merely to become familiar with it, then to understand it, then to work it out and carry it further.

With every significant discovery, the common people ask what is it good for, nor are they wrong to do so. For they recognize the value of a thing only through its usefulness.

The truly wise inquire into the nature of the matter and its relationship to other things, without regard to its utility, i.e., about how it can be applied to what is known and is essential for life, which quite different minds—sharp-witted, life-loving, technically trained and skilled—will discover soon enough.

From each new discovery the sophists try to extract some advantage for themselves as soon as possible, attempting to secure an empty fame, now by propagating the idea, now by adding to it, now by improving on it, by rapidly seizing possession, perhaps even by usurping it, and through such immature behavior they render true science uncertain and confused, and even its finest result, its practical blossom, withers on the vine.

The most harmful prejudice is the belief that any kind of scientific investigation can be proscribed.

Every researcher must regard himself as someone called to serve on a jury. He must attend only to whether the presentation is complete and set forth with clear proofs. He then sums up what he believes and casts his vote, whether his opinion coincides with that of the presenter or not.

In this process he remains just as calm when the majority agrees with him as when he finds himself in the minority; he has done his part, he has voiced what he believes, and he cannot control others' minds or souls.

But in the scientific world these attitudes have never prevailed; it is all a question of mastery and domination, and because very few people are truly independent, the crowd draws the individual along after it.

The history of philosophy, of the sciences, and of religion all show that opinions can spread en masse, but the ones that always prevail are those that are more easily grasped, i.e., are most conformable and comfortable to the human mind in its common condition. Indeed, anyone who educates himself in the higher sense can always assume that he will have the majority against him.

Were not Nature in her inorganic beginnings so thoroughly stereometric, how could she ultimately arrive at incalculable and immeasurable life?

The human being in himself, to the extent that he makes use of his sound senses, is the greatest and most accurate physical apparatus there can be; and that is the greatest disaster of modern physics, that it has effectively separated experimentation from the human element and recognizes Nature only in what artificial instruments can register, and indeed, wants to limit and establish thereby what Nature can achieve.

The same is true of calculation.—There are many truths that cannot be calculated, just as there is much that cannot be tested by definitive experiments.

But that is why man stands so high that in him can be represented that which is otherwise not representable. For what are a string and all mechanical divisions thereof compared to the ear of the musician? Indeed, one might say: what are the basic phenomena of Nature compared to man, who must first tame and modify them all in order to assimilate them somewhat to himself.

It is demanding too much of an experiment to expect it to accomplish everything. After all, electricity could at first be produced only by friction, while now its highest manifestation can be produced by simple contact.

As no one would contest the prerogative of the French language to spread and develop increasingly as the language of the court and of cultivation, so it will never occur to anyone to question the merit of the mathematicians, who, treating of the most important matters in their own particular language, earn the world's gratitude by knowing how to regulate, determine, and distinguish everything that comes under the heading of number and quantity in the higher sense.

Every thinking person, when he looks at his calendar or glances at his clock, will remember to whom he owes these benefits. Even if, however, we reverently concede them this honor in time and space, they will recognize that we are aware of something far beyond them, something that belongs to everyone, and without which they themselves could neither act nor have any effect: *the idea* and *love.*

As one of our merry researchers asks, who knows anything about electricity except when he strokes a cat in the dark, or when thunder and lightning crash and light up the sky? So then how much or how little does he know about it?

We can use Lichtenberg's writings as a most curious divining rod; wherever he makes a joke, a problem lies hidden.

Lichtenberg has also planted an amusing notion in the vast empty space between Mars and Jupiter. After Kant had carefully proved that these two planets had consumed and incorporated whatever matter could be found in that space, the former asked in his usual witty way: why should there not be invisible planets as well?—And was he not perfectly right? Are not the newly discovered planets invisible to the entire world, except for the few astronomers, whose word and calculations we must accept?

Nothing is more pernicious to a new truth than an old error.

People are so overwhelmed by the endless conditions of appearance that they cannot perceive the one source of all conditions.

"If travelers find great delight in scaling mountains, I find something barbarous, even godless, in this passion; to be sure, mountains give us a sense of the power of Nature, but not of the beneficence of Providence. Of what use are they to mankind? If you should venture to live among them, in winter an avalanche, or in summer a rockslide will bury or sweep away your house. The mountain torrent will drown your herds, the wind will blow down your granaries. If you attempt the smallest journey, every ascent is the labor of Sisyphus, every descent Vulcan's fall. Your path is daily blocked with stones, while the torrent is unsuitable for navigation. Even if your stunted herds find meager feed, or if you gather scanty hay for them, they are snatched away either by the elements or by wild beasts. You live a lonely and wretched vegetable existence, like moss on a gravestone, without comfort and without society. And these jagged ridges, these repellent walls of rock, these misshapen granite pyramids, which cover the most beautiful latitudes with the horrors of the North Pole—how should any man of goodwill take pleasure in such things or a philanthropist praise them!"

In response to this amusing contrariety of a worthy man, one might say that if it had pleased God and Nature to develop and extend the original mountain ranges from Nubia westward as far as the great ocean and then to cut through those mountain chains from north to south, valleys would have been created in which many a patriarchal Abraham would have found his Canaan, many an

Albert Julius his Felsenburg, so that their descendants could have increased, easily rivaling the stars in number.

Rocks are mute teachers; they render the observer mute, and the best thing one can learn from them is to keep one's counsel.

What I truly know, I know only for myself; a spoken word rarely proves helpful: mostly it creates antagonism, hesitation, and stagnation.

Crystallography, considered as a science, gives rise to some very curious views. It is not productive, it is only itself, and leads to no conclusions, especially now, when so many isomorphic bodies have been discovered, which prove highly diverse in their composition. Since it actually has no utility, it has developed its great complexity on its own terms. It offers the mind a certain limited satisfaction and has such variety in its details that one may call it inexhaustible, for which reason it attracts superior men and holds them so long under its spell.

Crystallography has something monastic and celibate about it, and is therefore sufficient unto itself. It can have no practical influence on life, since even the most exquisite products of this field, the crystalline gemstones, must first be cut and polished before we can adorn our women with them.

The very opposite may be said of chemistry, which proves to be of the broadest application and most boundless influence on life.

The concept of origination is completely and utterly denied us; for which reason we think, when we see something in the process of becoming, it must have been there already. Therefore the system of pre-formation makes sense to us.

How many significant things we see constructed out of parts. When we look at works of architecture, we see regular and irregular masses piled together; hence the atomistic concept comes readily to mind, and hence we do not hesitate to apply it even to organic situations.

He who cannot grasp the difference between the phantastic and the ideal, between the predictable and the hypothetical, is in a bad way as a natural scientist.

There are hypotheses where intelligence and imagination take the place of an idea.

It is not good to remain too long in the realm of the abstract. The esoteric does harm only when it attempts to become exoteric. Life is best taught through that which is alive.

The superior woman would be she who could take the father's place with the children when he is gone.

The inestimable advantage that foreigners will have, since they are only now beginning to study our literature carefully, is that they will be instantly whisked past the childhood diseases through which we have had to suffer for most of the century, and, if they are lucky, can obtain a wonderful education from us.

Where Frenchmen of the eighteenth century are destructive, Wieland is teasing.

As much poetic talent is given to the peasant as to the knight; all that matters is that each should take his own lot and portray it with dignity.

"What are tragedies but the versified passions of people who make external things into I know not what."

The word *school,* as it is understood in the history of art, where one speaks of Florentine, Roman, and Venetian schools, can henceforth no longer be applied to the German theater. It is a term which perhaps could still be used thirty or forty years ago, when, under more limited conditions, one could still conceive of an education in conformity to Nature and art. In precise terms even in the plastic arts the word *school* applies only to the beginnings, for as soon as it has produced highly talented men, its effects are felt far and wide. Florence exerts an influence on France and Spain; the Dutch and the Germans learn from the Italians and acquire more freedom in mind and spirit, instead of the Southerners learning more successful technique and great precision from the North.

The German theater has reached the final stage of development, in which the general level of cultivation extends so far that it no longer belongs to any single place, can no longer radiate from one particular point.

The basis of all theatrical art, as of every other, is truth, fidelity to Nature. The more significant this is, the higher the level at which dramatist and actor can grasp it, the higher the quality the stage will be able to boast of. In this respect Germany has derived great benefit from the fact that recital of superior literature has become more common, and has even spread outside the theater as well.

All declamation and mimicry depend on recitation. Since in reading aloud all attention and practice is directed toward the former, it is clear that such readings must be training grounds for truth and naturalness, if the men who undertake such a task are imbued with the value and dignity of their profession.

Shakespeare and Calderon have supplied a brilliant introduction for such readings; still we must always consider whether this overwhelming foreignness, this talent intensified to the point of unnaturalness, might not be harmful to German development.

Characteristic expression is the beginning and end of all art. Now each nation has a special individuality that diverges from the universal character of mankind; at first it may repel us, but eventually, if we accepted it, if we submitted to it, it could overwhelm our own characteristic nature and stifle it.

How much falseness Shakespeare and especially Calderon have visited upon us and how these two stars of the poetic heavens have led us astray is for the literary critics of the future to establish historically.

I cannot countenance complete emulation of the Spanish theater. The sublime Calderon has so much that is purely conventional that a fair-minded observer would have difficulty distinguishing the dramatist's great talent from all the theatrical etiquette. And if you present something like this to an audience, you presuppose goodwill on its part, such that it will be inclined to accept unworldliness, to enjoy foreign attitudes, tones, and rhythms, and temporarily to abandon its own sphere.

Yorick-Sterne was the wittiest spirit who ever wrote. Anyone who reads him instantly feels free and better. His humor is inimitable; not every form of humor can liberate the soul.

"Moderation and a clear sky are Apollo and the Muses."

Sight is the noblest of the senses; the other four instruct us only through the organs of touch: we hear, we perceive, smell, and feel everything by way of contact. Sight, however, stands infinitely higher, rises above matter, and approaches the capabilities of mind.

If we could put ourselves in the place of others, the envy and hatred we so often feel toward them would evaporate; and if we put others in our place, pride and conceit would be greatly reduced.

Someone once compared reflection and action with Rachel and Leah; the one was more charming, the other more fertile.

Except for health and virtue, nothing in life is more precious than knowledge and learning. Moreover, nothing is easier to achieve and less expensive to obtain. The entire effort consists of being calm, and the only expenditure is time, which we cannot save without spending.

If we could put aside time as we do cash, without using it, this would more or less excuse the idleness of half the world. But not entirely, for this would be like a household living on its capital, without caring about the interest.

The more recent poets mix a lot of water in their ink.

Among the many remarkable inanities of the academies, none seems to me so utterly absurd as the battle over the authenticity of ancient texts, of old works. Is it then the author or the text that we admire or censure? It is always simply the author whom we have before us; what do names matter when we are interpreting a work of the mind?

Who will assert that we have Virgil or Homer before us, when we read the words that have been attributed to them? But we do have the writers before us, and what more do we need? Indeed, I think the scholars who set to work meticulously on this superfluous matter seem no wiser than a very pretty woman who once asked me with the sweetest possible smile who had been the author of Shakespeare's plays.

It is better to do the most insignificant thing in the world than to consider a half hour insignificant.

Courage and modesty are the most unequivocal virtues. For they are such that hypocrisy cannot imitate them; they also share the quality that both express themselves with the same color.

Of all the rabble of thieves, the fools are the worst; they rob you twice, of time and of temper.

Morality leads us to respect ourselves; good manners require us to value others.

Art and science are words that are often used and whose exact difference is seldom understood; one is often used for the other.

I am also not satisfied with the definitions people give for them. Somewhere I saw science equated with wit, art with humor. I see more imagination than philosophy here; it may give us some notion of the difference between the two, but not of what is characteristic of each.

I think one might call science knowledge of the general, distilled learning; art, by contrast, would be science applied to action; science would be reason, and art its mechanism, for which reason it could also be called practical science. And so, finally, science would be the theorem, art the problem.

Perhaps someone will object here: poetry is considered art, and yet it is not mechanical. But I deny that poetry is an art; nor is it a science. Arts and sciences are both arrived at through thought, but not poetry, for it is inspiration; it was conceived within the soul when it first began to stir. It should be called neither art nor science, but genius.

At this moment every cultivated person should once more take up Sterne's works so that we of the nineteenth century may also see what we owe to him and understand what we might yet owe to him.

As literatures progress, what was once influential falls into obscurity, and what grew out of it becomes dominant, for which reason it is good to look back from time to time. What is original in our own work will be best preserved and appreciated if we do not lose sight of our ancestors.

May the study of Greek and Roman literature always remain the basis of higher education.

Chinese, Indian, and Egyptian antiquities are always mere curiosities; it is highly commendable to acquaint oneself and the world with them, but they will contribute little to our moral or aesthetic education.

The Germans run no greater danger than matching themselves with and against their neighbors; there is, perhaps, no nation better equipped to develop entirely out of its own resources, for which reason it has been of the greatest advantage to them that the rest of the world was slow to take notice of them.

If we look back over half a century of our literature, we discover that nothing was done for the sake of foreigners.

That Frederick the Great wanted nothing to do with them upset the Germans, and they did their best to amount to something in his eyes.

Now that a world literature is beginning to evolve, it is the Germans, to tell the truth, who stand to lose the most. They would do well to heed this warning.

Even discerning people fail to notice that what they want to explain are basic experiences, concerning which one should keep still.

Yet this, too, may have its advantages, for otherwise inquiry might be abandoned too soon.

From now on, anyone who does not apply himself to an art or a craft will be in sorry straits. Learning no longer advances us, with the world moving so fast; by the time we have taken notice of everything, we have lost ourselves.

The world imposes a general education upon us in any case; we need not make any particular effort in this regard, rather, we must master the particulars.

The greatest difficulties lie where we least suspect them.

Laurence Sterne was born in 1713 and died in 1768. To comprehend him, one must bear in mind the moral and religious teachings of his age; in this connection, it is well to recall that he was a contemporary of Warburton's.

A free spirit like his runs the risk of impudence if a noble benevolence does not restore moral equilibrium.

With his sensitivity, everything in him developed from within; through perpetual conflict he distinguished the true from the false, held firmly to the first, and ruthlessly opposed the other.

He felt a distinct hatred for solemnity, because it is didactic and dogmatic and easily becomes pedantry, of which he had an absolute horror. Hence his aversion to terminology.

In the most varied studies and reading, he always found elements of the inadequate and comical.

By Shandyism he means the impossibility of thinking about any serious subject for two minutes at a time.

This rapid alternation between gravity and wit, between sympathy and indifference, between sorrow and joy is supposed to be part of the Irish character.

His sagacity and penetration are boundless.

His cheerfulness, contentment, and patience on the road, where these qualities are tested to their utmost, are not easily equalled.

However much we are delighted by the spectacle of a free spirit of this sort, we are reminded precisely in this case that we must not adopt any of it, at least not most of the things that delight us.

The element of sensuality, which he treats so delicately and deftly, would prove the ruin of many others.

His relationship to his wife, as to the world, deserves attention. "I have not made use of my miseries like a wise man," he says somewhere.

He jests charmingly about the contradictions that make his situation ambiguous.

"I cannot bear preaching. I fancy I got a surfeit of it in my youth."

He is in no respects a model and in all a guide and an awakener.

"Our participation in public affairs is mostly only philistinism."

"Nothing should be treasured more than the worth of each day."

"Pereant, qui, ante nos, nostra dixerunt!" Such an odd statement could be made only by someone who imagines himself to be autochthonous. Anyone who considers it an honor to be descended from rational ancestors will attribute at least as much common sense to them as to himself.

The most original authors of modern times are original not because they produce something new, but only because they are capable of saying things as if they had never been said before.

Hence the best mark of originality is that one can develop a received idea so fruitfully that no one could readily guess how much lay concealed within it.

Many ideas first emerge from the general culture like blossoms from green branches. During the rose season you see roses blooming everywhere.

In fact everything depends on people's dispositions; where these are, thoughts also come forth, and as they are, so too are the thoughts.

"Nothing can be easily represented with complete impartiality. One might say the mirror offers an exception to this, and yet we never see our face quite accurately in it; indeed, the mirror reverses our form and makes our left hand the right. Let this be an image for all observations about ourselves."

In spring and autumn we do not readily think of having a fire, and yet it is so that, if we pass one by chance, we find the feeling it communicates so agreeable that we are inclined to muse on it. This may well be an analogy for every temptation.

"Do not be impatient when others do not accept your arguments."

Anyone who lives for a long time in a significant milieu does not, it is true, encounter all a person can encounter, but something analogous, however, and perhaps certain things without precedent.

Notes

Conversations of German Refugees

P. 15, In those unhappy days . . . threatening everyone of any distinction. The cycle begins in the fall of 1792, immediately after the failure of the Duke of Brunswick's invasion of France, described by Goethe in *Campaign in France 1792* (see vol. 5 in this edition). The family flees eastward.

P. 29, the Abbé began as follows. The following is based on an anecdote reported to Goethe about the French actress Hyppolyte Clairon, later reported in her own memoirs, 1799.

P. 34, no real account is taken of the midnight hour. In Goethe's day Italians still counted the hours from sunrise and sunset, not from noon and midnight; thus midnight was not necessarily marked. Goethe explains the system and remarks on the advent of evening as the focal point of the day in *Italian Journey*, entry for Verona, September 17 (see vol. 6 in this edition).

P. 36, a story . . . that could never be explained with complete certainty. Based on an anecdote circulating orally in Weimar.

P. 37, an example of Röntgen's best workmanship. David Röntgen (1743–1807), most successful German cabinetmaker of his day, best known for the intricate mechanisms in his furniture.

P. 39, Marshal de Bassompierre. François de Bassompierre (1579–1646), French courtier from whose memoirs (first published 1665) the following two anecdotes are translated.

P. 42, an old story that I have always been rather fond of. The following was translated from the anonymous collection *Cent Nouvelles nouvelles*, first published in 1482 and repeatedly reprinted through the eighteenth century.

P. 55, family portraits. Popular genre of middle-class tragicomedy in the later eighteenth century. The following novella has no known source.

Wilhelm Meister's Journeyman Years

P. 117, cross-stone. Chiastolith, variety of andalusite.

P. 139, Beccaria and Filangieri. Marchese Cesare Beccaria-Bonesana (1738–1794) and Gaetano Filangieri (1752–1788), major contributors to eighteenth-century discussions of penal reform.

P. 150, William Penn. Penn (1644–1718) founded Pennsylvania as a Christian state on a Quaker model in 1682.

P. 155, Homann volumes. Homann, Nuremberg publishing firm famous for its maps.

P. 158, Anton Rover. Play on the title of a novel by Goethe's friend Karl Philipp Moritz (1756–1793). *Anton Reiser* (Reiser=Rover), published 1785–1793, was an immediate predecessor of Goethe's own *Wilhelm Meister's Apprenticeship.*

P. 165, William of Orange. King William III of England (1650–1702).

P. 185, 'The Silent Ones.' Pietists. Pietism was a movement within eighteenth-century German Lutheranism that combined emphasis on Biblical doctrine, vigorous conduct of a Christian life, and involvement of the laity in the running of the church. It was closely related to the religious groups that settled in Pennsylvania.

P. 255, Mignon's fate. Mignon is a mysterious poetic child adopted by Wilhelm in *Wilhelm Meister's Apprenticeship* (vol. 9 in this edition). After her death she is revealed to be the kidnapped granddaughter of an Italian marchese whose seat on the Lago Maggiore Wilhelm has now come to visit.

P. 263, Know you the land . . . Beginning of Mignon's most famous song in the *Apprenticeship* (here in the translation of Hal Draper; see vol. 9 of this edition, p. 83).

P. 294, Reflections in the Spirit of the Wanderers. These aphorisms and the similar group at the end of Book III are to be understood as a collection, many by Goethe, many gathered from a wide variety of sources ranging from Plotinus to a popular eighteenth-century collection attributed to Laurence Sterne.

P. 305, Lessing. Gotthold Ephraim Lessing (1729–1781), leading thinker and dramatist of the German Enlightenment. Goethe has in mind here Act I, scene 3 of Lessing's last play, *Nathan the Wise.*

P. 316, Red Mantle. Ghostly barber in the fairy tale "Speechless Love" from the collection *Fairy Tales of the Germans* by J.K.A. Musäus (1735–1787), professor, satirist, and leading literary figure of Weimar until 1772. The odd conditions placed on Wilhelm's visit at the inn, the figure of St. Christopher, the mysterious noise (presumably St. Christopher snoring), and many motifs in the barber's story below play on this tale by Goethe's old friend. The collection remained popular through the nineteenth century.

P. 319, Alfieri. Vittorio Alfieri (1749–1803), Italian tragic dramatist.

P. 340, Ambrosius Lobwasser's four-part psalms. Translations made in 1573 of Huguenot singing versions of the psalms, used by German Calvinists into the nineteenth century. That they are being sung at home locates the action in pietist circles.

P. 343, Melusine. Heroine of the chapbook of the same name, who leaves her husband periodically to return to her natural form of mermaid; when her husband discovers her true form she leaves him.

P. 351, King Eckwald. Dwarf King in the chapbook *Horned Siegfried.*

P. 355, Röntgen's ingenious writing desks. See note to *Conversations of German Refugees*, p. 37.

P. 366, Yorick. Allusion to Laurence Sterne (1713–1768), who adopts the name of Hamlet's jester for the pastor in his novel *Tristram Shandy*, and who was widely understood in the eighteenth century to have portrayed himself in that figure. Goethe also has Sterne's other novel, *A Sentimental Journey*, in mind here.

P. 391, Kleist's 'Springtime.' Albrecht von Haller (1708–1777), Salomon Gessner (1730–1788), and Ewald Christian von Kleist (1715–1759), the most popular landscape poets of the German eighteenth century, each named here with his most influential work.

P. 391, the great danger of lukewarm faith. Revelation 3:14–16.

P. 403, Philine and Lydie. Minor characters from the *Apprenticeship*, as is Werner, mentioned below.

P. 422, heautognosis. Self-knowledge.

P. 422, heautontimorumens. Self-tormenters; *Heauton Timorumenos* is the title of a comedy by Terence (based on one of the same name by Menander).

P. 428, Lichtenberg's writings. Georg Christoph Lichtenberg (1742–1799), professor of physics and satirical writer.

P. 429, Felsenburg. In *Felsenburg Island* (1731–1743), an imitation of *Robinson Crusoe* written by Johann Gottfried Schnabel (born 1692, died after 1750), Albert Julius is the father of the isolated family.

P. 430, Wieland. Christoph Martin Wieland (1733–1813), leading poet and novelist of the generation before Goethe.

P. 431, Shakespeare and Calderon. Goethe was an enthusiastic participant in the German romantic revival of the Spanish dramatist Pedro Calderón de la Barca (1600–1681), and was not alone in declaring him equal to Shakespeare, who had been a major influence on German drama since the seventeen-seventies.

P. 434, a contemporary of Warburton's. William Warburton (1698–1779), Bishop of Gloucester; contentious opponent of Deism.

GPSR Authorized Representative: Easy Access System Europe - Mustamäe tee
50, 10621 Tallinn, Estonia, gpsr.requests@easproject.com

www.ingramcontent.com/pod-product-compliance
Lightning Source LLC
LaVergne TN
LVHW102150101026
849957LV00026B/152
9780691292373